Justin McCarthy

Dear Lady Disdain

Justin McCarthy

Dear Lady Disdain

ISBN/EAN: 9783337119263

Printed in Europe, USA, Canada, Australia, Japan

Cover: Foto ©Andreas Hilbeck / pixelio.de

More available books at **www.hansebooks.com**

DEAR LADY DISDAIN

BY

JUSTIN McCARTHY, M.P.

AUTHOR OF

"MISS MISANTHROPE," "CAMIOLA," "A HISTORY OF OUR OWN TIMES," ETC.

A NEW EDITION

London

CHATTO & WINDUS, PICCADILLY

1890

CONTENTS.

DEAR LADY DISDAIN

A ROOM on the ground floor, octagonal in shape, with an old
and picturesque fireplace filling up one of the narrower sides—
stopping up the corner, if one may say so—and with windows
in two of its sides, is filled with the morning sunshine. The
room and its furniture make an odd contrast, for the furniture
is new and the room is old. The chimney-piece is of tiles that
tell in their pictorial ornamentation many a scriptural story.
The ceiling is painted in colours once gorgeous, now faded. A
broad-backed and large-limbed goddess floats there, half clad in
volumes of bright blue drapery, upon clouds solid-looking as
her own substantial frame, and amid bulbous Cupids and masses
of hothouse flowers. The walls are of a dark and closely-grained
wood, and are all in panels of various sizes—two panels to each
side of the octagon—and pictures, no doubt, once filled each
compartment. The windows look upon trees and foliage so
thickly set that a stranger suddenly dropped down in the room
might fancy himself in the apartment of a palace adorned by
Verrio, and planted in the midst of courtly park. He might
have been right enough as to the palace, but a glance from the
window will quickly dispose of the park. The trees are set in
the gardens of the Thames Embankment, and the octagonal room
with the goddess floating on the ceiling is on the ground-floor of
a house in one of the streets running to the river from the
western end of the Strand.

The present occupant of this room was immensely proud of
it. He was almost in love with it. Hunting about for lodgings
which should be conveniently central for the West End, the

B

theatres, and the British Museum, he had seen the word "Chambers" in one of the windows of this house, and he was attracted by the trees in the gardens of the new Embankment. But when he went in and saw the chambers; when he looked at the chimney-piece of tiles and the painted ceiling; when he found that every room in the house had its history, that famous nobles and foreign princes had occupied that room, that celebrated beauties had swept up and down those broad staircases; he entered into possession without more words, and felt as proud as it he had come into some great inheritance. The suite of rooms consisted only of this one and a bedroom that opened out of it; but the present occupant wanted no more. There were not many residents in the house besides himself. Every chamber was occupied, but most of the occupants only used the place for office business of some kind, and went away in the evening.

Breakfast is laid upon a sadly modern and common-place table in the middle of the room; breakfast is the only meal the tenant has in his chambers, and it is supplied to him by special stipulation, and as an extra, or "hextra," by the elderly person in charge of the house. A newspaper lies on the table along with some letters. These latter are nearly all addressed to "C. J. Pembroke, Esq.," but one in a woman's hand is addressed fully and formally to "Christmas John Pembroke, Esq.," and Christmas as a man's first name is not seen every day.

Enters from the bedroom a tall, slight, and boyish-looking young man in an old velvet coat. He has brown hair and a dark complexion, and a moustache not yet very thickly grown on a face that otherwise is smooth as a girl's. He does not look like a Londoner—perhaps the wrist that shows itself from the sleeve of a coat which has shrunk, or which he has outgrown, is a little too brown and muscular for London rearing. Besides, he looks rather fresh and contented with himself and with life generally for a London youth. He gazes up at the ceiling and all about the room with irrepressible admiration. He has not nearly got over the proud sensation of ownership. He has to stop and think about it, in fact, to take it all in. Then he looks out at the trees and at the glancing river. It is June, and London is delicious. Since he arrived there have been hardly any wet days, and since his coming into these chambers absolutely none at all. And yet he is not merely London's lover, but London's devotee.

Then he looks at the letters on the table, and he is about to open one of them, which is evidently an invitation of some kind, when he sees the letter which is addressed in the handwriting of a woman. He is just at the age when the sight of his own name in a woman's hand sends a thrill through him. He ought first to have wondered who the woman could be, for he did not know

of any lady in England who was at all likely to write to him or
who knew his name so precisely. But the first idea which comes
to him is an odd little feeling of wonder whether, with the progress of the movement for woman's equal rights, women will
insist on writing in the same sort of character as men, and quite
an earnest hope that it may not be so—it is so interesting to see
a letter addressed to one in what we know to be a woman's hand.
Then he sets himself seriously to wondering what woman it can
be who writes to him, and he wonders about this, and turns the
letter over and over, and tantalises himself, and is positively
afraid that when he does open it it will resolve itself, as so many
of his letters do since he has had his name painted on the side of
the hall door, into a circular inviting him to buy cheap sherry,
coals, or shirts.

At last he opens the letter.

It was dated from a place which, as well as Christmas could
make out the word, was called "Durewoods," in one of the
southern counties on the sea.

"I have seen in the papers the name and address of Christmas
John Pembroke, described as a young man. I never heard of
any Christmas John Pembroke but my old and dear friend who
left England when I was young, and of whose death I read a
year ago. If you are his son, will you kindly write a line, and
I will write to you again? You must have heard your father
speak of me, if I am not addressing a stranger. If I am, pray
excuse what must seem a very odd intrusion; and let me add
that I am now an elderly woman, and am only seeking to hear
of a very old acquaintance."

The letter was signed "Dione Lyle;" and if Christmas is not
a very common name for a man, certainly, in our day, Dione is
not a familiar name for a woman. Dione! The young man
started when he saw it.

He read the letter over and over again, and, although he was
alone, with glowing cheeks. It sounded like a mild and melancholy reproach. His father had asked him to find out if he could
a certain lady—an old friend—in England. This was on that
mournful journey towards home, when his father was breaking
down, and began to be conscious that he was not destined ever to
see the country of his youth any more. When the young man sat
by his father's dying bed, the last words that came clearly from
his lips were "Dione, Dione!" and then the dying man murmured
hastily—oh, so hastily and unintelligibly—some counsel, some
instruction, something which poor Christmas could not make
out, and then sank back and all was over. That was a year ago
—already.

Never in the course of all the years during which Christmas had lived with his father—they two alone, so far as anything like home life was concerned—had he heard him say anything of this lady until it became clear enough that the elder man was destined not to reach England. Even then, in the first instance at least, he had only said that he hoped when Christmas got to London he would find out a lady who had been an old and dear friend, and whom he should like Christmas to know. Christmas remembered this, but was not prepared at once to connect that association with the name which was breathed from the dying lips—the one strange name. Now the name lay there before him; and he felt at once that some sad sweet story must have blended it with his father's latest memories. Christmas had almost no recollection of his mother, except that she never took any interest in him or seemed to care about anything; and she died long ago. She died at Nice, where the boy's earliest distinctness of recollection settled itself around her. Then his father, who was a scientific engineer, took the boy out to California, where he engaged himself in railway making while Christmas went to school in San Francisco. The opening up of Japan invited English skill and science, and the elder Pembroke resolved to go there; he took Christmas with him and educated him without help of other teachers. He was a very kind and even affectionate man, but he always seemed absorbed in his business when he was not occupied in the education of his son. One day he told Christmas calmly that he knew he could not live much longer, and that he should like to see England once more, and should like Christmas to live there always. It was on the voyage to San Francisco that he found himself dying, and then he told Christmas so, and quietly said that he had expected to be able to return to Japan after a short stay in England, and after having settled Christmas there, and had left his business affairs unarranged—that Christmas had therefore better return from San Francisco to Japan, and arrange matters as well as he could before going to England. He gave him some names of persons he was to see in London, and various counsels and recommendations, and at last the end came, and he cried out the name of "Dione, Dione!" Then his grave was made without hands in the Pacific, and Christmas was alone. He only remained in San Francisco for the next steamer to Japan. He arranged his father's affairs, closed his accounts with the East, crossed the Pacific again, and then the Atlantic, and was now preparing to think about beginning a career in London.

It was with a start of surprise that the lapse of time now suddenly impressed itself on him. His father was a year dead. A whole year since he heard that cry of "Dione!" So many weeks to return to Japan, so many months there, so many to get to London, with short delays in America, and a year was gone, and it must be owned that during all that time he had hardly once thought of his father's old friend. How indeed could he have possibly found her, or even gone about finding her? The chance that allowed her to see his name was the mere fact that he had intervened in a street quarrel and been summoned as a witness in a police-court, and had given his name and address, which accordingly got into the papers. Never before had he been a witness in any law court; never before to his knowledge had his name appeared in print. How many years might he have lived in London and never encountered such a chance? Why on the very night which brought his name into publicity, if as he hesitated in Pall Mall, he had turned up St. James's Street instead of walking on and then turning up the Haymarket, he never would have had to appear as a witness, and his father's friend might never have known of his existence! "I begin to believe in Destiny," Christmas said to himself, pleased as we all are to think that Destiny has a particular eye upon us.

He held the letter open in his hand, and thought of all these things, and felt, in the odd way of mortals, a small and trivial difficulty presenting itself most prominently to his mind amid so many serious reflections and saddening memories—a little difficulty which pushed itself out with absurd proportions as in a badly adjusted photograph a hand or a foot projects itself into grotesque dimensions. This was the question of the manner in which he was to address the lady; whether he was to assume that she was married or an old maid—Mrs. Lyle perhaps or Miss Lyle; and he asked himself whether in the event of the conjecture which he would have to make turning out a mistake, it would be better to err on this side or that. Would it be safer to run the risk of addressing an elderly and unmarried lady as Mrs., or an elderly and married lady as Miss? He decided that it would be better to write to Miss Lyle. A married lady would not take great offence at being mistaken for a Miss, but an elderly spinster might well feel uncomfortable if she were addressed as a matron.

The whole thing put him out a little for the moment. It made him feel remorseful, as if he had neglected something. He thought, too, that he had no right to be there enjoying the novel delights of London when his father was so lately dead.

He forgot his breakfast, and was about to begin a reply at once to his unexpected correspondent, when he heard a quick heavy tread outside, and then a knock at his door. He called "Come in," and a head appeared at the door, which was presently followed by a stalwart body. The visitor was a tall soldierly-looking man, with a fresh florid face, short thick yellow moustache, bright blue eyes, and very short yellow or sandy hair. He wore a frock coat buttoned across his broad and somewhat swelling chest, and a crimson tie, and carried an umbrella tucked under his arm, as a man might carry his sword. His waist was tightly drawn, and as he entered the room and bowed he clicked his heels together. This was Captain Cameron, the hero of the quarrel with the police in which Christmas had interfered and which brought his name into the papers.

"How do you do, sir? I'm afraid I have intruded at an awkward hour—too early a call?"

"Not at all," said Christmas, glad perhaps to be interrupted at the moment. "Won't you take a chair? Have some breakfast; I haven't begun."

"Breakfast, eh? Well, I don't know, I don't often eat breakfast—what you English fellows call breakfast."

"We English fellows? You are English, surely?"

"Not I, sir. I'm a Highlandman—a Hielan'man, sir! I represent a great clan. But I've been out and about the world so much that—I am a good Highlandman in heart, mind—I hardly know what to call myself in habits. I'll tell you though what a Highlandman never could learn to be—and that is, ungrateful! I've not forgotten how you interfered to help me out of a scrape—and took some trouble too : and that's why I've called to offer you my cordial thanks."

"Don't talk about it—'twas nothing."

"Nothing to a gentleman—that's true enough—and of course you couldn't help yourself—you had to behave like a gentleman. I didn't think there were any gentlemen left in England. I thought the race was extinct here, like the wolf and the wolf-dog, and the ghost, and all the other grand old things that made the place worth living in. But I see your breakfast is getting cold. Now I insist on your going on with your breakfast, or I shall think myself in the way and go."

"All right—if you really won't join me."

"No, I thank you. But if you don't mind my smoking a cigar?"

"Not the least in the world."

"Won't interfere with you at all—sure?"

"Quite sure."

"Then I'll just puff a little and we'll talk. I say, what a charming place you have here! How did you get at this place? That ceiling—I tell you, sir, that ceiling looked down on some Court beauties once. It's Verrio, no doubt. Merry Monarch, and Castlemaine, and, what's her name?—Stewart—and that sort of thing. But I wouldn't have that furniture, you know, if I were you—not that modern sort of thing. Regular London lodging-house sticks. I'd clear that lot out."

" But I don't know any better."

" No ? Just let me put things to rights for you. I know
man now up in Holborn—by the way, how they have ruined
Holborn; I'd never have known it again! What was I saying?
—Oh yes, about the furniture. I know a man in Holborn who
would give you just the right things—genuine furniture of the
very date, and very cheap. He wouldn't do it for you perhaps—
I mean if he didn't know you; but he'd do it for me. This is
really a charming place of yours; it must have a history. I
should so like my sister to see it—my sister, Mrs. Seagraves.
She'll be delighted to know you. I'll take you to her house."

" You are very kind, I am sure," murmured Christmas.

" Oh, she'll be delighted, and you'll be charmed with her I
know. Everybody is. We're very fond of each other, although
we don't agree about anything."

" Indeed ? "

" Not about anything, sir—anything! She's a Radical, and
an advanced thinker, and God knows what other stuff. I don't
mind—women must have their nonsense, and she's been a good
sister to a confoundedly wild brother. Well, you told me you
had been a long time out of London, like myself ? "

" I have been out of London since I was a boy. I had almost
forgotten its very streets."

" Well, how do you like it, now that you are here ? "

" I am delighted with it—I love London! I walk miles along
the streets—every name brings such associations with it. I
want to see every place that has any memory about it. I rush
to the theatres, no matter what is going on. I ' tear round,' as
the Americans say. I can't settle to anything yet. I—oh, I beg
your pardon."

He thought Captain Cameron was going to say something,
and he stopped, a little ashamed perhaps of his enthusiasm. The
gallant Cameron was leaning his chin gravely on one hand, which
he supported upon the handle of his umbrella, as if it were the
hilt of a sword; and with the other hand he had removed the
cigar from his mouth. It was this action which made Christmas
think he wanted to say something.

" No, I beg *your* pardon," said Cameron; " I did not mean to
interrupt you. I like to hear you talk in that way—it's so fresh.
It's like—now what is it like ? Like hearing some old air that
one hasn't heard for ages; or the smell of something—lavender,
perhaps—that used to be about the bedrooms long ago, when one
was a boy! Jove!—what a difference twenty years can make! "

" Then you don't like London quite so well ? "

" Like it? I am sick of it! I hate it! There hasn't been a
gentleman born in London for the last twenty years. The age of
gentlemen has gone, sir, and of gentlewomen! What does a

London girl talk of to-day? Radicalism and blasphemy—nothing
else. What is society in London? Freethinking schoolmasters,
and the literary puppies of Radicalism! Look here, now, I'll
give you an instance. I went the other morning to have my hair
cut, in a barber's place that I knew well twenty years. ago. The
name was changed, of course—I didn't mind that. Everything
changes here now-a-days? The fellow who cut my hair, sir—a
fine strapping young fellow, too, nearly six feet high, and with
the air of a soldier about him—I found out that he was a Volunteer—what do you think he discoursed about while he was cutting
my hair?"

"Radical politics, I suppose, taking London on your account
of it."

"The doctrine of Evolution, sir—Darwin and Huxley, and
the lot of them—hashed up somehow with the good time coming,
and the universal brotherhood, and I don't know what else!
Think of that! That's progress, I suppose! My sister says so.
I told her, and she wants to go and have her hair dressed by my
philosophic barber!"

"Then you are a Conservative?" said Christmas. "I don't
know much about English politics yet."

"Good heavens, my dear sir, neither do I! What could I
know or care about their confounded pettifogging parochial
affairs? I serve the cause of gentlemen all over the world. I
fought for the Turk against the Russian, and for the Pole against
the Russian, and for the Southern gentlemen against the Yankee
pedlars and wooden nutmeg sellers. Now I am engaged in my
own particular cause again. I am going to serve the King!"

"The King!—what king?"

"There are only two kings in Europe," said Cameron, rising
solemnly from his chair, as if to do reverence to the sacred names.
"His Majesty King Henry the Fifth of France, and his Majesty
King Charles the Seventh of Spain!" Here he raised his umbrella with the action of one who gives a military salute with a
sword. "I would serve Henry the Fifth of France if he would
only make a trial of his rights in the field, sir; but failing that I
give my services, such as they are, to the King of Spain."

"You are fighting for the Carlists, then?" Christmas asked,
with some curiosity. He had a vague notion somehow that the
Carlists only existed in newspapers and telegrams; and to meet
one face to face in London seemed almost as interesting as meeting with a Crusader.

"Well, yes. I am going to fight for them. I have been over,
and his Majesty was very kind; but these Spaniards are so
jealous of foreigners. I want to do something here which would
give me a claim—raise money, get arms—so that they must give
me a position equal to my rank. I was a brigadier-general in

the Confederate army. I resigned my commission because they wouldn't take my advice and I saw that things were going to the dogs. I knew it. I told poor Lee. He wouldn't see it. I resigned. No matter; I can't take a lower rank than that now anywhere. The King can't refuse me that. He ought to know how to treat a gentleman; don't you think so? I ought to get that rank."

" Certainly, certainly," Christmas answered, hurriedly, perceiving that something was expected of him.

" You think so—you really think so? You think I am not wrong in insisting on my proper rank? "

Christmas again muttered something which might be taken for assent, although he could hardly understand how such great devotion to the cause of Legitimacy could be reconciled with the gallant champion's anxiety about his own personal dignity.

" I am glad to hear you say so," Captain Cameron said, extending his hand and exchanging a solemn and formal grasp with Christmas : " I am very glad to hear you say so. The dignity of the military profession shall never be degraded in my person, whatever England may do. I *was* in the British army, as you are probably aware. I was once proud—proud, sir—to hold a captain's commission in the British army. I need not tell *you* that I am no longer proud of it. I have left that service, sir. You will not regard me now, if you please, as a British officer. No; I beg of you not."

" Certainly not, if you don't wish it. But I really don't know why."

" Good heavens! Don't know why? A gentleman, as you are, not know why another gentleman should not choose to be considered a British officer now? Of course you've been living out of civilisation; that explains. Why, sir, the British army now is to be officered by shoeblacks and potboys."

" Oh, come, that won't do even for my ignorance," said Christmas.

" It's the same thing. What is there to hinder it? I tell you, my dear fellow, your tailor's apprentice might have a commission now if he could only get up a little patter of knowledge and pass a ridiculous examination. And don't you see these are the very fellows to have the impudence to try for commissions; and they'll get them too, by Jove! Wait till England gets into a war, though, and see if she doesn't miss her gentlemen. Well, let who will stand it, I'll not; and so, my dear young friend, I serve his Majesty the king of Spain."

Again he raised his stalwart form and saluted the absent monarch with his umbrella.

" Well, sir," he said, about to take his leave, " we must see something of each other. I know the town, and can be useful to

you. I'll get you the furniture we talked of whenever you like;
and you must dine with me and come and see my sister. I shall
be in London for a few weeks yet. I think I shall have to take
an office—a room, you know ; quiet, and all that—recruiting.
Don't you see? Somewhere in this quarter. I wonder now
couldn't they give me a room in this place ; it would suit my
book capitally. I'll ask the housekeeper as I go out. But you
haven't fixed the day to dine with me and be introduced to my
sister. I know you'll like her ; she's a remarkably clever woman
—just in your line."

Captain Cameron must have been peculiarly quick of discern-
ment if he had already discovered what Pembroke's line was.
Certainly our young friend himself had not yet found it out,
although he had been trying hard for some time. But he was in
the delicious Cherubin age, which sees in every petticoat a possible
divinity—that charming poetic season just following, by so
strange and sudden a revolution, the schoolboy time which detests
and despises all girls. To Christmas the very name or thought
of a woman was interesting, and he therefore listened with far
greater attention to Captain Cameron now that he had heard of
a clever sister.

Captain Cameron stood meanwhile holding the handle of the
door ; and while still speaking to Christmas he heard footsteps
in the passage outside, and with his habitual quick-glancing
curiosity he looked over his shoulder through the half-open door.
Suddenly he flung the door wide open, plunged into the passage,
and called " Sir John! Sir John!" and Christmas saw him shaking
both the hands of a tall and portly personage.

"Come in, Sir John! Come in!" and the gallant Captain
with gentle force drew his friend into Christmas's room. "Now,
my dear fellow," he said "I do ask you to observe this extraordinary coincidence. Here is the very man of all others that I
want. I hadn't the remotest idea where to find him, and when
I come to make a call on you—whom I saw for the first time the
other day—I rush into the arms of my old friend. Let me make
my friends acquainted. Sir John, this is my young friend Mr
Pembroke. Pembroke, I am sure you cannot but know the name
of Sir John Challoner ; it has a European—no, by Jove! a world-
wide celebrity."

" Although you didn't know where to find me," said Sir John
with a soft smile.

Sir John Challoner was one of those men whose presence seems
to fill a room. Captain Cameron was tall and sinewy ; Sir John
was tall and full. He had a splendid head of dark hair, and his
beard and whiskers were glossy in their darkness. His forehead,
his teeth, the one hand which was ungloved were very white.
He looked a little too large for a lady's doctor, and a little too

well dressed for a banker. He might have been a president of the Royal Academy, or the chairman of a School Board perhaps. There was something at once grave and gracious about him which diffused an atmosphere of dignity through Christmas's little room.

"We are very intrusive, Mr. Pembroke," Sir John said, in a full sweet voice. "I have had the pleasure of seeing you before now, when your door happened to be open, and I could not help glancing in at your painted ceiling. I attend the board meetings of a company which has chambers on the first floor. We have a painted ceiling too; but not, I think, so fine as yours."

"Won't you come in and look at it?"

"Thank you, not now, certainly, while you are still at breakfast. We have disturbed you too much already."

"And how are you all at Durewoods—isn't it Durewoods?" Captain Cameron asked. "And how's my Lady Disdain?"

Sir John smiled quietly.

"She has grown a tall woman now," he said. "But we must not intrude on Mr. Pembroke any more just at present. Will you come upstairs with me, and I'll then accompany you with pleasure?"

So they took their leaves at last: Sir John with a gracious urbanity which left in the innocent mind of our English lad from Japan a vague impression that the great man—for Christmas was sure he must be a great man—had taken a special liking to him.

When they had gone, Christmas read over again the letter of Dione Lyle. He did not know that he quite liked the prospect it opened up to him. It was almost painful, in one sense, to think of meeting this unknown old friend—perhaps old love—of his father's. It was like the lightning on a record of some weakness which marred the sacredness of his father's memory. Then the unknown Mrs. or Miss Lyle—she must be elderly, and perhaps would be withered and dull. Perhaps, too, he did not quite relish the prospect of having to leave London so soon, when he found it so very delightful. Besides, he shrank from the chance of being questioned about his family affairs—he knew so little about his mother. On the whole he felt uncomfortable—filled with a vague presentiment of something chilling and discordant.

Yet he sat down at once and wrote a genial answer to the letter, and expressed his desire to be allowed to visit his father's old friend. He said but little in the letter about his father. He thought he would wait for all that until he saw the lady, and could form some opinion as to the probability of his father having really cared about her. As he addressed the letter it struck him for the first time that the place which Cameron had mentioned to Sir John, and where he assumed the latter to be living, had a name which sounded very like that of the place from which Dione Lyle dated. That surely, he thought, would be the very oddest of odd coincidences, and who, I wonder, is my Lady Disdain? For his quick Cherubin ears had caught that name.

He threw himself upon his sofa, looked at his painted ceiling, and thought.

CHAPTER II.

"IN A BALCONY."

Two or three days after the visit of Captain Cameron, Christmas found himself comfortably alone in a first-class carriage of one of the railway lines that connect London with the south-west coast. He had received a letter from "Miss" Lyle, as he now assumed her to be, asking him to pay her a visit of a few days, and he had plunged into the expedition at once. He had prepared for the visit mentally as for something melancholy and almost funereal, but just at present the sun and the scenery were too bright for anything gloomy to keep in the mind, and the run southward on the railway was a revel of delight to our youth. He had to change from his train to one upon a branch line less known to travel, and it was near to evening when he found himself deposited on a little pier in a nook of a broad blue bay, all glittering in the sun, and there seemed no way of getting any farther. When he asked a railway porter what he was to do next, he was told that the *Saucy Lass* would be up presently, and he waited for the coming of that ill-mannered demoiselle to help him to his journey's end. Very few passengers had come with him in the train, and of these only one apparently, a tall rather good-looking young man, who carried a rifle case, and had a sort of soldierly air about him, seemed to be going farther. This young man had come all the way from London, for Christmas remembered seeing him on the platform in the morning. Several persons were waiting for the boat who had not come in the train, for it need hardly be said that the *Saucy Lass* proved to be the little steamer that presently came puffing up to the pier, and having put ashore her passengers landward bound, turned round, took on board Christmas and his companions, and promptly plashed and spluttered out into the bay again.

The *Saucy Lass* churned her way pleasantly through the waves, and Christmas stood in her bow smoking a cigar, and very much enjoying the scene, the air, the water, the sun beginning to sink upon the tremulous sea, and the half-romantic novelty of the whole expedition. It was a huge bay that the steamer was crossing, a bay with islets rising here and there one covered with trees and soft verdure, one rocky and bare; another with some buildings on it like a fort or barrack of some kind. The *Saucy Lass* stopped at one or two little fishing villages and landed a passenger on a small stone pier, or, where there was no pier, screamed with her steam whistle for a boat to come off and relieve her of the traveller who desired to go ashore just there. The land ran up in considerable acclivity from the sea. It was well covered with wood in some parts, from amid which could be seen some pretty turrets or imposing roof; and a yacht lay at anchor here and there, an appanage doubtless of these pleasant residences. Where the bare soil appeared through wood or grass it was of a deep soft red. Everything was beautiful, and yet Christmas Pembroke hoped, as the steamer stopped at each place, that that would not prove to be his destination. For he saw no spot that seemed to him likely to be the retreat of his father's old friend. He could not associate her in his mind with turrets and a stately mansion and a yacht, and he could as yet see nothing between these and cottages of the poorest kind. And now looking westward to the horizon he could see nothing but the broad open sea, over which the sun was hovering in preparation for a plunge. By this time the boat had given out nearly all her passengers. Two or three women with heavy baskets, and a respectable looking personage in black, whom Christmas at once set down as a Methodist preacher, made up, with the tall young man already mentioned and Christmas himself, almost the whole of the company. Pembroke preferred to ask no questions about his destination. The mystery was far too pleasant to be voluntarily dispelled. If there were really some fairy islet just under that glowing sunset, and now hidden in its glow, all the better.

The steamer, however, suddenly turned from the sunset, and ploughed into a deep indentation of the shore, which was completely hidden by hills and trees until its opening actually presented itself. This proved to be a bay opening out of a bay—a small bay from a larger. The water darkened between the hills that now almost shut out the sun. The hills themselves seemed more sombre in their foliage. It was like a sudden passing from sunlight into evening shadow. The plashing of the steamer sounded noisy and intrusive in these quiet waters with their twilight shores. Christmas felt glad that there were other persons in the boat bound for the same place as he. He would not have liked to be solely responsible for the boisterous and bustling invasion of the puffing, vulgar *Saucy Lass.*

Christmas was yet of that age when one always feels a litt

nervous about arriving at any new place. He had not lived long enough or learned to think enough about himself in order to come to the conclusion that all people and places are very much alike when one comes to know them, and that it is not worth while troubling one's self beforehand with what he is certain to know all about in a few minutes or hours. He was now beginning to feel uncomfortable, and to wish that his destination were reached and the novelty of the thing over, anyhow. It was a relief to him when he saw at last a pier projecting itself into the water; and he could make out, in the gathering twilight, some white cottages a little way off, and roads rising high among the trees on the hill, and in the distance the roof of what seemed a large hall : and he knew that he had arrived. In a moment a plank was run out, and there was a little bustle of men on the pier, and the women dragged their baskets on shore. Christmas seized his little portmanteau, and strode on to the pier, with a delicious sense of fragrant hedgerow smells and summer evening atmosphere, and the breathing of trees and the salt savour of the water all blended with an odd feeling of perplexity—not quite knowing where he was or what he was to do next.

Nobody expected him, apparently, or paid the least attention to him. As he stood on the pier a little confused, and looking vaguely around him, a small open carriage drawn by two ponies rattled down the pier, and he saw that a lady was driving. For a moment he wondered whether this could be his father's old friend; but he soon saw that the lady was young, and that the other person who sat with her in her carriage was apparently her maid. The carriage stopped at the steamer, and then Christmas saw the respectable person he had taken for a Methodist preacher come out, dragging a hamper towards the carriage, and he was clearly only the young lady's servant.

"Not coming after all!" he heard her say when the man in black had answered some eager inquiry. "How very disappointing! What am I to do?"

Her servant apparently had no suggestion to make, for he only began fastening the hamper into the carriage, and he then turned the horses' heads round.

By this time it was clear to Christmas that nobody was waiting for him. He saw the captain of the steamer coming ashore, and he was just about to ask him whether he could direct him to the house of the lady who was to become his hostess. But the lady in the little carriage had seen him, and evidently remarked his forlorn and embarrassed condition. She whispered to her maid, and they both looked at Christmas, and then the lady spoke to the man in black, who presently approached, and touching his hat, asked him gravely if he would mind speaking to the young lady.

Christmas did not mind speaking to the young lady—or, perhaps, we should rather say, he did mind speaking to her, for he was a good deal confused, and was concerned more than a travelled youth ought to have been by the thought that he was in an awkward position.

" Pray excuse me," the young lady said, leaning forward as he approached; " I think you must be the gentleman Miss Lyle expects."

" Judging by appearances," Christmas replied, " I must rather be the gentleman whom Miss Lyle does not expect."

" Than you are he; I thought so. She doesn't expect you to-day, I know. Will you get in and let me take you to her ? We pass the gate."

" You are very kind," murmured Christmas, " but I ought not to give you any trouble."

" There isn't any—we shall pass her house, and I could not for her sake leave you drifting about here."

The maid and the man had by this time seated themselves behind. Christmas got in beside the young lady feeling that his adventure was beginning very agreeably.

" Let me relieve you of the reins," he said.

" Thank you; but hadn't I better keep them ? You don't know the way, and it grows dark. Now, then !"

She shook the reins, and the ponies rattled off. They clattered along the stony little pier, and struck off to the right. The village, or rather cluster of houses, lay on the left of the pier, for eyes looking inland. The lights were already beginning to twinkle a sort of thick yellow colour, as village candles by the seaside usually show. The hills and trees behind the village threw an immature darkness over the evening, and left to our new-comer only a confused and delicious sense of foliage, and sweet scents, and soft sky, and twinkling lights, and smoke ascending straight from the chimneys into the quiet air, and a throbbing sea. Along the verge of the sea they drove for a few minutes, and then turned up a steep road or lane nearly thatched over by the intertwining trees. The horses slackened their pace a little here.

Christmas could not manage to see his companion's face, for she had her veil down, but he was sure he saw her eyes sparkling brightly through the veil, and the girl wore a very pretty straw hat with a drooping feather, and she had no chignon, and all her movements were free and graceful, and she seemed perfectly mistress of herself and of the situation, and her voice was sweet, fresh, and animated. He was quite sure, therefore, that she must be a lovely creature, and he felt excited and interested and happy.

" You know Miss Lyle ?" he asked, as the pace of the ponies

allowed him a chance of being heard. "Perhaps you are a relative?"

"Oh no—only a friend."

"Do you live here?" Christmas was longing to ask, but he repressed himself.

"You have never seen Miss Lyle?" she asked.

"Never."

"How strange! But you are a relative of hers?"

"No, indeed. My father and she were old friends."

"Yet you have never seen her?"

"I have been living out of England for a long time. I only returned a short time since."

"She will be glad to see her old friends again," the young lady said thoughtfully. "She is just the woman to have friends."

"There are no old friends to be seen," Christmas answered. "My father is dead."

"I am very sorry," she said, looking at him quite earnestly. "My father is all the world to me."

"She has no mother," Christmas thought.

They reached the top of the hill, turned again to the right, rattled a few yards on, and stopped at a gate.

"This is the place," said the young lady. "Ring the bell, Martin, and loudly;" this was to the servant. Then to Christmas, who had descended, and was beginning to thank her: "Not a word of thanks, please. Good night. I shan't wait to see Miss Lyle now—I should be only in the way. Good night."

And so she gave her bridle reins a shake again, and the little carriage disappeared in the gathering dusk, and Christmas was left, portmanteau in hand, standing at the gate.

The bell had been rung so loudly that Christmas felt as if the responsibility of its shrill echoes was rather too heavy a burden for him to bear. But it was echoing for some time before any particular effect seemed to come of it. Christmas had no opportunity of forming an opinion as to the style of Miss Lyle's residence, for only an ivy-grown wall and a small gate or door of solid wood presented themselves to the road on which he stood. At last he heard a strong heavy lumbering sort of tramp ascending apparently some steps on the inner side of the wall, and the door was opened by a tall, grey old man dressed somewhat like a boatman. Christmas asked for the lady of the house and gave his name. The man listened apparently with great attention, but said nothing. He simply took Christmas's portmanteau and with a courteous gesture invited him to enter. A covered passage; a sort of arcade, with many steps and full of ferns and flower-pots, led downwards, and was lighted by the soft glow of an oil lamp. Christmas at first supposed that his guide was deaf or dumb, but as he began to descend the steps

with careless foot, and eyes wandering over the flowers and
ferns, the old man touched him on the arm, and said with great
deliberation—

" Mister ! Slow—None-quick. All right ?"

Christmas was less concerned about the kindly admonition to
take care of himself in the descent than relieved to find that his
escort's sententiousness apparently only came from a limited
knowledge of English. So far there was not much of commonplace about the household. From the depth of the covered
approach he was shown directly into the house, and passed
through a circular hall, softly lighted, into a reception room,
where he was left alone a moment or two, and began to glance at
books and engravings without seeing them. Then a pretty fresh-
cheeked and neatly-dressed country maiden came in, and told
him her mistress had not expected him that day, but that she
was very glad he had come, and please would he like to go to his
room? So he went to his room, which was up one flight of
stairs, the whole of the little house having apparently but two
floors ; and he found his room a very comfortable and rather
luxurious little apartment, with a window that opened on a
balcony ; and his mind was distracted from the work of dressing
by the books, engravings, bits of old china and Salviati glass
with which tables, shelves, and chimney-piece were crowded.

He hurried, however, to get dressed, for he was growing more
and more impatient to see his hostess. When he left his room he
met the little maiden again, who asked him would he please to
come into the balcony-room. He followed her into a room on
the same floor, the whole front of which apparently was balcony.
Here he was left alone for a few moments. Then he heard steps
—some very heavy—and the door opened ; and the old man he
had seen before came into the room, bringing with him and
supporting on his arm a living picture from Gainsborough.

The lady stood there in the faint light of the lamps—a lady
with full fair hair, and complexion at once bright and delicate,
and large deep eyes. She had a shawl of some soft light-blue
material thrown around her, above a dress of grey silk. There
was something old-English, pictorial, uncommon about the effect.
Where Christmas stood he could hardly perceive, what with the
faint light and the softly rounded outlines of her face, and the
fair complexion and the bright hair, that the lady was not young.
It was only when he approached that he could see the cruel lines
beneath the eyes which told that Age and Decay had opened their
intrenchments. A strange feeling of admiration, compassion,
and reverence came up in the young man's fresh and boyish
heart.

She held out her hand and welcomed him—with gesture and
look rather than words. Then she spoke a few words to the old

c

man in a dialect Christmas did not understand, and the man led
her to an arm-chair and seated her there, and left the room.
There was a moment of silence.

"Now," said Miss Lyle, "come near, and stand up and let me
look at you. Yes, you are like your father! You carry your
name written on your face—but he was handsomer, I think,
when he was your age. I have not seen him for many years. I
never saw him since he was young—since we were both young.
That seems so short a time—and now I am talking with his son!
We were great friends, and I must be fond of you for his sake.
Did he ever tell you anything about me?"

Christmas shook his head.

"Never talked of me?"

"Never—until—until he felt himself dying, and then he told
me that there was a lady in England, a friend whom he valued
highly, and he wished me to know her."

"And he told you my name, then?"

"Not even then."

"Then"—and her voice grew rather tremulous—"how do
you know that I am the friend?"

"Because," said Christmas, looking down and speaking in a
low tone, "he called out your name twice just before he died."

A flush passed over her face, and she remained silent for a
moment or two.

"That is enough," she said at length; "come nearer—stoop
down."

Christmas approached and bent down. She drew him towards
her, and kissed his forehead.

"That is for your father's memory, and for his sake," she
said quietly. "I hope you will be like him, my dear. They tell
me young men in London are very different now from what they
were when he was young, and I. He was very poor when he was
young, and so was I. He had great gifts—he might have made
a name, perhaps; but he had too pure a heart for much ambition.
We went our ways—things ought to have been different. I
suppose," she said, almost sharply, "your father appeared to you
quite a common-place, unheroic sort of person—the elderly man
who gave you money? That, I am told, is the way with London
lads now."

"I am not a London lad," said Christmas, with some resent-
ment in his voice. I'm very fond of London, but I know nothing
about it, and my father was the only friend I ever had. He
didn't talk sentiment, perhaps——"

"As other people do?" said the lady with a faint smile.
"No: he did not—even then—I mean ever. But he was the
truest gentleman and the noblest creature I ever knew. And if
you think I oughtn't to talk about him I can only say that he

was an older friend of mine than of yours. Well, and so you
have been all over the world? You must tell me all about your
travels. I don't want to known anything about your family
affairs or your private life in the past, though I hope you will
make me a little of a confidant in the future. Now you must
have some dinner. I hope you are not an epicure, like the young
fellows in the clubs of whom they tell me."

Christmas murmured something about not giving trouble.

"But you must dine. There was nothing to be had on the
way here, I know. I will keep you company, although I dined
earlier, for I did not expect you so very quickly. I thought you
would be too much engrossed with London to come away all at
once and entomb yourself in the country with an elderly woman
—an old woman I suppose you think me—just because she once
knew your father."

"I hope I have not come too soon. I ought to have given
you some longer notice, perhaps," Christmas said, for there
seemed a certain tone of perplexity and dissatisfaction in her
voice.

"Oh, no." She touched a bell near her; "Janet, some dinner
at once, and wine—you know: only don't keep Mr. Pembroke
waiting too long. Oh, no (again turning to Christmas), not too
soon for me, but I thought perhaps in a few days the place would
be quieter."

It seemed quiet enough to Christmas now; he did not know
what need or opening there was for greater quietness.

"I thought, perhaps, to have studied you all to myself a
little—no matter. But that is the reason why you were not
expected, and why no one went to the steamer to receive you.
Apropos, I hope you had no trouble in finding your way?"

"I was very fortunate, on the contrary: I met a young lady
who showed me the way."

"Met a young lady? What young lady? Is that a
chivalrous youth's fine way of talking of a fisher-girl?"

"Oh, no; a young lady who wore a hat and feather, and
drove in a pony carriage."

"*She* showed you the way?"

"She brought me to the gate very kindly in her carriage."

"Mr. Christmas, I begin to think you are not quite so modest
a person in the presence of young women as you seem to be in
the company of their elders. What on earth made you address
that young lady without any manner of introduction? Are
these the manners of Japan?"

Christmas laughed and coloured a little. "In fact, I didn't
address the young lady at all. She saw that I was a stranger
and didn't know what to do, and she sent her servant to me, and
then she said she knew you, and she offered me a seat in her
carriage."

"And you took it of course! Well, how do you like her?"

"I didn't see her face well," said Christmas; "It was growing dark, and she had her veil down."

"Indeed, and didn't once throw up her veil—just for a moment?"

"Not even for a moment."

"What a pity! But you'll see her face to-morrow, without a veil—*that* I can promise you! What an odd chance that she should have been there just at the time. Well, it can't be helped now."

"Will anything dreadful happen?" Christmas asked, with a smile.

"Nothing dreadful will happen to *her*, I am quite sure."

"She seems a very nice girl," said Christmas, plucking up courage.

"She is a very nice girl, Mr. Christmas—if you will use words in a wrong and slangy way. She is a very nice girl to *me*, and a very good girl. But I am a friend and a woman—a woman thirty years too old for rivalry. My old follower Merlin—the man who gives me his arm—I am a feeble walker—adores her, and so does Merlin's dog. They all spoil her—*I* don't; but she is fond of me all the same, I *think*. But Merlin and Merlin's dog and I may be very happy and safe where other creatures are in danger. Dinner, Janet? Thanks. Now, Mr. Christmas, if you will give me your arm, and let me lean rather heavily on your shoulder as we go down stairs, we can do without Merlin for once. I used to be a good walker long ago. When we have dined we will come back here and sit in the balcony."

The *tête-à-tête* dinner was at first a little trying to Christmas, who was rather a shy youth. His hostess did not eat, but sat and helped him and talked to him. Her manners were quite new and strange to him, and, indeed, he knew very little of the society of women. In Miss Lyle there was a curious mixture of the grace of youth and the easy, self-possessed confidence of age. When he listened without looking up, he might sometimes have thought that he was listening to a grandmother, and sometimes to a woman of five and twenty. Even when he looked at her, and her head was turned half away, and he only saw the fair hair, the softly rounded cheek, and the shoulder, he might have believed her still in the very prime of her womanhood. Her manner, too, puzzled him, and her allusions to her early poverty. Now she seemed like one always accustomed to something like luxury, and always used, too, to admiration. The disappointment which sometimes expressed itself in her manner was rather that of one who has won and found success itself a barren thing, than of one who has tried and failed. Certainly nobody could have answered less to Christmas's preconceived ideas of an old maid.

When dinner was over—and it was a very nice little dinner—they returned to the balcony-room as it was called, and they sat in the balcony. It was a soft, mild evening, and the air was sweetened by the smell of flowers and grass, and savoured by the keener breath of the sea. The night was clear, although no moon had risen; and from the balcony the eye wandered over trees and a scattered village down to the sea. The silver-grey of the sea was blackened at one point by the long pier, at the end of which the light of the *Saucy Lass* now "stuck fiery off." The balcony was low—but one short flight of stairs above the ground floor.

Miss Lyle settled herself in a chair in the balcony, and then, leaning over, called to Janet, who heard her from beneath, and brought her a shawl, in which she wrapped herself. Whenever she wanted any attendance she thus leaned over the balcony and called for Janet.

"I pass all the fine evenings in this balcony," said Miss Lyle. "I sit and dream here, and I live in the past and the present at once. Now I want to hear a great deal about yourself—what you have been doing, and what you are going to do. I have talked in the same way with your father!"

And Christmas soon found himself talking, as if to some confidential and sympathetic old friend of his past life, his education, his career, as yet unbegun, until it seemed impossible to believe that he had only left London that morning, and that he still hardly knew who his companion and hostess was.

A little pause came at one time, when Christmas had been giving some reminiscences of his life in Japan, and had made a casual allusion to his father's death. He did not like to touch upon the subject, for it affected him even yet almost as much as if he had been a girl thinking of her lost mother—for all his delight in London, his painted chamber there, and his holiday.

His hostess looked silently over the water, leaning her arm on the balcony, and her chin in her hand.

"It grows late," she said, suddenly, "and cold, I think. Our early summer evenings are chill here, and you must be tired. You were asking me something, were you not? about Merlin, I think—was it?"

Christmas did not remember that he had been asking her about Merlin, but he did not say so; and he was glad to hear something about the odd old man.

"Merlin," said his hostess, "is a Breton; he was a boatman and a fisherman. When I had a home in Brittany, in one of the places on the coast, I was fond of boating, and he and his son were my boatmen. The son had a fine voice and some musical taste, and I knew people then, and tried to help him to become a singer. He died, poor fellow!—he was drowned trying to save

some people; and Merlin had no one left: he was a widower.
I was coming here to settle, and he liked to come with me. I
couldn't do without him now—you will find him very useful.
He must take you out in a boat to-morrow. I hardly ever go
now. But you must humour his one weakness, mind, Mr.
Christmas."

"Only tell me what it is."

"He thinks he speaks English, and if he doesn't understand
what you say he will never admit it. Speak to him as if he did,
and he will generally catch up some idea of what you mean. I
can't help you to understand him—you must do the best you
can—for you don't understand his own language, I suppose.
His French is still worse than his English."

"I shall manage to get on with him," said Christmas. "It
shan't be my fault if we are not friends. I was afraid at first
that he was dumb."

"Oh, he has plenty of talk when he likes, and he thinks he
knows everything. He sometimes almost talks me to death, but
I don't mind. It comes naturally to me to humour him now,
and I suppose he finds it natural to humour me. He looks to
me altogether, and he is really attached to me. When you come
to my time of life, Mr. Christmas, you will perhaps understand
the value of having some one—any one—attached to you. But
I hope that you will not have had my experience, and that you
will have closer ties. Still, Merlin is better than no one!"

Her voice seemed to have grown old in a strange sort of way
as she spoke.

"How delicious the sound of that sea is," Christmas said—
to say anything.

"It tells you of the future," said Miss Lyle, looking kindly
at him, "and me of the past. That is why the sea is such good
company; it has a tone for every one's mood. It is better than
music, I think, for music jars terribly sometimes. Can you
sing?"

"After a fashion," Christmas answered.

"You shall sing to me, but not now; some other time. It is
late, and you want rest. Good-night, Chris!"

He had never been called "Chris" in his life before, but only
formal "Christmas." But there was something inexpressibly
touching in her tone, and he knew that she was not thinking of
him then.

CHAPTER III.

"CLAUDE MELNOTTE."

THERE was great joy on the night of Christmas's arrival—but not for that event—in the house of the widow Cramp, who lived in one of the best of the cottages near the sea. Mrs. Cramp's son had come all the way from London to spend a whole week of holiday with her. Mrs. Cramp had at one period of her life been a lady's maid, and then she married a ship carpenter, who settled her in Durewoods while he made his voyages: and he built the house for her in which she still lived. He was a careful, saving man, and when he died at sea he left her tolerably well to do—that is, above actual want—and with one growing son, who it had always been his wish should never go to sea. Mrs. Cramp had a step-brother in London, Professor Carpetts, of Camden Town. Professor Carpetts had, in the strictest sense, taken his degree and his title. He had conferred his rank upon himself, and was a professor of hairdressing. Professor Carpetts offered to bring up young Natty Cramp to his own calling, than which nothing could be more genteel; and young Natty was sent to London accordingly. Every year since that time Natty had come to Durewoods to spend his week's holiday with his mother; and so he came this year. He is a tall young fellow, naturally inclined to stoop, and therefore occasionally pulling himself up and standing with preternatural erectness. He has thick fair hair, and a growing moustache, to the development of which every secret known to Professor Carpetts' branch of science had been applied with zeal and hope. Natty has a good-looking but rather sheepish face, with prominent blue eyes and colourless eyebrows. He strode along to his mother's cottage with a military-looking black portmanteau in one hand and a rifle-case in the other. He was, in fact, the tall young man who had been a fellow-passenger with Christmas in the *Saucy Lass*, but the moment the steamer reached the pier he leaped ashore like another Protesilaus, without the catastrophe. So he had not seen what became of Christmas.

Mrs. Cramp had been watching the approach of the steamer from the first moment when its smoke was seen above the headland that guarded the inner bay. She was waiting at the door for her son, and gazed with full delight and pride at his tall, swaying figure as he drew near.

"Why, Natty, how you have grown, I do declare. Never!"

"Five feet eleven and a half, mother.   All but six feet. Think of that!"

"Your poor father was five feet ten in his stockings—and you've outgrown him!   Well, well."   And a tear of maternal pride sparkled in her eyes as she wished his father could see him now.

They had entered the house now, and Natty was putting down his portmanteau.

"Now I know what's in that," said his mother, glancing proudly from the portmanteau to the son.

"Yes, mother," Natty replied, with a sort of blush.   "It's the uniform.   To-morrow I'll put it on.   You haven't an idea how well it looks.   And the sword bayonet."

"The gun isn't loaded, Natty?"

"Loaded!   Oh, no.   Mustn't carry one's rifle loaded at ordinary drill or parade, mother," Natty replied, with an air at once careless and soldierly.

Natty Cramp had, it is almost needless to say, become a Volunteer.   He had marched in Hyde Park before royal personages.   His mother was perfectly convinced that the Queen must have looked at him and singled him out from all the rest. Natty laughed at this nonsense of his mother's, but he had a secret modest hope, which hardly dared to acknowledge its existence, that he was not quite wrong when he fancied one memorable day that the Princess of Wales did cast a glance at him.   Natty was that day driven into a mood of passionate loyalty.   He had read of the Swiss Guards—he had read many books—and he thought no success on earth could be more enviable than the pride and delight of giving up one's life in defending the threshold of some (we do not say which) lovely princess.

"Now, Natty dear, you'll have your supper," his mother said, soothingly.   "You must be tired and hungry.   You'll not mind having your supper in this little room to-night, will you, dear? But you don't know where you're going to be put to-morrow, I'll be bound.   Come now."

She was a comely woman, verging on fatness, and had dressed herself for this occasion, so that she looked quite the lady, as all her neighbours would have willingly said of her. Indeed, they looked up to her greatly as one who had seen in her day the interior of grand houses, and could speak beautiful English.   Natty surveyed her with eyes of no little pride; although, needless to say, *he* had seen ladies.   In his occupation one sees ladies pretty often, and ought to know what they are like.   He was studying his mother's *coiffure* with something of a professional air, and his attention was therefore a little distracted from her question.

"No, mother: I don't know."

"You are to have the drawing-room and bed-room all to yourself. I wouldn't let them, Natty, not to any one this week. No, says I to myself, my son is a man now, and a Volunteer, and when he comes for his holiday once in the year his mother isn't going to let him play second fiddle to any lodger. There, Nat!"

Nat's face glowed with good-natured pride. Since his earliest days that drawing-room, as it was called, had been a sacred apartment in his eyes. Mrs. Cramp had always helped out her means of living by letting that room and bed-room to such lodgers as might happen to come that way during the summer and autumn, and while it was not so occupied she still held it ready for any emergency. There were one or two families of wealthy people near who might sometimes find that they had a guest too many for their accommodation, and would send a young bachelor now and then to sleep for a night or two at Mrs. Cramp's. Therefore the front room and bed-room were always chambers of great distinction in the eyes of Nat, and his own installation there now was a tribute to his dignity of manhood and position such as a gracious Sovereign could hardly have surpassed. He made some weak and stammering protest about his mother putting herself out for him, but was immensely delighted.

Then supper was prepared, and Mrs. Cramp looked on happy to see her son eat. The supper was a little of a trial, too, to Nat's good nature and filial devotion. His mother had taken unspeakable trouble to heap the table with all the dainties which Nat had loved from his childhood. There was the strawberry jam which she had for years and years regarded as identified with the rejoicing of his annual holiday. There was the cake which she always made with her own hands, and according to his particular fancy. She could not believe in a holiday of Nat's without that cake, and she had often been haunted with cruel misgivings that his wife, when he got one, would never know how to make that cake, and would not allow his mother to make it for him. Alas! Nathaniel Cramp, the Volunteer, the romantic student and reader of books, had outgrown that jam and that cake! He smoked cigars now, and had coloured a meerschaum, and had succeeded to all the embarrassing and mournful dignity of manhood. But he knew how his mother had striven to please him, and he would have suffered any inconvenience rather than allow it to be seen that she had taken all her trouble for nothing. He did his best. He trampled down the pride of rising manhood, and he endeavoured to discipline his rebellious palate. But though he could eat the jam and the cake, he could not put on the old air of boyish relish. His mother saw it and felt a little pang. The pride of having a grown-up son has its alloy, too!

The scent of the strawberry jam had for the moment something oppressive in it to her. It brought her heart, as she might have said, to her mouth. For the first time she realised to herself the truth that she must lose her boy.

The mother's pride, however, turned itself again to rejoice in the son who was a man, and she began to ask after his affairs and his prospects.

"And so you've gone into Wigmore Street! I remember Wigmore Street so well—when we were living in Harley Street—that's when I was with Lady Sarah. It must be changed now ever so much. Wigmore Street! That's a great step for the Professor, Nat."

"For Mr. Carpetts, mother." Nat moved about in his chair rather uneasily. "He don't call himself Professor now, you know."

"No, Nat? Why not?"

"Well, you see, Professor won't do in a place like Wigmore Street. Professor is all very well for Camden Town or the Surrey side—they wouldn't know, But in the West End people know that a hairdresser ain't—I mean isn't a professor. People would only laugh at him. No respectable person would enter his cutting-room. It's vulgarity, mother—it's only fit for a Cheap Jack. I told the governor—I mean, I told Mr. Carpetts—so. It's absurd, you know," continued Nat, waxing angry. "When we talk of professor now in London, we mean a man like 'Uxley—like Huxley, mother—or that sort—not hairdressers."

"Yes," said his mother, "I suppose so, Nat." But she was sorry for the loss of the title. "Then you'll not call yourself Professor Cramp when you come into the business."

"Mother," said Nat, gravely, "don't you deceive yourself. I'll never come into that business."

"No, Nat! Good gracious, dear, why not?"

"That's no business for a man—for one who feels that he is a man! I can bear it for the time, but not for ever. Is this an age when a man—a man!—ought to spend his life dressing the heads of a parcel of women?"

"Are they very vexing, Nat dear—hard to please, and all that?"

"Who, mother?"

"The ladies, you know, who come to have their hair dressed. I know something of them, Nat; but you mustn't mind them, dear. They're all like that, you know."

Nat fidgeted much in his chair, and looked at his mother uneasily, and with a little impatience. He could hardly stand, even from her, any allusion to the dressing of ladies' hair—the particular branch of his calling in which he was most successful and of which unluckily he was most ashamed.

" Oh, it ain't that, mother—I mean it is not that." Nat had imposed upon himself the penalty of always deliberately correcting himself when he said anything which he considered ungrammatical or vulgar. "I don't care about that in particular. I hate the whole business. I'll cut the whole concern. I am not made for *that*. Is this an age, mother, when a man with feelings and a soul, and no end of aspirations, ought to be cutting people's aair ? "

"But, Nat, my dear boy," his mother pleaded, alarmed at these tokens of a rebellious spirit, " somebody must do it, you know."

"Let 'em do it—anybody who likes! There are cads enough who are fit for nothing else ! Let old Carpetts do it! Mother, your son is made for something better. We live in a great age, mother."

" Yes, dear."

" An age of progress and of science! The old world, mother, is gone up in fire ! " Nat exclaimed fervently, adopting some words of Carlyle which had stamped themselves deeply on his memory.

" Good gracious," murmured Mrs. Cramp.

" A new order of things is coming; and the priesthood oᶠ greatness is to have its turn. What are ranks and classes when compared with Immensity ? The creed of the new world is Evolution and the Brotherhood of Man ! "

" Nat, my dear, I don't like to hear you talk that way."

" You don't understand, mother," and he now spoke in a lordly and protecting sort of way, " and it would only trouble you if I tried to explain. But this isn't a time for a man who feels that he has thoughts and a brain to spend the fruitful years of his life in a hair-cutting room. Don't be alarmed, I shan't do anything rash; but when your son comes next year you shall see before you, mother, a man—a man who has proved his title to manhood—and not a barber's boy ! "

He rose with the fire of his eloquence and emotion. But in rising he knocked over a tea-cup and felt rather foolish, for he saw his mother look alarmed at her fallen china.

" 'Tisn't broken, mother," he said, and he put the cup un‐injured in its saucer. But the spell was broken if the cup was not, and he could not resume his interrupted outpouring of soul. "After all, she couldn't understand me," he thought. " I should only alarm her."

Indeed he had alarmed her. She kept glancing at him uneasily every now and then. She saw that she and he could understand each other no more, and that her boy was drifting out on some sea where she could no longer be his guide or even companion. It might perhaps lead to glory and greatness. Why

should not her boy become a great man? But anyhow the days
were gone when she could receive all her son's confidences in his
holiday and be his provider of joy. Nat had relapsed into silence.
Mrs. Cramp rose and took up the pot of strawberry jam, out of
which so little had been eaten, and put it away with a sigh.
The action was sadly symbolic. The little sweet-meat pot
became for the moment consecrated into a sort of funeral urn in
which the ashes of a happy anxious time were enclosed.

Mrs. Cramp felt no wonder, hardly any new shock, when,
after she had told him a good deal of local gossip, Nat rose,
stretched himself, and said he would smoke a cigar on the road
to the pier.

" And don't you wait up, mother. I'll lock the door."

In that quiet place the hall-doors usually stood open until
the latest inmate was going to bed. Even if that latest inmate
should forget to lock the door it would not matter much.

Mrs. Cramp obeyed the orders of her son now as she used to
obey those of his father. Perhaps she had never since her
widowhood began felt so keenly how much she missed her husband. She felt so helpless and ignorant, so powerless to do
anything but see her boy drift away from her. She had a vague
idea that perhaps he was in love with some lady above his
station. She could not sleep for perplexing and profitless
conjecture.

Meanwhile Nathaniel soothed his lonely spirit by walking
down to the sea and smoking a cigar. His mother's conjecture
about a love affair was wrong. Nat was not in love as yet with
anybody but himself, and not in love with himself in the strict
sense, but only with the possibility of himself, a sort of glorified
Eidolon of himself which he had constructed, and up to the
standard of which he hoped to bring himself one day. He had
never felt any pulsation of love for one of the ladies who came
to have their hair dressed in Camden Town or even in Wigmore
Street. They were not generally young in either place, and
when they were young they were not always pretty ; and even
if they were pretty they did not look so with their hair down
and their peignoirs around their necks. Moreover, those in
Camden Town he usually looked upon as ignorant and vulgar
young women who probably went with excursion parties to
Epping Forest, and those in Wigmore Street were coldly insolent
and evidently looked on him as what Shelley calls (Nat read
Shelley) a " mechanised automaton."

Nor was there any particular purpose indicated in Nat's
eloquent outpourings. He was only a cleverish untaught young
fellow who, by force of reading everything he could get at, had
read himself into self-conceit and discontent, and who was therefore in imagination constantly striking the stars with his sublime

head. For a long time poor Nat had been compelled to lead two lives quite distinct from each other. There was his real life when he worked and drudged faithfully in the calling which grew every day more and more distasteful to him. There was his ideal life when he sat up of nights in his bedroom reading " Locksley Hall " and " Clara Vere de Vere," and Mrs. Browning's " Lady Geraldine," and Robert Browning's " Evelyn Hope ; " studying Darwin, and Mill's " Liberty," and Carlyle's " French Revolution," and any of Huxley's lectures that he could get ; and he mixed the whole up together in a *mélange* of half-comprehended poetry and quarter-comprehended philosophy and science. It was a delightful part of his ideal life, too, when he joined a Volunteer Corps and wore a dark green uniform and carried a rifle with sword-bayonet, and marched at Wimbledon and was inspected in Hyde Park. These days of military masquerade were a sort of heroic heaven to him. Other young men whom he knew were but Tom, Dick, and Harry in their Volunteer uniforms. Nat in that garb was a hero of romance, a splendid soldier of fortune, a Quentin Durward, a D'Artagnan, a Claude Melnotte, a wild-Mahratta-battle warrior. Of late he had indeed begun to feel some scruples. He attended scientific and quasi-religious lectures on Sundays, and he had spoken in the discussions of broad-thinking philosophical societies ; and he was not quite sure about the fitness of the hero's trade for the great service of humanity and the future. Still the uniform had its fascination, and the heroic dream was not all dreamed out yet. These were Nat Cramp's two lives. We have called the one real and the other ideal ; but Nat was convinced, and so perhaps should we be, that the real Nathaniel Cramp was the hero of the ideal life and that the other was only his soulless, bloodless shadow.

CHAPTER IV.

"MY LADY DISDAIN."

DUREWOODS was, generally speaking, the name of the place in which Christmas found himself quartered for the hour. But it was not easy to say that there was any particular district or area specially covered by the name of Durewoods, or, indeed, any particular place to which the name strictly applied. The little arm of the sea, the narrow inlet from the great broad bay, at the inland end at which the village stood, was never called Durewoods bay or creek, or anything of the kind. Probably the

beautiful growth of trees that covered the slope of the rising
shores on either side had once been called Durewoods, and hence
the name had spread itself over the whole place. But these
woods were not now called Durewoods; they were simply called
" the plantation." Neither was the village called Durewoods;
people only spoke of it as " the cottages." The village had, in
fact, no corporate existence, no soul, and no name. It never did
anything as a community; it never acted together, or had any
apparent consciousness that it was a whole. The cottages were
there—had been built there somehow for the convenience chiefly
of the fisherfolk ; and that was all that anybody knew. The row
of tenements in front of the water was called " the cottages," the
few residences of a better class that stood on the hills were
spoken of as " the houses," and the one large and pretentious-
looking mansion was the Hall. Probably this had once been
called Durewoods Hall; but, if so, the name had lapsed into
disuse. Yet the place, taken collectively—Hall, houses, cottages,
and all—was called Durewoods. The *Saucy Lass* came and went
between " Durewoods " and other places, and she lay generally
of nights off " Durewoods " pier.

There were very few families of what might be called social
position living in and about Durewoods. One or two retired
officials of the Customs had come thither from the large seaports
near and settled for the quiet and the cheapness. A clergyman
and a Dissenting minister, and a doctor who was attached to a
neighbouring dispensary were there; and the captain of the
Saucy Lass walked home to his family abode there among the
trees every night. These and a few other residents occupied
"the houses." The Hall had been for many years unoccupied
until it came by some legal process or other out of the hands of
its ancient possessors into those of a clever, handsome, portly
gentleman from London, who was vaguely known down there as
having something to do with companies and finance. This gentleman came to Durewoods several times before he made up his
mind to occupy the Hall himself. He brought down architects
and surveyors, and various men of business from London, and
studied the matter a good deal. At last he made up his mind,
had the place put into repair, closed up half the building, furnished the rest, employed gardeners on the grounds, which were
not large, and spent great part of one mild winter there. Presently he brought his daughter there, his only child—he was a
widower—and settled her there with a housekeeper and a
companion; and he used to bring friends down every now and
then. The clergyman, the minister, the doctor, the retired
Customs' officials, and the captain of the *Saucy Lass*, all thought
Mr. John Challoner a great man, and were delighted to be in his
favour; but Durewoods, as a whole—if we may speak thus of

it—never took to him. To Durewoods he was always a stranger;
and he sealed finally its mind against him when he decided upon
occupying only half the Hall. In time he became Sir John
Challoner, Baronet; but Durewoods did not care. Of course, in
Durewoods we do not, in this sense, take in Mrs. Cramp. She
herself was but a settler and a stranger. She had been a lady's
maid; she had been frequently called in to assist Sir John's
housekeeper at the Hall, and she had a sort of professional
devotion to her social superiors anyhow.

Another stranger and settler was Miss Lyle. The pretty
little place which she occupied now had been discovered and
bought up for her by Sir John Challoner, and the house was
altered and almost rebuilt to suit her peculiar tastes and habits.
She came there with her trusty henchman, Merlin, several years
ago, and hardly ever stirred outside her own gate, unless when
she went upon the water with Merlin for her boatman. So far
as people knew her, they liked her, and the parents of Janet—a
Durewoods lass—and Janet herself, were greatly attached to her.
As for Merlin, his popularity was soon universal. He fell in
with the ways of the fishermen like a brother of the craft, and
would pass hours with them lounging along the shore, examin-
ing their boats, and helping to mend their nets. How any
interchange of ideas was at first effected it would be hard to
guess, but Merlin and the fishermen seemed from the first
to understand each other, as dogs or horses do. Merlin used
to stroll round to the cottages when the husbands were at sea,
and reassure the wives if the expeditions proved long and dangerous, and sing strange wild songs to the children, and tell
thrilling stories of adventures which had befallen himself on the
waves. These were nearly all narratives in pantomime, sharp
fizzing sounds being understood to represent flashes of lightning,
vehement undulatory motions of the hands being unmistakable
symbols of the mountainous billows, and, of course, the dullest
spectator could not fail to comprehend the final *tableau*, which
pictured Merlin himself swimming heroically to the wreck, or
rowing his boat thither, and saving somebody under conditions
of difficulty unparalleled. Merlin soon became an authority,
and a rather dogmatic one, upon most things, and acquired such
a hold over the respect of his neighbours, that even the fact of
his being seen to cross himself and tell over his beads like a
faithful Catholic, did not unseat him from his position of dignity.
There was, indeed, one legend which he was particularly fond of
telling, and which might, under other conditions, have wrought
him harm with his compeers. This was a tale of a fearful storm,
in which some fishers, and it was generally understood Merlin
himself among them, had become involved off the coast of
Brittany, and in which their lives were positively forfeit, until

suddenly the skies opened, a light shone on them, and a lady appeared in the heavens—beyond doubt the Virgin herself—and guided their boat safely to a peaceful creek where the storm raged no more. But, luckily for Merlin, the description of the lights "on the top," by which he meant "above," and the frequent repetition of the word "she," misled his auditory, and, aided by the happy effect of his gestures, they always understood that at the critical moment the lights of a Channel steamer hove in sight, and that the imperilled boatmen were quietly taken on board. So that the story, however thrilling and dramatic, did not tax their powers of sound Protestant belief any more than the melodious narrative of the vessel's rescue in the Bay of Biscay.

Merlin's popularity reflected itself a good deal upon Merlin's mistress. She was understood to have been a very great person of some sort, and to have lived in some splendid world whereof Durewoods had but a vague conception, and to have now retired into a sort of half-penitential privacy. Sir John Challoner and his guests always treated her with great respect, and whenever an artist or a group of artists came—as sometimes would happen in the summer—to make sketches at Durewoods, they always sent up their cards to her house, and were generally received by her. Durewoods was in a sort of way a little proud of this.

In this place had Miss Marie Challoner spent some seven or eight years. She had for society first her governess or companion, and then Miss Dione Lyle. As she grew up, being an independent and spirited young woman, not, perhaps, very easy to please in friends, she got rid of all professional companionship, and pleased herself by not even having a housekeeper, but taking the reins of domestic government in her own hands. It amused her to learn how to regulate and order things, and even to make mistakes and find out by experience of mistake the way to the right. When she was in any household difficulty she consulted Mrs. Cramp, and when she was in any intellectual perplexity she betook herself to Miss Dione Lyle. So her life went on, its highest effort at variety being when her father took her for a few days to Ostend or Paris, or, perhaps, Brighton; for he was a busy man, who rarely cared to go beyond the distance of a night's post from London. For the most part, she had to find her own intellectual and moral food as best she could around her; to live on the green leaves of her own trees, so to speak, like the sloth, whom otherwise she did not in the least resemble.

Miss Challoner had driven to the pier on the night of Christmas's arrival for the purpose of meeting her father. She found, instead, only his servant, who brought a message to tell her that he could not come for some days, and that he would then bring a few guests with him. This was a double disappointment to her; first, because her father had not come at once, and next, because when he was to come he was to bring guests with him. Miss Challoner did not greatly care, as a rule, for her father's guests. They wanted colour, she said.

My Lady Disdain was an early riser, although by no means given to early going to rest. On the contrary, she revelled a good deal in the unholy pleasure of sitting up till all hours in her bedroom, reading of nights. She had a great deal of spare time when her father was not at home; and it would have hung terribly upon her hands sometimes but that she had a very active intellect, and was fond of reading. She knew nothing, as yet, of a London season. Her father had preferred to keep her in the country thus far, but he talked now, as she was nearly twenty years old, of setting up a regular establishment in town, and introducing her formally to London life. She had, hitherto, only known London as a child knows it; as a place where she was taken to theatres, and had drives in parks. She had gone through the earlier part of what is understood to be a girl's education in Bath and in Paris, and when she was twelve years old she settled down at the house which her father had bought at Durewoods. Here she had no companionship when she had got rid of her governess but that of her father when he could absent himself from town, and that of the visitors he brought with him, and the school friends who occasionally came to spend a few weeks with her, and, for some years, the frequent association with Miss Lyle. Therefore, this young lady lived a good deal of her time in romance, in looking out for adventures, of which she was to be the heroine, and in wondering that nothing particular was ever happening in life. She would sometimes have welcomed anything almost, even pain itself, which varied a little the sweet monotony of her existence. So whenever a new acquaintance came in her way, she eagerly approached him or her, sought out for something refreshing and remarkable, generally failed to find it, and then let the new comer pass. She was perfectly sincere where sometimes people thought her insincere; utterly unaffected where censors occasionally complained of affectation. She had no more idea of deceit or fickleness when, having welcomed a new acquaintance yesterday, she turned away from him or her to-day, than one who, seeking to arrive at a particular place, and thinking he has found the right way, turns down a certain street in eager hopefulness, and then, seeing that he is mistaken, turns back and tries another. Has the street he leaves a right to complain that it has been treated badly? If not, then neither had any of Miss Challoner's acquaintances a right to say that she had treated them ill, when, finding that there was nothing specially interesting or fine about them, she showed no further care for their society.

D

This morning of which we are now talking, Miss Challoner felt rather anxious to know what sort of person Christmas Pembroke, Miss Lyle's guest, might turn out to be. She was pleased with the chance-meeting at the pier, and she took him under her charge out of pure good-nature. This was the more good-natured on her part because in the evening dusk he seemed to her at first only an overgrown boy, and she was not fond of boys. Their shyness, their brusque indifference to all topics but their own, their big hands, their stolid or boisterous egotism, their savage blindness to all beauty of scenery, sun, or sky, their clumsy prosaicism of nature, hurt her sensitive æstheticism. When she first took up Christmas Pembroke she assumed that he would prove to be only a stupid boy. But the few words which they interchanged, and the one or two glimpses into his past life which his words gave, and particularly the manner in which he spoke of his father's death, showed her that he had at least had some of a man's troubles, and touched her quick sympathies. Even if he was little better than a boy he had not been brought up as English boys are. He must have some other topics besides those which the boys have in *Punch.*

However, the duties of life had to go on, and the young lady set herself to perform her part of them. She would have to make some preparations for her visitors, and she thought the best thing she could do would be to go at once to the cottages and consult Mrs. Cramp. So she ordered out her little pony-carriage, and with the Methodistical Martin seated behind, she drove along the pleasant roads under the trees. She was fond of driving, and indeed of all exercises—riding, walking, swimming, and rowing. Likewise she was fond of doing things for herself, as she had preferred to be her father's housekeeper rather than have the duties handed over to somebody else. Many of her energetic and independent ways might have earned her in London the reputation of eccentricity, but here in Durewoods she could do as she liked, and she was one of those happily moulded women who cannot do anything ungracefully.

The little carriage rattled up to Mrs. Cramp's door, and Marie Challoner leaped lightly out, and threw the reins to her servant. The door stood open, and the visitor came plump into what might be called Mrs. Cramp's parlour. But Marie suddenly stopped on the threshold, for an unexpected sight met her eyes, and an unwonted form obstructed her progress. This was a tall, martial figure in dark green uniform, with a belt and a cartouche-box and a sword-bayonet, and wearing a smart kepi. The warrior was exhibiting himself as on parade for the benefit of Mrs. Cramp, who looked on with delighted eyes. The rustle of Miss Challoner's dress disturbed the parade. Mrs. Cramp stepped forward, all beaming with pride and welcome, to receive the young lady, and the soldier turned round, started, blushed, plucked off his kepi, let it fall, made an effort to pick it up, missed it, and looked remarkably confused.

Mrs. Cramp was only happy and proud.

"This is my son, Miss Challoner; my son Nathaniel. You used to know him, but he's outgrown everything this year or two."

Nat, it must be owned, looked rather abashed for a warrior; and hardly raised his eyes to meet the large, deep, friendly eyes that turned so suddenly on him.

"This your son—this my old friend Natty?" the young lady exclaimed. "Why, so it is! Natty himself, turned into a tall soldier—a field officer, or a general, or something! I should never have thought it! But now that I look at him I can discover some likeness of my old friend when he was a boy."

"He has grown, Miss Challoner, sure enough," his mother observed with pride, as Marie put her hand frankly into that of the awkward and palpitating youth.

"What am I to call you now—not Natty any longer, I suppose? Mr. Nathaniel? or Captain Nathaniel? That is a very becoming uniform—what is it?"

"It's the West Pimlico Volunteers, Miss Challoner," said Nathaniel, rising to a certain confidence in the pride of being a Volunteer, and picking up his kepi.

"You look quite a soldier, Natty—oh, I mean Mr. Nathaniel."

"Do—do call me Natty," the Volunteer pleaded; and he took courage to look up into her bright, kindly, and yet humorous eyes. "It sounds so delightful—just like old times."

"Well then, Natty!" the obliging young lady answered. "Natty! Yes, it does sound like very pleasant old times. Are you fond of reading still, Natty? He used to be quite a student, Mrs. Cramp—don't you remember? I used to lend him books— poetry, I think, for the most part. Yes, and he used to write verses! Do you still write verses, Natty? Yes—you do; I can see it in your look! You must show me something you have written—you must indeed."

"That he shall!" his mother declared.

"And you must come and see me—you must bring him, Mrs. Cramp. To-day will you come?—any time before three. I have some fine photographs—but you see all these things in London, I suppose, more than we do down here in the country. Mrs. Cramp, I want to talk to you a moment or two about things. Papa puts all sorts of arrangements on me that I don't understand in the least. I don't know what I should do, Natty, if I didn't have your mother sometimes at my right hand."

So with a pleasant smile she dismissed Natty, out of his own door step, as it would seem. Natty lounged round the house, got in at the back-door, stole up to his bedroom, and began to take off his uniform. He was, perhaps, rather glad that he had been seen for the first time thus arrayed; but he felt that the uniform had not, after all, produced much effect upon Miss Challoner. She had evidently understood quite well that poor Nat was only masquerading—showing off his fine things to his delighted mother, and she clearly did not regard him as a genuine soldier. How kind she was—and how beautiful! He should never have known her again. And what divine eyes! How frankly and sweetly she had spoken to him—and she had promised to call him Natty! His head was all on fire. Must she know that he was a hairdresser? Oh, his mother, he knew, would tell her everything! Would she countermand the permission to visit her when she heard of the calling he followed? Poor Nat felt as if the story of Aladdin were filling his mind, and he blushed and trembled to think that at that very moment his mother might be descanting to Miss Challoner on his good prospects as a hairdresser. Aladdin, to be sure, was a tailor's son; but then he was not himself a tailor; and he had such tremendous advantages in the way of supernatural auxiliaries over poor Nathaniel Cramp.

Meanwhile the Princess Badroulboudour (that surely was the name of Aladdin's princess) was not thinking at all about the Aladdin of the West Pimlico Volunteers. For the moment she had probably forgotten his very existence, for she was busily engaged in talking over some household arrangements to be made in preparation for her father's coming with his guests. But she was the kindest and most affectionate of girls, and she was really very glad to see Nat for his mother's sake and for his own, and she wanted to talk with him and show him some friendliness. She had no more idea of being constrained or formal, or even patronising, to young Cramp, than to the faithful old servant and friend, his mother. So when she was leaving she reminded Mrs. Cramp again that Natty was to be brought to see her; and she looked round for him near the door, and if he had been there she would have allowed him the privilege of helping her into her little pony carriage; but he was not there, and she got in very well without him.

Meanwhile Nathaniel, peering very cautiously from his bedroom window, watched her departure. He was in his shirt-sleeves; and he would not have been seen in his shirt-sleeves by HER—not for all the world. Kneeling on the floor, and peering with uttermost caution from beneath a corner of the blind, Nathaniel saw the back of her hat and the flutter of her feather as she drove away. Then he heard his mother calling him, "Natty! Natty, dear!" and he turned from the window in deep depression; which only began to be dispelled when his mother told him that Miss Challoner on leaving had renewed her invitation, and that he was to see her that very day.

That morning Christmas and his hostess were again in the balcony. She sat in her accustomed chair, which was moved for her according to the progress of the sun, so that she might always have the freest and finest view of the scene. Christmas was enjoying to the full the air, the trees, the sun, the breath of the sea, and the novelty of the whole situation. Miss Lyle apparently had put away the manner of almost querulous melancholy which had come over her the night before; and she was giving him some descriptions of the place and the people. He then learned for the first time that one of their neighbours was Sir John Challoner. Whereupon Christmas told her how he had had a chance introduction to Sir John Challoner a few days before in London. If he had been perfectly candid he would have told her likewise that it had given him a certain little thrill of surprise to find that he had already made the acquaintance of "My Lady Disdain;" but when is youth candid in such things? Christmas said nothing of My Lady Disdain, although he could hardly have told why he kept secret the small fact that he had heard of her by such a name.

"I beg your pardon," Miss Lyle interposed, suddenly, "is there not some one tapping at the door?"

Christmas stepped from the balcony into the room to see. Just as he did so, the door of the room opened, and a tall girl entered quickly; so quickly that her eyes met his before he had time to think that he had better not stare at her. He knew at once that it was his kindly guide of the night before—the seemingly undisdainful Lady Disdain. It was not by her face he knew her, for he had scarcely seen her face then, and he did not look long at it now. He was aware of the presence of dark eyes—of dark brown hair, coming rather low on the forehead, and gathering in thick, short curls around the neck; of a bright complexion, and lips that had a certain humorous expression about them; and, in short, a general influence of youth, and health, and high spirits, and originality; and he suddenly felt himself very young, and was convinced that he looked awkward. The young lady had not, for her part, the slightest shade of awkwardness.

"Pray excuse my coming in. I came to see Miss Lyle, and as no one answered to my tapping I took it for granted that she was in her balcony. I see you don't recognise me. I brought you here last night."

"It was dark then, and I hardly saw; but I thought it must be, and I hope you will allow me to thank you."

"Indeed I will not. I see she is in her balcony." And ther

Christmas saw the young lady embrace the elder, and settle around the shoulders of the latter her discomposed shawl and take a seat familiarly beside her. Christmas quietly added himself to the group.

"I knew you would come this morning, Marie, my dear," said Miss Lyle.

"You always say I may come any morning, don't you?"

"And you don't always come. But this morning I knew."

"Did you really? How did you know?"

"Shall I tell you outright?"

"Oh, yes; don't make any mystery."

"Because you were curious about my visitor, and you wanted to see what he looked like in the day. Come, Marie, confess."

"Indeed, it was. I mean that was the reason why I came. Now I have corrected myself in time, have I not? I saw you smile. But your friend can hardly understand this. I should tell you," and now she addressed herself to Christmas, "that Miss Lyle is always terribly severe on the way in which women answer questions. She says we always answer to something in our own minds, and not to the question. So I always try to correct myself in time. Let me see. What was it I was answering? Miss Lyle asked me to confess that I came here to-day out of curiosity, and I said at first 'Indeed it was'; which, I suppose, would hardly do as an answer in a printed dialogue, and so I corrected myself."

"We have not much to occupy ourselves with here," said Miss Lyle, "and I amuse myself now and then with playing schoolmistress to Miss Challoner, and correcting her spoken style; as I shall yours, Mr. Christmas. But you see what a truthful pupil she is, and how readily she confessed that it was curiosity and not friendship that brought her here so early this morning."

"I don't want to deny it," Miss Challoner said. "Why should I?" She looked to Christmas for reply.

"I don't know," Christmas answered, being thus appealed to. "We so seldom see anybody here—any new face—that a stranger of any kind is an object of wonder and delight."

"So there is no compliment to me?"

"Not the least in the world. But, Miss Lyle, I have had a double gratification for my curiosity already this morning. I have been up very early and caught two—I don't like to say worms for fear of seeming rude—perhaps glowworms, then."

"Who was the other victim?" asked Miss Lyle.

"Natty Cramp—dear old Natty Cramp turned into a British Volunteer, or grenadier, or whatever it is. I had not seen him for years. I was always away from Durewoods somewhere when he came to see his mother."

"My dear," said Miss Lyle, gravely, "you really must not bewilder poor Natty Cramp. Unfortified towns ought not to be bombarded, I believe. When is your father coming?"

"Not for a week now. I am very sorry; I am so lonely at home. And when he does come he is bringing some people, which will be just as bad."

"Not for a week?" Miss Lyle said, and she said it in a meditative, half-regretful sort of tone. "Then you, Mistress Marie, I suppose, are to be at large here for the next week?"

"She speaks of me as if I were a sort of wild animal— 'at large!'—some dangerous creature, like a panther."

"So you are, my dear," the elder lady said composedly. "I shall be very glad when you are sent to London and put through a season or two there. That will tame you perhaps. Meanwhile we have you here, and must only make the best of it."

"Do I seem a very disagreeable sort of a person?" Miss Challoner asked, turning her eyes fully on Christmas, and without the least appearance of coquetry or affectation.

"You seem very kind," the young man answered; "and you are very handsome."

Miss Lyle looked up amazed.

"Thank you," Miss Challoner said, with perfect gravity, and without lowering her eyes or showing the faintest light of a blush. "I am very glad you think so."

Christmas himself was much more confused by his abrupt compliment than anybody else. He had not meant to give out his opinion so bluntly, but it escaped him, and he now felt positively grateful to her for the easy and kindly way in which she had received it.

"I am always criticising her," Miss Lyle said, hastening perhaps to cover Christmas's confused retreat from the dialogue, "and finding fault with her—the way she wears her hair, and all manner of things. I want her to be perfection if she can. So she likes a compliment now and then."

"Now," said Marie, rising, "I have come to offer my services as a guide. If there is anything I specially delight in it is acting as a guide and showing a stranger all our beautiful places. I am a capital guide hereabouts, for I know all about everything."

"I intended to send Merlin out in the boat to-day with Mr. Pembroke, to show him some of our pretty inlets," said Miss Lyle. "If you insist on going, Marie—well, I don't know that I can prevent it."

"Will you not come?" Christmas asked her.

"No, thanks. The trouble of getting in and out of the boat is too much for me, and would be a great deal too much for anybody who had to endure my company. I look out upon

nature from my balcony—only too happy to have one. I once
used to look down upon a crowded street from a garret among
the swallows."

"I knew you would not go, of course," Miss Challoner said;
"and that is why I offered my services. Merlin can't talk to
Mr. Pembroke, and I can tell him everything—if he would like
me to go."

"I only wish I knew how to thank you for being so kind,"
said Christmas.

"She is a good girl," said Miss Lyle, "and kind, but I don't
know that it is only kindness in this case. She has to lead a dull
life of it here; and since you did happen to come at this time I
shall be glad if you can help to make a day or two pleasant to
her. My dear, would you mind going down and telling Merlin
about the boat? He understands you, and he isn't always
pleasant with Janet."

"I know I am being sent out of the room, as children are
when something is to be said about them which they are not to
bear," Marie said with a laugh as she went upon her errand.

"She has some sense," Miss Lyle quietly remarked, when the
door closed behind her. "I hope you have some sense too,
Mr. Christmas. I am very fond of that girl, but I told you I
would rather have had you here when her time was a little more
occupied. You have seen her father? What do you think of
him?"

"I couldn't well form any opinion. I only spoke to him for
a moment. He seemed a little pompous, I thought."

"Was there no sort of insight? You have been about the
world a good deal, and I thought young men knew everything
now. No matter, I shall leave you to judge of him for yourself—
only, Mr. Christmas, it was not by romance he came to own the
Hall. Your father and he started in life together, and so did I.
We three were all poor to begin with. Sir John, I suppose, is
rich now. You know whether your father became rich—I don't;
but if he did the money must have forced itself on him, or he
must have greatly changed."

"He never cared for money," Christmas said proudly. "I
am poor—I am glad of it."

"So am I, dear,—very glad. Well, then, keep to your independence. Be a friend of this romantic girl if you like—flirt
with her if she likes; but don't—don't make a fool of yourself—
that's all. Well, Marie, is Merlin ready?"

Marie stood on the balcony again, bright, eager, glowing with
youth and frank kindliness and beauty.

"You *are* growing a handsome girl," said Miss Lyle.

"A compliment from *you* is something to treasure, really,"
Marie said, and she kissed Miss Lyle on the forehead and blushed
at the compliment this time.

CHAPTER V.

"JUVENTUS MUNDI."

THE sun shone with the tender beauty of an English June, with mild bright warmth and poetical freshness which are so rare in other climates, and which may help to compensate the Briton for his want of the Italian sun's golden glory and the melancholy loveliness of the Indian summer—that gentle carnival of the season's sweets and tints which in the Atlantic States of the New World precedes the lenten frosts of winter. A fine June day in England ought to be consecrated to the youth of the world.

Christmas Pembroke felt its influence, although only in a vague and half-unconscious way, as he accompanied Miss Challoner to the boat. This was the first holiday on an English hillside in June, and it was the first—positively the first—time he had ever undertaken a ramble with a beautiful girl. To Christmas Miss Challoner was bewilderingly beautiful. There was no friendly critic near to point out her defects. Any half-dozen young ladies, or indeed almost any half-dozen young men, for that matter, might doubtless have shown how in every feature and tint and movement she fell short of perfection. Every such critic could perhaps have named some other woman who deserved admiration ever so much more; and who probably failed to get it. But as there was no such critic near to guide his taste, Christmas was left to the fulness of his own enthusiasm.

The way to where the boat was lying ready for them was a steep and winding path through Miss Lyle's little demesne. It was indeed a very little demesne for a region where lands and tenements were so cheap, but it allowed of a few minutes' delightful descent before the boathouse, the boat, and the water could be reached. Christmas had at first felt some dread that talking to a young English lady whom he assumed to be of high aristocratic rank and ways would be very embarrassing and difficult. But Voltaire's "Ingénu" himself could hardly have found much difficulty in talking with Miss Challoner. If that young lady had needed anything to set her at her ease her companion's blunt, fresh declaration about her being so handsome would have supplied the want. Here was no young London prig drawn by Leech, no stiff and heavy headed wallflower of the London season.

As they descended Miss Challoner stopped and looked back. Miss Lyle was seated in her balcony leaning upon her hand and looking after them. She smiled and nodded to them, and then relapsed into her former attitude and into an expression of quiet melancholy.

" She is a picture—always," Miss Challoner said to Christmas. " Everything she does seems as if it were done in an attitude for a painter, and she never thinks about it. She must have a story in her past life. Do you know it ? I don't ? "

" I know nothing but that she and my father were old friends. I am half bewildered to find myself here, not knowing why I am here, or why everybody is so friendly to me. I wonder sometimes if I am the real person at all—the person Miss Lyle takes me to be, or only an innocent impostor."

" Then you really know nothing of Miss Lyle ? "

Christmas told her in a few words all that he knew. He might as well do so at once, for he felt that he could keep nothing from her. She questioned him with an easy confidence, which was a hundred times more fatal to the life of a secret than the most ingenious inquisitiveness might have been. She listened with great attention and remained silent for a while.

" It is strange," she said, " and it seems sad. I don't well know why, but I can understand that she would naturally feel a great interest in you," and she threw a quick inquiring glance at Christmas, wondering whether he had sprung to the same conclusion as she had done. " I have heard," she added, after a pause, " that she was once a great artist—a musician or singer, and that she withdrew from the world very soon, and came and settled herself here. In summer she almost lives in that balcony. Papa knew her long ago, and he looks after her money affairs for her now, I believe ; but I don't think he would like me to ask any questions. Besides, I know enough. I know that she is a living, breathing picture, and that I am very fond of her, as you will be, if you are not already."

Here the discourse was broken in upon by a peculiar cry like part of the refrain of some monotonous uncouth piece of ballad music. It only came from Merlin, who waited for them in his boat, and thus signified his presence. They were now within a few paces of the boat, but Merlin always invited his passengers by the same peculiar cry which years ago had called his fellows about him when the fishing-boat was to be launched from the Breton shingle. As Christmas handed Miss Challoner in he looked back and could still see the balcony and Miss Lyle leaning on its edge.

That was a happy day for Christmas—a day that passed like a dream. He had come out to see the water and the scenery, with Miss Challoner for his guide, that he might miss no sight. Old Merlin rowed silently as the mysterious boatman made of metal in the Arabian Nights. The sun was bright ; the long narrow land-locked strip of sea was blue and glittering with the light of the sky on it; the woods sometimes crept down to the edge of the water. There were pretty places to be seen here and there, and there were little stories to be told, associations to be brought up, local anecdotes to be mentioned. But Marie soon fancied that her companion was a perfect Gamaliel as regarded these things. He hardly looked at the places she showed him, and he always, when he could, conducted the conversation away from the scene actually around him into some channel along which flowed naturally the memories and associations of her own life and the bubbles of her own fancies.

"You don't care about my explanations and descriptions," she said at last to the happy Christmas, who reclined in the stern of the boat, trailing one hand through the water, and looking at her. "I am a capital guide; I know all about this place, and you hardly listen."

"I prefer to hear you talk about yourself."

"But you have eyes for that beautiful little inlet there, with the birches growing just out of the water? You do see the beauty of things like that? If you lived here you would have to study tints and leaves and water, for we have nothing else to think of."

"I see the beauty of it all; but I care more for beauty—— " and Christmas confused himself a little, for he was actually going to say that he cared more for beauty like hers; but he checked himself in time, and said, "I delight in it all as a whole, but perhaps I am too new to the place to appreciate the details."

"You have not cared much for nature and scenery, I am afraid."

"I have been too busy with other things—helping my father, and being taught by him. Everything is new to me here; and all the novelties confuse me. Being absolutely my own master is even still the most confusing thing of any."

"But you will have some career to follow?"

"I suppose so. I must have when I find out what it ought to be."

"Have you no particular tastes? You ought to have some inclining of some kind already. How old are you?"

Miss Challoner always assumed a sort of superiority in tone, as if she were the elder person. This was lucky for Christmas, who was rather shy.

"Nearly twenty-two."

"So much as that! I never should have thought it! Why, you are quite a man!"

She turned towards him, and fixed her eyes upon him with a look of curious interest as she said this; and she really felt an additional interest in him because of her surprise. But the tame companions of Alexander Selkirk's solitude could hardly have shown less fear or shyness at the sight of a man than did Marie Challoner as she studied Pembroke's face.

"You ought to have found your path before this," she said, gravely. Tell me, now—have you no marked tastes of any kind?"

"Since I came to London I have been in love—with London. That is the most marked taste I have yet found in myself."

"I don't know London well; I hardly know it at all. But we are going to have a house there in the end of the year, or the beginning of next, or some time. You must show me London. Only I suppose we could hardly go about together in this sort of way—say, in a hansom cab."

"I suppose not," said Christmas, with, for the first time, a sinking heart, as he thought of the society in which she would be certain to move in London, which he assumed must be that of the very highest aristocracy.

"Then let us make the best of our time now—and we will land just here on this bank, and walk a little, and Merlin will wait for us. You must see some of the paths of these woods, for they are such favourite walks of mine. Are we not very fortunate in having this long narrow stretch of bay? You see it has all the beauty of a river, and yet it is the sea. Now I can actually see the horizon—of the great sea over which you have sailed from the East."

"Not exactly the same sea."

"Oh, I know all about geography, and the map, and Mangnall's Questions; but the sea is all one—it's just the same sea; it is the sea, and that's all about it. Half the pleasure of my life is in standing among these woods, on what seems to be the bank of a narrow green river, and looking out there to that horizon, and knowing that that is the same sea that washes the shores of Italy, and Greece, and Egypt, and Arabia, and——"

"And Japan and California," suggested Christmas, in order to bring himself somehow within her horizon.

"Oh, no; I have never thought of these places—they have no poetry or romance about them. Who cares for Japan and California? Yes, I do care for them now because you were there; one feels an interest, of course, in a place when somebody you know has been there. But still there is not much of the breath of poetry about them. I should never care to go to such places, or see them in day-dreams. Merlin" (and she spoke now in a peculiarly loud, clear tone, as the boat ran in to land), "Have you ever heard of California—the place called California?"

"Much things—yes. Have heard of much things—things here —many!" And Merlin tapped his forehead as the treasure-house of knowledge, with much complacency.

"Of California?"

"Ah—yes, yes, yes, yes! Much gold—aha! much gold. Down—in the floor"

" In the earth ? "

" Yes, yes, yes—earth—floor; the same."

" Would you like to go there ? "

" No, no, no! All black there—nigare. *I* know."

Christmas was interposing an explanation as to the complexion of the natives of California, but Merlin only shook his head, and repeated, " Black, black, all black—nigare. *I* know."

" You will find," said Miss Challoner, in a low tone, " that Merlin has caught up your words for all that; and he will soon get into talk with you as if by accident, and find out all about California, and astonish our natives here with it. He never could condescend to sit and be corrected in knowledge by you in my presence; but he will get it all from you afterwards; and then woe to the Durewoods ignoramus who shall dare to assert in Merlin's presence that the population of California are all negroes. Now will you give me your hand? Thank you. Merlin will wait."

They stepped ashore and began to ascend a winding path that mounted upwards through the woods, and Christmas entered upon his first walk under trees with a young woman. For the woods and the path, and the soft bright mosses beneath their feet, and the little streams that sometimes sprang from under green-covered stones and ran to meet them; for the sunny openings here and there between the trees, and the deep blue overhead, Christmas had no eyes. The sweet-singing English birds sang in vain for him. Yet not perhaps quite in vain. Perhaps some tone of music coming from some outer source, from the skies and among the trees, did blend itself into his consciousness. Perhaps the voice of a song-bird will always from that hour bring back to his mind delicious associations of happy expansive moments, when his soul seemed to be filled with exquisite emotion. Not quite in vain, perhaps, did the startled squirrel bound so prettily away, and then peer so knowingly from his shelter in the high branches. Not in vain was the sky so blue. All went to make up the hour, and the picture, and the dream. But Christmas did not then know it. He only knew that he was walking by the side of Marie Challoner, and that his heart was beating, and he could have vaguely said with Browning's lover, " Who knows but the world may end to-day ? "

If the talk had been left to Christmas, there probably would have been but little of it, but his companion, who was quite at her ease, talked of many things, and in particular pressed her questions about his inclinations and his career with an interest which almost finished by intoxicating the poor youth.

" You must not stay here long in this lotos-eating land," she said, " or you will soon become like the rest of us. Miss Lyle positively must send you away very, very soon."

Poor Christmas!

" I only came last night," he said in a remonstrating tone.

" Oh, yes, of course. I don't mean that she ought to send you away this evening; but soon. You ought not to waste too much of your time among us. Now let us stand here in this little hollow for just a moment. Do we not seem alone in the world here—as if there were no people on the earth but only you and I? "

Only you and I—alone in all the world! She had not the faintest thought of coquetry or of suggestive love-making when she spoke those tempting, thrilling words. She touched Christmas on the arm lightly, to call his attention, and she looked all round her and then inquiringly into his face to see if he, too, appreciated the peculiar and lonely beauty of the scene. It was very lonely. There was a sudden dip or hollow, a little dry basin, among the woods just there, and one could see neither the path that had been mounted nor any path yet to climb—only what seemed from that point of view illimitable trees around and the illimitable sky above.

Christmas could not venture to look into her eyes.

" I love this sudden bit of wild loneliness," she said; " I always bring strangers to see it."

Christmas was restored to himself for the moment by these simple words; and he praised the spot so warmly that his companion really thought his interest was in it.

" Now," she said triumphantly, as one who has extorted praise for some favourite object from unwilling lips, " now for the contrast. Just a little higher up—a little more climbing— and you shall see."

They mounted up higher and higher among the darkling trees. The path was a little steep, and Miss Challoner did not speak. Suddenly they emerged clear from the wood upon a smooth grass-grown hill. Higher still, up to the top, and then Marie turned round and showed him the great bay with its islets and its yachts and its vast horizon, while beneath them, on the side which they had ascended, were only trees to be seen. The narrow little inner bay and its village had disappeared. It seemed as if they stood on a peak in the ocean.

" There," exclaimed Marie, proudly. " Turn your eyes upon that broad sea, and think of the little nook of pathless wood we seemed to be in a few minutes ago."

" It is like San Francisco Bay," said Christmas. " I almost think I can see Saucelito or Alameda, or that I am looking out to the Golden Gate."

" The Golden Gate! That sounds like poetry. You must tell me all about the Golden Gate. But not now; some other time. I could not hear of anything which might compare too favourably with that scene just now."

"There are none of your beautiful English woods at San Francisco," said Christmas. "Dry sandhills are there."

"Then I am glad there is something in which our scene surpasses your San Francisco Bay you seem so fond of. I don't want you to forget this when you leave us, even for the memory of San Francisco."

"I shall not forget this," said Christmas quietly, "when I leave it."

"Why should not that bay, that lovely bay, have its Golden Gate?" Marie asked. "I feel as if I were looking through a Golden Gate now."

"So do I," said Christmas; and he meant it. He was indeed having his first glimpse through a golden gate through which youth is always eager to pass.

"I will sit on the grass for a moment," said Miss Challoner. "I feel tired, and it is so delightfully warm."

So she sat upon the grass, and Christmas threw himself beside her there, and they looked out over the sea and talked of anything that came up. Christmas began to develop to her a variety of views of life which an hour before had never occurred to him. He told her of his life and of the places he had seen, and she listened to him and stimulated him to more talk, and became greatly interested in his boyish simplicity and his masculine combinations of reading and experience.

"I am so glad you came here," she said at last, "and that I knew you. We are dull here now and then, and we are glad when an interesting new comer brightens our lives. I hope we shall be friends."

"Are you faithful in your friendships?" Christmas asked, plucking the grass up and not looking at her.

"Oh, did any one say I was not? Come, now, do tell me. I do believe somebody did."

"Nobody did. I only asked."

"I thought perhaps Miss Lyle had been warning you against me. *I* think I am very faithful in my friendships; but there are so few people whom any rational creature could care to have for friends. I am *her* friend, and that's one reason why I should like to be a friend of yours."

"Should we not wait a little?" Christmas asked. "You and she, I mean, until you see whether I am worth having as a friend."

"She believes that you must be, because of your father. And I——"

"Yes, and you——?"

"I take her opinion in everything. And besides——"

"Besides; yes?"

"You seem to me a friend whom I could like. But perhaps you don't like me?"

" I like you immensely."

" Do you ? I am very glad. But do you know that we
ought to have returned long before this ? I see that it is three
o'clock, and we have a long, long way to get back. And I forgot all about poor Natty Cramp. He was to have come to see
me, and he is probably there now; and only think of the time
he will have to wait! "

Christmas had a vague idea of having heard her and Miss
Lyle that morning talking of Natty Cramp, and he felt very
angry with Natty, and cordially wished that he were in some
other and distant part of the world—say at Saucelito, within
sight of the Golden Gate.

They were very pleasant, however, and full of talk as they
came down the path through the woods, and Miss Challoner
talked with such openly avowed perplexity about her embarrassment on account of Natty Cramp that Christmas at last grew to
have only friendly feeling for poor Natty. When they reached
the strand a little embarrassment awaited them. They found
Merlin gesticulating and calling to them.

" None-quick! Slow—all right—halt! "

The tide had fallen, and the boat could not get so far up on
the shore but that a yard or two of clayey surf several inches
deep lay between the dry part of the strand and the little craft.
Merlin's gesticulations and his rapid preparations showed them
that he was trying to get the boat into some favourable position
preliminary to doing something, Christmas did not know what.

" It's nothing," Miss Challoner said, composedly. " Merlin
will come out and carry me in when he has got the boat all
right. It often happens; but I am sorry for you. Do you mind
having your feet wet ? "

" Come with me," Christmas suddenly said, the colour all
rushing into his handsome boyish face. He lifted the girl off
her feet, and bore her in his arms through the surf, stepped into
the boat, and did not put her down until he could place her
securely in the stern. She looked a little surprised and amused,
but was not all discomposed.

" Thank you," she said. " I did not mean to have given you
the trouble; but you are very strong."

Christmas had never felt such a thrilling little moment before,
and he was thankful for his strength.

CHAPTER VI.

"ONE WRIT WITH ME IN SOUR MISFORTUNE'S BOOK."

POOR Natty Cramp had, indeed, a good long wait of it. The worst thing about his waiting, or, at all events, one of the worst things, was that he did not precisely know in what capacity he was waiting. His mother, who accompanied him, was in a manner free of the house, and went down among the servants at once, and made herself quite happy. But Natty was left to wait in the library, and was shown in there evidently as a matter of favour to his mother, instead of being allowed to remain, as he had modestly proposed to do, in the hall. He found the long delay very trying. He might have felt happy enough if he had been an ordinary visitor; but there was his mother going about among the servants, and he had already been presented to the servants as "My son Natty—don't you remember Natty?" All this was humbling. To be called Natty by Miss Challoner had a certain delight about it, even though it reminded him of the social gap between them; but to be called Natty by the cook had no delight in it at all.

So Natty walked up and down the library, and now and then took up a book and tried to read. He could not read. Every sound he heard seemed to him to announce the coming of Miss Challoner, and made him start with fear and hope. There was a great deal of fear mingled with the hope, for poor Natty trembled at the thought of being alone with her, and not knowing what to say to her, and stumbling over his words, and seeming uncouth and clownish. There in that library how many imaginary conversations did he not go over, in each of which he said fine things, brilliant things, witty things; in which he proved that he had a lofty, aspiring soul, and convinced Miss Challoner that, despite low birth and iron fortune, he had in him the material that makes great men! As time wore on, however, and she did not come, the style of the imaginary dialogue began to change, and he found himself growing rather sarcastic and proudly scornful, and saying bitter things, to let the disdainful lady of rank know that Nathaniel Crump held himself not inferior to those on whom fortune, and not their own desert, had conferred the accidental boon of social position.

"This is no country for a man to live in," Nathaniel at last exclaimed. "I'll not be the slave of caste! The Old World is used up. For men of spirit and soul, the only home is the giant Republic of the West. She shall hear this—— Oh, I say!"

E

His mother had interrupted him, coming softly into the room.
" Were you saying poetry, Natty dear? You must say one of
your poems to Miss Challoner."

" Perhaps she isn't coming," Natty faintly said, with sinking
heart, and all the proud resolves gone at the sound of her name.

" Oh, she'll come, dear; for she said she would. She's quite
too much the lady not to come. Something has kept her unexpected ; but she'll be here soon."

" Mother," Nat exclaimed, bitterly, " you don't understand
these people!"

" What people, Nat ?"

" People who boast of their rank—people like her ! What do
they care for us?"

" My dear boy, why do you talk in that sort of way? Me not
know my Miss Challoner ? Why, God bless you, I knew her
since she was a child ! Of course she cares for us—that she does,
believe me. We're not like her in rank, Nat, but we're content—
and she don't mind, bless you."

" Contentment," replied Nat, " is the virtue of a slave."

" Gracious ! " exclaimed his mother.

" Of a slave," repeated Nat; " and the days of slavery
are—— "

He stopped in his eloquence, however, for a civil maiden
appeared at the library door, and said Miss Challoner had come
in, and please would Mrs. Cramp and Mr. Natty walk upstairs.

Natty's face grew red, and his hands became nervous ; and he
followed his mother upstairs as unheroic a being, to all appearance,
as ever hugged a chain.

Miss Challoner was in a little room, her own, which looked
over the gardens and the trees. The Hall ended off at either side
with a rounded projection, which might, perhaps, be described as
a tower, and in one of these projections Miss Challoner had
chosen her room. It looked, therefore, inside like a room in a
castle or a turret, with its rounded form and its windows opening every way ; and this peculiarity enhanced immensely in
Nathaniel's eyes the romantic effect of his presentation to the
young lady in her home. The furniture was somewhat massive
and heavy, newly made for Sir John Challoner after the most
approved mediæval fashion. The fireplace was low, broad,
antique; the curtains were dark; the glass in the windows was
of lattice panes. It seemed to Nat as if he were introduced into
a castle chamber at the bidding of the châtelaine. There was the
châtelaine herself. She had been reclining in a great tall-backed
arm-chair, with one of her feet on a footstool, and as she entered
and rose to receive him, Nat could see the foot itself in a pretty
shoe, with a high heel, and a great buckle and rosette of ribbon
across its instep ; and then she stood up and rested inadvertently

one hand upon an ebony table, whereon it looked white enough
to have belonged to the white-armed goddess herself of whom
Nat had read in Pope's translation. But at that moment Nat
was not thinking of anything classic. His soul was filled with
the Middle Ages, and with castles, and with sweet peerless ladies,
who smiled even on lowly squires from the sombre surroundings
of feudalism. Miss Challoner stood with such unconscious ease
and dignity, and smiled upon Nat with such kindly dark eyes,
that he saw in her a very châtelaine and Lady of the Land, and
a benignant patroness ; and when she held out the white hand to
him, he felt as if he ought to have dropped on one knee and
pressed the hand to his lips.

Miss Challoner's friendly words, however, and much more the
voice of his mother, in unconstrained though very respectful
fluency of talk with the châtelaine, recalled him to modern life,
and he was able to take a chair and enter into conversation, and
show himself, as his mother afterwards told him, quite the
gentleman. Miss Challoner was fond of good photographs of
foreign buildings, and from picture galleries, and had many fine
specimens to show him ; and Nat's discursive reading furnished
him with something to say about each of them. She had, also,
a book filled with photographic likenesses of living celebrities ;
and this proved a great thing for Nat. He had seen nearly all
the eminent Englishmen, and she had seen none of them. He had
had orders again and again for the Strangers' Gallery of the
House of Commons, and he had attended all manner of public
meetings in St. James's Hall and Exeter Hall ; and he had heard
all the great preachers, and never, when he could help it, missed
a chance of hearing Professor Huxley, and he knew Mr. Carlyle
and Mr. Browning by sight. Therefore Natty started off in a
description of each one of these great persons, whom Miss
Challoner only knew by reading and by hearsay. He told her
whether each photograph was a good likeness or not, and if not
wherein it differed from the original; and whether or not it
accurately conveyed the expression of the original, and how that
expression varied when the original was speaking, and so forth.
Nathaniel's favourites were the poets, the preachers, and the
philosophers. But he was especially eloquent and instructive
about the preachers and the philosophers. He had heard them
preach and lecture, whereas he had only seen and read the poets ;
and he generally contended mentally with the preachers, and
strove to be the faithful appreciative disciple of the philosophers.
He had, therefore, a great deal to say of both these classes of
public instructors, and he grew quite warm and animated in his
descriptions.

Miss Challoner listened to him with a great deal of genuine
interest, and envied him his chances of seeing and hearing such

men in London. Mrs. Cramp afterwards declared that to see her there listening to Natty, quite interested and respectful-like, as if she was learning from him, was something she could never have believed.

It was beyond measure delightful, inconceivable to Nathaniel When in the course of his description his eyes suddenly looked into hers, and he saw in these such kindly, genuine evidences of interest in what he was saying, a new page of life seemed to open for him. How many times after did he recall the memory of that bright day! Indeed it never left him. Surely My Lady Disdain or the Princess Bradroulboudour had made two youths very, very happy that day! If so, she ought to have all the praise, for she meant nothing else.

But Natty's mother gave him hints that he must not take up Miss Challoner's time any more, and Miss Challoner herself thought perhaps that the visit had lasted long enough. So Natty rose in a sort of alarm and confusion, thinking he had stayed ever so much too long and done something dreadful. And then Miss Challoner felt impelled to say something to reassure him, and to show that she really felt an interest in him. So while they were standing up, she said—

" I don't think I asked your mother what you are doing now, Natty ? What is your occupation ? I hope it is something that suits you, and not too much work."

" He don't like his occupation, Miss Challoner," Mrs. Cramp hastened to explain. " He don't like it at all, and he wants to give it up."

" I have given it up," Nathaniel said, in a firm and almost stern tone. " It never suited me. But it was not your fault, mother ; you meant it for the best."

" What is it, Mrs. Cramp ? " asked Miss Challoner.

" It's the occupation of a hairdresser, please miss."

" Of a hairdresser ? " said the young lady. " A hairdresser ! Oh, no, Natty, you are quite right. That certainly is not the kind of work Nature intended you for, I am quite sure."

" Thank you, Miss Challoner," said Natty, gravely—and he threw a proud glance at his mother—" I thought you would say so."

" It's a very light business," pleaded poor Mrs. Cramp ; " and it's very respectable. And such good prospects—and a relation of my own, too. Natty would be as good as certain of succeeding to the business."

" But Mrs. Cramp, Natty wouldn't care for succeeding to such a business as that, or for succeeding in it. No man of spirit would—I wouldn't, if I were a man."

" Oh, but you, miss—of course it's different."

" Still, Mrs. Cramp, your son is quite right. I like his sense and spirit. Oh, no; he must not be a hairdresser. It would be absurd—a tall strong young man like that; why, he might as well be a milliner! I am so sorry I did not know of this long ago;" and the young lady put on as grave and earnest a face as though she could have known of anything very long ago.

Nathaniel hardly knew whether he was any longer treading upon firm earth, so elated had he become.

"I don't want to be vain, Miss Challoner," he proudly said; "but I do think I am capable of something better than that."

"Oh, yes; I know you are."

"And pray, Miss Challoner, don't suppose it's any feeling of shame—of false shame, that is—at my lowly station—that impels me. I hold that in whatever station of life a man may be born, he may act a noble part in it."

"Indeed he may, Natty; you talk very sensibly. The time has gone by, I hope, for stuff of that sort—I mean for stuff about station and caste, and all that."

Natty's eyes lighted, and he stood more erect than before. Why, what was this but an avowal from Miss Challoner's own lips that she shared his theories of man's natural equality? Which, indeed, she did—as theories, so far as she had thought about them. But now she only meant that the time had gone by for stuff about a man's being kept down in the world and prevented from seeking his proper place by any supposed oppression of caste and class and bloated aristocrats. For the moment, however, more than all this, she was thinking of what she could do for Natty.

"I don't know much about business, and occupations, and careers," she said. "I wish I did. But I do know that the dressing of hair cannot be the natural and proper calling of a tall, strong young man, who has intelligence, and cleverness, and ambition—I do know that much. I will talk to papa the moment he comes; he knows all about such things; and he shall find something more fitting for you, Natty. He will do it, I am sure, for me."

Mrs. Cramp was longing to explain that Nathaniel having served through all his long apprenticeship had only now his career and its profits fairly opening upon him, and that he could hardly afford to begin all over again. But she was borne down by the resolve of Nathaniel and the warm encouragement he met with from Miss Challoner.

"Meantime, I'll speak to Miss Lyle too, I think, about this," said Marie. "She knows a great deal about life, and she would sympathise, I am sure, with your son's desire to find some better occupation. Mr. Pembroke perhaps, too, ought to know something of the world; he has been a great traveller for so young a man. Have you heard of him, Mrs. Cramp?"

"No, miss."

"He is in Durewoods, on a visit to Miss Lyle, now. He is the son of a very old friend of hers, who is dead. He must be about Natty's age—a little older perhaps, and he is about Natty's height. I like him very much. I have been with him in the woods to-day showing him all our beautiful spots, Mrs. Cramp, and that is the reason I was so late and kept you waiting so long."

"Oh, please, Miss Challoner, don't name it," the polite Mrs. Cramp interposed.

How Nathaniel Cramp wished she had not named it! How dark his horizon suddenly grew! In the woods all day with a young man—a stranger; a gentleman, no doubt, who would dare to despise any fellow man who could not boast of rank, and a stranger who had travelled all over the far lands which he, Nathaniel Cramp, so yearned to see! For him poor Nat had been kept waiting all that time. Alas, what wonder! He was not a gentleman; he had not travelled.

"I—I beg pardon, Miss Challoner," he said, "I haven't the pleasure of the gentleman's acquaintance."

"No, Natty, I know that; but I am sure he would be glad to make your acquaintance, and to tell you anything. But perhaps you would rather not!"

"I think, Miss Challoner, I would rather not."

"You are very independent, Natty, I see. Well, I like you all the better for it; only I thought that perhaps a young man about your own age, who had seen the world—and he is not a tremendous person—a bloated aristocrat, and that sort of thing, as people call it, don't they? Still, you don't like it. Very well, but you don't mind my speaking to papa."

"You are very kind, I'm sure," Nathaniel began, "and I can't express my thanks, but then—— "

"Natty's very much obliged, Miss Challoner," the prudent and propitiating mother hastened to interpose; "and I know he'll be only too proud of anything you can say of him to your papa. You may say he is a good young man, Miss Challoner, and has been a good son and a comfort to his mother. Your papa will be glad to hear that of him, I know."

"Indeed he will, Mrs. Cramp, and I could have believed it, even if you had not told me. Well, Natty, perhaps you will leave it in my hands! I will take good care of your spirit of independence, for I like it; but you must let me speak to papa about you. I am quite determined you must not be a hairdresser. Please let me have some share in helping you to find work more fit for you."

"Oh, Miss Challoner, Natty can't be too thankful, he can't say what he feels."

" Who can, Mrs. Cramp? One should be a great poet, I suppose, Natty, to say all that he felt ; perhaps even great poets can't always do it. But you must both come and see me again before Natty returns to London."

So Miss Challoner talked on to stop all expressions of gratitude, and so she pleasantly bowed her visitors out, if bowing them out be not indeed an unreasonably formal mode of describing her frank and friendly way of dealing with Nathaniel and his mother. She was perfectly sincere and good-natured in every word she said to them, and was filled with a determination to do something which should put Natty in the way of making his fortune. She was in great spirits, and was longing to do good to somebody, to help in making somebody happy, because she herself had been so happy that day. There was much in Christmas Pembroke which impressed her sympathetically, and her whole sensitive nature vibrated to sympathies. She had always yearned for some friend about her own age, and she had now a vague, sweet hope that Christmas Pembroke might prove the long-looked-for friend and brother of her regard. For she led usually a lonely life enough, this poor Lady Disdain, as some of her acquaintances called her ; and she wanted some one to think about, and now and then exchange ideas with. Therefore she was for the time very happy in thinking that she could serve Natty Cramp, and that she would probably like Christmas Pembroke much, and could concert with Miss Lyle some way of serving him too.

These two young men ought to have been very happy when so handsome and so clever a girl had set her heart on serving them. Christmas Pembroke, of course, did not know of her kindly purpose. She could not offer to speak of him to Sir John Challoner, and find some occupation for him. Yet some words which she had heard from him made it clear that he was not rich, that he had his way to make ; and although his way would, of course, be something much more lofty and brilliant than poor Natty Cramp's, yet she was not quite without a hope that she, too, might be able to influence it. That, however, must be thought of carefully, and Miss Lyle must be consulted. But to Natty Cramp she could talk out, with no concealment, about his prospects and what she hoped and resolved to do for him.

Meanwhile, the object of all this kind purpose accompanied his mother silently as she left the Hall. Natty was not happy. Even if he had not heard of the stranger with whom Marie spent the earlier part of the day, and of his travels, he still would have felt dispirited and broken down. The very kindness of Miss Challoner's manner, the warm frankness with which she talked of speaking to her father on his behalf, oppressed him. His position was made so clear! How different things seemed when

they were looking over the photographs, and he told her of this
or that great personage whom he had seen, and she listened; she
really did listen. Since then the disillusion had been terrible.
That was delicious poetry: this was dry, grim prose.

" You ought to be very much obliged to her, Natty," his
mother said, as they came out on the road ; and there was a sort
of remonstrance in her tone, as if she would imply that he had
not shown himself sufficiently obliged.

" Mother, I am obliged to her."

" Don't you think she is a dear, darling girl ? "

" We do not know her," Nathaniel answered, coldly. " People
of our station cannot know her."

" Why, Natty, how you talk ! Nobody could know her better
than I know her—bless her ! "

But Natty remained silent, and his mother, wondering at his
manner, could only sadly conjecture that his holiday was dull
now down there, and that he was already longing to be back in
London.

That night Nathaniel Cramp again wandered from his
mother's cottage, and tried to divert his thoughts by smoking
a cigar on the pier. The night was soft and warm, with faint
promise of a later moon, and even still some tinge of light low
down by the horizon where the sun had sunk. Natty lounged
along the pier and listened to the waves, and looked up at the
sky, where a star here and there was shining, and he chafed
inwardly that there was not a storm—a wild, driving mass of
clouds scurrying across the sky before the wind, a scared and
ghost-like moon, and a wreck. Something Ossianic would have
been in keeping with the temper of his soul, and with what
seemed to be his fate. He would have liked a wreck, and to
stand there and see a spar drifting on the water, with a white
arm clasping it, and a pale face pressed to its tossing side; and
then to have plunged into the waves and breasted and battled
his way to the aid of the victim, just as her relaxed hands were
loosing their hold ; and to have saved Her or died with Her—
for, of course, it would and must be She ! Or he would have
liked to die anyhow. Death comes in with delightful ease and
welcome in the dissatisfied dreams of robust youth. Nat would
have liked that he had perished in some heroic effort to do something in the sea, and that his body had been washed ashore—and
that she might hear of his fate. Suddenly, however, he remembered his mother, and thought how sorry she would be and lonely,
and he made up his mind rather sadly that he must scheme out
his dreamings so as to absent him from felicity awhile, and in
this harsh world draw his breath in pain. Then he wished that
he could see a ghost ; that some dread messenger from another
sphere would come to him, and by his presence make Nathaniel

Cramp a different being from ordinary men. If anything out of the common would only happen—anything, anything, so that life should not go on as it had done before the eyes of the châtelaine had rested kindly on him!

He was now at the seaward end of the pier, communing, poor fellow, with his own absurd, fantastic thoughts, and becoming, in his egotistic extravagances, akin with all the heroes and all the fools. He turned round, and was walking slowly inward, when he saw a spark of light in mid-air, just before him. It was nothing supernatural, however : only the light of a cigar. Presently a man came along, smoking. Natty would have avoided his fellow-being just then, but on a long and very narrow pier, when one stands at the seaward extremity, it is not easy to avoid a new-comer. Natty stood still and looked at the sea, in the hope that the promenader would simply walk to the end, turn back, and go away. But the promenader with the cigar stopped too and looked over the sea. There was a moment of silence.

" Will the fine weather hold ? " the newcomer asked, speaking right out, in a frank and social sort of way.

" I should think not," Nat answered, slowly and gloomily ; " I should say, certainly not! a storm is coming. There will be wrecks! "

" Do you think so ? I shouldn't have thought that. Do you learn that from the red light on the horizon ? "

" There is," Nat solemnly said, " a lurid light on the horizon ! "

He was thinking of his horizon.

" And you think that threatens a storm ? In this latitude and in such weather I should never have supposed that. But I dare say you know this place ? "

" I know it," said Natty, " too well."

The new-comer—it was only Christmas Pembroke—looked at him with a little surprise.

" It's a beautiful place," Christmas said. " I don't think I ever saw a more charming place. I think a man might be very happy here."

" Happy ? Here ? Is any one happy anywhere ? What is it to be happy ? "

" I have been very happy here," Christmas said, with a pang going through him as he thought how soon he should have to leave the place ; " but I don't live here. You do, I suppose ? "

" No! I don't live here. I don't live—— " " Anywhere," Nathaniel was going to add, but he checked himself, and merely added, " I don't live here now."

" Will you have a cigar ? " Christmas asked, presenting his case.

"Thanks. Much obliged. You're very kind, I'm sure. I've smoked my last," and he laid a melancholy emphasis on the word "last."

"You can light it by mine. I haven't any matches left."

Their heads approached each other, and their faces were for the moment illumined by a little throbbing circle of fire. Natty saw a young and handsome face with a moustache, which moustache he owned, with a thrill of pain, was much better than his own. The little aureole of fire in which both their faces were circled for a moment, like the faces of the wan pair in Love's aureole, whom Mr. Dante Rossetti tells of, flashed now a sort of revelation on Natty's soul.

"I—I beg your pardon," he suddenly said, drawing back, and stammering with excitement; "but did you say that you were a stranger here?"

"Certainly—yes. So I am."

"You came down, perhaps, yesterday from London?"

"I did. To be sure, I remember now. Didn't I see you in the train?"

"It doesn't matter," Nat exclaimed. "Enough that I saw you! Perhaps you are staying at Miss Lyle's?"

"I am staying there," said the amazed Christmas. "Why do you ask? Have you any objection?"

"Take back your cigar—I want none of it! Take back your cigar!"

"My good fellow," said Christmas, coolly, "people don't usually take back lighted cigars which other people have begun to smoke."

"Then let it perish!" Nathaniel exclaimed, and he flung the cigar wildly out to sea, and stared with excited eyes.

"Let it perish by all means; but the next time anybody offers you a good cigar let me advise you to make up your mind first whether you mean to smoke it and be civil before you take it in your hand. Now may I ask who you are? No, though. I don't want to know. You are the rudest and most uncivil person I have ever met. But I suppose you have been drinking."

"Drinking!" Nathaniel cried. "Drinking! It's false! You insult me! It's a lie!"

Christmas made an angry movement, but he checked himself in a moment, reflecting that he had to do with some absurd country bumpkin who was probably half tipsy.

"You are a remarkably odd and eccentric sort of young man," Christmas said quietly; "and I should strongly recommend you to go home at once. There are no police here, I suppose, or you would run some risk of being locked up."

Christmas turned and was about to walk away, when the excited Natty interposed—

"No you don't! You don't get off in that sort of way, without apologising to me for the words you have used. Apologise! apologise! or you don't leave this spot!"

He seized Christmas by the breast of the coat. The young man not knowing now whether he had to do with a genuine manaic, flung him roughly off with a push—a very strong and sudden push, though certainly not a blow. Christmas was far stronger than Natty, and Natty staggered back, slipped, recovered his footing, plunged again awkwardly, and at last, to Christmas's utter consternation, tumbled backwards off the pier into the water. A wild cry came from Natty as he disappeared into the dark and heaving sea. Christmas sprang to the edge. Happily the tide was full, and the fall was not much. In a moment Christmas saw a wild, pale, affrighted face with its eyes starting appear above the water some yards away; and that moment he flung himself into the sea.

Christmas had learned swimming in seas where people grow as familiar with the water as with the land, and he saw at a glance that the owner of the affrighted face could not swim a stroke. He had taken in, too, at a glance, the whole situation. There must be a very strong current seaward to have carried Natty so far from the pier in an instant, but, on the other hand, there was a great iron ring attached to the pier, and once get to that and all difficulty would be over. Let the sinking man blunder his worst, and clutch and cling his awkwardest, Christmas thought he could manage that, as he dashed into the water.

It seemed remarkably cold, even for night, in summer, and Christmas for a moment felt himself borne vehemently outwards, and could see nothing. One confused second, and he found himself entangled in Nathaniel Cramp's bewildering legs and arms.

"Don't cling about me too much," Christmas roared, "and I'll get you in! Don't drown us both!"

Nathaniel had full consciousness, and tried hard to be heroic. There was not indeed one atom of the coward about him, but Alexander the Great, if he were in the sea and could not swim, would have found it hard to keep from clutching anybody who came to save him. Natty positively did try. He made almost superhuman efforts of will that he might not grapple round his rescuer. That was a moment never to be forgotten—the darkness, the noise of the waves, the water dashing over his head, the helpless feet plunging wildly for a foothold, the agonising effort not to clutch at the rescuer, and the seemingly endless endurance of the trial. Christmas seized Natty by the neck with one hand, and then with one or two desperate exhausting efforts dashed at the ring, missed it, and both went down; came up again, still holding his prey, saw the ring once more, apparently dancing up and down before him, and clutched it firmly this time.

" All right now," he said, cheerily; " we're safe enough. See if you can't scramble up my shoulder and get on the pier." He was beginning to form a better opinion of his companion's sanity from the manner in which the latter had behaved himself in the water.

Natty scrambled up pluckily and easily enough, and then, kneeling on the pier, held down a hand for Christmas.

" Take my hand; do take my hand!" he exclaimed.

" If I pull you over?"

" Give me your hand," Nat screamed.

Christmas caught his hand, and for a moment they very nearly did go over. But Nat stuck fast, and in another second they were both on the pier dripping and puffing side by side.

" Will you ever forgive me?" Nat pleaded, heedless of his river-god condition. " Can you ever forgive me? I beg your pardon again and again. I was a savage and a beast. I don't know what took hold of me."

" I'm glad I was able to take hold of you," said Christmas. " Never mind about the rest," and he began to laugh.

" But I didn't mean what I said. I didn't indeed. Something put me out, and I thought—— I don't know what I thought. Do forgive me."

" No matter now," said Christmas. " We must get away from this; then we can talk."

" But you do accept my apology? I am not like that—— I want to be like—like a gentleman. Will you shake hands? Do!"

" To be sure I will," said Christmas, holding out his dripping hand. " Fellows who have clasped hands as we did just now ought to be good friends. But, I say, you know this place; can't we go somewhere and get ourselves dried? Is there any sort of inn or public-house? I can't walk home to Miss Lyle's in this state."

" Come to my mother's," said Nat, eagerly, delighted to be of any service. " It's quite near, and we'll have the place all to ourselves. She'll be in bed, and there's a fire."

" Come along," Christmas said, right joyously; and they ran along at full speed.

The high powers had heard Natty's prayer in part. He had been in the waves, but he had not rescued anybody. His body had been brought ashore, but not dead; only wet. He had had an adventure, but it was not romantic or heroic.

CHAPTER VII.

THE SPARTAN BOY.

CHRISTMAS and Nat had a brisk run to the widow Cramp's, stamping the water out of their clothes as they ran, and laughing a good deal. The whole adventure gave Christmas downright pleasure, for his mind was beginning to be perplexed and disturbed by doubts and pains hitherto unknown to him, and he found it a relief to be torn for the moment away from himself—from brooding, into any kind of action. The accident had done Nat a world of good; it had brought him to his senses—at least for the hour.

A fire was still burning in Mrs. Cramp's house. The nights usually turned rather cold in Durewoods until the summer had advanced farther on its way. The glow was very welcome now to our dripping youths. Nat brought down all the clothes he had and all the towels, and the pair scrubbed themselves dry, and then Christmas put on some of Nat's ordinary clothes, while Nathaniel himself mounted, for lack of any other, the proud Volunteer uniform. Then Nat discovered a bottle of brandy, and they had each a glass to keep off cold, and they found that Christmas's cigar case had kept its contents dry through all the fight with the waves and the current, and they sat one at each side of the fire and smoked, and were very cheery.

" Better not talk about this thing," said Pembroke; " people would only laugh at us."

" It ought to be told," Nat answered conscientiously, " how you showed such courage, and saved my life—and I didn't deserve it of you."

" Of course any fellow who could swim was bound to do that; I don't care to have that told; we shall only look foolish."

" But I behaved so badly," Nat ruefully went on; " I was so rude, all about nothing. The truth is this, and you may laugh at me if you like—I hate my occupation, and my mother was a servant once, and I keep thinking everybody is looking down on me, and I heard of you knowing Miss Lyle, and—and—Miss Challoner and that—and I took it into my stupid head that you must look down on me too; and so I made a fool of myself."

" My good friend," Christmas said coolly, I have only just come to England after living nearly all my life in places where people know as much about the distinctions of English society as they do of what is going on in the moon. Let me tell you that the world doesn't concern itself half as much as you think about what people say and do in London."

" But we are in London now—I mean we are in England—and that makes all the difference, you know," Nat said with sad conviction.

" It does make a difference," Christmas owned, with a consciousness that only that very day he had been thinking of the possible barricade that might arise between Sir John Challoner's daughter and himself when they were all in London. " It makes a confounded difference, and I sometimes wish I were back in San Francisco or in Japan."

" Then you won't blame a fellow too much if he sometimes loses his temper thinking of these things," Nat said. " Remember that I'm ever so much worse off than you. You are a gentleman, anyhow—I am not."

" Then why don't you go where people think less of these ridiculous distinctions?   Why do you stay in a place like this ? "

" Where can one go ? "

" Go ?   Anywhere.   Go to Japan—go to America and get out West.   What do they care for gentlemen out there ? "

" I have thought of it," Nat said, rubbing up his hair with his hands. " I have dreamed of it many a night.   But I have hoped for a time here when manhood would assert its proper place—I have even dreamed of helping in the coming of such a time; I do try to help it all I can."

" A man must have some fair amount of self-conceit, mustn't he, to believe that he can do much towards the bringing on of the good time coming?   Take my advice, and don't wait for that; it will come without your help or mine if it is to come," Christmas said rather sententiously, for he began to think his companion's ideas of himself a little absurd.

" I have great faith in the future," Nat declared with a vehement effort to pump up again his old enthusiasm.

" So have I—so much faith that I don't think it needs any guidance from me.   Anyhow I must go now—I only hope I shan't find the house locked up."

" Shall I walk with you and show you the way ?   Then if the house is locked up you can come back here, you know."

" Oh, no, thank you.   I mustn't bring you out of your home so late.   I know the way quite well."

Nat came out with him to the door, and they crossed the threshold together.   The moon had just begun to show itself above the trees amid which the Hall was standing.   Both the young men looked in the same direction—perhaps at the moon, perhaps at the trees that were now so dark in their outlines beneath it on the hill.

" You don't feel that sort of thing ? " Nathaniel said suddenly.

" What sort of thing ? "

" That discontent with life and classes and wealth, and all that? You don't ever sit and think of a better time when equality and humanity shall prevail ? "

" I have been too busy," Christmas said, " and too much out of the world—I mean out of your world here—and I haven't had time."

" How happy you must have been out there ! You have come back to a country where everything is sacrificed to caste and the ascendency of rank; where the aristocrat is everything and the man is nothing."

This was a rather favourite period of Nat's, and he waxed sonorous in the delight of rolling it out to new ears.

" Rather odd," Christmas said; " you are the second person with whom I have exchanged a word on the condition of England since I came to this country; and the first man said exactly the opposite of all you are saying now. He insisted that England was given over to Radicalism and Red Republicanism, equality, socialism, the rights of man, and I don't well know what else, and that there were no such things as gentlemen in the country now."

" But I suppose he was an aristocrat himself ? "

" He seemed to think he was or ought to be; I don't know."

" There it is, you see; he growls because humanity dares to approach too near to the bars of his privilege! If he felt the realities as we do! If he knew what caste still is here ! " and Nat gazed wildly in the direction of the moon or the Hall—it might have been either. " But it's no matter. The thing must end some time. There is a world elsewhere."

" You seem to me to be cut out for an orator," said Christmas, smiling.

" I have sometimes tried to speak—but it's no matter. No more of that. I detain you. Good-night."

Christmas bade his new friend a hasty good night and hurried away. He did not want Nat Cramp to accompany him. He wanted to walk alone in the moonlight up that road under the trees, and he meant to pass Miss Lyle's gate, late though it was, and go on until he should reach the gate of the grounds, amid which the Hall stood. What to do there ? Nothing, except to pace up and down slowly before the gate a few times, and look in and see some trees and shrubs. In one sense he was farther from the Hall there than if he had been at Nat Cramp's door, for now he could not even see the roof or any part of the Hall. But he could see the trees which perhaps now *she* saw, and he was nearer to her by a few hundred yards than before—and what need to explain more fully how Christmas delighted and teased himself with the absurdities which have teased and delighted all genera-

tions of men ?   One sensation had lingered with him all the day,
pervading and suffusing all his other emotions like a perfume:
the thought that he had carried her for a moment in his arms.
He wanted to be alone, too, that he might think over something Nat Cramp had said.   "You," that is, Christmas, "are a
gentleman, anyhow."   This was exactly what now tormented the
mind of our *ingénu*.   Am I, he asked himself, what people here
would call a gentleman ?   He was not without a full conviction
that in the better sense of the word his father's son was a true
gentleman, or ought to be.   His father had always seemed to him
the very type and picture of a dignified, self-reliant gentleman,
with high culture and refined tastes; and Miss Lyle had called
him the finest gentleman she ever saw.   Christmas knew well
enough, from his reading of English journals and books, that the
education his father had given him was much broader and better
than that which young English gentlemen usually receive.
Christmas knew several languages and their best literature, and
he had had a good scientific education too.   He knew something
of music ; he knew a good deal about trade and commerce, and
had ideas on steam and machinery and navigation.   He was
perhaps a little vain of having seen so much more of the round
world than most young men of his age.   Therefore he was by no
means wanting in modest good opinion of himself.   But would
all this do much for him in English society if he had not birth
and position?   Would he, in short, be received on equal terms
among the London people whom Sir John Challoner knew?   He
had been very philosophical about distinctions of class where Nat
Cramp was concerned ; but his philosophy could do little to fence
his own breast against doubt and vexation.

Of all this he had never thought in Japan, or even in London
when he first came there.   He had looked upon London as the
playground of his first great holiday; and he had loved it and
his free life and his chambers and the goddess on his painted
ceiling.   He envied not a king; he was the equal of any man.
Only a few hours have passed away and a girl has smiled a
kindly smile upon him; and already what a craven he is becoming, and how he vexes himself about his position, and his lack of
position, and what people will think of him, and all the rest of
it !   Is this the first flower of that passion of love which is, or is
supposed to be, all ennobling ; and does Love in this case begin
by threatening to turn a brave young man into a snob?   Alas!
it is to be owned that the birth even of love takes place amid
some ignoble associations, and is not an event all poetic and
sublime.

This sort of feeling, however, was only Christmas's nightly
tormentor as yet.   Every night it came out of its cave within his
breast, like the hag out of the chest in the room of the merchant

Abudah, in the "Tales of the Genii," which people once used to read, and vexed and tormented him. As yet it scarcely ventured to brave the light of day and the voices of bright companionship. For if earth ever held a happy youth, that fortunate boy was Christmas Pembroke during the few enchanted days that followed his arrival in Durewoods.

This was the programme of his occupations. After breakfast he walked or drove or went in the boat with Miss Challoner After luncheon he walked or drove or went in the boat with Miss Challoner. Late in the evening Miss Challoner sat in the balcony with Miss Lyle, and he stood behind them. He then accompanied Miss Challoner to her gate, and perhaps even to the door of her house; for although sometimes her manservant and maidservant together came to escort her, and the latter was never absent, and the roads about Durewoods on a summer's night were as safe as the corridors in Miss Challoner's own house, yet Christmas could not think of allowing the young lady to brave the dangers of the outer world without his protecting arm to ensure her safety. Added to all these occasions of happy meeting, Miss Challoner more than once came and dined with Miss Lyle.

Miss Lyle looked on at all this with eyes of half-melancholy amusement, blended with a certain distrust. But she saw nothing better for her to do than to let things take their course. She knew that Marie Challoner was not a coquette in any sense of the word, and she did not believe the girl had any sort of inflammable matter in her heart. Marie had a free, friendly, half-boyish sort of nature which at least for the present seemed to turn with impatience and even contempt from sentimentalisms and love-making. It was Miss Lyle who, observing the scornful way in which the girl was accustomed from her very childhood to drop the acquaintances she had suddenly taken up if they proved un-interesting, and her indifference to flirtations and sentiment, had called her Dear Lady Disdain after Shakespeare's Beatrice. Some time, Miss Lyle thought, she will really be touched to the heart, and then her love will perhaps be profound and passionate, but the time is not yet. It was clear that Christmas Pembroke had not touched her, and Miss Lyle thought that since they had come together somewhat against her inclination, the safest course she could take was to let them meet freely as friends without even a hint of danger. In any case the danger would only be to poor Christmas's heart: and he—well, he must only get over it. He is very young, she thought, and he will have time and chance enough to recover and to form new impressions; and men survive deeper wounds—and women too, she thought.

Meanwhile, Sir John Challoner, who had always kept his daughter secluded away at Durewoods in order that she might not come upon London until he had settled all the conditions

F

under which she could best make an impression and had the people in his mind whom she was to impress, heard without any alarm of her acquaintance with young Pembroke. Marie wrote to him a long letter every morning, and as every letter contained a great deal about Mr. Pembroke and his goodness and his cleverness and so forth, Sir John was easy in his mind. Had she mentioned him once and then not again perhaps her father might have been a little uneasy, but the free and frequent descriptions of the new acquaintance set his mind at rest. Perhaps if he could have seen his daughter seated on the grass while this handsome young man reclined near her and looked into her eyes when they were not turned on his and looked away when they were, he might not have been quite so tranquil. Perhaps if he had seen the expression of deep interest with which she listened while Christmas warmed into eloquence about his future career and the great things he hoped to do under the impulse of an inspiration which he did not venture to define—perhaps Sir John might have seen good cause to hasten his coming to Durewoods. Yet there would have been no need so far as any interests of his were concerned. Marie Challoner's bosom rose and fell with regular and tranquil respiration, her pulse temperately beat time and made healthful music.

But poor Christmas! Never in life was youth more profoundly and passionately in love. He was so happy now and had such free access to her society that he did not yet know all the depth of his wound. He will feel it soon: he will know that he has it in his heart. Now his new happiness keeps his pulses stirring and life is all ecstasy—in the day. When he walks out late of nights to smoke a cigar as he did on the night when he literally fell in with Nat Cramp—for Miss Lyle allows of no cigars in her little cottage—he is stricken by a terrible foreboding of the blank sort of life he is to lead when he goes back to London and has the painted goddess on the ceiling—the ceiling he was proud of the other day—for his only present divinity! A sickening sensation passes through him as he asks himself what possibility there is for him but disappointment. Our young hero is not merely a young fool. He knew the strength of his own feelings just as he knew what weight he could lift or what distance he could walk. He knew that his present emotion had nothing to do with the light and passing sentiment which a raw young man mistakes for first love.

Miss Lyle was wholly mistaken when she rested her hopes for his safety upon Marie Challoner's untouched heart. He would have had a hundred times more chance of escape in the beginning if the girl had been a little in love with him or had been flirting with him. She would have been timid, embarrassed, reticent in the first instance, unreal in the second. But now she gave to

him in their conversation with entire unrestraint all the full
freshness of her intelligence, her broad liberal nature, her
emotional sincerity. A girl in love cannot help, consciously or
otherwise, deceiving her lover. Her timidity compels her to
half-concealment, or her longing to please him leads her to assume
what she has not. Marie Challoner had no such need or way.
Christmas saw her intellect and her nature exactly as they were.
And even had he not loved her, he must have admired her, and
must have felt sure that such a woman could give him the life
companionship which his nature would have sought. There are
first-love natures, if one may use such a phrase—natures that
never take fire until the one, *die Eine*, comes with the torch.
These are rare natures anyhow—and when they are found, are
found more often, perhaps, in men than in women; but they do
exist, and are very practical realities. Such a nature will move
on for twenty years from the supposed first-love season, and
never glow under any influence until the right one, *die Eine*,
comes, and never glow at all if she does not come. But let her
show herself when he is at the first threshold of youth, and the
inextinguishable fire lights up that moment. There is a story of
a beautiful alabaster lamp which would allow no candle to burn
within it, and the king and the queen and all the princesses,
sages, courtiers, magicians, priests, and what not, came to try
what could be done, and they could do nothing; and so the
beautiful lamp was given up as a bad job in lampmaking and lay
neglected on the table, until one day a stranger girl, there for the
first time, took it up and breathed lightly by chance on it; and
suddenly its taper burned, and could never after be put out.
Doubtless had she come that way the very first day it would have
answered to her inspiration just as well.

For the present, however, Christmas Pembroke is happy—in
the day. Sometimes in their walks they—he and she—come upon
Nathaniel Cramp, glooming about in lonely places; and Marie
is always friendly and sweet to him, and Nat's face brightens.
Nat and his mother have been up to the Hall once again to see
Marie, and Marie has taken good care to be punctual this time,
and not to keep them waiting for her. Also Nat has been invited
by Miss Lyle to tea, and Marie is there—and Christmas of course
—and Nathaniel has at first comported himself with a proud
humility rather odd and absurd to see, but he has thawed under
friendly influences, and been happy; and Christmas and he went
that night in companionship to smoke their cigars, and Nat cannot help liking Christmas and thinking him a nice unaffected
fellow—and Nat is very miserable.

One memorable morning—memorable at least to Christmas—
Miss Challoner brought a piece of news which everybody ought
to have expected.

"Papa is coming to-night, at last, Miss Lyle; and bringing all manner of people with him. I am so delighted, and disappointed. I wish he had come alone."

"Do you expect him to settle down quietly in the country with no companionship but yours, my dear?" Miss Lyle asked.

"I do expect it sometimes; but I suppose it is an idle thought. I could always be so happy with him. We have always been such friends, Miss Lyle, he and I. We can talk of everything; and he suits me so well because he allows such splendid liberty of opinion, and never wants people to think in grooves."

"You will have to think in grooves when you go to London, Marie."

"Then I shall exhibit my ideas performing in grooves for the outer world, and relieve my mind when I am alone with papa. I don't know that I am delighted at the prospect of a London season, but I suppose I shall get used to it. I do know that I shall always be glad when the time comes round for returning to Durewoods—and to you, Miss Lyle."

"People always say that sort of thing—girls, I mean," said Miss Lyle. "The day you are leaving for London, Marie, find your favourite spot in Durewoods, and look long at it, and take a tender farewell of it. You will never see it again!"

"Never see it again—my Durewoods? Miss Lyle, do you sit there so calmly and smile so blandly at me and prophesy my death before I even come of age?"

"No, dear, not so. What I mean is that the same girl who now looks at Durewoods will never look at it again. That's all. But you have to dree your weird, you know, like all the other young women."

Marie made no answer, and there was silence for a moment. Then Miss Lyle, looking up, saw to her surprise that there were tears in Marie's dark eyes, and that she was trying to conceal them. This was a sensitiveness for which Miss Lyle had not given her credit.

"My Durewoods!" Marie murmured in a low tone as if to herself. They were now in the balcony, and her eyes seemed' to absorb the scene with the eager, craving gaze of an affection which is about to lose the loved object.

At that moment Christmas Pembroke entered, and interrupted the conversation. Miss Challoner and he were going out together. In that irregular little colony Miss Challoner might be said to call for her cavalier of mornings instead of being waited on by him; the reason was that as Miss Lyle hardly ever went out it had long been Marie's habit to call in upon her any morning at any hour—and the visit of Christmas Pembroke made no change in their ways.

Christmas heard the news of Sir John Challoner's coming, and he felt that his time of abiding in a terrestrial paradise was gone. He looked from the balcony over the scene, and the sky seemed somehow to grow dark.

" I think we are going to have rain," he said.

" Oh, no ; the sky looks bright and beautiful," Marie remonstrated, still mentally hugging her Durewoods.

" Does it ? " He looked moodily down. Miss Lyle looked keenly at him, and believed she read him like a book.

" Who are coming with your papa, Marie ? "

" Captain Cameron—you remember him, Miss Lyle—and Mrs. Seagraves, his sister, and one or two other persons too tedious to mention."

" Anybody in particular ? "

" No ; I think not. Some people whose names I don't know."

" Names of men, dear, or names of women ? "

" Of both, Miss Lyle. I hardly noticed who they were. I shall have enough of them soon."

" Very likely. Now don't lose this bright morning. I don't want Mr. Christmas here to miss any chance of stamping Durewoods on his memory."

Thus admonished they went forth, and found the faithful Merlin waiting in his boat for them. Christmas was moody and sententious for some time.

" Will you come to the hollow in the wood, where we went that first day ? " he said, abruptly.

" If you wish. I am always glad to go there."

Merlin made for the shore, and admonished them as they were getting out with his favourite caution, " None quick," which was his way of advising people to go not quickly but slowly.

" Short—none long ! " he added. " High tide, *la limonade* ! " and he gesticulated dramatically to signify that the water would soon be high and billowy.

Christmas thought of the happy chance which on that first day enabled and emboldened him to bear Miss Challoner in his arms through the surf. This day he did not believe he should have the courage even if need were.

They entered the wood and began the ascent, he rather silent, she doing her best to keep up a conversation, but now and then glancing in wonder at him. They reached the little hollow.

" I am tired," said she, and sat on a great moss-covered stone.

" Of the walk ? " he asked gloomily.

" Of the walk up-hill. And perhaps of the day altogether. You are not a good companion, to-day, Mr. Pembroke. Why is that ? "

"I am sorry I cannot amuse you better," he began.

"So am I. Why are you so strange?"

"I ought to leave this place," he said, not looking at her. "I am passing my days here in idleness. I ought to have been in London long before this doing something."

"You ought not to stay too long here," she said, "that is certain. This place is not for you—I mean for any young man of spirit and energy. But I suppose Miss Lyle would have been disappointed if you had gone any sooner. And you have not been here much more than a week, after all."

"I shall go to-morrow—early in the morning."

"Oh! please don't do that, or I shall be so disappointed. You will not? Miss Lyle won't let you if I ask her."

"Why should you ask her?"

"Because I want you to know papa, and him to know you, and you both to like each other. I have set my heart on that."

"You are very kind," murmured poor Christmas sullenly, and wondering how he could be sullen with such friendly dark eyes looking earnestly at him.

"You don't seem glad that papa is coming. Why is that? I thought you would have been glad."

"It is because I am selfish," Christmas said, with gallant self-conquest, "because when Sir John Challoner comes, and his friends, I shall not see so much of you."

"Why not, if you wish? Papa will be glad to see you every hour of the day if you like. He likes everybody whom I like—not a great demand upon his good nature, for I don't like many people."

Christmas was softening.

"But we can't walk together, and come to this place this way," he said. "There will be always people. Your time will be always taken up. And then I must go to London. And then this is the first holiday I have ever had, Miss Challoner, and it is nearly over."

"Yes," she said gravely, "it is nearly over for both of us; but we could not be always making holiday. I envy you, who are going to London to do something. I am going to London soon, and Miss Lyle has been filling me this morning with the saddest forebodings. She speaks as if I were to be transformed into a different creature the moment I go to London, and were never to care for this place any more."

"I suppose it must be so," Christmas said, gloomily, and in the tone of one on whom a long experience of London life had wrought a stern conviction.

"You are as melancholy a prophet as she! I defy augury. No power on earth can change me to this dear place."

"I am afraid I was not thinking of Durewoods." He spoke

with his eyes turned away, and he kept harpooning at the mosses of the rock with Marie's parasol, which he was carrying for her.

"Of what, then, were you thinking? and what is it that must be?"

"I was thinking that when you go to London your time will all be occupied; and you will have so many friends; and you will forget me."

"Why should I forget you? I have often told you that I don't care about people in general; and I thought we had sworn an eternal friendship."

"Do such friendships last?"

"With me, I think so. I haven't had much experience, but I think so; if people trust me, and believe in me. Why should I forget you, and these days? I propose to myself to follow your career always, and to be glad when you do great things. We shall see you in London often, of course."

Christmas looked imploringly into her eyes. He could not, boy that he was, mistake the earnest and friendly expression that he saw there. She was very kind to him. She wished indeed to be his friend—and he was in love with her! If there had been one gleam of alarmed emotion in her eyes, if one tinge of colour had risen too quickly on her cheeks, if her eyelids had drooped even an instant as he looked at her, the poor lad must have broken out in a rhapsodical declaration of his love for her. How near she was to hearing the first avowal of a man's passionate love for her, and as wild a torrent of love delirium as ever insane mortal poured forth! One instant of struggle went on in the young man's heart, and then his chief desire came to be that she should not know it. There, if she could only have understood, was the first step in his manhood's career—earnest, truly, of honest things to come. He had conquered his emotions —at least he had stifled them. He crushed them down in his heart, trampled on them, stamped them into silence, and she knew nothing then.

"I'll love her all the same," he seemed to protest to his own heart. "I'll love her as much as I like. She can't hinder that; and she shall never know."

So he talked of their meeting in London, and of things in general, and the place and the scenery, and what not; and they turned to leave the hollow. A little sweetbriar branch had entangled itself in the sleeve of her dress; he removed it for her, and when she was not looking he hid it in his breast. They went down the hill together, and found the boat waiting for them, and there was no need to lift Marie into it this time.

Nat Cramp was wandering moodily among the trees. He saw the youth and maiden coming down, and he fled from the sight into the woods. Despite the honesty of his better nature, he was inclined to gird and swear against the haughty and happy young swell who might walk with Miss Challoner. "He *is* a handsome fellow," Nat owned with bitterness of heart; and he fiercely envied Christmas Pembroke, who began to feel as if it would be a relief to him to be ordered for execution.

CHAPTER VIII.

A PRIESTESS OF THE FUTURE.

THAT evening Christmas, sitting with Miss Lyle in the balcony, talked to her of his speedy return to London.

"You are right to go, my dear," she said, "and it would be only selfish of me to wish you to remain here any longer. But we have established a friendship, Chris, and every now and then you will come down here and spend a day with me. You will not feel that you are alone in the world, at all events; nor shall I. It makes me happy to have found the son of my old friend. I owe him so much, and I can only try to work the debt out by doing my best to help his son. That is the steamer coming in, is it not?"

Christmas had, despite of himself, been closely watching the approach of the steamer. But when she got to the landing place on the pier she could not be seen from the balcony, and therefore Christmas could neither know whom she brought nor who went to meet her.

"I suppose Sir John Challoner is in her," Miss Lyle said. "I want you to know Sir John Challoner; he could be very useful to you in London."

"I don't think I care to know people who are very rich," said Christmas, "and proud, and all that. I suppose he is a proud sort of man, and I don't want to be patronised, Miss Lyle."

"Still, I should like you to know Sir John Challoner. You will find him interesting; he is a remarkable man. I don't say that you will like him in everything."

"Do you like him?" Christmas asked bluntly.

"My dear Mr. Christmas! an acquaintanceship like that of Sir John Challoner and myself is not to be wrapped up in the word like or dislike. I couldn't finish him off in that easy sort of way. You might as well ask me if I like or dislike the ground, or the trees, or the lapse of years, or the law of gravitation, or something of the kind. *You* are free to form any

opinion, and to like or dislike him as the impression comes. I
have heard of his doing many good things; I never heard of his
doing anything bad.. He is a successful man, Chris—very successful—they say."

"I suppose so. My father knew him, I think you said, Miss
Lyle?"

"Your father and Challoner and I started in life together;
we were all friends, and we were all poor. We separated, and
went on our fool's-errands—some of us. Two of us sought
success after our own heart and found it, and I hope it has done
us good. It was a fine thing when it came, and worth the
sacrifice truly! One of us declined to push for any success;
and if life were a fairy story, Chris, he would have been sure
to find it first and best of all; but then he didn't. You will
know all about it some time, but for the present I want you to
judge Sir John Challoner for yourself. How do you like his
daughter?"

Truth to say, Christmas had been expecting some question
about Miss Challoner all the time, and had been schooling himself to bear it. He looked boldly up into Miss Lyle's face and
said—

"I like her very much. She is a very clever girl, I think,
and quite unaffected. I have known so few girls, Miss Lyle,
that it isn't much of a compliment to say I like her the best of
any I ever met, but I do all the same."

"I am glad to hear it." Miss Lyle had looked somewhat
anxiously into his face. "Nothing could have pleased me more.
I hope you will always be friends. I believe, for all people say,
that there can be friendship between man and woman; and you
and she ought to be good friends."

So the subject passed away, and Miss Lyle was evidently
relieved. Christmas felt, with a certain drawback of shame and
with much pain, that his pious fraud had succeeded, and that he
had played with success thus far the part of Spartan boy, which
he had imposed upon himself. When he left Marie Challoner
that day he had rigorously made up his mind that come what
would he would not move through life a disappointed lover
craving for compassion.

Perhaps there are occasions when the Hercules-choice of a
man's whole career depends not so much on what he really is as
on what he gives himself out to be, even to himself. A modern
soldier, whose name has become almost proverbial for reckless
dash in battle, has left it on record that he was terribly afraid in
his first battle, but that he pretended to be fearless, forced himself to believe accordingly, and so learned to get rid of fear in
the end. Suppose he had been perfectly sincere from the first,
might he not have remained a coward to the last? The necessity

of keeping up the reputation which he had voluntarily assumed
rescued and, in time, regenerated him. Something like a similar
crisis had now presented itself for the choice of Christmas Pembroke. If he had given way and confessed himself, it is only
too likely that the strength and backbone of his character
would have given way, and he would have been a limp and
nerveless creature all his life through. There may have been
within him some instinctive knowledge of this inspiring him.
He may have thought, "It is Now or Never with me; yield now
and yield ever." It may have been wounded youthful pride, so
infinitely more sensitive and exacting than the tempered pride of
later years, toned down by many shocks. It may have been
some melancholy conviction that his father had, for whatever
cause, dispensed with the reward of love, and borne his modest
life with patience and without complaint. Be the cause or
causes whatsoever might be, the Hercules-choice of Pembroke's
life was made.

Nothing said by anybody, even by Miss Challoner herself,
could alter the reality. If she loved him their future might look
difficult and cloudy enough, for she was rich no doubt, and her
father was said to be ambitious, and he, Christmas, was com-
paratively poor and had all his way to make; but the future
would at least be their future. But now he had simply to walk
his own way alone. No power on earth could alter the plain
fact that she did not love. The one only thing left for him to do
was to conceal his wound, and let none be distressed by it but
himself.

To himself, however, Christmas made full confession. He
recompensed himself for his Spartan-boy endurance when other
eyes were on him, by crying out, metaphorically at least, to himself. Next day he went out and mooned about the woods. He
did the shabbiest things, we are ashamed to say, and we only tell
of them because he too had the grace to be sometimes ashamed
of them, and to try and not to do them again. For example, he
ought to have resolutely avoided coming in the way of Marie,
and yet he hung that day about the places where he might
perhaps meet her, even though he knew that if he were to see
her then she must have some companions whom he would have
hated to meet. He started when he heard a sound of footsteps,
and felt as if the most painful and humiliating thing that could
occur to him would be to be found by her and her friends lurking about her father's gates. Then he grew angry with himself,
and went away; and again he told himself that he didn't want
to meet her, didn't wish to meet her just then, and that there
was not the least chance of his meeting her; and so he passed
by the gate again defiantly. Such odd blendings of strength and
weakness had this poor young lover, such brave and resolute

self-repression, such sudden fits of incapacity to struggle against himself. Many of us were young once, and may remember some such unheroic moments.

Meanwhile, during his fluctuations and wanderings, Marie Challoner did pass out of her father's gate, bright, happy, and full of pleasant talk; and Christmas missed seeing her. She was going with her father and two of his friends to pay Miss Lyle a visit. They stayed a long time; so long, that when Christmas returned to Miss Lyle's he found them there still. Fortunately, he was told by Janet when he entered that such visitors were with Miss Lyle, and that she wished to see him, and so he was prepared for the little ordeal. The room seemed full of flickering faces as he entered, among which he only saw distinctly that of Marie Challoner, with her beaming eyes of friendly welcome. He had a vague consciousness of being called up to Miss Lyle by Miss Lyle herself, and being presented to Sir John Challoner, and hearing Sir John say that they had met by chance before, and that he knew Christmas's father long ago. Then Christmas dropped out of the group somehow, and Miss Challoner gave him her hand, and said something friendly; and he saw that Sir John, bending over Miss Lyle's chair, was engaging himself wholly in conversation with her, and he was wondering vaguely who the strangers were, when one of them, a man, turned round, and there was a mutual recognition.

" Hullo! " exclaimed Captain Cameron, " this is a surprise! My friend Pembroke here? My gallant young friend and auxiliary! Why, Miss Lyle, there is a magic about you which produces these things. Now this gives me an opportunity I had long been looking for. Pembroke, oblige me—this way. I want to present you to my sister, Mrs. Seagraves. I say, Isabel? "

Isabel turned round and showed to Christmas a somewhat faded and thin but rather pretty face, with cheek bones a little high, probably in evidence of her Scottish origin, and large hollow eyes. She wore her reddish yellow hair in a kind of elaborate unkemptness over her forehead like a thatch. Her waist was so arranged by nature or art as to seem to begin immediately beneath her arms, and her dress descended long and lank from girdle to heel. As far as one might judge she seemed to have reduced her attire to the minimum of possibility in the matter of petticoats, and might be described as sheathed rather than draped in the tawny-green garment which covered the uninterrupted slenderness of her long form. Mrs. Seagraves usually held her head on one side and spoke from under eyes half covered by their languid lids.

" Isabel," said Captain Cameron, " allow me to present to you my very dear young friend Mr. Pembroke, of whom I have often told you. Pembroke, my sister is an advanced woman, as she

calls it, and I dare say you agree in all her views : all you young
people do now, I believe."

" I hope Mr. Pembroke is of advanced views," said Mrs. Seagraves, extending her hand with especial graciousness. " Indeed
I know he is ; I can read it in his eyes. Miss Challoner—but
please mayn't I call you Marie ? Oh, do let me call you Marie ;
it is so sweet. I may call you Marie—may I not ? "

While appealing to Marie for her consent, which had been
asked and readily accorded two or three times that morning,
Mrs. Seagraves held Pembroke's hand in hers and would not
release it, and Christmas began to feel awkward and to fancy
that he must look ridiculous. Marie being thus appealed to,
looked round, and Christmas could see a gleam of humour in her
expression. She almost smiled at him, and he could not help
smiling in answer. Mrs. Seagraves was too much occupied in her
own conceits even to suspect that anybody could see anything to
smile at in her.

" Marie, then—oh, yes, Marie ! You can see by his eyes—
Mr. Pembroke's eyes—that he has enlightened views of things.
Don't you like his eyes ? "

Mr. Pembroke seems to have good sight," said Marie.

" Yes, thank you, I have pretty good sight," the inspected
young man acknowledged.

" But your views, Mr. Pembroke ? You are advanced, I
know. You have thought of things—you are not like other
young men. I do so like young men who have thought of things."

" I don't know that I have thought very much of anything,"
said Christmas; "and what are advanced views, Mrs. Seagraves ?"

" Oh, *you* know. Not limited views ; not narrow. Boundless,
you know—free. No cramping conventionalities. Freedom from
the world's restraints and trammels ! Of course I don't mean
freedom from all restraints—oh, no, that would never do, and I
am the last person to approve of that. But from some restraints—
some restraints—those that cramp; those that repress—— "

" Didn't some great man say that only in law can the spirit
find freedom ? " Marie asked. She knew it was Goethe, but did
not care to seem too learned.

" Did he ? Only in law—is it ?—can the spirit find freedom ?
How very delightful !—I *do* like that. No, I don't exactly like it,
because I don't quite agree with it ; but of course we must have
law. Not narrow law—that we protest against—but free law—
the law of freedom ! Yes, that is it, the law of freedom. That
is what we want." Mrs. Seagraves was quite happy at having
found a phrase. " That is what your great man meant, Marie—
the law of freedom. Don't you think so, Mr. Pembroke ? "

" I should say that was exactly what he meant," said
Pembroke.

"Marie, you hear? Mr. Pembroke agrees with me that that was what he meant, your great man."

"I am sure Mr. Pembroke is an authority," Miss Challoner said gravely.

"Of course he is, dear. Anybody with such an expression, and such clear, enlightened views, would be an authority. You see our great difficulty of the future is to reconcile freedom *and* law. But if you have the Law of Freedom the problem is solved. Freedom *and* Law—law *in* freedom—don't you see? That was what your great man meant. You must find me out his name?"

"I think it was Goethe," said Christmas, whose father had well grounded him in great authors and sayings.

"Goethe! Of course, how very like Goethe! I do so love Goethe!—at least I used to love him long ago; but now I don't love him; oh, no! I don't like him at all! That is, I like him, you know, of course—we all do; but I don't believe in him quite so much. A conservative intellect, a little narrow—no, not narrow—perhaps I shouldn't say that; but narrow for him, narrow for what he ought to have been. We are so very advanced now, I have quite given up German philosophy of that time—not given it up, you know; I don't mean that—but I don't read it quite so much. You have read a great deal, Mr. Pembroke, I am sure."

"We had nothing to do in Japan but to read. We had hardly any society. But I ought to have read more than I did."

"Japan! You have lived in Japan! How very delightful! How I should like to live in Japan! No, not to live there, of course; but to see it, to travel there. I don't think I should though; they have strange ways there. Don't the ladies there—haven't I read something very strange, and some people would call it shocking, perhaps? How very strange! Perhaps you have seen them yourself? But I am sure you have not, and then, perhaps, it's not true."

Christmas could not well say whether it was true or not, as he had not the least idea what Mrs. Seagraves meant.

"But things are very much advanced in Japan, are they not?" she went on. "I am told that the advancement in Japan is something marvellous. Not what *we* call advancement, of course. Oh dear no! Of course not. But still advancement, you know. We have been advancing here, Mr. Pembroke, during your absence, with giant strides. Well, not perhaps exactly with giant strides, because when one comes to think of it, we really ought to have done a great deal more than we have done, and it makes one despondent sometimes. I often think we are not advancing at all—indeed I do. But we *are*, you know. Oh, yes, we are! It would be very sad if we were not making progress."

" I am afraid Mr. Pembroke has not quite formed his opinions yet," Marie said. "Perhaps he doesn't even know which is advancement and which isn't." She was maliciously amused.

" I don't believe anybody does," Captain Cameron interrupted. " Tell you what, Isabel, you ought to adopt some plan like that they have, or used to have, in the French army with the raw recruits to teach them to know right from left: twist a wisp of hay round one leg and something else round the other, and call out 'hay!' when they wanted the fellow to move the right leg, and the name of the other thing, whatever it was, when they wanted him to move the left. Let a wisp of straw be worn by the advanced people."

" My brother is such a reactionary," Mrs. Seagraves said, smiling sweetly on Pembroke. " I despair of *him.* At least I don't despair of him. Oh, no! not quite so bad as that. I have good hopes sometimes for him, if he would amend."

" Like auld Nickie-ben," said Cameron. " I aiblins might, we dinna ken, still hae a stake."

" Oh, for shame, Robert! How can you speak in such a way? Not that *I* mind, of course; but still the allusion to auld Nickie-ben—Miss Challoner might not like."

" Pooh! My Lady Disdain doesn't understand a word of it. What do people of this generation in England know about Burns? You may bet your pile, as the Californians say, that Miss Marie hasn't a notion of who Nickie-ben is."

" I am very fond of Burns, and I know that Nickie-ben is— Pluto, shall we say!" Marie promptly replied.

" Oh, I do love Burns! and I love auld Nickie-ben, Mrs. Seagraves said. " Not love auld Nickie-ben himself, you know. Of course not—what an idea! But the thought, I mean. So generous, so enlightened! Not advanced, of course—oh dear no! Very much the reverse, in fact. There is no Nickie-ben for *us,* Mr. Pembroke!"

" I am delighted," Christmas answered.

" Oh, yes! I foresee that you and I shall agree in most of our opinions. You will come and see me in London? Robert has pledged himself for you. I mean to take you with me to the Church of the Future."

" Why don't you call it the Paulo-post future?" asked Captain Cameron.

" Robert, how can you? Mr. Pembroke, I know will be greatly interested. We hope to do great things with the Church of the Future; and I shall enlist Mr. Pembroke. Miss Lyle, do you know I have already enlisted your young friend, Mr. Pembroke, for my Church of the Future? What a very delightful young man he is, and such a charming talker! But one mustn't say so—one mustn't let him hear one say so ; he might be spoilt :

young men are so easily spoilt. No, not spoilt, you know. I would not say *that*; but vain, perhaps—vain you would say."

"He shan't become vain here," Miss Lyle said, "for I shall devote myself to undermining any good opinion of himself that you may have helped him to form, Mrs. Seagraves."

"You can't say that he isn't a charming talker," Mrs. Seagraves said, smiling benignly, and with full sincerity, for she really believed that she had had quite a delightful conversation with Christmas, whom she had scarcely once allowed to open his lips.

"Christmas," said Miss Lyle, "Sir John Challoner wishes very kindly that you would dine with him to-day. I have told him that as this is your very last day here I could hardly spare you all the evening, but I have promised for you that you will accompany him and our friends, and take luncheon at the Hall."

"Then this is your last day—your very last?" Miss Challoner said.

"My very last."

"Just now," Sir John said, with gentle correction. "You will come, Mr. Pembroke?"

"Oh, yes, he must come," Marie ordered.

"I must come, indeed; I am delighted," said our young lover, really filled with delight, and saying to himself that as he had made up his mind to bury his love in the most secret and profound depths of his heart, the more friendly he appeared the better. Perhaps in those depths of his heart there was a feeling of unspeakable relief that Captain Cameron was the only man present besides Sir John Challoner and himself. There would be no pang in seeing Captain Cameron paying friendly attention to Lady Disdain.

As they were going out, Christmas was about to take his place straightway by Marie's side, and indeed she invited him with a look of friendly peremptoriness. But Mrs. Seagraves said—

"Such steep steps! Mr. Pembroke, do please give me your arm. I want to talk with you. Robert, dear, do give Miss Challoner your arm."

"Thank you, Captain Cameron, but I don't need any support," said Marie. "I am accustomed to these steps."

"Of course she disdains my support," said the brave Legitimist. "The old story! I never could win the favour of My Lady Disdain! Challoner, why don't you have this girl tamed?"

"I suppose we have all helped to spoil her," Sir John said sweetly. "With me she does as she pleases. It *is* the old story with me, Cameron; this is the second generation of it with me, Mrs. Seagraves."

"Give me your arm, Captain Cameron. I ask it now that

I may show how good I am," Marie said, as they came out on
the road; Mrs. Seagraves, Pembroke, and Sir John Challoner
together, Marie and Captain Cameron behind. As they sauntered
along, Mrs. Seagraves pouring forth her double stream of talk,
which now laved this side of a question and now that, they came
upon Nathaniel Cramp lounging drearily along the road. Christmas nodded a friendly salute.

"Surely," Mrs. Seagraves said—"oh, surely yes! I *do* know
this gentleman?"

Nat bowed with semi-martial grace, and raised his hat, and
murmured that he had had the honour of being presented to
Mrs. Seagraves in Avenir Hall, London.

"Why, of course—how could I have forgotten?—so eloquent a speaker, so profound a thinker! This gentleman—
Mr. —— "

"Cramp, madam," Nathaniel said, driven to bay, and full of
deep regret that he could not give any name which had at least
two syllables in it.

"Cramp of course—Mr. Cramp. How could I have forgotten?
Such a very remarkable name! No, not remarkable though, oh
no, not remarkable in any disagreeable sense, you know—quite
the contrary; but still a name that one ought not to forget,
don't you think so? 'Mr. Pembroke, this gentleman is one
of the most earnest supporters of the Church of the Future."

"Good morning, Natty," said Marie, now coming up, and
giving her hand to the blushing lad. "You never told me
anything about your Church of the Future."

"Why—hullo;" exclaimed Captain Cameron; "if this isn't
my freethinking——" he was just on the verge of saying
"barber" when he checked himself; "friend of Wigmore Street!
I say, young man, haven't we met in Wigmore Street?"

"I have seen you there," said Nat, with lips compressed, and
defiant; "I'm not ashamed of it."

There was an involuntary smile all round. Nat only meant
to convey that much as he disliked his abandoned profession, he
did not blush for it; but his words sounded as though he meant
to disclaim any inclination to blush for having met Captain
Cameron.

"Much obliged, I'm sure," said Cameron, with a jolly laugh.

"I beg your pardon," Nat said, conquered by the good
humour; "I didn't mean *that.*" (A slight inclination to
renewed mirth was visible. Marie remained now, however,
perfectly grave.) "I only meant that I'm not ashamed of
having been *there*—but I've left it now. I don't care for an
occupation like that."

"You are quite right, Natty," spoke up Marie from the
gallant Cameron's arm. "Papa, you know Natty Cramp—Mrs.
Cramp's son? I want you so much to know him."

Hullo, my Lady Disdain?" Cameron interjected. "I say, young fellow, you look a good deal more like a soldier than like a——like a civilian, I mean. You ought to come with me and serve the King."

"I am a Republican," said Natty; "I don't believe in kings."

"How delightful!" Mrs. Seagraves said; "how very nice not to believe in kings!"

"Pish!" Captain Cameron objected; "What does it matter whether you believe in them or not, as long as they are there? My good fellow, what's the use of being a Republican where there isn't a Republic?"

"True," said Nat, "I admit that." He spoke with a personal and grim significance.

"Right!" exclaimed Cameron, in mistaken triumph over a supposed concession. "I thought I could bring you to something. I could make a man of you; I know I could! Never mind your father, my Lady Disdain. This young fellow is made for war, not finance, I know. He's in my line, not Sir John's. Come and fight for a real king and a good cause, Claude Melnotte."

This was an unconscious home-thrust, for poor Nat had lately been yearning in his secret heart for some such possibilities as those that dawned upon the darkness of Claude Melnotte. But he thought of the Republic, and the Church of the Future, and he resolved.

"You're very kind," he stammered out, "and I am very much obliged; but I'm a Republican on principle."

"Good-morning, Natty," Marie said, coming to the rescue, as the patronising Legitimist now turned scornfully away. "We shall see you again—you must come up very soon."

"That's my Radical barber, Isabel," Captain Cameron said, recovering his good humour as they moved away. "That's the fellow I told you of. He seems an honest fellow, though a fool."

"A barber!" said Mrs. Seagraves. "How charming—what a very delightful idea! I do so love to know a barber—when he has intellect and high thoughts—not a common barber, of course. I never knew that barbers had such advanced views. I shall always love barbers for the future—not love them really, you know; but feel that they are men and brothers. So very, very refreshing!"

G

CHAPTER IX

"HER FATHER LOVED ME—OFT INVITED ME."

"I KNEW your father so well," Sir John Challoner said, "that I feel as if you and I were old acquaintances, Mr. Pembroke. Miss Lyle has told you, of course?"

"She told me that you and my father began life together," said Pembroke.

This conversation took place in the library of the Hall, to which Sir John at once led Pembroke, leaving Cameron and somebody else, whose name Christmas did not quite catch, "to amuse the ladies while we begin—or might we not almost say revive?—an acquaintance."

"She didn't tell you that we were rivals at one time, did she? No? Well, I think we were; and I was not the favourite one, Mr. Pembroke, as you may suppose! We were perhaps a little estranged at one time, but I think we remained friends always. I certainly never changed my opinion of your father. He had great talents, but no ambition. I had—well, not much talent, and great ambition. It was perhaps the old story—the old fable; the hare and the tortoise. Your father ought to have made some way in life. He could have if he cared about such things."

"He was thought very highly of in his own profession," said Christmas. "I have seen his name mentioned in newspapers since I came here."

"No doubt, no doubt. I heard his name mentioned every now and then. But what I mean is that he might have got on here in England if he had tried."

"But why should a man trouble himself to try for what he does not value?" asked Christmas.

"A very sensible question. I have put it often to myself. I suppose people say I have succeeded in life, Mr. Pembroke—don't they?"

"Miss Lyle has told me so. I hardly know anybody else in England."

"Well, I have succeeded in a certain sense. I never dreamed, when I was a boy, of anything like this," and Sir John threw a comprehensive glance around him, taking in, apparently, not merely the library and the Hall, but his whole worldly position and possessions. "I was a little disappointed in early life ; and I turned my attention then to making a way in the world. Will you be shocked if I say that I was mainly impelled by a spirit of disappointed rivalry with your father? I will show him, I said, that I can succeed in something. Strange, is it not? Well, I got on. I went into the great field of modern adventure—railways and finance. I married, Mr. Pembroke, for money—strictly for money; and I dare say I was happier on the whole than if I had married for love. My wife has long been dead, but her daughter has taken her place. I hope you like my daughter?"

"Everybody must," Christmas replied.

"Glad to hear you say so—I think her perfection, of course. People say she is good-looking, and I know that she is good. She is clever, too, and will have ambition when she goes a little into the world and sees what life is. Well, I employed my wife's money for our common advancement. I got into Parliament. I made myself useful, and I made myself troublesome; and I am, accordingly, a baronet. I am not content; I have two things yet to accomplish. I want to be in the House of Lords, and I want—as a first step—to be of society."

"But you are in society already, surely," said Christmas, conscious in his heart of a vague wish that Sir John was not in society.

"*In* society, yes; but I said *of* society. You perceive the difference? It is considerable; but you have not yet been in the way of observing our trivial distinctions. Well, Mr. Pembroke, I don't mind telling the son of an early friend that though I am *in* society there, I am hardly yet *of* it; and I mean to be. Many things were against me hitherto. I was known to have risen from the ranks, of course, and my wife was not a person of birth or great culture, though very good and sensible, and clever too. My daughter has education as well as talent, and she may perhaps—of course, one can't say—she may marry somebody in and of society. That would be a good thing, but of course she will always be free to make her own choice. I should not pretend to control her in the least. You see my ambition, Mr. Pembroke, and perhaps you don't think very much of it."

"Oh, I don't say that; I suppose a man must have ambition of some kind—here in England at least," Christmas answered despondingly, and almost regretting he had ever come to the land where it is not even enough to be in society if one be not also of society.

"You'll find it so, believe me. Even our aristocracy here have found it out. The idle days of being a gentleman and nothing else have gone by. A duke toils at the head of some Government department. A marquis's heir works night and day—Whitehall in the morning, the House of Commons at night. Not only that, but the younger sons of the aristocracy are actually pushing themselves into business—into finance, and even into trade."

"I am glad to hear it," said Christmas, resolving to overwhelm Natty Cramp with this knowledge on the first opportunity, but longing all the while to be in the drawing-room with the ladies.

"There's a young fellow inside, Ronald Vidal, the younger son of Earl Paladine, a very old Norman family—you will meet him in a few moments—who seems to me to have a positive genius for finance; I am bringing him out. He is a very clever fellow; at one time he thought of giving himself up to art, and he shewed great promise, but now he is taking to finance. He wants money, Pembroke, but he is of society; I have money, but—well, I said that before. Yes, I know a younger son who is a newspaper correspondent and another who is a partner in a coffee warehouse. Well, that is a change since your father's early days and mine! That brings me back to your own affairs. We must have a long talk over them when I return to London; we should not have leisure and quiet to-day. You have a profession?"

"I suppose I might call myself a railway engineer, but I don't much like the business, at least here," said Christmas. "I think of going back to Japan, or to India."

"Oh, no; at least we will think over things first. I can perhaps help—or at least advise you. I can tell you many things —I observe life a good deal in intervals of occupation. I want you to regard me as a friend, Pembroke, and to consult me freely. No, no, don't let us talk of thanks—your father's son has a claim. Come, I wanted just these few words of talk; the rest will keep for London. Shall we find Mrs. Seagraves and Marie?"

This conversation did not run on as smoothly as it has been set down here. Sir John kept moving about the library, taking down a book here and there, and inviting Christmas's attention to this or that particular edition. Sometimes he picked up from a table or a cabinet some little object of art or curiosity and showed it to his visitor; once or twice, as if unconsciously, he took a letter that lay open on his desk, and, asking Christmas if he cared about celebrities, remarked that it was in the handwriting of some great Minister or other eminent personage. This might be kindly good-nature wishing to amuse its visitor, or it might be the ostentation of a *nouveau riche*. Even a more critical observer than Christmas might have found it not quite easy to decide which was the impulse. Perhaps Sir John was inspired by neither one feeling nor the other, but was only anxious to find out what were the tastes of his visitor, as Ulysses tested the inclinations of the disguised Achilles.

"If you were staying longer in Durewoods," Sir John said, "I would ask you to make this library your place of study or lounge. But you will come here again: you will come here again."

As they left the library, and passed through halls and corridors, Sir John still kept drawing Pembroke's attention to this
or that object of interest or object that ought to be interesting.
But if his design in such a course were to discover what Christmas's tastes were, he must have been disappointed, or must have
come to the conclusion that Christmas had no tastes at all. For
the poor youth had so much to do with keeping down his feelings
on other subjects that he could not get up any decent seeming of
interest in pictures, books, or curiosities. Every sentence of Sir
John's friendly and confidential exposition of his own hopes and
plans seemed to put Christmas more and more distinctly outside
the threshold, so to speak. Marie Challoner had talked so kindly
and openly to him, that Christmas had felt within his own breast
something of the gloomy grandeur of a disappointed lover. Sir
John seemed to have, in the easiest and most unconscious manner,
conveyed to our hero a conviction that even in holding such a
thought in his secret heart he was guility of a preposterous
absurdity.

Sir John often leaned in an almost affectionate way on
Christmas's shoulder. They came thus to the door of a drawing-
room, were they heard sounds of music. Sir John was talking
with Christmas in the friendliest confidence. Suddenly, as they
entered the room, as if reminded of himself, he withdrew his arm,
and resumed at once his habitual manner of composed and somewhat cold urbanity. The change was that which would naturally
be made by a man of warm and genial friendship who nevertheless did not choose to wear his heart upon his sleeve. It thus
impressed Christmas, and he felt grateful for the sincerity of the
friendship it implied. He was glad of a little friendship just
then.

Mr. Ronald Vidal was seated at the piano, on which he had
been playing, while Mrs. Seagraves and Miss Challoner stood near.
Captain Cameron was leaning with his manly back against the
chimney-piece, and looked as if he had had enough of music.
The moment Sir John and Christmas entered the young man
stopped his playing and twirled himself quickly round on his
piano stool until he faced the company. He was a bright, handsome, yellow-haired young man, with a soft complexion, and a
face almost feminine in its outlines, although his figure looked
solid and strong enough, and he had very white fat hands. He
wore a long silky, light brown moustache, and no beard. He was
the sort of person whom an admiring young woman might take
as a model for a troubadour in a picture. If this was embryo
Finance, then Finance seemed happier than most divinities in
her power of disguise.

" No more of that from yours truly," Mr. Vidal promptly said.
' I know how Challoner feels when people are playing music at
him."

"I don't think I ought to be charged with ever showing a want of patience," said Sir John, smiling.

"No, but of course one feels that one isn't in tune when everybody is not as much of an enthusiast as Mrs. Seagraves, for example. I know Cameron hates music; but then we don't mind him—he has to suffer."

"I like music immensely," Cameron said, "but not that sort of effeminate music—only fit for boys and girls fancying themselves crossed in love. I like 'Scots wha hae,' or the 'Flowers of the Forest.' There was a piper in our regiment—long ago, in the good old days before Progress—if you only heard him—oh!" And in despair of conveying any adequate idea of what this musician could do, Captain Cameron stopped short abruptly.

"I believe it is not usual to introduce people now," said Miss Challoner; "but I do it—— "

"Therefore you do it, perhaps," Captain Cameron interrupted.

"Therefore I do it, if you like," said dear Lady Disdain, graciously. "Mr. Vidal—I want to introduce Mr. Christmas Pembroke and you to each other. Mr. Pembroke has lived in Japan, and grown familiar there with all the hideous things that you have been trying to persuade Mrs. Seagraves and me to admire."

"Oh, but I do admire Japanese things," said Mrs. Seagraves. "I think everything Japanese is so very lovely. Not everything, of course; because, as Marie says, some Japanese things are hideous. But we need not admire the hideous; we may select and keep to the beautiful. Now the colours of that fan which Mr. Vidal so admires, could anything be more lovely?"

"But that isn't Japanese," Christmas said, to whom Mrs. Seagraves had handed the fan; "that thing was never made in Japan." Perhaps he was not sorry to have an opportunity of contradicting somebody.

"Oh yes! surely yes! that is Japanese; Mr. Vidal says so." Mrs. Seagraves pleaded as earnestly as if she were appealing to Justice against some darksome wrong.

Christmas shook his head. "That thing was never in Japan, I can assure you; unless somebody took it out there and brought it back."

"So much for enthusiasm," said Cameron. "Let me look at it. Why, of course it isn't Japanese—unless the Palais Royal is in Japan. Is this your connoisseurship, Vidal? Eh? Am I to judge of your music by this—your—what d'ye call him—Chopin?"

"Oh, Chopin is divine, a divinity!" Mrs. Seagraves exclaimed.

"I hope he is; for some of you would be simply Atheists without him," her brother remarked.

"I do so love Atheists," said Mrs. Seagraves—"at least I like, them, they are so very interesting; but of course one is sorry for their opinions, you know—only they are so nice! I know such very delightful Atheists!"

Mr. Ronald Vidal lapsed out of the general conversation the moment anybody who professed to know anything intervened. He drew Marie away, too, and began to describe the Wagner music to her. He talked with immense vivacity, and he knew a good deal of many things; but he never thought any point worth arguing, and he had no faculty of improving his own knowledge by any supplementary information. If he did not seize upon the right idea at the first flash, he never got at it afterwards. He liked to be an authority upon everything, and to direct people how they were to think. He was a good-natured youth, with a manner which seemed brilliant, because he talked very quickly, and passed with a leap from subject to subject. But he never said a very clever thing, and never understood a joke. He got on particularly well with women, who liked his quick talk, and his free familiar ways in which there was not a hint of impudence or anything offensive. He was free with women, almost as if he were one of themselves; and most of them liked his ways and petted him. He could play on the piano wonderfully, sing finely, was wild about Chopin and Balzac and pre-Raphaelitism; and could tell ladies exactly how to think and talk on these subjects; and how to arrange their china and their Salviati-glass; and how their dresses ought to be made, and what colours harmonized with what; and what flowers were allowable in one's bonnet or one's hair.

Christmas observed him with half contemptuous sullenness, thinking him a fribble and a sort of epicene creature, and growing every now and then ashamed to find how like his own sentiments towards the British aristocracy were becoming to those of Nat Cramp. Christmas was wrong in his judgment. The Hon. Ronald Vidal was no fribble. With all his superficial way that young man was really very clever, and he was profoundly in earnest in everything he talked about. If he lectured ladies occasionally on dresses and bonnets it was as the exponent of a deep theory in art which prescribed a purpose and a colour for everything, from a fresco in a church to a ribbon in a girl's hair.

Sir John Challoner drew Christmas into the recess of a window.

"You will like to observe things," he said. "You see in our friend Ronald Vidal an illustration of a new figure in our age. There is the son of an earl, brought up to do nothing, who is sometimes, I can tell you, my master in bold and subtle financial combinations, and who once, when he had cleared twenty thousand pounds at a stroke, spent the whole of it in becoming lessee and manager of a theatre because he thought he had discovered a new Siddons, and had a theory of his own about the drama of modern life. He has founded no end of amateur musical societies, and he has sung as first tenor in an Italian theatre. He knows the ways and the people of the House of Commons, of which he isn't a member, better than I do; and he knows a hundred times more about the fashions in ladies' dress than my daughter. A few centuries ago he would have been a crusader and a troubadour."

"That is progress indeed!" Christmas said, beginning to think that he found a fine quality of satire and cynicism developing within him.

"From a crusader to a financier?" Sir John asked with his quiet smile.

"To a stage manager, I meant."

"The crusades were on a larger scale certainly," Sir John said. "In that way we *have* degenerated. But I am glad to see an earl's son in business—and he and I are in a sort of partnership, did I tell you? His father and mother asked me, Pembroke —made it a positive favour on my part."

" *That* is progress," Christmas felt impelled to say, but he was not quite certain whether Sir John had been speaking seriously or satirically. He had been observing Marie's father as closely as his condition of feeling allowed, but he could not yet make up his mind as to whether Sir John was a cynic or a sycophant in his dealings with the families of the peerage.

The visit was disagreeable to Christmas. He had hardly any chance of speaking to Marie at luncheon, and Mrs. Seagraves bored him. He got away at last as quietly as possible, saying nothing which could remind any one that that was the last day of his visit to Durewoods. Marie did not even notice his going, as Mr. Ronald Vidal, full of spirits, was telling her something very interesting apparently at the time. Christmas passed quietly out of the house and out of the grounds. He found Miss Lyle in her balcony, leaning over and talking to Merlin. She told Merlin that Mr. Pembroke was going away to-morrow, and added, "We shall be lonely here, Merlin, shan't we?"

"No, no, none-lone; none-lone!" the old man said in earnest and almost angry remonstrance. "Mademoiselle, no!"

"Why not, Merlin?"

"Mademoiselle have me!" and he smote a great blow on his chest to indicate apparently that there he was and there he remained, like Marshal MacMahon.

"Merlin doesn't endure any rivalry, you see," Miss Lyle said with a certain gratified expression.

Meanwhile Merlin, who was, as will be understood, underneath the balcony on the grass, was apparently in some embarrassment. He was looking downwards, as if searching for something. He had a dim idea that what he´ said must have grieved Christmas, and he was trying to find something consoling and complimentary to say, and English words to put it in. Suddenly he caught the idea, and looked up.

"Mademoiselle Marie lone. Oh, yes, yes! Mademoiselle Marie, she lone! Yes, yes! Mademoiselle Leel none-lone. No!"

"Mademoiselle Marie seemed very happy just now," said Christmas, in explanation to his hostess, for Merlin had not waited for any answer or comment, but disappeared into the house.

"I am not sorry to hear it," said Dione. "I was a little afraid—shall I confess it? that you might fall in love with her, Chris; but I am glad to see that you are heart-whole; that shows some sense, and I think the more highly of you. It would never do, Chris, believe me; and if you are at all like your father, I should be sorry to see you made unhappy for the best woman that ever lived!"

Never hero bore up better than Christmas did all that evening under trying conditions. He was hurt to the quick, and he could not and would not complain. Why should he complain? he asked himself. He was only an acquaintance, like another; he had helped Miss Challoner to pass her time for a few dull days, and now livelier companions had come and he was naturally forgotten. It served him right, he told himself, mentally. Had he always remembered the sweet, kind woman—his father's friend—seemingly his own only friend—when a pretty girl smiled on him?

So he rallied up, and pulled himself together, and made himself as agreeable as he could to Miss Lyle, and was prepared to leave Durewoods the next morning with a heart steeled firm by philosophy and rigid endurance. Alas for the philosophy and the endurance when, as Miss Lyle and he sat in the balcony after dinner, and looked over the sea, a flutter and swirl of rather impetuous petticoats was heard in the room, and presently Marie Challoner was with them on the balcony, looking brilliant with motion and haste and friendly good nature.

"Am not I a wild girl, Miss Lyle? I don't wonder if you scold me. I have left my people, and escaped for a moment, all alone, and with this shawl over my head. I had not a chance of saying one word of good-bye to Mr. Pembroke to day, and he vanished somehow, and I couldn't let him leave us in that way."

"You are a good creature, Marie," said Miss Lyle; "but isn't this rather an escapade?"

"Oh no! I shall be back before I am missed by any one. I shall fly back. But to part in *that* way would have been so unfriendly."

Pembroke stood silent. He was overwhelmed with emotion. He could not speak as yet, and he knew that both the women looked at him.

"Good-bye, Mr. Pembroke—no, not good-bye, but *au revoir*. We shall see you in London."

"Don't forget me," stammered Christmas, trying to smile and look pleasant.

"Come to us, and don't allow us to forget you—*au revoir!*"

"I must see you safely home."

"Indeed you must not! Have I not broken bounds, evaded, escaped, to say a parting word, and to pledge you to see us in London? Would you betray me?" Good-bye for the present; good night, Miss Lyle: don't be too angry with me!" and she kissed her, then wrapped her shawl again over her head, and there was an undulating of skirts and a rustle of silk, and she was gone.

"Those girls!" said Dione. "But why do I talk of girls? No girl but herself would have done *that.*"

The moon just then rose, and Christmas remained silent.

Next day Christmas stood in the stern of the *Saucy Lass*, and looked back upon the place where he had been so happy. He could see the roof of the Hall, and the trees that sheltered it; and could trace the double row of trees that marked the steep road up which he had driven with Marie Challoner that first night, and the woods that sloped down to the water—the woods which held the broad, lonely hollow, where he and she had stood side by side! Only a few days ago—he could hardly convince himself that days so few had passed. And everything—the very sunlight included—had been changed for him. He felt exalted into a kind of sublime wretchedness. He was half wild with love and the struggle for self-repression and boyish shame. He felt as if he could not leave the place. He had half-crazy ideas of leaping ashore and hiding himself in the woods—in that fatal hollow— and waiting there in the hope that *she* would come there, perhaps that very day, and seeing her once more. If she had any feeling for him she must come there—she would come; and he should see her, and speak with her once more—even once: and what matter if he died then? For his was the happy melancholy age of egotism when we believe in our hearts that Fate must surely be willing to make our lives into something dramatic, and to bring down the curtain for us at any moment when we give the signal.

Perhaps he might even have committed some absurdity of the kind he meditated, but that the *Saucy Lass* rang her bell, blew her steam whistle, and moved away from the pier. She moved slowly seaward a few hundred yards, and then, as if the Destinies meant to torture poor Christmas by keeping him still

in sight of his lost Elysium, she suddenly came to a stop. There
she remained motionless. A bank of clay, which sometimes at
low water obstructed the little estuary's course, had lately been
increased in bulk by the washings of some unusually high tides,
and now the tide being far on the ebb, and the *Saucy Lass* rather
heedlessly steered, she had run her bows and her keel into it,
and stuck fast. So there stood Christmas, while the captain and
crew were striving to get her off; and he could see the roof of
the Hall still, and could, in the words of a once famous adventurer, have " flung a biscuit ashore "—and he could not get
there. He was kept there, neither living nor dead. To think
that all this time he might as well have been on shore; that he
might have seen *her* once again; that perhaps that very moment
she might be in that hollow of the woods! He chafed and fretted
against the powers above, and the mud bank, and the *Saucy Lass*,
and Destiny.

An hour went on, and the *Saucy Lass* had not gone off. She
must wait now for the rise of the tide, it seemed, and that would
be some time yet. Meanwhile the weather had begun to change.
The sun, which had looked with unpitying brightness on poor
Christmas's pain, was now covered with clouds, and a little chilly
wind blew, and presently the heaven was all grey. Then came
a heavy dull drizzle, and the sea became of lead under a leaden
sky; and the sea birds flew low down to the water, and sent forth
dreary cries. The Hall and the woods and the village were seen
no more: went out in mist and in gloom. Then it rained heavily,
and everything seemed miserable.

Christmas felt a dismal satisfaction in the new aspect of the
scene and the condition of the weather. They suited with his
humour. Besides, they settled the question of returning to the
shore. He might wander in vain through the dripping woods
on such a day as that! He must go his way—all he asked now
was that the *Saucy Lass* would go hers, and take him from that
place.

At last the movement of the steamer's paddles told him that
she was about to work herself free. At the same moment he
heard the sound of oars, and saw that a boat had come up to the
side of the steamer. In an instant Nat Cramp, portmanteau,
rifle-case, and all ready for travelling, scrambled on board, and
Christmas and he exchanged a greeting.

" I wasn't quite certain about going back to-day," said Nat;
" mother would have liked me to stay. But where's the use, and
having to go at last? And when I found that the steamer hadn't
got off, I took it as the hand of Destiny, and I came."

Christmas was a little amused at the thought of Destiny's
hand troubling itself to make a special sign to Mr. Cramp. But
he had been thinking, vaguely, perhaps, but still thinking, about

Destiny's interference in his own affairs, which seemed quite a natural and proper sort of thing for Destiny to do.

"Going to London?" the one child of Destiny asked of the other.

"I'm going to London—yes, in the first place," Nat said gloomily; but I shan't be in London for long. I have made up my mind, I told my mother so; and that's one reason why I was glad when the boat stuck, you know, and let me get away. I couldn't stand her sorrowful face the whole day, you know."

"No," said Christmas, "I suppose not." But he was not thinking of the face of Nat's mother.

"I can't stand this place—I mean England—much longer," Nat said; "oh—we're going at last."

The *Saucy Lass* was quite free now, and she splashed her way towards the grey waters of the broad bay. Christmas and Nat · stood in the streaming mist and looked back, and tried to see the shore and the woods.

"Yes, I'm going away," Nat said, returning with a half audible sigh to his own affairs. "I mean to leave this old used-up country. I'm sick of it! Nothing but classes and ranks, and aristocracy, and caste, and all sorts of things like that! What way is there for a man of any spirit here? None, sir—none. I hate the whole thing. I shall seek out a career for myself."

"Where are you going?"

"To the West of course, the New World. I'll take your advice. The young Republic beyond the western waves!" And Nat flung the arm which did not hold the rifle-case proudly abroad, as if he were doing homage to the Republic that "rears her crest unconquered and sublime above the far Atlantic." Indeed, the poetic youth had those very lines of Byron's in his mind at the time, and he would have burst out with them if he had not feared that Christmas would smile. For poor Nat had a terrible fear of being laughed at by persons whom he presumed the world regarded as his social superiors. Thus, Republican and democrat that he was, he paid the tribute of his enforced homage to worldly position and rank twenty times a day. He was afraid of it even when it presented itself to him in the modest disguise of so unpretending a person as Christmas Pembroke. Thus in the classic days people were vaguely conscious of the presence of an awful deity, and were moved to fear even though the god showed himself in the form and aspect of some ordinary mortal.

"Going to the States? Quite right," said Christmas. "Of course it's the best thing you can do; you will be sure to get on there. Go out West—that is your place."

"I'll make a name there," the enthusiast exclaimed; "and people here shall hear of me before I come back to England again."

" What would you come back for? What do you want here? "

" I don't know," Nat said wildly, not daring to confess that he felt himself in imagination dragging at each remove a lengthening chain, and that all his dreams were of bursting in some day upon the stage of English life a splendid personage with name and money from the Republic beyond the Atlantic.

" Don't think of coming back," the kindly Christmas went on, in the full belief that he was giving the best possible advice. " Go out there determined to stay. Send for your mother when you get settled, and have her out there."

Nat looked a little gloomy. " Are you remaining here? " he asked, tentatively.

" I have to remain here for some time. I don't know what I shall do with myself yet. My father wished me to live in England —why, I don't know. I sometimes wish I never had come here," Christmas added, desperately. " Does it always rain like this? Is the climate always so detestable? I hate that sort of sky and an atmosphere like this."

The *Saucy Lass* rounded the headland and was in the broad bay, and Durewoods was extinguished.

Meanwhile Marie Challoner, weather-bound, was endeavouring to the best of her power to amuse her father's guests. She played a game of billiards with Captain Cameron, and she showed her prints and photographs and music to Mrs. Seagraves; and she played chess with Mr. Ronald Vidal, and he sang to her, and she sang to him. She was sorry Christmas had gone, but glad on the whole that she had known him; glad, though his coming had brought with it some little forebodings perhaps of perplexity and pain. She thought of him with kindly memory, and with hope to meet him again, and she even missed him, and wished that she had had him for a brother, or even a cousin perhaps. And if the day had been fine and she could have got away she would in all likelihood have gone to the beautiful little lonely hollow in the breast of the wood where she had been with him. But if the day had been fine she would probably have taken Mrs. Seagraves and Mr. Ronald Vidal too.

CHAPTER X.

"IS DUREWOODS NOT THE SAME?"

MOST of us believe in an ideal Self—something moving dimly in advance of us in life and kept apart from us continually by practical business, or by fits and starts lost sight of as the real man wanders away after temptation, but still to be seen every now and then in glimpses. This is perhaps the Genius of the Roman mythology which pertained to every individuality. It is the image of what one would have been if everything had gone exactly as it ought to have gone : if we had not been so poor when we were young, or so rich when we were young; if this person who has hardly any excuse had not tempted us; or that other, who has absolutely no excuse had not thwarted us. The world and the flesh and the other influence must have taken a terrible hold of a man when he is not allowed sometimes to catch a glimpse of this ideal Self.

The world and the flesh had not so blurred the eyesight of Sir John Challoner but that he sometimes saw, or fancied he saw, this ideal Self. It was visible dimly when he read in his library, but far more clearly and certainly when he was in the company of his daughter. It pleased him to think that in her company—that is, when they two were alone—he was then and only his real self. Perhaps a critic, if he could have known of this belief and analysed the evidence that supported it, would have said that Sir John Challoner, in his daughter's company, was only performing a part in order to hold her esteem and affection and be a hero in her eyes. But Sir John always told himself that with her he was what he would have been in the world and in life if things had gone otherwise; if he had not been driven to take up with ambition; if getting on in London were not so exacting a pursuit; and if a man who sprang from nothing had not so much to contend with. The unhappy artist in Murger's " Bohemia " cries out over the coffin of his mistress that it is his youth they are burying; if Sir John Challoner had been doomed to stand beside his daughter's grave he would have felt a similar pang of tortured egotism, and bewailed his ideal Self buried along with her.

Sir John was late in going to rest and early in rising. He accommodated himself to at least half the proverbial conditions of amassing health, wealth, and knowledge. His daughter, as we know, took after him in sitting up late, and—sometimes—in rising early. Sir John knew that while he was in London Marie was in the habit of sitting up in her room reading for hours after every other creature in the house and in Durewoods had gone to bed. He never advised her against such a practice or even suggested to her, as elders are wont to do, that late hours and lamplight were likely to wither the roses of her youth. He never crossed her in anything, and hardly ever gave her any direct advice. He had an idea that elder people commonly lose their influence over the young by boring them with advice which young people never take except under coercion. Besides, he told himself that he was by no means sufficiently certain about anything to make it worth his while to lose the full confidence of his daughter by preaching to her this line of conduct rather than that. When Sir John married he found that his wife had strong religious convictions. He had none himself; he did not care much either way, he said, for that sort of thing; he was far too active and busy to have time to think about such subjects. So he told his wife that she was free to bring up the children in any way and to any faith she liked. That was only fair, he thought, as she had some decided opinions, and he had not. If her creed proved to be right in the end, the children would clearly have gained by it; and of course if he proved to be in the right they would be none the worse. "The children" turned out to be only Marie, and when Sir John was in Durewoods he went to church with Marie on Sundays if she wished it.

The result of all this was that Sir John always seemed a delightful companion and a sort of hero to his daughter, and that he had a genuine influence over her, which would have weighed heavily upon a man endowed with a profounder sense of responsibility.

The night of the day when Christmas left for London Marie sat up reading in her turret chamber, the room in which Nathaniel Cramp had done honour to the châtelaine. Two soft lamps lighted the room, and, though the rain was still falling heavily, one of the windows stood open, and the sharp little wind that had blown all day switched a long branch every now and then dripping across the opening. Marie put down her book occasionally and looked out across the wind-shaken trees and over the gusty sky with its hurrying and ghost-like clouds. She felt very happy in the poetic variety of the wild wet night. In the country you must live on sensations or be content to vegetate; and Marie could not vegetate. So after a lovely summer day there was delicious variety in the stormy anachronism of wind and rain; as company pleased her after solitude, and then when the company had gone, welcome to solitude again. It amused and pleased her father often to observe how many of his peculiarities she had.

Marie was expecting her father to come to her room. She

knew he would come when the latest of his guests had left him. About eleven o'clock he made his appearance and settled himself down, as was his wont, for a talk.

"You are never sleepy at night, Marie—still the same?"

"Never, papa. Is that a very bad thing?"

"I suppose so; you are like your hapless father in that way. We can't help it, dear; and we still live. Good people always go to bed early."

"So I have always heard. But it is so delightful to read at night."

"It is—and you look wonderfully well, Marie. How do you like Ronald Vidal?"

"Well, I don't know. He is very new to me; and he is odd, and he seems clever. Is he old or is he young?"

"Doesn't his face tell his story?"

"He is handsome! and of course he looks young. But he seems to have withered up prematurely—he reminds me of the stories of changelings—Welsh fairy stories, are they not? And Breton, I think—old Merlin has told me of such things."

"Old heads are on many young shoulders in London now, Marie—shoulders of girls, dear, as well as of boys. I sometimes think we of the elder generation are the only young people; and I would insist upon it everywhere but that I am afraid to argue myself young now would only prove me old."

Marie looked with a smile of admiration at her tall, handsome, dark-haired father.

"Mr. Ronald Vidal must be about a century and a half older than you, papa. We count time by heart-throbs, you know—so Festus says—was it not Festus?"

"Then you think palpitations of the heart have made Vidal grow prematurely old? I shouldn't have thought that, Marie; but I am glad if you think so."

"Heart! No, I didn't mean that; I applied my quotation badly. I don't suppose he has any heart to speak of."

"Perhaps he doesn't wear it on his sleeve for young women to peck at."

"Daws I think it is in Shakespeare, papa; but daws and young women I suppose are pretty much the same."

Sir John smiled.

"He is a very clever young fellow, Marie; he has plenty of brains."

"Yes, I suppose so. But why does he talk of lace?"

"Of lace, dear?"

"He talked to me a great deal to-day about lace and old china."

"Well, old china wasn't so bad perhaps. This age of progress, you know, has discarded Greek art for old china, and we have

thrown over the Venetian school of colourists for the artists of
Japan. Vidal always likes to be abreast of the latest intellectual
developments."

" And the lace ? "

" That was to please you, I dare say. He doesn't talk to *me*
about lace. Men of a certain order of mind always mean to pay
a compliment to a woman when they assume that she only cares
about lace and that sort of thing. But if you show Vidal that
that is not your line he will very soon find some other subject.
I'll tell him, if you like, that you are a very clever, intellectual
young woman, and that you care no more about lace than he
does."

" Oh, please don't do that—it would frighten him ; he would
think me a sort of Minerva, and I shouldn't like that. Let him
think me as silly as he pleases. I like him very much as he is ;
he is quite an odd and curious study—and when is he going
away ? "

" He never stays long anywhere. But you will see him very
often in town. How do you like young Pembroke ? "

" Very much. There is something about him so fresh and
unstudied. He seems so young ; and yet not stupid and awkward
like a boy."

" He is the son of one of my oldest friends—you know,
Marie ? "

" He told me, dear ; and Miss Lyle too. I hope you mean to
be very kind to him."

" I think I shall take him under my charge altogether, if I
can—if he will fall into my ways. He is very young——." Sir
John hesitated.

" But he will grow, dear,—he will grow. I am so glad to
hear that you will help him on. I was going to make it my
humble petition to you—on my knees, if you insisted—that you
would do something for that good, clever boy. I suppose he is
poor—at least not rich. He told me *that*."

" Making you his confidant already, Marie ? "

" Oh yes, papa. I think I asked him to tell me all about
himself ; and he told me everything—everything ! But your
suspicion is wrong, papa, for all that."

" My suspicion, Marie ? " Sir John asked, a little uneasy that
she should think he had any suspicion.

" Yes, dear ; I saw you smile ! You think he was trying to
secure my influence with you—that was your idea. Confess."

" Sir John smiled again—this time a good deal relieved.

" You were quite wrong indeed, papa. He had nothing of
the kind in his mind. On the contrary, I think he is full of a
sort of fierce independence—like some wild bird. We must be
very cautious with him or he will fly away."

"Well, Marie, we will respect his spirit of independence. It is not a fault which troubles us too often in modern life. I am so glad to find that you like this young fellow, for we shall see him pretty often in London; and I meant to ask you, Marie, as a favour to myself and for the sake of times that you can't remember, to be specially friendly and attentive to this poor lad."

"How glad I am that I know him and like him so much already! I have grown quite attached to him; and this is not—I see you smile again—this is *not* one of my sudden likings, and I shall not drop him in a moment. I have made him a study, and I am sure I know him thoroughly; and I feel convinced that I shall always like him."

"I hope so, Marie. Why I want you to be especially civil to him is this—we shall have many men among our acquaintances in London of very different position and fortunes and prospects from poor Pembroke; and men of course of far greater talent—men of name and mark and all that; and I should be sorry if he thought that we looked down upon him, whatever they—I mean whatever others—might do."

"No one ever shall think that of me," Lady Disdain said with generous warmth.

"Nor of me, dear."

"Oh, they couldn't think it of you. You are always doing generous things. Nobody thinks you could be impelled by any mean feeling. But women are so ungenerous sometimes—I don't mean to be so, and people shall know it."

Sir John then turned the conversation away to other things. Marie did not forget to ask for his influence in some way or other on behalf of Nat Cramp; and Sir John, promising that from what he had observed he fully believed Nathaniel to be an inflated young idiot, promised nevertheless. It was Miss Marie's sincere opinion that her father could make the fortune of any one whom he pleased to patronise. They then talked of books and new poets. Sir John always took care to keep up with the new things, and to profess to admire them, whether he did or not, if his daughter did, lest he should seem in her eyes uncompanionable or elderly; and he always took care to avoid professing undue admiration for things which "were so in his time." At last he rose to go away. His daughter stood up, threw one arm around his neck, and kissed him. He held her apart for a moment, and looked with admiration and a sort of wonder, real or assumed, at her tall and finely developed figure.

"Why, Marie," he said, "you are a woman at last—a grown and even a tall woman! You were a little girl the other day, and now you are fit to be married! When we go to London in the winter you will have suitors enough, I dare say. But we mustn't take up with the first comer, Marie—you and I. You are far too clever and too handsome a woman not to have ambition."

"Is ambition so fine a thing?" Marie asked thoughtfully, and without noticing her father's praises.

"Is anything fine?" Sir John said, with a slightly cynical movement of his shoulders. "I don't know, Marie, if anything in life really deserves to be called fine. But ambition survives most things in certain natures; in people, perhaps, like you and me. And when one has great influence one can do great good."

"That is true," the girl said slowly, "that is quite true."

"People rail at ambition, my dear, who have not the capacity for success. If I had not been ambitious, Marie, how could I ever have been in a position to do any good, or lend a helping hand to mortal? I have done some good in my time, and shall again, and so will you. You will have influence and power some day. I see it! And you will use it well! Yes, love, you are quite a woman! At last—so soon! Good night, Marie."

He kissed her affectionately and left the room.

Marie stood for a short while where he had left her, and alone though she was, her face seemed to glow. The long, sweet, blank days of girlhood were over, then, and she was a woman! And there was a great world in which she was promised a career, and influence, and rank, and power of doing good. She might be of herself a benefactress and an influence, and be looked up to, and feel that she was something in existence. She had not thought of such things for women. A man may know or dream that he is on the threshold of a career; but the life of a girl is so different. And yet now here are promptings and counsels which tell her that she, too, may have ambition and success. Her heart palpitated.

She turned to the window and looked upon the tossing trees and the wild waste sky.

"I wish the night were fine," she said half aloud. "Is Miss Lyle right—already? Is Durewoods not the same?"

That night Marie dreamed of being a great princess, and of becoming a splendid patroness of Christmas Pembroke and of Natty Cramp.

Sir John went down to his library meanwhile, and began to turn over a number of business letters, proposals, and sketched-out projects, which he had put aside in the day for more deliberate consideration. But he seemed to have less than usual the power of turning his mind full on to these drier matters of business. He had a plan more intimately concerning himself in his thoughts, which he meant to work out if he could. So after a while he put his papers away, and nursed his knee, and thought over things. The more he thought the more he felt satisfied that he had hit upon the right policy to bring about the results at which he was aiming. The appearance of Christmas Pembroke upon his scene had been to him a very unwelcome and ominous apparition. The young man was handsome, attractive, fresh and winning in his ways, and he presented himself under romantic circumstances as the son of an old, long-lost friend and rival, and he came under the picturesque patronage of Dione Lyle. Here was something quite different from an ordinary young fellow turning up in the beaten way of London society; and Challoner knew that his daughter was impulsive and romantic, and he had little doubt that she could, under certain conditions, be self-willed.

Besides he had a strong conviction that Miss Lyle had brought forward this youth with a set purpose. He felt sure that Dione had brought his daughter and Pembroke purposely together. Dione had loved the lad's father, and she was full of romantic ideas, and Sir John always suspected that she owed him a spite because of the efforts he had made long ago, when he cared about such things, to keep her and her lover asunder. He did not know that Dione, or anybody, had ever found out what stratagems he had employed for the purpose; but he assumed that she had, and that even when she was most civil to him she cherished a spite against him. For himself, of course, he had long ceased to have any ill-feeling to anybody on the subject. He was now exceedingly glad that Dione Lyle had not married him, and he was rather sorry the elder Pembroke had not married her if he really cared about her so much as all that. But women, Sir John always understood, never forget any sentimental injury. He had for a long time been doubtful whether she really suspected the injury, but now that she had so suddenly brought this lad from Japan plump on the scene Sir John was convinced that she knew it all, and that this was her revenge. So like a woman—so remarkably like a woman! Romantic and malign at once—exactly a woman's scheme! Sir John thought it thoroughly out, constructed for himself the whole labyrinth of a woman's mind, and then explored it from end to end. He smiled to think how completely and easily he had discovered the plot. He settled it for himself that Dione Lyle was resolved to punish him, to mar his ambitious schemes, and to reward the son of her old lover by marrying Marie Challoner to Christmas Pembroke. Considering the peculiar life his daughter had led, her loneliness, her blended cleverness and innocence, he owned to himself that the thing was shrewdly thought of, and that under favourable circumstances, and with guardian-eyes less watchful than his own, it possibly might have succeeded.

The one part of the scheme which he thought clumsily

worked out was the story about Dione Lyle having only learned of Christmas Pembroke's existence by a chance paragraph in the newspapers. That he thought was poor—it was too obviously absurd. It was thoroughly feminine. It amused him to think of his old love fancying she could get him to believe that. He had no doubt young Pembroke believed it; for the boy was evidently quite ingenuous and simple, and it was the sort of romantic thing which a boy would like to believe. But Sir John Challoner had lived rather too long in the world to be thus deceived, and he felt sure that Dione had watched for years over the career of her old lover's son, and probably had been the means of inducing the elder Pembroke to start with the boy for Europe. Sir John was a clever man, but in studying human nature his light was not sufficiently dry, to adopt Bacon's phrase. He came to every subject with a previous theory, to which all inquiries and discoveries had to fit themselves. That theory was that everybody had a motive. For the not inconsiderable number of persons who even where their own interests are concerned are incapable of devising a secret motive, or keep it in force half an hour, who never think of deciding anything until the decision has to be made, and who then do just what they think right and fair—for this happily not inconsiderable class he made no allowance.

Seeing the plot, then, how was he to countermine it? Not certainly by the silly and vulgar old devise of endeavouring to keep his daughter and Pembroke asunder. He was not enough of an old stager to have any faith in that sort of thing now. That is the way, he well knew, in which blunder-headed parents have over and over again driven girls into objectionable love affairs and odious marriages. Sir John made up his mind at once to bind Christmas Pembroke to him by the strongest ties of gratitude and interest, and thus to become the boy's master, to press the lad on Marie as an object of friendly and patronising attention, and at the same time to keep gently touching, thrilling, causing to echo with long vibrations, the chord of ambition and of self-love which he believed to be in his daughter's heart as in the heart of every woman. To do him justice, he was too fond of his daughter to be content with the mere prospect of preventing a foolish match. He was anxious to save her from the pain and disappointment of a foolish love. Thus far, he thought, things had gone very well. He drew a good augury from the manner in which he had seen his daughter's eyes light up and then sink when he spoke to her of ambition.

How incalculably stronger ambition was than love the successful man well knew. *He* had outlived all the emotions of his youth in regard to love affairs; but Ambition, though she had little of the virgin, had always kept her lamp burning in his heart. He knew quite well now that if he had married Dione Lyle when he was young she would long ago have wholly ceased to interest him, even though they might have led never so happy a life together. In his proposed policy with regard to Christmas there was a considerable amount of genuine good nature; for although he felt towards his daughter an almost painful, almost distracting affection, yet he thought any youth to be pitied who, without wealth or position, could persuade even her to marry him for love. Not only would it be infinitely happier for Marie not to marry for love, but it would be happier likewise for Marie's lover. He was convinced that in the depths of his daughter's dark eyes he saw the germs of a fire more powerful and enduring than that of love. Once set that fire of ambition burning, and it would leave no place for feebler lights.

CHAPTER XI.

"GATHER YE ROSES WHILE YE MAY."

WHAT was the curious, hardly explicable impulse which kept Marie from visiting Miss Lyle for some days after Christmas Pembroke had left Durewoods? Miss Lyle herself would probably have smiled in her good-natured, half-melancholy, half-satirical way, and assumed that the absence of the handsome young man was explanation enough even if Marie had not new guests at home to amuse and distract her. Dione would not have been offended or annoyed. Girls must be all like that, she thought; and she was rather pleased that Marie should have liked the son of her old friend so well as to think the balcony a different place when he was not there. But perhaps Marie's kindly friend misjudged her. Marie may have kept away for another reason. She drew back for the moment from Miss Lyle perhaps as a Roman Catholic who feels subtle doubts arising in his mind about the truth of the faith in which he has been nurtured might shun the presence of the teacher whose counsels he begins to fear are no more for him.

"What is ambition?" Marie asked aloud one morning at breakfast. Only Mrs. Seagraves, Captain Cameron, and Mr. Vidal were with her. Sir John had breakfasted earlier, and was writing letters in his study.

Captain Cameron was engaged with a radish, which constituted the staple of his ordinary breakfast. Mrs. Seagraves sipped some tea, with her head drooping gracefully to the left. She wore a morning dress of pale blue muslin with white lilies curiously enwrought.

Everybody looked up as the question was propounded. Mr. Vidal did not burst forth with a rapid dissertation to settle the matter, as he usually did when any one had a doubt on any subject; and as the company generally expected explanations from him no one said anything. So Marie gravely repeated her question—

"What is ambition?"

"A conundrum, Miss Challoner?" asked Mr. Vidal lazily. "If so, I give it up."

"No; I ask for information, as the people say in the House of Commons or at public meetings, I believe. What is ambition?"

"It's the last infirmity of noble minds," Captain Cameron explained, being driven to bay.

"But what does that mean, Captain Cameron? what does that tell me?"

"Nothing, I suppose. I never looked much into the meaning of it; but everybody quotes it."

"What is the last infirmity of noble minds?"

"Why ambition, of course. Didn't I quote it for you?"

"Yes; but what does that mean?"

"There you have me," the Legitimist said gravely; "but I think ambition is a splendid sort of thing. I don't believe a man is worth his salt who hasn't a touch of ambition."

"Oh, I love ambition!" Mrs. Seagraves said, with enthusiasm, and with her head more than ever on one side, and one taper finger lightly supporting her chin. "It is the nurse of everything great. I should like to be ambitious—it must be so nice! Of course I shouldn't like to be ambitious in the wrong sort of way. I hate that sort of ambition—Napoleon and Alexander the Great, and people like that. I used to love them once—when I was a girl. I was quite in love with Napoleon— oh! quite in love, I declare. Not really in love—downright love —and besides he was dead; but in love as girls are with heroes. But I don't love that sort of ambition any more."

"Ambition in a man I understand," said Marie, not greatly enlightened by this last expression of opinion; "but in a woman! What has a woman to be ambitious for?"

"You are quite right," Captain Cameron approvingly answered, though in fact no opinion had been offered; "it's absurd and ridiculous and unladylike. There won't be a lady left in England soon if that sort of thing goes on."

Captain Cameron was evidently regarding feminine ambition as a new development of woman's rights. Mrs. Seagraves broke out with a fresh burst of enthusiasm for woman's ambition. Mr. Vidal, who did not care for discussions, or general conversation, said nothing. And Marie found that she could hardly get her question satisfactorily answered just then.

Indeed she had not started the subject with any idea of obtaining enlightment for herself, but partly because it was pressing on her mind, and partly because she was curious to know whether Mr. Vidal was himself an ambitious man. Sir John Challoner's words had left a deep and in many ways an alarming impression on her mind, and they seemed somehow to chime in with Miss Lyle's prediction—that once she left Dure-woods she would never return to it with the same feelings as she had now. It may be that Marie was only too conscious within herself of the first throbbings of an emotion which had started into life, at her father's words.

Mr. Vidal was a disappointing person at first. Marie was left a good deal in his company, for her father took charge of Mrs. Seagraves, and Captain Cameron generally went off on restless excursions of his own. Vidal apparently did not care a straw for woods and water and scenery. He hardly looked at anything out of doors. He talked almost incessantly; and talked a great deal about art, about pictures, and even about land-scapes; but he never seemed to allow his eyes to rest upon anything in nature. He told Marie all about the present season of the Royal Academy, and the past seasons, and the Salon in Paris; and he assured her that somebody of whom she had never heard before was by far the greatest English artist now living, and that somebody of whom she was equally ignorant was a mere charlatan and trickster whom all the world now was finding out. He told her how very absurd Lady Letitia Severance was making herself with her collections of china, which were not the right things at all, and in fact were absolutely worthless. He had brand-new opinions upon everything. Any celerated artist of past or present time whom Marie in her innocence happened to mention with admiration he assured her was cared for by nobody now, and was found to have a thoroughly false method. He rattled off the names of strings of poets and other authors of whom our untutored heroine had never heard, and he assured her that these were the persons who now absorbed public attention; and he went into fluent and æsthetic dissertations upon their respective merits until Miss Challoner felt perfectly ashamed of her ignorance. It was the same thing with music, of which he convinced her in the easiest and most offhand way that she knew absolutely nothing, or rather that she was much worse off than if she had known nothing, inasmuch as all her ideas were wrong, and her teaching had been imparted on a false method. Then he went on to the opera, and told her all about that; and then he analysed the merits of various theatres and actresses, and explained an

entirely new dramatic principle, to which he meant to give a
chance as soon as he could get hold of a theatre and raise the
money somehow. In the famous fateful little hollow among
the woods he engaged in a voluble and earnest dissertation on
the absurdly erroneous principle on which some people were
now decorating their ceilings.

Mr. Vidal was an entirely new creation to Marie Challoner.
He seemed wonderfully clever, she thought, and he appeared to
know everything and every one; and he was necessarily, therefore, interesting if you could only keep your attention fixed all
the time. But that was not easy in the open air for a girl who
was fond of the effects of light and shade, and trees and water,
and who was longing at every step to call attention to something
that she thought worth looking at. It was true that Christmas
Pembroke, too, seemed at first to have no eyes for the scenery,
but then he could see things when they were pointed out, and
his ways and talk were all more sympathetic. Christmas seemed
very young to her; Ronald Vidal appeared very old. She remembered what her father had told her about Vidal's talent for finance
and his love of enterprise and speculation, and it became a marvel
to her how he contrived to find time in life for so many things,
and for the elaborate culture of so many various fields of knowledge. She gave up the sun and sky for the moment, and set
herself seriously to study this new phenomenon.

"You seem to know everybody, Mr. Vidal—poets, painters,
authors, politicians, actresses."

"Yes, I know a lot of people; I like to know people. Of
course one doesn't know life if one doesn't know the men and
women who make it up. Look at the things you read or the
things you hear said in the House sometimes about foreign
politics by fellows who only pick up their notions out of books.
Things can't be known in that way. Go to the places; meet the
people; talk to the men; smoke a cigar with them; set them
talking—that is the way to understand questions. Men study
history—all right of course; very good. I make a point of going
and hearing a few debates in Berlin or Versailles, and I have a
few chats with Bismarck and Thiers and Gambetta. It's the
same thing at home. I want to see things from everybody's
point of view. I know Bradlaugh, and I know Odger."

"And all the poets and authors? Some of them I am
ashamed to say I am not at all acquainted with."

"I know them all. Some of them, you know, one meets in
society, quite often; but a lot of them live rather to themselves,
in out of the way places, and people don't always know how to
get at them. But I find my way among them easy enough, for I
know ever so many of the newspaper men—in fact, I write a
good deal for one or two of the papers."

" How can you find the time for all that ? "

" Why not ? There is plenty of time in life if people only were quick and knew how to make use of it."

" And in all these pursuits now—art, literature, journalism, criticism, finance—and Japanese fans and old china—which really is the one that most attracts you? I am positively curious to know that, if I am not rude in asking ? "

" You couldn't be rude in asking me anything, Miss Challoner. Well, you see, as to that, none of these things is really in what I consider my vocation."

" Indeed ! not even finance, in which papa says you are so clever ? And do you know, Mr. Vidal, I am not sure that I quite understand what finance means ? "

" Oh, you wouldn't care to know. It wouldn't interest you at all. But as to my special vocation—you were kind enough to ask ? No, it's not finance. My game of life, if I had my way, would be politics."

" Indeed ? But you are already engaged in politics, I thought ? "

They were now on the top of the hill, from which the view extended at one side broad over the outer bay, to the horizon beyond which lay, in Marie's favourite fancy, the shores of the wondrous lands of poetry and romance, and the children of the sun.

" You really must look at that view," she said almost pathetically. " Every one admires it. Is it not wonderful? "

" Beautiful, beautiful ! I have seen something like it some-where—can't quite remember where; perhaps it's in one of Saltmar's pictures; year before last, I think. Yes, it was in that. Very fine view indeed! You are very fortunate. A little windy here, isn't it ? Your veil was near going. Don't you like the tawny-green veils, with the Egyptian gold on the edges ? You haven't seen them ? You would be sure to like them. Tell Challoner to send you some. I'll let him know the place to get them. They are made specially, and a great many nice women have taken to them lately.

" Well, we were speaking of politics," Marie said, giving up the view from the hill for good and all. " I was rude enough to be curious about your vocation."

" Oh, yes. Well, Miss Challoner, my strongest desire is for political success. I want to be in the House of Commons."

" At last he is in earnest," Marie said to herself, and she was glad of it. Vidal had stopped short as they were descending the hill, and he looked with a certain strength of resolve on his handsome face.

" But I suppose you could easily get there," she said. " It surely is not difficult for one like you."

" It isn't difficult to get in, perhaps, although it costs a deuced lot of money—excuse the expression, Miss Challoner, it slipped from me—a great deal of money in these days; and I haven't much money, as you know I dare say—almost nothing of my own. I did make some few thousands once or twice under Challoner's directions; but I muddled the money all away on theatres and fads of that sort; and perhaps might do the same again if I had the chance. But it isn't merely getting into the House. I know I could get in there. I want—to tell you the truth—to be Foreign Minister. That is my ambition."

" Ambition! Then you too have ambition ? "

" Every one has, I suppose. *You* have, I am sure."

" Why do you think so ? "

" I don't know that I could give a very clear answer. Some-thing in your look, perhaps. And every woman of spirit who is worth anything has ambition."

" But ambition for what ? What can a woman be ? "

" She can be an influence—a power. She could be the wife of a statesman, and do great things in politics herself. She could be a queen of society. Oh yes, a woman might do great things —and help a man to do great things too."

Marie became thoughtful for a moment, and Mr. Vidal too was silent. Then she started a different subject.

" You who know so many artists, Mr. Vidal, and are so fond of music, ought to pay a visit to Miss Lyle—Miss Dione Lyle. She is a delightful woman, and a picture in herself."

" Challoner has told me of her—of her being settled here I mean. I always thought she was living in France somewhere."

" Did you know her, then ? "

" I remember having heard her—years ago, when I was very young."

" Indeed ? " Marie asked eagerly. " What was she—a great singer ? "

" The greatest concert-singer of her time—English singer, I mean," he said. " At least so I am told. But her style is quite out of date now."

" She retired very early and unexpectedly, did she not ? "

" I believe so ; there was some romantic story about her, I think ; but I have forgotten what it was, if I ever heard it. I should think her voice must have been going ; women don't give up a career like that without good reason, you know."

" But she is not like most women, I fancy."

" No ? Perhaps not. Of course you can't count on what some women may do."

" Then she really was a success ? " Marie said meditatively. " She really reached the height of her ambition—in the career that she had chosen ? "

" Well, yes—I believe so."

" And stepped down from the height again? "

" For some reason or other—yes."

" And is forgotten now ? "

" I should think pretty nearly forgotten."

"So much for ambition! Was it worth the trouble, I wonder ? " Marie asked rather of herself than of him.

" One can't help it; one has to go on."

" What does it come to in the end ? "

" Why, what does anything come to in the end ? " Mr. Vidal asked. " Nobody thinks of that in the beginning. And if he did it wouldn't matter three straws—he would go on all the same—if going on was his way, I mean."

" I have an idea—I don't well know why," Marie said, striving to interest him in Miss Lyle's story, because just now it filled her own mind greatly, " that she made a sacrifice—of some kind—to her ambition, and that now she thinks it was not worth the sacrifice."

" I dare say—very likely. But then if she had done the other thing she would probably think now that that was the sacrifice."

" Men might," Marie began, " but a woman—I don't know," and then she stopped, thinking it absurd to set about discussing sentimental problems of life with Mr. Vidal.

" There's a good deal of nonsense in the world about the peculiarities of men and women," said Vidal. "I have studied women a good deal, and I think they are just about as practical and ambitious as we are, in the long run. Anyhow life is a tempting game, and some people, man or woman, can't keep out of it. They can't sit on the bank and look on ; they have to go in, even if they make a muddle of it and have to sneak out beaten in the end."

" I don't believe it," exclaimed Marie. " Yes, I do, though," she quickly added.

" That's as Mrs. Seagraves might have put it," Vidal said and then they both laughed, and the subject was not brought up again. Marie started her companion off on some other topic whereon he could dissertate uninterrupted until they returned home. She felt wearied and depressed somehow after her walk ; but she was now satisfied that there was more in Mr. Vidal than she thought when he talked to her of lace.

Not many days after this Dione Lyle received a parting visit from Sir John Challoner and his daughter.

" We are going sooner than I intended at first," Sir John said. "I shall take Marie to Pau for a short time. Cameron is to cross the Pyrenees, and I shall go with him that way as far as I can. I should like to have a look at things in that region. Partly business, partly pleasure—so men like me have to combine things, Miss Lyle."

"Has Captain Cameron talked *you* into Carlism?" Dione asked.

Sir John smiled. "Oh no; I am only a man of business, not a political partisan. But he wants me to do things which would be fairly enough in my line if I could see my way. Anyhow Marie will have a holiday, and then we can settle down for the winter and the season in London."

Marie had hardly spoken thus far.

"I do so much want to get one of those roses, Miss Lyle, from your hedge down by the water," she said. "May I have one?"

"Of course, dear. Shall I tell Janet to get you as many as you like?"

"Thank you, I should much prefer to go down and get them for myself."

"As you please, Marie."

Marie rather hastily left the room, and was presently seen near the rose bushes at the water's edge. Dione and Sir John both looked for a moment in silence at her.

"Marie grows a beautiful girl," Miss Lyle said. "Take care of her, John."

"You don't think she looks unwell, or delicate?" he asked anxiously. "You don't mean that, Dione?" These two never addressed each other in so familiar a manner in the presence of any listener.

"Oh no, she seems to me in the full glow of health. I mean to take care of her happiness."

"Do you think anybody could care as much about her happiness as I do, Dione?"

"No; but you may not be the best judge of what constitutes a woman's abiding happiness. Look here, John Challoner, you are a sort of hero in that girl's eyes—try to keep up your character. Don't teach her to sacrifice herself to your ambition, or to hers, I don't care which."

"'All for love' or 'the world well lost,' I suppose is your motto now, Dione? It was not so once, I think. But I'll take care of her. I am going to take care of your young friend, too—Pembroke's son. I mean to help that lad to make his fortune if I can—for the sake of old acquaintanceship. We don't lose all our human feelings in the City, Dione."

Miss Lyle looked up with surprise in her soft melancholy eyes.

"Are you really going to be so kind to him, John, for the sake of old friendships?"

"Why should you doubt it?"

"I ought not to have doubted it, perhaps; but I am glad to hear it—and I believe it, and I think there is a great deal of good in you, after all! Well, I have some schemes of my own vaguely shaping themselves for him too."

"I know you have," Sir John thought, with the quiet satisfaction of one well on his guard, but he said nothing.

"And I will tell you of them some time, when I hear from you how he gets on, and all that. I feel really grateful to you, and I think," she added, smilingly, "I may trust your daughter's happiness to you, after all."

At that moment Marie entered the room with her freshly gathered roses and memories.

"And you are going into the great world, Marie!" Miss Lyle said. "Do you know that I feel a little like the old broken-down discharged soldiers I used to see in French villages taking leave of some bright young conscript? Well, you must be sure to come back unwounded and tell us of the wars."

Marie hardly spoke. She was much more moved than she had expected to be. A kindly embrace, a glance backwards, and the parting was over.

So Durewoods is to remain a lonely place for some time to come. Dione Lyle, sitting in her balcony, is to watch the trees growing browner and redder under the darkening skies of autumn, and is at last to retire from her balcony altogether, and look through the glass of her windows at the rain-beaten sea, where in the winter months the *Saucy Lass* makes but one passage each way every day, and the wind tears spitefully through the now bare and ragged branches on which lately grew the roses gathered by Marie.

CHAPTER XII.

THE CHURCH OF THE FUTURE.

THE happy days when we were so miserable! Will Christmas Pembroke at some later time look back and think the days happy when he was so miserable in his chambers, under his painted ceiling, after his return from Durewoods? Certainly he then thought himself very unhappy, and he sometimes envied with a bitter envy the French artist in the story whose only love was for a lady who lived then, and who lives still, in the Louvre, and who is called *La Joconde.* How he wished that he could love the goddess who floated on his ceiling! And when he first came to London he almost loved her, though her limbs were somewhat large and her face rather wanted for expression. She was then a part of the whole new chapter of his life—of his freedom, which, however, melancholy its cause, brought his first great holiday—of London—of an opening career—and of hope, and morning, and youth, and brightness, and all the rest of it. Now she was rather irksome to him, for she was so very very unlike Marie. Twenty times a day he wished he had never gone to Durewoods—had never seen Marie Challoner—had never come to England. For many a spell he found himself in good truth sick of life. We smile at these love-pains in later days ; but, good Heaven, how real they are, and how cruel they are! A young man vexed with them is many a time more sincerely ready to welcome Death than the serenest old philosopher who has grown into a conviction of the worthlessness of life.

"I suppose my father bequeathed this sort of thing to me," he said to himself once with that complacent mournfulness of consolation which comes to us when we think that Destiny has marked us out. "It's our luck, I suppose. He had to go through life disappointed, I know now ; and why shouldn't I ? He was a hundred times a better man."

If Christmas had but known it, his love, hopeless as it seemed, was his best stroke of fortune. Coming as it did so early, and taking so powerful a hold, it purified and dignified his youth. Heaven knows what temptations in his London holiday and his freedom might have proved too much for him, but for this strong love of his. "Lord of himself—that heritage of woe !" Christmas was no longer lord of himself. The memory of a girl whom he had known for a few days held him in bondage, now bitter and now sweet; but always saving. He chafed against it often, and asked what he had done to deserve such pain and the barren promise of a life withered apparently in its spring—but he never broke away from it. Probably, too, his love was all the stronger because he desired no confidant. There are young men, as there are young women, who must tell the story of their feelings to some one, and whose load is really lightened by such effusion, and who are fain to hear the one loved name repeated anyhow. Our Spartan boy from Japan had hardly any of this sentiment. He could tell his tale to no one, and he feared even to hear her name mentioned lest he should start and betray himself. He did his worship in the catacombs.

It is a Sunday morning, still in the summer, although London's season is fading. The day is fine and sunny, the church bells are tolling, the chapel bells are clinking, and the peculiar population of the London Sunday are abroad. There are the girls in their finery, with their gloves so admirably fitting, and their bonnets so exceedingly chaste, and yet in each of whom the most casual glance recognises Mary Jane of the kitchen dis-

guised as a lady and going to meet her young man. There is
the young man himself with shiny tall hat, and gloves which he
carries in his hands, and a cigar, and the way in which he holds
that cigar between his lips tells, one knows not how, that it is
a part of his Sunday get-up, and that a clay-pipe is his more
familiar solace. There are the pair, to look at whom would surely
have filled the heart of the author of " Sally in our Alley," with
sympathy and compassion—the tiny milliner girl and her tiny
lover ; the little, full-grown, slim woman and the little stunted,
full-grown, pale young man with the weak moustache and the
narrow chest. With great pride the little maid looks towards—
even she can hardly look up to—the little man. She belongs to
a milliner's dressmaking-room, and he is perhaps an assistant at
a clothier's, They are very happy now as they go for their
Sunday walk. They will marry with fearful prematureness, and
she and he will soon trundle a perambulator on the Sunday ;
and presently she will have to stay at home and mind the other
babies, and the husband is far too decent a fellow to seek after
the ideal in drink and the public-house ; and so he and she put
through a wan monotonous life, and will probably die early.
Even the police-court and the leading articles trouble themselves
not about him and her.

Some part of the Sunday crowd passes along the Embankment under Christmas's windows as he smoked a cigar and looked
out and indulged in easy moralising, and glanced again and again
at a kindly letter from Dione Lyle. One phrase in it touched
him keenly and curiously. Miss Lyle was describing something
new or altered in her house or garden, and she used the words
" When you were here." When you were here ! The words
seemed to Christmas to be charged with unspeakable pathos.
When you were here !—when things were as they cannot well be
again ; before the gates had closed behind you ; before the time
of roses was over. He put the letter down, and happening by
chance to look up thought the smug face of his floating goddess
detestable, and half resolved to have her painted out.

Christmas had luckily something particular to do this Sunday, and he took up a card that lay on his chimney-piece to
remind himself once more of the time when he had to keep his
engagement. The card was an invitation to attend at noon of
that Sunday a meeting of the worshippers of the Church of the
Future, Avenir Hall, Hope Place, West Centre. Pembroke had
not yet worshipped in the Church of the Future, although he
knew some of its leading disciples or prophets. Indeed, he had
paid a good many visits to the house of Mrs. Seagraves, who
received her friends on Sunday afternoons during certain months
of the year. She had come to have a sort of interest in his eyes
from the fact that her brother had gone off in the company of

the Challoners towards the Pyrenees, and she might perhaps any day chance to have news from Marie. Of Nathaniel Cramp, too, Christmas had seen something. Nathaniel now had absolutely severed himself from the haircutting, and was preparing for his grand enterprise. Christmas rather liked him, and liked the memories of Durewoods which his very presence brought; and was amused and yet sympathetic when Nat hinted, in a dark and gloomy way, at misprized affection and the pangs of hopeless love. He was too much engrossed, however, in his own thoughts to allow his curiosity about Nat to get any farther than a vague wonder as to whether it was a Durewoods lass or some Wigmore Street shop-girl who was working such ravage in the heart of his forlorn friend.

"What a lucky ass he is," Christmas thought, as he left his lodgings to attend the meeting at noon, "with his Church of the Future! I suppose that sort of thing occupies him and consoles him, and makes him fancy himself a high priest and a prophet, and I don't know what else! I wish I had a Church of the Future, and were a prophet."

For the occupations with which Christmas endeavoured at once to open up a career for himself and to drive away thought were rather of a dry and prosaic nature. He had become a member of the Institution of Civil Engineers, and he read a good deal in the British Museum, and he was preparing something very elaborate on the prospects of railway extension in Japan, and he attended meetings of the Geographical Society and the Society of Arts, and he sometimes had wild ideas of trying to get attached to some African exploring expedition. So far, however, he was living on his modest income, and had not yet earned a sixpence; and decidedly it is a loftier sort of business, and more grateful to the heroic soul, to be engaged in founding a Church of the Future than in speculating as to the extension of railways in Japan.

The Church of the Future did not look a very inspiring institution in the present stage of its existence. Of course it was only beginning; and Rome looked a poor thing enough when Remus leaped its wall; and every one laughed at the ugly duckling. The Church of the Future was yet in the ugly duckling stage of its growth. The meetings or services were held in a shabby little hall of a shabby street in the West Centre; a hall which was habitually used in the week as a dancing-school, and occasionally hired as a concert-room or a place in which some personage, misled by a mournful ambition, attempted to attract an audience to a course of lectures. The little platform had a dismal transparency behind it, the forms whereon could but dimly be made out in the wan daylight that underwent a process the reverse of filtration through the dull window panes;

I

and when studied carefully, as Christmas now had leisure to study them, they proved to be a circle of gentlemen in blue swallow-tail coats, light yellow trousers, white stockings, and dancing "pumps;" and of ladies in lank semi-transparent garments clinging to their limbs, and slippers so very much cut off the foot that it was marvellous how they held on at all. This melancholy crew was supposed to be emblematic of the delights of the dance, and had thus been an emblem since at least the childhood of Madame Vestris. Rows of seats were arranged down the hall, and there were two private boxes level with the platform. Very few votaries of the Church of the Future had come when Christmas took his seat. There were two ladies with short-cropped-hair, of whom one wore spectacles; and there were three or four young men who looked like overworked and sickly artisans; and there was one elderly man with long grey hair thrown back, and eager moving eyebrows, who would to a more matured and better informed observer than Christmas have suggested associations of the old days of the People's Charter. Christmas was thinking of backing quietly out and waiting in the street until more people should come, when Nat Cramp bustled in, all nervous and hot.

"We're not very punctual here always," said Nathaniel, "but they'll come in before long. We have been holding a council meeting—and, in fact, I'm afraid there's only too much likelihood of a schism."

"Indeed? How is that?" Christmas asked, making the best effort he could to seem deeply interested.

"Yes;" and Nat rubbed his hair wildly. "It's the difficulty about a definition, you see."

"A definition? Definition of what?"

"What constitutes membership—don't you see? Some of us think the Church of the Future ought to open its arms to all the world—all the world!"

Christmas could not help glancing round at the benches, still almost as empty as before. A straggler just at that moment looked doubtfully in and then withdrew—

"It's for the future, you know," Nat said as if in answer to Christmas's glance—"and here are some people, you see." (Three more came in.) "But we must build for the future."

"Shingle out into the fog?" Christmas said, quoting an old joke from the Western States of America about a fog so thick that a man engaged in "shingling" or roofing his cabin went on unconsciously thatching the fog for yards beyond the roof.

"What's that?" Nat asked sharply.

"Oh, nothing of any consequence. Just a Western way of putting the thing. Excuse my interruption."

"There's Mrs. Seagraves," whispered Natty, bowing and

blushing confusedly as that lady with three or four companions entered one of the private boxes. Mrs. Seagraves smiled sweetly upon Christmas, and then held her head much on one side and contemplated three lilies which she bore in her hand.

"Well, the schism—the definition?" Christmas urged.

"There are some," Nat went on solemnly, "who hold that no one who believes any of the tenets of the older Churches can be a member of our Church. I don't say that there isn't a great deal to be said for that view of the case, mind you—but I think it is better that we should set the example of being broad. I don't see that a man is necessarily disqualified for being a member because he believes in a future life."

"Certainly not," said Christmas, gravely and much amused. "Perhaps he can't help it, poor fellow. It may not be his fault—he may have been badly brought up, you know. And then he may repent."

"Yes, yes," Nat said rather hurriedly, and perhaps not quite sure whether Christmas was serious.

"Besides," Christmas added, "if you only receive those who already agree in everything, how are you to make any converts?"

"Well, anyhow, I'm afraid there's going to be a secession," Nat said ruefully. "There'll be a second Church. The worst of it is that old Mr. Tyas, of Hornsey, is at the head of the secession, and it's he who has always made himself responsible for the hire of the hall and the gas and all that. It soon won't matter much to *me*, you know—I shall be far away. But I don't like to see a cherished hope fade—another hope—and just as my lecture has come on to be read at last! Good morning; I must join the council—we ought to be beginning."

Nat nodded gloomily and withdrew.

By this time a few persons more had dropped in, and the hall was now about a third full. Presently the council emerged from a side door. Nathaniel Cramp was among them, and looked preternaturally sheepish, bashful, and withal self-conceited because of the paper he held in his hand, and which he was soon to have the honour of reading. The council consisted of ladies as well as gentlemen, and oddly enough, all the former were of what would be called good social position, while the men were either artisans discontented with existing Churches and social arrangements, or retired tradesmen who had taken late in life to the study of Strauss and Huxley. Mrs. Seagraves, though she might be called a Lady Patroness of the Church of the Future, did not take a seat at its council board. The ladies of the council were four in number; three elderly and for the most part of imperious manner, as they came in a little heated by discussions in which working men had differed in opinion from

them, or, as the ladies would themselves probably have put it,
contradicted them. The fourth was an unmarried girl of twenty
at most; a pallid pretty girl, with quivering eager lips and
bright eyes. A sort of murmur went round the audience as
this lady took her seat. She was evidently regarded as the
young Hypatia of the movement. She was understood to be
one who had no patience or pity for illusions and wrong opinions,
and who in her zeal for Science and Truth tore off Nature's veil
with fearless hand.

Each visitor on entering had been presented with a little
programme of the day's business, and Christmas now glancing
at his saw that the proceedings were to be opened with vocal
music, that a gentleman whose name was unknown to him was
to read a " selection " from the works of great thinkers, also
unnamed ; that Miss Sybil Jansen was to address the assembly
on the Oneness of Life, and that Mr. Nathaniel Cramp was to
read a lecture, after which music again ; and so the close of the
ceremonies. Christmas felt not the slightest doubt that the pale
pretty girl with the eager lips and eyes was Miss Sybil Jansen,
and he began to feel a little more interested than before. He
therefore grew observant. He noticed with some curiosity the
different demeanour of the young woman and the young man
while both were waiting for their turn in the performance. Miss
Sybil was evidently impatient for her hour to come. She bit
her lips ; she clenched her little hands, one of which was ungloved and very white ; her little bosom heaved, and she glanced
every now and then at the singers or the speaker, longing to
know if their part of the business was nearly over. Poor Nat
Cramp sat clutching his manuscript and his hat, a very picture
of awkward and self-conscious misery, every now and then turning pale and sickly of hue, and moistening his dry, hot lips with
a restless tongue. She waited as if for a triumph ; he as for an
execution. Is this the superior self-reliance of woman, Christmas asked himself; the natural awkwardness and diffidence of
man ? Or is it that she really has something to say and is
absorbed by the zealot's longing to deliver her message, while
poor Cramp only thought of showing off his talent, and now at
the critical moment is losing faith and courage ?

The singing was mildly didactic; with a good deal about
brotherhood in it. The selections from great thinkers were bits
from Herbert Spencer, Mill, Richter, and Walt Whitman. At
last even this was over, and Miss Sybil threw back her hair from
her forehead, shook out her skirts, and sprang to the front with
the introductory words, " Men, my brothers ! "

She had a singularly musical voice, with a sort of metallic
vibration in it, and it was so clear and sweet that it saved the
excited maiden any need of screaming, which it is to be feared

she would have done if need were. She seemed very angry with life and law generally, and her short pretty upper lip had really a sort of scornful turn upwards, which Christmas assumed to be the curl of pride, so familiar to the lips of the heroines of literature. For a while he paid no attention to what she was saying, and listened only to the musical impassioned voice, and watched the sensitive features all aflame with emotion. It was as if he were listening to some orator or actor who spoke a foreign tongue. The mysterious, almost magnetic, influence which at once brings speaker and audience together, and which more than any quality capable of clearer definition constitutes the difference between oratory and the very best kind of speech-making, seemed to be possessed by this excitable young person.

A square-browed young fellow, evidently a mechanic, who sat next to Christmas, followed every sentence with panting chest and with a low smypathetic murmur. They did not applaud in the Church of the Future. He once glanced at Christmas as if he must find some sharer in his admiration.

"Isn't she splendid?" he asked in a whisper behind his hand.

"Very remarkable," Christmas murmured, and he spoke in all sincerity.

"Did you never hear her lecture on Joan of Hark?"

"Never."

"You should hear it. Talk of Spurgeon!" and he gave a contemptuous growl. "But she's fine to-day. I tell you her blood's up to-day."

The young lady's blood probably was up, but it scarcely gave much tinge of colour to her cheeks. All her blood must have gone into the indignant tones of her eloquence, and perhaps into her flashing eyes. Christmas tried to follow the discourse, which appeared to be quite extemporaneous, but he soon lost himself in its whirling clouds of words. The speech appeared to be a rhapsody of denunciation against everything as it is, and of ecstatic faith in the all-healing virtue of having no faith. So far as Christmas could understand, it was the passionate proclama-tion of a dogma to the effect that nobody must have any dogma. About the speaker being thoroughly in earnest there could be no doubt. Christmas could see that tiny beadlets of perspiration stood on that excited upper lip. She glowed with indignation against the world's ways and sects and principles and laws, and she insisted that "man was taught to sell his manhood for an illusory and unattainable bribe," and that "woman was pur-chased like flesh in the shambles." She grew yet more passionate against Churches and superstitions, and, fired with the heat of the dispute in which she had lately fought alone against all the other ladies of the council, she declared with burning side glances

at them that all Dogma was Superstition, and that Superstition
meant the Living Death.

"That's it!" Christmas's neighbour approvingly murmured,
"that's right! Now she's thrown away the scabbard!"

Christmas did not understand the merits of the quarrel well
enough to know whether he ought to applaud or condemn this
policy of desperate war. He had, indeed, only a very faint idea
of what the young lady was talking about, or what it had to do
with the Oneness of Life. But he found it remarkably odd and
interesting to sit under the preaching of a pretty and angry girl
of twenty with a sweet strong voice, and to hear her pouring
from her dainty and delicate white throat such impassioned
words of eloquence against things in general, including the
Hereafter.

Christmas could not help wondering where Mr. and Mrs.
Jansen were all this time, and whether they approved of this
performance on the part of Miss Sybil. But however that might
be, Miss Sybil brought down the house, if such language may be
used of so small and decorous an assembly. When she finished
in a blaze of half-poetic rhapsody, like the bouquet of a display
of fireworks, and then dropped all palpitating and with tear-
flashing eyes into her chair, there ran a genuine thrill of emotion
through the little assembly, and of honest wonder and compassion through the unaccustomed heart of Christmas Pembroke.

Mrs. Seagraves, from her box, cast two sudden and successive
glances at our wondering and pitying hero. The first said as
plainly as words could have expressed it, "Is she not a splendid
creature?" and the next instantly added, "But you must excuse
her, you know!"

There was one in that assembly who could hardly excuse her,
and that was not Christmas. It was Nathaniel Cramp, for when
he rose, all confused and stammering, to read his lecture, the
worshippers of the Church of the Future began to melt away.
The gentleman who had read the selection from the works of
great thinkers rose, and somewhat unluckily perhaps, intervened
to solicit a full hearing for their friend and brother Mr. Cramp,
on the ground that this was probably the last time that brother
and friend would appear among them, as weary of the Old
World, its kingcrafts and superstitions, he had resolved to seek
the freshening air of the Great Republic of the West. So the
audience put up with Nat, but did not care at all about him.
His sentences were long-winded and full of commonplaces. He
read very badly; he could not raise his eyes off his manuscript;
he stammered and went wrong, and had to try back; his lips
grew dry and he choked; he could not get on quickly; he did
not know how to condense or skip a page, and the lecture was
very long. It closed with a quotation from a poet of the day

whom the lecturer did not name, and whom Christmas con-
jectured to be Mr. Nathaniel himself. The citation seemed only
to recommend humanity to "press forward into the future,"
which Christmas thought humanity could not very well help doing
anyhow. Nobody took heed. The Church of the Future had
ceased to listen to its brother's admonitions. Nat's essay was an
unredeemed and ghastly failure. He sat down, or rather he
collapsed. Then there was more singing, and the ceremonies
were over.

Christmas lingered a moment, and Nat came to him, trying
to look calm.

"It was a failure, my lecture," he said, with a dismal smile.
"They were all against me. *Her* chatter carried the day. It
was in vain for me to strive. I wish I hadn't read the lecture.
I ought to have spoken it."

Christmas had no idea of what the controversy was, or indeed
what Nat had been lecturing about. He only thought that Nat
had been very dull, and that the young lady certainly had not
been dull.

"She is very pretty," Christmas said, "and of course that
counts for a great deal. But I don't like to see a girl make a
display like that."

"Nor I," said Nat, who had always before been a devotee of
woman's mission to speak in the churches; "it isn't her place.
But I don't know that speaking is *my* gift, at least to an audience
like that. They are ungrateful; I sometimes almost wish I
had taken Captain Cameron's advice and joined the Carlists!"

"But you are a Republican?"

"Still," said Nat gloomily, "it is a Cause, you know. It is a
grand thing to have a Cause to fight for."

"If one believes in it, yes."

"Belief," said Nat, "is Fate."

"Very likely; but how does that help you?"

"Well, I am going to the United States, and I may find a
career there. There at least——"

His words were cut short by Mrs. Seagraves, who had now
emerged from her private box.

"Mr. Pembroke, Mr. Pembroke! You are coming to me this
afternoon?"

"You are very kind, Mrs. Seagraves, but——"

"Oh, no, don't say the word. You must come—you really
must. I do so want to introduce you to my dear young eloquent
friend, Miss Sybil Jansen."

And Pembroke glancing involuntarily towards the entrance,
saw the colourless pretty face, the tremulous lips, and the sparkling eyes of the young Hypatia. Curiosity prevailed, and he
promised to make his appearance in Mrs. Seagraves' drawing-
room that afternoon.

"She didn't ask *me*," Nat Cramp said as the ladies disappeared, escorted by one or two men whom Christmas did not know. "I could have told you beforehand that she wouldn't. Oh no, sir—not likely! The Church of the Future is all very fine, but will they ask a poorer member under their roof, sir? Tell me that!"

"I don't see that your Church of the Future is very different from any of the little congregations of the present or the past," said Christmas—"in point of liberality, I mean. You appear to me to wrangle over dogmas quite as much as your neighbours."

"She might as well have asked me to-day, though," Nathaniel continued, still brooding over his private grief. "She knows I am going away, and she needn't be afraid I'd trouble her too often. But it's no matter!" he added, in the tone of one who thinks the world ought to come to an end.

They were now nearly alone, and they moved towards the door. Christmas was rather pitifully impressed by poor Nat's outspoken egotism, and the manner in which Republicanism, Church of the Future, and all, resolved themselves into Natty Cramp's personal ambition, and Natty Cramp's longing to get invited into any manner of society.

"Which way are you going?" Nat abruptly asked.

"I am going towards Portland Place, but I am in no particular haste to get there."

"True," Nat said with subdued scorn. ".Mrs. Seagraves lives in Portland Place. I suppose she thinks that's a grand aristocratic quarter; but it ain't—I mean it isn't. I tell you that, Mr. Pembroke, as you are a stranger. Don't you be deceived. Portland Place isn't by any means an aristocratic quarter."

"I'm very glad," said Pembroke. "It suits me all the better."

"Will you turn into Regent's Park before you go to your friends? I shan't see you any more perhaps."

"Come," said Christmas, feeling sorry for Nat's condition of general discomfiture. "I am glad you gave me a chance of having a talk with you before you go. I know two or three people here and there in America, and I want to give you a few letters of introduction; it may do you some good—anyhow a man can't have too many friends in a new country."

"You are my only friend," said Nat, effusively; "you saved my life, and do you know I wish sometimes you hadn't saved it?"

"Saved your life? You mean that I was the cause of your nearly losing your life."

"You brought me out of the waves off Durewoods pier——"

"Having awkwardly upset you into the waves off Durewoods pier."

"No, no," said Nat with a wan smile. "It's very kind of you, but it won't do! It's very good of you to forgive me, but I must remember that it was in defending yourself against my stupid rudeness that you upset me. I'm not ungrateful. I try not to be, though I am afraid sometimes I was born with a very ungrateful heart. If you only knew the things I think of sometimes!"

"My good fellow, if we all only knew the things each of us thinks of sometimes I suppose we should all be very angry with each other."

"But you are so happy. You have everything."

By this time they were in Regent's Park, and in a place tolerably sequestered for the Sunday.

"In the name of the Devil, Cramp," said Christmas, seating himself in one of the iron chairs, "how do you know that I am happy? And why are you always going on as if I were some favourite of fortune—some fellow born with a silver spoon in his mouth? I have my way to make as well as you, and I have neither kith nor kin; and I haven't a friend in the world but one kind woman, who knew my father before I was born."

"I am unhappy," Nat pleaded; "I am not fit for my sphere; I was born for something better; and I am condemned to obscurity. A cloud hangs over me; and then my life is darkened —there are hopeless obstacles!"

Christmas felt no doubt that he was now approaching the tender subject of the love affair, and he knew well enough that his friend only wanted to be allowed to pour out his griefs into some confidential ear. But Christmas, as we have already said, had a strong dislike to such confidences. They seemed to him unmanly and craven. He especially shrank from them among men. If he could voluntarily have made any confession of his own love pains, it would probably have been to some kindly woman. But effusive confidences were not much in his way, and he did not want to hear Nat Cramp's story of his love and his disappointment, and the girl from Wigmore Street whom Christmas's imagination had created as the cold and cruel heroine of the romance. So he put away the subject of conversation and confidence thus offered to him, and he began to speak of Nat's prospects in America and the people who might be of service to him, and the letters he was to have, and at last they parted and Christmas knew nothing of the love-story of his blighted friend's life.

It did Christmas some good to observe Nat Cramp's absurd weakness and egotism. "I must do my best," he thought, "not to make an idiot of myself, and go about the world whining over my disappointments and wrongs, and trying to get people to pity me."

He turned and looked back at poor Cramp's tall and stalwart, though rather loosely-built figure, and thought he could see feebleness of character in his very walk as he slowly sauntered away amid jostling perambulators, nursery maids, long-legged privates of the cavalry, artisans carrying babies, and lads smoking Sunday cigars. "I dare say I could be just as great a fool," Christmas thought, "if I hadn't *him* for a warning;" and with this invigorating reflection he braced up his energies as with a tonic, and, determined to keep all brooding thoughts about himself as much as possible out of his head, he strode rapidly towards Portland Place.

Mrs. Seagraves lived in a large, handsome, old-fashioned house. She had a good deal of money, and she might be called in one sense a young widow. But no suitors came around her, for it was well known to all whom it might concern that Mrs. Seagraves would never marry again. A young Scottish girl of good family, and with a marvellously slender income, she had attracted the attention of a more than middle-aged barrister from London, a Queen's Counsel in large practice at the Parliamentary bar, who during a visit to Edinburgh was charmed first with Miss Isabel Cameron's skating, and next with her vivacious and delightful conversation. He married her and took her to London, and died ten years after, leaving her a considerable fortune, which, however, was to cease to be hers in the event of her taking a second husband. Mrs. Seagraves had not the most remote idea of making any such sacrifice. She was very happy with her freedom and her fortune; and with her usual brisk communicativeness she told every one the condition on which she had her money, and her determination not to forfeit the money for any of the children of Adam. So she had no end of acquaintances and no beginning of suitors.

Mrs. Seagraves' house was crammed with pictures, busts, books, curiosities of all kinds, old china, Japanese fans, and such like. It might have reminded the visitor, as he entered, of one of the curiosity shops in Holborn which Thackeray so loved. The history of the fads of a whole generation or more might be traced out by a careful excavation of the contents of that building. The investigator could dig his way down through stratum after stratum of whims embodied in substantial remains. Mr. Seagraves had been fond of collecting pictures—old masters, or what he believed to be such—old engravings, and rare editions of books. He and his wife went to the East, and brought back a perfect store of shawls, pipes, swords, and clothes of all kinds from Turkey and Egypt. Mrs. Seagraves took for a while to potichomania, then, to photography, then to collecting postage-stamps, then to bicycles, then to spiritualism and flower-drawings by spirits, then to old china, and then to articles from Japan.

If you wanted the monuments of her energy and enterprise you did not even need to look round, for you could hardly help stumbling against them everywhere. The old masters which her husband had collected were gradually being edged out of their places by the revivalisms of a newer school which claimed an older origin. Round-faced Madonnas, with no particular expression about them, were impinged by gaunt demoiselles whose waists began immediately under their arms, whose gowns were of a dull tawny green, clinging to them like the wetted drapery of Canova's figures, and who generally bore lilies in their hands. Even these latter now were threatened rather seriously by an invasion of almond-eyed and weak coffee-complexioned beauties in robes as clinging, but of varied and gorgeous hues, who typified the contribution to European decoration made by the art of the land which had been until lately Christmas Pembroke's home.

Mrs. Seagraves' Sunday evening receptions were generally well attended, but chiefly by people whom nobody ever saw anywhere else. They had a sort of little fame in their way—the power of which was exactly opposite in its quality to that of the heat of a fire, and increased proportionately with the square of its distance from the source. The people even in Cavendish Square probably had never heard of them, but French artists and poets had talked of them in Paris, and owing to the descriptions given by several correspondents of the journals, New York was under the impression that Mrs. Seagraves' receptions were about the most remarkable thing in London, while Chicago firmly believed them to be the principal object of a visit to Europe. The people who went to them were not vapid people, at all events. Everybody was more or less of an original; had done something remarkable, or at least ridiculous; or had some theory or mission; or led some school or had just abandoned and renounced some school; or had views on Life and Hereafter or the marriage contract which the general run of his or her neighbours did not share.

When Christmas entered the drawing-room it so happened that the first objects which met his eyes were the sparkling eyes of Miss Sybil Jansen. She was standing up near the chimney-piece talking to two or three persons, and with her back turned to the door. It was in the mirror over the chimney-piece that her eyes met those of Christmas. Miss Sybil immediately looked away, and turned with her side to the mirror. But presently Mrs. Seagraves glided amid her clinging draperies up to Christmas, and saying, "I am so glad you have come—I do so want to introduce you," drew him along by the hand, and presented him to Miss Sybil Jansen.

CHAPTER XIII.

" ENDYMION ? "

SIR JOHN CHALLONER had a house in one of the finest and newest parts of South Kensington. It was built of grey stone, or material which looked like stone; it raised its massive proportions above a wall of stone, and it had a broad carriage drive. It stood with others in a private road which had gates and a lodge, and a painted board stuck up to warn everybody concerned that cabs and tradesmen's carts were not to make a thoroughfare of that dignified enclosure. Sir John Challoner's house displayed a little square tower or belvidere or some such erection on its roof, and looked very fine and imposing, albeit a trifle new, cold, and crude. Perhaps it would not be too much to say that an intelligent observer might have seen Modern Finance in every outline of it.

If the exterior looked rather new, the furniture on the contrary looked very old, or perhaps it would be more proper to say did its very best to look old. Everything had been ordered regardless of expense from upholsterers who had a special gift for the revival of mediævalism. The necessity of conveying ideas compelled scholars, while Latin was still the language of European culture, to introduce a great many mock-Latin words in order to give names to things which were not in existence even when Apuleius wrote. So the genius of these gifted upholsterers had to supply them with mediæval ways of constructing articles of furniture and ornament of which the Middle Ages knew nothing. The effect was highly pleasing and artistic to those who regarded things with properly-tutored eyes, but to those not so trained it was somewhat angular, uncomfortable, and out of keeping. It gave to the uninitiated something like the sort of impression which might have been produced by the spectacle of a noble guest in armour endeavouring to eat one of Gunter's ices through the bars of his helmet.

The house, however, had a fine library well fitted up, and it was in this library that Christmas Pembroke found himself about five o'clock one March evening several months after the occurrences mentioned in the last chapter. Christmas now was a regular *attaché*, if we may use the expression, of the financial house of which Sir John Challoner was the head, and his special occupation and province was the supplying his chief with ideas and facts on the subject of railway extension in Japan and in the East generally. Into this work Christmas had thrown himself with tremendous energy, and he had developed a great deal of talent and judgment. He worked hard, partly out of gratitude to Sir John, who had been very kind to him, partly because it was his nature to throw his soul and energy into any task he undertook, and partly because in the literal over-taxing of his energies he found the best means of striving against the love which was so hopeless. He was almost becoming used to think of Marie Challoner only as the daughter of his chief, who was soon to marry a man of social rank and to make a figure in society.

Marie herself he had not lately seen. Her father left her with some friends in Paris when he returned from Pau, and during three months or more Pembroke was free of Sir John's house, and was often there, without dread or hope of seeing her. She returned in January, and made for a few weeks some acquaintance with London society, but it so happened that just at that time there were some arrangements to be settled, some people to be seen and talked to, in the North of England, and Sir John entrusted the mission to Christmas. When he returned to London Marie had gone into the country on a short visit to some of the family to which Mr. Vidal belonged, and before she returned Christmas had been sent off somewhere else.

Thus it happened that when Christmas came back to London on this particular evening he assumed that Miss Challoner was still in the country. All the previous night he had sat up writing out a memorandum on one of the special subjects in which he was concerned for Sir John Challoner's use, and he got into the train at the northern town whither he had been despatched about seven in the morning. He reached London at four, and having gone to his chambers he then set out forthwith for South Kensington, believing that the library there was the most likely place in which to find Sir John at such a time, and eager to show him his work.

Sir John had not come in yet. Christmas, as we have said, was free of the house, and he went into the library to wait for his chief. The lights were burning, there was a cheery fire on the hearth—the whole place looked bright and inviting; and Christmas sat in a great easy chair, which the spirit of mediævalism had happily permitted to pass in unchallenged, and he began to read over his manuscript again. Perhaps it was the subject; perhaps it was the style; perhaps it was the labour of the previous sleepless night; perhaps all combined; that fell heavily upon the lids and the senses of our young hero. Anyhow, after a while he lay back in the chair, and the manuscript dropped from his hand, and he fell fast asleep. He sank into a confused dream, during which he passed from Japan to Durewoods, and from Durewoods to Saucelito in San Francisco bay,

and thence to the City, London, with all the time the rattling
and the motion of the London and North Western Railway
dinning in his ear. Every now and then, too, Marie Challoner
came and looked at him, or from various disguises looked out
upon him. Once the floating goddess of his ceiling gazed down
upon him with the face and the eyes of Marie Challoner. Then
the form of the goddess and all her surroundings faded away,
and only the eyes of Marie Challoner remained, and there looked
so fixedly, so piercingly into his that in his dream he said to
himself if they continued thus to look at him he must awake.
And he did awake, and there, sure enough, were Marie
Challoner's eyes turned upon him. Before they could change
their expression he caught the look of kindness and of something
like compassion, and then he sprang up ashamed of having been
found asleep.

For Marie had returned home the night before, and had
entered the library not knowing that he was there and saw him,
asleep in the chair, and could not help looking at him with eyes
of kindly interest. He seemed so pale, she thought, and wasted
—very handsome, indeed, and far more masculine in appearance
than when she saw him last; but so pale, and even in sleep so
earnest and thoughtful! She did draw near, and even bend a
little towards him, noting the lines of his face ; and she, too, was
a little embarrassed when he awoke so suddenly.

" Oh—Miss Challoner ! "

She held out her hand. " I have not seen you this long, long
time ! " she said.

" I am ashamed of having been found asleep," Christmas said,
ordering himself into composure. " But the truth is that I was
writing all last night " (he stooped and picked up his manuscript),
" and travelling all the day, and I came in here to wait for Sir
John Challoner, and so I fell asleep."

" You were writing all night ? Are you becoming an author ?
I should be so glad."

" Oh no ! only doing some work about railways and that kind
of thing. You wouldn't care about it. I mean no lady would
care about it."

He thrust the manuscript rather confusedly into his pocket.

" You seem to me to have changed a great deal—and in such
a short time," said Marie.

" I have been working pretty hard," said Christmas ; " and I
suppose I grow, as the little French conscript promised to do,
in the presence of the enemy."

" Have you heard from Miss Lyle lately ? I think of her at
this moment because the very last time I saw her she compared
me to a French conscript going to the war. I remember it well.
Now you compare yourself to a conscript in the war.

"I didn't borrow the comparison, however," said Christmas, smiling in rather a constrained way.

"No, I don't mean that; but it is a coincidence, or an omen perhaps. Is real life then actually a sort of war?"

"I suppose so; but I like it."

"You don't work too hard, I hope?"

"No; oh, no. I can stand any quantity of work. It does me good."

"But you were writing all last night. I am afraid you are overworked," she said, kindly, and making a sort of approach to the familiarity of their earlier acquaintanceship.

"You are very kind," Christmas said; "but I am really not at all overworked."

There was a pause. Both were standing. Christmas held the back of the chair in which he had been seated when she came in.

"I hope," Marie said, gently, "that you like papa."

"Nobody ever had a kinder friend," Christmas replied, in a tone of genuine enthusiasm, and much relieved to be able to give full expression to his feelings on any subject. "I thank Heaven for having sent me such a friend; and I thank you too," he added, in a tone of some diffidence.

"Marie slightly coloured. "Then you really like him—I am so glad; but I knew you would."

"Like him?" Christmas exclaimed. I only wish there was something I could do for him, Miss Challoner—or sacrifice for him: and he should see—and you—whether I liked him or not."

"Indeed it makes me happy to hear you say so. You know that he and I have been always alone together, and we are so much attached to each other. And now, up here in the world, I have begun to find out, or to guess, or suspect—I don't know how—that——"

"To suspect what, Miss Challoner?"

"That—well, that papa has enemies; or at least that there are people who don't like him. That seems so strange to me."

"But every one has enemies; every one who is worth anything," Christmas said, with genuine and youthful warmth. "Of course Sir John has enemies! I should be sorry to hear that he hadn't. He has to deal every day with stupidity and cunning and craft and selfishness, and he is determined to be truthful and outspoken and kind in spite of the whole lot of them, and how could he escape having enemies? Why, Miss Challoner, I know that his very kindness to me has made some fellows jealous and angry."

"Has it really? Then I am glad he has enemies—if such things make enemies."

"You may be proud of it. I wish I had the chance of dealin

with some of his enemies," said Christmas, pushing away his chair, and throwing out his chest significantly.

" I wish you had," Marie answered, with the brightest smile that had yet come on her face; "and I am delighted to think that he has such a friend. But don't work too hard. I hope we shall see you often. We ought to be very friendly; and we don't seem so friendly as we were. Do we? "

" Don't we? "

" No—I think not. You seemed to me older than you were, and changed a little. I don't know how. And you have not ever asked me how I liked my long stay in France—or London life—or anything."

" Have I not? Well, I have not had a great many opportunities. Will you tell me all about it now? "

But at that moment, when they were both softening into something like friendly ease, a servant entered the library and told Miss Challoner that Mr. Vidal had called and was in the drawing-room.

Marie coloured slightly for the second time. " You know Mr. Vidal? " she said, turning to Christmas.

" I see him often. I don't know him very well."

" He is very clever—don't you think? "

" I believe so—he talks very well, and a great deal."

" He is very much liked," Marie said tentatively.

" Liked—by whom, Miss Challoner? "

" By people in general, I mean."

" Yes, I should suppose so," Christmas answered carelessly. " I should think he, now, hasn't any enemies."

" You are mistaken," Marie said warmly. " He is not by any means the frivolous person that some people think him."

" I don't think him frivolous," said Christmas; "on the contrary, I think him very shrewd."

" You say it in an unfriendly sort of way. I have heard it said and read it everywhere that women don't like each other, but I think men don't like each other."

" I can't like people until I know them very well," Christmas said. " What is the good of that kind of liking? "

" I have liked people sometimes without knowing them very well," Dear Lady Disdain replied. " I suppose it is a mistake. Good evening, Mr. Pembroke; I am *so* glad to have seen you."

She left the room, and Christmas seated himself astride upon a chair and leaned his hands upon its back and his forehead upon his hands, and gave himself up to torment of thought. He had offended her who was so friendly and good; he had been guilty of the meanness of speaking against the man who perhaps would prove to be her accepted lover. He had been very near betraying his own sad secret, and in any case she must now despise him. What reason had he to sneer at Vidal? Merely because Vidal was rich and of good family, and was loved by her. "Oh, good God!" he groaned audibly—"loved by her!"

Then he sprang from his chair and walked up and down the library, stopping strangely enough every now and then to look at names on the backs of books, and suddenly finding himself thus vacuously engaged, and wondering what he was looking at, and walking up and down the room again. "Oh, but he is not worthy of her," he repeated to himself, trying to cheat himself into the belief that that alone was his reason for disparaging Vidal. "He couldn't appreciate her; it isn't in him. He's a man about town; a man of the world; a speculator for the excitement of making money. He wouldn't care if he ruined half a population so long as he did a clever thing on the Stock Exchange. Aristocrat? Is that aristocratic—to be a Stock Exchange gambler, and to manage theatres, and to fix the salaries of ballet girls? Talent—culture? Is talking about old teapots and showing women how their milliners ought to make their dresses—is that talent and culture? Yes; he is of society, and he may make love to her, and will marry her I suppose—and I may not even think of her."

Then he asked himself bitterly what use there would be in thinking of a girl who loved somebody else; and whether it was not handsome conduct on his part towards Sir John Challoner to go on in this way secretly railing at his daughter's accepted lover. "They say it is a fine ennobling thing, love," he said to himself with grim irony. "I find it so! It's turning me into the meanest, most jealous, most pitiful cad!"

He went quietly out of the library. As he passed into the hall he heard the sound of music coming from the drawing-room; and then the music suddenly stopped, and he heard two or three voices in conversation, one of which was that of Marie. Mr. Vidal, then, was not the only visitor? "What is it to me? what do I care?" he murmured to himself; and he left the house unperceived, glad that not even a servant had seen him.

When he got into the street he walked along for a considerable distance without having any idea of a particular destination or knowing what he meant to do with himself. He had not dined and did not think about dining. He turned into Kensington Gardens, and sat there for awhile vacantly observing the lights through the trees in the direction whence he had come, and wondering—after the immemorial fashion of the homeless—whether in all the houses there were any creatures as unhappy as himself. For he felt himself homeless. His heart, his affections, his ambition, had no home. The sight of Marie Challoner that day and the words he had exchanged with her had upset all his system of self-discipline. He had been schooling himself

K

of late into a sort of iron self-control, and had been applying
himself to work and to study with a positive ferocity of energy,
and he had even begun to fancy himself cured; and five minutes'
talk with her—they two alone—had brought his fit again, and
banished all his reason. "What *am* I to do?" he asked of his
tormented mind. "This can't go on—I could not stand it—I
must break down in some way. Should I tell Sir John Challoner
all—all—and beg of him to pity me; and let me go back to Japan,
and not to tell Miss Lyle—and not to tell Her? No—I'll not do
that yet. I'll try to bear it—I'll make myself bear it—I'll cure
myself of this madness somehow—anyhow! I'll not give in!"

He jumped up and left Kensington Gardens. He had of late
been accustomed to spend his nights in the most eccentric way
when he was not working or engaged with Sir John Challoner.
He kept absolutely aloof from acquaintances, and his whim was
to range London streets in all directions until some far advanced
hour of the night. He wandered anywhere as the fit took him.
He turned into a West End theatre, perhaps, and remained there
until he was tired of the performance, which was generally very
soon; and then, perhaps, he wandered away until he found himself
near an East End music saloon, and he went in there and had a
little rest, and took to the road again. He spent evenings in the
regions round Leicester Square, and supped at French or Italian
restaurants among conspirators and Communists. Sometimes he
explored the haunts of the Italian organ-grinders in the Hatton
Garden region. He found himself sometimes, with a sense of old
acquaintanceship drawn from his memories of San Francisco,
among the Chinese of the low-lying regions of the far East End.
He talked to anybody and everybody; it relieved him to talk to
people he did not know, while he shunned any manner of companionship with any of his acquaintances. He used to walk
miles and miles and return quite wearied to his chambers, where,
when he lit his lamp, his painted goddess smiled down upon him
with her smile of vapid and provoking self-consciousness. These
nightly excursions were his only period of anything like rest, his
nearest approach to enjoyment. To this had his great holiday in
London already come!

This night, however, after he had sat in Kensington Gardens,
he did not set out on one of his familiar and purposeless tramps.
Some idea seemed to have struck him, and it was then that he
jumped up and went his definite way.

Meanwhile Marie Challoner had for her part been disturbed
in a vague way by her talk with him. It was strange the sort of
barrier which seemed to stand up between them now. A broad
distance appeared to have suddenly opened to divide them.
What had become of the bright, clever youth to whom she meant
to be so kind, and with whom she had sworn an eternal friend-

ship? Only a few weeks, it seemed to her, had passed since she
dreamed that she was made a princess, and that she had given
some brilliant appointment to Christmas Pembroke. Now she
found that she could hardly even be friendly with him. He was
the same surely—and yet not like the same at all. It reminded
her of some grim old story she had read—an uncanny story
suggestive of shuddering—about a youth who left his home, and
after a while there came a being who said he was the youth,
and who looked like him, and knew all the things the youth
ought to have known, and could answer every question the
youth ought to have answered, and so was accepted by the parents
—aye, and even by the sweetheart !—as the wanderer come home.
But the exile returned was cold and melancholy, and his presence
always had a gloom and a chill about it; his shadow darkened
the household hearth; and the dog—his own favourite dog—
always so loving and faithful—would not recognise him, or come
near him, but growled and shrank away at his approach. In the
end it came out that the youth was really dead—lying dead far
away, and this gloomy and gruesome visitor was but a spirit of
evil who, for some malign purpose, had put on his likeness.
Where had she read that uncanny story? Why did she think
of such nonsense now? "I am sure I never could have been
deceived by any goblin," she said to herself, putting herself
unconsciously for the moment in the place of the sweetheart.

Anyhow, the strange and shadowy change in the relationship
between herself and her handsome *protégé* of Durewoods—the
boy whom she took charge of that first night—puzzled and
pained her. She seemed to have lost something that helped to
make life friendly and bright. London now appeared to have
become very lonely. She went to see her visitors—Mr. Vidal
and one of his friends—with a good deal of inward reluctance,
and she never listened with less interest to Vidal's talk or his
music, and she was very glad when they had gone. Then she
passed the library door and looked in, and seeing no one there
she went in, and resolved to wait there for her father. He always
sat there for a while before dinner.

She had not long to wait, for Sir John Challoner presently
came in, and she rose with her light vigorous movement—the
healthful, energetic movement which fathers gladden to see—
and ran to meet him.

"Mr. Pembroke has been here, papa."

"He has returned then? He often comes and reads here. At
least he has often done so. Was Ronald Vidal?"

"Yes, he has just gone; and Mr. Lycett——"

"Lycett of the Foreign Office?"

"Yes, he who dined here one day lately."

"Oh yes, young Lycett. How do you like him, Marie?"

" Very well—I think."

" I don't see anything in him, Mariè. Vidal thinks a great deal of him. His father is a man of some brains; but I confess I don't see much in the son."

Marie's thoughts were not in young Mr. Lycett evidently Suddenly she said—

" Don't you think he has greatly changed, papa? "

" Who, my dear? "

" Mr. Pembroke. He doesn't seem like the same being to me —the same that he was when we first knew him."

" Well, Marie, he has become a man of business since then— and a very good man of business too; and we grow solemn down in the City, you know. Men's minds are kept on the strain there, and boys soon turn into men."

" But it never seems to have any of that effect upon you, nor upon Mr. Vidal. You are always cheerful; and he is always full of talk and spirits and nonsense."

" I am an old soldier, Marie, and used to it—I take things coolly now. Vidal is only, after all, a sort of volunteer on the staff—he hasn't any sense of responsibility. He only goes into financial matters for the amusement of the thing, to occupy himself. But it is different with our young friend Pembroke."

" Why is it so different with him ? "

" To begin with, he is new to the thing, and of course he throws his soul into it strenuously—you should see how terribly earnest he can be where business is concerned. He has often sat up all night writing out a memorandum which would have been in time enough a week after."

" Yes; he told me he had been writing all last night."

" Just so; I never saw any young fellow who could so com- pletely bury himself in business. Then, you know, he has his way to make, Marie. He must get money, dear, and he has the good sense to know it. Young fellows don't usually acknow- ledge any such necessity—think it unpoetic and unromantic, I dare say—as you do, Marie, in your secret heart—confess."

" I have not thought much about it. I suppose it has to be done. Then that bright, poetic boy is changing already into a grim and grasping money-maker? I am so sorry—I liked him so much. Is money worth all that—is life worth it ? "

" My dear child, if you were a man you would find—and indeed you'll find it soon enough, although a woman—that when people of spirit and energy go into a game they play it to win. They play it to win ! They can't help it."

" So Mr. Vidal always says. I am sorry—I think I could keep out of such a game."

" Keep out of it—perhaps. I don't say you might not do that, Marie; but once having gone in, you can't keep from play- ing your very best."

" And that is what *he* has come to already—so soon! I never could have expected that! It was I, papa, was it not, who first begged of you to put Mr. Pembroke in the way to make a career for himself? I wish I hadn't done so—I do indeed! What is the making of some money in comparison to the free, fresh life he has left behind? I would rather live on next to nothing and look at the world like Dione Lyle from a balcony, and love the sunshine and the trees, and the stars and the poets, and have delicious dreams of something better than all this—and be happy and poor."

" You never were poor, my dear," Sir John said, smiling at her earnestness; " and I suspect that he was—as I was. Dione Lyle moralises poetically over life with a substantial balance at her banker's, I dare say. Besides, Marie—to tell you the full truth, dear—you mustn't blame our hard City ways for all the change that you may see in young Pembroke. There are other emotions which impel young men to make money besides the accursed thirst for gold, my dear."

" Oh, yes; I know. Ambition, of course—the central sun of everybody's universe now, I believe."

" No, Marie; not *that*. Ambition, I fancy, our young friend rather renounces."

" Then what is it, dear ? "

" A handsome, impressionable youth of three and twenty; and you ask what is his prevailing emotion! I thought you read poetry, Marie, and that you still made use of our subscription to Mudie's."

Sir John looked quietly but very attentively at his daughter. She did certainly colour a little and her eyes drooped, but no girl of her age hears any allusion to love without some such passing tribute. She looked up immediately and answered almost as if carelessly—

" Oh, that is the cause, then? The sweet youth's in love! I never thought of that. He always seemed to me so like a mere boy."

" I believe there is something of the kind going on, Marie. I don't pay much attention to these things, and people don't consult me very often about them; but I believe there is something. Mrs. Seagraves has hinted to me, as I dare say she will to you, dear."

" I dare say she will. Is she herself the object of his vows ? "

" Nonsense, Marie."

" Really I didn't know. Who is the lady? Do I know her—is her name a secret ? "

" I don't suppose there is any secret about it. You don't know her, though you may have seen her. Did you ever hear of Miss Sybil Jansen ? "

" Sybil Jansen ?—oh, yes ; a woman who makes speeches at meetings ? But that can't be—that is too ridiculous ! Isn't she very old ; and doesn't she wear spectacles and brandish a cotton umbrella ? "

" She is very young and pretty, I am told, and she has bewitched our young Japanese. So they say, at least. I needn't tell you, Marie, that this is not to be spoken of or hinted at by you."

" Papa ! As if I would—— "

" Well, dear, you girls don't always know, I suppose, what you would or would not, and so it is right to give you a word of warning in time. I need hardly say that I don't like this poor young fellow to take up with a girl like that, but he hasn't breathed a word to me as yet. I dare say he will soon— if there is anything in it."

" And what will you say if he does ? "

" I shall give him just the same advice as if he were my own son. I shall tell him that I think he is too young to marry, and that he ought to secure a position for himself first, and give himself time, and see if he knows his own mind. I shall tell him frankly that to marry a girl with such opinions and such a kind of distinction around her will be practically the sacrifice of all his social prospects. You can't drag a woman like that into good society—it's out of the question."

" But if he—if he cares about her," Marie asked, with hesitancy, and without looking at her father—" if he thinks her worth such a sacrifice—it is not much surely. Why should he care about society ? "

" Very good. If he understands the sacrifice, and is willing to make it, that is enough ; but he ought to be told plainly what it is—he doesn't know anything about English life."

" And if he should persevere—if he really does care about her—that would not change you to him, papa ? You would not cease to be his friend ? I certainly should not."

" No, dear. He may marry whom he will for me."

" You don't mean that you don't care—that you will take no interest in him after ? "

" No, Marie. He shall have my friendship always—and yours, I hope. Any woman he marries shall be received by me."

" And by me," Marie said, emphatically. " I don't care what her opinions are, or whether she makes speeches. I shall like her because of him—at least I shall try to like her." The last words she spoke rather sadly.

" So shall I. But we can only speak for ourselves, dear ; and you won't always be able to speak even for yourself, I suppose. Well, there is the story. Give it an understanding ; but no tongue ! Keep it to yourself until I remove the bar of silence and secrecy ;

and now go and dress for dinner. You see that the City isn't all
to blame if young men grow a little grave and pale sometimes."

" I should like to see her," said Marie, thoughtfully. " Can't
we get to see her ? " She meant Miss Jansen.

" Easily—if you care to go to one of Mrs. Seagraves' Sunday
afternoons."

" I don't much care for Mrs. Seagraves. She is too ridiculous.
She doesn't even amuse me any more. But I like her brother,
for all his nonsense about kings and divine right; and I hope he
won't get himself killed in Spain. Do you know, papa, I think
if Captain Cameron were to ask me to marry him I should have
to say yes."

" My dear, how can you talk in that way ? "

" Yes, I think I should have to accept him. Could you give
him a hint, dear? Would it be proper ? "

" Marie! I don't like to hear you talk such nonsense. What
do you mean ? "

" Women are not generally supposed to have much meaning,
I believe, in what they say. But I have some meaning too. I
think Captain Cameron is the only real man I know—of the
unmarried, I mean. He seems to have some purpose in life fit
for a man—he has not surrendered his existence to the making
of money—or the chasing of butterflies."

" Butterflies, Marie ? "

" Silly and frivolous tastes, then. I don't know which I dislike the more, the work or the play of the agreeable gentlemen
whom we count among our friends. In their business moods
they are precocious usurers: in their hours of idleness they are
ladies'-maids a little overgrown."

Sir John looked up at his daughter in some surprise. He
had always encouraged her to talk out her mind as she pleased.
And he had often seen her in satirical moods. But she seemed
more bitterly in earnest now than was usual with her.

" I should have known even if you hadn't told me of Vidal's
being here to-day, Marie."

" Indeed, dear! How should you have known it ? "

" By your outburst against frivolous youth. I suppose he
was trying to amuse you after his own fashion. I really must
let him know what a wise young person we have here, and
recommend him to keep his levities for young ladies of feebler
mould."

" I think they would suit old ladies still better, papa. I
don't know anybody who would make a better attendant for a
careful old maid of quality with a taste for discoloured laces and
cracked china."

Sir John Challoner never lost his temper, and would not let
even his daughter see that he could be annoyed by anything a

woman could say. For though he adored his daughter as his
daughter, he no more considered her a creature equal to man
than a lady who loves her toy-terrier believes that toy-terriers
stand in the order of creation as high as West End ladies.
" You don't understand Vidal yet, my dear," he said, kindly.
" I don't wonder. His is a very complex character—women
don't readily make it out. But you will see some day—before
long I hope—that he has something in him."

Marie ventured no farther then, and was sorry she had
ventured so far. She went to dress for dinner, feeling miserably
out of humour with the world, and not knowing why. She sat
for a long time listless in her room, thinking what a stupid thing
life was, and how mean people's pursuits and ambitions seemed
to be, and moralising over existence in general, as young men
and women always do when they are unwilling to confess to
themselves that it is only some particular existence which concerns them. Many things, however, she acknowledged to herself
had disappointed her. She was sorry that *he* too should be going
in for the making of money—that he too was going to turn out
like all the rest—" he too " being Christmas Pembroke ; for she
really had liked him always, she said. Mr. Vidal's conversation
had been especially out of tune with her mood that day, and she
did not like to hear her father lay such stress on the necessity of
making money. She used to hear but little of such talk from
him at Durewoods. She began to have a shadowy, half-acknow-
ledged idea that her father making holiday at Durewoods was a
different person from Sir John Challoner the successful financier
in his ordinary life in London.

Besides—for she was a very clever girl, with eyes of keen
intelligence—she began to think that people in general did not
respect her father as she respected him—for the qualities which
she desired to respect in him. She did not like the way in
which Ronald Vidal commonly spoke to him, or of him. The
young man greatly admired Sir John, and looked up to him
evidently, but only as an eager young adventurer looks up to a
master in the craft. That was not the sort of admiration Marie
would have wished to see. In a vaguer way, too, her womanly
susceptibility to slight impressions, and her womanly observation of trifling shades of difference between one thing and
another, were teaching her already somewhat of the lesson which
Sir John Challoner himself had frankly explained to Christmas—
that a man with plenty of money may be in society without
exactly being of it. All these thoughts were pressing on her
when she suddenly and unexpectedly came upon Christmas
Pembroke in the library that day, and while his changed appearance and his seeming growth of years repressed her and
kept her at a distance, she felt her heart open warmly to him as

he spoke with such generous devotion of her father. Here at least, she thought, is genuine friendship and real sympathy—here is, thank Heaven, an unspoiled human heart. And now, behold, he too was grubbing in the City for money like the rest; and he was in love with a girl who screamed on platforms for Woman's Rights! Against such trials that day Dear Lady Disdain could at first find no rampart but in her disdain. She seemed to be in a fair way now of earning her nickname.

CHAPTER XIV.

SEEKING A PLIANT HOUR.

WAS Sir John Challoner then mistaken when he believed that in his daughter's eyes and nature he could read the evidence of a slumbering spirit of ambition and energy which could be aroused and made to play with fervour the game which has social success for its stake? Was Dione Lyle mistaken? Was Ronald Vidal, who was of society and knew life, and who really admired the girl, and believed that if she would marry him she could be trained into making him a splendid wife? As a younger son Vidal was determined to marry for money, and had long looked about among Manchester manufacturers and Liverpool merchant princes for a presentable daughter, content even with such a prospect; and he now sprang with eagerness at the chance of so handsome and brilliant a girl as Marie Challoner. Were these all mistaken in believing that she had spirit and ambition? Was she really made by Nature only to be a happy shepherdess of Arcadian Durewoods?

Probably they were not mistaken. But Sir John Challoner perhaps was unwise when he sounded the praises and the glories of ambition too much in advance. Everybody knows how a prudent mother secures her son against captivation at the hands of some pretty girl who is likely to be thrown in his way. She praises and puffs the girl so much in anticipation, and so excites his curiosity and eagerness about her, that when he sees her he is certain to be disappointed. Sir John Challoner had piqued and roused Marie's expectations too much on the subject of Ambition. When she saw it she was disappointed. It seemed a poor thing, such ambition as he could show her. She had seen very little of London society as yet, but she was quick to form impressions, and she was disappointed. If her father had been a great Parliamentary leader, and had eminent public men around him, Marie would probably have warmed to the large and thrilling game of life in which they were engaged. If he had been in the centre of a circle of literature and art, and she had listened to the talk of historians and poets, and novelists and painters, she might have felt the ambition to be the queen or the princess of such a coterie. But Sir John's Parliamentary colleagues were only men who used the House of Commons as a place in which to push their various "interests." The one or two peers who came on familiar terms to Sir John's dinner-table were promoted bankers. Ronald Vidal's father had not yet been persuaded to give his presence. The ambition was an ambition to push financial and railway schemes, and to make money. The people seemed to Marie stupid, the "interests" peddling and vulgar. Even when she still almost shrank from the expectation, she had expected something infinitely finer and more nobly alluring than this. The very house they lived in, which Sir John believed to be imposing and superb, impressed her with a sense of something crude, false, and almost vulgar.

Sir John said well when he said to her, "You never were poor; and I was." Mere costliness did not impress her as it still impressed him. She had always seen money freely spent around her, and she never thought about it. Dione Lyle's little house at Durewoods charmed her with its picturesqueness and its serene artistic taste, but her father's great new mansion in Kensington chilled her almost from the first. If every one is born either an Aristotelian or a Platonist, so everybody, be he king or be he cobbler, is born of the artist or the *bourgeois* class. Marie was of the former class, as her father was of the latter, and she could not help looking on all things in life, great and little, from the artistic point of view. The career which her present life seemed to open to woman's ambition had nothing picturesque or thrilling—in a word, nothing artistic about it.

All this produced its effect upon her mind, and its effect, combined with still newer things, shaped itself in thoughts more or less distressing and melancholy as she was dressing for dinner on that day while Christmas Pembroke was devouring his way through London streets and thinking of her. One thought was perhaps uppermost in her mind, the idea that she at least would be a friend to any girl whom Christmas Pembroke loved. More than once the tears came into the generous eyes of Dear Lady Disdain as she determined on doing heroic things to befriend that pair and make them happy. How very happy he must be, she thought, to have found the one he loves so soon, and to be loved by her. And she too—she must be very happy and must love him. "I will tell her," thought Dear Lady Disdain, "some day—how *I* liked him—from the very first."

Generous resolves within ourselves beget generous construction of others. Marie began to believe that Christmas was really working in the City only for his love, and not for the mere greed of money-making. She softened towards him and she became more and more anxious to see Miss Sybil Jansen.

Sir John had two or three heavy men and their wives to dine that day, and they went away early, and then he took his daughter to an evening party. Mr. Vidal was there, and was looking very handsome and bright, and was talking to everybody. He soon found his way to Marie's side, and seemed anxious to make himself conspicuous by his attentions to her.

Suddenly Marie broke in upon some criticism he was offering upon the music to which she had not been listening—

"Mr. Vidal—you know everybody. Do you know a lady—a Miss Sybil Jansen?"

"Sybil Jansen? Oh, yes, certainly. I have met her often."

"Indeed. Then you know her?"

"You say I know everybody! I have met Miss Jansen at one or two places. She is a sort of person whom some people take up, you know. You must go to the right place to meet her. People who like curiosities and so on sometimes make a point of paying her some attention. You wouldn't meet her here."

"Is she pretty, or is she clever? Tell me something about her."

"She is pretty in a sort of way. She has nice eyes and teeth, I think—a pale little girl; very young, and with her little head turned rather by self-conceit and the notion that she has a mission."

"She makes speeches—does she speak well?"

"Yes, I think so—for that sort of thing. I don't care about women's speeches—in public I mean, Miss Challoner. She talks like a little whirlwind: would give you a headache to hear much of it, I should think."

"Did you ever tell her what you thought of her speaking?"

"Well, no; not exactly. That would be rather rude, wouldn't it? I haven't quite the courage of old Lady Jervis—the old woman; mother of the young fellow Sir Dudley Jervis; *you* know.

"No, I don't know; but what did she do?"

"She took a liking to hear little Sybil, and got some one to take her to a lecture somewhere. When it was over somebody offered to present Miss Sybil, and the old lady blandly consented. So the poor girl was brought up, and Lady Jervis calmly studied her through her eyeglass, and then said 'Miss Jansen, if you were my daughter I'd whip you and send you to bed!'"

"What a detestable and cruel old woman! Yet I don't know that it was not better to speak in that way than to praise the poor girl to her face—oh, I know from what you have said that you did praise her to her face!—and then make a jest of her.

I suppose she is very much in earnest. I think now that I should like her."

" No, you wouldn't care about her."

" I mean to see her and make her acquaintance, for all that."

" That will be easily done if you really wish to know her and Sir John doesn't object. But I don't think he cares much about speech-making women, does he ? "

" Speech-making women seem to you a class something like dancing dogs," said Marie.

" Well, Dr. Johnson did make some sort of comparison like that, didn't he ? " Vidal asked.

Marie dropped the conversation, or, indeed, to describe matters more properly, shook it off. It offended her to hear any earnest attempt of an enthusiastic woman talked of in such a manner. " I had rather a thousand times be a man who could fall in love with her," she thought, " than a man who could only laugh at her. Why should she be laughed at ? She is trying to do some good in the world : and *I* am not. She has some purpose in living beyond making money and getting into society. I don't see any other purpose in most of the people I know."

Perhaps if Ronald Vidal had greatly praised Miss Jansen, Marie might have been more inclined to doubt her mission and her merits. But with all his supposed knowledge of women Mr. Vidal went wrong in assuming that every girl likes to hear other girls spoken of with contempt. He quite misunderstood Marie Challoner at all events, for she always had the generous weakness which inclines one to defend the assailed even without much inquiry into the merits of the question. If the nature of woman always loves to exercise itself in contradiction, as people say, the contradiction which Dear Lady Disdain found herself tempted to indulge in was only that which speaks up for the weak or the unpopular.

Ronald Vidal saw that he had not quite pleased Marie by his criticism of Miss Jansen, whom he would have praised with the greatest readiness if he had known that it would give her any gratification. He was a good-natured young man, who never cared to injure anybody ; but he generally found that conversations are more freely carried on by means of censure than by means of praise. His active mind seeking everywhere for knowledge of persons, had led him to where Miss Jansen was to be heard—and of course he took care to be presented to her, and no doubt he had praised her to her face and disparaged her (he was not much given to laughter, and had very little sense of humour) behind her back. But it is only fair to say that he would have pointed out the defects of his own sister with equal openness. Marie Challoner was probably the only woman who impressed him with any sense of genuine respect and admiration.

He greatly enjoyed talking scandal to other women, as he liked time-bargains with men or chaff with actresses; but he came to Marie always with better hopes and topics.

This night he had evidently had the hint which Sir John Challoner promised to give him. He left Marie discreetly for a while after the talk about Miss Jansen, but he contrived to come near her again before long.

"So glad to find you again," he said; and he managed to intercept others who were near her. " I have something to tell you—stay, here is a chair—in this quiet corner."

Marie was afraid perhaps that she had been a little abrupt in the matter of Miss Jansen, and she welcomed him with a propitiatory smile, and took the chair which he was offering to her.

" I am going to do something at last," he said—" something definite, I mean. I think you will approve of it. I am going to start upon a regular career in public life."

" Oh! I am very glad; I think you are doing quite right. Every man of talent ought to do something of the kind."

" Thank you," he said, much more warmly than the implied compliment deserved, and evidently determined to make the most of it. " Thank you! you are very kind and encouraging. Yes, there is an opening—did you hear them talking of it to-night?—in Lord Barbican's borough—and there would be a chance for some one who would come boldly forward on thorougly independent principles, and try to get the seat out of the hands of the insufferable Barbican family. One runs a risk and makes enemies of course; but I don't care. You see it's this way——"

And then he drew a chair beside her, and began to give her an account of how Lord Barbican and his family had for generations domineered over the borough, and how there was a good chance now, with the ballot, of wresting the representation from them, if a really independent candidate came forward who was not afraid of the Barbicans. Every woman warms to the prospect of a combat, and feels some interest in the champion who runs most risk; and Vidal soon saw a sparkle of ambition and encouragement in Marie's eye. Before he had talked to her very long she began to regard the borough as a sort of Andromeda, Lord Barbican as a devouring sea-monster, and the handsome Ronald Vidal as a rescuing Perseus. He did certainly look very handsome, and he talked, she thought, very eloquently. Perhaps she had really then misunderstood and undervalued him. Perhaps the levity was but the indolence of a gallant spirit waiting for its opportunity. Perhaps it was once more a Sardanapalus rushing from his revel to the battle, or Prince Hal renouncing Eastcheap to offer challenge to Harry Hotspur.

Marie's rather vague ideas of political contests happily enabled her to contemplate the coming struggle for Lord Barbican's borough with other eyes than those of an election agent.

"I thought you would approve of this," he said, in a low appealing tone.

"Mr. Vidal, it gives me great pleasure——"

"I have been thinking of it this long time, and especially since that first day when we walked up the hill among the trees at Durewoods. Do you remember?"

"I remember the walk," Marie answered, a little pleased, despite of herself, to know that he remembered it.

"Well, we talked then of political life and ambition, and you seemed to encourage my desire to make some sort of a name for myself in politics."

"Did I? That was very rash of me, Mr. Vidal, for I knew nothing about political life then, and I know very little now. Did I really venture to give an opinion?"

"Indeed you did? *I* have not forgotten it. And from that moment I determined to show you that perhaps I deserved a better opinion than you had of me."

"But please don't say that! If I was so rash as to urge you to anything, it was only, I suppose, because I had a better opinion of you than you had of yourself."

"Thank you—thank you. I'll do my best. I'll have your good opinion if I can. I'll win my spurs. The truth is, Challoner spoiled me—your father spoiled me!"

"I am sorry to hear that my father has spoiled anybody?"

"I don't mean, seriously, of course; but he has such a head for business and finance and all that; and he always told me I had too: and he is such a thorough man of the world, you know; and has such a tongue that he can make people do whatever he likes. I never saw such a fellow to talk people over as Challoner is. Never, I give you my word."

Certainly this was not the sort of panegyric which Marie would have cared to hear pronounced upon her father.

"I know so little of these things," she said, rather coldly. "I always lived so much out of the world down at Durewoods. My father always appeared to me in so different a light! I don't recognise him in your praise even, Mr. Vidal."

"Of course," said Vidal, "our fathers always appear to us in an ideal light. It's a merciful dispensation of Providence. We could never get on if we regarded our fathers and mothers as ordinary human beings. But you must not mind my nonsense, Miss Challoner."

"I don't mind it at all, Mr. Vidal."

By these words Marie probably meant to say that she knew she ought not to mind it, and that she would not mind it if she could. But she did mind it for all that. It jarred heavily on her feelings, and even on her nerves. Was this, then, the character which her father bore—the character of a pushing, plausible, grasping man of the world? It was not thus she thought of him when they read together and rambled in the lanes together at Durewoods, and when out of the vague hints she had heard of his early acquaintanceship with Miss Lyle she had woven together the threads faint and light as if spun from sunbeams, of some romantic story in which he must have played a noble, heroic part. Even if it was only Vidal's nonsense it hurt her to hear such nonsense spoken of her father.

Vidal could not make much further way that night. Passing through one of the rooms presently he met Sir John Challoner.

"I say, Challoner, look here," he said, and he drew him into a corner. "I've been putting my foot in it with your daughter."

"Indeed ; What have you been saying ? "

"Well, she was very kind, and I was telling her of all my plans, and, by Jove! I never saw her so friendly to me—when in an evil hour I began to excuse myself by saying that it was you who drew me into money affairs and all that, and that you were so clever a man of the world—— "

"Well ? "

"She didn't seem to like it at all. I thought if I could put the blame on you it would be all right—that she would excuse me all the more readily, and of course you wouldn't care. But she grew quite cold and distant at the bare suggestion that you weren't exactly like that particular one of King Arthur's Knights who found the Holy Grail."

"Marie has a very high opinion of me, Vidal."

"But I say—you know—what an absurd idea it is to bring up one's children with the notion that one is a sort of divine being! That sort of thing must burst up one day or other, you know. I can assure you I never had any such an idea of my father, although there could hardly be a better man of his kind. Anyhow, Challoner, you ought to have warned me beforehand that I was to think of you as a Bayard of Whitehall and a Fenelon of Lombard Street, and I'd have done my best to cheat myself into the delusion."

"You don't understand women yet," Sir John said with his quiet smile. "Women are not to be studied merely by sitting next to them at dinner parties, or waltzing in a crowd—or composing the quarrels of rival actresses, Vidal."

"I wish I understood your daughter a little better. She's the only woman I know who is worth the understanding."

"You must make allowance for her country bringing up," Sir John said with the slightest possible flavour of sarcasm in his tone. "*You* don't often meet such girls, Vidal. But in any case you ought to know that women don't as a rule care to look at things as they are, but only as they would like to think them. Even if a woman knew in her secret heart that somebody—her father if you like in certain cases—was not an ideal personage, she would always prefer to have him presented to her as if he were."

"I suppose that's true," said Vidal. "In any case it's advice I shall act upon for the future. But, good Heavens! to think of a clever, quick girl of to-day having such ideas about her father!"

"It is absurd," Sir John said, smiling in his peculiar way "but they are only children, you know, Vidal. Men of brains like you and me must humour their pretty little ways."

"I only hope I haven't made an utter mess of it."

"Oh, no; I don't fancy it can be quite irretrievable. I'll do my best by restoring myself to restore you too."

So they parted for the hour.

CHAPTER XV.

HYPATIA AT HOME.

SYBIL JANSEN lodged in a quiet street which branched off from a considerable thoroughfare in the West Centre of London. The houses there had been spacious mansions occupied by people of quality in other days, but had come gradually down in the world. Professor Huxley has expressed some regret, in one of his lectures, that we have not in our society, along with the arrangements which enable meritorious and gifted persons to rise from lowly state to high, some mechanism to facilitate or cause the regular descent of the unmeritorious and ungifted from high estate to low. It is a pity that the defect is not supplied, if only that we might be allowed periodically to watch the edifying spectacle of the deserving and undeserving person passing each other, as in an ascending and a descending bucket, the one mounting heavenward to Belgravia, the other mournfully going down for his sins to New Cross. Some such process may, however, be observed in our streets and houses. There the descent in the social scale may be watched by the easiest observer. The house sinks in the street; then the street sinks in the quarter; then the quarter sinks in the city. Only it is hard to trace out the moral. What were the sins that doomed the house, the street, the quarter, where Miss Sybil Jansen lived to go down in the social rank—what the virtues which earned for South Kensington its title to go up?

Most of the houses in this street had their lower floors occupied by solicitors, doctors, or dentists. The upper rooms divided themselves among lodgers. Thus the houses still kept up a sort of dignified appearance of being offices and chambers; not hack London lodging-houses. A good many artists lodged in that quarter, and the passer-by occasionally met some brown-checked Roman women with gold ear-rings and snowy chemisettes, with supple forms and superb walk, who were the models for peasantry of the Campagna to the rising pencils of the region. Not far was the British Museum, whence flowed after four o'clock each afternoon a stream of readers and students of both sexes, alike rather careless of dress, and alike for the most part somewhat ungainly of figure. Not all, however, were careless of dress or ungainly of figure, for Miss Sybil Jansen read in the Museum, and her pretty face, slender form, and artistic dressing were the admiration of many a student of the one sex, and the envy of many even among the most learned of the other.

It was in the British Museum that the acquaintance between Sybil Jansen and Christmas, begun in Mrs. Seagraves' drawing-room, had ripened into something like friendship, at least on his side. Miss Jansen had gone in for renovating the world on the basis of free opinions and the equality of the sexes. She hugged to her heart and often repeated to herself the statement in which the feelings of George Eliot's latest heroine had just been set forth—viz., that when any good was to be done for anybody, the heroine would have thought any allusion to the sex of the person concerned wholly irrelevant. Miss Jansen told herself in the fullest and purest good faith that where friendship, beneficence, and a good cause were concerned, a question of sex was irrelevant. If the question did not actually become irrelevant the moment it was philosophically proclaimed to be so that was no fault of Miss Jansen. Much more pretentious and important schemes of philosophy than hers have been founded on the principle of calling things irrelevant which yet prove themselves every now and then to have a sad and unalterable relevancy to our life. This principle of Miss Jansen's is only mentioned here to explain the readiness with which the young Hypatia struck up a friendly league with our hero and walked often in his company of evenings from the British Museum to her own door. Sybil thought no harm, and neither surely did our often preoccupied youth of the gloomy brow. He was lonely, and her frank friendship pleased him. There was a good deal sympathetic between them. He was now a little at odds with the world; and so she seemed to be. Some things had gone wrong with him; to her the whole scheme of the universe

L

seemed out of gear. He was unhappy, and certainly Sybil Jansen was not happy.

She had often asked him to pass a few hours of the evening with her and her mother, and he meant some time to accept the invitation. He had once or twice entered the house with her, and had been greatly pleased with his reception in his simple boyish way. He had not seen her now for many days (so far astray was Sir John Challoner in his conjecture), and he had hardly thought of her in his work and his rushing hither and thither. As he looked across Kensington Gardens this night he suddenly thought of her, and he resolved to go and see her. "They are friendly to me," he thought—and observe that even in his thought it was "they," not "she"—"and I think they would be glad to see me—nobody else cares particularly in London that I know of." In this mood he made his way— a pretty long way—to the street where Miss Jansen lived; and he saw lights in the windows, and the elderly woman who opened the door and took general care of the offices and apart- ments told him that she believed Mrs. and Miss Jansen were at home, and would he walk up, please? For this was no lodging-house, be it understood, with a common servant to wait on everybody. This was a collection of offices, chambers, and apartments, and the elderly housekeeper who took charge of the concern in general had nothing to do with admitting you or piloting you into any particular department of the building. You went your way and knocked at whatever door on whatever floor you wanted—almost as if you were in Paris; and you could not possibly be so lost to all impression of dignity as to suppose you were in an ordinary and commonplace Bloomsbury lodging- house.

So our youth found his way up a broad and very dimly lighted stair until he came to the floor on which the Jansens lived. He had been there before in company with Miss Sybil; that is, when he had escorted her home—or walked with her, for she did not care about escort—he had gone upstairs with her once or twice, as has been said, and had been presented to her mother. He had learned or inferred from Miss Jansen's conversation that they lived on some very small income which had remained to her mother, aided by Sybil's own hard work in translating for publishers, doing occasional magazine articles, and delivering lectures. One of Miss Jansen's faiths or dreams was that when women got the suffrage they would be able to command for their literary and other work reward equal to that of men. Christmas had mildly endeavoured to question with this hope, but had little success. He thought now, as he ascended the half-lighted stair, that Sybil's dreams were hardly to be wondered at, and that it would be cruel to deny her the pleasure of hope.

He tapped at their door, and a servant told him the ladies were in, conducted him across a small passage to the door of a room which was dark, scraped a match and lighted a lamp in the room, showed him in, then asked him his name, did not wait for his card, and disappeared apparently in some bewilderment.

Christmas was left for a few moments to occupy himself in looking over the books and papers which lay on the table. The word " Scrap-book " in gilt letters on one volume attracted his attention, and he wondered much how a young lady of Miss Jansen's vigorous and exalted turn of mind could care for a trivial and feminine compilation of that kind. He opened the scrap-book and found that it contained only a collection of cuttings from newspapers referring to the lectures and the speeches of Miss Sybil Jansen.

There was a melancholy interest in this poor little collection of criticisms. No journal of which Christmas had ever heard the name before had honoured the young Hypatia with a notice. But the *Peckham Chronicle* compared her to Corinna; the *Deptford and Isle of Dogs Gazette* said she reminded him of Sappho; the *Woman's Champion* declared that Miss Jansen was the priestess of a new gospel. There were pages and yards of this sort of thing cut out with scrupulous neatness, and preserved as though they were works of art. A feeling of compassion came up in Christmas's mind, as he thought of the poor girl trying to feed her heart on this sort of food, and believing that the voice of the *Deptford and Isle of Dogs Gazette* was fame. Fame itself, wise people say, is incense that only godlike hearts can feed upon without withering into atrophy; but fancy a sham-fame, the dulled reflection of a soap-bubble in a cracked glass !

While Christmas was thinking over these things there entered the young Hypatia herself. She was dressed gracefully and simply as was her wont—in black silk, high to the throat, and short at the ankle. She looked very pale and very pretty, and in the dimly-lighted room she gave the idea to Christmas that she was all eyes. She entered the room in the dubious way of one who expects to meet a stranger, and then recognising Pembroke, a very wave of welcoming expression passed over her face—

" Mr. Pembroke! Now this *is* kind, and I am *so* glad to see you ; " and she emphasised words here and there in her energetic little way; " but I had no idea it was you. Our new servant bungled over your name. Mamma will be so glad to see you."

" I have long been promising myself the pleasure of coming to see you," said Christmas, " but I have been a good deal out of town lately."

" You have just come in time for tea. I see you were looking over my notices. I ought not to have left that book out."

"Was I wrong in reading it? Surely not?"

"Oh, no; I don't mean that; but it looks like vanity; and men always say we women are vain. It is not vanity, however, Mr. Pembroke—at least in my case. I am not vain, but I hope I care for the cause which I represent; and any praise given to me must be of service to that. So you have been reading some of the notices? Some of them are very good! are they not? I wonder if you happened to read what the *Trumpet of Putney* said. Will you call me vain if I show it to you and ask you just to glance at it?"

She took the book from him with her nervous, quivering hands, and fluttered its pages over until she found the citation from the *Trumpet of Putney*. Christmas's heart sank as he glanced over it. It was an enthusiastic suburban reporter's rhapsody written in penny-a-line English, no word under three syllables, and the adjectives generally applied inaccurately. It spoke of Miss Jansen's talents as "transcendental," and said that her voice was as "potential" as it was musical. Yet this girl, of much talent and considerable culture, admired it and was delighted with it.

"I cried with joy when I read that first," she said. "It is too much praise, perhaps, you think; but I welcomed it as a sign that men were at last beginning to do justice to women. You don't feel with us, I know, and I am sorry for it, and I don't understand it. The generosity of your instincts ought to bring you to us."

"I haven't studied the question much, so count me as neutral, Miss Jansen."

"No. You can't be neutral. You must declare for right or wrong—for truth or falsehood. No, no; you are under some influence—the influence of some woman, I know, who persuades you that we are unwomanly. Oh, how we suffer from these cold creatures of society—these traitresses to their own cause!"

Miss Sybil's eyes gleamed and her breast heaved, and her little thin fingers closed as if around the hilt of some weapon wherewith to pierce the hearts of her treacherous sisters.

"Come," she said, suddenly changing her tone, and removing, or rather snatching, the book of criticisms from Pembroke's hand; "you don't care about all this sort of thing, I know, and I am only boring you to no purpose. I don't want to be a mere bore, Mr. Pembroke; but if you knew how much I think about these things! Come into the other room. Mamma will be delighted to see you. She likes you so much; and we will give you some tea."

Her voice sounded gratefully in Christmas's ears. He was glad to be where he knew that he was welcome, and he had been growing into a compassionate liking for poor young, lonely Sybil, with her futile aspirations and her barren ambition, and her morbid susceptibility. He had never before met any one so terribly in earnest.

Sybil led him across the little passage, and into a room where her mother and she usually spent their evenings. It was a large old-fashioned room, very neatly kept, and furnished in a style which, to a quick and observant eye, would have told a somewhat pathetic story. There was, for example, a superb old-fashioned piano, and there was a beautiful little ebony table, old-fashioned too; and there were two or three fine portraits in oil which had been done by a good hand, and had cost money in their time. But the carpet was of the newest and cheapest kind, the chairs unmistakably suggested a second-hand shop and "This Cheap Drawing-room Set"—the mirror over the chimney-piece had beyond doubt once been marked with its price in chalk in the front of some small auctioneer's store; the little time-piece was evidently of similar origin. The same discrepancy was in the books. There were two or three very fine and costly old editions, and there were many of the very cheapest of modern reprints, with their thin paper and their small over-worked type. Everything bore evidence of scrupulous neatness and of refined taste. The story told itself. The Jansens had once had money, and now they were poor.

Mrs. Jansen was a feeble and wasted woman, with a manner of somewhat faded and old-fashioned elegance, like that of one who, long withdrawn from society, had fallen behind the ways of the present. She was dressed with much greater effort at elegance than her daughter, and might have passed off in dim light, or to not very keen eyes, as up to the fashion in evening costume. She gave Christmas a cordial welcome and a kind smile. She would be very glad to have the monotony of her life brightened occasionally by the visit of an intelligent and agreeable young man; and if she had any dim, undefined thought deep down in her maternal bosom about Sybil, who shall blame her?

"Have you looked at mamma's portrait?" Sybil asked; and she held up a lamp for him to see the painting. "It was done by Westwood—he was an Academician, you know." (Christmas did not know, but was ready to believe.) "Is it not a wonderful likeness?"

Christmas saw the portrait of a slender, soft, handsome woman, wearing a hat and feathers, and a dress unfamiliar to his memories of female costume. It might have been one of the famous Miss Gunning's or one of Sir Joshua's beauties, for all he could have told. It certainly seemed to him to have little that even memory or imagination could connect with the worn and prematurely aged woman who sat near the hearth where the

little brass kettle was standing. But he praised the picture
cordially, evading the question of likeness, for he was a terribly
truthful and ingenuous youth.

"I can see that you do not think it a good likeness," said
Sybil, in a disappointed tone. "I know all Mr. Pembroke's
ways, mamma. He never can be got to say anything he doesn't
believe—he never will pay a compliment. Oh, if men were all
so truthful and honest!"

And yet Sybil seemed somehow as if she could bear a compliment or two now and then well enough.

"My dear, how could Mr. Pembroke see any likeness in that
to what I am now? You forget the number of years and the
changes. I was only Sybil's age when that was painted, Mr.
Pembroke. I had just been married. It was like me then, I
believe—very like. I am old enough to be able to say that now
without affectation."

"It seems wonderfully like, to me," Sybil said, holding up
her lamp, and gazing fondly at the picture. "I cannot see any
change. The farthest memory I have, mamma, is of you just
like that; only not the same kind of dress; and I cannot see
any change."

"One good thing about common misfortune," said the elder
lady, "is that it keeps up a sympathy and love that perhaps
other people don't have. Sybil is everything to me, Mr. Pembroke; and I suppose I am a good deal to her. Sybil, dear, will
you make tea?"

Sybil bestirred herself very gracefully and prettily, and
Pembroke watched her with interest. She poured some hot
water into the tea-pot to heat it; then she poured that off again,
then she put in some tea, after a momentary mental calculation
of the additional quantity required by the presence of the
visitor; then she poured water on the tea; and then she put the
tea to draw. As she moved about he could not help observing
now and then that she had a very white and pretty arm, and he
even had a glimpse more than once of a bronze slipper, a very
neat ankle, and a scarlet stocking. An instinctive politeness
made him talk chiefly to the elder lady; but he was not thereby
prevented from following the movements of the younger.

He could not help remembering that he had more than once
heard disparaging criticism of the young Hypatia, on the ground
that she defied society—that she went everywhere without escort,
and that she lived independently, and alone—"as if she were a
young man, and not a young woman," one censor remarked. It
was true that Sybil did go to places alone, and return alone; but
Christmas thought that anybody who saw her quiet home and
her attention to her mother might have excused many of her
acts of independence, and put at least the best construction on
her doings.

Sybil left the room once on some domestic purpose, and the elder lady, as if she had been following Pembroke's thoughts, said—

"My Sybil leads a strange life, Mr. Pembroke, or what would have been thought a strange life in my younger days. I do not cross her, and I do not even advise her against it, for she has been a most devoted daughter to me, and her life has been a trying one. I encourage her in going out to places alone, for how else could she go? And she would pine if she remained always within these walls."

"Nobody has a right to complain of what she does, if you approve of it," Christmas said warmly, and forgetting that it was not the best thing perhaps to tell the mother that people did complain.

"I suppose people do find fault with her," she said; "and with me. But a great many people—you can't think how many —praise her, and say that she has a duty to fulfil. And she is really a very clever speaker—they all say—and I am glad to see her throw herself into some public cause, for then she goes about and speaks, and is praised, and it makes her happy; and if she did not think she was doing some public good she never would leave me; and what sort of life would that be for a young woman? It is no vanity of hers. She is not vain in the least, I assure you."

Christmas was deeply touched by these evidences of affection on the part of mother and daughter. The girl still saw a likeness in the brilliant portrait to the worn elderly woman; the mother could not see the little touches of unrepressed vanity in the daughter which actually sprang to the eye of every passing stranger.

"And then," Mrs. Jansen went on with a little energy in her usually feeble manner, "if Sybil is warm about women's rights and women's wrongs, she and I, Mr. Pembroke, have both suffered much from a man. We have been cruelly treated. Why is that child poor and hardworked in her youth? Because of a heartless man! I am not a widow, Mr. Pembroke, though you may have thought so. My husband, my Sybil's father, is living, and—— "

She was leaning forward in her chair and speaking in tones of keen and concentrated anger. Sybil entered, and Mrs. Jansen leaned quietly back again.

"Sybil, my dear," she said, "I don't know if Mr. Pembroke would like a little cold meat with his tea. Perhaps he has dined early or not dined at all. Young gentlemen, I know, are apt to be careless."

Mrs. Jansen belonged to the days before gastronomy had come to be the special boast of every young man's education, and when young men were still called young gentlemen.

"I hope he would like some," Sybil said, "for I have had no dinner, and I am going to have some cold meat." Christmas had instincts far too kindly not to declare at once that he had eaten no dinner and that he should like some cold meat, of all things. Poor fellow, it was quite true that he had not dined, but true also that he had not thought about the matter, and now he did begin to feel hungry. Sybil left the room again.

Mrs. Jansen at once resumed her story to Christmas—

"Few women have suffered more at the hands of a bad and selfish man than I have, Mr. Pembroke—except Sybil—for, however, her father may have conceived that he had a right to wrong me, he had no right to desert that innocent child. Were you going to ask me why I tell you this?"

This was a painful question, but Christmas felt inspired with an answer which was at once truthful and soothing—

"No, Mrs. Jansen, I was not going to ask you that. I suppose you tell this to me because you think me better worthy of your confidence than a mere chance acquaintance."

"That is the reason partly; but partly, too, because I should like you to know that if poor Sybil seems to you strangely eager to see women righted, it is because she, more than most other human beings, has seen how women are wronged. Thank you, Sybil, dear. Shall we have some toast?"

Then Sybil set to making some toast, and Christmas offered to relieve her, and with a few hints of instruction did efficiently relieve her. In return for his education in the art of making toast, he gave some information relative to Chinese and Japanese ways of making tea, which was received with interest. No women could be more easy and self-possessed than this mother and daughter. It was clear that they did all such lighter work as belonged to the tea-table for themselves, and left their servant only what may be called the heavier duties. They never seemed other than perfectly well-bred women—ladies, as the phrase is—when thus engaged. Christmas could hardly recognise the fierce and palpitating little prophetess of the platform in the kindly, genial girl who bustled about her modest rooms and made tea and laid plates and was so feminine and winning.

After tea Christmas, who had a good baritone voice and some knowledge of music, sang to Sybil's accompaniment several songs, and he also endeavoured, without Sybil's accompaniment, to give the ladies some idea of what Japanese music and singing were like; and they looked at photographs, and they kept off the woman question, and were very pleasant. Once or twice Christmas was reminded that he was under the roof of an agitator or a woman endowed with a mission, when a number of letters from the post were brought to Sybil, and begging to be excused, she tore them open and found that they contained invitations to meetings and lectures, questions to be answered, and other such incidental intrusions on the peace of those who come before the public. Once or twice Sybil begged to be allowed to withdraw into the other room to answer letters that scarcely admitted of delay.

"Another word, Mr. Pembroke," said the elder lady during one of these absences, returning with trembling lips to her former painful subject. "There is another reason why I have told you of our misfortunes. I know well enough what a cloud hangs over a woman in this country who for whatever reason is separated from her husband. I know that if she were as free of fault as an angel there are people who would hold her in suspicion and would shrink from her. I avoid that, for I shrink from them. But as you are kind enough to come to see us, I think it right that you should know I receive no one under false pretences. Now you *know;* and I shall not trouble you any more on the subject."

This was, indeed, the chief reason of Mrs. Jansen's confidence. She had acquired in her wrongs and her loneliness a sort of fierce independence, and if she had, poor woman, any faint far thought that possibly Christmas and her daughter might come to like each other, she was quite resolved that he should know from the first of the cloud, as she called it, that hung over them.

Sybil re-entered the room with some letters which she had written, and Christmas offered to post them for her as he went homeward.

"If you don't object," Miss Sybil said, "to making yourself an instrument in forwarding such a cause as ours—for I warn you that they have to do with our cause and with speeches—to be made by *me.*"

"But I really have hardly any view either way——"

"Oh, yes; I am sure you have."

"My dear Sybil. Mr. Pembroke says he has not."

"He says it only in a qualified way, and out of good nature. The influence I dread is not the opposition of men, but the opposition of women through men. I fear that Mr. Pembroke is expressing the views of some thoughtless and happy woman—thoughtless because she is happy, and who does not consider how very different may be the lot of others—of thousands and thousands of others. That is the influence I dread."

Miss Sybil was growing eager, earnest, and rhetorical again. Christmas could not imagine why she kept charging him with thus taking his tone from some woman.

"I assure you, Miss Jansen," he said, almost as earnestly as she had herself spoken, "I don't believe I ever exchanged a word on the subject with any woman but yourself—oh, yes; except with Mrs. Seagraves, who is all on your side."

"What a kind, good-hearted woman, so generous and un-fettered! I like her. I know people sometimes think her affected and ridiculous—I don't care! Oh, yes; she is with us. But I think her friend Miss Challoner is against us."

The colour rushed into Pembroke's face. He felt himself red and hot; he could not wholly keep down his emotion.

"I don't know what Miss Challoner's opinions are on that subject," he said, trying to speak composedly. "I don't think she ever said anything to me about it. Anyhow, I'll post the letters for you with pleasure, if you'll allow me. Perhaps the carrying them in my hand may convert me to your side."

Sybil herself lighted him to the door when he was going. Her thin white hand felt cold and tremulous as she placed it in his.

Christmas left the house full of kindly feeling and generous sympathy for the woman who had been so friendly, and touched with a special compassion for the girl thus hopelessly beating her soft bosom against the bars of conventionality. He had not spent so human, so friendly an evening for a long time; and he felt less desolate, less like a savage, and he was grateful for the little glimpse of a quiet home which had brought him this relief.

It was very late when he returned to his lodgings, for in the intermediate time he had walked to Kensington and paced in the silent shadow of Sir John Challoner's house, and waited lounging there until he actually saw a carriage come up, and under its flashing lamps saw Sir John hand out his daughter; and then, but not at once, Christmas quitted his place of refuge in a near doorway, and lighted a cigar and went his way.

When he had left Mrs. Jansen's room Miss Sybil did not return to her mother at once. After a few minutes she came in silently.

"What a very charming young man!" Mrs. Jansen said. "I like him very much; he has such a bright smile, I am sure he has a good heart. Any one can see that he has not been brought up in London; London makes young men so artificial and puppyish."

Sybil still said nothing.

"You like him, Sybil; don't you?" her mother asked, sur-prised at the silence.

"Oh, yes, dear, I like him. I suppose I ought not to have spoken about Miss Challoner," she added hesitatingly.

"Who is Miss Challoner, dear?"

"A friend of Mrs. Seagraves—at least, Mrs. Seagraves knows her—very beautiful, and very clever, and very rich."

"And why should you not have spoken of her?"

"Because he—is—in love with her."

"My dear, how do you know?"

" I know from his look when I mentioned her name."

Sybil sat down and silently took up some work. Her mother looked at her wonderingly at first, then sadly, and thought of new clouds perhaps to arise upon their pale, grey sky.

Sybil looked up suddenly :

"She is so rich," said the girl, " and we are so poor."

CHAPTER XVI.

" DEMETRIUS LOVES YOUR FAIR—OH HAPPY FAIR ! "

IT was perhaps an unfortunate thing for Christmas Pembroke that he should have passed all the earlier part of his youth in such isolation from the influences which surround a young man's growing years in ordinary life. An Englishman of his age might indeed have had no grand passion before, but he would almost certainly have had some little anticipatory passion, some affair of pickets and outposts suggesting an idea of the greater ordeal to come. At twenty-two or twenty-three years of age most men have glided through many emotions which at first seemed to be genuine love, but were not. They have looked into the eyes of girls, and fancied for the hour they saw all heaven there ; they have touched tremulous hands, and whispered meaningless words, intended to express ineffable meaning ; they have thought themselves happy, they have thought themselves wretched—they have awaked to find themselves neither wretched nor happy ; they have come to look back on these past emotions and their passing heroines with as mild and mellowed a regret as Francois Villon bestows on Bertha with the large foot, and the good Jehanne whom the English burned, and Heloise, and the snows of other winters. They have thus become acclimatised to emotion, and when the grand passion comes (we are now thinking only of young men pure and strong enough to have a grand passion) they can rough through it with less of a strain upon their heart and nature. But to Christmas Pembroke it was all new, and it tried him terribly. It was as if he had never seen a woman, or known of woman's existence, until he came under the influence of Marie Challoner. So the passion which he felt for her seemed as if it must tear his unprepared heart asunder.

A discontented person has left it on record as his complaint against the ways of Providence that he could always get on very well until he allowed himself to be persuaded that he ought to do something for the benefit of his health, and then all went wrong. Does it not sometimes seem as if things were going very

well with us until we took it into our heads that a sublime
moral duty bade us to follow some unwelcome course, and then
forthwith we disturbed and distracted everybody ? Marie Challoner had been urged by natural kindness, by sense of right, and
by an unexpressed idea that there was something in her own
heart requiring to be kept down and disciplined and punished
—she had been urged by all these impulses to show herself
especially friendly to Christmas since she had heard her father's
account of him. When they met after that day in the library
she always smiled on him so sweetly, and gave him her hand so
kindly, and put herself in his way to talk with him so winningly,
that the poor lad's head and heart were all aflame. There were
times when he felt as if he must take her in his arms and kiss
her. There were moments, ecstatic and agonising, when he
thought that if he had done so she would not have been very
much displeased. He used to lie awake of nights and think
over her words, her looks, at this moment or that, and asked
himself was it not possible that he had long mistaken her, and
that she was inclined to love him ? If Marie Challoner had been
the most heartless coquette she could not have perplexed and
tormented our hero more thoroughly than she did with her
generous resolve to be his friend and to do him kindness. For
in her heart, all the while, Dear Lady Disdain envied this pair
of young lovers, as she believed them to be, their romantic and
unselfish love ; and looked forward each day more and more with
vague and grey presentiment to a brilliant marriage in which
she would have to persuade herself, as well as she could, that
she was gratifying her own ambition along with that of other
people.

One thing Marie had made up her mind to—that she would
see, speak to, and be very friendly with Miss Sybil Jansen. She
told her resolve to her father, and he agreed, not over-delighted
at the prospect, to take her to one of Mrs. Seagraves' Sunday
afternoon receptions in the hope that she might there meet Miss
Jansen. The day came and Sir John had to go.

" I'll leave a message for Vidal, Marie," he said, " to follow
us to Mrs. Seagraves', if he should call while we are out—he
sometimes goes there, I believe. He is amused by that sort of
thing." The affinity between Sir John and Vidal was only on
their business sides. To Sir John all amusement was weary
work, and he could not understand why anybody should impose
more of it on himself than was made compulsory by the laws of
society.

" Now this *is* kind of you, you dear darlings, both ! " Mrs.
Seagraves exclaimed with fervour, as they entered her drawing-
room, and she swirled towards them in her trailing tawny-green
silk with pale yellow flowers worked into it. " Yes, I call you

dear darlings both of you, Sir John as well, for coming to see me. And Sir John so busy too—with finance and companies! I do so wish I understood finance. It must be so nice. But exacting, isn't it?—oh, yes, very, very exacting.—That makes it so kind of Sir John, Marie dear, to break away from all his occupations and come here with you."

"But we don't look after our finance and our companies on Sunday, Mrs. Seagraves," Sir John gently interposed.

"No? Is that so? How very good of you! I never thought you cared for any of those things in the City and business and all that. Only women I thought kept up those usages. But I am so glad to know: one ought to know these things. And so you are all such Sabbatarians in the City, and so pious? How very strange and touching, I think! There is something in that quite Druidical—or perhaps Puritanical rather? Yes, I mean Puritanical, of course. I used to love the Puritans once; and now I am sure I shall love them again."

Marie left to her father the business of conversation, and was searching with her eyes through the rooms, as yet without recognising anybody. As far as she could judge by one or two hasty glances, most of the company seemed to be studying blue and white plates.

"Now, is there any one here you would like to know?" Mrs. Seagraves asked, observing that Marie had been looking round the room. "There are some very charming people here. There is a delightful young man; a Communist; I believe it was he who wanted to blow up Paris. Should you like to know him? There is a pre-Raphaelite poet; I do so love the pre-Raphaelite poets—at least I used to like them. I don't think I do now. Where is Sir John?"

Sir John had escaped, and was conversing with somebody he faintly remembered having seen somewhere once, and whose acquaintance he was under present circumstances glad to claim.

Mrs. Seagraves brought up two or three people in rapid succession to Marie, hardly allowing one to open a conversation before she extinguished him with a successor. Presently, Marie heard her addressing a new arrival affectionately as her dearest Sybil, and she saw that her hostess was talking with a very pretty pale girl, whose hair was thrown back from her forehead, and in whom she felt certain that she recognised the young Hypatia. Marie, while carrying on as well as she could her conversation with the newest of the new acquaintances whom Mrs. Seagraves had presented to her, watched Miss Jansen with close interest. "She is very pretty," Marie thought, "and she looks intellectual, and she is unconventional—I shall like her." Marie observed, too, that Miss Jansen's sparkling, restless eyes were turning every other moment eagerly towards the door.

"Looking afar," Lady Disdain said to herself, trying back upon her Byron, and persuading herself that from her passion-less attitude she was only amused at such weaknesses—"looking afar if yet her lover's steed kept pace with her expectancy and flew."

"Do poets call horses steeds nowadays?" Marie asked of the young poet with whom she was talking.

Naturally he did not understand the meaning of the question, and he thought the young lady was speaking scorn of poetry, and thereby implying a special contempt for his poetry. He had heard that she was the daughter of a rich man, and he set her question down to the purse-proud arrogance of pampered wealth —and Marie had made an enemy.

As Mrs. Seagraves was passing at the moment, Marie touched her arm.

"Is not the lady you have just been speaking to Miss Sybil Jansen?" she asked in a low tone.

"Oh yes—such a dear friend of mine! You would like to know her, I am sure, dear Marie. I should so like you to know her."

"I should like to know her very much indeed," Marie said earnestly.

"I'll bring her to you"—and Mrs. Seagraves was swirling away when Marie gently restrained her.

"Please no, Mrs. Seagraves—I'll go to her with you," and she put her arm within that of the tawny-green lady, and was led across the room to where Miss Jansen was seated in eager talk with one or two men. These Mrs. Seagraves promptly dispersed.

"My dear Sybil, I am so glad to have the opportunity of bringing together you and my very dear friend Miss Challoner—Miss Marie Challoner. I always call her Marie. She wishes to know you, and I am sure you will like each other—oh, love each other! Two such noble minds—such souls!" and Mrs. Seagraves thereupon left them and floated away in ecstasy.

Marie held out her hand, which was small and plump, and Sybil gave hers, which was small and very thin, and which trembled at the kindly touch of Lady Disdain. It must be owned that the little priestess of the Church of the Future hated her new acquaintance at that moment. Priestess and prophetess as she was, her eyes first of all took in every detail of Miss Challoner's dress, and she found that Marie's dress was very costly, while she knew that her own was very cheap. In Miss Challoner's frank manner she read insolent patronage.

"I have been wishing for a long time to know you, Miss Jansen," said Marie, "and I came here to-day in the hope that I should see you."

Miss Jansen threw a look of defiance into her manner as she replied coldly—

" You do me a great honour, and I ought to feel much flattered. May I ask whether we agree in our general opinions?"

" I hardly know," Marie answered with a smile; " I have not formed any very serious opinions. I was anxious to know you for yourself. I think, rather than for your opinions."

" Friendship, I believe, is best founded on agreement of opinion as to the purposes of life," Sybil observed ; and Marie could not help wondering that so pretty and bright-looking a girl should care to speak exactly as if she were making a little speech out of a book.

" What are the purposes of life ? " Marie asked undismayed, and indeed rather amused.

" Have you never considered them ? "

" Not very deeply, I am afraid."

" Then you have no purpose in life ? "

" I should like to make people happy, if I could. Is that any purpose ? "

" In itself," said Sybil, " it has little meaning."

" Then you shall teach me all about it," Marie said, determined to be pleased, if she could, with this odd little book in petticoats. " I'll learn of you, Miss Jansen, to have a purpose."

Sybil contracted her little eyebrows.

".You have no need and no impulse that way. You would not learn. You are among the fortunate; you know nothing of life's trials and struggles. Leave the purposes of life to those who have to bear its strain."

" I have not had much to do with the struggles of life, indeed, or with real life of any kind so far. But I am sure I can sympathise with those who are not so fortunate."

" Oh, no—your place is different. Keep to it, Miss Challoner."

" An uncivil little person ! " Marie thought; but she was not discouraged.

" Well, for the moment I have no other object, Miss Jansen, than to make your acquaintance, and to say that I believe we have some friends—and one or two very dear friends—in common; and I wanted to say a friendly word or two to you. If you don't like me I will go away," Marie said, with her usual independent frankness; and I shall not be offended even if you say that you don't desire my friendship. But I shall be sorry."

" You are very kind," said the little Sybil, feeling her breath come and go with the quick emotions of her fighting soul. She could hardly resist the genial way of the noble-looking girl who evidently meant to be so kind—and yet what, she asked, was that very kindness but pity ! At that moment each of the girls seated there, side by side, became aware of Christmas Pembroke's presence in the room. Each, too, was aware—could not but know—that when he saw them a light and then a shadow passed over his face, and that he blushed like a boy.

" He sees *her*," Marie said to herself, and her heart was filled with a strange sympathy, compassion, and melancholy kindness.

" He sees *her*," Sybil thought, and her heart beat fiercely with jealousy and with anger.

Christmas's glance had indeed taken in both the girls. In a moment he assumed that Miss Challoner was friendly with Sybil out of pure kindness, and probably because she had heard that the girl was poor, and that some people laughed at her. How noble she looked, he thought, that superb and queenly girl, and how her form and her features made a splendid contrast to the slight, pale, and nervous girl who sat beside her! The contrast told heavily against the poor little priestess of the future, and Christmas felt sorry for her, in all his pride in the beauty of the woman he loved. Yes, as he looked across and saw her there, he was proud that he loved her, and once again the thought passed through him—could it be possible that she might ever come to care for him? How many times within the last few days had that strange, sweet hope flashed upon him!

People did all sorts of odd things at Mrs. Seagraves' receptions on the Sunday afternoon. They sang and played, and were otherwise eccentric, *du parti pris*. Somebody began to sing just as Christmas came in, some "dear divine creature," Mrs. Seagraves said, " whom you *must* listen to," and whom she adored, " not really adored, you know ; " and therefore Christmas had to remain where he was, and seem to listen. He was almost glad of this, for he could look across the room at Marie, and had not yet to break the spell of the strange hope and pride with which he regarded her. Never before had he felt like this. There was something in it like the pride of ownership—like the pride of the accepted lover who knows that she is his own whom all the world admires. Is it an omen—a presentiment? How, his heart said, if this very day, here in this room, some word or look or touch of her hand should tell me——? He hugged himself in his dream, and dreaded even the close of the song lest something should happen to awaken him.

Before yet the song was ended Christmas saw Mrs. Seagraves glide from her place near the piano to welcome with special eagerness some new comer. Strange with what a chill Christmas awakened—he could not tell why—from his dream. It was Ronald Vidal. For some little time past Christmas had not seen much of Vidal, and had begun to think that perhaps he had mistaken Vidal's position with regard to Marie; or that perhaps Vidal's recent and sudden plunge into political life had been the result of disappointed hopes as a lover. Mr. Vidal's appearance now was the most ill-omened sight our poor young hero could have seen.

"So very, very kind of *you* to come," Mrs. Seagraves said, having detained Ronald's hand in hers until the song was over; "in the full flush of your success too; and all the world talking of you! I am proud of this. Everybody wants to know you—but everybody does know you as a public man now."

"We have a saying in our county, Mrs. Seagraves," said the good-humoured Vidal, "that more people know Tom Fool than Tom Fool knows!"

"How very delightful!" Mrs. Seagraves said, not quite understanding. "And so you are going to be a great public man, and you are an orator. I so love orators! I should like of all things to be an orator. I wish I could be an orator! We are all so proud of your success—and I know one who is proud of it! Oh, I know why you come here to-day; but I am obliged to you for coming, all the same."

Vidal murmured a word or two of thanks for her compliments and escaped, and Mrs. Seagraves, turning round, found herself near Christmas.

"You know Mr. Vidal? Is he not a very charming young man? Oh, yes, of course you know him; you see the Challoners so often; and don't you think his speech was very clever?"

"Very clever," Christmas answered, who had never read the speech, and did not know now what he was saying.

"And is this true they tell me? You ought to know—you are so much with the Challoners. But perhaps you don't wish to tell anything about it? You are so very discreet—and I like discretion above all things myself—especially in young men—oh, yes—especially in young men."

"It is not discretion in this case, Mrs. Seagraves," Christmas said bluntly; "only that I don't know what you mean."

"This about Miss Challoner and young Vidal—you know. They are engaged, people tell me. Quite a delightful and romantic story—they say." She leaned towards Pembroke and whispered with great appearance of mystery, "They say that she promised to consent only on condition of his giving up all his frivolities and things—you know—what young men waste their time in—and going into Parliament and making a success there. And now he is in Parliament, and has made the success there. Isn't it delightful?"

"Very delightful!"

"Like something in a romance! I do so hope it's true! It's like a knight going to a tournament and conquering everybody to please his ladye-love. I do so love romantic things like that. At least I used to love them once, when I was young, but now of course, I don't love them any more. I have grown practical

M

ι nd sensible. Yes, I only care to be practical now ; but not all
practical, of course. One must have some feeling of the romantic
left, Mr. Pembroke ? "

"Must one ? "

" Oh, yes. *You* are all romantic, of course—all young
people are. And some day you will be making some great success too, to please some fair ladye. That will be so charming.
Then I shall wish you joy. Have you spoken to Miss Jansen
yet ? "

Ronald Vidal meanwhile had established himself at Marie's
side ; and after saying a few words to Miss Jansen, had managed
to allow somebody else to engross that young lady for the
moment, and thus had Miss Challoner all to himself.

Christmas watched them for a moment or two. There was a
look of proud humility on Mr. Vidal's handsome face as he talked
to Marie in a low tone ; and our hero owned to himself that he
did look confoundedly handsome and like a troubadour, and just
the sort of man whom many women would be fond of. Still he
had thought somehow that Vidal was too much a combination of
business and pleasure—the City and the green-room—for the
higher nature of Lady Disdain. But he was mistaken—that was
only too plain. Besides Vidal had made a political success, he
had everything on his side—family, good looks, and now even
political distinction. No wonder Miss Challoner listened to him
with downcast eyes, and cheeks that coloured as he spoke !

Ronald Vidal had accomplished one of the few great successes
which remain still to mark with a note of admiration some passage in the life of an ordinary Englishman. He had made a
decided hit, an unquestionable success, in the House of Commons.
He had seized a happy opportunity during some debate on a
question of foreign policy, and had displayed great fluency, great
knowledge of the subject, the places, the people whom it concerned ; he formed his sentences clearly and well; he said some
sharp, bold things ; and when he had occasion to introduce two
or three Latin words he pronounced them with that curious
inaccuracy and astounding disregard for all the possibilities of a
Latin tongue which is deemed to be the essential condition of
good form in the English universities and the House of Commons.
He had the peculiar good fortune of all fluent and ready speakers,
and because he had done well without elaborate preparation he
was set down as capable of doing really great things with preparation. In a word he was a great success, and the House saw
in him a predestined Under-Secretary to begin with.

It would not be reasonable to suppose that Marie Challoner
could hear people talk of this swift success without feeling some
pride in it. Mr. Vidal really had gone in to do this for her
gratification and to win her approval as avowedly as any knight

ever went into the lists of the tournament to win the smile of his
lady. She had not seen him since the success, which was won in
the debate of a Friday afternoon, and of which all the daily
papers of the Saturday were talking. She had not heard the
speech, and had not expected that he would speak that evening;
and now he was telling her that even if it had been a premedi-
tated attempt, which it was not, he would not have forewarned
her, for he declared that he never should have had the courage
to make a successful first speech if he had known that she was in
the Ladies' Gallery listening.

"You see if I had failed the first time," he said modestly, "I
could have retrieved myself perhaps the next attempt, or the
next. But if you had heard my failure, I never should have had
the heart to try again."

No flattery could be more alluring to a girl like Marie
Challoner than just this plain and straightforward acknowledgment of her influence. Ordinary compliment would have been
utterly thrown away upon Lady Disdain. She would have received
it with cold contempt or laughed at it. But here was this
brilliant, successful youth of distinguished family and name con-
fessing that her applause was so precious to him that the tongue
which could address the House of Commons in accents of un-
faltering fluency would have been tremulous if she had been
listening. It is no wonder if Marie coloured a little and looked
down.

Christmas Pembroke still, through whatever torturing
ordeals of conversation, kept his eyes now and then on Marie.
Once he positively started, for he saw a sudden emotion pass
tremblingly over Marie's face, and he saw her eyes droop and
her lips press together, and then she said a word or two to Mr.
Vidal, who presently rose and left her, and on Vidal's face, as our
hero thought, was the light of pride and triumph. Well', he has
it—all!

What had passed was only this. Mr. Vidal hastily observed
that he had an engagement; that he had only rushed in to Mrs.
Seagraves' drawing-room to see her—Marie; and then he asked
in a low tone—

"May I call and see you to-morrow afternoon—about five?"

What was there in these words that made Marie turn suddenly pale, and feel chill and strange? It was then that Christmas
started as he looked at her. She was silent and embarrassed for
a few seconds. Then she said, "Oh yes, I shall be at home,"
without looking up, and Vidal went away without another word
to her.

"To-morrow at five," Vidal said to Sir John Challoner as
they shook hands in passing. Sir John smiled and nodded.

Christmas felt like one who has received a sunstroke. Some

heavy weight seemed to rest upon his brain. He never knew how
the next few minutes passed or whether they were only minutes.
He knew that he talked to some people and laughed a good deal.
Presently a hand touched his arm gently, and, awaking again into
clear consciousness, he saw Marie Challoner. She was leaning
on her father's arm; they were going away; but some one had
stopped Sir John and engaged him in talk, and Marie, seeing
Christmas, turned and touched him. There was a strangely
weary and harassed expression upon her face, which Christmas
recalled to memory long after; but she looked cruelly beautiful
to the young man, and her eyes had a bewildered softness and
sweetness in them.

"You did not come and speak to me," she said, "and now
we are going away."

"You are going soon?" Christmas asked, uttering any
inanity that his lips can form. "I hope you are not tired?"

"I think I am tired—a little perhaps."

"The room is warm," said Christmas, with a bursting heart.

"It is. I have spoken to Miss Jansen, and I like her very
much. Will you tell her so—from me?"

"I will." He had not sense enough left in him even to
wonder why he was selected to convey the message to Miss
Jansen.

"Good-bye?" and Marie held out her hand. Good-bye!"
and it rested for a moment in his. It then did not strike him as
strange that they should have said a sort of farewell.

"Glad to see you, Pembroke—good evening; we are going,"
Sir John said looking round. "Can we take you anywhere?"

"No, thanks, Sir John."

"No; you are not going yet of course. Good evening."
Sir John nodded, smiled, and made his way with his daughter
through the crowd, the curiosities, and the crockery.

"Is she not charming? Oh, *so* charming! Don't you think
so?" Mrs. Seagraves asked of Miss Jansen.

"Who?" Miss Jansen coldly asked.

"Marie Challoner. She is the sweetest of girls—so fresh and
unconstrained."

"She is the sort of woman," Sybil said, emphatically, "who
keeps us as we are."

"Is she really? Does she really? Keep us as we are?"

When Mrs. Seagraves did not quite understand what somebody meant she repeated the words generally, turned them over
in a kind of puzzled delight as if she meant to say that she
liked the idea very much in advance, and was sure she would
like it still better when it was more fully explained.

"Yes. She is one of the women who, having all they want
themselves, declare that women have no wrongs to complain of.

and get praised by men for saying so. Men may admire that sort of woman—*I* don't."

"Oh, but you are too severe, my dear Sybil—far too severe—and on my sweet favourite, my model girl! No I don't mean that, you know, not a model girl by any means. I should hate a model girl: pattern of propriety and all that. Oh, no, Marie isn't a model—quite the reverse in fact. Of course I don't mean quite the reverse, you know; but you understand—and she really is such a sweet girl. Mr. Pembroke—Mr. Pembroke, do come here and defend my favourite."

Christmas was coming to speak to Miss Jansen, conscious that he ought to have done so long ago. She received him very coldly, and he assumed that she thought him guilty of rudeness. He was sorry if he appeared so, for he felt himself so shut out of life and lonely that he could ill afford to lose one friendly look.

"Mr. Pembroke of course admires her," Miss Jansen said. "All men do, I suppose."

Christmas felt as if he were being put to the torture. He knew that the blood was rushing to his face.

"You mean Miss Challoner?" he said, with desperate effort. "She is very handsome, and she is very kind—I have always found her——" and he could not get any further.

"Is she to be married to that young man who has just been here—son of some lord, people tell me?" Miss Jansen asked. Mrs. Seagraves had disappeared.

"I don't know; I suppose so."

Sybil took a cruel pleasure in tormenting him and watching his wincing, while she tormented herself as well.

"Is she in love with him, do you think?"

"How should I know?" Christmas said, with a gallant resolve to seem easy and indifferent. "Do women fall in love now, Miss Jansen?"

"Not women of that sort I should think—unless loving a title and rank be falling in love. Don't you wish you were the son of a lord, Mr. Pembroke?"

"Not particularly. Why should I?"

"Then you might have a chance, you know, of competing for Miss Challoner. Now you look angry—I like to make men angry—it is a sort of triumph."

"Miss Challoner sent you a very friendly message," Christmas said, determined that the spiteful ltttle priestess should have no such triumph over him.

"Indeed! Through you?"

"Through me."

"Truly! What was it?"

"She asked me to tell you that she liked you very much."

"How kind of her—so patronising!"

"No, no, she didn't mean it in that way; you don't understand her."

"No? Perhaps not. Will you take a message from me to her in return?"

"I may not see her again—soon," said poor Christmas.

"That would be a pity. But if you should see her, will you tell her that she is very kind, and that I prefer not to be patronised, and that she and *I*, holding such very different opinions, could have nothing in common?"

"I shan't tell her that," said Christmas. "I shan't tell her anything. And I know you don't mean what you say."

"Well, I am going," Miss Jansen said; "I am tired of this place." She looked very pale and weary.

Christmas made no effort to be her escort. He was sorry for her, disappointed with her. "Is this the way, then, of all women?" he asked himself. "Are they like this: bitter, fanatical, so wedded to their own little theories and crotchets that they must hate and detest all who differ from them? Or is it simply a miserable jealousy because she is rich and fortunate? Are women all so mean and miserable?"

Perhaps it would have gratified his mood at present if he could have thought so. But he could not. He had heard from Marie Challoner sometimes satirical and scornful words, but never the expression of one small ignoble thought. But then she is so happy! She has everything. And poor Sybil has so little. "Why should I blame her?" he thought. "Envy comes into our hearts in spite of us; only women, I suppose, cannot shut it in there and hide it."

Still, as he walked away from Portland Place, he felt really sorry that Sybil should have shown herself so malign—merely because Marie Challoner did not share her opinions on woman's rights, or was richer and happier than she. The contrast set off Marie with a lustre which was positively oppressive to him now. How handsome she looked! How sweet she was! He had never loved her more passionately. How often now he thought of Dione Lyle's warnings against allowing himself to be fascinated by Marie Challoner! What is the use of such warnings? He could not even flatter himself that he had been deceived or trifled with. Marie was his friend from the first, and she was his friend now—just the same. No coquette that ever falsely smiled men's hearts and senses away could have been so fatal in her companionship to Christmas as that sweet, serene friend. It was all his own fault.

That miserable Sunday Christmas walked miles and miles until he had walked himself clean out of London. But he could find no solitude. Even when one is fairly clear of street and suburb there is no solitude round London on the Sunday evening.

He went doggedly along and around, having a vague idea that if he made himself dead-tired the mere physical exhaustion would distract him from too much thinking. Men weary in the snow keep repeating the multiplication table, because they know that if for one instant they relax the exercise of the mind they must fall into the sleep of death. Christmas kept his limbs in unceasing motion, fearing that one instant's rest would allow him to fall into the terrors of thought and memory.

The poor young Hypatia, too, had a weary time of it. She was miserable and bitter, and her mother wondered what mournful change was coming over her girl. Sybil went to a Sunday evening meeting somewhere and delivered an impassioned address all about the sensibilities and the sufferings of woman; about the bird beating itself to death against the bars of its cage; about the heedless strength and thoughtless cruelty of man; about the tyranny of rank and class; and a great deal more to the same effect. More than one earnest young mechanic or clerk fell profoundly in love with her, and thought her an angel of eloquence, and spent half the night thinking of her, and found their lives and their surroundings mean and narrow and odious because of her. She went home and tried her very best to be cheerful and pleasant to her mother, and not to make short or pettish answers; and when she was in bed, and everybody else in the house was asleep, then she almost drowned herself in tears.

Christmas came late to his chambers, to the painted goddess on whose ceiling he now hardly ever turned a glance. He sat for a while and made up his mind to something. Then he went to his desk and took therefrom, preserved with tender and loving care, the little fragment of sweet-briar which had clung to Marie's dress on the day when last they walked among the trees at Durewoods, and which he had treasured ever since. There was no fire in the grate, but he lighted up some paper there and made a great blaze and laid his bonny briar on it, and watched and watched it until it became only ashes.

CHAPTER XVII.

A PIOUS FRAUD.

SIR JOHN CHALLONER leaned against the chimney-piece of his library next day in a happy and hopeful mood. Things had gone well with him hitherto, and they were now promising to go still better. Ronald Vidal's Parliamentary success was an unmistakable fact, and a thing to be proud of; and it would settle the young man down for life. Marie's friendly ways towards Vidal left Sir John in no doubt about her answer to the question which was to be put to her that day. She would before long be the wife of the son of a peer, who bore an ancient and famous title. Sir John for a moment almost wished that his wife was living to share in the pride that was coming to them, until he remembered that after all she was not a woman to shine in society, and that she was probably much better off in heaven. He was thus reconciling his mind to her unavoidable absence when a servant brought him the announcement that Mr. Pembroke particularly wished to see him.

" Show him in—of course." He wondered why Pembroke chose to be so formal when he might have come into the library unquestioned. But he hoped Pembroke had some favour to ask. At present it would have relieved his mind to do a favour for somebody.

" Come in, Pembroke," he called cheerily, and Pembroke came in, looking pale and thin and troubled. This, however, was not evident to his patron, for, as we have said, Sir John was in a happy mood, because all things seemed to go well with him. There was something almost caressing in his manner as he welcomed Christmas. Indeed, he had begun to feel very parental to the young man of late, and to think as Christmas came and went that it must be very pleasant for a man to have a son who could be his confidant in business.

" Sit down, my boy," he said smilingly, and pushing a chair towards Christmas.

" I wanted to speak to you this some time back," said Christmas, " very particularly."

" Yes ? " Sir John said encouragingly and still smiling.

" It's not about business, Sir John."

" No ? " Sir John said with equal encouragement in his tone, and beginning to think that he saw his way to what was coming.

" I have been thinking over it this long time ; and I was not certain whether I ought to say anything about it to anybody—even to *you*. But I can't help it—I can't help telling it to you—you have been so kind to me that I don't think I ought to have any secret from you—even this."

"The young fool is privately married!" Sir John said to himself. "Well, Pembroke," he said aloud, "go on, my boy. We don't need so much preface, do we—you and I?"

"I'd give half my life, I think," said Christmas with energy, "to any one who could tell me whether I ought to speak of this to you, or ought not. I think I ought to speak of it—but I am so ignorant of what is the right thing."

"My dear fellow, I'll tell you without asking for any part of your life. If you would tell this story to your father, tell it to me."

"It's not the same," Christmas said; "you will soon know how different it is."

"Of course I don't mean to say that you could feel to me as to your father—you needn't tell me that, my boy. But you may put confidence in me as much as if I were."

"It was not that I meant, Sir John, at all—it was something quite different—you will soon see."

"Well, let me see as soon as possible, and don't have us guessing riddles, Pembroke—or shall I make a guess?"

"I want to leave England, Sir John."

"You want to leave England? I certainly did not expect that. What on earth do you want to leave England for?"

"I think of going back to Japan."

"But why, Pembroke? I thought that you had come to tell me that you were anchoring here for good?"

"Oh no, Sir John; I want to leave England because I am very unhappy here, and I can't endure life here any longer. There is the truth. I'll tell you all the reason, if you wish to know it—if you don't know it already."

"Indeed, Pembroke, I do not know it—but I am very sorry to hear of this—I thought you were very happy; and we are so anxious to make you happy—why should you leave us? I am so sorry, and Marie will be——"

A sudden ejaculation, a sort of groan, broke from the young man's lips; and his face grew crimson. He was standing now near the chimney-piece as Sir John wheeled his chair to look at him.

"Pembroke," said Sir John, gravely, "you had better come to the point and tell me in plain words what this is all about. It is clear that I was out in my guessing, and I don't care to guess any more."

"Well," Christmas said, with a kind of desperation, "there's nothing to be ashamed of. It's not my fault—I can't help it—

and it need not trouble any one but me. I—I'm—it's only this —Sir John, I love your daughter ! "

Sir John, too, stood up, with a flush of anger on his face.

" You may blame me if you like," Pembroke went on, now finding his tongue fluent enough, when the ice was broken and the worst was done, " I can bear all that—I don't deserve it; but you may not think so. I tried as hard as any human being could do not to give in. I have been trying for months. I never would have told a word to mortal if I could have got over it. But I couldn't, and now my mind is made up. I will go away, and not trouble any one. You may blame me, if you like. Why should you blame me ? I can't help having feelings."

" My good boy," Sir John said soothingly, " who talked of blaming you ? But of course I am taken by surprise ; and I am sorry. You know how useless this is ? "

" If I didn't know that how should I ever be able to make up my mind to go away ? I always knew it was useless—from the very first."

" And when," Sir John asked, with a faint flicker of a smile coming over his lips, " when, Pembroke, was the very first ? "

" The first day I saw her," answered Christmas, promptly. " No—not the first—I mean the second. The first time I hardly saw her : she had her veil down, and we only spoke a few words. It was the next day."

" You knew it then ? "

" Yes ; I knew it then ; at least I felt very strangely. I must have known it then. But I didn't know then how strong it was and how it would last. I thought I could conquer it and crush it down ; and I fought hard—you would not blame me if you knew how hard I fought—and it was all no use ! "

" One word, Pembroke, before we go any farther, although I hardly think I need say it. My daughter, I presume, knows nothing of this ! "

" Oh no, Sir John. How could she know ? "

" Well, of course, I know you would have said nothing without having told me first. I didn't mean *that*. But might anything in your manner have led her to suspect ? "

" No," Christmas said, shaking his head, and speaking in a tone of the profoundest conviction, " she has not the least suspicion. She never had."

" Well, I think so too. But how do you know so certainly ? "

" Because she has been always so friendly to me. Even yesterday," the young man added, with burning cheeks.

" I am sure you are right, and that at least is something."

" It is something," Christmas said, sadly. " If she ever suspected it she would be sorry for me ; and she would not be so friendly, and I should always feel as if I had been the means of giving her pain somehow. Now I shall not have that to think of. Well, Sir John, I feel more like a man, and less like a child or a coward, now that I have told you this, and that you know all."

"Sit down," said Challoner, "and let us talk this over a little."

They both sat down. Christmas buried his hands in his pockets and gazed downwards, his head bent on his breast.

"Of course this is bad enough," Sir John began, "but it might be worse. Pembroke, you are a very young man, and you'll get over it. I know such consolation is not quite in keeping with your feelings just now, but you'll live this down, my dear boy. You'll get over it."

Christmas shook his head.

"I'll never get over it, Sir John—never. You think people always say that? Perhaps they do, but some of them mean it and know it. We are a terribly unchanging lot," he said, with a melancholy smile that flickered on his pale face like a weak sunbeam on snow; "my father's last words were of the woman he—he cared about, and I hope mine will be the same."

"Well," Sir John went on, not caring to press that point, "at all events we may look at whatever good side there is to the thing. Suppose, let us say, that Marie had known of this, and were romantic and susceptible—and all that—and that she felt as you do——"

"Oh!" Another ejaculation broke from Christmas, and again the blood rushed into the face that a moment before had been white. The bare thought, the mere suggestion of such a possibility sent a wave of passion through him which seemed to surge directly up from his heart to his head.

"I say suppose that had been so. I talk to you plainly, Pembroke, as to a man of sense and of the world." (Sir John knew that even a young lover is flattered by being regarded as a man of sense and a man of the world.) "Suppose that had been so? What would have come of that? I presume that you have been studying my daughter's character. But you hardly know her as well as I do. Have you seen that she is ambitious? Most women are, but she is especially so. I have not seen in her much of what you young people call a capacity for love. She will go into society and shine there and be happy. I tell you, Pembroke, I love my daughter far more even than fathers generally love their daughters, and yet I say, with all my heart, that a young man like you would not do well in marrying her. Does this sound harshly? It is the truth, my boy. There are women whom mere love will not suffice; and Marie is one of them."

"I suppose so," Christmas said, blankly; "I don't know much about women—I should not have thought it."

"Of course you would not have thought it. My dear boy, to you a woman is an angel still."

Christmas shook his head.

"Not every woman," Sir John corrected himself; "but perhaps some one particular woman."

"I don't know about angels," Christmas said. "I never thought whether your daughter was an angel or not."

"They do in romances—the young men, I mean—don't they?"

Christmas winced under this dry, chill analysis, as he might under the touch of a cautery.

"I only know what I feel," he said, "and I could not put it into words, Sir John. I'll put it into acts! I know what your daughter seems to me to be."

"My dear Pembroke, you may be sure that you could not have a higher opinion of Marie than I have; but it is perhaps a different sort of opinion—taken from a different point of view. A father does not need to think his daughter is perfection in order to love her; but a young man looks at things differently."

Christmas made a somewhat impatient gesture, as if in protest.

"It's not that," he said. "I love Miss Challoner because I can't help it, and it's my misfortune—that's all. I have to bear the consequences, and I mean to bear them. But don't let us try any mental analysis, Sir John—I confess I am not equal to that." With all his grateful feeling to Sir John, a strange sort of hostile sensation was beginning to grow up in his heart.

"Well," said Challoner, "I only meant to show you for your own good, Pembroke, how utterly hopeless all this would be."

"I know all that. You couldn't teach me anything about that, Sir John—I always knew it."

"No, no," Sir John said, gently. "You really do not quite understand me, Pembroke. I am assuming for the moment that things were exactly as you would have them; that my daughter felt as you do, and that I saw my way to give my consent; I tell you frankly, Pembroke, that you would be doing a mad thing, that you would be marrying a woman of ambition and spirit too great for such conditions—you won't mind my speaking plainly? —and that before long she would regret it; and you? Do you think it strange that I should speak in this way of my daughter?"

"No," said Christmas, bluntly, "for I suppose it is like this you would wish her to be."

"It is; you are quite right. I wish her to be ambitious. I am glad she is now (and he laid some stress on the word *now*) on the threshold of such a life as suits her. But that doesn't hinder me from being sorry, deeply sorry, for you, my poor boy! I wish this hadn't happened to you in my house. I ought to have known—I ought to have foreseen."

He laid his hand kindly on poor Christmas's shoulder. Perhaps this lad's misfortune really did touch him. There was silence for a moment. Christmas turned towards the chimney-piece, and so concealed his face. He was very young, and he was hit very hard. He could not have looked in any sympathetic face just then.

"Well," said Christmas, after a moment; "the worst is all out now—you don't blame me?"

"I have so often wished that I had a son," Sir John answered, fervently. "If I had a son, Pembroke, I should like him—under such conditions—to have acted as you did."

He held out his hand, and Christmas grasped it. The great financier could have wished at the moment that his young friend were a good deal less strong—for Sir John's hands were soft and fat, and adorned with rings, and Christmas's emotional gripe was like the clutch of Goetz's iron hand.

"We'll talk of this again," Sir John said, bearing the grasp without showing sign of pain, but gently withdrawing his hand as soon as possible; "and I don't know whether it may be necessary for you to think about leaving England, or doing anything in particular, for some months to come at all events; and perhaps by that time you may look at things in a calmer light. I'll explain to you in a day or two. You see, we must do nothing rashly—we must not call people's attention."

"One word," said Christmas: "Sir John, under any circumstances, *she* is not to know."

Sir John laid his hand gently on Pembroke's—

"Trust all that to me. If you were my own son, your confidence could not be more sacred. To-morrow—or next day—I'll speak to you of this again. Now, good-bye."

Sir John turned towards the window, and when he looked round to the hearth again Christmas was gone.

To do him justice, he was sorry for Christmas, and he was sorry for what had happened. But at the present moment his principal anxiety was that there should be no going away, and farewells, and half-ostentatious renunciations of a career on the part of the young man. Some instinct told him that for the present it might be imprudent to have any manner of scenes or explanations. For all his praise of his daughter's ambition and his professed faith in it, he dreaded the possible consequences of her regarding this handsome, chivalrous young man as in any sense a sufferer or martyr. "One never can tell," he said to himself, "which will have the stronger fascination for women—success or failure—the man who is up or the man who is down." Also, according to his familiar fashion, he asked himself whether it was not possible that Christmas, single-minded as he was, might have some lurking motive of his own in making the confession he did. Suppose the poor lad had still a faint hope of touching Marie's feelings? Suppose the proposal to banish himself back to Japan were made with a vague idea of that kind? "No, he mustn't go," Sir John decided. "That would never do—we can think of something better than that."

He looked at his watch. It was half-past four o'clock. Ronald Vidal was to call at five. He left the library and went to his daughter's room.

It was a corner room like that which she had at Durewoods, and was chosen by her because of the likeness, and it had been fitted up at her wish in just the same way. Marie was seated at her writing desk when her father came in, and was looking over old letters, unfinished sketches, scraps of verse-making begun and put aside, and such other litter as people usually look at only in their rather melancholy moods. Sir John thought she was looking pale. She smiled very warmly for him, however, and put her papers down.

"I was looking over scraps of old verses, dear," she said. "In Durewoods long ago—when I was young, you know—I used to fancy myself destined to be a poet. I have been reading some of the verses now; they are such dreadful rubbish!"

"I suppose all young people write verses—it's the right sort of thing to do when one is young. Are you disappointed at not turning out a poetess, Marie?"

"Could a poetess get into good society, papa?—a real poetess, I mean; not a lady of fashion who writes verses.

"Why do you ask such a question?"

"Mr. Vidal thinks professional poets are only tolerated in society—like a sort of Christy's Minstrels, perhaps. Is that so? *I* don't know. I saw a poet the other night, and people all seemed very attentive to him, and women were fluttering about him. But Mr. Vidal says he doesn't call that sort of thing being actually in society"

"Well, Marie?"

"Well, dear—that's all. I only wanted to know. For I should not like to have sacrificed my career for the sake of writing poems. I shan't have to earn my bread, you know, papa, and I suppose my first duty is to be respectable."

Lady Disdan was in one of her cynical moods, which were becoming somewhat frequent of late. He did not like her present way of putting things. It seemed like a reproach to him, or at least a reminder that he was still under some conditions with regard to his place in society.

"I suppose people like us can afford to do as they please, Marie. I am rather too busy myself with the realities of life to have time to think much about poetry or poets. But I always thought that some of our poets were in very good society.

By the way, poetry makes me thinks of music, and music of Ronald Vidal. He is coming here at five to-day ? "

Marie coloured a little, but only said listlessly, " I suppose so."

" I have had a visit already from another young lover—I mean from a young lover," her father said, with an appearance of easy sprightliness. " Christmas Pembroke, Marie."

" Indeed ? "

" He came to make me his confidant. Do you remember I told you some time ago that I was sure he would keep no secret from me ? "

" You did, dear."

" Well, I was right. He came to-day and told me all."

" It was—as you expected ? "

This easy question, put in a tone of the quietest interest, apparently, was to Sir John like the sight of the instrument of torture to some prisoner of weak fibre, who knows that if pressed he will swallow shame and save himself. He was not a man of scruples in the beaten ways of the world, but to deceive his daughter by something even broader than an equivocation seemed an odious act. He did not expect so direct a question ; he had taken it for granted that his daughter would assume the purport of Christmas's confession and deceive herself. In the one flash of hesitation it came on him oddly and with a painful sense that if he had been bred a gentleman like Ronald Vidal he never could have hesitated. But this did not now give him pause, and he answered—

" Yes, Marie; it was as I expected, of course."

Then it is so," said Lady Disdain. " I should not have thought it—but how could any one judge. She seems to me so sharp and vehement—and—I don't know. I am glad if he is going to be happy—I am very, very glad."

" There are some difficulties in the way just yet," Sir John said, carelessly. " He does not think of marrying at once,—it would be out of the question at present. And Marie, my dear —this was only told to me—perhaps I ought not to have whispered it even to you—and by the way," he added, with a sickly effort at saving his conscience, " you will please to remember, dear, that I have not, in fact, told you anything of what he said to me, and of course you won't breathe a word of this to any one."

" You need hardly caution me, dear," said Lady Disdain, rising grandly ; " I am not likely to speak of Mr. Pembroke's love-secrets."

" You know," Sir John said confidentially, " one must not mind too much what boys of that age may say on such subjects. They hardly know their own minds. Our young friend may have changed his mind long before anything comes of this."

Sir John spoke with two purposes vaguely present to his mind. The one was to prepare his daughter for the probability that Christmas never would marry Miss Jansen ; and the other, to satisfy his own conscience that he was not doing wrong in treating with indifference an emotion which was possibly only the passing dream of a boy

"I should think Mr. Pembroke knows his own mind," Marie said carelessly. "She is a very pretty girl, and very clever. I don't think we ought to blame her if she chafes a little against the ordinary lot of women. We do play a very poor part in the world, I think."

"I hope you will play a brilliant part, my dear."

"I hope so. One ought to do something." There was some bitterness in her tone.

"It rests with yourself, Marie, I fancy," Sir John said quietly.

"I suppose she will give up declaiming against the world's laws," Marie said meditatively, and without replying to his words, "when she is happy. I suppose she is very fond of him."

"Oh, yes—I suppose so."

"And he is in love with her! So soon! It seems strange— I don't know why."

A servant entered with a card.

"Vidal is below," Sir John said. "You will see him, Marie? I have to write a letter."

There was half a moment of silence—he looked at his daughter.

"Oh, yes," Marie said at last, "I will see him."

CHAPTER XVIII.

"O VATER, LASS UNS ZIEHN."

MARIE CHALLONER knew perfectly well that Mr. Vidal had come for that day, and her father knew that she knew it. Mr. Vidal had been thrown so much with her of late, and evidently by her father's desire, that she had gradually grown to accept his attentions as a matter of course. When on a visit lately with two of Mr. Vidal's aunts she had heard hints plain enough on the subject of his admiration for her. Still, she seemed always to shrink from contemplating the possible result of all this, and drew back even from asking herself what answer she ought to make in the probable, or indeed almost certain, event of his asking her to marry him. She had put the thought away as a nervous man, unused to speech-making, still puts off collecting his thoughts, and persuades himself that the chairman of the public dinner will not, after all, call upon him to respond to any toast. Now the moment had come, and it was too late to think of collecting thoughts or making up mind. The response had to be given at once.

Sir John Challoner looked after her as she entered the drawing-room, and then he went to his library. He found himself unusually nervous, and he felt a little irritated for the moment with the providential arrangement which had made lads and lasses, and imposed upon fathers in his position the responsibility of seeing that their daughters married the right man. In financial affairs he was strong, cool, and fearless—his enemies sometimes said unscrupulous; but he was flurried now, in his own house, and a little abashed in the presence of his own daughter. He seemed to have lost his courage. He could not undersand why he felt so humbled and hurt because he had had to deceive his daughter a little, and in a matter which probably would have been to her almost unimportant. Nobody could say in any case that he had not acted properly and for her good. What would be the use of wounding her sensibility by allowing her to know that this poor boy was in love with her? Besides, he, Sir John, was solemnly bound not to reveal Pembroke's secret. To be sure, he had implied that Pembroke had a secret of a very different kind, and that certainly was going rather far. Still it was only a precaution of reasonable prudence under the circumstances, and women have always to be managed more or less by stratagem. "Good Heavens!" Sir John peremptorily asked of his unsatisfied conscience, " who ever dreams of telling all the truth to women?" But, again, not telling all the truth is one thing; telling something which is not the truth is another. And deceiving one's daughter, who looks up to him as a guide and a light, and Marie, who was so transparently truthful herself, and who seemed to be instinct from her very birth with that principle of honour which is so rare among women! In short Sir John felt that the subject had better not be thought over too much. He put it away from him with a resolute effort to lay the whole blame of the transaction on Providence, which had not created him with a clear, uncompromising soul and conscience like that of Pembroke's father, or at least set him from his birth with men of the class of Ronald Vidal, who must always speak the truth as a necessary condition of their education.

He was waiting in momentary expectation of Vidal's coming to him. He knew that Vidal would come to him the moment his interview with Marie was over, and he knew that whatever were the result Marie would be sure to disappear to her room and not be seen for some time. Sir John, usually so composed in all his

N

ways, was almost palpitating with uneasy eagerness while that
interview was going on. The evening was grey and unusually
dark, and lights had not yet been brought. Sir John paced up
and down the room, and lost himself in vague excitement and
expectation. His thoughts wandered back and back. Suddenly
he started—it seemed to him as if he heard the wail of an infant.
In a moment he returned to himself, and knew that it was but
some sound on the road outside, but he knew too why his
imagination had deceived him. He had never walked up and
down in a library alone and in such anxiety of expectation since
the evening when Marie was born. That was the infant's cry
which now rose up out of the past and reached his ears.

He rang for lights, and almost at the same moment with the
servant Ronald Vidal entered. He was coming hastily towards
Sir John when he saw the servant at the lamps, and he stopped
short, took a book from a shelf, and appeared to be engaged in
looking for some passage in it. Challoner noticed that Vidal's
hands were trembling, and this alarmed him. Could Marie have
refused him?

The servant left the room.

" Well ? " Challoner asked eagerly.

" Well ! " replied Vidal, coming over to the hearth and standing just where Pembroke had stood, with one foot on the fender,
while he pulled at the ends of his moustache and made them join
on his chin—" I believe it *is* well, Challoner—but I hardly
know."

" You hardly know ?   Did you ask her ? "

" Oh, yes, I asked her."

" And what did she say ? "

" Well, she didn't say no."

" Did she imply yes ? "

" She did—I think so—in a sort of way."

" What a bold suitor ! " Sir John said with a smile, feeling
now sufficiently reassured as to the result of the interview, " who
goes to propose to a lady and comes away without being quite
certain whether she said she will, or she will not ! "

" But that's just it.   Your daughter wouldn't say anything
for certain.   She is to tell me more distinctly in a day or
two."

" Meanwhile you are bidden to hope ? " Sir John said,
smiling, and thinking within himself what idiots even clever
young men of the world were where women were concerned.

" I suppose so," Vidal said ; " she was very frank—and awfully
collected, Challoner ; a deuced deal more than I was, I can tell
you.   She said she hadn't the least objection to me, rather liked
me, in fact—quite friendly and encouraging.   She said there
wasn't any reason why she should refuse me, but she would just

think it over. I suppose it's all right, Challoner—you ought to know—I never did that sort of thing before."

"Of course it's all right," Sir John said, almost angrily. " What I don't understand, Vidal, is what else you would have, or why you should think it is not all right."

" I don't know exactly, but the whole affair seemed so unlike what one expected, don't you know ? I expected something awfully emotional; wasn't it natural that I should ? I can tell you *I* was emotional enough."

" Can you remember anything you said ? " Sir John asked, rather amused.

"Not a word. I tried to be very eloquent and touching, but I broke down. Miss Challoner was so awfully composed—and she wouldn't help me out one bit! I am sure girls in general are not like that."

"My daughter hasn't been brought up like girls in general, Vidal."

" No, by Jove!" exclaimed Vidal, with something like enthusiasm in his tone—"if she had—if she were one bit like girls in general I shouldn't have been as much embarrassed as I was; but I am downright in love with her, and I only wish I could think, Challoner, that she was in love with me."

" Girls don't like to show their feelings too readily.'"

"It isn't that; I wish it were. I know a little more than that, Challoner—there wasn't a gleam of emotion about her. She is not in love with me, Challoner."

" All that will come in time—at all events she's not in love with anybody else.'"

" No; there's something in that. Then you think it's all right ? "

"Certainly. If Marie meant to refuse you she would have done so at once."

" I hope, you know, that she isn't merely taking me to please her father? We mustn't allow her to do that, Challoner."

" You are a more sentimental lover than I ever thought you were likely to be," Sir John said, smiling.

" Am not I ? " Vidal asked simply. " Yes ; you have no idea how queerly I feel about the whole affair. I never felt like this before—and I didn't think it was in me; I have done a great deal to try and please her Challoner—*you* know. I haven't a share of any kind in any theatre; and I've given up—everything in fact. I do hope she will come to like me a little, Challoner."

" I think I can answer for her; but if you like I'll ask her myself."

" I wish you would—I really wish you would, Challoner. I

can't bear the idea of our forcing her into anything. I sometimes think we seem like a pair of conspirators."

"We are only conspiring to make her happy if we are conspirators."

"I would rather make myself unhappy than her—I would
a thousand times," the perplexed Vidal exclaimed with energy.

Sir John got rid of the young lover as quickly as he could,
thinking that he had had rather more of love's raptures than he
was quite able to relish for one day. Ronald Vidal's account of
his daughter's composure and self-command pleased him greatly.
He was very glad to find that she was not one of your emotional
people, and he felt satisfied that she would make all the better
wife for not being sentimental on such an occasion.

When Vidal had fairly gone, Sir John sent for his daughter.
He had now nearly shaken off the uncomfortable impression
produced upon him by the pious fraud in which he had thought
it prudent to indulge. The first novelty was over.

"Vidal has gone, Marie," he said, as his daughter entered the
library.

"Yes; I supposed that he had gone, dear, when you sent
for me."

Sir John took his daughter's hand and drew her towards
him—

"Am I to congratulate Ronald Vidal?" he asked in a low
tone. "Your answer, as he described it to, me, did not leave
him quite certain—and of course he is very anxious, poor
fellow.'"

"Is he very anxious? I am sorry."

"But I may congratulate him, Marie, surely?"

"Oh yes, dear—if that is the right sort of thing to do. But
don't you think I ought to be congratulated rather than he?"

"Why so, Marie?"

"I am attaining the height of my ambition, papa—I am going
to be a great lady in society. I am going to be wedded to an
Earlie's son, like the girl in the ballad. What could be a greater
occasion for congratulation? But I don't see why he should be
congratulated."

"Not for getting such a wife, Marie?" And Sir John gently
put his arm round his daughter, and turned her towards the
mirror. She looked at herself very composedly.

"Yes," she said, "I forgot all about that. He is really very
kind and complimentary—in the most practical sort of way too.
I suppose he does see something attractive in me. If I were a
man I am sure that is not the sort of woman I should admire."

"What sort of woman, then might you admire, dear?"

"Something *petite* and sweet and gracious; full of affection
and tenderness—all that sort of thing. There are so many

charming girls I have seen who would just suit Mr. Vidal."

" He doesn't think so. His ideal wife is one of whom he can be proud, and whom every one will admire, and who will make a brilliant figure in society."

" Having been specially trained for that purpose, regardless of expense, in the fashionable circles of Durewoods," Marie said gravely. "Well, the greater my deficiencies the greater his generosity, papa."

" He is really very ardent and sincere in his love for you, Maria."

" Is he? I am very sorry."

" Sorry, my dear ? "

" Yes. I am not worth all that warm and strong feeling. It is thrown away on me."

" But you do feel some attachment—some liking for him, Marie ? "

" Oh, yes, dear—I think so."

" Remember, Marie, there is not the slightest constraint or pressure upon you. I have not even used a word of persuasion ; and your promise is not yet given. You must not marry Ronald Vidal if you don't like it."

" I will marry him, papa, if he wishes it. There isn't any reason why I should not. It will please him and I know it will please you—and why should I not do what you both would wish ? "

" I wish you would tell me exactly, Marie, how you feel about this proposal."

" Dear, I don't feel anything. That is what surprises me. I have no emotion at all. I don't care to be married particularly—I would rather remain as I am a great deal ; but I suppose I should have to marry somebody at some time, and I like Mr. Vidal very well, and no one could possibly be more kind and considerate."

" You have no stronger feeling of any kind either way ? "

" None, dear ; my mind is a blank—except for what I have told you."

" I am sure you will be very happy, Marie, and that you will have a good and clever husband."

" Oh, yes, I am sure."

She seemed almost absolutely indifferent to the whole subject Sir John was much puzzled.

" You seem unhappy, Marie."

" I am not so, dear, indeed. I am quite happy—I think."

" Not disappointed ? "

" With what, papa ? "

" Well, with your prospects, so far ? "

"No, I think not. Things are always different in reality, I suppose, from what people expect. Life looks a little more prosaic as we get to know it. I used to think of something more romantic and full of colour, and really I don't know what. I think I am a little disappointed in myself, perhaps. I used to think I had an emotional sort of nature, and I find that I have not—that is all."

"The better for you, dear child, in actual life. One cannot be too strong.'"

"I suppose so. It all seems so strange; I seem so unconcerned. This won't be very soon, papa?"

"This what, dear?"

"This marriage."

"Not if you don't wish it. Ronald, of course, will have arrangements to make. I have a great idea, Marie, for the meantime. How should you like to see America?"

"America? The United States?"

"Yes. I have a good deal to do with several projects in different parts of the States; and people on both sides have been urging me to go over and see things for myself. I have all but made up my mind to go; and if you would like to come with me, I will make up my mind at once."

Marie's eyes flashed, and her whole face brightened with delight at the prospect.

"I should love to go! I should love to go! There is nothing in the world I should like so well—to travel in America! Should we go far?"

"All the way across, dear—to San Francisco and the Pacific."

"And see the Golden Gate!" The words sprang from her lips involuntarily. With them too came an unbidden memory— a picture in the mind. In one moment she was standing on the height at Durewoods and looking over the bay, with its islands, and listening to Christmas Pembroke as he told of San Francisco and the Golden Gate. The time seemed so far off and so childlike somehow in its poetic happiness, that its memory filled her with sweet pathetic feeling, and tears started, she did not know why, into her eyes. She turned her head away.

"Ronald can't very well come," Sir John said meditatively; "but we cannot help that."

"We shall be all the happier to ourselves," Maria said eagerly, and without stopping to think; "it will be delightful, papa—you and I alone—like the old tmes!"

And now, as she looked up, her father could not but see that there were tears in her eyes. He was touched by her affection for him—surprised, perhaps, that there should be such emotion in one who seemed lately so cold; and he felt proud of it. He kissed her tenderly.

" Well, my love " (even to her, Sir John hardly ever used the word " love "), " you and I are very old friends and fellow-ramblers, and Ronald and you will have plenty of time to travel together. He won't grudge me this last holiday with you. Then that is settled, dear; and we will go as soon as ever you are ready."

" I am overjoyed at the idea. How long shall we be away ? "

" Let me see—it is a large place, and we shall have much to look at. Four or five months, perhaps."

" That will be delightful." And she went into all the details of the proposed trip with an eagerness which amazed and perplexed her father. She was all aglow with delighted expectation at the prospect of a trip to America, and she had hardly exhibited even a languid interest in her engagement to be married.

" Then you won't keep this poor fellow long in suspense, Marie ? " Sir John said, as he was leaving her.

" What poor fellow, dear ? "

" Ronald Vidal. You will give him his answer soon ? "

" Oh, yes, dear ; whenever you like. You may give it for me —that will be best, perhaps—to-day if you wish."

" I don't suppose he would like that quite so well, Marie," her father said with a smile. " I should think he would prefer to have his answer from your own lips."

" Very well, dear. To-morrow, or whenever you and he wish."

" You have always been the best and dearest of daughters," Sir John said, drawing her towards him and kissing her with an affectionate enthusiasm such as he did not often show even to her. " You cannot but make a good wife, my love, who have been such a daughter."

But she did not show any emotion in return, and her father found that her lips were cold.

He was a little sorry for that, but he had never supposed that she greatly loved Ronald Vidal, and therefore he did not expect from her any positive delight in the prospect of marriage. But he was as profoundly convinced as the most conscientious and disinterested father could be that he was securing his daughter's happiness while advancing his own ambition and hers. " The Honourable Mrs. Ronald Vidal," he said to himself over and over again after he had left her. Then at last he should see himself actually connected with the British aristocracy. Ronald Vidal had told him again and again, with the odd frankness which was part of his nature, that his people wanted him to marry a girl with money, and thought he ought to do so, but were terribly afraid of his either taking up with some unpresentable woman from Manchester or getting mixed up with actresses; and that they welcomed with delight the prospect of his getting such a wife as Miss Challoner. All his people, he said, thought her " perfectly splendid," and the moment the thing was settled there was no limit to be put to the cordiality with which they would take her up.

The American journey had been a flash of inspiration to Sir John just now. For some time it had seemed clear that he must go out and have a look at things in the States. At first, his idea was that Ronald and he would go together. Then Ronald took up with a Parliamentary career to please Marie and make her proud of her future husband, and of course he must stick to his work. Sir John himself had never gone in for politics, and was therefore by no means tied to the House. Then Sir John thought that he would go alone after the marriage of his daughter. But now this unlucky affair of young Pembroke's made it absolutely necessary that Marie should be taken out of the way for the present, or else Christmas would suddenly go, and there would be a parting and questions and all that kind of thing ; and Sir John held that women, like kings according to the Scottish saying, were " Kittle cattle to shoe behind "—there was no telling how they might bear with the operation which one considered the most needful for them. So while he was actually talking with his daughter the idea of going to America at once, and taking her with him, flashed into his mind and proved itself a success.

" Then, Marie," he said as she was leaving him, " you get yourself ready as quickly as you can, and we'll have such an exploring of the New World as Christopher Columbus never had."

"*O Vater, lass uns ziehn!*" Marie answered in the words of Mignon, and she went to her room murmuring to herself the sweet melancholy phrases of that ineffable outburst of vague longing. " Let us go ; oh, father, let us go. There, far away— lies our path ! "

Marie seemed to have hardly any feeling left within her but a longing for the American journey. She burned with anxiety to be going away, away, far away out of London and her present surroundings. She would not have cared so much for travel, no matter how far, on the European Continent. That would be too much like the usual kind of thing ; and people they knew in London might meet them there. But when once the Atlantic interposed to divide them from all old associations, then she thought she could begin to enjoy travelling, and the free air would bring healing on its wings. Healing from what ? She did not ask herself the question.

She only knew that she would enjoy the change and the travel and the freedom, and that four or five months of respite seemed now like a happy eternity—at least like a time into

which every possible hope and joy ought to be crammed, and to
the end of which one must not think of looking. Perhaps the
end would never come! Anyhow, it seemed to her now that
without that free holiday on the other side of the Atlantic she
must stifle as if for want of air.

She did not dislike Ronald Vidal. On the contrary, she liked
him much better than she did most other people. She had no
particular dislike to the prospect of being married. That was a
thing which must come some time, and it might as well be soon
as later. She was absolutely unconscious as yet that there was
any feeling in her heart which ought to prevent her from
accepting Vidal's proposal. For a long time, indeed, she had
looked forward to that proposal as certain to come. Her father
had in a quiet, vague way taught her, almost by imperceptible
degrees, to look to Mr. Vidal as the husband she ought to have.
A kind of net had gradually seemed to close around her, and she
had imperceptibly seemed to part with even the power to wish
to be free. There was no one else she would have cared to marry
or thought of marrying. Yet with all this kind of negative
content her heart seemed stifling as she thought of her coming .
life. The very absence of emotion was terrible. The future
looked so blank—it showed in anticipation like life without air.
All the romantic dreams of her girlhood had come to this reality!
" I have no love in me," Lady Disdain said sorrowfully to her
own heart, " I cannot feel as other women seem to feel. I
suppose I was born without any nature like that. I may as
well marry *him*—he is very good and clever; and I suppose he
likes me better than any other woman."

Thus she reasoned with herself as she sat in her own room
alone. She thought of Christmas Pembroke and Sybil Jansen;
and she envied those who could love and who were loved, and
thought of her own loneliness, and at last, in the grey of the
twilight, she burst into tears.

CHAPTER XIX.

" OH, SAW YE NOT FAIR INEZ ? "

THE *Saucy Lass* bore Christmas Pembroke one evening of early summer to the Durewoods pier. He had not visited Durewoods since his first stay there, and he had often been smitten with a sense of ingratitude towards his friend Miss Lyle. There were reasons why for some time back he had rather shrunk from coming under her eyes, and having perhaps to answer the kindly peremptoriness of her questions. But she, he thought, knew nothing of his excuse for avoiding her, and he feared she must think him ungrateful. The fear was confirmed when on writing to ask her if he might pay her a visit he received a reply which he could not but regard as a little cold and curt for her, telling him that he would be welcome. He started for Durewoods next day.

The Challoners had left England. They were to reach New York before the heats of summer set in, and, after spending a few days there and in Boston, to cross at once to San Francisco, where the months intolerable in the Atlantic States would be delightful; and when autumn came they were to return to New York again, visiting many places on their way. Christmas had not seen Marie before her leaving London. Sir John had taken care to keep him engaged in expeditions hither and thither in the northern cities; and Christmas knew it was for the best, although he chafed at it too. But he had made up his mind now that he would not see the Challoners any more. He would not see *her* married. He would return to Japan. It was especially to tell Miss Lyle of his determination to leave England that he was now visiting Durewoods. " Durewoods has been my Sedan," he said to himself.

The heart of the poor youth swelled cruelly with emotion as he began to see the pier at Durewoods, and the cottages, and the trees on the hill amid which Marie's home was standing. Durewoods without her was like the forlorn chamber when the coffin of the loved one has been carried away. It was like the ghost of Durewoods. Pembroke felt a pang of remorse at the thought that the dear, kind friend who still lived there was after all so little to him—that her presence did not remove the death-like atmosphere which for him now hung over the place.

But when the boat touched the pier, and he leaped ashore, and saw old Merlin waiting to carry his portmanteau, he brightened up, and gave the brave Breton a cheery shake of the hand, and asked him voluble questions about Miss Lyle and about himself, and the boat and the garden and the fisher-folk.

"Miss Leel well—beaut'fool well—alway well. Merlin take care of *her*. Miss Marie gone to Amerique—over the great sea—near the fisheries of the Newfoundland—many fishers go there, *I* know."

"Miss Lyle is lonely, perhaps, without Miss Marie ? "

"No—no, no—not lone. Miss Leel not lone—for Merlin take care of her. Merlin not gone to Amerique." And Merlin chuckled much over this pleasantry, and smote his brave breast.

"You grow tall," said Merlin, as they walked along.

"Tall, Merlin ? Not taller than before."

"Oh, yes. *I* know. Tall!—More like man. Tall—old ; very old. You grow very old ! "

Christmas smiled at this tribute to his completed manhood, for so he understood Merlin's words. But Merlin meant too to convey the idea that Christmas was looking paler and thinner than he had expected to find him.

Miss Lyle received Christmas with sweet and gracious courtesy. They dined together, and Janet waited, and every-thing was just as it used to be. But the news which Miss Lyle told him now and again suggested change. Marie Challoner had been in Durewoods for two or three days before her voyage, and Miss Lyle had seen her several times. There was discouraging news from Natty Cramp, whereat his poor mother was greatly concerned. He was not getting on so well as he had expected to do.

Then they went into the balcony, and Christmas praised the beauty of the scene, and thought to himself of the little hollow in the woods, lonely to him for evermore, as everything seemed to be now. Then he said to Miss Lyle that he had something to tell her, and she showed a friendly interest, and listened while he explained, as well as he could, that a life in London did not suit him ; that he didn't think he was a big enough man to make much of a success there, and that he thought he could do better on his old ground in Japan. At last he got to the end of the story somehow.

"Is that all ? " Miss Lyle asked.

That was all. Christmas thought it was a good deal.

"I didn't want to say anything until you had finished. Have you finished ? "

"Yes, Miss Lyle. That is all I wanted to say. As some of our American friends would say, I'm through."

"I don't understand slang," said Miss Lyle—"even English slang. I am not fond of it."

There was a pause. Christmas wondered if she were going to say nothing more on the subject of his resolve, and if the matter were to drop there. For a while she had seemed to be growing more friendly, but again there came a marked coldness in her manner. Christmas did not wonder at that. He felt with renewed pangs of conscience that he had been but an inattentive friend for some time, and must not expect instant pardon.

"Then you have made up your mind to renounce London and go back to Japan?" she said, at last, in a tone of some dissatisfaction.

"I have," Christmas answered, glad that she had said anything. "I am afraid you will think me a variable personage, Miss Lyle, without much of a mind to make up."

"It *is* strange," she said, following up apparently some train of thought of her own. "Your father was above all things a man of steady purpose. I begin to think you are not like him at all, Mr. Christmas, and that I have been rather mistaken in you."

"Well, Miss Lyle, you will do me the justice to admit that I never claimed to be like my father, or fit to be compared with him."

"Still," she said, in an almost irritable way, "it *is* strange how the sons degenerate. I don't understand it. Where *did* you learn these fickle ways, and that want of trust, which I can tell you I like still less?"

Miss Lyle, as Marie Challoner had said long ago, was picturesque in everything she did. Few people look dignified when out of humour, but in the gesture with which she drew her white shawl round her shoulders, as if wrapping herself in a garment of offended pride, there was something effective and dramatic.

"Want of trust—in *you*, Miss Lyle?"

"In me, yes. Do I not deserve your confidence? Did I not offer myself to you from the beginning frankly as your friend, and how could you doubt that I was so? I tell you, Chris Pembroke, I should almost have loved a lap-dog called by your father's name, not to speak of his son; and I did so wish to be your friend, for his sake; and this is what comes of it! To you, perhaps, it may seem ridiculous that I should feel in this way. Very well—at least you see that I *do* feel."

"But you are entirely mistaken, and you do me a great wrong. The thought of going back to Japan was only flickering in my mind for some time: and Sir John Challoner asked me to put off deciding for a little while. I did so. But now I have made up my mind, and I came to tell you. He does not know of it yet—I mean I have not yet written to him."

"You choose your confidants well," Dione said scornfully. "I don't mean merely your going to Japan, Christmas; but you confided to John Challoner your reason for flying out of England —you never told that to *me*. I waited to-day patiently to see if that would come out even now, and it didn't! No; your full confidence is kept for him."

Christmas grew red and hot. He could hardly believe his ears. Could it be possible that Sir John Challoner had actually betrayed his confidence—and for what reason? He looked at Miss Lyle in positive alarm and began to speak, and then became silent.

"I will spare your blushes," Dione said—feeling some pity for his confusion—"and I am glad you have the grace to blush, Chris; but you might have told me of this as well as John Challoner." Having, as she thought, compelled the young man to feel confused, she began to soften to him.

"Did Sir John tell you—Miss Lyle, are you serious? I can't understand this! But if he did, then at least you must know why I felt bound to tell him and not you——"

"I don't see that, Mr. Christmas. But let me ease your mind. It was not from Sir John I first heard the story—although when I asked him he didn't deny it."

"Not from Sir John? Then from whom—for no one else on earth could have—— "

"You ridiculous boy, don't you know that men of the world never keep anybody's secret absolutely? They always let drop hints. Why you should have insisted on any particular secrecy in this affair is as great a wonder to me as why you should have chosen him for a confidant. I presume you didn't suppose that the thing could have been kept a secret from us all for ever, even if you did retreat to Japan with her."

Christmas was now utterly bewildered. There was evidently some extraordinary misunderstanding somewhere.

"I don't know what to say," he broke out at last. "We don't understand each other, Miss Lyle."

"Come, I really begin to think you are more foolish than distrustful, Christmas. I suppose boys are shy of talking of these things even to elderly women. But you could have found no trustier friend than me—nor one less likely to care for social prejudices and that kind of thing. I don't believe your father's son could make a very bad choice. Well, I forgive you your secrecy. And so you have fallen in love, my poor boy, and are going to be married? So soon?"

Christmas started with such evident and genuine surprise that Miss Lyle was startled in her turn.

"Is this not true?" she asked, sharply—"are you not going to be married? Are we playing at cross purposes?"

"We are indeed," said Christmas, with an aching heart. "There never was such playing at cross purposes! Who told you that story, Miss Lyle? Not Sir John Challoner, at all events."

"But is that really not true? Have you not fallen in love; and are you not going to be married?"

"A man less likely to be married, Miss Lyle, is not to be found anywhere between this and Japan."

"Oh! Have you quarrelled?"

"Quarrelled with whom?"

"With the young lady, of course. I suppose we needn't now make a mystery of her name—Miss Jansen."

Christmas rose from his chair in amazement. In all his trouble of heart he was boyishly inclined to laugh.

"Is that the story, Miss Lyle—is that the mystery—the confidence?"

"But is it really not true? Is it all a mistake or a delusion? Are you more deceitful than I could have believed, or are people going out of their senses? Do let us come to some understanding."

"Miss Lyle, there isn't one single particle of truth or meaning or anything else in that story. I know Miss Jansen; but I never felt anything for her but friendship—and there is even much about her that I don't like; and I am not certain now whether she is not rather unfriendly to me than the contrary. As for any other idea, it never even occurred to me until this moment; and it would be ever so much less likely to occur to her. To begin with, she hates the whole race of men."

"Yes; I don't mind that," Miss Lyle said, quietly. "They soon get over that—girls, I mean. But if you tell me seriously that this is not true——"

"But, Miss Lyle, to say it is not true is nothing. There isn't the faintest conceivable foundation or excuse for it. The wonder is how any one could ever have thought of it. Did you say that some one told you this?"

"Oh, yes," Miss Lyle answered, composedly: "Marie Challoner told me."

"Miss Challoner!" Again Christmas's face burned with emotion; and at once there flashed upon his memory the fact, hardly noticed at the time, that Marie had sent with a peculiar expression of look and voice her friendly message to Sybil Jansen through him. He felt unspeakably wretched. Strange contradiction of human impulses! The one thing he dreaded most an hour ago was that Marie Challoner should know of his love for her. Now it seemed a thousand times worse that she should believe him to be in love with another woman.

" This is terrible," he said.

" Of course such things are always provoking; but one can't help them. This seems to have been a very singular misunderstanding."

" Did Miss Challoner speak of this as a guess on her part?"

" No. Marie Challoner, Chris, is an impulsive girl, so truthful that it is hard for her even to keep a secret: and she said something here which aroused my curiosity, I can tell you, and I am afraid I extorted the rest. Then she said that her father had enjoined secrecy on her—but Marie was never exemplary in the way of obeying injunctions."

" But it was not Sir John Challoner who told her this story?"

" Indeed it was."

" Miss Lyle," Christmas said gravely, " you are mistaken in that, I assure you."

" My good boy, I am not mistaken. The poor girl, conscious of having broken her father's trust, insisted, in her proud honesty, upon telling him that she had done so and asking his pardon, and I insisted on telling him that the fault was mine, and of course the whole story came out then."

" Sir John Challoner said I was in love with Miss Jansen? Sir John said that?"

" He did. At least I told him what Marie said; and he said Marie ought not to have told it to anybody, and he seemed greatly vexed at the whole affair."

Christmas was lost in confusion. It seemed natural enough that if Miss Challoner or Miss Lyle had made a guess of any kind Sir John might have allowed her to remain under a delusion rather than give any clue to the truth. But, as he understood Miss Lyle, there was something more than this.

" Did I understand you rightly, Miss Lyle? Did you say that Sir John told this story—told it himself—to Miss Challoner?"

" Certainly, Chris; he and she both spoke of it in that way. Sir John said, more than once, that he was to blame for having revealed to his daughter what you told him in confidence."

Christmas leaned upon the balcony and thrust his hands deep into his pockets. He was perfectly bewildered.

" But there must be something in all this,'" Dione said impatiently. " It can't be all midsummer madness. You did, surely, tell John Challoner something in confidence!"

" I did."

" And had it nothing to do with Miss Jansen?"

" Nothing."

" Was it any sort of love-confession?"

With eyes doggedly downcast Christmas answered, " It was."

"And in Heaven's name, Chris Pembroke, why did your father's son select John Challoner of all men on earth as the confidant of his love story?—Oh!"

The exclamation broke from Miss Lyle because of the sudden expression with which Christmas had looked up when she put her imperious question—an expression which was a revelation.

"You unhappy boy," she said in a low tone, and leaning towards him, "was *that* it?"

"*That* was it. Now you know all. Now you know why I told him, and why I didn't tell you."

"Did you know that she was engaged to young Vidal?"

"I did. I guessed it."

"Then what on earth was the good of your speaking to her father? What did you hope to get by that?"

"Nothing."

"You had better have told me a hundred times. You didn't suppose that John Challoner was a person to be touched by your romantic attachment, and to say, 'Take her, my boy! Bless you, my children'?"

"Miss Lyle, I imagined nothing, and hoped nothing. I couldn't endure the place any longer. I tried hard, and I found that I couldn't do it, and he had been so kind to me that I didn't like to seem ungrateful or changeable, and I couldn't invent lies. I thought the best thing to do was to tell her father all, and beg of him to help me, and to—to cover my retreat, in fact. I suppose it was an absurd thing to do—I thought it the most honest way."

There was a moment's silence. The evening was darkening. The scents of the flowers came more richly out, and the plash of the water below sounded sadly in the ears of the poor youth on whom Dione turned her pitying eyes.

"I am glad you did whatever you thought was honest, my boy," she said. "You never can be sorry for that. Well, well!"

Christmas did not speak. He could not pour out his soul readily, even to her. He was at once frank and shy, as nature and his early way of life had made him.

"This is a great misfortune, Chris! Tell me—do you know yourself—will this last?"

"Oh yes," he answered in a low tone, and without looking at her. "It will last my time, Miss Lyle."

"Of course all young people say that; and I shouldn't mind it much in your case, my dear, but for what I know. And so you got this wound under my roof, my poor boy? I wish I had never found you out, Chris, and brought you here, for this."

"No, no!" he said, eagerly; "don't wish that, Miss Lyle—don't wish that. I have your friendship—I couldn't wish to lose that, and I don't want to lose—the memory even of—anything that happened. I'll come all right—I mean I'll fight my way on through life."

"You would not be without the memory of your dream, then?"

"Would my father have given up the memory of his?"

Dione's lips trembled. She leaned back in her chair, and remained silent for a moment.

"Now, Miss Lyle," said Christmas, "you know all; you have got this all out of me somehow, which I never meant to have told to anybody but one. I am not sorry, but I don't mean to plague you any more with my troubles. I didn't come here to make you uncomfortable. I'm not going through life with an everlasting lament in my mouth. I am no worse off than ever so many better fellows."

"I thought it a bad omen at the time that you should have met her the very first moment you stepped ashore here. I didn't want you to meet her. Then, when the thing was done, I thought it best to say as little as possible, and seem to make light of everything. But I did give you a warning, Chris."

"You did, I remember. But it was too late then, and it wouldn't have been of any use in any case—not the least."

"I suppose not. You don't blame her, Chris?"

"Blame her! Her! For what?"

"You don't think she meant this—or trifled with you?"

"Oh, no. She is as true as light. She was my friend always; she is now. It is no fault of hers. She never suspected."

"I am glad. I should have thought so, but I am glad to hear you say so. One word more. You have not any lurking hope—about her?"

"Oh, no; no hope."

"You are right, Chris. I know Marie as well as any one can, and I know that all the world could not make her engage herself to Mr. Vidal if she cared for anybody else. But I am glad you have the courage to look that straight in the face. The only thing now is—what is to be done?"

"My mind is clear," said Christmas; "I'll leave England and go back to Japan."

"But why do that? why not stay firmly here and make an honourable career for yourself? A man has some other business in life than falling in love and brooding over it."

"I have other business, and I mean to do it, Miss Lyle, and not to brood. But if I remained in England I should be likely to brood on to the end of the chapter."

"There are other women too, Chris."

"There are no other women for me, Miss Lyle, and good

o

advice is thrown away on me I am afraid. Sooner than stay
here and see her—see her married, Miss Lyle, I would leap off
the pier below and swim straight out to sea as far as ever I could
go, and sink quietly down when I could swim no farther. It
wouldn't be half a bad thing to do—go down with the setting
sun."

" You won't do that, I know," Miss Lyle said. " You'll not
do that cowardly thing, Chris. That might do for Natty Cramp,
perhaps, or some egotistical fool of his kind; not for you. But
we'll say no more of this just now. It's a surprise, and I must
think it over. You used to like to smoke a cigar in the
evenings ? "

Christmas understood the very clear hint. She held out
her hand to him, and he saw that her eyes were filled with tears.
Heaven knows what boyish impulse made him kneel beside her
chair and press her hand to his lips. Then she gently laid the
hand upon his head. There passed through Dione's mind at the
time the sweet, strange, unspeakably tender saying of the
Duchess of Orleans about Dunois—that he was a child stolen
from her.

She was glad when Christmas left her, for there was something which puzzled her in all this, and which she had not
spoken of much to him. Indeed, the moment the question
arose in her mind she kept the talk, such as it was, away from
that. Christmas had told Sir John Challoner that he was in
love with Marie. Sir John had voluntarily, distinctly told
Marie that Christmas had made to him an acknowledgment of
love for Miss Jansen. There was no possibility of mistake or
misapprehension on either side, on any point. Why did John
Challoner tell his daughter that lie ?

Strange, she thought, if John Challoner's deceits should have
come between the son, as they did between the father, and the
woman he loved and might have married!

For there could be to Dione's mind no explanation possible
of Sir John's proceedings but an anxiety to render it impossible
for his daughter to think of Christmas, and thus to hurry her into
a marriage with Lord Paladine's son. He must have feared
that Marie might fall in love with Chris. That must have been
his motive.

But then Dione had talked with Marie only the other day in
full and warm friendship and confidence about her marriage, and
Marie had not given the faintest indication of any feeling that
could stand between her and it. She did not seem to have any
delight in the prospect, and it was only too clear that she had
no romantic attachment to Mr. Vidal. But even when Dione
spoke to her in some wonder of her seeming coldness, and lack
of interest in her future Marie assured her again and again that

she was marrying of her own free will, and at no one's persuasion, and that since she must marry she knew no one so acceptable for a husband as Mr. Vidal. Again and again, too, had Marie told her that she did not think she had a nature formed for the kind of emotion which is described in books as love.

"So many girls say that," Miss Lyle thought, "until the time comes. But I think it must be so with her."

John Challoner then must have been deceived—such was Dione's conclusion—out of excess of caution, as was his wont. Poor Christmas was right—Marie felt nothing for him but an easy friendship. There was nothing to be done. The boy must take his fate and bear it. The less said now about the misunderstanding and the perverted confidence the better. Let that all seem to be a misunderstanding, and let it drop. She would not argue any more against Christmas's resolve to go back to Japan; all things considered, it would be the best course he could take.

But she could not still help wondering over the strange stroke of fate, or whatever it was, which had brought the son of her old lover across so many thousand miles of earth and sea under her roof to have his heart pierced there by the daughter of his father's old rival.

CHAPTER XX.

"PROFESSOR NATHANIEL P. CRAMP."

THE Genius of young Liberty had indeed not yet proved propitious to Natty Cramp. He landed at Hoboken, on the New Jersey shore of the North river at New York, one sunny and lovely morning, and he gazed across at the somewhat confused and unalluring river front of the great city with the air of a conqueror. The fresh breath of freedom, he proudly said to himself, was already filling him with new manhood. But New York is in some ways a discouraging place to land at. There are no cabs; and there are no street porters; and to hire a "hack" carriage is expensive; and to track out one's way in the street cars and the stages is almost hopeless work for the new comer. Then the examination at the Custom-house was long and vexatious; and yet, when Natty got through the Custom-house, he felt as if he were thrown adrift on the world without any one more to care about him. As Melisander in Thomson's poem declares that, bad as were the wretches who deserted him, he never heard a sound more dismal than that of their parting

oars, so, little as Nathaniel Cramp liked the brusque ways of
the Custom-house officers, he felt a sort of regret when they
nad released him and his baggage, and he found himself absolutely turned loose upon the world and his own resources.
    This small preliminary disappointment was ominous. Natty
had come out with a little money and a great faith in himself
and his destiny. He had the usual notion that New York and
the United States in general are waiting eagerly to be instructed
in anything by Europeans, and especially by Englishmen. Having
failed utterly in London, he thought he must be qualified to
succeed in New York. His idea was to give lectures and write
books—poems especially. He soon found that every second
person in America delivers lectures, and that every village has
at least three poets—two women and one man. He had brought
a few letters of introduction from some members of the Church
of the Future in London to congenial spirits in New York, and
he made thereby the acquaintance of the editor of a Spiritualist
journal, of a German confectioner and baker who had a small
shop on Fourth Avenue (and Fourth Avenue is to Fifth Avenue
as Knightsbridge is to Park Lane or Piccadilly), and of a lady
who wore trousers and called herself the Rev. Theodosia Judd.
The influence of these persons over New York, however, was
limited, and although they endeavoured to get an audience for
one of Natty's lectures at a very little hall in a cross street far
up town, the public did not rush in, and Nat delivered his
lecture so feebly that a few of the few who were in went boldly
out again, and one elderly man produced from his pocked a copy
of the *New York Evening Mail* and read it steadily through.
Yet the Spiritualist journal had had several little notices preliminary of Natty, whom it described variously as Professor
Cramp and Doctor Cramp, the celebrated author and lecturer,
from London, England; and this was a secret delight to
Nathaniel, for the blind Fury with abhorred shears might slit
away his audiences, but not the printed and published praise.
It cheered him for a little while to be thus publicly complimented, and he said to himself, with great pride, that that came
of being in a land of equality, and that he would have been long
in London before the hireling and subservient press of that city
would thus have spoken of him.
    Still New York as a community was absolutely unawakened
to any recognition or even knowledge of Natty's existence, and his
money was melting away. He " boarded " very modestly in a
quiet little cross street where he paid but a few dollars a week,
but he was earning nothing.   There were awful moments when,
as he passed some of the showy hairdressing shops in Broadway,
and saw the richly dressed ladies going in and out, he began to
wonder whether he had not better take at once to the single

craft and mystery whereof he was really possessed, and do for the curls and chignons of Broadway what he had done in other days for those of Wigmore Street. But his pride would not as yet suffer this. He went home to his bedroom in the boarding-house and read over again the paragraph in the Spiritualist paper which spoke of his literary gifts, and he vowed that he would never stoop to curl heads of hair again—never.

Suddenly another chance opened up for him. His friend the editor of the Spiritualist journal came to him one day with the grand news that he had procured him an appointment to deliver a lecture in the Lyceum course of Acroceraunia, one of the rising cities on the north-western confines of New York State. Acroceraunia was beginning now to hold its head pretty high in the world. It had already celebrated the twentieth anniversary of its foundation, and as its neighbour and rival, Pancorusky City, had long been having its Lyceum winter course of lectures, Acroceraunia had at last made up its mind for a winter course of lectures as well. All the leading citizens had come forward most spiritedly, and so liberal were the promises of assistance that Acroceraunia put itself in communication at once with the American Literary Bureau of New York to engage a certain limited number of "star" lecturers, the other nights of the course to be filled up with local and volunteer talent, and any rising young lecturers who might be known to private members of the committee and might be willing to offer their lecture for a modest sum in consideration of the opening thus afforded. Now the brother of the Spiritualist editor was one of the most important men in all Acroceraunia. He edited the Republican journal of that city. He wrote to his brother in New York requesting him to recommend some promising young lecturer who would not object to take twenty-five dollars and his ex-penses. The "stars" would not any of them shine for an hour on Acroceraunia under a hundred dollars, and many of them could not even be tempted out of their ordinary spheres by such a sum as that; and some again were so heavily engaged in advance that Acroceraunia would not have a chance of getting them on any terms for many seasons to come. In fact Acro-ceraunia had only engaged two genuine stars for her course, one to open, and one to close it. There seemed a great deal too much local talent and Singing Society in between, and therefore some padding of a less familiar kind had to be sought out. Hence the offer to Natty Cramp.

Nathaniel jumped at it. He was beginning to fear that he never again should have a chance of testing his rhetorical skill ; and besides, twenty-five dollars, look you, are equivalent to five pounds, and would be a substantial gain to Nathaniel Cramp. It so happened, too, that Nathaniel suited the conditions of the Lyceum course of Acroceraunia very well. That season, and indeed for some seasons back, all the Lyceums had had some lecturer from London, England, in their course. But when Acroceraunia had secured, and with immense difficulty, its two American stars, there was not nearly enough of money still in prospect or possibility to enable it to get one of the British luminaries as well. Therefore Nathaniel Cramp was positively a godsend. "The celebrated English orator, Professor Nathaniel P. Cramp, from London, England," would look very well on the placards and advertisements. The people of Acroceraunia were in general a steady-going home-keeping community. They rose early, they worked hard, and when the gentlemen of a family came home in the evening they generally went to sleep on the lounge after supper, and were awakened by their wives in time to go to bed at a proper hour. They never dreamed of trips to Europe in the summer, and they did not take in the British journals. For half of them, then, the name of Natty Cramp would do just as well as that of any of the more distinguished Britons who were stumping the States that fall.

So Nathaniel accepted the offer, and when the time came he took the train for Acroceraunia. He travelled all night and arrived at Acroceraunia about eleven o'clock next morning. He was straining his eyes anxiously for the spires and domes of the city where he was to make what he really held to be his *début* as a lecturer in the States; but when the train stopped he could see no spires, no domes, no city. The land wherever his eye could reach was covered with snow; he saw nothing but snow. Natty was beginning to think this could not be the right station at all, when the brakesman at the upper end of the car, who had been madly straining and tugging at his piece of mechanism like a sailor set all alone to work at a capstan, suddenly dashed open the door and shouted "Acrocerauny!" and Nat had to bundle himself out, portmanteau and all, as quickly as he could, on the wooden platform of the station. He stood hesitatingly a few moments, expecting to find some one to receive him. But there was clearly no one there to escort him, and the train had gone its way.

He took up his portmanteau and walked slowly, doubtfully out of the station, wondering what he should do next. Outside the station he saw two staggery and ramshackle looking omnibuses waiting. One had in its day been a Fulton Ferry omnibus in New York, and bore on its side the well-known pictorial ornamentations, a little faded, which distinguish that conveyance as it rumbles up and down Broadway and Fulton Street. This omnibus now belonged to the "Acroceraunia House." The other was in the service of the "American Hotel." Natty thought as he had to choose he ought to give the prefer-

ᴠᴠᴄᴇ to the hostelry which assumed the name of the city which
ʰᵃd honoured him with its invitation, and so he got into the
ʲarriage of the Acroceraunia House, feeling very much out of
ʲpirits, and divided mentally between an anxiety to know where
Acroceraunia was, and a feeble wish that the moment of his
arrival might be postponed as long as possible.

There was no other passenger in the omnibus as it jolted
away. Nat was rather glad of that. He was rattled along white
road after white road until he began to wonder whether the town
had any right to consider itself as in any manner connected with
the railway station which bore its name. At last a few houses
appeared, each standing separately in its piece of ground. Most
of the houses were built of wood, and had bright green shutters
and little Grecian porticos, and every house had a clothes-line.
Natty must apparently have passed in review the " pantalettes "
of the whole female population of Acroceraunia as he drove
along. At last the omnibus turned into something which bore
resemblance to a street, or at least, was like a high road with
houses at each side. But Natty saw a little placard on a
wall as they were turning into this street or road, which for the
moment withdrew his attention from everything else, and made
him blush and feel shy, proud, terrified, and delighted. For he
could see on it the words "Lyceum Lecture Course," "This
Night," and "Professor Nathaniel P. Cramp, of London, England." Natty positively drew himself into a corner of the
omnibus as if every eye must have been looking out for him, or
as if he were Lady Godiva riding through Coventry, and had
just been seized with a suspicion of the craft of Peeping Tom.
But pride soon came to Natty's rescue again, and he felt that at
last he was coming to be somebody, that this was the beginning of
fame, and that the world comes to him who waits. He delivered
to himself in a proud undertone the closing sentences of his
lecture.

The omnibus stopped at last in front of a house of dark brick,
with a sign swinging above, and after a good deal of clattering
and stamping on the part of the horses, and cries of " Git up "
on the part of the driver, it backed up to the porch, and Professor Nathaniel P. Cramp got out. He made his way into the
office of the hotel, a gaunt, bare room with a stove in the midst,
a counter at one side, and a grave man behind the counter.
When Nathaniel walked up to the counter the grave man turned
round a huge ledger or register which lay before him, pushed it
towards Nat, and handed him a pen without saying a word.
Natty knew the ways of the New World well enough now to
know what this meant. He inscribed himself in the book,
Nathaniel Cramp, London, England. The grave man marked a
number in the book opposite to Nat's name, and handed a key

with a corresponding number to an Irish porter, who took Nat's portmanteau and preceded him upstairs. The porter opened the door of a small bare bedroom in a gusty corridor, and showed Natty in.

"Guess you'll want a fire built ? " said the porter.

"I should like a fire," Nat mildly answered.

The attendant put down the key of the room on the table, and Nat observed that the key was stuck or set in a large triangular piece of metal like the huge and ill-shaped hilt of a dagger.

"What do you have that thing on the keys for ? " Nat asked.

"To keep the guests from putting 'em in their pockets—don't ye see ? '

"And what matter if they did put them in their pockets ? "

"Then they forget 'em there, don't you see? When a guest is in a hurry he never rec'lects to give up his key. Last fall every key in the Acrocerauny House was carr'd right off one morning. Now we fix 'em that way, don't you see? They can't put 'em in their pockets anyhow."

And the porter took himself off loudly whistling as he went, " The Wearing of the Green."

Presently he came back with wood and lit the stove. Natty was too dispirited to talk. He looked out of the window at the one long street white in the snow. Opposite was a " dry goods " store with a liberal display of red and white " clouds ".(light soft shawls of fleecy worsted or some such material) for women, and with some spectral crinolines dangling at the door. Next was a shop where " rubbers "—india-rubber overshoes—were sold ; next was a hardware shop ; next a grocery store ; then a blank wall ornamented with a huge announcement of some sort of pill, and a small square bill which Natty knew to be the placard of his own lecture. It was now barely noon. Dinner, he had been informed, was at two ; supper at six. What was he to do in the meantime ?

A tap at the door. Natty called " Come in," and two men— one young, bright-eyed, handsome, and awkward ; the other tall, hard-featured, and of middle age—came in. Nat bowed.

"Professor Cramp, I presume ? " the elder visitor said.

Nat intimated that his name was Cramp, but he did not make it clear that he had no claim to the title of professor.

"Professor Cramp," the younger man struck in, " I have the pleasure of making you acquainted with the president of our society, Mr. Fullager."

Mr. Fullager and Nat solemnly shook hands.

"Professor Cramp," said Mr. Fullager, " I have the pleasure to make you acquainted with our secretary, Mr. Plummer, junior."

Nathaniel and Mr. Plummer shook hands.

"There was a little mistake with regard to our meeting you at the *depôt*," Mr. Fullager explained; and Nat luckily remembered that "*depôt*," in Mr. Fullager's sense, corresponded with "station" in Nat's. "The train was on time to-day, which it usually is not, and when Mr. Plummer and I got to the *depôt* you were gone, sir."

Nat affirmed that it didn't matter at all, and that he was much obliged. His visitors were now seated, and were waiting calmly in silence, evidently understanding that the responsibility of the conversation rested on him. He felt that he must rise to the dignity of the situation somehow. A sudden inspiration possessed him, and he said—

"Yours is a very charming town, Mr. Fullager. It seems to grow very fast."

"It is quite a place, sir—quite a place."

"What population, now, have you?" And the wily Nat crossed one foot over the other knee, nursed the foot with his hand, put his head sideways, and waited for an answer with the air of one who had studied populations a good deal.

"Well, sir," Mr. Fullager said, after some grave deliberation, we have forty-five hundred persons in this city."

"Forty-seven hundred," Mr. Plummer said.

"I guess not, sir,—not quite so many."

"Not if you take in the houses on the other side of Colonel Twentyman's lot, Mr. Fullager?"

"Ah, well; yes—perhaps if you do that we should figure up to forty-seven hundred."

"That is a remarkable population," Mr. Cramp said, patronisingly, "for so young a town." Nat hardly knew one population from another.

"We are only twenty years old, sir."

"Twenty years only! Wonderful!" Nat observed, with an air of dreamy enthusiasm.

Then there was another pause. The two visitors were perfectly composed. They gazed at the stove, and did not feel that they were called upon to say anything. They had come to pay their respects to the foreign lecturer as a matter of courtesy and politeness, and when they considered that they had remained long enough they would rise and go away. There are plenty of talkative Americans, no doubt, but the calm self-possession of silence is nowhere so manifest as among the men of some of the States.

But Nathaniel was much discomposed, and racked his brain for a topic.

"What kind of audiences do you have here, Mr. Fullager?" he asked, in another rush of inspiration.

"Well, sir (after some deliberation), I should say a remarkably intelligent audience. You would say so, Mr. Plummer?"

"Decidedly so," said Mr. Plummer, with a start, for he had been thinking of nothing in particular at the time. "Decidedly so, Mr. Fullager. Several gentlemen have told me that our audience is far more intelligent than that of Pancorusky City."

"Oh, yes. I should certainly have expected that," said Nat, with the air of one who was rather surprised to hear the comparison made and who would not on any terms have consented to bring himself down to an audience such as that of Pancorusky City. Nat was really developing a considerable aptitude for playing the part of distinguished foreign visitor.

"Would you like to see some of our institutions, sir?" Mr. Fullager asked. "The City Hall, the ward schools, our water power, Deacon Renselar's saw mills?"

Nat said he should like it of all things, and he remembered that he must call on the editor of the Republican journal, to whom indirectly he owed his renewed chances of fame.

"We'll call on them both, sir," said Mr. Fullager—"we'll call on the editors of both our journals—the Democrat and the Republican. We have no politics, sir, in our association, and they both, sir, have said kind words about your visit and your lecture."

Nat professed himself delighted to have the chance of being presented to both the editors, and felt indeed a great deal more proud than he would have cared to tell. If the people at home could only see him thus treated like a distinguished stranger and made a regular lion of, what would they say?

So Natty was conducted over the town and had all its growing wonders pointed out to him, and was presented to the editors of the rival journals, and was not invited to "liquor up," or, by any form of phraseology, to drink anything. This latter fact we mention with some hesitation to English readers, being aware of their preconceived opinions on the subject of American usages. It is an article of faith in England that every conversation in America opens with an invitation to drink. Nathaniel had already discovered that, outside the great cities where the foreigners abound and diffuse their customs, nine out of ten Americans rarely taste any liquid stronger than tea.

The day thus wore away pleasantly enough for Nat, who found it more and more agreeable to be allowed to play the part of distinguished stranger. But when he returned to his room in the hotel, and the evening came on bringing the hour of his public appearance terribly near, his spirits sank dismally. When the gong sounded at six o'clock for supper, and he went down to the lighted room where the guests were refreshing themselves on tea, hot "biscuit," and preserves, he had a nervous consciousness

that every eye was turned upon him and that he was looking
awkward. He thought it a very objectionable institution which
obliged the lecturer to take his meals in public and to be seen
swallowing hot dough, denominated biscuit, immediately before
his appearance on the platform. He would have liked so much
better to burst upon Acroceraunia all at once, and for the first
time, when stepping forward to deliver his harangue. He nearly
choked over his biscuit with blended nervousness and self-
conceit.

Opposite to him at the same narrow table Nat saw a handsome man with soft blue eyes, a bald head, and a full fair beard
and moustache, who was evidently regarding the distinguished
lecturer with interest. When Nat looked towards him the blue-
eyed man said—

"I think, sir, I have the pleasure of addressing Mr. Cramp?"
Nat started and awkwardly admitted the fact.

"I have heard you lecture already—in the Avenir Hall, isn't
it called?—in London."

"Oh, indeed," Nat replied, with an effort to be calm and
dignified, which was combated by three emotions rushing upon
him at once: a pang of home-sickness at the sound of the word
"London," a distressing consciousness that the stranger must
have heard him make a sad mess of it, and a sickening dread that
the stranger must have also learned that he was once a hairdresser.

"I was on a visit to Europe for some years," the new acquaintance said, "and I spent a considerable time in London,
and I went into Avenir Hall one Sunday and heard you
lecture."

"I didn't do very well that day," said Nat.

"You were evidently not used to public speaking, and you
were nervous, but I shouldn't think the worse of your chances
for that. If a man has anything in him he is sure to be
nervous."

Nat was glad to hear that anyhow, although there was an
easy patronising way about his friend which, as a distinguished
lecturer, he hardly relished.

"You live here, I presume?" Nathaniel said, anxious to turn
the conversation from his oratorical deficiencies.

"In Acroceraunia? No; I live farther westward," and he
mentioned the name of a town which Nat had heard of, and
where there was a large and well known State college; "I hope
to have the pleasure of seeing you there." And presently the
blue-eyed man, having finished his supper, rose from the table,
bowed to Nat, and left the room.

If Nat had been a little less deeply engrossed in the thought
of his lecture he might have been struck with the strange and

picturesque sights which met his eyes as he proceeded with his
friends Mr. Fullager and Mr. Plummer to the hall where he was
to confront his audience. The earth was white all around with
the crackling and glittering snow. The "red-litten windows"
of the hall seemed to have an unearthly colour as they shone
between the white of the ground and the blue of the moon-
lighted sky. The street and the houses were but sharp black
lines and cubes against the snow. The dark belt of a pine
wood, from whose depths, much thinned lately, the bear had
more than once made his way into Acroceraunian streets in
Acroceraunia's earlier days, girdled the valley all around, and
then above and behind it rose the hills, through the clefts of
which a melancholy wind swept down along the frozen roads.
The sleighs came rattling up to the hall from outlying farms
and villages, and the sleigh bells tinkled merrily, and the lights
in the carriages sparkled like fire-flies out of season. Never
had Nat seen such a waste of brilliant white as that upon the
earth, such a profound blue as that in the sky; for the sky was
not black with the hue of the night, even low down on the
horizon where the moon least lighted it, but a deep purpling
blue. It was strange to turn one's eyes up to what seemed the
awful solitude of the hills, and the belt of pine woods and the
horizon, and then to drop one's gaze suddenly to the little
luminous and bustling place just around the hall. As Nat stood
on the steps of the hall which was on the side of a slightly
ascending street, the town was lost, swallowed up in shadow and
darkness, and outside the sphere of light which radiated from
the windows of the hall there seemed nothing but the hills, the
pine woods, and the snow. Where did they come from—that
cluster of people with their sleighs and sleigh-bells, and lights
and furs, and rapid feet and pleasant talk? From the drear
waste of snow around, from the black pine woods from the cold
far hills? There was something strange, unearthly, uncanny, in
the sudden crowd and the twinkling lights thus starting up out
of shadow, out of darkness, out of nothing. At a breath one
might have thought the whole vision would disappear, the lights
would go out, the bright eyed lasses and tall sinewy lads, the
sober elders with the set faces, the stamping horses with the
rattling bells, all would vanish and leave the stranger alone with
the drear hills and the moaning pines.

   But Nat Cramp did not give many thoughts to these things.
His may be called a subjective mind, and he only saw a hall
where he was to give a lecture and a little crowd of people,
whom he thought with a certain terror he should presently have
to address. He had chosen a theme which he considered must
especially appeal to the sympathies of a Republican audience.
His subject was " The Worn-out Aristocracies of Europe.'

The hall was tolerably well filled, for people in Acroceraunia went to every lecture in their winter course regularly as a matter of duty. But they were, to Nat's thinking, sadly undemonstrative. American audiences, especially in country places, hardly ever applaud. They listen, if they are really interested, with a motionless and an awful interest. Nat kept his manuscript open before him, but tried to speak as far as possible without consulting the paper. But he soon began to feel afraid of facing the grave and silent audience. The echo of his own words alarmed him. He lashed the weaknesses and excesses of the effete aristocracies of Europe, and the calm audience betrayed no fervour of Republican enthusiasm. He narrated what he held to be a very good story, and *on ne rit pas*, as the French reporters used to say sometimes when an orator's joke failed to draw fire. He paused for a moment in one or two places for the expected applause, but it did not come, and he had to hurry on again abashed. He became cowed and demoralized. He forgot his task, and he hid his face in his manuscript and read, conscious that he was reading a great deal too fast, and yet thirsting to get done with the now hopeless effort. The essay was awfully long. Several persons quietly got up and glided out of the hall, the soft fall of their indiarubber-covered feet naving in Nat's ear a spectral sound. There was a pretty girl with beaming eyes whom Nat had noticed as she leaped from a sleigh at the door when he was entering the hall before the battle. He saw her too when he began his lecture, and the beaming eyes were turned upon him. Alas! the beaming eyes were now covered with their heavy lids, and the pretty girl was asleep. To add to his confusion and distress, Nathaniel saw that his friend of the supper was among the audience, and was broad awake.

At last the final word of the discourse was pronounced, and the released audience began to melt away as rapidly as possible. Nat sat upon the platform with downcast eyes, utterly miserable.

"Our audiences, sir," Mr. Fullager explained with grave politeness, "are accustomed to lectures of about three-quarters of an hour in length. You have occupied an hour and a half. They are early people here, and they make their arrangements accordingly. You will therefore not attribute the premature departure of some of our citizens to any want of respect for you. I have no doubt they all enjoyed the lecture very much."

"It was remarkably instructive," said Mr. Plummer.

Instructive! Nat had intended it for a burst of brilliant and impassioned eloquence, blended with scathing sarcasm.

As they came out Nat heard a young lady say—

"It didn't interest me at all; just not one bit."

"English orators don't amount to anything, I guess," was another commentary which Nat caught in passing. For him the sky seemed to have turned from blue to black, and the moon to have withdrawn her light.

He was sitting in his bedroom cold and wretched. He had got rid of his friends of the committee, and the fire in the stove had got rid of itself, when a tap was heard at the door, and his bald and blue-eyed acquaintance of the supper-table came in. For some unaccountable reason Nat particularly detested this man.

" Come," said his visitor cheerily, and going to the very heart of the subject at once, " you must not be cast down. You are not used to this sort of thing, and you don't understand our people here. In places like this they have forgotten all about the effete aristocracies of Europe, and don't care, as they would say, a snap one way or the other. I suppose an English village audience wouldn't care much for a lecture on the dangers of our Third Term system. Half our Acroceraunian folks have no other notion attaching to England than the thought that your Queen is an excellent woman and a pattern mother. Are you going to try again ? "

" No," said poor Nat bluntly ; " I'm not."

" Well, you know, it isn't every one who can hold an audience. I'm a wretched speaker myself, although I'm a professor. The mistake you English people make—excuse me if I say it—is in thinking that anything will do for us here in the States. Now I am a blunt man, as you see. Can I serve you in any way ? I see you have got on a wrong track, but I think there's something in you, and I love London, so what can I do for you ? "

" You are very kind—but there is nothing."

" Oh, yes, there is. Let me see. I am Professor Clinton, of the University of New Padua ; and I am going home to-morrow —a few hours in the cars. Come and pass a few days at my house, and we'll talk things over. We want all sorts of clever young fellows about our university, and who knows ? Come with me to-morrow."

He clapped Nat on the shoulder : Nat burst into tears.

CHAPTER XXI.

THE soft sunlight of the sweet melancholy Indian summer is already passing like the dream of a poetic renaissance over the woods and fields and waters of the town—the city we should rather say—of New Padua, in one of the middle States of America, when we meet Natty Cramp again. Several months have gone since the scene described in the last chapter, and Nathaniel is settled in New Padua, under the friendly protection of Professor Clinton.

New Padua is a university town. But let not any one be deceived by the name into fancying that New Padua is anything like Oxford, or Bonn, or even for that matter like Cambridge in Massachusetts, where the University of Harvard is situated. New Padua is the seat of what people in England would call a great popular college rather than a university; a college founded by the State, of which it is the educational centre, with special reference to the needs of the somewhat rough and vigorous Western youth who are likely to pour in there. The city of New Padua belongs to a State which not very long ago used to be described as Western, but which the rapid upspringing of communities lying far nearer to the setting sun has converted into a middle State now. The town is very small and very quiet; remarkably intelligent and pleasant. The society, and indeed almost the population, is composed of the professors and officials of the college, with their wives and daughters; the judges and magistrates; the railway authorities; the Federal officials; the students; and the editors of the newspapers. It is a sort of professional population all throughout. The professors of the university are mostly men of mark and high culture. One or two are Germans, one or two Italians; one is French. Of the American professors, two at least bear names distinguished even in Europe, and one of these is our friend Mr. Clinton, who is Professor of Astronomy and is in charge of the Observatory. Like almost all Americans, Professor Clinton is something of a politician. He contributes occasional articles to the *North American Review*, and writes not a little on European affairs in one of the New Padua journals.

It was this latter connection which enabled him to be of

service to Nathaniel. When the young man had been a few
days in his house, and he saw that there was really a certain
amount of literary capacity about him with a great deal of energy,
Clinton obtained for him an engagement on one of the New Padua
papers, told the editor he would find a useful man in Nat provided he worked him hard enough to work all the nonsense out
of him and get pretty quickly down to the good stuff at the
bottom. Thus Professsor Clinton started Nathaniel fairly in a
new career, liking the lad with a sort of good-humoured and half-
contemptuous feeling, and continuing always kind to him. Professor Clinton's house was always open to Nat. Many a night
when Clinton's wife and sister-in-law (he had no children) had
gone to bed, he would start out with Nat for a long walk by the
river, and would listen with kindly tolerance to Nat's theories
and hopes, and ambition and nonsense. Professor Clinton had
made in his own way all the success that was open to him, and
he regarded it modestly, knowing that in the world's eyes it was
not much, but finding it enough for him. It pleased him to do
kind things and to note the human weaknesses of those whom
he served, and Natty's absurdities had a sort of interest for him.

Nat might have been happy enough in New Padua. He did
all manner of work for the paper—reviews of books, descriptive
reports of local events, and leading articles on European affairs
—which latter seemed, to many people in New Padua, to show
quite a wonderful knowledge of the famous personages of the Old
World. His pay was small, but he could live on it and wear
decent clothes. He "boarded" at the "Franklin House" for so
many dollars a week, and had no cares in the way of making the
two ends meet. He went about a good deal; in the pleasant
society of New Padua through the influence of Professor
Clinton's introductions, and was thought by some persons to be
quite a remarkable and promising young man. He was constantly presented to strangers as " Mr. Cramp, one of the editors
of our leading journal," for in most of the American States any
one who contributes regularly to a paper is popularly rated as
one of its editors. He was the equal of anybody; and in New
Padua no one knew anything of his early career in Wigmore
Street. He began to concern himself greatly in State politics,
and already to lay down the law thereupon. He ought to have
been content with himself and happy.

One day, when Nat was at the office of his paper looking over
the "exchanges," he suddenly saw a paragraph in a San
Francisco journal which made him start and flush and tremble
and see the chairs and desks around him flicker and rock in
supernatural fashion. For the paragraph announced that
among the last arrivals in San Francisco were the distinguished English financier and member of Parliament the Hon.

Sir John Challoner, accompanied by his daughter; and then there were a few lines descriptive of the programme of civilities and attentions which the leading financiers and others of San Francisco were preparing for their visitor. In another journal of the same city Nat saw a long leading article about British capital and Californian resources *à propos* of the visit of the eminent British financier.

Poor Nat ! He hardly knew at first whether he felt delight or agony. He hardly knew, to use a vulgar phrase, whether he was on his head or his heels. Perhaps the predominant sense soon became one of pain. *She* was on the same American Continent with him; and he had not got over his insane passion for her one single bit. Was it posssible that they might meet ?—and if they did, would she speak to him as to an equal! He could feel, he could hear, a heavy, distinct throbbing in his head. He looked to the coming weeks now with heart-sickening longing and craven terror.

From that moment he studied the Californian papers with eager curiosity, and was rewarded now and then by a paragraph further reporting the doings of Sir John Challoner—and once by a line, a thrilling line, of " personal " news which concisely set forth that " Miss Challoner, the great English heiress, is said to be the most beautiful Englishwoman who has lately visited the West." Nat seized the sub-editorial scissors, cut this paragraph out, and kept it for himself.

Nat made " copy," however, and rather successful " copy," of the distinguished visitors. He wrote a long account of Sir John Challoner, his wealth, his dignity, his splendid country seat at Durewoods (which Nat described very fully), his town house (which Nat had not seen), and his beautiful and brilliant daughter. Even Professor Clinton was taken in and assumed that Nat must have been among the intimate friends of the Challoners in London. Another occurrence greatly raised Nathaniel's credit as an authority on European affairs. This was " The Cameron Affair," which seemed to New Paduan eyes likely to embroil Europe. It was the case of the gallant Captain Cameron, who, having in some way fallen into dispute with his Carlist chiefs, had flung up his commission, and was returning home in disgust when he happened unluckily to fall into the hands of the other side, and was in a fair way to be shot as a spy. Would England claim him as a *Civis Romanus?* Would she look tamely, aye, basely, on and submit to the murder of her gallant though mistaken son? This was the question which Nathaniel put in tones of varying indignation day after day in the pages of the New Paduan journal. Natty wrote columns about Captain Cameron, and was rather sorry when the news

P

came one day that the gallant Legitimist had been allowed to
return quietly home.

It was a great thing for Nat, however, and he made the very
most of it, speaking, when the news of the captive's release
came, as if it must have been the articles in the New Paduan
journal which, flashed across the cable wires to Madrid, had
effected the release of the hero.

"I was glad to say a word for poor Cameron," Nat would
observe loftily to all listeners in turn. "He pressed me very
hard to take service with him under Don Carlos. He was kind
enough to think highly of my military capacity; but of course
my Republican principles rendered that impossible. He is a
man of ancient family, Cameron, an honest fellow and a thorough
soldier."

So Nathaniel was winning quite a reputation in New Padua
as a man who had been pretty intimately conerned in the great
political movements of Europe, and he began to take on airs of
authority even with Professor Clinton.

One memorable day Nathaniel walked from the office of his
journal towards the university grounds. These stood on an
elevated plain a little outside the town, a simply laid out enclosure with broad oblong blocks of building, bare almost as a
barrack, but deriving a certain picturesqueness from the situation. For standing on almost any spot of the university grounds
one could look on the river winding between the hills and bluffs,
and dotted here and there with little islets, each feathered and
tufted with trees. The peculiarity of the scene was that the
town was set back from the river and sheltered in between the
bluffs which made the river's bank, and an inland range of low
and rolling hills. So when you stood upon the university
grounds and turned your back upon the university buildings
you saw only the river, lonely, with no sign of growing civiliza-
tion on its banks, looking as it must have looked when the red
man shot along it in his canoe. The very soul and spirit of
solitude might at certain soft sweet evening hours have seemed
to abide there.

The melancholy beauty of the Indian summer was on the
foliage and the water and in the sky this evening when Nat
Cramp entered the university grounds. As he passed along a
glimpse of the river attracted him, and he stood at the edge of
the collegiate demesne and looked upon the scene. Its beauty
touched him. He did not in general think much about inanimate
nature; his own concerns occupied him far too much. His little
self-conceits and strivings and humiliations filled his eyes and
blinded them against the charms of trees and water, skies, stars,
and flowers, as dust might have done. His poetry had always
been only egotistical emotion put into inflated rhythm, and his

eloquence was phrase. But he was for the moment stolen from himself by the quiet charm of that scene. The river flowing slowly eastward seemed to speak to him somehow of home, and there began to descend into his soul, mingled up with much feeling of baffled egotism and of hopeless love, a kind of salutary sense that he, Nathaniel Cramp, was in general little better than a sham and an Ass.

How far this healing mood might have grown upon him is not likely to be known by us. A friendly hand touched him on the shoulder and startled him.

" I have news for you," said Professor Clinton, his large blue eyes smiling benignly. " Your friends the Challoners are coming to New Padua."

Had Professor Clinton announced to him that his crimes were discovered, and that the English detectives were in New Padua to arrest him, and had he committed any crimes to merit arrest, poor Nathaniel could not have looked more confused. He had now and then contemplated this as a possibility. New Padua lay not far out of the track of the great Western highway, and it was a place that strangers liked to visit. Nat had had secret visions at night of Marie Challoner coming to New Padua, and of his meeting her there—he no longer a London barber, no longer the mere son of a Durewoods housekeeper, but the son of his own works, and a rising citizen of the rising university town— a man who might hold himself as good as the best. But when the event seemed close at hand his nerves were shaken. Would Sir John Challoner speak to him? Would he tell people who Nat was? Would Marie call him " Natty," and bring him, *coram publico*, news of his mother, and treat him as a kindly, proud English girl treats the son of her old servant ? And the unfortunate lad felt, amid all these ignoble considerations, that he loved her more wildly than ever. The one manly, unegotistic, refined emotion of his whole nature was just his absurd passion for her.

He stammered out some awkward word or two expressive of delight.

" Yes, they are coming to stay for a few days with our president " (the president of the university), " and they are going to see all our sights. Professor Benjamin is to tell Sir John Challoner all about the mining resources of our State, and show him everything. You didn't know of this before ? "

" No," said Nat simply ; " how could I have known ? I didn't see anything in the papers."

" I thought they might have written to you, perhaps.

" No, they haven't written—yet."

" But they know you are here, I suppose ? "

" Well, I don't quite know," Nat answered slowly. " You see

I left England rather suddenly, and my people didn't half like my coming out here. I was always a Republican. I resigned my rank in the Volunteers because I couldn't bear arms in the service of a monarchy, you know," the young Republican added proudly.

" But why shouldn't you bear arms in the service of your own Government and your own country ? "

" Because I am a Republican, as I have told you."

" Stuff and nonsense! What's the use of being a Republican when you haven't a Republic ? "

" I remember poor Cameron saying just the same thing to me one day," Nat remarked with a forced smile, " when he was pressing me to take service under Don Carlos with him. But he couldn't persuade *me*. A principle is a principle. So I came out here."

" And very good of you, too," said the blue-eyed Professor, with a smile; "just like the others."

" The others ! What others ? "

" Lafayette, you know, and Kosciusko—and the rest; don't you see ? "

Nat did not see, and did not like that sort of thing.

" The president's going to have a grand reception for them," said Clinton. " I mean for your friends the Challoners, Cramp, not for your lamented predecessors Lafayette and Kosciusko; and you are to have an invitation."

" Am I ? " said Nat, with a growing redness and dampness ascending to his very hair; for every other emotion whatever was for the moment absorbed in the wild joy of the thought. " Then I shall certainly see her and speak to her."

" Yes, I took care of that. I told him that you were a personal friend of the Challoners, and that of course they would expect to see you   I didn't do wrong in that, did I ? "

For Nat's face betrayed the most unmistakable embarrassment.

" No; oh no. But I think, you know, I would rather nothing was said about me until—just until we meet. You see I don't know Sir John so very well, and I'm not so absolutely certain that he likes me—and he's an odd sort of man—and I know her much better."

" Oho," said the Professor, prolonging the word into quite a cadence of meaning—" is that the way ?   Now I begin to see—but you don't want to avoid them ? "

" No! no! no ! " Nat exclaimed with the most genuine eagerness, a horrible alarm seizing him that perhaps Clinton would tell the president not to invite him.   " I want to see her—them, I mean—of all things.   Oh, she is a lovely girl!   And she was so kind to me ! " he added in an involuntary triumph of his better nature and of grateful feeling.

" Well, well! all right," the genial Professor said. " You'll meet them; and the president, you know, isn't likely to say anything about you beforehand, for he hardly knows you, and he's all full of his own concerns; and I could give Benjamin or Benjamin's wife a hint if you like that you'd rather see how the old man was disposed towards you before you were brought back to his recollection. Yes! I'll give Mrs. Benjamin a hint. She's a bright little woman, and she'll understand the whole thing."

Professor Clinton had found a ready explanation of Nat's embarrassment. A good-looking, cleverish romantic lad, very poor; a pretty and doubtless romantic girl, very rich; a father purse-proud and great in finance and Parliament—it is easy to see why the lad should be at once longing to meet the girl and a little alarmed about the father. He whispered his ingenious romance to his wife and her sister, and to Mrs. Benjamin, the wife of the mineralogist, and it was generally understood that there were reasons why Mr. Cramp did not wish to be brought immaturely under the notice of his distinguished countryman, but that these reasons did not imply any rooted antipathy between Mr. Cramp and his distinguished countryman's daughter. The result of all this was that at least half a dozen ladies of New Padua had their interest in the approaching reception at the university considerably quickened by the hope of seeing a page from a living romance brought under their eyes there.

The day came. It was known through New Padua that Sir John and Miss Challoner had arrived at the house of the president the previous evening, but were not to be, so to speak, on exhibition until the reception in the university rooms. Society in New Padua seldom spread itself out much. People had pleasant evenings in each other's houses, where they ate ice-creams even in the depth of winter, and apples, and drank tea, and looked at engravings, and had bright, genial conversation— such genuine conversation, fair interchange of ideas on letters and art and things in general, as one only reads of now in England; and they went home early. The ladies came very plainly dressed on most of these occasions, and if a lady who had walked with her husband from her own home appeared in the drawing-room in her hat or bonnet nobody considered it odd or unseemly. Only on rare occasions did the gentlemen come in evening dress. But this reception of the English travellers at the university rooms was to be quite an exceptional thing, and every lady who had been to Europe that year, or who had got any dresses home from Paris, was delighted to have an opportunity of making a little display. Really the feminine beauty of New Padua was well worth looking at, even in its undress. Perhaps it ought

not to be called New Paduan beauty, for there were no born New
Paduans yet grown up. Twenty years ago there was no such
place as New Padua. The university had gathered a community
about it from all quarters. The principal judge and his wife
were natives of the State indeed, but came from its largest town
a hundred miles away. The president of the university came
from New York. His wife, still a fine woman, though passing
her prime, was from Maryland. Professor Benjamin was from
Ohio; his wife had drawn her early breath within sight of
Boston Common. Our friend Clinton was a Vermonter, married
to a lady from Illinois. The various foreign professors already
referred to had some of them foreign wives; and the editor of
the journal to which Mr. Cramp was attached had once been
United States consul at Athens, and had brought home to New
Padua a countrywoman of Sappho as his wife.

Nat was invited to accompany the Clintons on the momentous
evening, but he preferred to glide into the rooms of the
reception alone. Need it be said that he dressed with care? He
had always saved and scraped enough out of his earnings to keep
himself well dressed, but his pride was his evening costume,
which he had hitherto had no occasion of displaying in New
Padua. In his bedroom by the ineffective light of a kerosene
lamp he took this evening costume out and surveyed it with a
melancholy affection. When all his preparations were nearly
made for leaving London he indulged in the wild luxury of
ordering a full suit of evening costume from a first-class tailor.
Then he believed himself going out to conquer the New World.
It did not seem unlikely that the costume would display itself at
the dinner table of the White House at Washington. It appeared
certain that it must delight the eyes of many a brilliant assembly
crowded in lighted halls to hear the young Republican orator
from the Old World. Alas! Nathaniel had never yet had a
chance of displaying that well-made suit of clothes. In the
States there is no uniform proper to lecturing, and audiences
rather mock themselves of the white tie and the dress coat—
despite the singular theory so devotedly maintained in England
that American men always wear dress coats. There was something Nat thought strange, significant, weird, fateful, in his
putting on that costume for the first time that night. What
might not that portend?

Nat studied himself fondly and yet critically in the glass.
He certainly was not a bad-looking fellow, and he looked
browner, straighter, more independent, and less sheepish than
he was wont to do under the burthen of his detested occupation
in England. The coat was superb; the trousers were faultless.
As to the vest there was so little of it that it hardly called for
remark; but the expanse of snowy and glossy shirt front was

unexceptionable. The little studs of pink coral had a sort of poetic or romantic aspect, and the flower in the buttonhole spoke of emotion.˙ Natty felt almost as he used to feel when he was new to the uniform of the West Pimlico Volunteers, and the parades in Hyde Park and on Wimbledon Common, under the eyes of royalty.

It was a pity that he could not call a hansom cab, leap into it, and rattle up to the hall of the reception. But there were no hansom cabs in New Padua, nor as yet even street cars, and people who had not vehicles of their own went afoot into society. In winter they put on " rubbers," but it was not winter as yet, and the night was fine and the roads were dry. So Natty issued forth in his shiny boots and with a heart quick beating. Would she know him; would she recognise him; would she be friendly? Would Sir John snub him and let every one know of poor Nat's humble beginnings?

The gravel of the walks within the university enclosure was echoing everywhere to wheels and hoofs and hurrying feet as Nat entered the grounds. The reception was to take place in the library, which was blazing with lights : its windows were squares of flame against the night. Many guests were going in, and the sounds from within indicated a crowd already. All the graduates had had invitations, and such of their female relatives as happened to be resident in New Padua, and so there was a goodly gathering. Nat had remained purposely late. As he set his foot upon the steps of the outer door a terrible thought pierced him. Suppose he had come too late; and that she had already withdrawn? Or suppose she was unwell or fatigued, and could not make her appearance at all?

With a freshly perturbed heart he entered the library, greeted as he entered with a friendly shake of the hand by the president and his wife, both of whom shook hands as a matter of course with every one, and neither of whom at the moment remembered who Nat was. Nat was not sorry for that. He glided past into the crowd. He actually passed Sir John Challoner, passed him quite closely, brushed against him, and was not recognised or even seen. Sir John was engaged in animated conversation with two or three professors and a judge. Nat breathed more freely.

Had he had time for such emotions he might have wondered at the transformed appearance of the library; at the lights, the flowers, the green wreaths and festoons of leaves—above all, the company. Could these be the quiet and unpretentious dames and demoiselles of New Padua, these ladies of the floating silks, the jewels, the bracelets, the laces, the wonderful structures of hair? Nat felt doubtful whether he should be justified in speaking to Professor Clinton's sister-in-law, unless she should previously recognise him—she looked such a different sort of personage in a blue silk dress and a train, and with white arms bare. True he had often seen the white arms still more bare than that, when she was engaged in her simple and undisguised occupation of helping to make bread and piecrust, and to cut up apples in Professor Clinton's modest household. What a grand lady she looks now, Nat thought. But indeed, she looked a lady always, he said to himself; and in her home of late he always called her "Minnie" as her folks and friends did.

While he was thinking whether it would be right to call her Minnie in her blue silk, and while he was still casting uneasy eager eyes this way and that, it suddenly seemed to him as though the lights danced and twinkled, and the floor rocked, and some heavy, dizzying sounds were dinning in his ears. For in one of the recesses in the library—a recess set out with a table, whereon were engravings and photographs, and gaily ornamented with ferns and flowers—there at last he saw Miss Challoner. She was seated, and was looking, or affecting to look, at photographs, and Professor Benjamin was acting as showman; and a thrill of absurd delight went through Nat's heart as he saw that it was Professor Benjamin and not a young unmarried man. Mrs. Benjamin was there too, and round-eyed little Miss Benjamin. It was clear that Miss Challonor had withdrawn for the time with these two or three friends from the central throng. She looked weary, Natty thought, and *distraite*, and very pale. But how beautiful she seemed to him, with the dark hair thick around her neck, and coming somewhat low upon her forehead ; and the eyelashes long and dark, under which now her eyes were hidden !

"Isn't she real splendid !" a youth near Nat asked of another.

"I expected to see an English girl more ruddy-like," the other replied, a young Western giant overlooking the crowd. "She looks proud and stuck-up rather."

"Mrs. Benjamin says she's just lovely," the other rejoined emphatically, and using "lovely" as English people employ 'amiable."

"She don't seem like it," the young giant remarked. Natty turned round and glared on him, but the young giant did not observe the glare.

Now, Nat said to himself, was his time—now or never ! Now, while she was thus secluded and only the kind Benjamins were near. He pushes his way through the crowd ; he is near ; he is nearer ; he is within the recess ; he is close to the table ; the Benjamins already see him, and smile on him, and interchange significant glances with each other. Nat's forehead is hot, and his tongue is dry, and falters ; but there is no escape now, and he desperately says "Miss Challoner !" and Lady

Disdain looks up and turns the deep light of her eyes on him.

A moment of doubt and wonder, and then "Natty!" comes from between the surprised and parted lips, and Dear Lady Disdain, all astonished but kindly, holds out her friendly hand to the palpitating youth.

"You didn't expect to see me here," the tremulous, delighted Nathaniel said.

"No, we have been so long away from home, and your mother did not know when I saw her last. But I am glad to see you, Natty—Mr. Cramp, I mean." Lady Disdain corrected herself with a gleam of brightness coming into her smile.

Then she bade Nat to tell her all about his adventures, and said her father would be glad to see him, and in a moment was conversing quietly with him like an old friend. But in the intervening moment the Benjamins had seen enough. For nothing could be more clear to them than the fact that the first sight of Nat had filled Miss Challoner with emotion. Confused and palpitating as Nathaniel was, she was far more obviously and deeply moved. The colour rushed at first into her cheeks, and her voice failed her, and then her eyes drooped and her lips trembled, and Mrs. Benjamin declared afterwards that she saw the tears come into the dear young lady's eyes, and that she thought she was then and there going to faint. Marie did not faint however, but recovered her composure very soon. Yet was kindly Mrs. Benjamin not wholly mistaken. For the unexpected sight of poor Nat had been to Marie like the arising of a ghost from some far dim grave. It was not Nathaniel Cramp she saw, but the place, the past, the memories of which Nat's was a chance and incidental figure, yet charged with all the full force of irresistible association. She saw Durewoods and her home and her girlhood; she saw again her dreams and longings; she saw youth and emotion and the hope of love, and Dione Lyle, and Dione Lyle's warnings, and the hollow in the woods—and Christmas Pembroke!—and at the same moment there came on her, drawn by an inseparable link of contrast, the shadow of the life that was awaiting her in London, the marriage, with no love in it on her side, the barren ambition, the dull self-repression, the drilled and disciplined heart, and all the unsatisfying succession of empty, monotonous to-morrows. All this and much more came rushing on Marie as she saw the poor lad from Durewoods standing there before her, and her colour did deepen, and her lips did tremble, and it may even be that a tear did start into her eyes.

But a very pretty little chapter of romance began to circulate in the library of the New Padua University that night.

CHAPTER XXII.

LOOKING THROUGH THE GOLDEN GATE.

MARIE CHALLONER had seen many strange, delightful, wonderful sights in the New World before she arrived at New Padua. She had looked upon Niagara, and had crossed the Mississippi; had been among the Rocky Mountains and passed through the superb canons, and along the edges of precipices having more than Alpine steepness and grandeur, as her way led her through the gorges of the Sierra Nevada, in California. She had watched the soft Pacific steeped in its sun-streaked mist as it heaved slowly to and fro through that Golden Gate of which she had dreamed so much. From the sandhills of San Francisco, and from the balconies of the Cliff House where the visitors crowd to watch the never diminishing swarm of seals barking and struggling on the rocks, she had looked across those sleepy waters, and in sight of the Pacific remembered Durewoods. The Golden Gate had a marvellous fascination for her. When her journey turned back eastwards again, she seemed as if she were parting from some dear familiar scene of childhood.

Sir John Challoner could not understand the change in his daughter's manner. She was alternately listless and satirical. Sometimes it seemed as if nothing could interest her. She lay back in her seat in their "palace car," and for hours together hardly looked at anything. Again she would sometimes suddenly engage in conversation, and talk and laugh and say sharp bright things in a way which much perplexed him. A sort of distance seemed to be opening between him and her. It made him sometimes angry and sometimes gloomy to observe this. "I suppose children are always ungrateful," the successful man of the world said to himself, and he sometimes almost wished that he never had a daughter. At least he sometimes wished that he had come out on his journey alone; he often wished that he was back again with his offices and his City companies, his clubs and the House of Commons. Then, when he saw Marie occa‧ sionally looking so bright and handsome, and so much admired, he was delighted with her and proud of her, and felt terror-stricken at the thought of her possibly sinking into bad health. She was always sweet and good in her manner to him—only not so affectionate, not so confidential, as she used to be. It was not the same thing—and why?

"I am sorry to leave San Francisco because of the Golden Gate," she said languidly to him one day when they were in the railway on their return towards the east.

" San Francisco disappointed me," her father remarked. " I didn't expect to see it such a sandy and dusty place. It seems like a little London set in sand."

" I don't care about San Francisco, but I love the bay, and Saucelito, and the rocky islands, and the Golden Gate."

" Why the Golden Gate, Marie? "

" Perhaps because it reminds me of Durewoods, dear."

Sir John smiled. " How on earth can anything near San Francisco remind you of Durewoods? "

Marie hesitated a moment, and then said, without replying to his question—

" How strange it was to sit in the balcony of that hotel—the Cliff House, wasn't it?—and watch those seals perpetually scrambling up the rocks and then plunging down into the waves, and always barking and restless! Some of them never seemed to keep quiet. One would scramble and fight his way up to the very top of a rock and then only plash down again. They seemed to me very like human creatures—only, I suppose, every one has said that already."

" Yes; people find out resemblances in particular seals to particular men. Don't you remember that they told us one seal was called after —— " a well-known American politician whom Sir John named.

" Oh, yes; and I think I detected several striking likenesses to people whom we know at home. But it was not that I meant; I was thinking of mortal ambition and projects, and that sort of thing. Almost everybody is trying to scramble up to something; and when he gets there he will want to get to some other place—unless he splashes down before he is halfway up and disappears altogether; and the human race, too, is noisy all the time. Why not rest in the sunlight, or be happy to sink down, down in the soft waves? "

" I didn't know that you were moralizing so much when watching the seals; I dare say I could have helped out your comparison."

" The moralising was much too simple and commonplace to disturb you with then—I feel rather ashamed of it. It is too like Sturm's Reflections."

" Still you have not told me why the sight of the Pacific reminded you of Durewoods; I don't see anything to remind you."

Had Marie been evading the question? Not consciously, perhaps. But now, when she did answer, it was with a little hesitation.

" I think because I was on the hill at Durewoods one day, looking out over the bay, when that poor boy, Christmas Pembroke, began to tell me of the Golden Gate. I believe I told him then I didn't care much to see it ever. I wish I hadn't said that."

This was a particularly irksome turn for the conversation to take, so far as Sir John was concerned. They had a little chamber or compartment of the palace-car all to themselves, and Marie had taken off her hat and was leaning back with her head and her ruffling hair against the crimson velvet that covered the back of the seat. She looked strangely young and almost childlike to her father at that moment. He could not tell why. Perhaps it was the half-languid, half-impatient way in which she moved her head from side to side, regardless of the condition of her hair, which gave him the impression.

"Why do you wish you hadn't said it, dear?" he asked tentatively, and in something like the tone one might use to a child.

"Because it must have seemed so cold and careless, and he loved the place so much, poor fellow!"

"Why poor fellow, Marie?"

Sir John's smile was now a good deal forced, and he studied her expression with sudden anxiety.

"I don't know. I suppose because he's going to be married. There will be no more cakes and ale, I suppose, when he is married."

"I presume he likes it," Sir John said, with affected carelessness.

"I suppose so. Is he not very young to be married.

"N—no, I don't think so," Sir John said, with an appearance of easy deliberation. "I rather think not, Marie. I think he must be older than I was when I married."

"Yes, that is true. But then you married very young. And you were very happy?"

"Very happy, dear."

"I hope he will be happy."

Then there was a pause, and it may well be imagined that Sir John Challoner did not feel greatly inclined to renew the talk on the former ground. He thought long and deeply over his daughter's words, and a new fear came on him.

Meanwhile he had in his pocket a letter from Christmas Pembroke of which he had said nothing to his daughter. The letter had only reached him the very morning of their departure from San Francisco. It was short, friendly, and melancholy, written soon after Christmas had been to Durewoods, thanking Sir John for his many acts of kindness, but expressing a desire to leave England, and a wish that Sir John would, if convenient, release him from whatever engagements they had together, and so allow him to go at once.

Nothing could now happen better, it seemed to Sir John,

than that Christmas should leave England and betake himself
to Japan or any place out of the way of some of his friends. A
terrible suspicion was beginning to pass through Sir John's
mind. He had before this feared and guarded against the possibility, remote and wild though it then seemed, of his daughter's
coming to take too deep an interest in the young man. To guard
against this possiblity he had deliberately deceived her. Now
the fear struck painfully to him that his precaution had been
taken too late and that his deceit had been in vain. He was
enraged with himself—almost with her, and certainly with Christmas. He chafed to think of the possibility of such a boy, without name or money, or any place whatever in society, interposing
for a moment between his daughter and a marriage with a man
like Ronald Vidal.

Especially was he made angry by the simple directness of a
short postscript to Christmas Pembroke's letter :—

"I have heard with a great deal of pain that there is an
absurd story about my being engaged to a young lady here in
London. I need not tell *you* how utterly untrue that is, but I
should take it as a great kindness if you would contradict the
story whenever you have an opportunity of doing so, with deli-
cacy, of course. You will understand how painful such a foolish
story is to me."

This was poor Christmas's almost despairing appeal. It was
written in the sad hope, that if, owing to any misunderstanding
or any false idea of thus preventing the truth from being discovered, Sir John had allowed Marie to be deceived by a wrong
guess or a foolish rumour, he would at least undeceive her as to
that—now that Christmas was not likely to see her any more.
It made Sir John feel doubly annoyed, this throwing on him
an insufferable responsibility. It seemed like forcing him to
remember and admit that he had told a falsehood. "I must get
this fellow out of the way at all risks before we return to London,"
was the resolve in his mind which made him compress his lips
as he studied his daughter's face and wondered whether his
terrible suspicions could really be well founded.

"We may be looking forward to London already, Marie,"
her father said after a while, fearing that the journey was weari-
some to her.

"So soon, dear? Oh, surely not. Our holiday can't be
coming to an end yet?"

"It hasn't been much of a holiday to you, Marie, I am
afraid."

"Dear, I have enjoyed it very much all the time; I don't
think I want it ever to end."

"You seem to be weary somehow, and not to enjoy things."

"And you are hurrying home to dull and dreary London on

my account? I know I am driving you home. Will you stay
longer here if I show that I really do enjoy everything? Only
promise me and you shall see ! "

"I am a busy man, Marie; I can't afford long holidays.
Don't you want to return home at all? "

"No, dear. At least not to London ; I am very well at home
here. Home?—that is you and I—is it not? We are here, papa,
and remarkably well off, I think."

"And Ronald? " Sir John tried to seem easy and playful.
Marie coloured a little.

"Ronald is very busy and very happy, I dare say—and he is
a good kind creature," she added, hastily.

"He is giving up everything for you, Marie," Sir John could
not help saying."

"And I have nothing to give up for him. If I had—— "

"Well, dear ? "

"I suppose I should not be so magnanimous as he."

"Have you answered his last letter, Marie? "

"Not yet, dear, but I will when we stop at some place; only
I don't well know what to say. It's of no use doing guide-book
work. Guide-books in print are bad enough, but in writing!
And no one cares to hear about anybody's travels. I didn't
listen to half the things poor Christmas—Mr. Pembroke, I mean
—used to tell me at first, though I see now that he described
places wonderfully well. Did you like Miss Jansen, papa? "

"I hardly noticed her."

"I wish you had; I should like you to have told me what
you thought of her. Was it not strange that he never should
have told Miss Lyle? "

Sir John was glad when they reached Sacramento, the first
city at which they were to make any stay on their way eastward.
From Sacramento he wrote to Christmas Pembroke, and Marie
wrote to Ronald Vidal. Thus they came in process of time to
New Padua, where they met Nat Cramp, and where Marie's
·reception of him diffused the little romance we have already
mentioned.

How proud that reception made Mr. Cramp no words can
tell. When he had been seen to sit beside Miss Challoner and
talk to her, he walked the rooms with the air of one who belongs
to another world. He went boldly up to Mrs. Clinton's sister
and called her " Minnie " in the full face of her blue silk; and
he patronised her and everybody, and put on airs at once romantic
and lordly. He alternately looked or tried to look pensive and
sentimental, like one of Angelica Kauffmann's heroes, or proud
and grand. Poor Nat was always ready to soar from abject
depression into ridiculous exaltation. He delighted to be questioned about Miss Challoner, and to put the questions aside with
a mysterious and somewhat of a wounded manner.

" Who is your friend, Marie ? " Sir John said to his daughter as they were leaving the university rooms—" your young English friend ? I can't remember his face, but I know I have seen him before."

" Papa ? Not to know Natty Cramp ! "

" My dear, who in the world is Natty Cramp ? "

" Oh, for shame—to forget Sarah Cramp, our faithful old Sarah Cramp—of Durewoods, you know."

" Was that old Mrs. Cramp's son—that young man ? "

" Yes, dear, that is Natty himself."

" He has greatly changed, improved, I think—he used to be an awkward, sheepish looking cub, Marie—was it not so ? "

" Oh, no, dear, at least not very awkward, and not at all a cub. A good poor fellow; clever, I think, in a sort of way ; and shy and rather ridiculous; but I used to like him. You must really promise me that you will try to do something for him here, papa. You will speak to somebody, won't you ? He looks upon me as a sort of protector of his, and I should like to be so. I am afraid I rather like to play the part of a lady patroness."

Sir John was glad to have a chance of pleasing her.

" Anything I can do, Marie, I'll do gladly, and I suppose we may be civil to him out here. Nobody knows, I dare say—— "

" Knows what, dear ? "

" Well, about his mother, and his early condition, and all that."

" Oh, nobody would care here," Marie said, enthusiastically. " Here there is perfect equality. A man here is a man, and only a man. *He* told me. He says he is happy here because he is the equal of any man—and I should be happy too if I were he."

Sir John smiled.

" Very good, Marie—only, for all that, I think we will keep the mother and the hairdresser's shop to ourselves. *He* won't be sorry for that you may be sure."

Sir John and Marie were waiting for the carriage of their host and hostess, which was to carry them to the private residence of the president of the university across the grounds. Meanwhile the president himself came up, and at the same moment Mr. Cramp.

" Papa, this is Mr. Cramp," Marie said. I think you hardly caught his name when you met to-night before."

Nathaniel bowed with dignity. Even the haughty father could not abash him now. But to his surprise the father proved not to be haughty.

" Mr. Cramp, I am greatly pleased to meet you," said Sir John, extending a friendly hand. " You will forgive my not remembering you to-night at first. I have been seeing so many new faces lately, and I never expected to meet an old acquaintance here."

"Mr. Cramp is one of our rising young citizens, sir," the president good-naturedly observed. "We mean to be proud of him, sir, some day. I hear a great deal of Mr. Cramp through my esteemed friend Professor Clinton."

Mr. Cramp murmured his thankfulness and delight.

"Professor Clinton, sir," said the kindly president, "is coming to breakfast with me to-morrow, Mr. Cramp, to meet our distinguished friend Sir John Challoner. If you will give us the pleasure of your company, Mr. Cramp, we shall be delighted."

Oh, happy, happy Nathaniel! The noise of wheels scraping up the gravel, a light touch of gloved hands, a sensation blended strangely of dark eyes, rustling skirts, the sound of a carriage door shut to—and Nat was standing on the threshold gazing up to the stars at the end, or nearly so, of the happiest night he had ever spent.

Nat was not alone, however. The president was still there, he and his wife being bound to stay until all their guests had taken their leave.

"I shall be pleased to present you to my wife, sir," the president said; "she will be delighted to know you. I am sorry to say that hitherto we know you only by hearsay. We have only gentlemen at breakfast to-morrow; but after breakfast you must come and see the ladies of our family, and Miss Challoner, I have no doubt, will be pleased to see you."

Up came Professor Clinton and his womankind.

"Cramp, my boy," said the blue-eyed Professor, "will you take my wife and Minnie home? I want to arrange one or two things here with the president; but if you wait for me at our place I shan't be long, and we'll have a walk and a star-gaze together."

Nat had proposed to himself a walk round and round the president's house, and a star-gaze for some particular window which he could fancy to be Miss Challoner's. But he was so happy this night that he could have done anything with pleasure. There was a certain soothing sensation, too, in the thought of walking home with these two kindly, simple women, in whose eyes Nat knew that he was by this time established as a sort of hero of romance. They looked very pretty, both the women, with their heads and shoulders enveloped in soft and fleecy white "clouds"—the time for furs and overshoes had not come as yet. Miss Minnie carefully, and without any affectation of indifference, gathered up her blue silk all round, and with fond deliberation arranged it over her arms so that its skirts should not by any chance descend to touch the gravel and kiss the earth. Thus kilted, and with a great display of white petticoat, she gave her arm to Nathaniel. Ladies in Chicago and New York may be prodigal of their dresses, and Saratoga may be reckless about a blue silk once or twice worn, but in the small and inland towns the lasses do not find that blue silks come home to them every day; and they are almost as careful of their little fineries as a Swiss lady might be. Nathaniel's lofty soul was a little disdainful of Minnie's neat and careful adjustment. Despite his principles of equality and of democracy, his admiration and homage went up more readily to ladies who had no need to think about saving their silks, and who moreover went home in carriages at night when their revels were ended.

CHAPTER XXIII.

NAT IS CRUSHED.

THE few days that the Challoners spent in New Padua promised to be the most delightful that Nathaniel Cramp had ever known. Nay, they were, until the close, an ideal time to him. They soothed every vanity, gratified every sense, and inflated him with the most fantastic hopes. He could hardly believe his senses when he found himself one of a small company of men brought together to breakfast with Sir John Challoner. When Sir John appealed to him at breakfast once or twice to confirm his recollection or impression of something in London, Nathaniel felt his ears tingle with pride. Sir John was particularly gracious, partly because Marie had asked him to be so, and partly because, since Nathaniel had been somehow assigned to them as an old acquaintance, he thought it judicious to make the most of him, and so avert any suspicion of Nat's lowly rank. Sir John himself was far too new a comer into the upper air of society not to be a little nervous about his companionships. Therefore he was specially friendly with Nat. Once he referred to "my friend Cramp." Nat felt his heart sing with joy.

Nat often saw Marie. Wherever her father and she went now he was always, and as a matter of course, invited to make one of the party. His consideration in New Padua begun to go up immensely. His natural hesitancy and alarm when he heard that the Challoners were coming there was now misinterpreted in a sense particularly delightful for him. He was considered to be remarkably modest and reticent about his intimacy with the British aristocracy, for of course Sir John Challoner was popularly regarded as a man from out the very heart of the British aristocracy. Many people called his daughter Lady Challoner or

Q

Lady Marie Challoner, and there was some discussion as to whether it was proper to address her father as the Honourable or Right Honourable Sir John Challoner. Natty explained all that. He had not sprung from the servants' hall or curled hair in a West End saloon for nothing. He acquired new consideration by his precise knowledge of the manner in which British titles are distributed and applied. If the Prince of Wales had paid a visit to New Padua soon after, it would have been the confident expectation of most persons that Mr. Cramp would prove to be an old and intimate friend of his Royal Highness. To do Sir John Challoner justice, he had a kind of idea that it might serve Nat in New Padua, where he assumed that the lad was about to stay for the rest of his natural life, if he was understood to have been on terms of friendship with great British financiers. It would probably help Nat, and it could not, Sir John thought, harm *him* in any way.

Marie, on the other hand, was moved solely by simple kindliness and good feeling towards the young man who used to be a sort of humble playfellow of hers when she was a little girl, as yet uninstructed as to differences of rank and social state, and who was the only son of a faithful old servant. She was undisguisedly friendly with him. Everything, therefore, conspired in Nat's favour, or rather conspired against him.

One day, when the stay of the Challoners was nearly at its end, there was an excursion to some mineral treasure or other which was giving evidence of its existence near New Padua, and of which Professor Benjamin was particularly proud. It was but a short distance, and everybody walked. Some dozen or more of professors and professors' wives were there, with a sprinkling of daughters. They followed the windings of the river. Nathaniel placed himself resolutely by Marie's side and walked with her. There were two or three others with her also ; Professor Clinton, for example, and Mrs. Benjamin, and little round-eyed Miss Benjamin ; and therefore Sir John did not mind his daughter having Nathaniel as one of her escort. Probably Nat walked rather quickly. Somehow or other, no one could tell why, the remainder of the escort dropped behind, and at one winding of the path Marie found herself alone with Nat. She was glad of a moment's opportunity to ask him all about his prospects, that she might bring a full and true report to his mother ; and she had not hitherto had any chance of making a direct inquiry.

Nat's heart beat too violently, when glancing backward he saw that they were alone, to allow him readily to begin the conversation. But Marie saved him all embarrassment by beginning at once—

" Then you are settled here for good, Natty ? "

" I don't know that, Miss Challoner ; I like this place, and the people are kind to me—but it is narrow and small. Not much of a career here, Miss Challoner, for a man's ambition; and in this country one feels that he has a career open to him if he has intellect and courage," Nat added, with careless grandeur.

"Oh, I didn't mean New Padua. I didn't suppose you would stay here always, although it seems a delightful little place. So full of quiet and simplicity; and people only caring about books and education, and not about making money and getting on in the world. But I know, of course, that men must have ambition" (and Natty for the moment whimsically presented himself to Marie's mind in the form of one of those seals swarming up and down the rocks near San Francisco), "and I only meant that you were settled in the States."

"I don't know that I can be called settled anywhere yet, miss —I mean Miss Challoner. I should like to make a name and a fortune, and go back then to Europe; I should like to show England what manhood can do elsewhere."

Marie was amused in a pitying sort of way by Nat's idea about astonishing England's weak nerves in the person of her unprized son, successful in a more appreciative land. But she was in a soft and indulgent mood, and in a strange sort of way she seemed almost to cling to Nathaniel Cramp for the sake of the memories that his presence brought.

"I am so glad to hear that you are likely to do well," she said, gravely. "We heard rather discouraging accounts at first; your mother was greatly alarmed."

"Things did look bad at first," and Nat remembered, with a twinge, that the first difficulties had overwhelmed him with as unreasonable a depression as the first little movement upwards had elated him with an absurd self-confidence. "They did look bad at first. The Americans with all their many great qualities —which no one is more proud to recognise than I am"—Nat interjected oratorically—"are a little jealous of strangers. Not unnaturally, perhaps."

"I should not have thought that. People always tell us that they are anxious to get all manner of help from the Old World."

"In a manner, certainly. But there may be, in certain cases, a little jealousy too—in certain cases, I only say. They like their own orators—I don't blame them, Miss Challoner; far from it. But I have got over all that, I am happy to think. It was indeed but momentary I may say. Now my way is clear," the rising youth said proudly. In fact, Mr. Nathaniel, with his few dollars a week in a village, saw himself already swaying the destinies of parties, editing leading journals in New York, making and unmaking Presidents, and perhaps eventually accepting the post of United States Minister to the Court of St. James.

His confident manner quite imposed upon Marie as it had imposed upon himself, and she felt a throb of generous gladness.

"I am delighted to hear of all this," she said; "I shall tell your mother, Natty, and I can see her joy already. She has no idea of anything so good. I suppose you did not like to tell her too much until things became quite certain, lest there might be any disappointment?"

"You have divined my motive, Miss Challoner," said Nathaniel, grandly. "One must not announce a victory before he has won it."

"Still, Natty, I think I would have told her something of the good news. I would have prepared her a little; it would have cheered her up. She suffered a great deal, I know."

"Men must work, and women must weep," said Nat, with dignity.

"But she is not young, and suppose anything had happened and she had died not knowing of your success? Could you ever have forgiven yourself?"

Nat modestly confessed that he could not, but he pleaded that it was only very lately that his prospects had begun to open with such a roseate glow.

"What a beautiful scene this is!" said Marie, suddenly. "And this is winter with us. That sunlight is more beautiful than summer sunlight; it is so soft and mild. It is the moonlight of the year, I think."

"It is—just that," said Nathaniel, who had not been observing the sunlight.

"I don't see any of our company. We must have walked very quickly. I think we had better turn back, Natty."

"May I offer you an arm?" Nathaniel said with sudden courage, and hearing his heart beat loudly the while.

Marie would have had no hesitation in saying to any one else that she did not need support and preferred not to take an arm. But she was afraid that if she said this to Nat he would have been hurt, and would have thought, quite wrongly, that she refused his arm because he was the son of her old servant. So she thanked him and leaned on his arm, and they turned to walk back. Nat moved very slowly.

"How strange it is," he said, "us two—I mean we two—walking in this way—on this side of the ocean—and your arm leaning on mine! Miss Challoner, it's like a dream."

Marie looked up at him in wonder.

"I don't know how it is to you," the infatuated Nat went on, "but to me, Miss Challoner, to me it's Heaven!"

Never woman could have been more amazed than Dear Lady Disdain. She did not as yet think of being angry or quite know that there was any reason why she should be so. Her first impression was that her unfortunate companion was really out of his wits. It came on her like a flash that his talk had been marvellously grandiloquent and full of pride and confidence, for which she did not understand that there could well be any justification. Could the poor creature really be out of his wits? In the same instant Marie's kind heart thought of his mother.

"Natty," she said in a tone of soothing remonstrance; and perhaps for the first time in her life with a tremor of timidity in her voice as she glanced eagerly around. There was no one near.

"Oh, hear me out!" the wretched Nathaniel went on; "I can't stop now—I must speak—you have a sympathetic soul, you are above the miserable ways and prejudices of meaner minds. I know you are. You do not look down upon me as others do— as others did at home; you do not despise me because my birth was lowly and my occupation was at one time mean."

"No, Natty, certainly not. I always thought the higher of you for endeavouring to raise yourself. *We* were always friends, Natty; but I don't think any one we ever knew was mean enough to think less of you for—for not being rich."

Marie now believed that she was only soothing an outburst of the morbid and half-crazy egotism of a self-conceited lad smarting under the memory of fancied humiliations. She would as soon have thought of her groom, or her Newfoundland dog, or old Merlin at Durewoods making love to her, as of Mrs. Cramp's Natty.

"Oh, yes, I have suffered; but not from you—never from you. Now things are changed. Now we are in a free and equal land, where a man may make his way to anything and be equal to anybody. Here, Miss Challoner, I may dare to say—with you leaning on my arm——"

Marie quickly withdrew her arm.

"Don't be afraid. It's only this—we two alone, and I must say it here—under this bright heaven," Nat exclaimed, wildly, "that I love you—oh, Miss Challoner, yes—that I love you!"

Marie was bewildered by this outburst. She was not sure at first if she had understood him rightly. Then, when there was no possibility of further misunderstanding, she was startled, angry, full of shame and pity, and withal vexed by a shocking inclination to laugh.

"Natty, how can you speak in such a way?" she said at last. "I could not have expected this, or believed it of you. I was always friendly with you. Is this my return?"

"I can't help it," he exclaimed, passionately; "I love you: I 'ave always loved you" (in his emotion he went back to the pronunciation of his early days, and he became conscious of the fact in a moment, and it added new agony to his sufferings); "I loved you since I was a boy——"

"Why will you speak in so foolish a way," she said, more gently, "and so prevent me from ever being friendly with you any more? Your mother was a dear old friend of mine, and I am sorry for this—for her sake.

"Ah, but there it is," he broke out, wildly; "that's where it is—that's why you despise me! My mother was a servant—a servant—a servant—and I'm only like a dog in your eyes. But you are wrong, Miss Challoner. I ain't—I mean I am not—a dog here. This is not your country of aristocrats and caste and class. A man is a man here."

"A man ought to be a man anywhere, and not a fool," Lady Disdain said, likely to lose her temper now.

"Is a man a fool because he loves a woman above him in rank? Half the best men in the world have been fools, then! I am not ashamed. Call me anything you like—I must love you all the same. You despise me because I am poor and low! Oh, but if you have a woman's heart at all you might feel for me, and make some allowance for me, and not trample on me, trample, trample on me, just because I come of humble people.

The unfortunate youth was trembling and shivering from head to foot with emotion. His cheeks were lividly pale, and his eyes, always rather small and lustreless, were winking and watery with tears. He seemed, indeed, like a half-mad creature; like a loving dog whom his master spurns and curses. Lady Disdain looked at him with alarm, and her anger all melted away and only pity remained.

"It is not because you are poor, indeed," she said earnestly, and trying to soothe him; "but you know how absurd all this is; and it is wrong of you to expect me to listen to it. I ought not to allow you to talk to me in such a way; but you are an old friend, and I know you only forgot yourself for the moment and that you will never do so again. Come, Natty, say that we may be friends again as we used to be. Did you not know, you foolish boy, that I am engaged to be married?"

"Engaged to be married!" he stammered.

"Yes, Nat, I knew you never could have heard of it, or you would not have talked such nonsense. Come, let us bury all unkindness and forget it——and never speak of this folly any more."

"Engaged to be married to *him?*" Nat asked fiercely, and following out a track of his own ideas.

"Indeed yes, Nat, to *him,*" she answered, following out a track of her own ideas. "And so you see you are late in any case," she added, with a smile, trying now to make as light of the whole affair as possible.

"But *he* ain't a gentleman neither," Nat interposed

vehemently. "At least, he isn't what you would call a gentleman. I don't see why he should look down on me and give himself airs. What was his father but a civil engineer—what is himself ?"

"Nat," said Lady Disdain turning rather pale, "you don't know what you are talking of, and I deserve anything for having listened to you so long."

"Then it isn't he; it isn't that Japan fellow—he saved my life though," Nat struck in, with sudden penitence. "Oh, but don't go until you say you forgive me. Oh, don't despise me and hate me. Oh, Miss Challoner, you have made my life so wretched—so awfully wretched ! "

"If I have, she said, "I am sorry for it; I would have been your friend gladly. I—I am not so very happy myself. But I will not listen to any more, Nat, and I will not stay here."

"Don't tell any one," he pleaded, with a pitiful last outburst; "don't set them laughing at me !"

"I shall tell no one," she said, unable wholly to suppress her contempt for him. "I suppose if it were told they would laugh at me more than at you; and I deserve it."

So she was turning from him, for she felt anger and scorn in one moment. She pitied him again, for the unfortunate wretch had flung himself grovelling on the ground, and clasped his hands over his head as if he would shut out the sense of his disappointment and his humiliation. She glanced at him and then along the path where their friends might soon be expected to appear.

"Natty! Get up, you foolish fellow, and show yourself like a man. These peeple will come along soon—do you want them to see you, and have all this talked of? What do you think my father would say? Get up, and help me to conceal this ridiculous affair. I promise to do my best to forget it, if you will."

Dear Lady Disdain was growing so impatient and alarmed at the prospect of their friends coming up that she felt inclined to rouse her grovelling admirer with a thrust of her parasol.

Nat got slowly up, looking wild, haggard, and scared.

"What am I to do ?" he stammered.

"Here," and a flash of inspiration enlightened her, "you see that little tuft of—mallow is it ?—no matter what it is, down there, just at the water's edge—no, no, not that way—down the bank just beneath us. Climb down and get me *that*. There's no danger—I could do it myself," she added, with an emotion of irrepressible contempt; "it will give you time to get composed, and will turn away their attention."

Poor Nat obeyed as a frightened child might do, hardly yet understanding why she wanted him at such a moment to perform a feat of climbing. He was awkward enough at it, too, for his boots were new and very tight, and he had his gloves on, and the clayey, crumbling bank was rather deep, and there were only little brambles and branches to cling to. But Marie's point was gained. If Nat were now found puffing and excited there would be sufficient reason for it. He was already nearly down to the water's edge when Professor Clinton, Mrs. Benjamin, and Miss Benjamin appeared.

"Thank Heaven!" Lady Disdain mentally ejaculated. The thought came into her mind that that was the first piece of deceit she had ever practised, and she began to think that the cynical things said of women by old-fashioned railers must be true, and that the gift of ready deceit is the heritage of all Eve's daughters. She felt terribly inclined to laugh, with a natural revulsion of feeling, as she saw poor Nathaniel's awkward and floundering attempts to get up the bank again.

"Mr. Cramp is a gallant cavalier," she said to Professor Clinton, who, with his companions, seemed to be looking in some wonder at Nat's performance. "I admired the little tuft of flowers below, near the water, and he has kindly gone to get it for me. Oh!" for at that moment Nat's foot slipped, and he seemed destined for a plunge in the stream.

"He'll fall right in!" said little Miss Benjamin, breathless.

"No, he's all right," Professor Clinton coolly said. "But I say, Cramp, you're not much on climbing—banks of clay at least. Here, hold on to that."

He extended to Nathaniel the crooked handle of the walking-stick he was carrying. Nat glanced up at first with eyes that meant indignant rejection. But at that instant he felt the smooth hard soles of the new boots beginning to slip again, and in despair he clutched the handle of the stick, and the stalwart Clinton tugged him safely up.

"You are not used to our clayey banks yet, Cramp," Clinton said, smiling. "I dare say you have often scrambled down there, little Mollie?" he asked of Miss Benjamin.

"Oh yes, Professor Clinton; we all do it," was the prompt answer of the little round-eyed maid. "We all coast down that bank when the river's frozen."

"Coasting," it should be explained for the benefit of British youths and maidens, is lying upon a little "sled" or sleigh which rushes of its own impulse down some steep and frozen descent. Usually the owner of the "sled" brings it to the verge of the descent, gives it a push, and then, when it is in motion, flings himself on it, and is borne along with tremendous velocity. The regular thing is to sit or lie on it feet foremost, but it must be owned that the daring spirits of both sexes (up to the age say of twelve) find joy in flinging themselves face downwards, head foremost, on the flying car.

" Well, I dare say you have. Feet foremost or head foremost, Mollie ? "

" Oh, feet foremost, Professor Clinton—mostly ; but sometimes head foremost," added the little lass with a slight blush, and yet with a certain pride in her daring.

" I thought as much ! Never mind your mamma—I dare say she has run as great risks in her time. You see, Cramp, your feat wasn't very great."

" I don't want to have Mr. Cramp's services and gallantry depreciated, all the same," said Marie. " Thank you, Mr. Cramp, I am greatly obliged. What very beautiful flowers—and peculiar, at least they seem so to me. Now, Professor Clinton, I want you to tell me all about these flowers, for I don't think we have any-thing quite like them at home."

Thus Marie succeeded in changing partners, so to speak, with Mrs. Benjamin, and she kept with Professor Clinton for her escort until the whole party came up. No one suspected that Nat had been making so painful an exhibition of his passion and his folly. Nat disappeared soon from the party, making some stammering explanation about " journalistic labour," as he called it, that had to be accomplished, and he hurried to his quarters in the Franklin, the most wretched of all self-conceited and humiliated men.

CHAPTER XXIV.

" GO AT ONCE!"

CHRISTMAS PEMBROKE came down one morning at the beginning of winter to his breakfast in the room with the painted goddess on the ceiling. The moment he entered the room he saw one particular letter among others lying on his table, and he knew the handwriting of Sir John Challoner. His face flushed. He seized the letter eagerly ; and then held it a moment unopened in his hand.

This letter he knew must be in answer to that one which months ago he had sent out to the States, and which, after wandering from place to place, always arriving just after Chal-loner had left, reached him at last the very day when he was leaving San Francisco. It was written by Sir John from Sacra-mento, the first town at which he and his daughter stopped on their way eastward. For this letter Christmas had waited and waited. It seemed out of all possibility, not to say propriety, that he should take French leave of one who had been so kind to him as Sir John; he must first have his formal sanction and release. That was the reason Christmas gave to himself and to Dione Lyle for lingering so long in London. But in his heart there was another reason, which the postscript of his letter to Challoner had dimly indicated. He would not leave England for ever until he knew that Marie Challoner did not believe him to be in love with Sybil Jansen. It seemed one of the most ridiculous of all vanities that he should wish to be assured upon that point, and yet he would not leave England without being assured of it. In his heart there was "a kind of fighting" that would not let him rest about that story which Sir John Challoner had told or sanctioned—the story of his engagement with Miss Jansen. Christmas had not told Miss Lyle half what he thought of that strange story; and we know that she had taken care not to tell him all she thought. Why had Sir John Challoner told his daughter, or encouraged her in believing, such a story? The thought wounded Christmas in many ways. Did Sir John think so little of the confession Christmas had made to him—the confession of his hopeless love and his broken heart—for broken he poor lad believed it to be; did he think so little of it as to make a jest of it? Was he so cruelly deceived in Sir John, to whom he looked up with so much regard, and whom he believed to be so sympathetic? Or could it be possible that Marie Challoner's father really had some deliberate motive in trying to make his daughter believe that Christmas Pembroke was in love with another woman? This was the doubt that sometimes made Christmas tremble with wild fears and angers, and wilder hopes. Many a sleepless hour of the night, many a dreamy abstracted hour of the day, had that thought cost him.

"Here is my sentence," he said to himself, taking Sir John's letter in his hand. This is what he read:—

"MY DEAR PEMBROKE,—Since you have made up your mind to leave England, I agree with you in thinking that any further delay would be a waste of time. Do not let anything stand in your way so far as the offices are concerned. I write by this post in order that arrangements may be made for supplying your place. I think if I were you I would return to Japan by the overland route, and so have a passing glimpse at India, etc., which you may not soon again have an opportunity of seeing.

"Good-bye, my dear boy; and God bless you! I need not say how glad I should have been if I could have kept you always with me. But as you find that your own interests require another course, it is only for me to speed the parting guest. It is a great pleasure to me to have made your acquaintance, and I shall always look back with interest upon the time we spent together.

"I hope you will write to me when you get settled in Japan.

" My daughter joins me in kind regards and good wishes.—
Ever, my dear Pembroke,

"Your sincere friend,
"JOHN CHALLONER."

Christmas put the letter down. Then he took it up again,
and read it over—scanned every word of it. No new meaning
shone through it. It was not so much a farewell as a dismissal.
Had Sir John Challoner been turning from his doors an over-
importunate dependant, he could not have been more coldly
imperious in his tone. There was no getting over the bitter
reality. Christmas was simply thrust out of the circle of Sir
John Challoner's acquaintance and bidden to begone.

The blood rushed into Pembroke's face. Good God! what
had he done to deserve this? What change had come over the
man who had always professed such friendship and affection for
him? Or was Challoner simply insincere from first to last?
Often and often had Dione Lyle hinted as much, and he could
never be brought to believe it. Now?

" My daughter joins me in kind regards and good wishes."

" She never said that!" Christmas cried out to his solitude.
" She never knew of it. She never would have sent me off with
two or three cold words. She would have said something warm
and friendly, or she would have written a few lines of her own.
I know she would! Unless he told her what I, like a fool, confided to him. But even then why should she not feel some
compassion for me, and say a kind parting word, when I am
never to come in her way again? Oh, no!—she knows nothing
about this letter."

Christmas sat himself resolutely down to think this all over,
as if it were some baffling problem. "There is deceit in that
letter, somehow," he thought, "and it must be found out.".
Suddenly he jumped out of his chair.

" I'll not go!" he exclaimed. "I'll not stir from England
until I have seen her and spoken to her. There's some infernal
treachery at work in all this. Why did he tell her a lie? Why
didn't he tell her I was leaving England? Why does he want
to get me out of the way before she comes back?"

Then there came a depressing reaction, and he asked himself
what was the excuse for the wild sort of hope that would keep
burning within him—the hope that Sir John Challoner had some
strong motive in preventing Marie from seeing him any more.
We don't live in the days when flinty hearted fathers can compel
their daughters to marry, and Miss Challoner did not seem the
sort of girl who could very easily be coerced in any case. Still
there remained the unmistakable fact that for some reason, be it
what it might, Sir John Challoner was playing off a piece of
deceit—even of treachery.

"No, come what will," Christmas vowed once more, "I'll not go until I have seen her. I can only make a fool of myself and be laughed at, and I don't care about *that.*"

A new life and courage seemed to animate him. It was strange how completely he had become possessed all at once with the conviction of Sir John Challoner's treachery. He had not the faintest doubt on that point any more. "Perhaps if I were wise and self-denying," he thought, "I would go away all the more quickly, and not interfere any more. Suppose I find out that her father is an insincere friend, will that please her or make her think any the more of me? Can I do anything but mischief by remaining?" Yet he could not shake his own resolve. "I will not go!—I will not go!" he said again and again.

A whole hour must have passed away before he thought of looking at the other letters on his table. One was in the writing of Miss Jansen:—

"DEAR MR. PEMBROKE,—Mamma has been very ill, but is now better. She wonders that you never came to see her; but perhaps you did not hear. She would be glad if you could come to-night, as she wishes to ask your advice about something. She sends her kind regards.

"SYBIL JANSEN."

"What an idiot I am!" Christmas thought, "and a shabby, ungrateful idiot 'at that——'" and he mentally used an Americanism. For he had to confess he had rather avoided the Jansens of late, feeling a little sore about the absurd stories which connected Sybil's name with his, and being ashamed to meet Sybil's eyes. Our youth had been brought up so far away from modern civilisation that he was strangely and perhaps savagely modest about women, and assumed that every pretty girl could have her pick and choice of lovers, and that, therefore, Miss Jansen could not possibly care to have her name connected with his. Therefore, he had kept out of her way, fearing lest she should think he had been vain enough to encourage such reports. Besides of late he had felt little inclination for women's society of any kind. The small needful gallantries and courtesies irritated him, and he preferred to nurse his pain in sullen solitude.

A loud and resolute tapping at his door disturbed him. Christmas opened the door, and the martial figure of Captain Cameron entered. Our hero had not seen the Legitimist since his somewhat unsatisfactory return from the wars. The Dux redux looked in no wise disconcerted. His manner was as jaunty, self-reliant, and good-humoured as ever. He might, so far as all appearances went, have just seen Don Carlos seated in triumph on his ancestral throne.

" Delighted to see you, Pembroke, my dear fellow," Captain Cameron said, as he grasped Pembroke's hand. " I have been resolving to look in upon you this some time. Having breakfast —eh? I think you are always having breakfast. You young fellows now have such healthy appetites."

Christmas expressed his satisfaction at the sight of Captain Cameron, and he thought with a pang that his first acquaintance with Sir John Challoner was made in that room through Cameron's introduction.

" But I say, you are not looking all right," Cameron said. " Growing thin, I think, and pale. Ceasing to be a boy, eh? Man's estate; and a very pretty estate it is to succeed to! I am disgusted with the world, Pembroke; disgusted, sir!"

" Well, I don't know that I am greatly charmed with it," Pembroke said.

" Poof, my dear fellow! what do you know about it? What does a fellow of your years know about disappointment and ingratitude and treachery and all that? A smile from a pretty girl, I dare say, would raise you into the seventh heaven. Wait till you come to my time of life! Wait till you have your soul in some great cause, and work for it and sacrifice your time and your money—and your blood, by Jove!—and see everything going to the dogs—and your advice neglected and yourself put aside. Well, well!"

" The Carlist affairs are going badly?"

" Badly? Wretchedly. Shamefully. They are blind,.sir, mad! *Quos Deus vult*—but that's an old quotation. I give you my word, Pembroke, that if my advice had been taken, the King would have been in Madrid before now. Look here; I'll show it all to you. You know Spain?"

" No—I am sorry to say I don't."

" Never been there? Well, no matter. Just see now—follow me. Here are the mountains—this toast-rack. Very good. Here are our head-quarters; yes, this cruet-stand. Now the advance of the *Madrilenos* is just there—jammed up there, sir; in a cleft stick. Now, you see what our course ought to be." Captain Cameron paused and looked triumphantly at Christmas.

Christmas studied the field of battle with an air of profound interest.

" Of course you see it; a school girl couldn't miss it. There's the way to the capital thrown right open—clear as the Thames embankment, by Jove! Just make a feint here—swing round your left—keep the fellows engaged—easy work; and then on with your main force slap into Madrid! I showed it to them, sir; I showed it to them just as clearly as I am showing it to you now!"

Christmas thought if that was so he could perhaps excuse the Carlist generals for not seeing it precisely at a glance.

"And they couldn't see it?" he asked.

"Couldn't see it? They wouldn't see it, sir. It wouldn't suit the book of some of them—oh, no! What would become of the influence of certain persons—I mention no names—of certain persons over his Majesty" (and Cameron performed a military salute in honour of the absent prince), "if a foreigner, a mere foreigner, were to be allowed to show the way to victory? No, no, that would never do. You have no idea, Pembroke—you can have no idea—of the jealousy of these Spaniards where a foreigner is concerned. I believe they would rather be whipped by a Spaniard than led to victory by a foreigner. So I left them. What could I do? You heard that I was taken prisoner by the other fellows?"

"Yes, I heard that. It made some stir over here."

"Stir? I should think it did. But England is of no account now. I almost wish they had shot me, Pembroke, just to see whether anything could arouse England to a sense of her degradation. We are pigeon-livered, my good fellow, and lack gall to make oppression bitter—Shakespeare, you know. You can have no idea what they think of us in other countries. They laugh at us. This affair of mine created quite a sensation in the United States, I can tell you."

"Indeed?"

"Oh, yes. Isabel—Mrs. Seagraves, you know—has had some American papers sent to her with some splendid leading articles on the Cameron affair, as they call it. I have the papers—published in a city called New Padua—evidently a very important journal—pitching into England terribly for her want of spirit. I have a strong notion myself that the articles were inspired, you know, from the White House. General Grant must know my name well enough; he must have heard of me when I fought under poor Robert Lee for the flag of the Stars and Bars; and I know he wants to pick a quarrel with England."

Christmas had received some newspapers containing articles with Natty Cramp's name written in Nathaniel's handwriting at the bottom, and coming from New Padua. He therefore did not feel quite so confident about the inspiration of the White House. But he was not inclined to get into any discussion, or to dash Captain Cameron's opinion of his own international importance.

"Well, all that is past and gone," the brave Cameron resumed; "and I looked in to talk about you and not about me. Isabel tells me you are leaving England."

"Yes, I think so—before long."

"Quite right, my boy! England's no place for a man of spirit any longer. Where are you going?"

"Back to my old ground. Japan, I think."

"Japan? Well, yes—let me see. Japan? To be sure; why not? I have an idea of offering my military experience and services somewhere. I thought of Siam—and I thought of China; and I have been thinking too a good deal of Brazil. I wonder would there be a good opening in Japan? There's nothing to hold me to Europe any more. I am afraid the cause of Legitimacy is lost, Pembroke, for our generation! Have you heard from the Challoners?"

"I had a letter from Sir John this morning," Christmas said, with a pang shooting through him.

"They're coming home very soon, Vidal tells me. You know she's going to be married to him——Dear Lady Disdain, we used to call her."

"Yes; I know."

"I suppose it's a good match for both parties? Challoner has plenty of money, and the young fellow has family and rank, and all that. But I don't know; I shouldn't like it if I were her father—I think. Should you?"

"I don't know much about *him*."

"Oh, he's all well enough for our time. He ought to be a gentleman; but what does a gentleman want mixing himself up with stock-jobbing speculations, and theatres, and actresses, and harlequins, and all that sort of thing? Let a man be in business—if he can't help it; all right. But if you are a gentleman, continue to be one, I say. It's all right, however, I dare say. They know best. He's well enough for our time. But I shouldn't have thought Marie Challoner would care about him."

"He's a good-looking fellow," said Pembroke, generously; "and clever, I believe."

"Good-looking!—yes, like a fiddler or a dancing-master. Clever!—a sort of cross between a stockbroker's clerk and a third-class painter. And that's the son of an earl, the scion of a noble house, sir, now-a-days! And that's to be my dear little Lady Disdain's husband! Well, it's no affair of mine. I say, Pembroke, why the deuce didn't you make love to her yourself? You're a deuced deal more like a gentleman and an earl's son than he is. Tell you what, you might have had a chance. Think of Jock o' Hazeldean."

Pembroke made no answer to this suggestion, and Captain Cameron took his leave after a while, promising to look in again very soon and talk with his young friend on the possibility of there being a good opening in Japan for the brains and sword of the experienced soldier of a lost cause.

"Everything fails us in life," Pembroke thought, "but self-conceit! If all else fails with me, I shall try to persuade myself that the world was unable to appreciate me. I believe a man is capable of dying consoled alone in a garret if he has self-conceit to comfort him. That is really humanity's last friend!"

But Pembroke was now far from being all unhappy, even though the thought that Sir John Challoner had been treacherous was bitter, and seemed to shake the realities of things. A new hope was exciting his brain and filling his heart. There was something yet to be done before he wholly succumbed and disappeared. If Sir John Challoner had been treacherous to him, he was released from all fealty. His heart echoed again and again the words of Captain Cameron, and he did not believe that Ronald Vidal was worthy of Marie, or that she could have loved him. A thousand little memories crowded back upon him, conspicuous among them the memory of her pale, weary expression when he saw her last, that day in Mrs. Seagrave's house, and of the touch of her hand when she said "Good-bye!"

"She doesn't care for him," he said aloud, in his excitement. "I am not an idiot—any more. She does not care for him; I know that much at least!"

He felt a strange lightness all through him; the exalted sensation of a man who finds that there is one last chance, yet one blow to be struck, one decision to be given; and that, let it fall out as it will, all the old chapters of life are closed for him. Let it end this way, let it end that, a new life begins. If only the time would pass quickly over! It is the interval that is hard to bear.

Christmas went down to the City treading upon air, and took formal leave of his business connection with the house of Challoner, and ascertained the exact date when Sir John was expected to return to England. He was pervaded and sustained by a strong resolution which he could not have set forth in plain words for the life of him. Did he propose to rush in at the last moment and carry off Marie Challoner like young Lochinvar? Did he think to break in on her bridal party like Edgar Ravenswood? Did he expect that an inundation would arise somehow and wash Marie Challoner out of her engagement with Ronald Vidal and into the arms of him who conceived himself a worthier lover, as happens to one of Mr. Charles Reade's heroines? No, he did not propose or expect anything of the kind. All his excitement and his recklessness of meaner considerations came out of his resolve—that at least he would speak with her once again, that she should know how he loved her, and that he would live and die loving her. Then he would take what happened. Let her then dismiss him to the other end of the earth. At least she would have known that he loved her, and only she would have spoken his sentence.

CHAPTER XXV.

ANOTHER PIOUS PARENTAL FRAUD.

Poor Sybil Jansen sat long and wearily at her window waiting that evening for the coming of Christmas Pembroke. The once ardent and disinterested priestess of the future, whose whole soul was concerned in the mission of women and the perfection of the human race, had grown very morbid and discontented. She found her hopes of the coming time as unsatisfying as the applauses of Avenir Hall. She had not seen Pembroke for some time. He never went to Mrs. Seagraves' Sunday afternoons now, and was seen no more at Avenir Hall. But Sybil had heard that Miss Challoner was soon to be married to Ronald Vidal, and there was just enough of comfort in that to prevent her from ever settling down contented to take up the thread of her old career.

Mrs. Jansen had seen her daughter's condition. She understood it only too well. But the mother and daughter never spoke on the subject. Mrs. Jansen watched her daughter's eyes as they turned eagerly now and then of evenings towards the door when a knock was heard. He did not come, and Mrs. Jansen went so far as to try a pious little fraud. She invented to herself some excuse of believing that she wanted Mr. Pembroke's advice, and she bade Sybil write to him. The mother had something of a reward when she saw her daughter's cheek colour with pleasure and a kind of shame. What was the good of asking him to come for one evening, one hour, more? Only somebody in love, or the mother of somebody in love, could tell. What was the good of that last ride together, which yet Mr. Browning's lover thought better worth than all the dreams of poet, artist, or statesman?

Well, Christmas Pembroke came that evening. His own excited and exalté condition made him animated and sympathetic. He looked very handsome. There was, with all his masculine strength of frame, and what seemed to the Jansens his world-wide travels and experiences, a certain boyish simplicity and freshness which made him peculiarly attractive. He seemed to be absolutely without affectation or even self-consciousness. Mrs. Jansen, for her own part, had conceived a sort of maternal affection for him, and felt his absence, and thought that his friendly smile, generally with a tinge of a boyish blush accompanying it, lighted up their melancholy little room. But Mrs. Jansen had clear enough eyes, for all her mother's partiality, and she did not see

R

in the young man any sign of more than friendship for her
daughter. Yet she had practised her pious little fraud, and
induced him to come that evening, and was glad when he came.
The business on which she wished to consult him was not much
—did not even look to be much. It concerned the investment
of some small, small savings in some Eastern railway project,
which made Christmas tremble to hear of. Heavens! with what
superfluous elaboration of argument and energy of description
he showed Mrs. Jansen that such a scheme could not by any
possibility begin to pay for at least fifty years, supposing it ever,
by any rare combination of fortune and skill, to be made to pay
at all. Christmas had not the least suspicion that any *arrière-
pensée* or pious fraud lurked in the mind of the good and anxious
woman to whom he was expounding the principles on which
alone such projects could be made to pay. Sometimes, in en-
forcing his argument, he addressed himself to Sibyl, in order to
have her assent and attention too.

"But Miss Jansen doesn't care for all these dry unpoetic
details," he said, fearing that he was wearying the young woman.

"Sybil is very, very fond of hearing anything that instructs
her," Mrs. Jansen hastened to say.

"You explain it all so well," Sybil herself said, gently. "I
oegin to be afraid we women have not the heads for business
that you men have." This was a meek propitiatory concession
to the stronger sex, which a year ago the young Hypatia would
not have believed herself capable of making. It was something
very like a hauling down of the colours.

"Well, you see, this is the sort of thing I have always been
working at," the unconscious Christmas replied. "In Japan
perhaps a project like that may work well. I may be able to
give you some information, or put you in the way of doing something." (He was really quite concerned about the small means
which their frank disclosures showed them to have. He considered himself poor, but he was a young Crœsus compared with
Sybil Jansen.) "I shall be a good deal in that line when I go
back to Japan."

"But are you going back really?" Mrs. Jansen asked.

"Oh, yes; I intend to go back very soon."

"You are tired of us already?"

"No, indeed; but I don't seem to find my right place here;
and I feel somehow as if I were driven back. It's just that, Mrs.
Jansen. I can't stay."

The little servant came in at that moment and brought some
message to Mrs. Jansen, who thereupon excused herself, said she
would return immediately, and left the room.

Sybil had risen, and was standing near the hearth. Christmas
was seated at the table, with the papers which he had been looking

through lying before him. He rose and went towards the hearth also, where the fire was burning brightly, and Sybil was busying, or seeming to busy, herself in preparing tea. His heart was touched with regret for the kind and simple friends whom he was so soon to lose for ever; the modest and quiet little household of mother and daughter, who were so poor, so good, so friendly to him, and whom he was not to see any more.

"Yes, I am sorry to leave England," he said.

"Why should you be sorry?" Sybil asked, without looking up. "I wish I were a man and could leave England."

"Where do you wish to go?"

"Anywhere, I don't care—anywhere out of this—away, far away."

"Well, I suppose we are restless beings, most of us. But I feel sorry, too."

"I don't see what you have to be sorry for. You lose nothing."

"I lose some very dear friends," the young man said, softly.

"Oh, friends are nothing. You will soon forget your friends."

"I shall not forget *you*——"

Sybil's cheek glowed and her hand trembled.

"Nor your mother."

Sybil shrugged her shoulders.

"You will not think much about us. It is not we, Mr. Pembroke, who are driving you out of England."

"No, indeed! Who ever thought of such a thing? Why should you drive me out of England?"

"I said so," the young Hypatia went on viciously. "I said it was not we who are driving you away."

"Why, of course not. Nobody is driving me away."

"Oh, yes; somebody is." And Sybil shrugged her shoulders again. "I know quite well."

"Come now, tell me what you mean."

"I know that you are brokenhearted and despairing, and that you are flying to the desert—and—all that. You are off to the wars again, like the sentimental youth in the song, because the lady you love is to be a bride with a diadem on her brow! What feeble creatures you men are! You are always making yourself ridiculous about some woman. There now—you are angry!"

"No, I am not angry," said Christmas, feeling, however, a good deal embarrassed, and wondering why a kind and clever girl could descend to such commonplace and trivial teazing; "and this is an old story of yours, Miss Jansen—I am used to it now. It doesn't disturb me."

"I don't want to annoy you," she said, "especially as you are going away—and we have not so many friends. *We* are not rich and sought after like the lady who is to be a bride with the diadem upon her brow! Well, let us say no more about her— only it is no use your trying to conceal from me the real cause of your returning to Japan. That sort of thing may deceive mamma, but not me."

"But I don't want to deceive any one, and least of all such friends as you and your mother."

"Then why invent excuses? Why evade? Have men ·no courage? If I were a man, I should not feel ashamed—— "

"But—Miss Jansen, in Heaven's name," Christmas asked warmly, " ashamed of what?"

" Ashamed of being in love and of being disappointed—thrown over for a greater lover—for the son of an earl! There! Of course I know that you are in love with her—with Miss Challoner ; and that you are leaving England because you can't endure the idea of seeing her married to Another, as the romances say."

Sybil's eyes were sparkling, and her lips were trembling. It must be owned that at the moment Christmas thought her an ill-natured and vehement little person, and wondered why, if she believed all she said, she did not sympathise with him rather than thus rail upon him. He drew a great breath, and then faced the situation boldly.

"If I were in love with her," he said, gravely—" I'll not mention her name, Miss Jansen—I don't think we have any right to mention her name in talk like this—if I were in love with her, and were thrown over as you say, that would be a great misfortune for me, would it not ?"

"I suppose so."

"Suppose you had a brother, and it were his case—it might be, you know ; would you not feel sorry for him and try to cover his misfortune, and to lighten it if you could? Yes, I know you would, for I know that you have a good heart."

" How do you know?"

"I can see what you are to your mother, and I know well enough. Put me in your brother's place—— "

" Oh, in one's brother's case one would know the truth."

" Well, you may know the truth from me, if you will. I am not ashamed, and I had rather you did know the truth than hear you talk—in that way. I never was thrown over for a richer ¹over. It never entered into Miss—into *her* mind—to think of me as a lover. I never thought of putting myself forward in such a way. I never thought myself worthy! But if you will know all—well I can't conceive how any man could be brought so near her and so often as I have been—without loving her! There, you have the whole truth; and that's all! "

Christmas stared doggedly at the fire. Poor Sybil was cold, pale, and trembling. Her excitable temperament had so nearly betrayed her! She felt penitent, ashamed, degraded; and yet, as he stood there, so full of jealous pains and futile anger and love.

"You'll not forgive me," she said at last, in trembling tones, "for speaking in such a way! You think me mean and malicious."

"Oh, no," Christmas said, turning to her, "I am not so unreasonable, Miss Jansen; I don't bear malice."

"You mean that *I* do?" she said piteously.

"No, no; I didn't mean that; I know that what you said was only mere *badinage*."

"I didn't know," the poor little priestess pleaded, "how serious it was. I didn't know that you cared—for her—so very much—as all that."

Christmas took her hand in signal of complete forgiveness. It was very cold. She drew it quietly away.

"I should not like you to think badly of me," she went on; "I am not mean and spiteful and small minded, Mr. Pembroke —like so many women. At least I try not to be. But I am unhappy in many ways; and disappointed; and people don't like me; and think I am unwomanly—because I make speeches and all that—and I am not unwomanly! Oh no—only much too womanly, I think, and you think now, perhaps?"

"I never thought you unwomanly," said downright Christmas; "I told you this moment that I knew what a kind good heart you had."

"Thank you very much. Well, I am glad you are not angry with me. Now, when mamma comes back she will ask you, of course, to stay this evening with us and have tea."

"Yes?"

"Well—please don't stay. Don't! You must have some pleasanter place to go to; and we should be so dull."

Christmas was beginning an energetic protest.

"No—please don't stay. I had rather you didn't. I am not very well—and you don't mind?—you are not offended? Thank you a thousand times. We shall see you some other time— perhaps—before you go."

So when Mrs. Jansen returned and asked Christmas to stay, he excused himself and went away. That night poor Sybil sobbed and cried a good deal in her mother's arms, and her mother for the first time was allowed to know all without pretence at concealment.

That was the end of poor Mrs. Jansen's pious little fraud.

CHAPTER XXVI.

FAREWELL TO NEW PADUA.

For some days after the walk by the river the Clintons saw nothing of Nathaniel Cramp. At the departure of the Challoners eastward they were accompanied to the railway station by a large concourse of friends—the president of the university and his wife, the professors and their wives, the various officials, the ministers of religion, the editors; but Nathaniel Cramp was not there. Clinton's womankind soon began to urge him to go and see whether Mr. Cramp was not sick, or whether something strange had not befallen him.

Professor Clinton was superficially something of a martinet and disciplinarian with his womankind, but in the end it was found that they generally had their way. They looked up to him as intellectually the greatest man in all the world, and submitted meekly to his discipline as regarded their general opinions, their reading, and their parts of speech. In the latter respect obedience sometimes brought its trials with it. For Professor Clinton was rather a purist as regarded the use of good Saxon English, and he rigorously forbade his wife and sister-in-law to use any of the euphemisms with which certain half-educated classes of persons in the United States, women more especially, are fond of disguising their ideas. If Jessie or Minnie had any occasion to speak of the lower limbs of herself or anybody else she was compelled to say "legs" plumply out; and if she proposed to go to bed she had to say she was going to bed, not "retiring"; she had to speak of "undressing," not of "disrobing," and so on with many other phrases which seemed very shocking indeed to some of the ladies of New Padua. Likewise they were forbidden to speak of any of their acquaintances as "a very lovely lady," or "a very pretty lady," but were told by Professor Clinton that at all events where the person under discussion had to be described by any qualifying adjective, complimentary or otherwise, she must consent to be spoken of as a "woman." In all these matters of discipline Professor Clinton's wife and sister-in-law were obedient at any peril of misconstruction. But in many or most other matters they generally contrived to shape their ends, and where questions of feeling were concerned the Professor was found at last a not unwilling subject of petticoat government. The two simple-hearted and kindly women were just copies of each other; an elder and a younger sister, no more; and Clinton was one of the men who like to have out with men all their intellectual and masculine talk, their arguments, dissertations, and speculations, and to have only sweet, familiar, easy conversation at home.

Gradually, therefore, the feminine influence had been working more and more on Clinton in favour of Nat Cramp. The women did not see anything ridiculous about him, and could not have understood how Clinton could laugh at him and yet like him at the same time. Clinton therefore of late ceased to invite their attention to any of what he considered Nat's absurdities, and only amused himself with them. In obedience partly to domestic urgency and partly to his own concern for Nat, he set out one evening for the Franklin House. He was told Nat was in his room, and he went upstairs and knocked. There was no answer, and he opened the door and looked in. There, to be sure, was Nat, bending over an opened trunk. He looked round in a startled way when he heard the sound of the opening door.

" Why, Cramp, my boy, what have you been doing with yourself? We have missed you all this time; and my wife and Minnie have been so much alarmed that I thought I had better come over and see about you; I called at the office; and of course you were not there."

Nat came forward, looking yellow and ghastly. He was in his shirt sleeves, and had clothes, books, and properties of various kinds heaped about him. He seemed as if he had not slept for a long time.

" You are looking very bad," said Clinton—" and what are you doing?"

" I—I'm going to Europe. I've had bad news from England. My mother's dead." And Nat began to toss things rather wildly from one trunk to another.

" Come, come," the kindly Professor said, taking him by the arm: " You are hardly in a condition for this kind of work just now; and you are not going to Europe to-day anyhow. Let these things alone; and put on your coat and come out with me for a quiet walk by the river. We are safe not to meet anybody at this hour, and you shall talk or be silent just as you like. I'm an older man than you; and yet it's not long since I lost my mother; and I felt like a child, I tell you."

" It isn't that," Nat stammered; " but I feel as if I was so ungrateful. And I was; I was ungrateful!"

Nat was indeed looking white and scared like a man thoroughly conscience-stricken.

" Well, I dare say we were none of us as grateful as we ought to have been either to our mothers or to the Power that gave us them and life," said the Professor soothingly. " But you don't seem a lad likely to have been any worse than the rest of us, Cramp. Come, walk out with me and tell me all about it; or as much about it as you feel like talking of just now."

But Nat drew back, and seemed like a frightened bat that could not bear the light.

"I haven't been out ever since," he stammered.

"Ever since?"

"Since I heard the news."

"Well, but look here—the mails from Europe only came in last night, and you appear to have been out of our sight for nearly a week. Why, I never saw you since the day we were out with the Challoners and Benjamin."

Nat looked confused and scared worse than ever, and he rubbed up his hair wildly, perhaps to hide his confusion. Professor Clinton had touched unwittingly the raw place of his remorse. It was not grief for his mother which had kept him hidden from the light of day. He had, indeed, only heard of her death the night before. He had been crushed by the weight of humbled self-love and of bitter disappointment. When after his abasement before Marie Challoner he had crept back to his lodgings he flung himself on his bed and lay there grovelling like a trampled worm. He hated the outer air. He believed that every one must be laughing at him and despising him. The whole story, he felt sure, would be all over New Padua. Sir John Challoner must hear of it, and in his anger he would be sure to tell that it was a hairdresser's apprentice who had made love to his daughter. Nat was not one bit a coward so far as physical courage went, and yet for two days and more he trembled and started at every sound upon the stairs. He had vague terrors of Sir John's anger and of Sir John's vengeance.

The shock of the news which told him of his poor mother's death came in positively like a strengthening relief to the pitiful tortures of his disappointment and his seared self-love. Much of his present agony of remorse was owing to his consciousness that his grief for his mother was swallowed up in mere selfish regrets and pangs. He tried to chastise himself into a more fitting mood of sorrow by thinking of her and of all she had done for him and suffered. And she was dead now—and long before this the grave had closed over her coffin. He remembered how she had nursed his childhood, and how fond he was of her and delighted to be with her once. He thought of the glad holidays when he used to hurry to Durewoods from London, and she used to do all she could to make him happy, and have her little sweets and preserves for him; and how he used to rejoice in making her his confidante, and telling her every small hope and trouble and pleasure; and how, then, he began to think that she didn't quite understand him, and was not up to his mark intellectually; and how proud she was always of his uniform and of himself—proud of him whom everybody now despised! and how ungrateful he was. And now he should never see her any more! Thus at last he wrought himself up to the boiling point of emotion, and his feelings broke into the steam of tears, and, disregarding all Clinton's efforts at consolation, he flung himself down upon his half-packed trunk and cried like a child.

The Professor let him have his way. In truth, he thought all the better of Nat for his irrepressible burst of grief, not knowing by what mental process of irritating the feelings this wholesome relief had been brought about. Grief for a mother is the emotion with which an American, like a Frenchman, finds his heart most readily sympathise. In the sentimental and pathetic song-writing of the country the mother's name is the special Open Sesame of the feelings. Even the songs of the war were most often laments for or by absent mothers. Professor Clinton looked on sympathetically, and resolved to tell his wife and Minnie what a good heart young Cramp had, and how he was not by any means the merely egotistic and feather-headed young fellow he, the Professor, had sometimes suspected. "The women are generally right in these things," Clinton mentally acknowledged, remembering how his wife and Minnie had always stood up for young Cramp.

The tears did poor Natty great good. They relieved his feelings and his conscience both. How could he any longer accuse himself of being ungrateful to his mother, or failing in profundity of sorrow for her, when he had felt his own hot tears run down his cheeks at the thought of her? The tears came again and again, until at last he rose, relieved, and told Clinton he was going to be a man once more.

"A man's never more of a man," the Professor said, "than when he is lamenting for his mother. But it's as well to rouse yourself, Cramp, if you can, and think of what you have to do. Come, we'll go into the open air. Put up all these things for the moment, and you will tell me why you are going to Europe, and when, and all about it."

Nat allowed himself to be persuaded to dress and to shut up the lids of his trunks for the moment, and the Professor and he walked out together. They made a little circuit to avoid the town and the grounds of the university; and to use the language of the place, they "struck" the river a little higher up. They walked on by the bank of the stream in silence for a while. Evening was coming on and was growing a little chilly. The skies were very clear, and the sun, sinking on the one horizon, was beginning to be reflected in saffron, violet, and purple on the verge of the other. When Nathaniel was yet new to the place and fresh from the more misty and less luminous skies of England, the Clintons used to "chaff" him mildly because he often mistook the glowing mirage of the sunset that showed

itself in the east for the genuine pageant that was burning like
a superb sacrifice in the west.

Clinton put his hand gently upon his companion's arm, and
they stopped for a moment. Clinton looked along the path of
the river, sunlit between its quiet hills.

"And are you really going back to Europe?" he asked
gently, turning Nathaniel to look upon the peaceful and lonely
beauty of the scene, as if in remonstrance against the thought
of his deserting all that so soon for the noise and smoke of
London.

"I must go back," said Nathaniel in a tone of melancholy
dignity. "My poor mother has—has left me some money in
fact, and there are things to look after. I must go back at
once."

"But only *en congé*, I hope? You will come back to us?
You can easily arrange things with the paper so as to have your
place kept open for you. They'll do that for me, I know; and
if you like I'll arrange it all."

"I—I really don't know—I haven't thought of it—taken so
suddenly you see—and all that. I can't tell, Professor Clinton,
what may happen to me. I don't see what I want here or anywhere—or in life at all."

"You think so now, and that's natural enough. But you'll
soon live that down. I hope we shan't lose you, Cramp."

"You're very kind," Nat answered gloomily, "but I am well
aware that I ain't much—that I am not much of a loss anywhere."

"My good fellow, don't be too modest. I assure you that
you are well liked here. My wife, and Minnie (and he gave a
curious look out of his blue eyes at Nat), like you ever so much,
and would be sorry to lose you, and so should I. You seem to
have taken hold here, as we say, remarkably well."

Truth to say the Professor and his kind little wife had lately
begun to suspect that in Minnie's quiet bosom there was growing up a sort of tenderness for the tall and fair young Englishman who sometimes talked so eloquently and poetically. Clinton
himself even when he amused himself with Nat's little vanities
and nonsense liked the young man; and liked Nat all the more
because he had so served and befriended him. Clinton assumed
that nothing ever would or could come of Nat's passion for Miss
Challoner; and he thought little Minnie, who would always if
she were allowed the chance look up to Nathaniel as a great
man, would be a far more suitable partner for him than the
brilliant young English heiress—even if there were the remotest
possibility of such a partnership as the latter ever being accomplished. So he gave a quick experimental glance at Nat when
he mentioned his wife—and Minnie.

"I have been very happy here," Nat said, "but I suppose a man must follow his destiny."

"Hum—ha—I fancy we can all generally make our destiny for ourselves, my boy—barring accidents, at least. Are you ambitious of trying your fortune in the great city,—in London,—again? Do you think that the only stage worth playing to?"

"No," said Nat, with some hesitation, "it isn't that exactly."

"Well, I once thought no stage in life was worth playing to but that of some great city. I tried it, Cramp—in New York when I was much younger; and in London not so long ago. I might have settled in London: I had strong inducements. Your great scientific men are just too kind for anything; and they nearly turned my head with their friendliness and their attentions—which I never expected, you know—and they told me if I remained in London I should be a sort of little great man. I had made one or two hits, you know—stumbled on an odd asteroid or two—watching and calculating here of nights in the observatory yonder, and they made much more of me and my doings than I deserved. But I came back here."

"I think I'd have stayed," said Nat.

"If I had been a younger man perhaps: and yet I don't know. I should always miss those quiet bluffs and the sound of that river; and I like our pleasant peaceful ways here. I tell you what, Cramp—I have made a moderate success in my own way—more than ever I dreamed of when first I came a poor lad out West thus far; and I have had some little triumphs—such as I told you. But the sweetest memory I have is just the memory of the evening walks that Jessie and I used to have among the trees and along the bank here before we were married. And we'll have many evening walks here yet, please God! And she is not a very brilliant woman—my Jessie—she doesn't know quite as much about astronomy as your Mrs. Somerville, and she couldn't write like your Mrs. George Eliot, but she's made me so happy."

"That's all very well," said Nat, with a wan smile; "but there is no one to make me happy."

"You don't know, my boy—you don't know yet. Come, let's get on a bit; I want to show you our new lot."

They walked on a little farther, drawing at every step nearer to a spot surcharged with recollections peculiarly painful to poor Nat. The "new lot" which Professor Clinton wished him to see was a piece of ground which Clinton had lately bought, and on which he was going to build a new house. He was very proud of the spot he had chosen, and had often spoken to Nat about it, and told him that when he first came to New Padua he had fixed upon that particular spot as the place where he should like to have a house if ever he could afford to buy land and build. Now he was at last about to gratify his ambition.

" Our house is all right enough at present," Clinton explained, as they walked along, " and it suits us quite well; but it hasn't such a view as this new one will have ; and besides, this has been a dream of mine so long that I may as well gratify it. You see we haven't any children, and so we may as well indulge our whims, Jessie and I. We shan't sell the old house though."

" No ? " said Nat, interrogatively, and trying to seem as if he were listening with interest.

" Well, no. We feel more like keeping it among us. Very likely we'll give it to Minnie as a wedding present when she marries. She'll be marrying, one of these days. She's a dear good girl, Minnie."

Professor Clinton glanced again at Nathaniel; but the young man was only becoming more and more depressed and embarrassed. Clinton said no more on that subject. Suddenly he touched Nat's arm and said—

" Stay, Cramp, my boy. This is the place—— "

" Come on ! " Nat said, hurriedly.

" No, no. This is the place."

" Do you think I don't know it ? Do you think I forget it ? "

" Well, I didn't think you knew it. Anyhow, take a look at it and tell me what you think of it."

" I don't want to look at it—I won't look at it; I've seen enough of it ! " Nat exclaimed, wildly. " Come on—what did we come here for ? "

" Well, this is my new lot, you know, that I've been telling you about. I'm afraid you were not listening to all my gossip, my poor boy."

" Oh," said Nat, coming to himself and sinking at once from excited nervousness into deep depression—" This is your new place ? Yes, yes, to be sure. It's very nice."

But he only looked at the spot and its surroundings in a furtive, timid, unwilling way, as a murderer in some old story might try to look with seeming indifference and ease at the hollow in the wood beneath the mossy earth of which he has buried his victim. For this was the very spot where he had broken out with his fatal love declaration to Miss Challoner— Clinton's new homestead was to rise on the very ground where Nat had grovelled in his shame and agony. He wondered how Clinton could have forgotten that it was just near this he helped him, Nathaniel, up the steep and clayey bank. But that incident was not fastened into Clinton's mind as into Nat's by the spearhead of a painful memory, and Clinton just now remembered nothing about it.

" Well," the Professor said believing that Nathaniel's grief for his mother was too heavy on him yet to allow him to withdraw his thoughts for a moment to the concerns of others—

" we'll come and have a look at this place another day. Anyhow, you'll carry the place in your mind, Cramp, if you do go away: and you'll remember what it looks like—and that some of your friends are living there."

"Aye," Nat said, gloomily; "I'll remember. I shan't forget this spot."

"And you'll go back to the old country?—there's no way of inducing you to stay?"

"No; Professor Clinton—I must go back."

"Tempted by the big stage and the world for an audience, eh? Well, Cramp—still you know the big stage requires a great strong actor, my boy! You haven't got the big buskins of rank and wealth to raise you up and add to your size, remember. I don't want to discourage you—far from it; but it takes great lungs to fill that theatre!"

"But it isn't that, Professor Clinton. It isn't that, I do assure you. I haven't any ambition in me any more. I may have had aspirations once—I don't say I didn't have them. I may have thought there was something in me," and Nat smote his breast energetically; "and I may have hoped to make the world hear, not without respect, the name of—my name, you know," he added, somewhat hastily, for it suddenly struck him that "the name of Cramp" would not close a period with dignity. "But all such ideas are dead within me now—dead; I am crushed!"

"Oh, no; nothing of the kind."

"I am crushed!" Nat repeated, solemnly. "I only ask now for one thing, and that, Professor Clinton, is death!"

Nat was theatric, and so far was a sham in his way of expressing his emotions. But there cannot be a greater mistake than to suppose that sham expression always denotes sham emotion. Nat's feelings were well nigh those of despair. He was scorched by love and hate, by the bitter agonies of mortified self-conceit, by grief and shame. He was just in the mood when the old stories would have made a man sell his soul for the promise of satisfaction to vanity and vengeance. If the false and baffled suitors could have presented themselves with their perfidious device for taking in the proud beauty now, this Claude Melnotte would probably have jumped at it no matter how preposterous.

Professor Clinton might have chaffed Nat openly about his tragedy airs at another time, and he might have smiled even now, but for the young man's miserable expression, haggard cheeks, and twitching lips. "This is not merely the grief for a mother," he thought. "I suppose the poor young fellow really is in love with that handsome English girl. What a hopeless look-out!"

"Well, Cramp," he said quietly, "if you only want Death, I

guess you might as well wait here and spare yourself the trouble of going to Europe. He'll come and find you here, you may be sure, if you only wait long enough. Seriously, my boy, I doubt whether you will do any good in any way, Cramp—in any way," he repeated, with emphasis, ".by going to Europe. I know something of England, and what the differences are of money and position there ; and take the advice of a friend, Cramp, and think no more of *that*—you know what I mean."

" Professor Clinton," Nathaniel said, solemnly, " If you think I'm going to thrust myself on people that don't want me, you are mistaken. If you think I don't know what British purse-pride is, and what the barriers of class—of money, that is—are in a country like mine, you are mistaken ! But a sacred duty calls me to cross the ocean, and perhaps a Fate! You may chance to hear something of me. I don't know. But think well of me, if you can. Think the best of me you can."

Despite all the grandiose inflation of Nat's language (a style to which Clinton had indeed grown somewhat accustomed of late) there was a certain earnestness, a sort of desperation, in his manner, which impressed the Professor and made him think of it long after. They walked home presently, and almost in silence. It had grown quite dark by the time they reached New Padua. Nat hurriedly declined an invitation to step in and see Clinton's "folks," and went to the Franklin House alone.

The next evening, when Clinton and his wife and sister-in-law were sitting down to their modest supper (the final meal of the day was called supper there, and took place at least three hours earlier than an ordinary London dinner), a letter was brought to him from the Franklin House, accompanied by a parcel.

" This is from Cramp," he said to his wife, and both glanced ominously at Minnie.

The letter told in a few confused lines, written evidently under the influence of some excitement, that the writer would, " before this reaches you," have left New Padua. It thanked Clinton for all his kindness, and declared that he was Nathaniel Cramp's best and only friend. It conveyed the writer's kind and grateful regards to Mrs. Clinton and to Minnie, and finally begged that Clinton would accept the copy of the Girondists, by Lamartine (Bohn's translation), sent herewith, that Mrs. Clinton would accept the photographic album, and Minnie the copy of Miss Jean Ingelow's poems, also sent in memory of their devoted friend Nathaniel Cramp.

There were soft tears in the eyes of both the kindly young women. It was like Nat Cramp's luck, or, as he would have preferred to call it, his Destiny. A sweet and pretty girl might have loved him and looked up to him always, and he never knew it.

"Poor fellow!" Clinton said, "he has taken his mother's death greatly to heart."

After his supper Professor Clinton went to the Franklin House to find out something about Nathaniel. He could only learn, in addition to what he knew already, that Nathaniel had gone eastward on "the cars," and had had his baggage "checked" for New York. He had not said anything about the probable time of his return. The people at the Franklin House assumed that he was only going to be absent for a few days.

So Professor Clinton went home and told his womankind.

"He'll come back soon, I dare say," he added, cheerily, although somehow he did not expect to see Nat return.

The misgivings were prophetic. When the train plunged into the deep cutting just outside the town, and Nat instinctively ran to the end of the carriage to get a glimpse at parting of the university buildings on the bluff above the river, he saw New Padua for the last time.

CHAPTER XXVII.

"WHY WEEP YE BY THE TIDE, LADYE?"

WILD and whimsical were the purposes which filled Nat Cramp's mind as he journeyed back to New York—his career all over, he said to himself; the star of his fate declined. It may be questioned whether to youthful self-conceit there is any pleasure of sense or soul more exquisite than that of despair.

"Is it even so?"—says Romeo—"then I defy ye, stars!" Nat Cramp felt all the way as one who could defy the stars. The petty annoyances, discontents, disappointments of life troubled him no more. He was released from all responsibilities. He hugged to his breast with all the satisfaction of mortified self-conceit seeking redress the thought of an early death and of the sensation it must cause and the tragic dignity it must shed over him. "They won't laugh at that," he said to himself.

But death will not come by mere asking; and Nathaniel was not quite clear as yet how it was to come to him. He had always been fascinated by the manner in which the hapless hero of Victor Hugo's "Travailleurs de la Mer" contrives to finish his career—standing on a rock which the rising tide must cover, so that just as the ship bearing his beloved away, the wife of another, sinks below the horizon, the water—the same water which bears her—closes over him. If he could do that! If he could stand upon some rock near Durewoods—far from help and yet within her sight—and thus be submerged! But it would be hard to bring about all the conjunction of favouring circumstances which alone could render possible so effective a catastrophe. Nat felt even some painful misgivings that he might not at such a moment have control enough over his nerves and instincts to enable him to cling to his rock and not to make unseemly struggles for dear life—that dear life that he detested. He had therefore at present some vague idea of finding out the steamer in which the Challoners were to sail from New York, taking a passage on board it, suddenly when in mid-ocean presenting himself before Marie, once more declaring his love, and then plunging into the sea beneath her eyes. Something, he felt assured, must happen, or be brought about. The career must close dramatically; the curtain must fall at the right time. Thus alone could ridicule be changed into respect and failure be converted by the glamour of tragedy into something as fascinating as success.

His poor mother had, as he told Professor Clinton, left him some money. He had put it rather vaguely and grandly to Clinton as if it were a sort of property. It was really a good deal to Nat—two hundred and fifty pounds in money, and the little house in which she had been living. A day or two before her death she had sent him an order on a New York house for fifty pounds. She had only then learned that he was in New Padua, and she feared he was not doing well, and she therefore sent him that money and begged that he would come back, as she feared she was growing weak and ill. The same steamer brought him the news of her death and of the fact that she had left him what little she had managed to save and scrape together. Long before he reached England the grave, he knew, must have covered her. He had been attached to her in his way, and he thought now with many a pang that lately he had been ashamed of her. Now somehow he laid the blame of her death on the same blighting influences of adverse fortune and caste and class and Destiny, and all the rest of the cruel agencies which had marred his own career. He had now no consolation left on earth but the despair which was only self-conceit driven to bay.

Mingling up with all his misery was a curious sense of satisfaction in having for the first time in his life money which he could freely spend. The fifty pounds which had been sent by his mother would pay for a first-class passage to Europe in one of the Cunard steamers in which he assumed that the Challoners would travel, and would keep him in New York at some first-class hotel until the time of his departure. Then when he got to England—if he did ever reach England—he should find money there—" quite enough to last my time " he grimly and complacently thought. He had some idea of having a marble monument erected out of his mother's savings over his mother's grave, with the inscription, "By her unworthy but penitent son, Nathaniel Cramp." But for all that there was yet time enough. Meanwhile he could do as he pleased with what money he had; and he would at least be a gentleman, in whatever despair, for the remainder of his time.

How much of this was nonsense and idle self-delusion, and how much was the set, unconquerable purpose of despair which makes dignified even frivolity itself when it comes to that with frivolity, the course of this story does not allow us to know for certain. It is true that no emotion by which men's hearts are swollen—not love, not patriotism, not thirst of money, not craving for revenge—has ever inspired more desperate and dogged deeds than mortified self-conceit. It may be that Nat would have held firmly to some suicidal purpose none the less because he felt a pride in ordering a hack when he reached New York and driving at once to the Fifth Avenue Hotel, and in dressing rather carefully when he got there, and then in descending to stand with air of lordly Briton among the group who lounged in the hall and at the entrance.

He stood there for some time and looked vacantly enough over the bustling and varied scene—a scene which now, when evening had refined whatever of the commonplace and the colourless was in it, showed singularly bright and picturesque. Through the broad stretches of Madison Square the many lamps glittered like fireflies among the dark trees. At one side, as he stood at the entrance of the hotel, extended the monotonous stately length of Fifth Avenue, its solemn gentility scarcely disturbed by even the passing of a street omnibus, its rows of brown stone houses making a line of contrast with the animation, rattle, and flashing lights of Broadway (which here suddenly slants across it) and of Madison Square, not unlike that which a dark and silent canal might make between populous quays and glittering windows. An unceasing rattling, bell-ringing, stamping procession of heavy street cars, and of little staggering, restless omnibuses or "stages," was in motion before the doors of the Fifth Avenue Hotel; passengers were always jumping off and jumping on the cars; the whole population of New York seemed to stream up and down that one great channel of Broadway. The hall and entrance and the steps of the hotel were alive with New York loungers; with solemn, sallow Southerners, always seeming to be oppressed somehow with a sense of offended dignity; with dark-skinned Cuban swells, tremendous for shirt-fronts, and diamond studs; with Irish porters and negro barbers, and "helps" of all kinds. Noise, clatter, light, bustle, were everywhere. No street-scene in London gives the same idea of restless and exuberant vitality. It impressed Nat Cramp rather

s

sadly. He thought of the time when he first looked on Broadway and believed he had come there to conquer fortune and fame. He could not endure the crowd and the noise and the glare. He knew New York well enough to know what a city of sudden contrasts it is. He walked down through the solemn silent dignity of Fifth Avenue, then dining grandly inside its brown-stone fronts, until it declined mournfully into the vast, gaunt, and desolate expanse of Washington Square ; and there he sat on a bench under a dismal tree and looked at the stars burning in fullest lustre from the deep purple of the evening sky, and he was as lonely to all intent as if he had been in some midnight mountain pass. Nat never knew how long he remained in that drear inclosure ; but when he returned to his hotel the doors were all closed and he had to ring for admittance.

Next day he was astir early, and set himself to work to find out something of the Challoners. This was an easy business in a city like New York, where everybody's movements are in the papers, and where the registers in the hotel-offices are open to all eyes at any moment. He found that they were in the city, that they were to remain there or in the neighbourhood for a few days more, and that that very evening they were to leave the city for the purpose of paying a visit to a distinguished scholar and author who had a home in one of the islands. He also learned the name of the steamer by which the Challoners were to return to Europe, and he hastened to the office and endeavoured to secure a passage on board her. His attempt was hopeless. Every berth had been taken long since. That mad whim, at least, was not to be gratified.

Then another whim seized him. He would accompany the Challoners unseen on their visit to their friend in the island, and he would look on her again. This whim, at least, was easily gratified. He had simply to ask at any of the ferries (it may be well for the instruction of English readers to remark that New York is girt with water almost as completely as Venice itself, and is therefore ringed with ferries—walk straight on in any direction and you come to a ferry-gate and a steamer just on the point of starting), and it was easy to learn what steamer went to the island, and to that part of it where the Challoners were to be entertained. It was one of the longer trips, and the steamer only went a few times in the day. Nat spent the rest of that day watching the departure of the boats.

Evening was coming. It was still the Indian summer. Except that the air grew chilly after sunset, there was scarcely yet a hint that such a season as winter could be expected. Soon over the New Jersey shores the sun would begin to go down. Even the rough, prosaic, unadorned, grimly-unpicturesque piers and wharves around the river-front of New York were glorified into something poetic and beautiful by the magic of that atmosphere and those skies. Even Natty, as the soft sunlight fell upon him, began almost to think that life ought to be worth something. Evening is coming, and there is the last steamer, and people are already going on board. Should he go and risk being disappointed? Perhaps it was all a mistake; and she is not coming? The sun will soon begin to sink, but long before he sinks that steamer will have pushed out into the broad Sound. Ah!—and see, there is fair Inez to dazzle when the sun goes down!

For at that moment a carriage drove up to the ferry-gate, and Sir John Challoner got out, calm, portly, and dignified. Then a tall gentleman with a long grey beard and a snowy head gave his hand to Marie Challoner as she dropped lightly down. There was the châtelaine of Durewoods again—there on those rugged, dusty paving-stones, amid those bustling, hustling crowds, amid baggage and carts and porters and hackmen and negroes! How beautiful she looked in her hat and feather, and with that all unconscious expression of pride in her eyes and on her lips which poor Nat but too well knew was ready to give place at a word to the bright, fresh look of kindly sweetness. She took the arm of the grey-haired man, and they hurried on board. The skirt of Marie's dress almost touched Nat as she passed him in the crowd, for he had not a moment's time to withdraw from the spot where he had been standing and hide himself. But he had not been seen—she would never have expected to see him there. Nat paid his fare and went on board; and stationed himself for the present behind a huge pile of baggage, where he could easily see without much chance of being seen by those whom he was watching.

The steamer soon left the ill-paved, dusty, noisy wharves, and struck out straight for the sunset. Then she turned her side to the sun and glided swiftly along among small islands and large, by shores which lay low and soft under young trees from amid which every now and then a spire looked up, past great ocean steamers and vessels lying at anchor, and tiny tug-boats puffing with supernatural impatience and hurry. Nat saw from his retreat that Marie Challoner was walking up and down the deck leaning on the arm of her stately grey-haired host. Sometimes they passed quite near him—close to him, even—and he could hear them speak. Once he heard the grey-haired gentleman ask Miss Challoner if she had ever read Cooper's "Water Witch," and when she answered that she had read it long ago, and used to be very fond of it, he stopped in their promenade and pointed to one of the islands and told her that there was the spot where the *Water Witch* was supposed to be lying when the story opened. Nat looked out from his lurking-place that he might see the island and the whole scene for himself. For one moment he

almost forgot his love, his shame, his wretched failure, in the
memories that came back upon him. Oh, the days when he read
the "Water Witch," and delighted in it, and longed for a world
of adventure like that world of story ! Oh for the happy boyish
days when illusion could still seem to be the soft-creeping
shadow of the reality coming on, and the romantic dream might
be interpreted as the faint saffron light heralding the early
dawn !

An Irishman, a labourer, apparently, of some kind, but well-
dressed and independent-looking, was standing near Nat talking
to a companion. Doubtless they were going over some recollections of old days at home, for the first man, looking out across
the purpling waters, said, in a low tone and in words common in
his country, and thrilling with all the half-poetic, half-devo-
tional fervour of the Celt—

"Well, God be with the old times ! "

Nat only faintly caught the meaning, perhaps, but his soul
sadly echoed what it did receive. Oh, God be with those old
times when he was yet only reading romances, and his poor
mother lived !

The sun was gone, and there was no twilight, and a faint moon
arose. The skies were wan and chilly. Most of the passengers
had entered the great saloon, which, with its sides all window,
covered a large part of the deck, and within which lights were
burning and stoves were glowing. Nat could see that Sir John
Challoner was there reading letters and newspapers. But Marie
and her companion remained on deck and walked up and down,
and looked on the skies, and the shores, and the water, and
talked. It was so dark now that Nat could emerge from his
hiding-place and, with his hat over his forehead, look boldly
around him, having little fear of being observed. It was strange
to be so near her ! Never before had he such a time to feed his
senses in gazing on her and thinking of her. Whenever she
turned he saw her face looking pale in the faintly rising moonlight. Sometimes he could not see the outlines of her stately
figure, but only the pale face and the dark hair against the
deepening shade of the evening. A beautiful face it seemed to
poor Nat, and melancholy, divinely melancholy, he thought. He
could hardly feel angry with her any more, although he had
abased himself through her and she had been so cruelly kind to
him, and his life had been so ruined and made hateful because
of her. He felt a kind of ignoble satisfaction as she looked so
pale and melancholy, for he sprang to the conclusion that she
did not care about the man she was going to marry—and then
suddenly another conviction pierced him like the puncture of a
dart, and he had almost screamed out with rage at the thought.
It remained with him and tormented him, and he began to hate
her again.

"That's why she's so pale—that's why she's unhappy!" he repeated to himself. "She's got to marry somebody else, and she's in love with that fellow from Japan!"

The steamer now drew near to a long, low, softly-outlined shore covered with young trees almost to the edge of the water, and sparkling here and there with the lights in homesteads and little villages. Close by the shore the steamer held her way, and Nat could hear from the woods the shrill double-throb of the katy-did, which seemed to him to have a doleful and boding sound, congenial with the darkling hour and his own condition. The shore was indented by many little bays and creeks, and sometimes the steamer ran into one of these and landed some passengers. Each time Nat shivered with excitement, he knew not why, believing that they had come to the end of their voyage. What he proposed to do when they did come to an end of it he had not yet asked himself.

At length the steamer splashed into a bay or inlet, running apparently rather far inland. The moon had now risen in stronger light, and Nat could see that they were narrowed in by shores on both sides, so that for a time there was nothing but trees and water and sky; the white gleam of the moon above, and the yellow glow from the saloon windows below.

Marie Challoner and her companion stood close to him now.

"We are near the end of our voyage," her companion said.

"I don't know whether I ought to be glad or sorry," she answered. "It has been such a delicious little voyage among those islands, but this place is most beautiful of all. I love this place."

"I am so glad you like it," her companion said, smiling at her enthusiasm—"for this is my home."

"Is it wrong of me," Nat heard outspoken Lady Disdain answer, "if I say that I love it already because it is so like *my* home?"

And now a pier was seen, a rude, somewhat rickety wooden pier, with twinkling lights, and sound of bustling men and stamping horses. Sir John Challoner came out from the saloon, and Nat drew back again to escape observation. The boat panted, puffed, stopped, backed, went on again, and finally settled at the pier, and planks were run out. Two negro servants leaped on board and bustled up to Miss Challoner's companion, and took some orders from him. Then he and she and Sir John went ashore. Nat followed them with a little crowd of other passengers. He saw them get into a carriage with flashing lights and drive away.

Natty's first impulse was to run after the carriage. He thought of himself, however, before he had ventured on this ridiculous proceeding, and was content to walk leisurely in the direction it had taken. There was only one road that he could see, and therefore there could be no going wrong. When he had mounted the road, which ascended gently, far enough to be clear of the little crowd around the pier, he came to a stand for a moment and endeavoured to get his thoughts into order. What did he mean to do—what did he want to do?

All his ideas resolved themselves into a vague purpose to see her again. He strode on without thinking any more about the matter—doggedly, and with his head down. He crushed the fallen leaves under his feet, and looked neither to right nor to left. The sound of feet coming towards him soon caused him to look up, and he saw in the moonlight a little boy and girl trotting hand in hand down the hilly road. He asked them where the host of the Challoners lived. Everybody in that region knew him by name, and the children both in one breath told Nat to go "right on," and that he would see the gate in a few minutes. Nat went right on and came to the gate, opened it, and went in.

He followed the path of an avenue, dark between young trees. He heard no sound but that of the katy-dids and the murmur of the woods. The moonlight hardly made its way to the path he trod. He was ready, if he heard a step anywhere, to plunge into the plantation at either side, but no footfall sounded except his own. Suddenly the path ended, and a scene opened before Nat the beauty of which even at that moment he could not fail to see.

A broad expanse of lawn, valley, and water lay before him. An amphitheatre opened among the trees; its sides made of grassy lawn, its basin filled with a beautiful lakelet fed by a stream that descended under a pretty bridge from amid the trees on the side opposite to where Nat was now standing. On the lawn stood a long, low, wooden house with windows all round, and a great verandah or "stoop" on which were seats, and which was reached by a broad flight of steps. The house and the verandah were almost embowered in plants and shrubs and fruit trees. Grape-clusters hung in huge masses along its sides. The tulip tree and the hemlock, and the enormous willow—so unlike, in dimensions, the willow which Nat associated in memory chiefly with burial grounds at home—were planted here and there near the house. The lake glittered, pure and cold in the now chilly moonlight. The yellow lights streaming from the windows of the house filled Nat with a wild yearning for shelter and friends and welcome, and a bitter sense of his own desolation. The whole scene made up fitly the home of a poet—even Nat was conscious of a sense of its beauty borne in upon him with a rush of thought that the world was full of such homes and scenes, and of happiness, and success, and brilliancy—and love; and that he was out in the cold from everything.

He wandered round and round the house, and even ventured to peer in through a window here and there, but the blinds inside were all drawn down, and he could see nothing. He could hear many voices, however, and animated talk, and after a while he heard music. Then some of the windows on the verandah, which opened level to its floor, were raised, and people came out on the verandah and the steps. Nat hid himself behind a little clump of trees in the shadow.

Marie Challoner came out with her host and stood on the steps. She had a white "cloud" round her head and shoulders. Nat could hear her voice, though he did not catch the words she spoke, and she seemed to be animated with a sort of reckless good spirits. She brought her host down to the verge of the little lake, and several of the company followed them there; and she insisted, apparently, on getting into the boat. Nat could see that Sir John Challoner and their host appeared to remonstrate with her good-humouredly, but that she would not be persuaded out of her enterprise, and so she got into the boat, and another girl with her—a slight, fragile American, looking like the ghost of a girl beside the full, noble figure of Lady Disdain. Lady Disdain took the oars and practised the craft she had learned of old Merlin in Durewoods waters when she was a little girl, and with a few light, strong strokes, sent the boat shooting across the little lake and under the bridge and up to where the water grew narrow in its basin, and where the feeding stream poured in. So the boat disappeared out of the moonlight, and was lost among trees and shadows, but when it had gone Nat could hear that Marie was singing in her full, deep contralto voice. How happy she is—how happy they are all! poor Nat thought, and he almost hated her for being happy, because she had scorned him.

Again he heard the plash of the oars, and he saw several of the company run round the edge of the lake and station themselves on the bridge to see the English girl shoot her boat beneath. Nat emerged boldly and stood upon the lawn. There were several stray spectators lounging about, and there were gardeners and "helps," and Nat had no fear of being noticed by any one except Sir John Challoner, whom he would take good care to avoid, and Nat had eyes like a lynx. Straight under the bridge and into the moonlight shot the boat, swift and black, across the water. Marie as the rower had her back turned to Nat. Her "cloud" had fallen round her shoulders, and her thick hair was seen. Then as the boat darted in towards the bank the rower suddenly rested upon her oars, and turned quickly round to see whither she was impelling herself, and Nat saw her face full in the moonlight, with the pale forehead and the careless hair coming low on it, and the sparkling eyes and the lips firmly set with the eagerness of her exercise and her responsi-

bility as a rower. Then the boat touched the shore, and before
any one could come to her help Marie had leaped out and taken
her fragile companion under the arms and landed her lightly on
the bank.

Nat drew back to the shelter of his clump of trees, and he
heard laughing and talking and moving feet, and in a few
moments the lawn and the verandah were lonely and silent
again.

He hung about the house, about the plantation, and on the
lawn for hours. He heard music now and then, and some men
occasionally came on the verandah and smoked and talked. Nat
saw Sir John Challoner among the rest. Then all these disappeared, and the sounds from within the house grew less and less,
and at last the lights in the room where the company had been
were put out, and Nat saw negro helps bustling about here and
there, and he crouched on the ground among the trees to escape
discovery. All was quiet at length. Lights twinkled in rooms
on the verandah level and above, which Nat assumed to be bedrooms. He felt very miserable, and wished now that he had not
come on this idle expedition. What was the good of seeing her
for a few moments? Where was he to go now? Suppose he
should be found lurking like a robber, near the house, and treated
as a robber, or turned from the grounds with ridicule and disgrace?

At that moment a window on the verandah opened and Marie
Challoner herself came out and stood in the moonlight. She
leaned on the railing and looked over the scene. Dear Lady
Disdain was not inclined to sleep. She had forced herself into
spirits all the evening, and now the reaction had come. Perhaps
it was merely the physical reaction which affected her. Perhaps
it was the resemblance which she fancied that she saw between
the whole place and that Durewoods home from which and from
all its sweet associations she now began to regard herself as
parted. She was very melancholy—depressed almost beyond
endurance, and she had panted to be alone for a moment, and in
the open air—the cold, clear night air.

Nat Cramp was quite near to her—so near that if he emerged
for one moment from behind his trees into the moonlight of the
lawn she might have seen him—perhaps must have seen him.
He was so near that he could hear every rustle of her dress as
she moved, so near that he held his breath lest she should hear
him breathe and take alarm. Sometimes an insane desire seized
him to come boldly forward and speak to her, and then he thought
of her anger, her scorn, the certain exposure and ridicule. More
than once he thought of going down into the little lake and lying
there; and it fascinated him to picture the sensation which would
be created when next morning his body should be found, and she

at least must then know that his feelings were deep, and that he hated life, and knew how to die.

She bent her head down upon the railing of the verandah, and he suddenly knew that she had burst into tears. He heard her sobbing. He gave a cry of rage and despair which startled her very quickly from her hysterical mood, and made her stand up ashamed, affrighted, with wonder and excitement. But he heeded nothing. He had lost even all sense of dread at the possibility of discovery. He ran through the plantation, crushing among the trees in his blind wild flight. He reached the avenue and tore furiously along it until he actually ran against the gate. He scrambled over somehow, and gained the open road, and threw himself down there, panting, exhausted, indifferent for the moment whether he were pursued or not, discovered or not.

But he was not pursued. Nobody thought of him. When Marie's first alarm was over, and she could see nothing, and only heard a crash among the trees, she thought it must have been some dog or other animal loose in the plantation. She retreated very quickly to her room, however, and waited for a while with beating heart; but as she heard no further sound outside the house, and heard within the house the subdued, reassuring tread and voices of servants, she thought little more of the occurrence which had startled her. So when he had lain long on the road outside the gate poor Nat got up and slowly dragged himself to the steamer pier. He would hang about anywhere until the morning, he thought, and then go back to New York by the first steamer, and return to England to see his mother's grave. Even his death now, he believed, would hardly interest Miss Challoner, for he told himself with agony that she was sobbing because of " that fellow from Japan."

CHAPTER XXVIII.

IN THE SAME BOAT.

Two or three weeks after the time of the last chapter, Christmas Pembroke was in London one streaming night of rain and wind. He had been leading a strange sort of life lately. He had severed himself from all association with acquaintances, and passed a moody, lonely, semi-savage existence. He had not for some time even written to Dione Lyle, and for aught she knew he might have been on his way to Japan. He had deliberately abstained from writing to her because he feared that she would try to prevail on him to leave England before the Challoners should return, and he had not the courage to confess to her the hope and the purpose which kept him in London and upheld him in life. He felt himself for the present a sort of enemy to the human race, so bitter had he grown in his exaggerated sense of the treachery of Sir John Challoner.

This particular night he turned into a colonial club, of which he was a member, to see something about the mail steamer next expected from New York. As he was passing out again through the hall he suddenly ran against Mr. Ronald Vidal. Of all men he, Christmas, would have avoided him. They ought to be enemies, Christmas thought ; it would be a relief to him if they were ; and yet they were not.

On the contrary, Mr. Vidal was more friendly than usual, for instead of passing on with the genial " How do ? " and graceful nod which constitute our warm-hearted English way of acknowledging an acquaintance, he came to a stand, and had evidently something to say to Christmas. It ought perhaps to have been a mortal defiance in order to fall in with Christmas's mood ; but it was not.

" Seen the Challoners yet ? They've come, don't you know ? " Vidal added, observing that Christmas looked as if he did not quite understand.

" Have they come ? I didn't know—you didn't expect them this week I thought."

" No ; Challoner had to cut things a little shorter than he intended. They came by Havre."

" Oh ! Are they in London ? "

" No ; they have gone to Durewoods—only passed through town. Challoner will be here to-morrow or next day. Miss Challoner won't come to town—just for the present."

Christmas thought he knew what that meant, and his heart beat fiercely.

"I hear you are going back to Japan—is that so?" Vidal asked.

"Yes; I am going back."

"You don't like us here—can't stand our winter fogs, I suppose? Well, such beastly weather as this would make one glad to get out of England anywhere. We shall see you before you go, I hope?" Mr. Vidal added with a faint consciousness now growing up within him that Christmas being considered as a stranger in London he really ought to have been more attentive to him and to have had him to dinner at his club or Greenwich or somewhere.

Christmas said something civil in reply, and they went their ways. Short as their conversation was, it was about the longest they had ever carried on together. They had never seemed to approach each other in the least. From the first our young hero had felt a dislike to Vidal, not unnaturally, although perhaps very unreasonably. He disliked him first because he was a young man of position whom Sir John Challoner would evidently like to have as a husband for his daughter; and more lately because Vidal was apparently destined to hold that place. On this substantial basis of antipathy it was easy to construct many little separate objections and dislikes, and Christmas found great fault with a man who cared about lace and old china. Mr. Vidal had not the slightest ill-feeling to Christmas, about whom indeed he hardly ever thought at all. Like most persons who are quick in observing externals and noticing little weaknesses, Vidal had scarcely any perception of character or faculty of arriving at the real feelings of others, and he had never supposed that his approaching marriage with Marie Challoner could concern Pembroke in any way.

Christmas felt his heart beating so quickly as to be painful and almost unbearable when he left Vidal. They had come then, and she was in Durewoods again, and evidently she was soon to be married—and meantime what was he to do? How hopeless, how insane now seemed that purpose which had kept him alive while yet the ocean was between them and the purpose was only a vision! What a romantic madman he must prove himself to be! People would pity him, or laugh at him. She would blame him perhaps, and he should have to leave England with her words of blame and the knowledge that he had offended her for his farewell!

No matter. Blame or contempt, anger or laughter might fall on him—what did it matter to him now? After all, what he was going to do was very simple. It was only to ask a girl who had always been kind and friendly beyond measure to let him see

her for a few moments and say good-bye to her in person before
he left England for ever, and then while they were together just
to tell her in plain simple words that he was not in love with any
other girl, that he had never dreamed of marrying any other girl.
And even if he should be carried a little further and should say
he had loved and did still only love her—what harm would that
do to her? What kindly-hearted woman would think the worse
of him for that? He would leave her in a moment, and she
would be troubled with him no more. Why should she be
angry with him for his tribute of a hopeless love that asked not
even a word of kindness in return?

Christmas hurried to his lodgings, and packed up a few
things and wrote a few letters and put his affairs, such as they
were, as much as possible in order. For he was determined that
his leaving London—when he had seen her for the last time—
should be rapid as a flight. He would go to Durewoods to-
morrow by the earliest train, he would endeavour to see her at
once, and that interview over he would hasten to Miss Lyle's,
say a few words of good-bye, then back to London, and fly thence
across the Continent to take passage for the East in the first
steamer that would receive him on board. Dione Lyle knew
nothing of his rush to Durewoods or its purpose. When it was
over she might guess it if she would, but there would be little
time for guessing anything then.

He smoked many cigars and walked up and down his room
and thought a great deal and burst out every now and then into
wild fragments of song and felt very much as a man might do on
the eve of a battle or a duel. He did not go to sleep until very
late and he had to be up early. He anticipated his hour of
rising several times, fearing he had overslept himself, and sprang
out of bed and turned his gas full on and looked at his watch
only to find that there were hours yet, between him and the time
for starting.

At last he got up and found that it was six o'clock. His
train was to leave at half-past seven. The station was but a few
minutes' walk from his chambers. He tried to look out of his
windows, but there was a driving rain plashing against the
panes, and a fierce wind was shaking the trees and rattling the
window-frames, and there was outside a denser than midnight
darkness. It suited his mood of mind, this furious winter
weather, this wind and this fog; he was grimly glad it was not
summer or even a bright winter's day. He wondered to himself
how the hollow among the trees at Durewoods where he and she
had stood alone that first day—would look on such a day as this.
He determined that after he had seen *her* for the last time he
would go and stand there—and so bear with him into his exile
a memory of the place not gladdened by summer and soft blue

skies, and her sweet companionship, but lonely, wintry, scourged
with rain and tossed with cruel wind.

"It's a pity I can't see her there to-day for the last time," he
said half aloud in his excitement, and bitterly. " That would be
something like what they call the irony of fate indeed ! "

Then to be prepared for everything and make sure that no
time should be lost, he sat down and wrote a few lines to Miss
Challoner, saying he particularly wished to speak to her before
he left England, and asking if he might see her. He made his
request as simple and friendly as possible, avoiding all appearance of high-tragedy airs. He put the note into an envelope,
and wrote on the envelope her name and address. Then he tore
off that envelope and burned it at the gas ; and he wrote on
another only the words "Miss Challoner," without any address.
For he thought that in the remote possibility of his losing the
letter on the way—the most unlikely, surely, of all imaginable
contingencies—or of the train breaking down, or anything whatever happening to prevent him from presenting the letter at the
Durewoods Hall himself, would be much better that it should
not be found and sent on by any other person. Then he put the
letter into the breast pocket of his overcoat, and opened his door
and went out.

Such a morning for a trip to the sea-shore ! The streets were
deserted, although it was past seven ; the wind blew the rain in
sheets along them ; the jets of gas in the lamps winked and blinked
every now and then as if they shrank and cowered before the
gusts. The great railway station looked utterly forlorn ; it
seemed hardly possible to believe that there could be any evidence
of such life and activity as the starting of a train on such a
morning. Christmas really had an absurd misgiving as he
entered the station that the officials would tell him there was no
train for Durewoods that day. This misgiving, however, was
not realised. The train was to go its way independently of
wind, darkness, and the pains of wild young lovers. Christmas
got into a carriage and tortured himself with wishing that the
moment was come for the train to start. It wanted not quite ten
minutes of the half-hour ; but Christmas chafed about these
ten minutes as if the train was doing him some personal injustice
by not starting before its time, or as if it mattered in the least
to him even though it were an hour behind it.

The ten minutes did at last pass away, and the train left the
station. All was blackness outside except where a flash of gas
now and then streamed across the windows and allowed a
glimpse of rain-beaten roofs and chimney tops. There were two
or three other passengers in Christmas's carriage, but he spoke to
nobody. Could it be that through this wind, rain, and darkness
it was possible to arrive at Durewoods, and its memories of the

sun and the bright water and Marie Challoner? Could it be
that Marie Challoner herself was now there? Could anything in
life ever be bright again?

The livid spectral morning at last crept over the fields. The
rain gradually abated, and towards noon a dismal glint of ghostly
sunlight broke through the clouds. Then this again was lost in
masses of heaped-up cloud which the wind drove together. The
rain and wind seemed to be contending which should put down
the other. At present the wind appeared in a fair way to
succeed, although every now and then a reinforcing gush of rain
occupied the landscape to show that the contest was not
yet over.

The train reached the junction where Christmas had to leave
the main track and take the little branch line which led to the
sea. Only one other passenger besides himself got out here.
Christmas did not look at the other, but the other looked at him
curiously, wonderingly, and then came up to him, and Christmas, to his amazement, recognized the face and figure of
Nathaniel Cramp.

"Why, Cramp! What on earth brings you here? I thought
you were four or five thousand miles away."

"I have come back, Mr. Pembroke—as you see. But I
thought you had left England before this."

"Take your places, gentlemen," cried the railway guard.
" Train for Baymouth " the little port from which they were to
cross to Durewoods.

"Are you going to Durewoods?" Christmas asked as they
took their places, with a faint hope that Cramp was perhaps not
going there, and very reluctant to be troubled with his or any
other society just then.

" Yes, I'm going to Durewoods," Nathaniel answered grimly.
" Are you? " And he chafed at the notion of Christmas going
there.

" I am going there—yes. But what on earth has brought you
back from the States, Cramp? I thought you were getting on
famously there."

" So I was. My way was open there. But a sacred call has
brought me back; and I am going to Durewoods to perform a
sacred duty."

Christmas looked up surprised.

" I am going to see my mother's grave and to raise a monument to her."

Christmas's heart was touched in a moment. He had not
heard of the death of Nat's mother—indeed he had for some
time been engrossed solely with his own affairs and disappointments. Now he felt repentant for having wished to get
rid of poor Nat, seeing that Nat had lost his mother. There-

fore he did his very best to show that he could feel for the poor
fellow's loss.

"I am very unfortunate, Mr. Pembroke."

"Never mind the 'Mr.,' Cramp. We are brothers in misfortune I think—in many ways."

"I believe we are," Nat interposed, with an emphasis which
even then struck Christmas as a little odd. But almost everything about Nat was odd, and Christmas thought the loss of his
mother had made his manner particularly wild now. Even grief
somehow failed to render poor Cramp quite tragic or heroic.
There was always a dash of the ludicrous about him.

Christmas drew him to talk about his mother, and his prospects and plans. Nat spoke with vague and awful foreboding
about some mysterious fate, which he seemed to regard as
certainly impending over him. All that did not much impress
our hero, however. He remembered with mingled pain and
humour his meeting with Nat on the Durewoods pier, when Nat
talked so grandly and tragically and they both presently fell into
the sea.

As the train neared Baymouth they ceased to talk. Christmas
found his anxiety and impatience become almost intolerable, and
Nat remained buried in gloom. The sea came in sight. It was
tossing in sharp broken waves, and was a livid greenish grey
under a grey sky, from which even the wind that still blew
fiercely could not pack the clouds away.

"Looks wild, don't it?" said Nat.

"Very wild indeed. I wish we were across," Christmas said,
in an impatient and vexed tone, not thinking about any danger
in crossing, but only of any possible difficulty or delay.

"Perhaps we may not get across ever," said Nat, tragically.

"Why not? Of course we shall get across."

"These waves are deep and wild," the prophet of evil
gloomily remarked.

"Why, Cramp"—and Christmas laughed an impatient laugh
—"you've crossed the ocean twice, and you must have seen
rougher seas than that. You ought not to be alarmed."

"Oh, *I* ain't alarmed!—I am not alarmed, I mean. No, not
in the least. The waves don't matter to *me*."

"Baymouth!" called the guard, as the train ran up to the
little station. Christmas leaped out and made for the pier, not
waiting to see whether Nat followed him. Pembroke's mind
misgave him, and he tormented himself by conjuring up obstacles
and difficulties to prevent him from getting on. The first sight
of the pier confirmed his forebodings. No *Saucy Lass* or other
steamer was there. But that was nothing, he thought. She was
delayed in her trip from Durewoods by the wind and weather.
She would be here presently. The delay was vexatious, however.

But Nathaniel, who had not hastened so wildly from the station, had time to get some news there, which he brought to Christmas now with the morose satisfaction of one who is rather pleased by anything that crosses the mood of any one else. The *Saucy Lass* had received a severe injury to her machinery that morning owing to the weather. She had been rescued from utter destruction by a chance steamer of much larger size, which had towed her into a little port near, and there she was helpless for the present. There would be no steamer to Durewoods that day, and possibly not even the next day.

Christmas assailed the railway-guard and station-master, who were, however, utterly indifferent, and who blandly explained that their company and their line had no more to do with the steamer traffic than he, Christmas, had. Were there no people about who had anything to do with the steamer? No, the officials thought not; they had probably gone round to the port where she was now laid up. Moreover, the station-master calmly expressed a doubt whether " anything much " would come of their being near at hand, seeing that they certainly had no other steamer ready. Further, he informed Christmas that the *Saucy Lass* often did not move from the pier for days in winter, when the weather was bad, " like now "; there were so few people who wanted to cross to Durewoods in such a season.

" But if people want to go, and have to go—what then? "

Then he supposed the *Saucy Lass* could take them. But she couldn't take any one to-day, anyhow.

" Surely you don't mean to say there is no way of getting to Durewoods to-day? "

There was the road; but that went all round the bay—a matter of thirty miles and more.

" Come, that can be accomplished. Is there any sort of carriage or conveyance to be had in this confounded place? "

The answer was decisive. There was none whatever.

" Great heavens! what a place; what a country; what a people! Think of this,—Cramp—you who have been in the States! " Christmas exclaimed. Thereupon the station-master set them down as two Yankees disparaging the institutions of Old England, and he withdrew from the consultation.

" A boat," said Christmas, " can't we have a boat? " But he thought of the hours it would take to cross to Durewoods with such a sea running, and such a wind blowing; and he began to despair.

A friendly porter offered a suggestion. The bay took an immense stretch inland—just there. If they could get a boat— if any one would give his boat in such weather, they could run across that stretch of sea to Portstone pier—a matter of five miles of water, and that would cut off more than twenty miles of road. They then would be less than ten miles from Durewoods, and they might get a carriage at Portstone. Besides, if they only ran in for Portstone pier they would have the wind right behind them all the way.

Christmas was delighted with the suggestion, and thrust a crown-piece into the hand of the man who had made it. Filled with gratitude for this generosity the porter set to work to help him to get a boat. This was hard work. The fishers were all at sea—had been out some days. There was only one small boat available anyhow, and only a couple of boys to row it, and their mother seemed a good deal alarmed at the thought of their venturing out in such weather, although the lads themselves were eager for the enterprise and the pay.

Christmas and the railway porter and the boys declared that there was not the slightest danger. The wind was falling, and anyhow it would be with them for Portstone that far.

"You don't want to go to-day particularly, Cramp," said Pembroke, turning to him. "You needn't come if you think there is any risk. I have a special reason for going to-day."

"Have you, Mr. Pembroke?" Nat said, with deepened emphasis. "Then so have I. I'm going in that boat." And he wildly waved all objection away.

"Well, then, look here; if you will go——"

"I will go. I have said it."

"Very well—can you pull an oar?"

"I used to pull an oar often—on the lake in St. James's Park."

Christmas shrugged his shoulders.

"Well, no matter. I don't think it will be much a matter of rowing at all. With any scrap of a sail—I'll manage it—we'll run across as quickly as a bird; and we needn't take these lads at all. We'll leave the boat at Portstone, and have it sent back to-morrow."

"That's the best thing to do," said the railway porter, with an approving nod.

The proposal was a great relief to the mother and a corresponding disappointment to the boys. Christmas gave the lads a shilling a-piece and that reconciled them to safety on shore. He paid what the woman asked for the hire of the boat, which was not very much, for she was an honest creature who declined even to consider the possibility of her boat being lost or injured.

"Do you really think that there is danger?" Nat asked in a low tone, and with a tremor of the lip, which Christmas set down to fear.

"Why do you ask me that?"

"Not taking the boys, you know."

"I don't think there's any danger. I have told you that I

T

particularly want to get to Durewoods to-day—and being drowned would not bring me there. But if you think there is any danger, Cramp, why on earth do you go? It will be a case of a straight run under sail; and if the boat doesn't turn bottom upwards she can't help getting over to Portstone, and I don't want anybody."

"I am not afraid of the danger," Nat replied, with a sickly smile. "It isn't that, Mr. Pembroke; you are quite wrong; never were more out of your reckoning in all your life."

"Come along, then! Now, boys, to launch her." A little crowd of boys and girls had got round. "You had better get in, Cramp, and sit in the stern. I'll jump in after."

"Watch your time," the railway porter recommended, "watch your time. There's a stiff wave coming." He, too, prepared to lend a hand. The oars were put in, and the little mast shipped, and the sail—a small square thing—reefed up for the moment, and Nat scrambled into the boat and sat in the stern.

"Take my coat, Cramp," Christmas called out, as he pulled off and handed to Nat his thick Ulster overcoat, which threatened to be in his way during the rough work of launching the boat. "Now, then, lads, all together."

Christmas and the railway porter and the two boys, with various amateur assistance, ran the boat down to the very edge of the surf.

"Lie down, Cramp," Christmas called, "it's the best thing you can do for the moment; " and Nat threw himself down. Then with a rush they sent the boat sliding on the back of a receding wave, and when Christmas had given a final push he sprang upon its bow, and got lightly in and seized an oar, ready to push off from the shore if needs were. But the wave took them fairly out and tossed them all dancing and whirling round to another wave; and wind, sea, and all were making for them, so that when Nat Cramp struggled into a sitting posture they were already a long way from the line of little figures still gazing after them.

"Are our things in, Cramp? "

"The two portmanteaus? Oh, yes; and your coat, Mr. Pembroke? "

"I shan't put it on. Holding this sheet and managing this sail will keep me warm enough. I think, Cramp, I had better steer unless you are quite sure of yourself? "

"It's so very rough—it tosses one so."

"Well, it isn't like St. James's Park. No matter; I can manage it all. In fact there's nothing to do but to keep her head up and run right for Portstone with such a wind and sea as this."

The wind had abated somewhat, but it was still strong, and

the sea was very rough. Christmas now had got his little sail all right and was seated in the stern holding the sheet and managing the rudder at once. Cramp sat in the bow. The stout little boat tumbled about a good deal, and Nat, despite his longing for death, sometimes started a little when the bow was deep down in a greyish green valley and some great wave seemed about to fall upon it. Christmas felt his spirits rise immensely. There was something exhilarating in this battle with the sea and the knowledge that so much depended upon his eye and hand. For there was enough of wind and sea to make a small boat with a square sail a dangerous vessel for a clumsy hand or an uncertain eye.

The two companions did not speak much at first; it needed something like a shout to be heard through the wind and waves.

"It's very cold!" cried Nat.

"What do you say?" his fellow-voyager shouted.

"It's very cold!"

"Put on my coat, Cramp; I don't want it—I couldn't wear it —I am very warm; put it on."

Nat managed to put it on, not without greatly shaking their little ark.

"But I say, don't jump about in that way, Cramp, or you'll capsize us! It wouldn't take much to do it."

Nat crawled along the seats until he had got his head under the sail and within easier speaking distance of Christmas. He looked particularly livid and ghastly, and Christmas assumed that he was terribly frightened.

"I wish you would keep quiet, Cramp," he said. "There isn't the remotest danger as long as you keep quiet and don't capsize us."

The sky was all grey and dark, and the dull green of the sea, brightened by no ray or relief from above, had something funereal and boding in it.

"Wouldn't it be an odd thing," Nat said, "if you and me— I mean to say you and I—were to be drowned here to-day?"

"It wouldn't be at all odd if you keep moving about in that way."

Nat laughed defiantly.

"You saved me once off Durewoods pier, Mr. Pembroke. You couldn't save me in that sea now."

"No, Cramp—nor myself."

"Not much chance for us there?"

"Not any, I should say."

"I saw a sail—far off yonder. She couldn't save us?"

Christmas shook his head.

"Even if she saw us we should be down among the dead men long before she could bear down upon us, I fancy. For which reason, my good fellow, keep quiet."

" But, Mr. Pembroke, I don't know why I should want to live I'm sick of life—I hate it all."

" Well, Cramp, I don't know that I have any great motive in living. But I want to live for this day anyhow. Wait till to-morrow or next day, and then perhaps I should care as little about living and be just as heroic as you."

Christmas spoke with a kind of contempt for Nat, whom he believed to be only in one of his familiar mock-heroic moods, a little swollen by the excitement of the situation.

" To-morrow ? " Nat screamed, like one frenzied with sudden passion and despair. " To-morrow! I know what that means ; No, no! To-day's our time! We'll never see Durewoods again, you and I. You will never see *her !* " And he jumped up in the boat and gesticulated like a madman, as he shouted " Hurrah, hurrah ! "

" By the Lord, Cramp, you've done it now ! " Christmas cried. He flung himself to the other side of the boat, tried in one terrible moment to keep her steady, to keep her head up ; was conscious of a bewildering sensation, as if the whole world were upturning, and the sky and sea crashing down upon him to-gether, and in another instant the boat turned over and the two young men were in the waves.

CHAPTER XXIX.

HOME AGAIN.

THE Challoners were home again in Durewoods. They had crossed the Atlantic in winter, and were lucky enough to have some calm seas; and Sir John observed with pleasure that on more than one clear and cold day, when the waters were quiet enough to allow of pleasant walks on deck, Marie showed unusually good spirits and seemed to enter a little into the enjoyment of existence again. He had watched her with some uneasiness as she sat on deck the day they were leaving New York. The steamer was crowded with friends taking leave of friends whom the vessel was to bear away, and there was a great deal of kissing and embracing, and there were many tearful eyes. Sir John observed with wonder and anxiety that his daughter sat there cold, apathetic, and silent, looking on the emotional crowd out of eyes that seemed hardly to take an interest in anything. His mind misgave him. Was she really unhappy, or was her once magnificent physical health giving way?

Therefore, when they were fairly on the ocean, and she brightened up, and talked to people, and seemed like her old self—perhaps a little exaggerated at times—he was greatly cheered. There was a handsome vivacious young French naval officer on board who seemed to lose his heart at once to Lady Disdain, and with whom Lady Disdain was pleased to talk a great deal—and if it were not Lady Disdain one might perhaps even say to flirt a great deal—and her spirits sometimes seemed to rise almost too high. But Sir John was reassured and delighted. "It's all right," he said to himself. "She will be perfectly happy yet. When she is married and settled in London life and moving in society she will be as happy as a queen." He felt little fear thenceforward even when her bursts of high spirits were followed occasionally by hours of gloom and apathy; even when he observed that the first sight of the shores of her own country made her start as if in repugnance or dismay.

Ronald Vidal met them at Southampton. He looked very handsome, and blushed in almost a boyish way when he saw Marie. She held her hand out to him, and said "How are you, Ronald?" and Ronald took her hand, but seemed somehow a little dashed by this reception, and he did not kiss her.

Ronald went off presently to see about having their trunks quickly through the Custom-house, and Sir John was left alone for a few moments with his daughter.

"I think you frightened our young squire, Marie."

"How so, dear?"

"Well, I don't know; you were not very warm in your reception of him, I thought."

"Was I not? I meant to be very friendly."

"He didn't venture to kiss you," Sir John said with a smile.

"Would it have been the right thing to do?"

"Well, I don't know whether there is much either right or wrong about it under the circumstances. But I should think he might have ventured."

"Oh, yes; if it is the right thing to do. But I really didn't know. I suppose he hardly expected me to kiss him. I confess I am not equal to *that*."

"He seemed a little discouraged, I thought," Sir John said.

"Some people are so easily discouraged," his daughter replied.

"Here he comes," her father said hastily in an undertone, rather glad that the conversation was brought to a close.

They got through the Custom-house, and Ronald had engaged a carriage for them in the express to London.

"Marie looks pale, I think," Ronald said when they were in motion.

"Everybody tells me I am looking pale," she said, with a touch of petulance in her voice. "I am perfectly well. I am in rude and vulgar health. But it is so cold and wet here—how could any one help looking pale? Has it been raining all the time, Ronald?"

"A good deal. It's been a very dreary time to me, Marie."

"Indeed? I didn't think you cared about the weather."

"You know I don't; and you know it wasn't that."

"What have you been doing all the time? I saw that you have been speaking: we got the papers—and I read the speeches, and liked them very much." A burst of kindness dictated her words, for she thought he did seem dashed, and she asked herself what earthly right she had to find fault with him and make him uncomfortable. "And you are quite a public man now! Leading articles in the papers about you! The *Times* insists that what you said was entirely inappropriate and unseasonable, and I don't know what else; and the *Daily News* declares that you said just the right thing at the right time. I agree with the *Daily News*."

Ronald was perfectly happy now. He started off with a full account of all that he had done and said, and why he did it and said it, and what everybody said to him about it: how his father told him that if he kept on that way and dropped his confounded play-houses ("And settled myself down in life," Ronald added, with a glance at Marie) he might come to something; and how Gladstone complimented him; and Dizzy was wonderfully civil in his reply; and how Bright came up to him in the smoking-room and told him he had made a fine speech, but recommended him to use shorter words, and to study the early English poets, and not to quote too much Latin—" And he's right, by Jove!" Mr. Vidal exclaimed, "and Bright's the only great—really great—artist in oratory that we have, Marie." He streamed away with a good deal more of political talk, and he was very much delighted with Marie and himself and everything else.

Marie's cheek brightened a little now and then. This did seem a fairer prospect than a life spent with financiers and the magnates of the railway and men whose talk was not of oxen, but of bulls and bears. She did think that it would be something to move in a society made up of great political chiefs and their followers. She had even across the Atlantic read with a certain kindling pride of the speeches made by her lover just towards the close of the Session, and of the comments and criticisms they called forth; and she felt convinced that there was in Ronald Vidal a capacity to rise in politics, and in herself a capacity to understand them. She told him in a few warm words how glad she was that he had made such a success.

" I owe it all to you," he said in a low tone.

Ronald Vidal should then, if he only could have known, and the fates and the railway had allowed, have taken her hand in his and kissed her boldly, perhaps twice, and gone instantly away and left her to think of him all the rest of the day and the evening, with a favourable recollection and with something like the sense of having willingly given up her life to make part of his. But Mr. Vidal did not know this, and did not think about it; and in any case the express was rushing along at full speed for London, and he could not possibly get out except with the result of making a corpse of himself. Therefore he remained by Marie's side and talked to her while Sir John read the newspaper.

Mr. Vidal was now made so happy that he became quite himself again, and fearing lest Marie should be bored with too much politics he passed on to personal news. He told her about various persons whom she knew, and ever so many more whom she did not know. He told her of the new actors and singers, and the winter exhibitions of pictures, and all the latest fashions, whimsies, and fads of society. He had no end of descriptions of this, that, and the other lady, and her dress, and her drawing-room, and her china. He talked of marriages which were coming off, and once or twice he began some story of private life in this or that family, and suddenly broke off in the middle and seemed a little confused; and altogether he did not show to so much advantage as when they were talking of politics.

Marie wondered how so clever a young man just entering on
so interesting and noble a career could care for all the things he
was now talking about. She wondered he did not ask her about
anything she had seen in all the travels that seemed to her so
marvellous and delightful: and she even asked him why he
didn't ask her anything of the kind. So he had then to express
a polite desire to hear everything : but he did not listen to anything long. Mr. Vidal was not good as a listener, and he did
not care a straw for travel, except as a means of meeting new
men and women. There was hardly anything Marie had to tell
him about people he cared to hear of, and he was always begging
pardon and breaking in upon her description of something just
to tell her about the absurd house that Lady Jervis was having
built, lest he should forget, "and everybody is talking about it
—old Lady Jervis, you know"—or some recital of equal interest.
Marie thought of the day when she walked with him up the
Durewoods hill, and tried to get him to look at the scenery and
talk about it, and could not succeed. She gave up any further
attempt to interest him now in what she had seen, and she
listened with all the attention she could give to everything he
had to tell, and Mr. Vidal became happy again.

When they reached London, Marie saw a lady get out of the
train whom she knew to have been a fellow-passenger of hers
from New York, and in whom she had taken a great interest,
although she saw her but once or twice. The lady had been
very sick nearly all the way, and was seldom visible. She was
very handsome, Marie thought, although she looked a little
wasted. There was a shade of darkness round her eyes which
gave her a melancholy and romantic aspect. She had a superb
mass of golden hair, and a very stately presence. Now as she
got out at the station she was giving directions to her two maids
and a man in livery, and two or three friends were in waiting for
her, and she seemed to Marie like some foreign princess or other
such distinguished person. In the little bustle about Sir John
Challoner's carriage, and servants and luggage, Marie saw that
the handsome lady saluted Ronald Vidal, who went up and shook
hands with her and spoke a few friendly words.

" Who is that ? " Marie asked, when they were in the carriage
and driving away—" that lady with the beautiful face ? I do so
want to know who she is."

Vidal laughed.

" That's Rosamunda Shirley—Mrs. Mattocks is her real name
now. So she's been your fellow-passenger ? She's been starring
it in the States—making a lot of money, she tells me. She'll
want it all, I dare say—Mattocks plays like anything—can't
stop—always loses."

" But who is Rosamunda Shirley ? "

" Oh, she's an actress, you know. We had her for a season at the Mayfair—I mean the people who owned the Mayfair then engaged her. She married a man named Mattocks, who used to be in a cavalry regiment; he had to sell out—a regular black sheep—he lives upon her now. But he wouldn't go to the States with her, all the same."

" She looks very unhappy," said Marie. " I knew she had some melancholy history. Is she a great actress, Ronald—does she play in tragedy ? "

" Tragedy! oh dear, no. Burlesque—tights—that sort of thing. No, she isn't much of an actress, but she can sing a little and dance a little, and she has a fine figure, and looks very well on the stage. That hair isn't her own, you know," the candid youth continued.

" Oh! I thought I should like to know her so much; but if she is not really an artist, I don't think—— "

Vidal looked amazed.

" Oh, *you* couldn't know her," he said. " She's all right enough—I never heard anything much said against her, but they are a queer lot, husband and all."

" In any case," Sir John remarked coldly, " I don't suppose ladies usually make the acquaintance of burlesque actresses."

Sir John was rather displeased that this incident had occurred, and Ronald now began to see for the first time that it had probably been an unlucky affair. Vidal hardly ever made account of any point of view different from his own, and it had not occurred to him as possible that Marie could be displeased at his knowing a burlesque actress whom she, of course, was not to know. " There never was any harm in poor Rosie," he thought: and his mother and sisters knew perfectly well that he had lots of acquaintances in Rosie's world, and they never cared.

" I haven't seen her—Mrs. Mattocks—this long time," he hastened to say. " Our acquaintance was very slight. I always thought him a black sheep."

Nobody said anything more on the subject, and Ronald talked of something else. The rain streamed down, and Marie thought London looked unspeakably dismal. She looked from the carriage windows, and wondered once or twice whether there was any possibility of her seeing Christmas Pembroke in the streets as they drove along. She was more than once on the point of asking Mr. Vidal if he knew anything about Pembroke, but some reason which she could hardly have explained to herself kept her from putting the question. Vidal never said a word about Pembroke because, as it has been remarked already, he rarely remembered that young man's existence.

At last the drive came to an end, and Marie was at home in Kensington. Not long, however, did she remain there. Her father hurried her off to Durewoods, and she was glad to go—perhaps all the more glad because Ronald Vidal was not to accompany them. He was to follow them soon : " when things had been arranged." He took leave of Marie again with a pressure of the hand she held out to him, and he did not venture to kiss her.

The Challoners went by train to Baymouth, and thence went all the way round by carriage, avoiding the sea passage, although the *Saucy Lass* had not yet met with her accident. Sir John was unwilling to subject his daughter to the rough wind, the tossing sea, and either the drenching rain on deck or the stifling cabin of the *Saucy Lass.* They had a very dreary drive of it with the windows closed and the rain beating against the glass. They could see nothing of the country, and they talked but little. They approached Durewoods, it might be said, by the back way, and Marie had nearly reached her own gate before she knew where she was.

" Can this be Durewoods really ? " she asked, trying to peer through the mist and rain ; " this frightful place, so drenched and desolate ? "

" This is Durewoods indeed, Marie. Welcome home, dear ! "

" It seems a strange welcome home ! Can it be that the hill I loved so is hidden somewhere under that sky, and that dear Dione Lyle's balcony and her roses can be within sight ? Well—perhaps it is all the better."

" Why, Marie ? "

" It will be the easier to part from Durewoods, dear."

" You talk of parting from Durewoods as if you were going into exile, Marie. Durewoods will be here all the same—for you and Ronald always."

" Yes, it will be here," said Marie, and she stopped : and presently the carriage drove in through their own gate and along the avenue and up to the door.

" I shall be glad to see good old Sarah Cramp," said Marie. " If she knows that we are coming she will be here to meet me, I am sure."

But Sarah Cramp did not know that they were coming ; and one of the first pieces of news given to Marie when she entered the hall was that poor old Mrs. Cramp was dead and buried. Marie could not restrain her tears for her faithful old friend who was gone : and such was the condition of her welcome home to Durewoods.

But there were a great many things to do, and persons to see, and instructions to give and questions to ask, after so long an absence. Marie, as we know, had always liked to be her own housekeeper, and there was an understanding that after her marriage she was still to be housekeeper of Durewoods whenever she and her husband

had to be in the country. In town, too, she was to look after her
father's house a good deal, and was to sit at the head of his table
when he had to give dinner parties with ladies. Therefore let
us do justice to Dear Lady Disdain and admit that she did not
waste much of the active time of the day in mere regrets. In the
country—or at at all events in a place like Durewoods, where
servants are still a little primitive and simple in their ways, and
keep their eyes fixed rather wearisomely on the hand of the mistress—Marie had really a great deal of ordering, instructing, and
marshalling to do. She sometimes compared herself to Squire
Hardcastle drilling his domestics : and sometimes, when she was
inclined for a more heroic similitude, to Alexander Farnese, who
used to say that for ever so many years, the exact number of
which she had forgotten, he had never passed an uninterrupted
hour of day. Our heroine's sitting up late of nights became a
fashion with her chiefly because of this daily occupation.

Marie was greatly pleased to hear her father say that they
must at once have the carriage out and pay a visit to Miss Lyle.
" That must be done before dinner, Marie," he said. " She would
take it ill if we did not go at once."

This seemed very thoughtful and kind of Sir John, who of late
had not often time to indulge in thoughts of mere kindness. But
other feelings than those of old friendship were inspiring Marie's
father. He had been haunted by a dread of Christmas Pembroke
turning up in some inconvenient way, and by the fear of the young
man having perhaps told his whole story to Dione Lyle. Sir John
did not know whether the young man was still in England or not,
and he longed to know. If he had fairly left the country Sir John
would have been happy, and if he could have known this for certain while he was in London he would not have hurried his
daughter down to Durewoods and thus brought her within reach
of Dione Lyle. But he had not a chance of speaking to Ronald
Vidal alone, and even if he had it is doubtful whether he would
have asked Vidal a question about Christmas Pembroke. Sir
John's exaggerated caution made him dread to say anything about
Pembroke to anybody, lest that person should suspect something
or say out something which would set other people suspecting.
Sir John's knowledge of human nature and the springs of human
action was of a very simple kind, which yet passes off generally
for piercing sagacity. He came to his conclusions on the assump-
tion that everybody else was influenced by the same motives and
interests that influenced him, and in the same way.

Therefore Sir John was anxious to see Miss Lyle as soon as possible, and was determined that the first meeting of his daughter
and her should be in his presence. He had great faith in his own
power of averting the worst consequences in the way of awkward
disclosure or question by some personal intervention if needs

were, and by preventing things from being talked out to any
clear understanding. A timely muddying of the waters is often a
great advantage in such cases, and Challoner had great faith in
muddying of waters.

They visited Miss Lyle in a semi-formal sort of way, the for-
mality, however, being a little disturbed by Merlin's enthusiastic
joy at the sight of Marie, and by his first kissing her hand and
then shaking it several times vehemently from left to right. The
brave Merlin was especially proud of his knowledge of English
customs, and he always shook hands in this lusty fashion with
Miss Lyle's more favoured personal friends. Sometimes, indeed,
when a strange visitor came for the first time, if Merlin happened
to be in a very gracious humour he shook hands with the stranger
even before he allowed the latter an opportunity of inquiring if
Miss Lyle were at home.

Miss Lyle, of course, was at home, and she was delighted to
welcome Marie. These two women were really very fond of each
other, and faithful to each other. It seemed odd to John Challoner, but there was no mistake about it, and he was glad of it,
because he suspected that Dione Lyle disliked him, and distrusted
him, and owed him a grudge, and as a sensible man knows that
you can never tell when, where, or how some enemy may injure
you, he was pleased that Dione should be fond of his daughter,
for that would secure her to him—except, perhaps, in some
romantic and absurd love affair such as that of young Pembroke.

The visit was friendly and agreeable, and there was no bringing up of unpleasant associations. The hostess was not this time
in her balcony room.

"I hardly know you, Miss Lyle, out of your balcony room,"
said Marie. "May I go there and look out?"

"But the balcony is closed, dear, and it's so wet and miserable."

"Still, I should like to look out. I have not yet seen the
sea."

"I should have thought you had enough of sea, but, my dear,
do go and make the balcony look bright a moment by standing
there if you will."

"Take care not to catch cold, Marie," her father added.

When she had gone Dione turned to Sir John and said suddenly and sharply—

"John—do you know anything of Christmas Pembroke?"

"Nothing, Dione; I haven't heard anything of him since my
return; haven't had much time, you know. Has he left England?"

"I presume he has, but I don't know. I have heard nothing
from him. He has not come near me or written to me—not a line
to say good-bye even. I think that rather strange—ungrateful,

perhaps. He is a good boy, and there must be some cause. I thought somebody, perhaps, had been putting him against me."

"I know nothing of it. He wrote to me long since to say that he was going to Japan at once: I suppose he has gone."

"I suppose so: but—— Well, Marie, how do you like the view under these skies?"

Sir John went home with his daughter greatly reassured. Christmas had evidently gone, and Dione was not in league with him, and she was not inclined to talk to Marie about him. Sir John began to think that things were going very well.

CHAPTER XXX.

SHE WOULD AND SHE WOULD NOT.

THE rain fell heavily upon Durewoods next day, turning the roads into mere mud-channels, and shutting out sea and sky alike from the sight. Dione Lyle was sitting in the room which had the balcony: but the balcony itself had long ceased to be an endurable station. Miss Lyle was alone, and was seated near a little table, on which she leaned her elbow. It was evening, and the wind screamed among the trees like a screech-owl. Dione felt very much depressed. Suddenly she heard a sound, and looking towards the door of the room, which was open, saw Marie Challoner standing there.

"You looked so picturesque, Miss Lyle, that I could not help stopping for a moment to study you."

"I am so glad you have come, Marie. I was beginning to feel very lonely. I suppose we feel that sort of sensation more and more as we grow old—I used to like it once."

"But you never grow old; you are always the same age—like a picture. When you come to die, Miss Lyle, I feel certain that you will not die in the way that is appointed for us common people—you will simply change into a picture and ornament this house for ever."

"That is rather a pretty idea, Marie. Will you have a cup of tea?"

"Yes, please. I came for some tea—and to see you again. I was growing very lonely, too."

"Come near me, dear, and let me see how you are looking. Stay, I will ring for the lamps, it is so grey and dark."

"No, Miss Lyle: please don't examine me by the light. The dusk suits me much better: I couldn't stand an inspection by lamplight to-day."

" You don't look well, Marie. Why are you so pale and thin, girl? Your long travelling has done you no good but only harm, I think. What is the matter with you? "

"Nothing, Miss Lyle: I am very well; but it is such miserable weather. Nothing looks like itself now."

" You don't look like yourself, Marie. You look unhappy. Are you sorry to be back among us all again?"

" Well, Durewoods isn't the same. Do you remember telling me once that Durewoods would never be the same to me again when once I had left it for London life? I think you were right. It never has been the same to me since. When we were in America we went of course to see Niagara. Oh, what a lovely place! I don't mean the Falls merely, but the woods—Goat Island and its delightful woods—no, I'm not going to describe— don't be afraid! It was such beautiful weather—early autumn! Well, when we were returning to New York in the winter somebody persuaded us that we ought to see Niagara in that season too. How I wish we hadn't gone! The trees were naked: the air was cold: the woods were like grave-yards: the skies were black with the promise of snow; the whole place was dreary, gaunt, and wretched. It was the same place and not the same. It was Niagara under crape: Niagara's corpse lying in its shroud. It was a Niagara of the under world—it was *schauder-haft.*"

" You are growing quite eloquent, Marie," Miss Lyle said, with a smile.

" Because I felt it so much! Very well: to me now Durewoods is just the same. It is the melancholy ghost of my Durewoods."

" You ought to be pretty well used to Durewoods in winter, Marie."

" But I don't call this winter merely: this is Durewoods in decrepit old age, just about to die. Everything seems to tell me of death here. I feel like the hero of ' Maud.'"

" I think the lamps would make us a little livelier."

" Let us just wait a little yet. To tell you the truth, Miss Lyle, I don't want you to examine me under the lamps just yet, until I have had some hot tea and plucked up my spirits a little. I don't want to be told that I am looking pale and wretched. Merlin has just kindly informed me that I am looking bad, bad —none-good."

" Well, I suppose you are a little anxious just now," Dione said, gravely, " on the threshold of a great event, dear."

" Oh, no: it isn't that. I have had that before me long enough to get used to it, I should think. Do you know it was a great shock to me the very moment I reached home here in Durewoods to be met with the news that my poor old friend

Sarah Cramp was dead and buried? She was such a dear, kind, good old creature, and I have such happy memories associated with her name. And I met her son—that absurd, foolish creature—in America, and altogether it seemed so miserable."

Marie felt her colour come as she remembered unfortunate Natty Cramp and the exhibition he had made of himself when last she saw him. It made her doubly sorry for his poor old mother.

" Is he likely to do any good, that creature? " Dione asked.

" Oh, I don't know—I'm afraid not, but I hope so," Marie said, not very coherently; "but the news of poor Mrs. Cramp's death was a great shock. The whole place seems like death."

" You ought to have other thoughts, surely, Marie! "

" I suppose so. Well, I will try. Let us be merry."

" I should like to see you a little brighter, dear, I confess. If I were—some one—I should feel rather shocked at the thought of your seeming so miserable—at such a time."

" Nobody knows anything about it but you, Miss Lyle. I pour out all my dolefulness on you. I don't treat papa to it—or anybody. Men would not understand such unreasonable ways, I suppose."

" I am not a man, dear; and I confess I don't quite understand you just now. You are not really unhappy, Marie? Certainly I don't see why you should be—if you have always told me fairly."

" I ought to be the happiest of women, I suppose."

" You ought to be," said Dione, emphatically, " or else you ought to acknowledge that you are not, and—— "

" Well, Miss Lyle—acknowledge that I am not, and what? "

" And act accordingly."

" Act as if I was not the happiest of women? "

" Yes. Don't go on doing that which you have no right to do unless it makes you the happiest of women."

" But happiest of women is all nonsense—is it not? Why should I be happiest, or what right have I to expect to be happy at all? I am well enough. I am about as happy, I suppose, as anybody else, or as I desire to be. My wants are few, Miss Lyle. A house in Park Lane, I think: or Berkeley Square, perhaps: a box in both Opera-houses: unlimited credit with Madame Elise: an acquaintance with three or four duchesses: a handle such as ' Honourable' to my name: old china and lace: and my own way in everything."

Dione moved her shoulders impatiently.

" That isn't much, Miss Lyle, and—yes, there is one little thing more. I should like the name for which I surrender my own to be a pretty one, and composed of four syllables: two names, you understand, of two syllables each. I should not like to be simply Mrs. Briggs. Well, in this too I am to be gratified. Therefore, oh! am I not happy? ' I am, I am '—as the dear little Peri says who is being admitted, like me, into the best circles of Paradise."

"I don't care to hear you talk in this way," said Dione, almost angrily. "It isn't real, my dear; and it is thrown away on me. If you were just a cold-hearted and ambitious girl I should give myself very little trouble about you. You don't put your cynicism on well, Marie. You lay it on too thickly, child; we can all see the paint. You are not ambitious, and you are not cynical."

"Indeed, Miss Lyle, I think you are wrong. I think I am a little ambitious, and I rather believe I am developing a certain gift of cynicism which will look very pretty when it has been properly cultivated. Our American journey a little dashed my ambition perhaps."

"Really? I was not aware that society in America was such a school of modest contentment."

"No, it was not in that way that my ambition became rebuked."

"How was it then?"

"One met with such hundreds of communities where they talked our language and read our books—and didn't comprehend our ambition."

"Yes?"

"What is a woman's ambition in London, Miss Lyle?"

"Really, my dear," Miss Lyle said, drawing her shawl around her and settling down in her chair with a less dissatisfied air, "you must tell me all about that. I have to be taught, and you say you understand the thing."

"Well, I take it that the ambition of a London girl means— putting it roughly, you know—living in Belgrave Square instead of Russell Square. These two extremes, I suppose, represent Victory and Defeat. I am speaking, of course, of people worth considering. You would hardly expect me to take Clapham or Hampstead into account at all."

"I have forgotten most of the landmarks of fashion, dear, but I'll take your definition if you like—on your authority. Well, what then?"

"Well, you see in America there are such millions of people who don't know the difference between Russell Square and Belgrave Square. It's discouraging. So many people asked me if I knew Herbert Spencer—and I didn't; and if I knew George Eliot—and I didn't. I felt rather ashamed; and it would not have helped me a bit to tell them—if I could have told them— that though I didn't know Herbert Spencer yet I lived in Belgrave Square."

" But," Miss Lyle said slowly, " they have their distinctions between their Belgrave Squares and their Russell Squares—or their friends and enemies sadly belie them."

" Oh yes, indeed they have. But there it is, you see. There is the rebuke to ambition conveyed in my satire—it is satire, you know. You don't understand the difference between Madison Avenue and Washington Place ? "

" No indeed, dear."

" Yet look at the difference to a New York girl of my age and expectations ! Well, there it is. What is the use of an ambition the symbols of whose triumphs are only understood in one's own parish ? "

" But, my good girl, all your argument is against yourself, and on my side. You tell me you see the folly of ambition, and all I said was that when you gave yourself out as ambitious you were only affecting it."

" I may have my philosophic moods, may I not, without being a downright practical philosopher ? I think I have heard of such a thing with men."

" My dear Marie, this is useless beating about the bush. I think you are not as happy as I should like you to be, and I think you are not satisfied with yourself—shall I go on ? "

" If you please, Miss Lyle."

" I don't like to see you going into this marriage—in this sort of way."

" How should women go into a marriage ? "

" I shouldn't mind an ordinary woman. I know she would be made happy by what people would call a brilliant match. She would have all she wanted : and I don't know that I should blame her for not stipulating for anything else any more than a woman who, not caring for a piano in her room, didn't stipulate for a piano. But you are different."

" You don't know. I suppose we are all much the same."

" Marie," said Dione, taking the girl's hand and looking into her eyes, " I have always seen in you something that young women don't have generally—something very rare among us altogether, I believe—a sort of thing that men call honour. Now if you will tell me on your honour—if you will for the moment suppose yourself a man—and tell me on your honour that you really are glad of this marriage because of the position you think it will give you, and that you are going into it willingly—I'll promise not to trouble you any more about it."

Marie gently withdrew her right hand and placed it on her breast.

" On my honour," she said gravely, " as a gentleman, I am going into this marriage with my eyes open and of my own free will."

Dione shook her head.

"Gentlemen, good Master Challoner, don't evade questions when on their honour. I asked you if you were marrying willingly for the sake of the position you expect to get in society."

Marie's eyes turned downwards.

"Miss Lyle," she asked, "what provision does the code of gentlemanly honour make for one when a question is put which he cannot answer directly without the certainty of being misunderstood?"

"That's answer enough for me, Marie. I don't want any more."

"But you don't quite understand—you don't indeed. I mean this. I don't myself know or care a great deal about society and all that. But I must marry some one—papa says so and everybody—and one might as well have a name as not. I am not marrying for money. Mr. Vidal—I suppose I ought to call him Ronald—hasn't a great deal. He brings the name, and I suppose I am to bring the money. So it isn't such a pitiful bargain on my part."

"Bargain!"

"Well, it is a sort of bargain, you know: but most marriages are, I suppose. One thing I do wish, Miss Lyle, with all my heart."

"Yes, dear?"

"That my father had a son. Then he must have most of the money, and he would be the hope of the family, you know; and all the responsibility would rest upon him; and I should have so little money that people wouldn't trouble themselves about me; and I might perhaps be allowed to marry my brother's tutor if he was nice, or some poetical young creature, as the good girls do in the books."

Dione looked at her silently, pityingly.

"Or, Miss Lyle, failing that, I do sometimes wish—shall I confess it?"

If you like, my dear."

"I do wish sometimes that as my father has not a son——"

"Yes—well?"

"That he had not a daughter either."

"I knew it," said Dione. "I knew that you were only a victim in all this."

"No, no," Marie said eagerly, and looking up so suddenly that she forgot how Miss Lyle must see the tears in her eyes, "indeed, indeed, I am not a victim. Papa would not for anything in the world urge me or press me. He has told me again and again that he would rather sacrifice anything than allow me to marry if I was not quite satisfied. I *am* satisfied—as satisfied as I could be with anything—since my father has a daughter and

she is expected to marry somebody. You know how good
Ronald Vidal is, and clever, and he is young, and handsome, and
everything."

"I never heard a word," Dione quietly observed, "said against
the County Paris—did you? He was good and clever—I suppose
—and young and handsome—and yet Juliet took poison rather
than marry him."

"Ah, but then there was Romeo," Marie said quickly, and
then she grew red and felt ashamed and wished she had not
said it.

Dione saw the blush, and was more surprised than she would
have cared to admit. "Can there be any feeling in this girl that
she is purposely keeping back from me?" she thought.

"And there is no Romeo in your case, my dear," she said
rather as a quiet statement of fact than an inquiry.

"None, Miss Lyle. Ronald himself is the nearest approach;
so you see the cases are very different."

"Suppose the Romeo should come after?"

"After—what?"

"Should come too late. Suppose some one should come a
year or two hence, who would have been just the Romeo if fate
had sent him sooner. I am not jesting, Marie, I am serious, and
I want you to put that question to yourself very, very seriously.
You are not a child, Marie, and mind, dear, I couldn't believe
in any wrong thought in either Juliet or you—only would not
your life then become miserable: and would ambition and the
world content you if you found that there was a man who might
have been—the one, the only one, you know? Just think of it,
dear, and answer the question—to yourself, Marie, and not to
me—I don't ask you for such a confidence as that. Don't be
afraid—ask it boldly of yourself, and answer it—to yourself."

There was a moment's silence.

"Shall I ring for lamps now, Miss Lyle?" Marie asked,
rising.

"If you please, dear."

"And I must go. I have kept the carriage waiting—papa
wants me back very soon, but I would come and talk with you."

The little maid, Janet, entered the room with lamps. When
she had gone Marie said—

"What a pretty girl Janet grows, Miss Lyle!"

"Janet is going to be married soon."

"Oh, is she? I am so sorry! I mean I am so glad, of course
—if she wishes it. But why does she get married?"

"What would you have her do?"

"Stay with you, of course, and be happy. I wish you would
let me keep house for you, Miss Lyle. I think Janet ought to
be the happiest girl in the world—I have often envied her of
late. Now I don't envy her any more."

Marie presently took her leave. Miss Lyle remained filled
with perplexity and much distressed. The thoughts and doubts
brought up by her conversation with Marie did not alone distress
her. Neither she nor Marie had in the course of their talk made
any allusion to the name of Christmas Pembroke. Yet Dione, at
least, was thinking much about him all the time. For he had
lately disappeared altogether from her knowledge, "dropped out
of the tissue" of her life. He had not written : he had not come
to see her : she did not know where he was, or what had become
of him.. She was sometimes alarmed and sometimes angry. She
was well inclined to make every allowance for a disappointed
lover, and his moods and sudden resolves and changes of purpose,
but still she could not help saying to herself that he might have
told her of anything he proposed to do, that he might have said
good-bye, even by letter, before leaving England. Anyhow she
was both perplexed and pained by his silence, and she would not
even mention his name to Marie.

The evening was peculiarly dull and trying to Marie. Her
father and she dined alone. At one time their having an evening together, all to themselves, was one of Marie's special joys.
But now things had changed. He did not seem the same person :
they were not companions now as they used to be. Sir John
treated her with an almost deferential politeness which irritated
her sometimes. He conducted himself a little too much as if he
was entertaining the Honourable Mrs. Ronald Vidal, not dining
alone with his daughter Marie. Sir John did this unconsciously,
but it is certain that his mind was filled with a sense of the
dignity which was now so soon to descend upon him. He thought
Marie looked handsomer than ever. His mind fed itself on the
satisfaction which fortune seemed to have in store for him. At
one moment it occurred to him that, after all, such things have
frequently happened—elder brothers often die young : and who
knows—Marie *might* one day be the Countess Paladine. The
thing was by no means impossible. He offered his daughter
some grapes with a graceful deference that seemed almost like
homage.

Then during the evening he talked a great deal about their
future arrangements. The honeymoon was to be spent at Lord
Paladine's country place. Lord Paladine himself was, at present,
in Sicily. The newly married pair were not to return to town
until the opening of Parliament. Sir John asked Marie a great
many questions about the house that was to be taken for her in
town—where she would like it to be, furnished in what way,
and all that sort of thing, which rather distressed her just at
present.

"I am very glad to leave all that to you and Ronald," she
said. " He knows all about these things, and I don't. He has

peculiar tastes too—very good tastes I dare say—and you know
I never had any in particular. I am sure you and he will
manage it all beautifully. I know I shall like whatever you do."

"Thank you, my dear. Still a woman's taste is often so
good."

"Not mine, dear. I scarcely know one thing from another."

"You see, Marie, you'll only want a small house. Young
people now all begin in nice little houses. Great establishments,
even if people have the means to keep them up, only look well
for middle-aged people. And then you know, my dear, you and
Ronald will have to live rather modestly. You really· haven't
much to spend. He has something from his mother, but not a
great deal—by no means a great deal—and then there will be the
interest on your fortune. Well, I don't see that you can possibly
have more—for the present, I mean—than two thousand five
hundred a year."

"Perhaps that isn't enough," Marie said, with a sudden little
display of interest and even eagerness. "Perhaps we ought not
to marry on so little—is it little? Does Ronald know? It
might be well to wait, perhaps, until we grow rich."

"What nonsense;" her father said, smiling. "It's plenty of
money for you two—you are not such a pair of spendthrifts."

"But is Ronald quite aware of all this, papa? He may not
think it much, you know."

"Of course he knows all about it. He is not such a mercenary
creature, Marie. It isn't money he wants, dear; it's *you.*"

"Oh!"

Marie had been leaning forward: she now subsided back into
the armchair, where she was rather languidly resting.

"Besides, look at the career he has before him: and then you
know, of course, all that I have will come to you—to you both—
some day."

"Perhaps you will outlive us, papa. I should not be at all
surprised."

"My dear, what an absurd idea! But now let us just turn
to this household business for a moment," and he branched off
into a variety of details, to which his daughter hardly even tried
to give much attention. At last he became a little impatient
when he could not help seeing her indifference.

"Marie, I believe you take no interest at all in these arrangements."

"Well, dear, not much; I think I would rather leave it all to
him and to you."

"But don't you think Ronald will expect you to show some
little interest?"

"Oh no: I think not. I think he would rather be let alone
—left to his own choice, I mean. He understands all that sort

of thing so well, and he likes it. I cannot do better than leave it all to him. I shall be sure to like whatever he likes."

Sir John almost sighed.

"Well, Marie, as you please. But I should have thought you would feel a little more curiosity even—— "

"It will come in time, I suppose; but I don't think I much want to anticipate the time. I think until it does come I would rather keep it out of sight, and not think about it so very much."

There was a pause in the conversation then, and Sir John gave up all idea of getting the prospective Mrs. Ronald Vidal to take any concern in the arrangements for her entrance upon married life in town.

A gust of wind sent the rain streaming among the trees outside.

"What a melancholy time it is!" said Marie, "nothing but rain and wind since we returned to Durewoods. Such a welcome to give to wanderers returned."

"This must be a bad night at sea," Sir John said. "I am glad we escaped this, Marie. This wouldn't be pleasant on the Atlantic."

"Yes; it must be terrible at sea now—everywhere I suppose. Will there be wrecks?"

"I fear so—off this coast perhaps in particular."

"I hope we have no friends at sea."

There was another pause. Marie sat thinking. Suddenly she looked up—

"Papa?"

"Yes dear."

"Do you know anything about Mr. Pembroke?"

Sir John did not show any of the irritation which he felt.

"No, Marie, I haven't seen him. When I go to town, probably—— "

"But he is in England?"

"I suppose so; I presume so."

"It is rather strange, Miss Lyle never said anything about him since we have come home."

Sir John was glad to hear it, but made no remark, and that conversation also dropped.

CHAPTER XXXI.

ANOTHER wet day Marie saw, as she looked next morning from her window over the tossing branches of the leafless trees. "I begin to think now I shall be glad to leave Durewoods," she said.

There was no use in thinking of going out in rain and wind among soaking shrubs and plashy grass. Marie had the best of it up in her turret, for whatever of the picturesque is in an English wet day, was to be found among the trees that beat against her window panes, and the grey clouds that seemed to rest like a canopy on the tree-tops. The height of her refuge did for the scene something like that which dim moonlight often does—it left the commonplace features and the mere details out of sight, and only showed the more grand and massive effects. Another time perhaps Marie would have delighted in looking through the rain-vexed branches and at the heavy grey curtain that hung around them; but now it all seemed too dreary to be endured. She had enough of melancholy within, and could scarcely bear it when nature chose to strike the same dismal chord without.

She set herself to a task which she had for a long time contemplated. This was the destruction of all her old letters—attempts at poetry, unfinished diaries, trivial fond records, and such relics as her desk contained, and which she thought—why she could not tell—she ought to get rid of formally before entering upon her new life. There was indeed no particular need of this holocaust. But it soothed and pained her to make it. It seemed a befitting ceremonial wherewith to take formal leave of her girlish life and enter upon a new existence. She opened her desk, drew her chair near to the bright fire, and began her work of sacrifice.

What trifles most of these scraps now seemed to her which once she thought important or interesting! There were ever so many things she had begun and never finished. Like every bright clever girl who has read a good deal and been a good deal alone, Marie had at one time fancied herself a poetess: and there were many scraps of verses here which then she had taken for the offspring of inspiration, but which now seemed palpable, passionless, cold, imitation. There were the verses done under the impulses of the first fresh delight in Tennyson; and here were some, all plaintive with early springs and stars and tears which came up when she was in love with the German mind poets; and here again were some heroine-like attempts to sound the iron harpstring of "Men and Women." There were the beginnings of one or two tragedies: and there were some hymns to "Marie, Star of the Sea," written when our heroine was under the influence of a young friend, a girl devotee from a French convent, who made Marie love to be a Roman Catholic and be glad that her own name was that by which her friend invoked her celestial patroness. This girl had given herself formally up to the convent now, and Marie envied her. There were the opening passages, too, of essays in which Marie felt called upon to set right generally the warped order of things, but which she had not completed. There were diaries in which at one time she had proposed to record all her thoughts, and in which for a time she did record them, until it occurred to her that they must be rather too much like the thoughts of everybody else, and that not much advantage came of her setting them down.

Then there were the letters. These were chiefly from girl-friends, most of them now well-nigh forgotten. The letters of the young devotee were numerous, and were even now interesting with the strange, pure, passionate white-heat of their devotion. There were no love-letters in Marie's desk—no love-verses, unless, indeed, such name may be given to one or two early attempts at poetry by Nat Cramp, which that unfortunate amateur had been prevailed upon years ago to submit to Marie for her judgment, and in which she now for the first time began to perceive certain allusions to respectful adorers not daring to lift their eyes to the stars, and other similar flights, which she clearly had not taken in their right sense before. Marie laid them very hastily on the fire, but was sorry for the poor fellow too—and hoped he would do well yet, and marry some one who would be fond of him, and would even think him clever.

But there were no love-letters. This beautiful frank fearless girl had had, without even knowing it, admirers without end, and had been friendly with all of them, but never one of them had got the length of a letter with her. Many a man will love again and marry, and be fond of his wife, and have his heart in his home, his children, and his ambition, and yet never hear Marie Challoner's name without a little throb of reviving emotion and romance; and she remembered none of them. She had never yet been kissed by a man except her father—not even, as we have seen, by her accepted lover. So her desk contained no secrets. Nothing but the ashes of the papers she was burning so fast lay smouldering in her grate. Yet it was not without a strange little heart-throb that she came on one letter amid her collection. She read it twice over, and thought at first that, perhaps, she would save it from the general burning, and keep it as a memorial of a bright, sweet, passing time.

" Shall I keep it ? "

It was a letter—a very short one—from Christmas Pembroke to her, written many months before.

Marie had often, of course, seen Pembroke's writing, but it so happened that she had only this one little scrap of it among her papers. Their acquaintanceship or friendship had been for the most part so close and so personal that there was hardly any need of a correspondence by letter between them. But she had received this little note from him on some unimportant subject, and she had written a reply to it, and put the note in her desk, where it lay until now, and she found it.

" I had better burn every scrap that belongs to the old life in Durewoods," she thought, " and begin quite new, with nothing to remind me of the past days at all."

Still she held the little letter in her hand, and looked at the signature, " C. J. Pembroke," and wondered whether he was married yet, and whether he would be happy ; and was holding the letter still, and looking at it thoughtfully, regretfully, when she heard a tap at the door, and, to her own surprise, she found herself starting and blushing, and in a moment her father entered the room. The sensation which Marie Challoner felt at that moment she had never felt in her life before. Never before had she known herself to start, and blush, and tremble at her father's coming, as if she were trying to conceal some guilty secret. The newness and wonder of the sensation added unspeakably to her confusion. It would have been impossible for Sir John Challoner not to notice her embarrassment. She held the letter crumpled in her hand : and the very action of so holding it only drew his attention all the more. His quiet look studied her.

" I hope I have not disturbed you, Marie," he said, very composedly.

Marie recovered herself and her fearless candour, and put the letter plainly out on her desk, but her colour was still glowing.

" No, dear ; only I did not know who was coming ; and I was looking over and destroying old papers—scraps of poetry—of verse, I mean—and letters."

" Shall I leave you to your work, Marie, and come in again ? "

" Oh, no ! I am very glad you came. You have come just in time. Papa, I have something to say to you."

Marie rose from her chair and went towards the fireplace and leaned her arm on the chimney-piece and looked into the fire. She had Christmas Pembroke's letter in her other hand. In the few moments or seconds since her father's coming disturbed her, and set her blushing and trembling, she had made up her mind. Sir John waited. He had a vague foreboding that he was to hear something unpleasant. There was a painful silence for

moment. Marie dreaded the results of her resolve, but the re
solve was made when she found herself trembling at the sound
of an opening door because she had a letter in her hand.

" Well, Marie, what is it ? "

" Papa, I can't marry Mr. Vidal! I must not do it! I can't
do it ! "

Sir John stood up. This was what he had expected. This
was what he knew was coming. He looked at his daughter for
a moment with eyes of blazing anger. But he had long schooled
himself into the knowledge that in our modern ways anger counts
for little, especially with women, since one cannot very well beat
them. So he moderated his looks and tried to speak with easy,
half-bantering composure.

" My dear, what is the meaning—pray, may I ask—of this
sudden change of mind? "

He was a good deal more stammering and less fluent than
usual, and he tapped the palm of one hand with the back of the
other nervously. He was afraid a trial of strength was in preparation, and he had never had such a trial with Marie ; but
there seemed something about her ways which told him that if
the girl once rebelled she would not very easily be put down.

" It *is* sudden, and I know you will blame me ; and *he* will
think I have treated him so unfairly—if he cares."

" If he cares, Marie ! You know how much he cares. It
may be very foolish of him, no doubt; but you know how he
cares, and I hope, Marie, you are not serious in this. You should
remember that you are dealing with a man, and that you are
not a child."

" I am very sorry and ashamed of myself," Marie said,
humbly ; and she longed to burst into tears. " I know I ought
to have found out my own mind long ago. But I have found it
out now—and it is not too late—— "

" Nonsense ! " Sir John interrupted, deeply regretting that it
was not too late. " What do you call finding out your mind ? Be
a little more distinct, Marie, if you please, and let us talk in the
language of reasonable people, dear, and not in the language of
flowers or romances. What do you mean by finding out your
mind ? "

" I know now that I *never* could care enough about Mr. Vidal
to marry him. I never could—if I say love him, you will call
it the language of romance ; but that is what I mean, and I
can't express myself any better." There was now a little of the
rebellious tone in her voice, and it admonished Sir John to be
cautious in his tactics.

" But, my dear child," he said, soothingly, " I don't know
that you ever gave Ronald Vidal to understand that you had
that kind of feeling for him. He knows quite well that you have

not. Don't give yourself any trouble about that. Ronald
Vidal hopes that that feeling—love—will come in time, and so
it will."

" Oh no—it would never come."

" Well, he is willing to take his chance and do his best. He
understands your feeling towards him perfectly, and he doesn't
expect too much. He is a very sensible and modest young fellow,
and he thinks himself very happy to get such a wife on such
conditions, I can assure you."

"I don't think so. I am sure he has far too much spirit to
take any girl on such conditions. I never could care about him
—never in all my life! Papa, it is no use. I will never marry
Mr. Vidal."

"But, Marie, this will be shameful—it will be a disgrace!
Do you think you can deal with a grown man in that sort of way?
Do please to look at his side of the question—do try to be a
reasonable creature for a moment, even though you are a girl.
You accepted this young man's offer deliberately months ago,
and on those very conditions. You never pretended to have any
romantic love for him, and he never asked you for it. I told you
over and over again not to engage yourself if you did not feel
quite satisfied. Did I not, Marie?"

"You did, dear," Marie answered, feeling that with every
word a wider gulf opened between her and her father.

"Well! Then—yet you accepted his proposal. Nothing has
changed since that time, and yet we hear all this nonsense."

"Oh, yes, something has changed."

"What has changed?"

"I have changed," said poor Marie.

"But, good Heavens! that is not his fault, and he is not to be
punished for that. Besides, you haven't changed. You never
said you had any love for him, and how could you have
changed?"

"It is so hard to explain," pleaded Marie, and she was very
meek and humble, for she felt in many ways ashamed and
conscious of unhappy weakness, "but I must try to explain it—
if you like. I promised him because I believed then—that—
that I had none of that sort of feeling in me, and that there was
no reason why I might not marry him—as well as another—
though I didn't want to marry any one. But now—it's different."

"In Heaven's name, Marie, how is it different? There is
nothing different."

"Yes, dear, I know now that I was mistaken about myself.
I know that I could have that feeling, but not for *him.* Now you
know."

With what an effort that confession was made—with what
slow, difficult, and formal words! It ought to have been sobbed

out on a mother's breast. It was made by Marie standing at one side of the hearth to him standing at the other, both erect and cold and separated. Marie spoke rather as a woman who, under the impulse of over-mastering necessity, explains to a doctor the symptoms of some physical illness than as a motherless daughter confides her heart's secret to the father who is her only friend.

"Marie," said her father, "you cannot have been deceiving me all this time. I could not believe you capable of that." He spoke with as much of the severity of austere truthfulness as if he never had deceived her; and for the moment he felt all that stern virtue.

"I have not been deceiving any one—except myself," said Marie sadly; "and even that I did not mean to do. You see that I don't deceive even myself any more."

"Then how long have you known—that you didn't know your own mind?"

"I came to know it—for the first time——"

"Yes, go on, Marie. For the first time—when?"

"Just as you came into the room—now!"

"What nonsense! Why, Marie, I never before heard such nonsense as this. My dear, you really must not behave so like a child. How could I tell Ronald Vidal such a tale as that?—what would he say? To tell him that for months and months you thought you knew your own mind, and that one fine day all in a moment you found out that you didn't!"

"It is true—just the truth, and it will have to be told to him. I will tell him myself if you think I ought to bear my own shame."

"You speak too lightly of this, Marie."

"Do I? I don't feel lightly about it. I never knew what it was to feel such pain and shame before."

"You don't seem to have thought about the matter at all. Do you fancy that he has no feelings?"

"Indeed, indeed, I have thought about him. Oh, I am so sorry for him—if he does really care for me. I would pray to Heaven, if that were any use, that he didn't care for me. But how could I do him a greater wrong than to marry him when I——"

She stopped, and leaned both her elbows on the chimney-piece and made a hiding-place of the hollow of her hands, in which she buried her face.

"Yes, yes, we know all that," her father said. "We know that you don't particularly care about him—love him—whatever it is; but we knew all that before."

She raised her head and looked at him imploringly.

"Oh, it isn't that—there is more than that. Oh, can't you guess? It isn't only that I don't care for him; it is that I do care for somebody—not him."

Sir John flung himself from his place by the chimney-piece.
"Good God, Marie! what do you mean, and what are you
talking about? It can't be."

"It is—it is."

"Where is that letter you had in your hand when I came in?
What is it? Give it to me."

She had put it on the chimney-piece now. It had been in the
hollow of her hands when she leant her forehead on them. She
took it up and gave it to her father without a word, but with
trembling hand and face all crimsoned by shame and resolve.

Sir John looked at the paper—the few lines of writing with
the signature of "C. J. Pembroke," and something like an oath
broke from his lips.

"When was this thing written?" he asked, with a tremendous
effort not to lose his self-control.

"I don't know—I forget. Months ago—a year perhaps."

"Have you been corresponding with him?"

"No," poor Lady Disdain answered. "I don't think I ever
had another letter from him."

"But you said you only found out all this—about your
feelings and so on—a few minutes ago?"

"Yes, that is the truth."

Sir John was now puzzled as well as angry. Let us give him
all the credit he deserves for his effort at self-control. He was a
sleek, portly, polished gentleman now, who had society and its
proprieties always before his mind to school and mould him.
But it would have relieved him now if he could have beaten his
daughter. He walked up and down the room once or twice,
blowing off the steam of his anger.

"Marie," he said, suddenly stopping, "I wish you would just
be good enough to explain all this to me in plain English—clear
words to everything—and as little romance as may be. I want
to understand, if I can. That letter—I don't see anything in it—
is ever so many months old. Yet you never thought of this—
this nonsense—until now. What *is* the meaning of that?"

"I don't know—indeed, indeed I don't. I never knew that I
cared about him in that sort of way. I was very, very wretched
lately; but I didn't know even then *that* was the reason. It
came on me now in a flash, the moment I took up that letter.
I couldn't help it—I couldn't understand it—and then you came
in, and I started so like one doing something wrong, and then I
knew." Her voice broke down in a little sob.

"This is the greatest misfortune that ever fell on me," Sir
John said, clenching his hands to keep down his anger.

"It is the greatest misfortune that ever fell on me," his
daughter pleaded.

"But, good God, you might have known your own mind!
What are we to do? Where is he—do you know?"

" I don't know."

"Has he left England ? "

" Oh, indeed, I don't know."

" Tell me—has he ever guessed at anything of this ? "

" Papa, how can you ask such a question ? " Marie said, with some of her old vivacity and energy coming back to her under the influence of what seemed almost an insult. " *I* didn't know —how could he know ? And if I did know—well, I would never have promised Mr. Vidal; but nobody then should ever have known. I would have kept that to myself. Oh, I wish I had known, for that very reason."

" I don't understand—what do you mean, Marie ? " her father asked sharply. In his confusion and anger he had forgotten his own fiction.

" You know *he* never cared about me," poor Lady Disdain pleaded piteously. " He told you himself that—oh, you know what he told you."

Sir John pulled himself together in time and remembered his pious fraud. He resolved to turn it to the best account he could.

" I am glad, Marie," he said coldly, " that you have common sense—and—and—well, yes, propriety, let us say, left in you to keep you from letting all the world know that you have fallen over head and ears in love with a young man who—to say no-thing of other considerations—happens to be in love with another girl. I am glad you have no idea of entering into the arena and competing for Mr. Pembroke."

" Oh ! "

He saw that he had stung her, and he was glad. He began to have a reviving hope from her wounded pride.

" Still, you know, Marie, people will talk, and your affairs and mine can't claim special exemption. Everybody knows that you are engaged to Ronald Vidal—there was a paragraph in the papers the other day—and of course if the thing is to be broken off there will be a talk. He will have to get some explanation of your very sudden change—he has a right to that, you know, after having been placed in such a position—and of course the thing will get about. We shall have the pleasure of knowing that everybody says you would not marry Vidal because you were in love with another person—who didn't care three straws about you."

Marie quivered as if she had received a stroke of a whip. But the words gave her renewed firmness. She now saw that she could look for no sympathy and even for no mercy from her father. She must act for herself and defend herself, alone.

" What would you have me to do ? " she asked, coldly.

" Do? Do what every sensible girl—yes, every modest girl would do. Conquer this silly sentiment—this sudden feeling that began, you say yourself, ten minutes ago. Stamp it out. It will die in a few days or weeks. Don't insult and ill-treat the gentleman—the gentleman—whom you have engaged to marry by throwing him over, and making a fool of him, and all in obedience to some ridiculous, romantic, schoolgirl whim."

" Papa, is that really your advice ? "

" Of course it is. It would be the advice of every sensible person. What nonsense ! "

Marie shook her head.

" Then I am glad I am not a sensible person, for I'll never do that. I'll never marry Mr. Vidal. Oh—well ? "

For Marie's maid had entered the room. Sir John walked towards the window, afraid some of their words had been overheard. He looked out upon the dripping trees blown by the wind that still, on the third day, fought its course against the rain. He was trembling with disappointment and anger. All his little world seemed to have been shattered by an impetuous touch from the hand of a foolish, romantic, headstrong girl.

" Please, miss," the maid began, " there's a person—a man—below who wants to speak to you particularly."

Sir John turned sharply round.

" To me, Sophy ? not to papa ? "

" No, miss; to you. He said he must speak to you particularly."

" What is his name ? "

" He said his name it didn't matter; you wouldn't know his name, he said."

" Is he anybody from Durewoods—anybody I have ever seen ? "

" I never saw him before, miss."

Marie looked inquiringly at her father.

" Send him up here," said Sir John; " I'll see what his business is." His mind misgave him : he was ready to suspect anything now.

" It must be somebody wanting money. A subscription, or charity, or something," Marie said, when the maid had left the room.

" I really cannot guess who it is," her father said, coldly, " but I shall soon know."

It took some time to bring the visitor from the hall up to Marie's turret-room. No word passed between her and her father in the interval.

" This is the gentleman, please miss," the maid said.

He did not look quite like a gentleman somehow, but he was a remarkably self-possessed, orderly sort of man, with formal whiskers and the air of one who declines in advance to consider himself an intruder anywhere.

"My respects to you, Sir John," he said, with half military decorum; "and I beg the young lady's pardon. My name is Sands."

"Yes, yes. I thought I knew your face. You are the police inspector from Portstone? Do you want to see me, Mr. Sands? The servant asked for my daughter."

"It *was* the young lady I wanted to see, but I am glad to find you here, Sir John; and glad to see you home again, sir. I hope it is not a painful duty, Sir John, but I am afraid I shall have to ask the young lady to assist us in a matter of identification."

Marie turned round surprised.

"Identification of whom, or what, Mr. Sands?" Sir John asked. "My daughter is very much engaged at present, and if it isn't a very important matter——"

"Well, Sir John, it may be important in a manner." He had now taken out a pocket-book, from which he took carefully a discoloured letter; and then turning to Marie he said—

"Perhaps, miss, you wouldn't mind telling me if you know that writing—and if you think it's meant for you."

Marie took the letter without a word. It was merely addressed to "Miss Challoner," but she knew the writing perfectly well.

"Where did you get this?" she asked.

"What is it, Marie? Do you know the writing? Say Yes or No." Sir John seemed even more disturbed than she.

"Oh, yes! I know it—it's Mr. Pembroke's."

Sir John gave her a warning look—a look of anger and caution. It seemed to say, "Recollect yourself now—no exposure, no scene. Remember it is you who have brought all this on us!"

"Then you think it is for you, miss?"

"I suppose so. Where did you get it?"

"Would you please to open and read it, miss?"

Marie opened it. It was wretchedly discoloured, and the ink had run; but it bore date the day but one before that day; and this was what it said:—

"My DEAR MISS CHALLONER,

"I cannot leave England without seeing you and saying good-bye. I have a strong reason for asking you to give me a few minutes of your time, and it shall not be more. You will not refuse me this, I know. I wish particularly to speak to you alone.

"Ever truly yours,
"C. J. PEMBROKE"

"But where is he? and where was this found?" she asked.

"Give me the letter, Marie. Didn't you know anything of this?"

"No, dear; how should I know? Where was this found? Papa, ask him where this was found."

"Well, miss, that's the painful part of it; but we mustn't come to think the worst all at once. This gentleman was a friend of yours?"

"He *is* a friend of ours."

"Yes, miss—leastways, I'm sure I hope so. Is he a young gentleman twenty-four or five maybe—tall, fair complexion?"

"He is—he is!" Sir John said impatiently. "But now tell us what this is all about, Mr. Sands."

"Well, Sir John, we've had bad weather here, and there must have been accidents round this coast, and a body's come ashore at Portstone——"

"Oh, God!" Marie cried.

Sir John put his hand firmly on her shoulder.

"And, of course, we tried for marks of identity, and found money, but no card-case nor letters—but *that* in one of the pockets. I knew Miss Challoner's name, and thought it best to come along. It may be all some mistake, you know, Sir John, and truly sorry I am if the young gentleman was a friend of yours."

"He was coming to see me, Marie said; "and he is drowned!"

"Well, miss," said the inspector, seeing with some pain the stony paleness of her face, "we never can be sure of these sort of things until we actually see, and that's what I was going to ask —whether you would mind coming to Portstone and just looking at the——I mean, seeing if it was the young gentleman. But as Sir John knows him too, perhaps we may spare you the trouble, miss."

"Oh, yes; Miss Challoner couldn't attempt it, Mr. Sands, nor is it necessary; I will go. My daughter feels this, as you see. It is a shock, of course. He was a very dear friend of ours."

"I'll go," said Marie; "I'll go with you if you please, papa. I—I must see him again!"

"If you'll be kind enough to wait for us in the library, Mr Sands, I'll come to you in a few moments and let you know what we think best to do." He was longing to have the man out of the room, for he feared that Marie's unnatural calmness must give way.

Mr. Sands bowed and backed himself out of the room. Sir John carefully closed the door after him, and then returned to his daughter. Marie was now leaning one arm on the chimney-piece and looking at the fire. There were no tears in her eyes,

x

but her breast was heaving abruptly like to one in physical
agony which she will not confess. When she spoke there was
a dry sob in her voice.

"He was coming to see me!" she said, "and now he's dead!"

"Marie, my dear," her father said, "this is a terrible blow,
and a very sad thing. But we can't help it, my—my love; and
it's the will of Providence, you know."

Sir John was not cut out for a religious consoler. He had
all through the successful part of his career gone in for strict
morality and propriety, but he had not given himself any religious airs. Indeed he thought that sort of thing in an active
modern financier savoured rather of hypocrisy and looked
suspicious; or at all events had an unprepossessing aspect of
Nonconformity or Wesleyanism about it, and would be bad form.
He was therefore a little constrained and awkward now in his
recognition of Providence, and he feared that he was not very
impressive: and made himself the less impressive by the fear.

"He was coming to see me," said Marie again. "Well, I'll
go to see him! I'll go with you, papa."

"My dear, we must be very careful. The thing is beyond
help now, and I'm very sorry for the poor young fellow—and of
course, Marie, I am not so unfeeling as not to symyathise with
you, after what you have told me to-day. But then, my dear
child, you cannot want to make an exposure of your feelings and
have people talk. You know how they would talk, and then
if you had been engaged to the poor young man it would be
different; but you must remember that at this very moment
you are engaged to Ronald Vidal; and that poor Pembroke
was——"

"Was in love with somebody else! Yes, you have told me
that. It always seemed so strange to me. Now *she* has lost
him. Ah, poor girl, how she must have loved him! What
will she do? And he was coming to see me! I wonder why he
rared to see me? I didn't deserve it."

Sir John looked at her in wonder. He always regarded women
as hysterical creatures with natures at once little and tempestuous,
who were easily shocked and made angry and made glad: who
cried at a word of contradiction, and hated all other women, and
when any sad news arrived screamed and threw themselves about
the floor or went to bed and drenched themselves in tears there.
He was surprised and alarmed at the stony composure of his
daughter. She was speaking in low monotone, and except for
the quick movement of her chest, and the occasional short sob
which now was hardly heard, there was no sign in her of any
overwhelming emotion.

"This will be sure to break down," he said to himself. "This
will never last."

"I really think you had better not come, Marie, dear," he said hurriedly. "We must think of others in this matter. We must think of Vidal, you know. It's no use having things talked of now which can be avoided. For your sake and for Vidal's, we cannot have it said that you were in love with one young man while engaged to another."

"Nobody shall know that. I don't care about myself—oh, not one single straw—what people say. I deserve anything for not knowing my own mind in time—well! well! But it is right on Mr. Vidal's account, I see *that*, and I owe him something. But I will go with you, please—and I will not make any scene. Nobody shall know—and I should only go mad if I were left alone here."

Sir John felt that there was nothing for it but to give way. His sympathy with his daughter was not so great as he professed. He was much rather inclined to be angry with her, but he knew that it would never do to show any anger towards a girl under such circumstances. The one uppermost feeling in his mind would have been best expressed, if it might be, in the angry question, "Why did she bring all this nuisance on me? What did she mean by being such a fool as to fall in love with that young fellow?" Never in his life did Sir John admire his daughter so little as since her confession. Before that he had been not merely a loving, but an admiring father. He was proud of his superb daughter, with her self-sufficing intrepidity and her ambition, and her prospects. He saw her in his mind's eye the peer and the rival of peeresses. Now there seemed to him some-thing mean in the love she had confessed. In his secret heart he was not sorry to hear that the waves had removed Christmas Pembroke out of the way. That matter was settled, at all events, and with good management he did not despair of being able to bring Marie to marry Ronald Vidal yet. His course for the present was clear, he thought. He must sympathise with this girl, humour her, give her her head in everything, try to induce her emotions, if possible, to flame and blaze themselves away un-seen before Ronald came down; and perhaps, after a while, when the thing was over, she could be brought to listen to reason. On the whole things were really looking better than they did an hour ago. There was no reason now why she should not marry Vidal; and Vidal was so sensible that he would wait another six months, if necessary; and even if Vidal suspected that she had had a little tenderness for Pembroke, he was so generous and so much a man of the world that he wouldn't think too much about it now that the poor fellow was dead. Sir John himself had a settled conviction that every woman had been profoundly in love with some other man before she accepted her husband, and he didn't see that they made any the worse wives for that.

It was well that the future seemed to him to open a little brighter than it did a few moments ago. He might not, with all his sleek self-control, have been quite able to conceal his anger from Marie if his plans were hopelessly spoiled. But now he showed himself very tender.

" Well, my dear, he said gently, " I will not cross you in this. I know I can trust to your self-control and your sense of what you owe to your own dignity as a woman. You shall go with me. I'll order the carriage at once to take us over. We'll be there before it gets dark. This is indeed a terrible trial for you, and, of course, it is all the heavier because you cannot indulge your feelings openly. My poor Marie ! "

CHAPTER XXXII.

WHAT THE SEA GAVE UP.

MARIE was alone for a few moments when her father left her room and went to make arrangements for their dismal journey. Something in his manner distressed her. In all her personal pain and grief she had a vague consciousness that he did not seem to her very sorry. His change in manner since the terrible news made her heart sink. She suspected that since Christmas Pembroke was now removed from the way he would try all the more to persuade her to marry Mr. Vidal, and she should have fresh arguments and new struggles. In a day or two perhaps Vidal would be in Durewoods, and nothing in life seemed to her now half so hard to bear as the thought of her engagement with him. She pressed her hands to her forehead. A resolve came. " I'll break it off myself ! " she determined. " I have a right ! My life is my own—and I will do it ! It is no shame now, since *he* is dead. I may love him now to my heart's content—and I could not even think of him while I remained still bound to Mr. Vidal."

" Marie," her father said, quietly entering the room, " get ready dear, if you will come. We shall start in half an hour exactly. I have a letter or two to write first, which must go to the post."

" I, too, have a letter to write," Marie thought.

" In half an hour I'll come," Sir John said.

" I shall be quite ready, dear," Marie replied with a composure which puzzled him.

The moment he had gone she went to her desk and began to write. The purpose that she had in writing kept her nerves calm

and steady. Her composure was surprising to herself now.
Even while she wrote she found herself coldly looking the
situation full in the face and resolving that this was the best
thing and the right thing to do. Her whole soul was now set
on being free of her engagement with Ronald Vidal—free to
think always over Christmas Pembroke and to own to herself
that she loved him. This step, too, would save her father the
pain of having to tell her story with his own lips to Ronald, and
it would prevent the possibility of his trying to induce her still
to marry Vidal. She grew sick at the thought of his cool and
man-of-the-world arguments all over again.

She felt, too, as if she could not look on Christmas Pembroke's
dead body until she had released herself from her engagement
with Mr. Vidal. That seemed an indispensable and sacred duty.
Not that she feared to indulge in any burst of grief over the
body of the young man whom she had known, all too late, that
she loved. Lady Disdain believed that, broken as she was, she
still had strength and pride enough not to betray herself before
vulgar lookers-on. But her soul would at least be free; and she
could own to herself that she loved him. A girl beguiled into an
engagement during the absence of the lover whom she was taught
to believe dead could not have panted more eagerly to free herself from it in order honestly to meet the lover come safely back
than Marie longed to be free from her engagement with Mr.
Vidal before she went to look on Christmas Pembroke dead.

This was the letter she wrote. She wrote it "at one stroke."
and as fast as her pen could go. Her mind was mistress of its
subject—

"DEAR MR. VIDAL,
        "This letter will give you pain to read, I fear. It
gives me pain to write, but I cannot help writing it; and I have
not asked the advice of any one about it. I wonder if you
already guess what I am going to say.

"I cannot keep my promise. I must ask of you, and beg of
you, that you will release me from it. When I promised I did
a great wrong to you and to myself; but I did it partly without
thought, and partly through ignorance of my own feelings. I
know now that I ought not to marry you. I know that I never
could care for you as you deserve and as your wife ought to care
for you.

"This is not all. Perhaps you might be generous enough
and hopeful enough to overlook that. But I am going to say
what, perhaps, no girl ever wrote before at such a time, and
what, perhaps, I ought to be ashamed to confess. I know now
what I did not know then—that there is some one I do care for
more than ever I can care for you or any other being. He does

not know this, and never can know it now; but I do. I loved him.

"I suppose this is an unwomanly confession. If so it will make you feel the less regret when you receive this letter. You could not care to make any girl your wife who could have written it. I shall be glad to believe that—if it is any relief to you to condemn and despise me. I don't know what the usage of the world may be, but I have made up my mind that there should be truth between you and me.

"I do not ask you to forgive me. I ought to have asked your forgiveness when I promised—not now when I release you from your engagement, and set you free.

"MARIE CHALLONER."

"When that leaves Durewoods," said Marie, "I am free!" She made up the letter, addressed it, went downstairs herself and placed it in the old-fashioned post-bag, and having met nobody on the way came quietly back to her room. There was a strange feeling of exaltation—almost of exultation—about her. All high emotions are in the same key; and with resolve there always comes some thrill of the exultant mood. When Juliet's lover knows all and has surveyed in mind the worst and made up his resolve, there is something like exulting pride in the declaration that now after all he will visit Juliet, and that very night. Our heroine thought with a kindred pride that now she was free to look on the face of the man she loved. At that moment came back to her the quiet, warning words of Dione Lyle the day before.

"Miss Lyle was right I suppose," she thought. "I may think of him so now at least, since he is dead. Even the poor girl whom he loved would not blame me now, if she could know."

Her father came and quietly handed her to the carriage, maintaining a dignified ease while in the presence of the servants, but relapsing into ostentatious sympathy when they were alone together and on their way. It was little more than mid-day, but the skies were covered and the scene was dim with mist. They had a long drive, and they did not talk much. The momentary elevation of spirit which Marie had felt when she made her resolve had passed away, and she had now only a sense of utter loneliness. She looked into the future and shuddered at its blankness: and she looked back on the past and wondered why she ever was happy.

For all the sympathy Sir John Challoner now expressed, his daughter could not bring herself to turn towards him in confidence and love. It was not merely that she could not bring herself to this; but it did not seem in the nature of things that she should make the attempt, or that there could be any confidence between them any more. Some vague idea that she had not been fairly dealt with floated across her mind. It had not much shape; but there it was. Why did Christmas Pembroke want so much to see her before he left England for ever? Why was he leaving England for ever? Why had he never told Miss Lyle about—all that about Miss Jansen?

Looking back now upon the past she wondered at herself, and that she had not sooner understood the secret of her heart. Now she knew. She had loved him this long time. She had unconsciously tried to close her breast against him when she heard that he was in love with another girl, but he had gone with her inseparable as her shadow everywhere. His memory had oppressed her always. The darkness in which she sat, the pain constantly in her heart, had been because of him. But for her father and for the sake of Mr. Vidal, to whom she owed something, she would not have cared now who knew it. She wished that she might go to Sybil Jansen and say:—"I loved him too. I may tell you, now that he is dead," and let them be sisters in misfortune.

What things that formerly were bewildering to her, as to her own moods, now seemed clear, and how strange many things appeared that concerned him! Why did he tell her father that he wanted to marry Sybil Jansen, and not tell Miss Lyle? Why did he always seem unwilling to hear anything about Mr. Vidal? That day—that last day—when she saw him at Mrs. Seagraves' house, and when she sent through him a message of friendliness to Miss Jansen—why did he look so blankly, as if he didn't understand? Why was Miss Jansen so cold and rude to her? Why did she hear of his love for Miss Jansen the very day when Mr. Vidal came with his proposal to her?

Thus vainly she tortured her mind, as people will do—as if dead were not dead—as if things might be set right yet—as if it mattered now asking why or how when all was finished for ever. Now and then she remembered with a sickening pang that it was vain to think of all this, and then she began to think of it all over again. Each moment she became more and more conscious of a creeping, chilly sensation of distrust towards her father. It was not strong and decisive enough to be suspicion—what was it?

She looked thoughtfully at him as he sat in the carriage, and she remembered the years when they were such companions, and when his coming always made her holiday, and she wondered why her heart should be so cold to him now. He looked up and her eyes met his, and his were full of pity she thought. She was touched, and she gently put her hand upon his arm.

" Papa, dear ? " in the old loving, childlike way which she had some time disused.

" Yes, my love."

" Have you any idea—can you think—why *he* wanted to see me before he left England ? "

For a moment perhaps Sir John was tempted to tell her the truth and give her in her grief the poor consolation of knowing that he loved her. She looked so wistful and eager and piteous. But Sir John was a prudent and calculating man. He had made most of his successes in life by the capacity to survey the whole of a situation in a moment, compare the " fors " and " againsts," and make up his mind. To tell her the truth would do her no good—it would only prevent her recovering from all this folly, and it would for ever damage him and his authority in her eyes. The present pain was only for the present. Did he not remember his own love pains about Dione Lyle? and now how absurd they appeared! So he decided.

" Well, Marie, we were always very kind to him—you particularly; and he seemed very grateful, poor fellow. It was only natural he should like to see you and say that he felt thankful ; and then, perhaps, he fancied I didn't quite approve of his throwing up his career in England in that hasty sort of way, and might have thought you would serve as a peacemaker. I should say it was something of that kind : very likely. Poor fellow—poor fellow ! "

Marie sank back again into her former attitude. It did seem likely—and yet!—and so all the vain tormenting questioning began over again.

They were passing some scattered outlying houses at last, and boats and nets, and posts with chains and ropes attached.

" Now, my dear," her father asked, in a tone of thrilling, startling, laboured gentleness, like that which tells the patient that the operation is about to begin, " are you quite sure that you can go through all this? A great deal depends upon your self-command. There is no necessity at all for you to get out of the carriage, and it will be so painful——"

" Are we at the place? "

" Yes; very nearly. I really think you had much better not get out."

" It seems to me at present," Marie answered, " that I have only one desire left in the world."

" Yes : well; what is that? "

" To see him once more."

Sir John shrugged his shoulders and felt bitterly angry. " This is what one brings up daughters and loves them for. Some young fellow comes from God knows where, and they have no feeling left in them for any one else ! "

" As you please, Marie—if you will. But remember not to make an exposure of yourself. Don't let us play a scene in a tragedy for the edification of Portstone."

" Why should I expose myself ? " she asked. " I know all that is to be known—the worst is over. I only want to see him now and to know that I have seen him."

The carriage stopped, and Mr. Sands opened the door. Sir John got out and gave his hand to Marie. She alighted with a firm and easy step, and glanced quickly around her. The look of the place, or as much of it as she saw, became stamped upon her mind. They were at a doorway in one of the three sides of what might have been called a square, if a quay and the water did not form its fourth side. The grey misty sea was plashing every moment over the quay side, and the rain was driving across the irregular pavement. The houses of the place were ancient and tumble-down looking structures for the most part. There were lights already blinking in the windows of some of them, although the evening had not yet set in. In one house there were red curtains drawn across the lower windows, which, with light behind them, gave the one cheery patch of colour to relieve the drear monotony and worse than wintry dismalness of the place. There were boats here and there, and there were posts with chains, and there were a few men in oilskin coats mooning about.

" Just this way, Sir John," Mr. Sands said, " this way, miss ; three steps down. The light here, Ruggles."

Ruggles, whoever he was, held a lantern, and Sir John and his daughter descended some steps into a long central passage or hall. Marie felt her heart beat painfully, but she kept her self-control completely. She was conscious of carefully holding up her dress that it might not trail on the damp and dirty steps.

" What place is this ? " she asked quietly.

" This is the police station and the fire-office, miss," the polite Sands replied. " We ought to have a deadhouse here, but we ain't got one yet."

Marie shuddered. This seeemed like enough to a deadhouse.

They went through the central passage, which was very dark, but which had rooms with stone floors on either side, that appeared tolerably well lighted with windows. Marie observed that there was a bird in a cage in one of the rooms.

Then they passed through a backdoor and crossed a little ill-paved yard, Mr. Sands obligingly holding an umbrella over Marie. They came to a sort of outbuilding like a stable or a laundry, and Mr. Sands, going on before, opened the door with a latch.

Marie drew back for one instant. She knew this was the place.

" You will be firm, my dear child," her father said imploringly. His whole soul was filled with the longing to get all this over without a scene. If he could once have her safely back in the carriage, she might faint then, or cry, or do anything she liked. He did not himself think now of the sight they were to see. It was nothing to him. If he had come alone and with a mind free there might be some room for a thought about the fate of his old friend's son. But now he could only think of the possibility of Marie's making a scene which might lead to gossip and talk and scandal. A girl in such a case might, for all he knew, throw herself on the body. He drew Marie's arm more firmly within his own, and they went in.

This place was better lighted than the more habitable part of the building. It had great sloping skylights that almost made a roof of glass. The daylight was tolerably clear yet.

There was nothing in the room but a broad bench; and on this lay something covered with a great rug or blanket. Marie held her breath. The time has come, she thought to herself now. A strange conceit passed through her. "I know now that I could walk quietly to execution—it wouldn't be half so bad as this!"

"This is the body," Mr. Sands said with superfluous explanation. The body covered with its rug seemed to lord it over the place like visible King Death himself. Mr. Sands spoke in a low tone as one might in the presence of a king.

Sir John and Marie looked on in silence. It seemed to her that her very heartbeats now stood still.

"Shall I?" Mr. Sands asked, putting his hand upon the rug and making a motion as if to remove it.

"If you please," Sir John answered.

Marie found herself murmuring some prayer—to whom, for what, she scarcely knew.

Mr. Sands turned down the rug. A pale, waxy face was seen. It did not look awful; it did not look human; it did not seem as if it ever had belonged to life at all; it was only like a waxen mask. Marie stooped over it for a second, holding her breath. Sir John bent down too, puzzled, amazed; and then Marie tore her arm from his and gave a great cry that rang through the gaunt empty room, "Oh, it's *not he!* Oh, thank God!"

"Oh, the young lady!" Mr. Sands exclaimed, and ran to lift her, for she had fallen all in a heap upon the floor.

"No; thank you, don't——I can lift her," Sir John cried furiously. "This has all been a confounded mistake, Mr. Sands! This isn't the person we supposed. Can't you get a chair somewhere? No; I say, don't mind. We'll come out of this place."

Sir John was a strong man still in his prime, and he made no more account of lifting and carrying his daughter than he used to do in the days when it was his delight to bear her himself to her cradle. But he did not feel tenderly to her now in his heart. He felt impatient and angry. He was angry with her for making what he would have called an exhibition of her feelings, and he was angry with Mr. Sands for having brought about the mistake; and with Christmas Pembroke for not being the dead body; and with the dead body for not being Christmas Pembroke. In his haste he had not seen whose body it was. He had not known that poor Nat Cramp was lying there with all his foolish story of vanity, ambition, love, and disappointment brought to a sudden end.

CHAPTER XXXIII.

" BUT NO MORE LIKE MY FATHER."

MARIE CHALLONER had been prepared for everything but for what she saw. She had schooled herself, steeled her heart and her nerves, and she could have looked without giving way on the cold, dead face of the man whom now she knew she had loved. She thought she could bear with anything rather than not see him for the last time. The last time—and also ‘surely the first time! She never saw him before in the true light—as the one she might have loved. She had torn herself free from her engagement in order that, when she had seen him for the last time, she might be able in the secrecy and solitude of her own room at night to indulge in her grief for him without feeling shame. But she had not been prepared for what she did see and for the wild reaction of joy that he was not dead. Therefore, a sudden stifling sensation seemed to cling upon her brain and her pulses, and there was an instant's, a second's intolerable struggle : strange lights flashed before her eyes, and there was an unearthly singing in her ears, and for the first time in her life she fainted.

She recovered very soon, and she found that her father had been wetting her forehead with a handkerchief dipped in cold water, and she smiled a faint thankfulness and said she was better—was quite well; and her father, who did not speak much, brought her to the carriage where he said she could rest more comfortably, and she reclined there feeling like a prisoner reprieved before his death sentence has been wholly carried out and who has not quite recovered himself so far as to understand his joy.

She saw her father and Mr. Sands talking together. She was now reviving rapidly and beginning to feel her relief. Presently Sir John came and took his seat in the carriage next to her.

" The young lady is better, I hope ? " Mr. Sands asked, putting his head (which he respectfully uncovered despite the rain) in at the carriage window.

" I am quite well now, thank you, Mr. Sands," Marie answered, glad to speak to anybody. " I never fainted before. But I was so glad to find that it was not the friend we thought."

Grief we all know is easier to keep in its place than joy. But it is especially hard to keep from talking of one's joy. Dear Lady Disdain found it a severe trial not to pour out to her father all the sense of gladness which had so completely overmastered her. Something told her, however, only too surely that he would not share her emotion, and it was therefore a sort of relief to her even to express them thus faintly to respectable Mr. Sands.

" From what Mr. Sands has been telling me, however, I fear we must not look on things as quite so certain," her father said, chillingly. " Two young men, you say, took a boat at Baymouth, Mr. Sands."

" Two young men, Sir John. Such is the information we have received—two young men take a boat at Baymouth; no one goes with them. *This* body is supposed to be one of them."

" I am sure he is not drowned," Marie said, in a low tone. " I know he is safe."

" Well, well, we needn't try to argue that point," Sir John said. " Of course we all hope he is safe."

" Odd, this one having the letter to the young lady in his possession," Mr. Sands remarked.

" No, not particularly odd," Sir John was quick to observe, for he did not choose to have it supposed that any odd things could happen where his daughter was concerned. " I dare say this poor fellow was a messenger. Mr. Pembroke's servant very probably. Do you know Pembroke's servant, Marie ? Was that he ? "

" Papa—don't you know ? "

Sir John thought she was hastening to explain that Pembroke probably did not keep a servant, and he considered any such explanation unnecessary.

" Ah, well—you didn't recognise him ? "

" But—surely—did not you ? The poor fellow. It seems cruel and heartless to have been so glad—seeing him there dead ; but I couldn't help it."

" Do you know who it was, Marie ? "

" Oh yes, dear. It is that poor unfortunate creature Natty Cramp. I should have been so sorry for him "—and Marie turned pale and felt sick at the thought of the dead body and of what it might have been.

" Nonsense!" Sir John said—" it can't be!"

" But indeed it is—poor Nat Cramp. So soon after his mother!" Marie tried to feel very, very sorry; but the knowledge that it was not Christmas Pembroke kept sorrow asleep for the present. "When sorrow slumbers wake it not," says the German song. Marie felt it a pious duty to stir her sorrow and try to rouse it; but it had drunk of an opiate and would not wake.

" Why, we left him in America the other day," Sir John said.

" One of the young men, it would appear, was understood to have come from America, Sir John," Mr. Sands explained.

"He would have come on hearing of his mother's death," said Marie. "But that is poor Natty. His dreams are all over."

" My daughter must be right," Sir John said. " This was the son of an old person lately dead who had been a servant at Durewoods, Mr. Sands."

" Very sad!" said Mr. Sands; " but we must all come to it."

" Wait for me, Marie. I'll just go with Mr. Sands and look again. I did not look very closely when I saw that it wasn't— it didn't occur to me."

Marie was left alone for a moment. The whole mystery seemed clear to her. Poor Nat Cramp was hastening to Durewoods on account of his mother's death, and Christmas had given him the letter to carry to her. The thought of their being together seemed to her out of the question. If they were together how could Nat come to have the letter intended for her? The suggestion did not even trouble or alarm her. Oh, no! he was alive! and she was happy. For the present she had not even time to think that if he lived he lived for some one else. It was enough now to know that he was not dead.

Sir John came back looking a little pale.

"It is poor Cramp sure enough," he said—"why the deuce didn't he stay in the States where he was doing well?"

Sir John was very angry with Cramp for not being Christmas Pembroke. Or it seemed to him perhaps that if Cramp had only remained in New Padua Pembroke then must have been drowned. He gave directions, however, to Mr. Sands that when all the formalities of the law were over, the body should be removed to Durewoods, and buried there near that of Mrs. Cramp, and that he, Sir John Challoner, would bear all the expenses. He also requested Mr. Sands to let him know if anything else came to light—about the boat and the other young man—and the carriage drove away.

" Why was this young fellow bringing a letter to you, Marie?" her father asked sharply.

" I don't know, indeed, papa. But I suppose Mr. Pembroke must have asked him to bring it to me."

Sir John shrugged his shoulders.

"It seems to me that there was a kind of plot going on all around me, and that everybody had some mystery, which was carefully kept from me. Was Dione Lyle mixed up in all this work?"

"In what work, dear? I don't know of any."

"All this letter writing and fetching and carrying, and love secrets and the rest of it. The whole parish, I suppose, will know that Miss Challoner was in love with some young fellow—while she was engaged to Lord Paladine's son. Good God! what a state of things!"

"Oh, but nobody knew it," Marie pleaded. "Oh, why can you not believe me? Nobody knew it. I didn't know it myself. Don't make me miserable by telling me that I have disgraced myself. I have not disgraced myself. Nobody ever shall know it, if *you* don't betray it."

"Marie, let me know this distinctly, once for all. Has nobody else ever heard of this?"

"Nobody else—oh, no!"

For the moment she did not remember that in her letter to Vidal she had made a confession which only wanted the name to be complete.

Sir John threw himself back in his seat with a sort of sigh as of one who mournfully resigns himself to the dubious consolation that things might have been worse. Marie was left to her own thoughts for the rest of the journey homewards. It was not her father's fault if she did not regard herself as a very wrong-headed young woman, who was bringing trouble upon her family and friends. All this kind of thing was very new to Marie, who had been a sort of princess in her home before this, and whom her father would have spoiled—if she could have been spoiled—by petting and by something like homage.

When she returned to her own room it came on her mind that there would seem to her father an inconsistency between the assurance she had given him that nobody knew of her secret but himself, and the sort of confession she had made to Mr. Vidal. He must come to know what she had written to Vidal, and she felt that it would be unworthy on her part not to tell him at once. She had written the letter with a set purpose which nothing could shake: and why should she be afraid to say that she had done so? What, indeed, could it matter now? She could not and would not do the only thing that would have pleased her father—what then did it matter whether his displeasure fell upon her a little more or a little less sharply, a little sooner or a little later?

Still she felt a kind of dread at her heart. She shrank back from facing the unknown consequences of what she had done

She was alarmed at the thought of seeing her father in some mood such as she had never known in him before. She had heard and read of fathers who were violent and fierce. Her father, of course, had never been like that. It was hard to believe in the possibility of his ever being like that. But he had spoken to her that very day as he never spoken to her before, and as she could not yesterday have believed it possible that anybody would ever speak to her. Who could say what might not happen next? All strange and inconceivable things had lately broken in upon her life. A great sea had rushed over it and swept all the old landmarks away. Nothing could be surprising any more. Therefore her heart beat quickly. Like all women she was inclined to tremble at the unknown and the possible.

But the one thing which she could not do was to deceive. " If this remains unknown to him one hour longer I shall have deceived him," she said. In that moment of confused emotion there came to her recollection that Dione Lyle had praised her for having something like a man's sentiment of honour. She went resolutely to her father.

She knew she should find him in the library. Only the other day it seemed when she used to run in and scramble into his arms, and sit on his knee and make him put away whatever book he was reading and talk to her. How kind and patient he always was! Again she remembered what a holiday his coming used to be! Now she was almost afraid to go to him. But she put her fear down and went in.

Sir John was leaning on the chimney-piece with his back turned to her, and looking moodily at the fire. As he heard the rustle of her dress he looked up and their eyes met in the glass over the chimney-piece. There was no sympathy in that momentary interchange of glances. Each looked away at once.

"Have I disturbed you, papa?" she began, with an effort at ease.

"No, Marie, I was not busy." This was said in a tone and with a manner which conveyed as plainly as any words could have done—"My mind was too painfully occupied with the trial imposed upon me by an ungrateful daughter to allow of my devoting myself to my usual occupations."

"I wanted to say something to you."

"Yes, Marie." There was a slight relaxation of the melancholy rigour of his face. "Has she come to announce submission?" he asked himself.

"I know you will be displeased——"

"Oh! Well, Marie?"

"I told you to-day that nobody could possibly know anything about—about all that—but you."

"Yes, you told me that—and I believed you. Well—was it not true?"

This harsh, cruel way of taking her up shocked Marie and almost made her repent of her candour.

"It was true," she said quietly. "At least I meant it for the truth. But I didn't remember then that I had told another person something of it."

"I thought as much, Marie," Sir John said with a half-triumphant, half-contemptuous smile. "You women never, I believe, tell the whole truth at once. Well, I suppose I know the rest. You told this romantic secret, of course, to Dione Lyle! I might have known it. I believe in my soul that woman was at the bottom of the whole affair. She hates me I know. Well, she has her revenge now. I can't deny that."

"No, I never told Miss Lyle," Marie said, surprised amid all her nearer personal emotions at the words he had spoken—the words about hatred and revenge. "She knows nothing about it."

"Then who in the name of the—— I want to hear who knows anything about it."

"I wrote to Mr. Vidal to-day."

"You—what? You wrote to Ronald Vidal?"

"I wrote to him to-day."

"Marie? You wrote to Vidal to-day—about what?"

"I told him that I couldn't ever marry him—because I didn't care about him—and because——"

"Well, go on in God's name and let me hear it all."

"Because, I cared—very much—for somebody else."

Sir John Challoner had been nervously turning in his hand a large vessel of Venetian glass which he found on the chimney-piece. He now dashed it on the hearth, where it broke in pieces with a crash that made Marie start and tremble. Women are greatly frightened by a dispute which begins with a loud noise and breaking of glass.

"Marie—you didn't do this. I don't believe it. You never would have dared to do it without telling me."

"Oh yes, I did it. I thought it very right to do——"

"Do you mean to say that you have actually sent that letter—sent it away with that shameful confession in it?"

"Yes: it is gone."

"Great God! What did you do such a thing as that for? Have you no sense of shame—have you no thought of me or of anything? Why did you not tell me?"

"Oh, because you would have tried to persuade me. And we should only have had useless arguments—and you don't understand how a woman feels—or, at least, how I feel. Papa, I am sorry if you are angry, but I couldn't help it. I felt that I must set myself free from this miserable engagement, and set *him* free too—good, kind Ronald Vidal—and the only right way was to tell him the truth."

" We are disgraced for ever ! "

"There is no disgrace," Marie said bravely—"but there would have been disgrace to me if I had married that kind-hearted, honourable man, when I had no love for him, but only for somebody else. Oh yes, that would have been disgrace. I am not ashamed of what I have done."

"I am, by God!" her father cried out so furiously that she started—"and I am ashamed of you! Yes, I am—and I ought to be! Did any one ever hear of such a thing? Why didn't you let me write?—if you must break off the whole thing—I could have put it in some decent light."

"I wrote because I wanted just the plain truth to be known."

Sir John looked at her with fierce inquiry. Could it be that she meant to imply anything against him—that he would not have told the truth? But his daughter had no such meaning.

"I knew," she went on simply, "that you would not like to tell that—and Mr. Vidal might still think that he was bound to press me, and might think there was nothing really in the way —and so I wanted him to know once for all that it would be impossible."

"My God, what deceivers women are!" Sir John cried in his indignation against the whole sex, about whom it was one of his articles of faith that men were not bound to tell them the whole truth in anything. "To think that you could be with me all this day, Marie, and never tell me that—and look me in the face and keep such a secret as that! Have you told Vidal his name as well as everything else ? "

"Oh no;" and she found the colour all mounting to her forehead.

"But, of course, he'll easily guess; and this will be the talk of the town! Marie, I am glad your mother is dead."

He walked up and down the room, and kept saying in a loud tone, "What are we to do? What are we to do?"

Marie felt nearly crushed. She had not before regarded her offence in this odious light. She had not supposed that it was an actual sin against womanhood to be in love even with somebody who was not in love with her—so long as she kept her secret to herself—and whose fault was it that she had not kept it to herself? Surely only theirs who would have her to marry a man whom she never could love. Therefore while she regarded herself as very unfortunate and beset by very peculiar trials, and was prepared even to own that she must now be a great trouble to her father, still she had not thought of herself as a mere scandal upon womanhood. But it is hard to hear one's self bewailed and cried out against as a shame to one's household and not to droop the head. A sense of one's innocence, we are told, sustains and consoles all the good people we read of. But there

Y

are some very good people who are not quite so complacently
satisfied of their own goodness, and who, therefore, when they
hear themselves vehemently denounced as guilty are startled for
the moment into almost fearing that they are not innocent.

Sir John suddenly stopped.

"I wish to God I had never had a daughter!" he said. "I
wish you had died when you had that fever long ago—and I sat
up all night—night after night, and I wouldn't let the nurse
watch you—I did, by God! I've worked for you more than for
myself. I have had ambition for you—I speculated and saved
and schemed and planned for you. A match-making mamma"
—he changed his tone for a moment to one of savage sarcasm—
"a match-making mamma couldn't have done more for her
daughter than I did for you—and now this is what it all comes
to!"

He was working himself up into a fury which Marie thought
terrible to look at. It was strange indeed to her, and had long
been strange to him. John Challoner had been born poor and
among the humble, and he had been born with a passionate and
in many qualities a vulgar nature. He had gradually risen in
the world; he was endowed by Nature with just the combination of faculties which mean rising in the world, and no more.
Getting up and up, he had schooled himself into the proprieties
and the manners of the people with whom it was his ambition to
associate, and he had disciplined his bursts of anger. But, as
we have seen, a certain taint of the original vulgarity of nature
always remained in him. So, too, the deep, coarse passion
remained down in his breast somewhere. It was always only
smothered—not extinguished. It broke out now and blazed;
and Challoner liked it to blaze. Now that there was nobody
looking on but his daughter—for whom, since she was not likely
to be the Honourable Mrs. Anything, he had no longer much
respect—he was glad to give his old nature its full way. It
relieved him, and his disappointment was almost unbearable.

Marie was startled and shocked out of all thought for herself.

"Oh, papa—dear, dear papa, don't speak and look in that
way? You are not like yourself. Oh, I am so sorry if I have
disappointed you."

She put her hand gently on his shoulder. He flung it off—
and flung her off so roughly that she found herself shaken against
the chimney-piece. Then he stood near her, with his face
purpling and his large white hand clenched, and her heart stood
still, for she thought he was going to strike her.

Then he drew back and tossed his arms loosely about as if to
shake off the temptation that beset him.

"Go out of the room!" he cried. "Get out of the room, and
don't stand there to provoke me! You are a disgrace to me."

He turned his back upon her and strode to a window, and stood there chafing and tossing his arms almost as wildly as the trees outside were tossing their boughs.

Dear Lady Disdain, white as ashes, went out of the room. She went to her turret-room where she had been so happy, where she had been such a princess. She could not yet find any relief to her agony in tears. She felt a dry, catching, choking sob every now and then rending her throat, but she could not cry. The whole thing was so frightfully strange. Was it her father—or a madman—or some hideous creature of a dream—who had heaped such insults on her, and flung her away with his hand, and driven her from the room? Her misery was too new for her to realise its shape as yet. One thing only was pressing down upon her—the consciousness that all was changed—that nothing ever again could be as it was for her. Where was her father—the kind, fond, petting companion of her childhood and her youth? That strange, wild, choking, red-faced man below, who flung his arms about and stamped and broke glass things and rated at her and flung her away?

Her heart leaped with a nameless, indefinable terror as she heard a tap at the door, and then saw it open and her father come in. Instinctively she drew back and almost cowered in the corner beside the chimney-piece. Dear Lady Disdain had never before known fear. She had never had anything to be afraid of: and the common terrors of deaths, storms, wrecks, and such like would have found her brave and brilliant. But she was for the moment cowed by this strong, furious man, who she supposed might beat her and kill her if he liked. If she was capable or conscious of any distinct wish or hope at the time it was that he would kill her in some quick way, and not strike and beat her first.

Sir John was now as pale as she, and he trembled more than she did.

"Marie—Marie," he said, "I have come to beg your pardon, my child. I—I want you to forgive me. I do not know what came over me—but I didn't mean what I said. I used to be very passionate once, but not this long time—only it came out then in a moment. Won't you forgive me, my dear?"

He mistook Marie's hesitation. She was too much bewildered and alarmed to collect her senses and reply, for this presentation of her father was as strange and dreadful as the other.

"My dear, my dear, do you refuse to forgive me? Good God! are you afraid of me? I'll go on my knees to you."

"Oh, my dear," the poor bewildered, heart-torn girl cried, throwing her arms round his neck, "don't speak in that way; it is like madness! I forgive you, dear. I forgive you, a thousand times. I know you didn't mean it—it was nothing. Do not

think about it any more. I am not afraid of you, dear—oh no,
not a bit. Why should I be afraid?"

She now petted and soothed him almost as one might a child.
He seemed, indeed, a sort of child to her. At first she feared in
her ignorance that he was really going mad, but at last she came
to understand things better. It was only the furious outburst
of a disappointed and a not noble ambition. This it was which
had made her father first rage and then grovel. Oh, how truly
she forgave him, and felt pity and regret all unspeakable for
him! How she prayed for him and wept for him that sad night!
But the dear, dear father of her girlhood whom she admired as
well as loved—the strong, serene, stately father on whose arm she
was so proud to lean, and whose smiling presence made her best
festival—that friend and father was gone for ever.

CHAPTER XXXIV.

ONE TAKEN—THE OTHER LEFT.

ONE of Nat Cramp's wild dreams had been realised. That far-off
night when he walked on the Durewoods pier he found a certain
delight in wishing that he had perished in the sea and that his
body had been washed ashore, and that *she* might hear of his fate.
A kind Heaven, pitying and indulgent even to his nonsense, had
granted at least half his prayer—as Apollo dealt with the hero in
the "Æneid." The sea has washed his dead body ashore and
brought it under her very eyes. It would probably have reconciled him to death in any case if he could have known for certain
that Marie Challoner would bend over his dead face and recognise
him. Poor Nat, what a pity he cannot know! Ah, it is humiliating to think that there is no heroism in life half so desperate
as the heroism of self-conceit! Yet suppose Nat could have
known? Suppose he could have seen Marie Challoner fall in a
faint from very joy that it was he who was dead and not Christmas Pembroke? Suppose he could have known that his life or
death would hardly be thought of by her, provided only that
Christmas Pembroke were alive? Surely, one might say that
the Devil himself could have invented no more cunning, cruel
trick than that—to entrap poor Nat into throwing away his life
only that his very death might show more clearly than ever his
utter insignificance in her eyes. To die for the sake of giving
her at least a pang; and to find that the pang was only one of
joy because he and not somebody else was dead! What but this
could be indeed "the fiend's arch mock?"

The sea keeps some of its secrets. It will always keep secret the answer to the question whether Cramp really meant that day to drown himself and his companion. Was his conduct only an ebullition of meaningless bravado? Was it merely the irrepressible extravagance of a fantastic, morbid mind strained to its utmost by excitement? Had he thought of what he was doing at all, or was he unaccountable for any freak and impulse as a drunken man might be? That cannot be settled. There was so much of self-conceit and sham and mountebankery about the poor youth at his best that he could never know himself how far he was in earnest. But it is probable that his condition then was desperate enough for anything, and there was always a preposterous amount of earnestness under his most grotesque folly. The one certain thing is that wilfully or otherwise, by blundering bravado or set purpose, he turned the boat over, and that next day his body lay cold under the eyes of Marie Challoner. All the dreams and hopes and romance, the nonsense, the Claude Melnotte visions, the Republic, and the Church of the Future had conducted him to this. His epitaph, perhaps, might fitly be embodied in the cry of joy with which Marie welcomed the discovery that it was he and not another whom the chilly, broken waves of the winter sea had washed ashore.

Meanwhile what of the chance companion who had come down from London with Cramp that day, and whose Bellerophon-letter poor, cold, unconscious Cramp had brought with him safely to land in order to torture our heroine and take all the tragic dignity out of his own fate?

When the boat turned over and flung Christmas Pembroke and Nat Cramp into the sea, the two parted company in a moment. Christmas rose to the surface at once, and kept his nerves steady and tried to look about him. The waves were sharp and rough, and buffeted him hither and thither as the gusts of sudden wind varied. They struck him in the face and beat him on the back of the head and blinded his eyes, and sometimes threw him clean over on his back. They seemed to own no regular rise and fall to which a stout swimmer might suit himself. Perhaps, in such a condition of things, if a man really can swim, he is apt at first to lose his temper rather than his courage. It is almost impossible not to be angry with the waves, very hard to keep from shouting at them and cursing them. They seem to play so unfairly; to give their enemy no chance; to fall upon him from all sides at once; to hit him when he is down; to fling themselves on him most viciously when he is most embarrassed. The swimmer becomes infuriated against them and hates them as if they were living, treacherous, pitiless enemies; and indeed there seems something perversely human in their malignantly boisterous behaviour.

If Christmas denounced or cursed them, however, it was from the teeth inwards. He had far too much sense to waste any of his breath and his strength in outcry when he had such a fight for his life before him. One passionate resolve filled him. He would not die: the waves should not kill him. He made up his mind to take things coolly. Swimming with any definite purpose would be a sheer waste of power. He did not know where to swim. The only thing he could do was to keep himself afloat with as little waste of strength as possible and hold as well as he could that position with regard to wind which would best save his face and eyes from the beating of the waves. "I shall do well enough for a good while longer," he thought, "if I don't freeze with cold." But heavens! how cold the water was! And how dreary the whole scene was—the grey sky: the black waves!

Christmas looked round everywhere when he could use his eyes to any advantage, but could see no sign of unfortunate Nat Cramp. It was probably a lucky thing for him that he did not see his late companion, for if he had he would certainly have tried to save him, and they would both in all probability have been washed ashore at Portstone together. Such a struggle for life, however, leaves no time for regretting lost companions. Every moment that Christmas tried to raise his head a little above the waves to see if anywhere he could descry unhappy Nat, he was so beaten and buffeted and flung about and fallen upon, that all his attention had to go back at once to himself alone. At one moment, however, he saw that he was very near the upturned boat. A thrill of hope and joy went through him. It was not easy to get to the boat without the chance of being dashed against her or sucked under her, and Christmas dreaded almost above all things a disabled hand or arm just now. Nor was it easy being near the boat to do anything better than allow himself to be dashed against her and take his chance. So he made for her anyhow, and presently he was flung forward and felt a sensation as if some giant had flung him up against a wooden gate, and uncertain whether his ribs were dashed in or not he found himself lying across the upturned boat and clinging to her keel. This was the moment for safety. It was at all events a relief not to keep his limbs and senses employed in the mere struggle to remain afloat. He was afloat now easily enough, and the only thing was to keep himself from being smothered by waves breaking against the boat, or from being torn away from her, or having his head beaten against her keel. "Luckily there are no sharks about here," our poor hero thought.

Far away he saw the sail of which Nat Cramp had spoken. The wind, however, blew from her to him, and he did not believe there would be the slightest chance of sending his voice across the gusts to her. So he prudently spared his lungs and did not try. It was raining and the sky was all clouds, and he did not think he could do anything to make her see him. Still he had great hopes from her, and while that sail remained above his horizon he felt that no chilling sea could cause him to give up the struggle. For he seemed to have made up his mind that the sea should not swallow him before he had given his last message to Marie Challoner. " Die here now," he thought, " and she never to know how I loved her? No—I'll not die! I'll never give in! I'll get to Durewoods yet!"

It was strange how queer and drowsy and dreamy he seemed to grow. He was lying now not very uneasily along the back of the boat and holding on to her keel and was nearly out of the water, and there was a warmish and thick drizzle of rain falling around him, and the tossing motion and the hoarse roaring of the waves seemed to dull all his senses. The sharper tension of the struggle was gone and his frame was relaxed, and he felt inclined to go to sleep. He seemed to himself less like one clinging for dear life to an upturned boat in an angry sea than like one who lies in his bed and dreams of being in such a plight. But that the light had not changed he would have thought he must have been hours in the water. It seemed half a lifetime since he left London in the pouring rain that very morning. Was it that morning or when? Had he really met Nat Cramp at all?

Sometimes he found his eyes closing, and he once must have dozed for an instant, for he thought he was travelling in the sleeping-car of a railway at night, and that the noise of the waves was the rush and rattle of the train. Then he came to himself with a start, fearing he was about to be washed off the boat. Sometimes his mind wandered and he fancied he was in Japan with his father; in San Francisco; in Durewoods with Marie Challoner in the hollow among the trees holding her hand, and he talked to her quite aloud. More than once when his tired, languid eyes closed, he fancied he was lying in the chair in Sir John Challoner's library at Kensington asleep, and he believed that he had but to open his eyes and see Marie Challoner bending over him. So he looked up and saw the grey sky and felt the tossing of the pitiless waves, and clung all the faster and with strength renewed to the slippery boat and compelled his nerves to keep under his control, for if he lost his self-discipline for even a single moment he knew full well that he should never see Marie Challoner again. These little half-unconscious moments, these fits of sleepiness, were probably his salvation. Perhaps without them his nerves could never have endured the strain put on them—the strain of watching his safety and holding on to the boat.

What gleams of pleasure were extracted from the most unpromising condition, like the sunbeams from the Laputan cucumber? A chance change of position bringing a sense of freshness and relief to the overstrained frame, to the uneasy limbs, was for the moment a delight, as it is to the sick man on a bed of pain. Then he allowed his mind to enjoy the respite for an instant, and it went off guard and stood at ease. Sometimes he found himself shouting out scraps of song in answer to the hoarse roar of the waters. Sometimes he talked to himself and sometimes he shouted to Nat Cramp. Then he grew lazy and languid again, and felt very cold, and when his mind was awake and active enough to take in the reality of his condition he began to fear that he could not hold on any longer, that he must drop off and die, and never see Durewoods more. But again some change of position gave him fresh relief and he presently found himself back in Durewoods among the trees talking with Marie Challoner. Then he grew so languid that even when he once became vaguely aware that the sail he had seen was much nearer to him than before he only made mental observation that it was a schooner and did not seem to be conscious of his having any personal interest in it. But he suddenly awoke with a start that nearly lost him his place on the boat, and he cast away this languid, dying mood, and, tossed by the waves and soaking in the rain and chilled in the feet and legs as he was, he found the lifeblood bubbling and dancing in his veins again, and his mind told him " I shall see Durewoods again, after all ! " and he shouted to the schooner with a lung-racking effort which made his voice little good for singing for many a day after. Again and again he shouted till he fell back quite exhausted, only able to wait for any fate.

Afterwards he had a consciousness of being dragged and heaved on board a vessel, of having some delicious, divine, reanimating, burning liquid poured down his throat—only brandy and water—of seeing several faces round him, of asking if any one had seen poor Cramp, begging them to look out for Cramp, and then falling asleep.

CHAPTER XXXV.

"YOU ARE AND DO NOT KNOW IT."

A NIGHT of broken rest, of short, horrible dreams from which it was a relief to start, and sweet dreams still shorter from which it was a pain to awake; a night which seemed long as a lifetime, which was divided into intervals and chapters that were like years, brought Marie Challoner to her next morning. Until the slow dawn had come and familiar objects could be seen, the sleeping and the waking alike seemed a nightmare. A profound sense of strange, immeasurable misfortune was over Marie all the night through. What was to happen to her now? What was to happen to her next? How were she and her father to live together henceforward? Was it possible or right that they should live together? For when all his passion had passed away and he had put on an apologetic and subdued manner towards her, it was still just as clear as before that he considered her to have broken up all his plans and spoiled his life. He had the manner of one prepared to bear anything that might fall on him by or through his child, but who could not quite conceal the cruel pains of his martyrdom. Marie felt already like a stranger in the house—like one who had no right to be there, who had forfeited her claim to her father's love and shelter. Could a high-spirited girl endure this long? Would life on such conditions be worth having?

What she felt was that she had not merely lost her father, but that fate had changed her father, given her a new and sadly different father—one whom she hardly knew how to speak to, whom she looked at with uneasiness and dread, who seemed to shrink from her and to dislike her even when he was most civil and kind in words. The changeling of the fairy story is always the strange, unfamiliar, uncanny child whom the perplexed parent cannot warm to—here the changeling was the parent. Seldom surely was a girl's heart more peculiarly tried. For the new vein of love which had been breathed in it, exquisite as was the sensation it brought, only seemed to have been opened that her heart might bleed to death. Her love was to be barren—an endurance, a miserable secret, not a blessing. She had found out that she could love and that she did love, only just in time to find out that she could not have a lover. If Christmas Pembroke was not dead—if that hope and belief brought a rush of joy, what a cold reaction followed it! His name was nothing to her but a name to make her blush. By the strangest combination of unhappy chances, love seemed to have brought to her nothing but the need of renunciation, of repression, and of concealment.

Yet in one way her heart and her spirit never changed. She was still glad that she had broken suddenly and decisively from her engagement with Ronald Vidal. She felt her cheek burn with shame as she thought of him. She could have thanked Heaven now that he had never kissed her. It was well to have any little sense of relief anywhere, for the background as well as the foreground of her thoughts was nearly filled up with figures of pain. When for one moment her anxious mind ceased to brood on the possible fate of Christmas Pembroke, or the future of her father and herself, it rested on the wrong she had done to Ronald Vidal and the pain she must have caused him, or on the stark dead body of poor Nat Cramp.

The storm that had swept the skies and the seas for so many miserable days was over. The rain had ceased and the clouds had broken. A pale mild sunlight shone from a cold blue streak of sky. There was something even in that. The world was not all given over to mist and rain and racking wind. The gleam of pale sun was a touch of inspiration to her sinking, sickening heart. It seemed to Marie like the long-withheld smile of God's compassion, and it brought tears into her eyes.

What a forlorn meal was that breakfast when she and her father sat together and tried to seem as if they believed they were the same to each other, and talked a little on indifferent topics, each well knowing what was at the other's heart! How often did each look up and find that the other's eyes were suddenly withdrawn!

"I have had a letter from Mr. Sands this morning, Marie," her father said at last. "I am going over to Portstone after breakfast. There is to be an inquest, and I am to identify poor Cramp. Then I shall have him—the body—brought here and buried properly near his mother. That will be only right, you know."

"The widow's son by the widow," said Marie. "Poor Sarah Cramp! She worked and saved—and loved—to little purpose."

Sir John shook his head.

"Yes," he murmured audibly, but as if unconsciously, "she did. We all work and save—and love—to little purpose, I think! Yes, yes—well, well! "

Marie's cheeks coloured a little, but she said nothing. She was not probably of an age or in a mood to make allowance enough for her father's point of view. He had, indeed, loved her much, in his own way, and had worked for her and saved for her, and was proud at the thought of having his life's ambi-

tion gratified through her, by her—and she had blown down all
his plans and schemes and hopes with the breath of what seemed
to him a girl's foolish whim. His ambition truly had not been
noble, but its dying agonies were keen, and the first passion of
disappointment over he did not bear them badly.

But if Marie did not yet make mental allowance enough for
her father's disappointment, she at least was reasonable enough
not to embitter it by any remonstrance, even if it did give forth
a petulant wail now and then. She only said—

"I am glad that we can show our kindly memory of her—
and of him too—even in that poor way."

"Then," Sir John went on, " I am going on to Baymouth at
once. I am going to town—I shall return here the day after
to-morrow, I think."

"You are going to London to-day ?" she asked, with
tremulous lip.

"This evening—yes. I must see Ronald Vidal at once, of
course—that is due to him—and put things in the best way I
can. There is no need of your seeing him any more. There is
nothing to explain—which I cannot explain better; and it would
be painful to you and to him. After all, the main fact is the
great thing—and explanation can't do much with that."

Marie had nothing to say. Perhaps she ought to have thrown
herself into his arms and poured out some words of regret for
his disappointment, and of tenderness and affection. But she
felt that she could not do this. There was a chilling distance
between them ; and in her heart she resented, more profoundly
even than she knew, the manner in which he would have disposed
of her in marriage. She said nothing.

Presently Sir John rose and looked about him irresolutely.
Then he said, without looking at her.

"I don't exactly know what I shall do, Marie. I have been
thinking ; but I haven't yet quite made up my mind. I don't
care, of course, to be seen much in London until all this thing
has blown over. And one's plans have to be altered in every
way. I think I shall let the house in town, and this place
perhaps. We might go somewhere abroad and live quietly
there for awhile. I almost think I shall resign my seat in
Parliament. It seems hardly worth while keeping on. But
I don't know yet."

"If you would let me go and live somewhere away," said
Marie, with her eyes full of tears,—"and you need not disarrange
all your life—or if you would let me stay for awhile with Miss
Lyle—or the Rivers in Paris "—some school friends of hers.

"I don't think Miss Lyle is much of a friend of mine," Sir
John said, coldly, " or that her influence has been so very happy.
Besides," he added, with the affected cheerfulness of a martyr,

"I am not going to turn you out of doors, Marie, in that way. I am not one of the flinty-hearted fathers you read of in your romances. But when all one's plans are altered one has, of course, to make new arrangements. I always said you must not be pressed to marry any one against your will; only it is a pity, of course, that you didn't find out a little sooner; but we have talked of all that, and it can't be helped now."

So he went away, and Marie was left for awhile to herself. She felt very miserable, and was oppressed with the conviction that the very servants must know that she was fallen from power and was in disgrace. It was in some sense a relief to her when Janet, Dione Lyle's little maid, presented herself with a message from her mistress to say that Miss Lyle would like most particularly to see Miss Challoner if Miss Challoner would not mind venturing out, as the day was fine. Miss Challoner would not have minded venturing out in very bad weather that day for a kindly look and a loving word from any one, and she promised to go to Miss Lyle at once. But she went with a palpitating heart, for she felt convinced that Miss Lyle's message must have something to do with Christmas Pembroke. "Perhaps he is lost! Perhaps I shall know in five minutes that he is safe, or that he is lost!" Marie said to herself; and come what might she must, for her own sake and for woman's dignity, not show what she felt too much. Then, again, Miss Lyle might have sent only to ask something about him, having heard vague rumours perhaps. And Marie must be careful not to alarm her too much where she could not yet believe there was serious ground for alarm; and still must not give her too much hope, where, after all, the worst might have occurred. Marie had been greatly touched always by Dione's affection for Christmas Pembroke.

And then Marie's own personal troubles—they must not be told. Her father's secrets and her own—they must not be told, even to such a friend as Dione Lyle. To no human heart could she reveal the melancholy truth that her father and she were divided for ever—that her father, as she had known him, was lost to her. Nor would she tell that she had broken with Ronald until Ronald himself had accepted the fact that their engagement was at an end. What secrets she went burthened with to meet the one only friend in the world to whom she would gladly open all her heart! And Dione had keen eyes and would see any sudden evidence of peculiar emotion, and would ask the reason, and if she did ask, what could Marie answer? There was nothing for Marie, she thought as she went along, but to school herself into the most absolute self-control, and let no surprise betray her into emotion or into inconsiderate words. Of all tasks that could be imposed on her, any task of concealment, the accomplishing of even the most pious fraud, was the hardest

strain to put on Dear Lady Disdain, whose words followed her
thoughts as the sound follows the flash.
., She found Miss Lyle alone, holding in her hand a half-
crumpled paper, which Marie knew to be a telegraphic despatch.
When one is in anxiety about a human life, the sight of such a
paper sets the heart beating, and Marie had hard work to speak
a few sweet composed words of ordinary familiar greeting to her
friend. Then Dione Lyle's first question nearly startled her out
of all her pre-arranged self-control. It came out quick and
sharp.
"Do you know anything of Christmas Pembroke—that unfortunate boy?"
"No," said Marie. "I—I very much wish I did. But I hope
he is well?"
She was going to say "I hope he is safe;" but she checked
herself, remembering that this would be to betray to Dione Lyle
her fears that he was not safe. So her sentence had to end rather
feebly.
"Yes; I hope he is well—and I hope he is in his right senses.
Have you heard nothing about him lately?"
All the composure vanished.
"Oh, Miss Lyle, *you* know something—I see that you do.
Pray—pray tell me—don't keep me any longer in suspense!"
"My dear, what in the world are you in suspense about?"
"About him. Where is he? Oh, do you know—is he safe?"
Miss Lyle opened her eyes.
"Why, Marie, you *do* know something about him, after all!
You know more than I do, for you know that he was in some
kind of danger. Perhaps you wouldn't mind telling me what it
was all about?"
"But he is safe—he is living?"
"He is living," Miss Lyle said, composedly. "At least he
was living when he sent me that message. But it doesn't at all
follow that he should be living now, for you see that the message
got to Baymouth and was allowed to toss about there until there
was a chance of somebody coming over here, who kindly put it
in his pocket and brought it along with him. You have an
energetic father, my dear, who is always busy in schemes for the
development of everything. I wonder he wouldn't apply his
mind to the task of getting a telegraph wire stretched along to
Durewoods."
Marie was not listening to these latter words. She had taken
the telegram and was reading it as well as she could, while it
fluttered in her trembling hands:—
"Don't be alarmed about me, if you should hear any reports.
I am all right; I will get to Durewoods as soon as possible. Do
you know what has become of poor Cramp? I hope he is not
lost, but I fear the worst has happened!"

"He is safe—I knew it!" Marie said, and a rush of tears blinded her eyes for the moment. Let us not blame her if in the very moment when the full knowledge of his safety sent such a thrill to her heart there came with it the recollection that he was not saved for her.

"Where did this come from?" she asked, with faltering tongue—when she could speak, and cowering rather under the keen clear eyes of Dione Lyle.

"If you look at the telegram in your hand, my dear, you will see that it comes from Calais. But why should he be in Calais, or why he should have poor Cramp with him—I suppose it means that young fellow from Durewoods—I thought he was in America—all this passes my understanding."

"He was with poor Nat Cramp then!" Marie said. "I did not know that. I should have been so much more alarmed if I had. He was coming to Durewoods in a boat, I suppose. They told us of a boat and two young men—and I suppose they must have been upset—and perhaps some steamer picked him up and carried him to Calais. Poor Nat Cramp is drowned, Miss Lyle."

"I am sure I am very sorry," Miss Lyle said; but she was evidently not thinking much over his fate just then.

"Such a strange escape! So wonderful! But I knew *he* was not lost. Something told me that he would come back safe—and he will come! Was it not a strange thing that I should have known it!"

"I should take a little more interest in the story," Miss Lyle said, "if I knew what it was all about. Why was he coming to Durewoods in so tremendous a hurry?—and how did you know that he was coming? I hope, Marie, you were not keeping up a correspondence with this poor boy?"

"We had no correspondence," Marie answered, with downcast eyes. "Why should we correspond?—or why should we not, Miss Lyle, if we had anything to say?"

"But you should have had nothing to say," Dione replied warmly. "What could you have had to say to him? You were engaged to be married—what had you to do with that boy? I do think there is something very mean about women. You haven't escaped it even. Why torment that poor young fellow? I wish you had never seen him, Marie."

"Well—so do I, Miss Lyle! It has made me very unhappy."

"And I don't wonder? You have spoiled his life for him. I knew you would."

"Miss Lyle, why are you angry with me, and what have I done? I don't understand a word. Surely you don't think I knew—oh, no. I didn't know that he was coming here to see me."

"Oh! He *was* coming here to see you, then?"

" So he said—in the letter."

" I thought as much! I knew he was coming to see you! I knew the whole thing had some such mad freak at the bottom of it! And what did he want to see you for ? "

" I don't know—to say good-bye as he was leaving England— perhaps," Marie said piteously. She felt weak and humbled, for everybody seemed against her, though she was not conscious of having injured any one except Ronald Vidal. She had come to Dione Lyle for sympathy, and found that there too she was looked upon as a sort of wrong-doer.

" I don't see what he wanted of farewells under such cir- cumstances. What good could come of that? He knew you were engaged to be married."

Marie plucked up a little spirit now. " I don't see what that has to do with it, Miss Lyle. I suppose people are not to be cut off from every word of kindness and friendship in this world because they are engaged to be married. We—we—liked each other always—he and I. We were friends. At least I liked him—of course I did—and I think he liked me. Why should he not wish to say good-bye to me when he was going away? It was very, very kind of him—and I don't think I deserved it."

" How would Mr. Vidal have liked it, do you think? "

" I shouldn't have thought it necessary to ask Mr. Vidal's consent even if I had known," Lady Disdain said, colouring. " I didn't know. But he would never have thought of objecting —why should he object? I am sure *she* would not have objected unless she is a greater fool than I hope she is, for his sake," she added, with one womanlike and irrepressible touch of bitterness towards " the other."

" Who is she ? "

" That young lady—Miss Jansen, of course."

" What has she to do with this, dear ? "

" The girl to whom Mr. Pembroke is engaged ? "

Dione had almost forgotten that old story, and in her present impatience she could not even pretend to believe in it. For the moment she really supposed that Marie was indulging in some little coquettish affection.

" Stuff and nonsense ! You don't believe that story, dear. You know you don't. You know very well that the poor lad cares no more for that girl than I do who never saw her."

Marie opened wondering eyes.

" But he did care for her—he said so," Marie faltered, almost breathless.

" Not he, dear ; he never told any such untruth."

" But, Miss Lyle, whom then did he care for ? "

Dione looked into her open, wondering eyes.

" Either you are a better actress than I thought, dear, or you are more innocent than some of us were at the age of ten. Did you never know with whom Christmas Pembroke really was in love?"

" Never — except Miss Jansen. Every one said Miss Jansen—— "

" And you don't know still—you don't guess even now?"

" Oh, I can't guess. I'll not try to guess," Marie said, growing very red; "and it couldn't be, Miss Lyle," she added rather inconsistently.

" It could be, dear—it was—and it is; and I can tell you I wish it had never been, for his sake. Indeed, I thought you must have known it."

" Oh!"

The exclamation was partly a protest: but it was also a cry of wonder and delight.

" And that was why I was a little sharp, my dear," Dione went on, " I thought you knew it, and were pleased with it—I mean I began to think this when I got his message to-day, and found that he had been trying to see you. I never thought it before, and I don't think it now. Yes, Marie, he was in love with you all the time."

" It can't be," said Marie, " I don't think it can be."

" He told me so, Marie."

Another irrepressible note of delight was heard.

" Yes, I extorted it from him. Poor fellow! Well, I am glad to tell you all this now, Marie, because it is better you should know. I wish I had told you before."

" So do I," Marie said in a low voice.

" Yes, you might have known better how to act. Now, you know, and your course is clear, Marie."

" Is it? I wish it were."

" Of course you must not see this poor lover of yours any more."

Marie started.

" You wouldn't surely think of seeing him again after that? What would be the use of it? Why should you torment him for no purpose? I think it would be very wrong of you, Marie; and I know you too well to believe you would do anything wrong. Promise me, Marie, that you will not see him."

Marie was silent. Her soul was too much absorbed in wonder and delight to allow her to follow the words of her friend. He loved her; and had loved her always! The strangest thing, perhaps, was that the longer it rested in her mind, the less strange it seemed to be. It seemed so natural—and yet she had never thought of it. It fell in now and fitted with and made part of every look and word and act of his that she could recall, and yet it never occurred to her then. After the first shock of surprise and doubt the doubt vanished and never reappeared. Oh, yes; it was all clear now as the sunlight. He loved her as she loved him. All the world now seemed filled with happiness for her. She was so happy that the tears came into her eyes at the thought that she might possibly die, or he, before they met again.

" You will promise me this, child ? " Miss Lyle said softly.

" You will trust me, Miss Lyle, won't you, without asking for any promise ? I'll not do anything that you will blame. I will think of what is good for him a thousand times more than of myself. Yes, you may be sure of that! But I didn't know of this; and it has come on me suddenly, and there is so much to be thought of. I can't speak of it now—even to you, dear, dear friend. May I go away? I will come again whenever you want me."

" When I send for you, dear," said Dione, kissing her forehead, " and not before! I will ask you to come when you may come. I see you have taken this as—well, as I ought to have known that my poor Marie Challoner would take it. We must think of him, poor fellow ! "

" We must, indeed," said Marie, looking up with a bright look through her tear-flashing eyes, that almost dazzled Dione; and then she kissed Dione and went away.

" She has a good heart," Dione thought to herself, " a kind, pure, generous heart ! She feels for him as a woman ought to do—in the right way. I wish things had been otherwise! I wish those two could have loved each other, and married, and been happy. Well, well ! "

The last two words she found herself speaking aloud in her solitude. Her mind went back to a time when two hearts, each alike devoted to the other, were torn asunder and sent different ways for nothing. Here, after all, there was but one heart to bleed ; and men get over these things sometimes, she said : and then she felt very lonely and melancholy, and the twilight seemed a pain to bear in such a mood.

CHAPTER XXXVI.

THEY STAND CONFESSED.

CHRISTMAS PEMBROKE had accomplished his resolve so far as
the getting to Durewoods was concerned. The day was bright,
clear, and cold, when the *Saucy Lass,* now in good condition
again, brought him safely to the little pier. The village looked
melancholy in the wintry sunlight, and a keen pang shot through
the poor youth's heart as he thought of the bright soft summer
evening when first he landed there; when the whole place came
up for him, rising beautiful and poetic like some Delos-island
over the grey monotonous waters of his life. He could see the
whole scene once more as he saw it then—and the pony-carriage
at the pier, and the dark eyes of Marie Challoner looking kindly
at him.

He had been wild with impatience to get to Durewoods, and
now he walked slowly up the pier, and turned to the left instead
of the right when he reached the road. He lounged along
"melancholy, slow" in the strict sense of "The Traveller," and
feeling unfriended too, although he knew that he had friends.
He stopped and looked at the cottage in which poor Mrs. Cramp
used to live, and he thought of the night when Nat and he,
dripping from the sea, found shelter there. He knew now of
Nat Cramp's fate: the captain of the *Saucy Lass* had told him all
about it, and how Nat had been buried near his mother; and
Christmas had communicated to the captain in return his part
of the story, which was news to Durewoods. As Christmas
looked at the house he felt almost as if he were guilty of Cramp's
death, because of the piece of curious misfortune which caused
them to meet at the station that unlucky day. He wondered
what disappointment or disaster it was which had given such
wildness to Cramp's manner, and was sure it belonged to love.
As Lear believes all miseries and madness to come of ungrateful daughters, so Pembroke naturally set down such human
trials to the pangs of disprized love. Then he turned quickly
back, wishing he had not come that way or passed Nat's house,
and thinking that if omens, good or bad, could matter to him
any more it would have been of evil omen to look on the place.

Now that he was in Durewoods he began to wonder why he
had come there so precipitately; why he had come there at all;
why he had taken such great trouble to save himself from the
sea with the hope of getting to Durewoods and seeing Marie
Challoner. When he did see her—if she would see him—what

was to come of that? What did it matter whether she knew the whole truth about Miss Jansen or did not know it? He felt at moments almost inclined to go back again to London. All the vague doubts and hopes and perplexing conjectures needing explanation, which had seemed to him when he was in London like a summons from Providence or fate bidding him to hasten to Durewoods, began now to wear a look of blank absurdity. Probably he would have taken flight and gone back to London but that he knew full well the moment he got back there the dreams and longings would all set in again, and he should have to follow whither they bade him to go. Being here now he would go through with it; he would see her for the last time.

He turned again and passed the pier, and held to the right, and mounted the little hill. Winter now brooded over that scene, and winter over all his hopes! The very ground was bare of leaves now. They had lain there in heaps in the little hollow on either side of the road for months until the rains rotted them into the earth or the keen winds scattered them far away. So, our young hero thought, had all his hopes—the hopes with which he entered London—been dealt with: so scattered and trodden into the earth of prosaic commonplace. He was in a sadly egotistical mood just now, after the fashion of the disappointed, and he could not help fancying that the wintry aspect of the place was purposely in keeping with his own desolate condition. Egotism alone, perhaps, could have soothed and consoled him now.

Yet the day was bright and cheery for a winter day in England. There was a light frost, and all trace of rain and mist was gone; and as Christmas turned to look back upon the sea, one great tract of it glittered with a smile of sunlight, and it might have been summer for the moment, and not winter, if one looked but on the heavens and the waves. Why not accept the smile as ominous when one is so ready to think of the grey clouds and the naked trees and the chill earth as symbolic? Christmas plucked up heart at the sight of the water and the gladdening sunlight. " Come," he said to himself, " I shall live all this down? I'll get this last meeting over, and then I'll go back to my old home, and work hard there, and never come back to England any more; and all this will seem like a dream, and I shall have her memory always. Why, that alone will make life worth having!"

So he went resolutely on, and even when he came to the gate of the Hall he did not pause and reconsider, or pass on as if he had no idea of going in, or were not quite certain whether he should look in that day, or play any of the other tricks of indecision. Certainly he did for one moment falter at the gate —the lodge-keeper's wife afterwards remarked picturesquely that

he " quivered on his foot like "—but he went in through the gate,
only asking as he passed if Miss Challoner was in Durewoods
and at home. His heart did sink a little within him as he
reached the door, but he assumed as well as he could the easy,
unconcerned air of an ordinary visitor, and he sent his card to
Miss Challoner.

He was shown into the library, which Miss Challoner was in
the habit of using as a reception-room when her father was not
in Durewoods. Christmas waited there with a beating heart for
what seemed to him an endless time and was in reality about
five minutes. Then Marie's maid came in smiling, and cordially
glad that Christmas was not drowned, and longing to say so in
frank country fashion; and she told him that Miss Challoner
would see him in a moment. Then Christmas looked at the
backs of books, and took a book out now and then, and opened
it and put it back in its place without noticing what it was :
and walked up and down the room, and trembled when he
thought he heard *her* step, and grew more nervous than ever
when he found himself mistaken and she did not come. What
a long, long moment that was! This time he was not mistaken,
for he looked at the clock on the chimney-piece. Ten minutes
already !

The delay came about in this way. Not long before his
coming, Marie had received a telegram from her father, sent on
from Portstone by special messenger, which at once relieved and
distressed her.

" I have seen R. V. and talked with him a long time. I have
explained all. He is greatly cut up, but admits that things are
hopeless and had better be considered at an end, and is going to
Naples to stay some months. Begs me to give you kind regards
and to say that he does not blame you, and will try to bear up.
I leave for Durewoods at once, but wish to let you know this
without delay. R. V. asked if you would like him to write; I
thought better not."

She was free then. She need not think of Ronald any more ;
and womanlike she began to think of him with great compassion,
and to blame herself for ever having listened to his proposal, and
to feel ashamed of herself, and ashamed even of being so glad to
be free. She was in the midst of all this self-reproach, and her
eyes were dimmed with tears, when the card bearing the name
of Christmas Pembroke was put into her hand. Quickly she
dropped the telegram and blushed, and started, and became half
wild with excitement, and it must be owned forgot all about
poor Ronald. When she sent her message to Christmas by the
maid she ran and plunged her face into water to wash away the
traces of the tears, and she looked at herself in the glass and
wondered what she should seem like in *his* eyes, and remembered

the day when in his blunt boyish fashion he told her she was handsome. Strange, at that time she was only amused by his brusque frankness, and now as she remembered it and looked at herself in the glass she saw that the mere thought of it made her blush. "I wonder will he think me handsome now?" she thought—and then she hastened with her preparations to meet him, for the absurd idea came into her head, "Suppose I keep him too long—and he has to go away—and goes to Japan without seeing me?"

Christmas waiting nervously below heard the rustle of a dress at last and a light quick tread, and then had a confused impression of dark eyes and a sweet, fresh voice, and a tall, shapely figure, and a hand with a kindly pressure; and Marie Challoner was with him. The whole place for the moment swam before his eyes, and he looked so pale and half distraught that Marie feared he must have suffered serious harm by his long wrestle with the winds and the waves.

"It is so kind of you to come to see me all this way," she said. "But, of course, you would come to see Miss Lyle."

"I have not seen her yet. I—I came to see you first."

"But you look very pale. We were all so glad to hear that you were not drowned; we never thought of asking whether you were hurt."

"Oh, no, I was only a little shaken—not hurt at all—nothing to speak of."

"How glad you ought to be—and in such a sea so long! Hours upon hours, was it not?"

"It seemed a terribly long time to me. I thought it would never have come to an end. But I don't think it could have been very long in reality."

There was a moment's pause.

"You had a wonderful escape," said Marie. "You ought to be very thankful."

"Yes," he answered, "I didn't want to be drowned just then."

"I hope it did you no harm—being in the cold sea all that long time."

"No; I don't think it did. I felt very stiff and stupid for a day or so, and not like myself: but it didn't do me any harm."

"How strong you are!"

"Oh yes, nothing does me any harm—nothing of that kind. Poor Cramp—you've heard, of course?"

"Yes, I have heard." She did not say that she had fainted at the sight of Cramp's dead body, or why. "What a terrible thing! He was so young, and I used to think once that he would come to something."

"It wasn't any fault of mine," Christmas hastened to explain.

"I didn't want him to come into the boat; I begged of him not to come. But he would have been perfectly safe if he had only kept quiet. I don't know what came over him, whether he was frightened out of his wits or not, but he seemed like a madman. Why, he would have been alive and well now if he wouldn't keep jumping up and going on like a lunatic. There wasn't the slightest danger. I do believe he was mad, and I hope he was; for I feel half guilty somehow of his death, although Heaven knows it was no fault of mine, and I would have saved him if I could—at the risk of my own life—not much to risk, certainly."

"I think you risked your life far too much as it was. Why did you get into a boat on such a day?"

"Well, there was no other way of getting to Durewoods."

"But why not wait until the next day; or until the weather was fine or the steamer was ready; or go round by the road? Why risk your life for nothing?"

"Yes, there was no need of so much impatience, indeed," poor Christmas said disconsolately. "I might as well have waited; but anyhow, Miss Challoner, I should like you to know that it was only my own life I wanted to risk—if there was risk—and not poor Cramp's."

"I know very well that you did not think of yourself. That is why I blame you so much Mr. Pembroke."

She felt it a delightful thing to be talking to him. He was very much embarrassed. She saw the end of all this, and he did not. So she trembled a little, but was very happy; and he stammered and was awkward and miserable. Now that he was with her he began to think there was not a great deal of purpose in his coming, and to wish he had stayed away. Yet he longed to linger still in her presence, trying to say the right thing and failing; resolved that at least she should know the truth about him, and yet afraid to come to the point.

"Well," he began with a rush: "I came to see you, Miss Challoner——"

"Yes, Mr. Pembroke?"

"Because—I am not taking up your time, I hope?"

"Not at all."

"Because—you are not particularly engaged just this moment?"

"No, indeed."

"If you were, of course another time would suit me. I could call later in the day."

"I am very glad to see you now or at any time, Mr. Pembroke: and I am not at all engaged. But will you not take a chair?"

"Thank you, no; I think not. While I keep standing it seems as if I were preparing to go."

"But why want to go in such haste? I have not seen you for such a long time."

"No; and you have been to America since. I hope you enjoyed your trip?"

"Very much."

"Do you like the States?"

"Very much. I liked San Francisco especially, and the Golden Gate."

She thought perhaps he would say something about the unforgotten day when he first told her of the Golden Gate. She had said the words to bring some answer from him, and she saw a sudden little shadow of emotion run across his face, as one sees a shadow cross a meadow. She knew that the words had touched him as she meant them to do. But he did not answer to the touch.

"Well," he said, "I have come to say good-bye, Miss Challoner, and to say how much obliged I am to you for all your kindness; and how I shall always remember——" He stopped.

"Then you are really going back to Japan, and leaving us all in England?"

"Yes; I have thought of it this long time, so I came to say good-bye."

"If you must go really—if it is for your advancement; and if we must say good-bye——"

"Now suppose—this sudden thought passed through her mind—suppose he shakes hands and says good-bye and is really going out of the room without another word—what am I to do then? Must I let him go?

"I couldn't leave," he said, "I couldn't leave, you know, without saying good-bye."

"Oh, no! I am sure you would not be so unfriendly as to do that."

But suppose, she thought, he only did come to say good-bye, and says nothing else, and goes away then—what am I to do?

"And besides," he went on in a hesitating way, "it wasn't only that."

She drew a long breath of relief. She was happy again, since it was not only that.

"There was something else I wanted to say to you—and I couldn't leave you for ever without saying it—something I wanted to explain. May I go on?"

"Oh, yes, Mr. Pembroke, if you wish! What was it you wanted to explain?"

"You won't be angry with me, Miss Challoner, if it seems odd? You will be a little generous with me, and believe I have a good motive, won't you? and you won't be offended?"

"Why, Mr. Pembroke, this is a terrible preface! Why should

I be offended? How could I possibly suppose that you meant to offend me?"

"Thank you—then I'll go on. I wanted to explain—Miss Challoner, you heard, I know you did, something about me and a young lady, whom I needn't name, about my being in love with her, and our being engaged. Didn't you?"

"Yes. I heard something of the kind."

"Did you believe it?"

"I suppose so. Why not? Was it not true?" She spoke with her best possible imitation of friendly carelessness.

"It was not true; there was not one single word of truth in it."

"How absurd of people to spread such reports! I cannot think how such things get about. But, after all, Mr. Pembroke, I don't see that you need complain very much. It is much more unpleasant for *her* to be talked about. She is a very pretty girl, I think. And was there nothing in all that, really?"

"Nothing at all. She never cared anything about me, and I don't care three straws about her."

"Come, now, what a very rude way to speak of a young lady; I thought you had more chivalry, Mr. Pembroke."

"Well, I only meant you to understand that there never was the faintest idea of anything like love between us. I want you, above all things, Miss Challoner, to believe that."

"Of course I believe it, since you tell me—but would it not have been a great deal happier for you if the story had been true?"

"It couldn't be true, Miss Challoner, and I came here to tell you why it could not be true. I know that it was told to you, and I do not know why. Not for anything on earth would I leave England until I had told you that that was not true, and showed you why it could not be true."

"And why could it—not—be true?"

"Now," thought Christmas, "I cannot stop; now all must be said."

"Because I loved *you*, Miss Challoner, and because I do love you, and shall love you all my life! Because I am all wild with love of you! No—don't draw away from me, or be angry. That's all I have to say. It is all over now—and I'll leave you this moment."

"But why do you tell me this?" Marie asked, all palpitating with fear and joy.

"Heaven knows—I don't know! Because I couldn't help telling you. I couldn't live if I hadn't told you. After all, what harm has it done you?"

"But if it were true—if you really felt all that for me"—she began, not unwilling, perhaps, to tempt him into saying it over again, that she might hear it again.

"If it is true? Shall I tell you a thousand times over, Miss Challoner, that I love you? I will say it a thousand times over rather than go away without knowing that you believe me I love you—I——"

"Oh, hush!" said Marie, almost borne down by his vehemence, and a little afraid of such emotion, which was so very unlike Ronald Vidal's way. "I do believe you if you say so. But why do you tell this to me? It must make me unhappy to think that I am the cause of your being unhappy."

"I should be ten thousand times more unhappy if I had not told you. Besides, it isn't any fault of yours. You can't help my falling in love with you. I insist upon my right," Christmas said, with an attempt at a smile, "to love you if I like, and as much as I like, and as long, and you can't prevent that. It's a free country! Well, that's all. I should be perfectly wretched if you thought I loved or cared a rush for anybody else but you; and so in listening to me, Miss Challoner, and hearing me out, you have done all you could do to make my life endurable."

"That is not much," said Marie. "You know I would do a great deal to make you happy if I could."

"Oh, yes!" Christmas hastened to say, with something like genuine and manly cheerfulness, "I know all that. I know that you never felt anything but the kindest friendship to me. Why, I should call you my dearest friend on earth, if I could only think of you in that way. And how good of you to listen to all this! I felt terrified, but you have made it so easy. I felt that I must tell you this, but I was afraid it was wrong to do and would offend you, and that you would be angry, and then I should hate myself and wish I had never told you. Now you know; and you are not offended——?"

"Oh, no; only sorry——"

"Sorry? for what? For shining like a light across a poor fellow's way, and giving him always something to remember, and an ideal; and so much that I can't put into words? Why, I shall have the memory of your kindness and your friendship always! I would rather have seen you and loved you—and know that you knew I loved you, and that you forgave me, than be a king—and I haven't lost you, after all," he added with a melancholy smile, "for I never had any hope of winning you. So I am all the gainer you see!"

"You deserve a better fortune, Mr. Pembroke."

"Don't think about that. You have done all you could to make me happy—and now I've said all I wanted to say—except good-bye."

"Good-bye," she said very faintly; "if we must say it;" and wondering what she was to do next.

"We must say it! Good-bye. I need not say how I wish you happiness. You and yours—and *all* yours."

"Yes,—thank you; and before you go—as you are going—should you like——?"

"Should I like Miss Challoner?"

"Should you like"—and an insane impulse carried her away,—"perhaps to kiss me?"

The blood rushed into Christmas's face and into hers; and they both trembled, and stood trembling. There was a moment's silence, and then he threw one hand into the air with the gesture of a man who flings away some last chance.

"No!" he said, "I shouldn't! I should go wild if I had to leave you then—and your kisses are not yours to give away!"

"It's not true," Lady Disdain replied with indignant emphasis. "You don't know what you say. They are mine to give away or I should never have offered them. You may be sure I never said such words before."

She was as angry with him and with his rejection of her offer as if he could have known the whole truth. She was angry with herself for having made the offer. She felt almost inclined now to let him go.

"I don't understand," he began.

"Of course you don't understand; men don't ever understand anything," and Lady Disdain found herself in her emotion parroting the commonplace sayings of angry women without thinking of it. "Do you suppose, Mr. Pembroke, that because I offered to kiss you I must be in love with you?"

"Oh, no, no," he exclaimed quite earnestly, and with fervent disclaimer—"how could I suppose anything of the kind? I assure you, Miss Challoner, such an idea never entered my mind—never!"

"Then why did you speak in such a way?"

"But I didn't—indeed I didn't. I knew you only meant good nature and friendship, and pity and all that; but I couldn't stand it, Miss Challoner, all the same."

"Well," and she drew a long breath, "it's no matter, I meant it well. And you are really going to Japan?"

"Yes. I am going."

"I wish you could take me with you."

"You wouldn't care to be there. You are much happier here." He thought she was only jesting about her love for travel and seeing the world.

"I shall not be happy here."

"But you have everything to make you happy—and when you are—married—you can travel again, and——"

"I am not going to be married. No,—you need not look surprised. It is quite true—I am not going to be married. I have broken all that off—this long time—yesterday—I don't know when. But I am free."

" Why did you do this?" the wondering youth asked.

" Why? Because I had made a mistake in life. Am I the first girl who didn't know her own mind? Because people persuaded me, and I didn't know myself—not in the least. Now I do—and I am free. But this is only personal talk—about myself, and I must not detain you. Good-bye, Mr. Pembroke."

Our hero was for the moment all puzzled.

" You changed your mind?"

" Yes. No, though—I don't think I did. I only found out my mind—found what I ought to have known long ago."

Was any faint idea breaking in now on the mist of Christmas's mind?

" What ought you to have known long ago? Is it wrong to ask you?"

" I ought to have known that I cared for—for somebody else."

Christmas was standing with his hat in his hand. He tossed the hat on the table near, and moved towards her half in hope, half in fear, hardly knowing what he did or felt.

" Yes," she said, " I am very sorry: it was very wrong and thoughtless of me to *him*: but I didn't know—and they told me you were in love with *her*—and—will you kiss me now? and I'll go with you to Japan or anywhere if you like!"

Then Christmas Pembroke for the first time kissed a young woman's lips.

CHAPTER XXXVII.

" CONTENT SO ABSOLUTE."

WHICH of these two young lovers was the more happy and the more in love? A question that probably the wit of man could not settle until at least the old and general question had first been settled—is man or woman susceptible of the higher happiness and capable of the stronger love? The wise person told of in classic story, whom the gods permitted to be changed for a time into a woman and then resume the form and the life of a man, is said to have reported as the result of his experience that the woman is more loving and the man more happy. If this be a true report, then let us say that Marie Challoner loved the more and Christmas was the more happy. The latter part at least would bear some seeming of truth, for in all her fresh delight of love and happiness Marie felt some painful thought about her father arising in her mind, while Pembroke's breast was filled with his joy, and he could spare no thought for obstacles—cared nothing about them, whether they were to arise or not. But, indeed, all one could say of these two is that he and she were just as much in love and just as happy as a man and a woman ever could be. Curious to note that their love had been of such strangely different growth. That of the man had lit up almost the first moment he and she met, and kept burning always. Her love had been of slow growth, long unrecognised, unsuspected, only gradually making its presence felt, until at last it broke and glowed into full flame.

Perhaps, if any romantic person could have looked into that library to see a living chapter of love and romance, he or she might have been a little disappointed and might have wondered that there was not somewhat more of passionate demonstrativeness. But, indeed, the two lovers were a good deal embarrassed and even shy. The suddenness of the new relation which they held to each other made them wonderfully timid.

"I wish we were up in the wood—in that dear delightful little hollow," said Christmas.

"I don't think I could wish anything to be but just what it is," Marie answered quickly, for the little hollow in the wood had to him only a memory of her, but she remembered that she had been there with Ronald Vidal too, and therefore held it less sacred.

"I can hardly believe in all this; it is too happy," he said. "The change is too sudden for me to realise it yet. And I am afraid, Marie—would you believe it?"

"Afraid? Of what?"

"That I am not half good enough for you, and can't make you happy enough, and give you the position you ought to have. You have been always used to such a home—full of luxury and all that."

"Yes. I have always been used to it, and so I don't care about it. What good has it ever done for me? I have always had money enough—or rather I have never had any money at all, but everything has been bought for me that I wanted, and much that I never did want—and now it would please me much more to buy things for myself. I know that I shall develop a perfect genius for domestic economy, and I shall be as delighted with it as a child with a new toy, so don't be afraid of *that.*"

"But I haven't much money."

"Oh, but you will get more, or we shall find what you have quite enough for us—and I don't care. It will not affect me. I am not talking like the romantic young women in the novels, Chris."

It sent a delicious thrill through him to hear her call him "Chris."

She saw the expression of delight that passed over his face.

" I think I shall always call you Chris. I used to like to hear Miss Lyle call you Chris. But I wanted to tell you that I am not like a girl in a romance. I do know the value of money, and luxury, and all that—to me ; and I know that it is just nothing, and that as long as you care for me I shall never care what kind of furniture is in the room, or what sort of carpet we are treading on. I know now that I never was happy, or could be—until I found out that I could love some one—and that you were the some one."

" Marie, suppose I had not come here to Durewoods, but had gone away—what should we have done ? "

" Oh, you couldn't have gone away—it's impossible. Heaven would never have allowed that. But don't call me only Marie—like everybody else."

" What shall I call you then ? " For he still was shy and almost afraid to call his own his own.

" I don't know—something tender and loving—something which will let me feel that you do really love me beyond all the world. Am I too outspoken and bold, Chris ? I can't help it. You have saved me from such a miserable life, and I want to be assured again and again that you love me and that I may love you."

And so all thoughts and plans for the future were put away for the moment, and their talk for awhile was given to mere assurances of love. It was the youth of the world for them again. They grew in courage both of them, and Christmas found that he could devise marvellously sweet and tender names for her.

Yes, it was for the hour a renewal of the world's youth and golden days so far as these two were concerned. They sometimes walked up and down the room, he with his arm around her waist and his tall, somewhat boyish figure bending a little down towards her, and his heart filled with a wonderful longing to be able to go out and fight lions or do something else for her to show how much he loved her. They seemed to have forgotten that they were not in Arcadia, but in the library of a London financier's country house, and that there were such things in the world as ladies'-maids and butlers, and preparations for luncheons and dinners, and possible morning calls. The latter events, however, were only possibilities in Durewoods, so far as Sir John Challoner's house was concerned when Sir John himself was absent. He brought his visitors with him from town.

So our lovers walked slowly up and down and talked and sometimes laughed in that old library as if it were their own safe retreat, wholly sheltered from the intrusion of the outer world. It was the striking of the clock on the chimney-piece which first brought them back to the details of common life.

"Can it be so late?" Marie asked. "Two o'clock!"

"I suppose I ought to go away?"

"I suppose so. I wonder if I ought to ask you to stay for luncheon at three?"

"I don't know. I haven't the least idea," the unsophisticated youth answered. "But if I go away now you must let me come again very soon—or let me see you somewhere."

"I used to go to see you at Miss Lyle's long ago without any hesitation," Marie said, smiling at the thought. "But I suppose I could not do that now. I wonder what Miss Lyle will say when she hears all this. She will put all the blame on me, I know."

"The question is," Christmas said, "what are we to do next? I suppose we shall have some difficulty with your father. I ought to go to London and tell him of this at once."

"He will be here, perhaps this very evening," Marie said, turning a little pale at the thought. "If he will not consent, Chris?"

"I don't care about his consent, so long as I have his daughter's. You won't break your word, I know."

"Oh, no—I'll not break my word—nor change. We must only wait."

"I'll not wait," said Christmas. "I'll carry you off by force if needs be—and then no one can blame *you*."

"I don't care about the blame. It is not that. I don't even care about his anger. I mean it would not alarm me or put me from my purpose; but I should be so sorry to give him any more pain, and I should like him to like *you*. He was always so good to me and so fond of me, and I used to be so fond of him, and of course this is a disappointment to him. If we are to be—married—you and I, Chris——"

"*If* we are to be married!"

"Well, *since* we are to be married, I should like our married life to begin in kindness with him, and if it might be, with his good will. We are both young, and you seem so very young, everybody says,—and we could wait. I should be happy, no matter how long we waited, while I knew that you always thought of me, and loved me. You will promise me this—not to have any quarrel with my father if we can—if we can avoid it by waiting a little. You will promise me this?"

She threw her arm over the young man's shoulder—it was the first approach to a caress she had yet made—and looked pleadingly into his eyes.

"My dearest dear, I'll promise you anything," he said. "I'll do anything you like that will make you happy."

With a blushing cheek and growing courage she kissed him.

"And then you know," she pleaded, "he has some right to

complain of me. Yes, and of you too, Chris! Why did you say that you were in love with that poor girl? Did you say that?"

"Oh, I never said it! I never said a word of the kind. How could I have said that?"

"Well, but he came to believe it somehow, and he thought you said so. How could that have been?"

Christmas had thought of this many times, even during their first flush of surprise and happiness. Was he to let Marie Challoner know that her father had been guilty of such a cruel fraud?

"I don't know," he said hastily. "He must have misunderstood somehow. I was awfully confused of course, and I suppose I didn't know what I was saying. I thought he would understand me, or that he partly guessed already. It was a very different love-story I meant to tell him."

"About *me?*"

"About you, love; and only you! See what a piece of work I must have made of it!"

"And what confusion it brought on everybody. If I had known then——"

"But you didn't care about me then?"

"Oh yes, I did. I know now that I did. I felt towards you even then as I never felt to any one else. I ought to have known. Oh yes, Chris. I was beginning to be in love with you then! But of course I closed my heart against you when I heard *that.* Do you remember the day in Mrs. Seagraves' house?"

"Do I remember it? Didn't I walk the streets half that night and think of killing myself?"

"I was very much in love with you that day, only I wouldn't allow myself to think of it. And that was the day when poor Ronald Vidal asked if he might come and see me."

"I saw him," Christmas said, "and I hated him then, and I should have liked to kill him. Now I suppose he would like to kill me! Well, I don't wonder at that."

"It was the next day you told my father."

"It was," said Christmas, hurriedly, wishing that her memory of that fact at least were a little less clear. "It was all my fault, that terrible misunderstanding. Well, my dearest dear, this time when I go to Sir John Challoner with my love-story I'll make my meaning clear."

"What will you say?"

"Sir John, I am in love with your daughter, Marie Challoner —in love with Marie Challoner, your daughter—as I do believe no mortal man was ever in love with a girl before! I am in love with a girl whose name is Marie Challoner, and who is your daughter! That will be clear enough?"

"Yes, I think that will be clear enough; but you may add something."

" What can I add to strengthen that ? "
" Only this : ' and Marie Challoner, your daughter, is in love
with me.' "
" Yes, I will tell him that too, although I can still hardly
believe in it myself! Shall we go together and throw ourselves
at Sir John's knees ? "
" I fear he would only laugh or say something satirical. I
have an idea, Chris—let us go together to Miss Lyle and tell her
all, and ask for her advice."
" Come," said Christmas, " we will go. You are not afraid to
be seen with me ? "
" I am not afraid of anything, except of being without you,"
said Lady Disdain.
The two lovers went boldly out together, and presently appeared hand in hand before the wonder-stricken eyes of Dione
Lyle.

CHAPTER XXXVIII.

" THE ASTROLOGY OF THE EYES."

ONE Sunday Captain Cameron strolled into his sister's house in
Portland Place at the hour when her afternoon reception was
going on. He did not very often go there, for his opinions on
most subjects—social, political, and religious—concurred with
those of very few who usually presented themselves in that
drawing-room. Besides, there were a good many visitors there
who had no opinions whatever on such subjects, and these
Captain Cameron regarded as worse than persons with any
sort of wrong and strong creeds. There were some artists and
poets to be found there who hardly knew what sort of Sovereign
or Ministry was in power anywhere, and would not have cared
a rush to know. Some of these persons, indeed, made a point of
frankly declaring that it was a matter of absolute indifference to
them what political principles were up and what were down so
long as there were pictures to paint and music to listen to ; and
one had even announced to the appalled Cameron himself that
he didn't care whether England's prestige was gone or not, and
that if half a dozen invading armies were to occupy London in
succession it would not give him the slightest concern so long as
they didn't interfere with the Dudley Gallery and Wagner's
music.
' This particular Sunday, however, Cameron had heard a piece
of news which interested and puzzled him, and about which he

thought he could probably learn the truth from his sister. With all his dissent from her opinions and the good-humoured chaff in which he occasionally indulged, Captain Cameron thought his sister a very clever and delightful person, and in her strangely-chosen sphere a queen of society, and he did not by any means see her as some even of her friends were pleased to do. He assumed, therefore, that nothing so strange as the news he had just heard could be true if Mrs. Seagraves did not know of it, and he therefore boldly plunged into the midst of her society.

A young lady, whose hair was wreathed in huge coils and complications of twirls on the top of her head, was singing some of Elsa's plaints from "Lohengrin" when Cameron entered. In that odd place the company usually listened when anybody sang or played. Cameron therefore stayed for a while at the door and looked for his sister.

He saw her standing near a table and resting one hand upon a huge blue china jar, while the forefinger of the other hand touched her chin; and her head leaned gracefully to one side in the attitude of a pensive listener. She was dressed in a dun-coloured silk, which clung so closely to her that it seemed a puzzle how she ever could have stepped into it, or could now contrive to step in it. Standing near her was a pale, pretty, and slender girl, dressed in quiet colours. The moment the music was over Mrs. Seagraves broke into raptures, which Cameron, making his way towards her, came just in time to hear.

"So glad I am, Robert, that you heard that enchanting music."

"Music, eh? I confess I like something with a tune to it."

"Oh, barbarian! Is he not barbarous, Miss Jansen—my brother?"

"Mrs. Malaprop says men are all barbarians," Captain Cameron observed.

"Does she really? Does she though? How very delightful! I should love her, I know! I am sure I should love Mrs.—who, Robert?"

Robert did not stop to explain. He did not expect that clever ladies of to-day would have read Sheridan.

"What's all this cock-and-bull story I hear, Isabel—about my charming little Lady Disdain and young Vidal?"

"So delightful, and so strange!" Mrs. Seagraves said, forgetting Mrs. Malaprop in her new enthusiasm. "At least, not strange—no, not by any means strange, but just what one ought to have expected, I suppose. One should always look out for the strange in these matters. But it is delightful! At least it is delightful to us who like it, and who love all the people—that is of course, the principal people. Of course it can't be delightful to Mr. Vidal—oh, no. I should say it must be quite the reverse

2 A

to him. And for that reason I am so very, very sorry. I was very glad at first, but now I am very, very sorry."

"But what is it, Isabel? I should like to know whether I am to be glad or sorry—or totally indifferent."

"Robert! Indifferent—totally indifferent—to anything that concerns the happiness of my dear, sweet girl, Marie Challoner! Oh, for shame! But I know you didn't mean it, and I couldn't think so badly even of a man. But men are very bad—oh, so very, very bad! Not deliberately bad, perhaps—no, I don't say that; but thoughtless, perhaps. Should we not say thoughtless? I hope you don't admire thoughtless men, Sybil dear? I think you girls generally do admire thoughtless men—and spoil them. I used to love thoughtless men once—I thought it made them like heroes. Now I don't like them at all."

"About Miss Challoner, Isabel? That's more to the point now."

"About Miss Challoner? Oh yes! Well, you know, she's not going to marry Mr. Vidal, after all!"

"Indeed? Well, I'm deucedly glad to hear it," the Legitimist said, "if it's true."

"But, Robert dear—our dear Mr. Vidal?"

"Well, he may be your dear Mr. Vidal if you like, Isabel, but ne isn't my dear Mr. Vidal. I never thought much of him. I like a gentleman to be a gentleman, and I'm glad to find Lady Disdain of my opinion at last."

"Oh, I think he is so charming," Mrs. Seagraves said, "so very, very charming. Not charming, perhaps—not exactly charming."

"No indeed—not by any manner of means charming, I should say."

"Well, perhaps not; but so clever, so very clever, and so handsome! At least, I used to think him handsome once, but now I don't know that he is so handsome as I thought him. He used to remind me of a troubadour, and I do so delight in troubadours. Sybil, my dearest child, you delight in troubadours, don't you? Oh yes—a girl with your eloquence and your eyes must delight in troubadours."

"I never saw any troubadours," Miss Sybil curtly answered.

"Never saw any troubadours? How very, very strange! No, though—I don't mean that it is strange, of course—it couldn't be strange, for there are no troubadours now any more, and you couldn't have seen any. Still the imagination does so much, especially with poetic natures; and I should have thought that you were just the girl to have loved troubadours. And I am so sorry, my dear Sybil, to hear that you really don't love troubadours. Robert, shouldn't you have thought Miss Jansen would love troubadours?"

The Legitimist bowed rather stiffly to the little Sybil.

"But I had quite forgotten," Mrs. Seagraves said, "that you don't know my dear friend Miss Jansen. How very strange! Dear Robert, how fortunate you are! Not fortunate in not knowing Miss Jansen—of course not that—what nonsense! But fortunate in having the opportunity now of being presented to her. My dear Sybil, will you permit me to present my brother, Robert—Captain Cameron? You ought to know each other, you two."

Captain Cameron was dignified, but not cordial. He had heard of Miss Jansen as a young woman who made speeches, and he considered that young women who made speeches were coarse, masculine, and rather indelicate creatures, utterly unladylike at the best. He had an impression that they were Atheistical as to their views on the subject of religion, and that they aspired to the wearing of trousers. When he heard Miss Jansen's name mentioned he looked in instinctive alarm downwards, and was relieved to see skirts and not pantaloons. " I look down towards her feet—but that's a fable," murmured the soldier, one of his few memories of Shakespeare occurring to him with a whimsical appropriateness.

" Now, Robert, I shall leave you to talk to Miss Jansen. You two are just made for each other—of course I mean for intellectual converse, for high argument."

" I never presume to argue with a lady," Captain Cameron remarked, with grim and stony courtesy.

" Arguments with gentlemen are usually thrown away, I fear," Miss Jansen said icily. " They do not consider us worth listening to, or answering."

" Oh, but my brother is not of that sort, I can assure you: he is far too chivalrous. Who is it—what great person—who says that friendship rests on similarity of tastes—is it? and differences of opinion? There are you two just pictured. I am sure your inclinations are both just the same—to do good. Oh, yes! to do good and to elevate humanity: and your opinions are so very different. Sybil, my dear, I leave to you the charge of converting my brother! I never could accomplish it, my dear, but it is reserved for you. Oh, yes! I know it is."

" But, Isabel, just a moment." She was swirling away. " You haven't finished telling me about Marie Challoner. Why won't she marry Vidal? "

" My dear Robert, you don't think she could marry two persons? "

" Gad! I don't know what you ladies mayn't think you have a right to do now-a-days, with your advanced opinions, and your rights, and so on. But I don't say that of her. Well! who's the other person—the one she wants to marry? "

" Wants to marry! What a very, very shocking phrase! I wonder at you, Robert. As if ladies ever wanted to marry—such an idea! How can you endure this, Sybil? Of course my Marie Challoner doesn't want to marry anybody."

"Just so: have it any way you like. Who wants to marry her, then?"

" Why, your friend, you know—the young man from Thibet, from Japan I mean—Mr. Pembroke."

" Hullo! Is that the way? And will she marry him?"

" Oh, yes! It's the most delightful thing you ever heard of! She was in love with him all the time, and he didn't know it; and he tried to drown himself several times out of love for her, and she didn't know it."

" Dear me," said Miss Sybil composedly, " what a very stupid pair they must have been!"

" But Sybil, my dear, stupid? My Marie Challoner stupid! Oh, you don't know her at all. The brightest girl! Why, my brother will never forgive you. He is downright in love with her, I assure you, over head and ears! Not really in love, you know, dear; that's only my jest, of course; but he thinks ever so much of her, I can tell you."

" So I do," said Cameron; " and I think if I were a matter of say five and twenty years younger, I would have tried for the belt—for the zone, anyhow—myself. Well, I am glad to hear your news, Isabel. He's a fine young fellow—not at all stupid, Miss Jansen, I can assure you, but on the contrary very clever; and he's every inch a gentleman, and she's every inch a lady, and two such rare beings in these days ought to be brought together."

" I didn't mean stupid in that sense," Sybil quietly explained. " I meant stupid in not knowing that they were in love with each other. I could have told them that story long ago. They ought to have come to me."

" You, my dear? Well, I always say you are an inspired prophetess! But how did you know?"

" I saw them both in this room," Sybil said. " It was enough to look at them, if one had eyes."

" But they didn't know it, Sybil."

" That's why I say they must have been stupid. I always knew that he was in love with her, and when I saw her I knew that she was in love with him."

" By Jove!—excuse me, Miss Jansen—I never dreamed of it," said Cameron, " and no more did Isabel. How on earth did you know?"

" I knew it by her eyes the moment he came into the room," Sybil said contemptuously. " I didn't want any more instruction. It amuses me to watch the little weaknesses of my fellow creatures, and I was greatly amused that day when I found her out."

" We must watch your eyes, my sweet Sybil," Mrs. Seagraves exclaimed, "one of these days, and we shall read some pretty story there, for all your marble coldness and your contempt of our poor human weaknesses. But not too soon; oh, no! not too soon. We can't spare you just yet; we want you and the world wants you for nobler work than marriage."

" You all seem to like marriage pretty well, though," said Cameron.

"And you don't, Captain Cameron, your sister tells me," Sybil said with a smile. " For shame not to have made some woman happy long ago! Women are only supposed to be made happy when some lordly man patronises them and holds out his hand."

" I am so delighted to hear you scold him, my dear Sybil. Oh, he deserves it, and I have often told him so. I am quite ashamed of him. Not ashamed really, you know, because Robert, for a man, is not bad at all; but ashamed that he hasn't been married. You must look in his eyes and tell me what you see there."

"I shall have to wear blue spectacles, then," the Legitimist said, not so ill-pleased with the conversation after all, and thinking Sybil not so very disagreeable a person as he had supposed.

" And so you found out my sweet Marie by looking in her eyes ? " Mrs. Seagraves went on ecstatically. " So delightful and poetic. Like second-sight, or fortune-telling, or the divining rod, or any of these charming things. I do so love superstition, and astrology, and alchemy. Oh, yes, alchemy above all things ! Don't you love alchemy ? I don't love it now though quite so much as I did : I think it is so deluding and bad, very, very bad. No, I prefer astrology. You must teach me how to read people's eyes. I shall call it the astrology of the eyes. Won't that be pretty—sweetly pretty ? You shall teach me the astrology of the eyes."

" Well, that isn't half a bad phrase," said Cameron.

" One makes such mistakes if one doesn't know. Why, Sybil, now that I remember, I really thought I saw in your eyes—or somebody's—that my young Japanese friend was in love with you, I did indeed."

" Yes, I knew you did," Sybil said quietly, "but I couldn't betray the poor young man's little secret. I knew he didn't want to have it known, and of course I wasn't going to put any one on the right track. He was so very honest that when I taxed him with his folly he confessed it all frankly; and then of course I would not betray him for the world."

" Bravo ! " Cameron exclaimed. " That's genuine and honest *camaraderie.* I like that. I didn't think women were capable of that sort of thing."

"Well, you shall teach me the astrology of the eyes," said Mrs. Seagraves.

"To begin with, let us see your own eyes, Miss Jansen."

"With pleasure."

They were very bright eyes, and Miss Jansen opened them slowly and looked steadily in the face of the Legitimist. He read nothing in them. "She's a nice little girl," he thought, "but cold and hard. I shouldn't like to be the young fellow who marries her. That's what woman's rights and such stuff bring girls to. It's like a Palais Royal flower of porcelain to the 'Flower of Dumblane.'"

He did not remain long near Sybil after Mrs. Seagraves had floated away. The marble hardness of the girl repelled him, although she was far more gracious to him and pleasant with him than was her wont where men were concerned. Some one else came up and spoke to Sybil, and Cameron drew away, and presently left the house and went to his club, where he sat down and began a long letter of congratulation to Lady Disdain and another to Christmas Pembroke. The brave Legitimist was almost inclined to be sentimental. He remembered that pretty poetic Nannie Langdale whom he used to know—well, perhaps a matter of thirty years ago. People used to quiz them both a good deal then about each other. Well, well! Who was this Nannie got married to? He did know all about it surely, but now he had forgotten. By Jove! Nannie would have married him then if he had only asked her. Perhaps he was a little sorry now he didn't ask her. He hummed a bar or two of " Oh, Nannie, wilt though gang with me?" but it was rather too late now, anyhow, and probably Nannie was better off as things were; and she presently passed out of his mind, which became perplexed with the thought of what sort of wedding present he ought to give to Dear Lady Disdain.

When Sybil Jansen had talked a little to this person and that, she too quietly withdrew from the room, and from the house, and walked homeward. She felt a certain pride in herself such as the Spartan lad might have felt before the teeth of the fox prevailed and he fell and revealed his secret. Sybil had succeeded completely in hiding the wound in her bleeding breast. She had freed herself fom the slightest suspicion of having been hurt. She could not perhaps have held out much longer, but so far she had succeeded, and she had a right to be proud. She tripped along the crowded Sunday streets quite lightly, and many an eye glanced as she passed after that neat figure and that pretty ankle. Her heart seemed bursting within her, and she walked so quickly because the streets seemed to rock under her and she longed to be safely home. When she got home she spoke to her servant with unusual softness and sweetness, and to her mother she was careful to show the gentlest temper and not on any account to make a short answer. As the bleeding away of a wound some, times changes fierce battle-natures for the time to a feminine gentleness, so Sybil's heavy heart seemed to have reduced to mild-ness and docility the impatience and occasional sharpness of an eager, feverish temper. Mrs. Jansen had had a headache in the morning, and Sybil asked so kindly and so much about it, and offered such suggestions of remedy and relief, that one might have thought her mother's headache was all the girl had to trouble her in life. She helped to arrange their modest little Sunday dinner and she tried to seem as if she was helping to eat it.

After dinner she remained a good long time in her own room. Mrs. Jansen did not go to her. She knew her daughter's ways and weaknesses. She knew that when Sybil remained alone it was better not to disturb her, and of course all Sybil's brave little play-acting had never deceived her mother for a moment. Her quiet watchful eyes had followed every motion of her girl, and she knew that something had happened. But she knew better than to ask any questions. She would let the girl alone, and in good time Sybil would tell her all.

That night Sybil had to speak at a little meeting in some one of the secluded, almost subterranean, buildings where on the Sunday evenings in London minds of an advanced order lay them-selves out to instruct the race. Mrs. Jansen was sitting by the firelight without a lamp, when Sybil came quietly in.

"Would you like me to light the lamp, mamma?"

"If you will, dear."

"Well, in a moment, just."

Sybil came and sat by the fire near her mother. Then she laid her hand gently on Mrs. Jansen's knee, and the mother laid her hand over her child's. Mrs. Jansen knew now that Sybil was going to say something.

"Mamma, Mr. Pembroke is going to be married."

This was what Mrs. Jansen had been expecting to hear.

"Indeed, Sybil? To that young lady?"

"To Miss Challoner—yes."

"But I thought she was engaged to some one else."

"She was—but she—was in love with him all the time."

"How very strange—how very wrong!"

"They say she is giving up everything for him," Sybil said. "People are happy who have something to give up."

"I hope she will make him happy," Mrs. Jansen said with a sigh. "I liked him very much."

"So did I," said Sybil.

Mrs. Jansen put her arm round her daughter's neck and said quietly, "You will get over this, my darling child: and there are worse things in life—and in love too—than such a disappointment as yours."

"I have been crying a great deal," Sybil said, "but I am better now, and I shall try not to think of it any more."

"Perhaps you had better not go to the meeting to-night. Perhaps you could not speak?"

"Oh yes, mamma, I must go. One ought to do any good one can. And I should only die if I didn't do something. I don't mean to be merely a good-for-nothing old maid."

Sybil tried to smile and look as if she were not utterly miserable. Her mother might be excused if she thought that night that fate had deal rather heavily with her and her daughter. So pretty a girl too, it seemed doubly cruel of hard fortune to lay its icy hand upon that pretty young head. Mrs. Jansen went with her to her meeting, and wondered at her fervour and eloquence, and clung to her and watched her with eager following eyes, as we watch some loved and frail creature whom we fancy death will take from us if once we look away.

Yet perhaps Sybil Jansen is not the least fortunate of all our people. She at least has something which can never be taken from her—an ideal. She has an ideal lover who never car change and can only die when she dies, and an ideal married life which is all unclouded and which calamity cannot touch. Of all our people she is henceforward the most secure against disappointment. May we not say too that she has another sweetener of life—not only an ideal love but an ideal grievance? The wrongs of women will wake her sympathies more than ever, and into their cause she will throw all the passionate energies of her fervid little soul : and be happy even in her wrath against the injustice of the world. For her sake at least let us hope that the suffrage may not soon be granted to women, that some little of man's tyranny may continue yet awhile to oppress his weaker companion, so that poor Sybil may have a cause to occupy her energies and to keep her attention distracted from her own lonely state. Meanwhile it is known that Sybil has refused many apparently eligible young men who have supplicated her; and it is generally believed that her sense of the injustices done to her sex by the oppressor is so keen that she has registered a vow never to marry while the least remnant of those grievances still remains. If she is to die an old maid, then it is at least understood that this fate is of her own deliberate choice. So she can cherish her ideal love in secret, and keep the fire burning at its altar where the breath of change can never blow it out, nor the smoke of human weakness or passion obscure its brightness.

CHAPTER XXXIX.

THROUGH THE GOLDEN GATE TOGETHER.

WHEN Sir John Challoner returned to Durewoods he was not surprised to find a letter awaiting him from Christmas Pembroke containing an earnest request to be allowed a few minutes' conversation with him. Sir John could hardly now be surprised at anything, and he knew what was to come, and had no idea of struggling any longer. His castle of cards had all tumbled down, and he knew that it was hopeless to try to build up another of the same kind. Perhaps a little compassion, or at least a little pity, may be spared for him. His ambition and his schemes had not been meaner than those of the average middle-class man, straining with all a life's fervour to reach the higher class; and he had been so very near to the fulfilment of his desires! Now that the whole thing was over, he especially dreaded the open proclamation of the little piece of treachery by which he had tried the more surely to compass his ends. Success bought by falsehood is not always enjoyable, even to natures more thoroughly case-hardened than Challoner's; but it is cruel indeed when the falsehood remains, having failed to accomplish the success.

As Challoner read over Christmas's letter, and saw that it came from Dione Lyle's house, he could not help thinking that there must occasionally be a sort of retributive justice in human affairs. Some five and twenty years ago or more he had succeeded by some treacherous devices and stories in separating Christmas Pembroke's father from Dione Lyle. It had profited him nothing. Dione did not marry him, and the time soon came when he was very glad that she did not. Dione never knew the worst part of Challoner's deceptions, but she knew that he had come between her lover and her. She forgave him afterwards, for she was of a sweet, soft, and yielding nature, and she did not know all, and he had pleaded for pardon in the name of his youth and of his overmastering love for her. In a strange way, too, she yearned a little towards him because he had been young with her, and to see him brought back the memory of the dear, brief days of her love. As he rose and rose in the world he still always showed himself a devoted friend to her; and he was a widower and lonely; and then there grew up the little Marie, whom Dione loved more and more. The disappointed woman who had won success and found it worth little, and quietly quitted the field in time, lived at Durewoods in a sweet melancholy retirement, in a condition of dreamy present happiness and memory of the past—almost a

sensuousness of the soul. As Marie grew, her fresh, vigorous
and vivid nature was very pleasant companionship, and Dione,
who called her Dear Lady Disdain, and fancied wrongly that she
could only inflict and not suffer love, was rather glad that the
girl should be spared from disappointments.

Now, behold!—time has come round, and the son of Challoner's old rival has come back from the other end of the earth,
and has ruined his plans, and is to carry off his daughter. In
his heart John Challoner still believed that Dione Lyle had
brought all this about, for he feared that she knew more than
she actually did, and he looked upon her as likely to show herself even yet his enemy. He was wrong, as we know, but he
told himself that she had had the best of it here, and he respected
her perhaps rather the more because she had won. Now he was
chiefly anxious to save some wreck of his old character and
authority in his daughter's eyes, and not to be mercilessly ex-
posed to her by Dione and by Christmas as a deceiver and—what
other word will serve?—as a liar.

He received Christmas with cold urbanity, and listened to
the young man's short, clear story. Then Christmas quietly
said, without looking directly at him—

"I am afraid you will think me rather blunt, Sir John, in
my way of putting this; but I want to be very clear this time.
I am afraid I must have made a sad bungle the last time when
I told you my story, and led you into a misunderstanding which
was near setting us all astray."

Sir John looked up quickly, and then their eyes met, and no
doubt the two men quite understood each other. Sir John drew
a long breath and felt relieved.

"I told Marie," Pembroke said—Sir John almost started at
the "Marie"—"what a bungle I must have made of it the last
time, and how I was resolved to be clear this time."

"Well, Pembroke, you certainly have been clear this time,
and I thank you for that." (Probably the two again understood
each other.) "Now what do you expect me to say to all this?
To give my consent? I presume Marie and you have given each
other away without asking me?"

"We do love each other very, very much, and I have not
such bad prospects; and even now, Sir John, she wouldn't be
quite poor: I have some means, and she does not care to be
rich. We shouldn't be paupers, you know. I am much better
off—you have often told me yourself—than lots of the younger
sons of your aristocracy—and I mean to make my way, and to
rise."

"I needn't have any hesitation in saying that this is a disappointment to me," Sir John said. "You know all that. I had
different views for my daughter. I haven't a word to say against

you personally, Pembroke, but you know—I told you from the beginning—that ambition and the world count for something with me. I am disappointed—I don't deny it."

" Still, when Marie has not the same kind of ambition her feelings ought to count for something."

" I think they have been allowed to count for a great deal in this instance," Sir John said, with a smile of melancholy irony. " I think her feelings have it all their own way, Pembroke. I am not a man to talk eloquently about ungrateful children and that sort of thing, but I was very fond of my daughter, Pembroke, and devoted to her—and—well, you may have a daughter some day, and devote yourself to her, and find after all that— well, find that you will understand better what I mean."

" But Marie is devoted to you—no better and more loving daughter ever lived," the young man protested warmly.

" Yes, yes, of course, we know all that. Still, Pembroke, I am a little cut up, you perceive. One can't help it; that's the way fathers are made. Well, let us pass over all that and come to the more practical question. Is there anything for me to settle ? "

" I don't quite understand—— "

" No. Well, I'll make it plain. Have you and my daughter already arranged all the details of your future life ? "

" Oh no. She wouldn't think of such a thing without con- sulting you, even if I had wished her to do so—which I never did."

" How considerate you young people are," Sir John said, with the smile of melancholy irony again, " when once you have settled the main point to your own satisfaction ! Well, then, really I think you had better carry out your original plan, Pem- broke, in the first instance. Go to Japan and see what you can do to set up a house there. Let it be in connection with ours. I wish that. Stay there for a while, a year say, and come back then. This thing will all have been forgotten by that time. Let me see—what with going out and coming back and all, a year and a half will have passed. That will do. The people we know in London will have forgotten by that time that I ever had a daughter ! Come, what do you think of that ? "

" A year and a half is a very long time—a terribly long time," said Christmas, with a gloom-stricken face. " Why, it's like a life banishment. One might die in the mean time. But you have met me fairly, I must say, and I pledged my word to Marie that I would try to do anything you asked."

" I am very much obliged to Marie. But I don't think you quite understand me, Pembroke—you clearly don't mean what I mean. I don't want you to go into banishment, as you call it, alone."

"Oh!" Christmas exclaimed, delightedly, and blushing like a boy.

"No. Take Marie with you—I dare say she would go."

"Oh yes," the lover declared, with fullest confidence.

"Yes. I suppose so. Very well; take her with you. My good Pembroke, how do you think my daughter and I could get on together all that time? I mean after what has passed. No, no; the best chance for all of us is to break up our little camp and go different ways. When we meet again we shall meet on a new footing, and perhaps we shall then be better reconciled to each other, and I shall have forgotten all this, and shall be glad to welcome Marie on any terms. Will that do?"

"It will do for me, Sir John, and I think I can speak for her."

"No doubt, no doubt. But we'll make that certain. We'll ask her."

Sir John touched a bell and bade a servant tell Miss Challoner that her father wished to see her in the library.

"Meanwhile," Sir John said,—"and not to bring girls into money matters—Marie, of course, shall have her fortune——"

"Not if I can prevail upon her," Christmas said, energetically. "Not one sixpence, Sir John—and I know I can speak for her in that. No one on earth shall say that I married Marie Challoner for money."

"My good fellow, how is every one on earth to know that you and she have not got the money? Every one on earth can't look at your account in the bank."

"Anyhow, Sir John, *you* shall know it," Christmas said bluntly.

"I never thought you were looking after her money. I know how little your father cared about money; how little he had of what people in the world would call wisdom. But we may put that aside for the present. I shall only insist upon your resuming your relations with our house, and you shall rise there as fast as you can. To tell the honest truth, Pembroke, I shall be glad to have my son-in-law in the house. And you know I always thought highly of you in business. For my daughter's sake you will make yourself valuable, I know: and you will rise—you will rise. Come, that's settled, at least—your fierce independence won't object to that?"

"I am only too grateful," Christmas said, "and I'll try to show that I am."

"Well that, you know, is as much for my interest as yours. I must push my son-in-law; and your being in the house is the one part of the arrangement that I like. You are not offended at my frankness, I hope? Ah, here comes Marie."

One evening in the early summer, some months after this, Dione Lyle was in her balcony, seated in her usual fashion with her side to its railings, on the upper bar of which she laid her arm, and looking through the delicate green of the young leaves across to where the sun was sinking in the sea. The weather was mild as yet, with only a gentle foretaste of summer heat, and the sky was of pale blue, with a silvery tone towards the horizon, and the moon and sun could be seen at once in the heavens. Old Merlin was doing some work in the garden below, among the roses from which Marie had gathered on the evening when she was leaving Durewoods for her first London season: and he looked up and pointed to the sun and moon, and said something with his abundant gesticulation about the beautiful evening and the coming summer.

"But I shall be lonely this summer, Merlin."

"No, no—none-lone," Merlin said, pausing in his work to make earnest and energetic remonstrance.

"Janet is to be married, you see, and I must have a new maid; and Miss Marie is married, and Mr. Christmas; and they are gone away—to the other end of the world, you know."

"Miss Leel none-lone," Merlin still protested, smiting his breast with his wrinkled brown hand. "No, no—Merlin not married, Merlin not gone to other world (he had not quite caught her words), Merlin always stay with Miss Leel! No, no—none-lone—none-lone!"

And he turned to his work again, still occasionally smiting his breast, and repeating to himself his reassuring formula.

Miss Lyle smiled good-humouredly, but seemed a little melancholy nevertheless.

"I wonder where they are now," she said to herself. "They were to have sailed before this. Well, it is just the sort of evening to begin sailing out into a new life."

Her thoughts began to wander back into the past, wherein now she lived so much. She remembered sweet calm evenings like this long ago, and the loves that seemed inseparable, and the hopes that were so bright and died so soon. She thought of the young lovers who were sailing away, and was gladdened amid all her memories.

"I am glad I made them promise me that," she thought. "They will always keep this place when I have left it; and they will sit in this balcony—and I do think that I shall somehow see them."

While the sun and moon together were thus looking down upon the waters of the bay at Durewoods, and trying to peep into the little hollow among the trees on the hill side, and throwing a gleam of soft, sanctifying light over the small churchyard above the village where poor Nat Cramp was lying, a girl looked out of a window in the West Centre of London—a pale girl with bright eyes. There was not much to be seen below but pavement and bustling passengers, and the roofs of luggage-laden cabs hurrying to railway stations. So Sybil Jansen naturally looked to the evening sky where the sun and moon were visible together.

" I wonder where He and She are now," she thought.

She looked into the sky a good while longer, only thinking about him and her, and where they were, and how happy they must be, and how sad life was to some, and all other such thoughts as almost every happy love-union must fill some breast with, until she heard the voice of her mother calling her, and then she drew quietly back into her room and showed herself cheerful, and only at times hung over little deep dark pools of silent thought, wherein she saw not her own image, but only " him and her."

Meanwhile the Cunard steamer for New York had cleared the bar at the mouth of the Mersey, and was leaving the long, low-lying Lancashire shore on the one side and the sand-hills and reddish projecting rocks and soft broad beach of New Brighton on the other. The vessel was throbbing through the great waters out to sea, and the sea seemed only more tremulous than the sky—not less quiet.

Marie and Christmas Pembroke had come from the saloon and paced from the stern quite up to the bow of the steamer, to be free of other passengers for the moment, and to look out over the water through which they were cleaving their way. They were silent for a while with the very fulness of their content.

" This *is* an evening to begin a voyage," Christmas said at last in a low tone.

" See—the sun and moon together in the sky ! " Marie said. " I wonder is that a good omen at the beginning of a voyage ? I hope it is."

" Everything must be a good omen to me," said Christmas. " You are all the good omens in yourself."

" I wonder is Miss Lyle in her balcony now, looking at that lovely sky, and does she think of us ? How selfish we are in our happiness! I should like to know that Miss Lyle was thinking of us now, and her to know, Chris, that we were thinking of her."

" She will believe that of us, I am sure, and she is so kind-hearted and sympathetic I think she wouldn't grudge us a little forgetfulness of everything but ourselves just for the moment. I know she would not blame me, for I only feel still as if I had carried you off somehow, and as if somebody or other might still come up to claim you. I can't realise it all yet. When we are far out at sea then I shall begin to believe that I have you safe!

Then we shall walk the deck of nights, and talk of her and of the people and the places we have left behind."

" Is it not happy that we parted from my father on such good terms, and that he is satisfied ? Is he not very kind, Chris ? "

She said this a little eagerly, for she wanted to be reassured about her father, and to have his broken image put together again as much as possible, now that she had had her own way and was so happy. Christmas did not fail to reassure her. Then, as was natural, they fell to talking of themselves again, and their happiness, and their prospects.

" I can hardly believe that we are going all across America, you and I together," Marie said. " If you knew what a sick, sad heart I had when I made that journey before! It seems wonderful to me now, but I did not know then why I was so wretched."

" Ours seems a wonderful story to me. So wonderful that I still ask myself—can it be true? The other day I was plunged in the very depths of despair, and now I am in a dream of happiness."

" And we are going off together for a great holiday in a wonderful new world, you and I alone, and we are to travel together, and live together, and come back together."

" And we shall stand, you and I together," said Christmas, " on the shore at Saucelito and look on San Francisco Bay, and think of Durewoods there."

" Yes," Marie added, " and we shall pass, you and I together, as we are now, through the Golden Gate!"

THE END.

PRINTED BY WILLIAM CLOWES AND SONS, LIMITED, LONDON AND BECCLES.

A LIST OF BOOKS
PUBLISHED BY
CHATTO & WINDUS
214, PICCADILLY, LONDON, W.
Sold by all Booksellers, or sent post-free for the published price by the Publishers.

Abbé Constantin (The). By LUDOVIC HALEVY, of the French Academy. Translated into English. With 36 Photogravure Illustrations by GOUPIL & Co., after the Drawings of Madame MADELEINE LEMAIRE. Price may be learned from any Bookseller.

About.—The Fellah : An Egyptian Novel. By EDMOND ABOUT. Translated by Sir RANDAL ROBERTS. Post 8vo, illustrated boards, 2s. ; cloth limp, 2s. 6d.

Adams (W. Davenport), Works by :
A Dictionary of the Drama. Being a comprehensive Guide to the Plays, Playwrights, Players, and Playhouses of the United Kingdom and America. Crown 8vo, half-bound, 12s. 6d. [*Preparing.*
Quips and Quiddities. Selected by W. DAVENPORT ADAMS. Post 8vo, cloth limp, 2s. 6d.

Adams (W. H. D.). — Witch, Warlock, and Magician : Historical Sketches of Magic and Witchcraft in England and Scotland. By W. H. DAVENPORT ADAMS. Demy 8vo, cloth extra, 12s.

Agony Column (The) of "The Times," from 1800 to 1870. Edited, with an Introduction, by ALICE CLAY. Post 8vo, cloth limp, 2s. 6d.

Aïdé (Hamilton), Works by :
Post 8vo, illustrated boards, 2s. each.
Carr of Carrlyon. | Confidences.

Alexander (Mrs.), Novels by :
Post 8vo, illustrated boards, 2s. each.
Maid, Wife, or Widow ?
Valerie's Fate.

Allen (Grant), Works by :
Crown 8vo, cloth extra, 6s. each.
The Evolutionist at Large.
Vignettes from Nature.
Colin Clout's Calendar.

Crown 8vo, cloth extra, 6s. each ; post 8vo, illustrated boards., 2s. each.
Strange Stories. With a Frontispiece by GEORGE DU MAURIER.
The Beckoning Hand. With a Frontispiece by TOWNLEY GREEN.

Crown 8vo, cloth extra, 3s. 6d. each ; post 8vo, illustrated boards, 2s. each.
Philistia. | The Devil's Die.
This Mortal Coil.

Post 8vo, illustrated boards, 2s. each.
Babylon : A Romance.
For Malmie's Sake.
In all Shades.

The Tents of Shem. With a Frontispiece by E. F. BREWTNALL. Crown 8vo, cloth extra, 3s. 6d.

Architectural Styles, A Handbook of. Translated from the German of A. ROSENGARTEN, by W. COLLETT-SANDARS. Crown 8vo, cloth extra, with 639 Illustrations, 7s. 6d.

Arnold.—Bird Life in England. By EDWIN LESTER ARNOLD. Crown 8vo, cloth extra, 6s.

Art (The) of Amusing : A Collection of Graceful Arts, Games, Tricks, Puzzles, and Charades. By FRANK BELLEW. With 300 Illustrations. Cr. 8vo, cloth extra, 4s. 6d.

Artemus Ward:

Artemus Ward's Works: The Works of CHARLES FARRER BROWNE, better known as ARTEMUS WARD. With Portrait and Facsimile. Crown 8vo, cloth extra, 7s. 6d.

The Genial Showman: Life and Adventures of Artemus Ward. By EDWARD P. HINGSTON. With a Frontispiece. Cr. 8vo, cl. extra, 3s. 6d.

Ashton (John), Works by:

Crown 8vo, cloth extra, 7s. 6d. each.

A History of the Chap-Books of the Eighteenth Century. With nearly 400 Illustrations, engraved in facsimile of the originals.

Social Life in the Reign of Queen Anne. From Original Sources. With nearly 100 Illustrations.

Humour, Wit, and Satire of the Seventeenth Century. With nearly 100 Illustrations.

English Caricature and Satire on Napoleon the First. With 115 Illustrations.

Modern Street Ballads. With 57 Illustrations

Bacteria.—A Synopsis of the

Bacteria and Yeast Fungi and Allied Species. By W. B. GROVE, B.A. With 87 Illusts. Crown 8vo, cl. extra, 3s. 6d.

Bankers, A Handbook of Lon-

don; together with Lists of Bankers from 1677. By F. G. HILTON PRICE. Crown 8vo, cloth extra, 7s. 6d.

Bardsley(Rev. C.W.), Works by:

English Surnames: Their Sources and Significations. Third Edition, revised. Crown 8vo, cl. ex., 7s. 6d.

Curiosities of Puritan Nomenclature. Second Edition. Crown 8vo, cloth extra, 6s.

Baring Gould (S.), Novels by:

Crown 8vo, cloth extra, 3s. 6d. each; post 8vo, illustrated boards, 2s. each.

Red Spider. | Eve.

Barrett.—Fettered for Life.

By FRANK BARRETT, Author of "Lady Biddy Fane," &c. Three Vols., crown 8vo.

Beaconsfield, Lord: A Biogra-

phy. By T. P. O'CONNOR, M.P. Sixth Edition, with a New Preface. Crown 8vo, cloth extra. 5s.

Beauchamp. — Grantley

Grange: A Novel. By SHELSLEY BEAUCHAMP. Post 8vo, illust. bds., 2s.

Beautiful Pictures by British

Artists: A Gathering of Favourites from our Picture Galleries. All engraved on Steel in the highest style of Art. Edited, with Notices of the Artists, by SYDNEY ARMYTAGE, M.A. Imperial 4to, cloth extra, gilt and gilt edges, 21s.

Bechstein. — As Pretty as

Seven, and other German Stories. Collected by LUDWIG BECHSTEIN. With Additional Tales by the Brothers GRIMM, and 100 Illusts. by RICHTER. Small 4to, green and gold, 6s. 6d.; gilt edges, 7s. 6d.

Beerbohm. — Wanderings in

Patagonia; or, Life among the Ostrich Hunters. By JULIUS BEERBOHM. With Illusts. Crown 8vo, cloth extra, 3s. 6d.

Bennett (W.C.,LL.D.),Works by:

Post 8vo, cloth limp, 2s. each.

A Ballad History of England.

Songs for Sailors.

Besant (Walter) and James

Rice, Novels by. Crown 8vo, cloth extra, 3s. 6d. each; post 8vo, illust. bds., 2s. each; cl. limp, 2s. 6d. each.

Ready-Money Mortiboy.

My Little Girl.

With Harp and Crown.

This Son of Vulcan.

The Golden Butterfly.

The Monks of Thelema.

By Celia's Arbour.

The Chaplain of the Fleet.

The Seamy Side.

The Case of Mr. Lucraft, &c.

'Twas in Trafalgar's Bay, &c.

The Ten Years' Tenant, &c.

Besant (Walter), Novels by:

Crown 8vo, cloth extra, 3s. 6d. each; post 8vo, illust. boards, 2s. each; cloth limp, 2s. 6d. each.

All Sorts and Conditions of Men: An Impossible Story. With Illustrations by FRED. BARNARD.

The Captains' Room, &c. With Frontispiece by E. J. WHEELER.

All in a Garden Fair. With 6 Illustrations by HARRY FURNISS.

Dorothy Forster. With Frontispiece by CHARLES GREEN.

Uncle Jack, and other Stories.

Children of Gibeon.

The World Went Very Well Then. With Illustrations by A. FORESTIER.

Herr Paulus: His Rise, his Greatness, and his Fall.

BESANT (WALTER), *continued—*
For Faith and Freedom. With Illustrations by A. FORESTIER and F. WADDY. Crown 8vo, cloth extra, 3s. 6d.
To Call her Mine, &c. With Nine Illustrations by A. FORESTIER. Cr. 8vo, cloth extra, 6s.
The Holy Rose, &c. With a Frontispiece by F. BARNARD. Crown 8vo, cloth extra, 6s. [*Shortly.*
The Bell of St. Paul's. Three Vols., crown 8vo.
Fifty Years Ago. With 137 full-page Plates and Woodcuts. Demy 8vo, cloth extra, 16s.
The Eulogy of Richard Jefferies. With Photograph Portrait. Second Edition. Cr. 8vo, cloth extra, 6s.
The Art of Fiction. Demy 8vo, 1s.

New Library Edition of
Besant and Rice's Novels.
The whole 12 Volumes, printed from new type on a large crown 8vo page, and handsomely bound in cloth, are now ready, price Six Shillings each.
1. Ready-Money Mortiboy. With Etched Portrait of JAMES RICE.
2. My Little Girl.
3. With Harp and Crown.
4. This Son of Vulcan.
5. The Golden Butterfly. With Etched Portrait of WALTER BESANT.
6. The Monks of Thelema.
7. By Celia's Arbour.
8. The Chaplain of the Fleet.
9. The Seamy Side.
10. The Case of Mr. Lucraft, &c.
11. 'Twas in Trafalgar's Bay, &c.
12. The Ten Years' Tenant, &c.

Betham-Edwards(M)—Felicia.
By M. BETHAM-EDWARDS. Cr. 8vo, cloth extra, 3s. 6d.; post 8vo, illust. bds., 2s.

Bewick (Thomas) and his
Pupils. By AUSTIN DOBSON. With 95 Illusts. Square 8vo, cloth extra, 6s.

Blackburn's (Henry) Art Handbooks :
Academy Notes, separate years, from 1875 to 1887, and 1889, each 1s.
Academy Notes, 1890. With numerous Illustrations. 1s. [*Preparing.*
Academy Notes, 1875-79. Complete in One Volume, with about 600 Illustrations. Cloth limp, 6s.
Academy Notes, 1880-84. Complete in One Volume, with about 700 Illustrations. Cloth limp, 6s.
Grosvenor Notes, 1877. 6d.
Grosvenor Notes, separate years, from 1878 to 1889, each 1s.
Grosvenor Notes, 1890. With numerous Illusts. 1s. [*Preparing.*

BLACKBURN (HENRY), *continued—*
Grosvenor Notes, Vol. I., 1877-82. With upwards of 300 Illustrations. Demy 8vo, cloth limp, 6s.
Grosvenor Notes, Vol. II., 1883-87. With upwards of 300 Illustrations. Demy 8vo, cloth limp, 6s.
The New Gallery. 1888 and 1889. With numerous Illusts., each 1s.
The New Gallery, 1890. With numerous Illustrations. 1s. [*Preparing.*
English Pictures at the National Gallery. 114 Illustrations. 1s.
Old Masters at the National Gallery. 128 Illustrations. 1s. 6d.
An Illustrated Catalogue to the National Gallery. With Notes by H. BLACKBURN, and 242 Illustrations. Demy 8vo, cloth limp, 3s.

The Paris Salon, 1890. With 300 Facsimile Sketches. 3s. [*Preparing.*

Blake (William) : Etchings from
his Works. By W. B. SCOTT. With descriptive Text. Folio, half-bound boards, India Proofs, 21s.

Blind.—The Ascent of Man :
A Poem. By MATHILDE BLIND. Crown 8vo, printed on hand-made paper, cloth extra, 5s.

Bourne (H. R. Fox), Works by :
English Merchants: Memoirs in Illustration of the Progress of British Commerce. With numerous Illustrations. Cr. 8vo, cloth extra, 7s. 6d.
English Newspapers: Chapters in the History of Journalism. Two Vols., demy 8vo, cloth extra, 25s.

Bowers'(G.) Hunting Sketches:
Oblong 4to, half-bound boards, 21s. each.
Canters in Crampshire.
Leaves from a Hunting Journal. Coloured in facsimile of the originals.

Boyle (Frederick), Works by :
Crown 8vo, cloth extra, 3s. 6d. each; post 8vo, illustrated boards, 2s. each.
Camp Notes: Stories of Sport and Adventure in Asia, Africa, America.
Savage Life: Adventures of a Globe-Trotter.

Chronicles of No-Man's Land. Post 8vo, illust. boards, 2s.

Brand's Observations on Popu-
lar Antiquities, chiefly Illustrating the Origin of our Vulgar Customs, Ceremonies, and Superstitions. With the Additions of Sir HENRY ELLIS, and numerous Illustrations. Crown 8vo, cloth extra, 7s. 6d.

Bret Harte, Works by:

LIBRARY EDITION, Complete in Five Vols., cr. 8vo, cl. extra, 6s. each.

Bret Harte's Collected Works: LIBRARY EDITION. Arranged and Revised by the Author.

Vol. I. COMPLETE POETICAL AND DRAMATIC WORKS. With Steel Portrait, and Introduction by Author.

Vol. II. EARLIER PAPERS—LUCK OF ROARING CAMP, and other Sketches —BOHEMIAN PAPERS — SPANISH AND AMERICAN LEGENDS.

Vol. III. TALES OF THE ARGONAUTS —EASTERN SKETCHES.

Vol. IV. GABRIEL CONROY.

Vol. V. STORIES — CONDENSED NOVELS, &c.

The Select Works of Bret Harte, in Prose and Poetry. With Introductory Essay by J. M. BELLEW, Portrait of the Author, and 50 Illustrations. Crown 8vo, cloth extra, 7s. 6d.

Bret Harte's Complete Poetical Works. Author's Copyright Edition. Printed on hand-made paper and bound in buckram. Cr. 8vo, 4s. 6d.

The Queen of the Pirate Isle. With 28 original Drawings by KATE GREENAWAY, reproduced in Colours by EDMUND EVANS. Sm. 4to, bds., 5s.

A Walf of the Plains. With 60 Illustrations by STANLEY L. WOOD. Cr. 8vo, cloth extra, 3s. 6d. [Shortly.

Post 8vo, illustrated boards, 2s. each.
Gabriel Conroy.
An Heiress of Red Dog, &c.
The Luck of Roaring Camp, and other Sketches.
Californian Stories (including THE TWINS OF TABLE MOUNTAIN, JEFF BRIGGS'S LOVE STORY, &c.)

Post 8vo, illustrated boards, 2s. each ; cloth, 2s. 6d. each.
Flip. | Maruja.
A Phyllis of the Sierras.

Fcap. 8vo, picture cover, 1s. each.
The Twins of Table Mountain.
Jeff Briggs's Love Story.

Brewer (Rev. Dr.), Works by :

The Reader's Handbook of Allusions, References Plots and Stories. 15th Thousand. With Appendix, containing a COMPLETE ENGLISH BIBLIOGRAPHY. Cr. 8vo, cloth 7s. 6d.

Authors and their Works, with the Dates: Being the Appendices to "The Reader's Handbook," separately printed. Cr. 8vo, cloth limp, 2s.

A Dictionary of Miracles: Imitative, Realistic, and Dogmatic. Crown 8vo, cloth extra, 7s. 6d.

Brewster (SirDavid), Works by:

Post 8vo, cloth extra, 4s. 6d. each.

More Worlds than One: The Creed of the Philosopher and the Hope of the Christian. With Plates.

The Martyrs of Science: Lives of GALILEO, TYCHO BRAHE, and KEPLER. With Portraits.

Letters on Natural Magic. A New Edition, with numerous Illustrations, and Chapters on the Being and Faculties of Man, and Additional Phenomena of Natural Magic, by J. A. SMITH.

Brillat-Savarin.—Gastronomy

as a Fine Art. By BRILLAT-SAVARIN. Translated by R. E. ANDERSON, M.A. Post 8vo, printed on laid-paper and half-bound, 2s.

Brydges. — Uncle Sam at

Home. By HAROLD BRYDGES. Post 8vo, illust. boards, 2s. ; cloth, 2s. 6d.

Buchanan's (Robert) Works :

Crown 8vo, cloth extra, 6s. each.

Selected Poems of Robert Buchanan. With a Frontispiece by T. DALZIEL.

The Earthquake ; or, Six Days and a Sabbath.

The City of Dream: An Epic Poem. With Two Illustrations by P. MACNAB. Second Edition.

Robert Buchanan's Complete Poetical Works. With Steel-plate Portrait. Crown 8vo, cloth extra, 7s. 6d.

Crown 8vo, cloth extra, 3s. 6d. each ; post 8vo, illust. boards, 2s. each.
The Shadow of the Sword.
A Child of Nature. With a Frontispiece.
God and the Man. With Illustrations by FRED. BARNARD.
The Martyrdom of Madeline. With Frontispiece by A. W. COOPER.
Love Me for Ever. With a Frontispiece by P. MACNAB.
Annan Water. | The New Abelard.
Foxglove Manor.
Matt : A Story of a Caravan.
The Master of the Mine.
The Heir of Linne.

Burton (Captain).—The Book

of the Sword: Being a History of the Sword and its Use in all Countries, from the Earliest Times. By RICHARD F. BURTON. With over 400 Illustrations. Square 8vo, cloth extra, 32s.

Burton (Robert):

The Anatomy of Melancholy. A New Edition, complete, corrected and enriched by Translations of the Classical Extracts. Demy 8vo, cloth extra, 7s. 6d.

Melancholy Anatomised: Being an Abridgment, for popular use, of BURTON'S ANATOMY OF MELANCHOLY. Post 8vo, cloth limp, 2s. 6d.

Caine (T. Hall), Novels by:

Crown 8vo, cloth extra, 3s 6d. each; post 8vo, illustrated boards, 2s. each.

The Shadow of a Crime.

A Son of Hagar.

The Deemster: A Romance of the Isle of Man.

Cameron (Commander).—

The Cruise of the "Black Prince" Privateer. By V. LOVETT CAMERON, R.N., C.B. With Two Illustrations by P. MACNAB. Crown 8vo, cl. ex., 5s.; post 8vo, illustrated boards, 2s.

Cameron (Mrs. H. Lovett), Novels by:

Crown 8vo, cloth extra, 3s. 6d. each; post 8vo, illustrated boards, 2s. each.

Juliet's Guardian. | Deceivers Ever.

Carlyle (Thomas):

On the Choice of Books. By THOMAS CARLYLE. With a Life of the Author by R. H. SHEPHERD, and Three Illustrations. Post 8vo, cloth extra, 1s. 6d.

The Correspondence of Thomas Carlyle and Ralph Waldo Emerson, 1834 to 1872. Edited by CHARLES ELIOT NORTON. With Portraits. Two Vols., crown 8vo, cloth extra, 24s.

Chapman's (George) Works:

Vol. I. contains the Plays complete, including the doubtful ones. Vol. II., the Poems and Minor Translations, with an Introductory Essay by ALGERNON CHARLES SWINBURNE. Vol. III., the Translations of the Iliad and Odyssey. Three Vols., crown 8vo, cloth extra, 18s.; or separately, 6s. each

Chatto & Jackson.—A Treatise

on Wood Engraving, Historical and Practical. By WM. ANDREW CHATTO and JOHN JACKSON. With an Additional Chapter by HENRY G. BOHN; and 450 fine Illustrations. A Reprint of the last Revised Edition. Large 4to, half-bound, 28s.

Chaucer:

Chaucer for Children: A Golden Key. By Mrs. H R. HAWEIS. With Eight Coloured Pictures and numerous Woodcuts by the Author. New Ed., small 4to, cloth extra, 1s.

Chaucer for Schools. By Mrs H. R. HAWEIS. Demy 8vo, cloth limp, 2s 6d.

Clare.—For the Love of a Lass:

A Tale of Tynedale. By AUSTIN CLARE, Author of "A Child of the Menhir," &c. Two Vols., small 8vo, cloth extra, 12s.

Clodd.—Myths and Dreams.

By EDWARD CLODD, F.R.A.S., Author of "The Story of Creation," &c. Crown 8vo, cloth extra, 5s.

Cobban.—The Cure of Souls:

A Story. By J. MACLAREN COBBAN. Post 8vo, illustrated boards, 2s.

Coleman (John), Works by:

Players and Playwrights I have Known. Two Vols., demy 8vo, cloth extra, 24s.

Curly: An Actor's Romance. With Illustrations by J. C. DOLLMAN. Crown 8vo, cloth, 1s 6d.

Collins (C. Allston).—The Bar

Sinister: A Story. By C. ALLSTON COLLINS. Post 8vo, illustrated bds., 2s.

Collins (Churton).—A Mono-

graph on Dean Swift. By J. CHURTON COLLINS. Crown 8vo, cloth extra, 8s. [*Shortly.*

Collins (Mortimer), Novels by:

Crown 8vo, cloth extra, 3s. 6d. each; post 8vo, illustrated boards, 2s. each.

Sweet Anne Page.

Transmigration.

From Midnight to Midnight.

A Fight with Fortune. Post 8vo, illustrated boards, 2s.

Collins (Mortimer & Frances), Novels by:

Crown 8vo, cloth extra, 3s. 6d. each; post 8vo, illustrated boards, 2s. each.

Blacksmith and Scholar.

The Village Comedy.

You Play Me False.

Post 8vo, illustrated boards, 2s, each.

Sweet and Twenty.

Frances.

Collins (Wilkie), Novels by:

Crown 8vo, cloth extra, 3s. 6d. each; post 8vo, illustrated boards, 2s. each; cloth limp, 2s. 6d. each.

Antonina. Illust. by Sir JOHNGILBERT.

Basil. Illustrated by Sir JOHN GILBERT and J MAHONEY.

Hide and Seek. Illustrated by Sir JOHN GILBERT and J. MAHONEY.

The Dead Secret. Illustrated by Sir JOHN GILBERT.

Queen of Hearts. Illustrated by Sir JOHN GILBERT

My Miscellanies With a Steel-plate Portrait of WILKIE COLLINS.

The Woman In White. With Illustrations by Sir JOHN GILBERT and F. A. FRASER.

The Moonstone. With Illustrations by G. DU MAURIER and F. A. FRASER.

Man and Wife. Illusts. by W. SMALL.

Poor Miss Finch. Illustrated by G. DU MAURIER and EDWARD HUGHES.

Miss or Mrs.? With Illustrations by S. L. FILDES and HENRY WOODS.

The New Magdalen. Illustrated by G.DU MAURIER and C.S.REINHARDT.

The Frozen Deep. Illustrated by G. DU MAURIER and J. MAHONEY.

The Law and the Lady. Illustrated by S. L. FILDES and SYDNEY HALL.

The Two Destinies.

The Haunted Hotel. Illustrated by ARTHUR HOPKINS.

The Fallen Leaves.

Jezebel's Daughter.

The Black Robe.

Heart and Science: A Story of the Present Time.

"I Say No."

The Evil Genius.

Little Novels. | A Rogue's Life.

The Legacy of Cain. Crown 8vo, cloth extra, 3s. 6d

Blind Love. With a Preface by WALTER BESANT, and 36 Illustrations by A. FORESTIER. Three Vols., crown 8vo.

Colman's Humorous Works:

"Broad Grins," "My Nightgown and Slippers,"and other Humorous Works, Prose and Poetical, of GEORGE COLMAN. With Life by G. B. BUCKSTONE, and Frontispiece by HOGARTH. Crown 8vo, cloth extra, 7s. 6d.

Colquhoun.—Every Inch a Soldier: A Novel. By M. J. COLQUHOUN. Post 8vo, illustrated boards, 2s.

Convalescent Cookery: A Family Handbook. By CATHERINE RYAN. Crown 8vo, 1s.; cloth, 1s. 6d.

Conway (Moncure D.), Works by:

Demonology and Devil-Lore. Third Edition. With 65 Illustrations. Two Vols., 8vo, cloth extra, 28s.

A Necklace of Stories. Illustrated by W. J. HENNESSY. Square 8vo, cloth extra, 6s.

Pine and Palm: A Novel. Cheaper Ed. Post 8vo, illust. bds., 2s. [*Shortly.*

Cook (Dutton), Novels by:

Leo. Post 8vo, illustrated boards, 2s.

Paul Foster's Daughter. Crown 8vo, cloth extra, 3s. 6d.; post 8vo, illustrated boards, 2s.

Copyright.—A Handbook of English and Foreign Copyright in Literary and Dramatic Works. By SIDNEY JERROLD. Post 8vo, cl., 2s. 6d.

Cornwall.—Popular Romances of the West of England; or, The Drolls, Traditions, and Superstitions of Old Cornwall. Collected and Edited by ROBERT HUNT, F.R.S. With Two Steel-plate Illustrations by GEORGE CRUIKSHANK. New and Revised Edition, with Additions, crown 8vo, cloth extra, 7s. 6d.

Craddock.—The Prophet of the Great Smoky Mountains. By CHARLES EGBERT CRADDOCK. Post 8vo, illust. bds.; 2s.; cloth limp, 2s. 6d.

Cruikshank (George):

The Comic Almanack. Complete in Two SERIES: The FIRST from 1835 to 1843; the SECOND from 1844 to 1853. A Gathering of the BEST HUMOUR of THACKERAY, HOOD, MAYHEW, ALBERT SMITH, A'BECKETT, ROBERT BROUGH, &c. With 2,000 Woodcuts and Steel Engravings by CRUIKSHANK, HINE, LANDELLS, &c. Crown 8vo, cloth gilt, two thick volumes, 7s. 6d. each.

The Life of George Cruikshank. By BLANCHARD JERROLD, Author of "The Life of Napoleon III.," &c. With 84 Illustrations. New and Cheaper Edition, with Additional Plates, and a Bibliography. Crown 8vo, cloth extra, 7s. 6d.

Cumming(C. F. Gordon),Works by:

Demy 8vo, cloth extra, 8s. 6d. each.

In the Hebrides. With Autotype Facsimile and numerous full-page Illusts.

In the Himalayas and on the Indian Plains With numerous Illusts.

Via Cornwall to Egypt. With a Photogravure Frontispiece. Demy 8vo, cloth extra, 7s. 6d.

Curzon.—The Blue Ribbon of the Turf. By LOUIS HENRY CURZON. Crown 8vo, cloth extra, 6s. [*April.*

Cussans.—Handbook of Heraldry; with Instructions for Tracing Pedigrees and Deciphering Ancient MSS., &c. By JOHN E. CUSSANS. New and Revised Edition, illustrated with over 400 Woodcuts and Coloured Plates. Crown 8vo, cloth extra, 7s. 6d.

Cyples.—Hearts of Gold: A Novel. By WILLIAM CYPLES. Crown 8vo, cloth extra, 3s. 6d.; post 8vo, illustrated boards, 2s.

Daniel. — Merrie England in the Olden Time. By GEORGE DANIEL. With Illustrations by ROBT. CRUIKSHANK. Crown 8vo, cloth extra, 3s. 6d.

Daudet.—The Evangelist; or, Port Salvation. By ALPHONSE DAUDET. Translated by C. HARRY MELTZER. With Portrait of the Author. Crown 8vo, cloth extra, 3s. 6d.; post 8vo, illust. boards, 2s.

Davenant.—Hints for Parents on the Choice of a Profession or Trade for their Sons. By FRANCIS DAVENANT, M.A. Post 8vo, 1s.; cloth limp, 1s. 6d.

Davies (Dr. N. E.), Works by: Crown 8vo, 1s. each; cloth, 1s. 6d. each.
One Thousand Medical Maxims.
Nursery Hints: A Mother's Guide.
Foods for the Fat: A Treatise on Corpulency, and a Dietary for its Cure.
Aids to Long Life. Crown 8vo, 2s.; cloth limp, 2s. 6d.

Davies' (Sir John) Complete Poetical Works, including Psalms I. to L. in Verse, and other hitherto Unpublished MSS., for the first time Collected and Edited, with Memorial-Introduction and Notes, by the Rev. A. B. GROSART, D.D. Two Vols., crown 8vo, cloth boards, 12s.

De Maistre.—A Journey Round My Room. By XAVIER DE MAISTRE. Translated by HENRY ATTWELL. Post 8vo, cloth limp, 2s. 6d.

De Mille.—A Castle in Spain: A Novel. By JAMES DE MILLE. With a Frontispiece. Crown 8vo, cloth extra, 3s. 6d.; post 8vo, illust. bds., 2s.

Derwent (Leith), Novels by: Crown 8vo, cloth extra, 3s. 6d. each; post 8vo, illustrated boards, 2s. each.
Our Lady of Tears. | Circe's Lovers.

Dickens (Charles), Novels by: Post 8vo, illustrated boards, 2s. each.
Sketches by Boz. | Nicholas Nickleby.
Pickwick Papers. | Oliver Twist.

The Speeches of Charles Dickens, 1841–1870. With a New Bibliography, revised and enlarged. Edited and Prefaced by RICHARD HERNE SHEPHERD. Cr. 8vo, cloth extra, 6s.—Also a SMALLER EDITION, in the *Mayfair Library,* post 8vo, cloth limp, 2s. 6d.

About England with Dickens. By ALFRED RIMMER. With 57 Illustrations by C. A. VANDERHOOF, ALFRED RIMMER, and others. Sq. 8vo, cloth extra, 7s. 6d.

Dictionaries:

A Dictionary of Miracles: Imitative, Realistic, and Dogmatic. By the Rev. E. C. BREWER, LL.D. Crown 8vo, cloth extra, 7s. 6d.

The Reader's Handbook of Allusions, References, Plots, and Stories. By the Rev. E. C. BREWER, LL.D. With an Appendix, containing a Complete English Bibliography. Fifteenth Thousand. Crown 8vo, 1,400 pages, cloth extra, 7s. 6d.

Authors and their Works, with the Dates. Being the Appendices to "The Reader's Handbook," separately printed. By the Rev. Dr. BREWER. Crown 8vo, cloth limp, 2s.

A Dictionary of the Drama: a comprehensive Guide to the Plays, Playwrights, Players, and Playhouses of the United Kingdom and America, from the Earliest to the Present Times. By W. DAVENPORT ADAMS. A thick volume, crown 8vo, half-bound, 12s. 6d. [*In preparation.*

Familiar Short Sayings of Great Men. With Historical and Explanatory Notes. By SAMUEL A. BENT, M.A. Fifth Edition, revised and enlarged. Cr. 8vo, cloth extra, 7s.6d.

The Slang Dictionary: Etymological, Historical, and Anecdotal. Crown 8vo, cloth extra, 6s. 6d.

Women of the Day: A Biographical Dictionary. By FRANCES HAYS. Cr. 8vo, cloth extra, 5s.

Words, Facts, and Phrases: A Dictionary of Curious, Quaint, and Out-of-the-Way Matters. By ELIEZER EDWARDS. Crown 8vo, cloth extra, 7s. 6d.

Diderot.—The Paradox of Acting. Translated, with Annotations, from Diderot's "Le Paradoxe sur le Comédien," by WALTER HERRIES POLLOCK. With a Preface by HENRY IRVING. Cr. 8vo, in parchment, 4s. 6d.

Dobson (Austin). — Thomas Bewick and his Pupils. By AUSTIN DOBSON. With 95 ch ice Illustrations. Square 8vo, cloth extra, 6s.

Dobson (W. T.), Works by : Post 8vo, cloth limp, 2s. 6d. each.
Literary Frivolities, Fancies, Follies, and Frolics.
Poetical Ingenuities and Eccentricities.

Donovan (Dick), Detective Stories by:
Post 8vo, illustrated boards, 2s. each; cloth limp, 2s. 6d. each.
The Man-hunter: Stories from the Note-book of a Detective.
Caught at Last!
Tracked and Taken.

Drama, A Dictionary of the. Being a comprehensive Guide to the Plays, Playwrights, Players, and Playhouses of the United Kingdom and America, from the Earliest to the Present Times. By W. DAVENPORT ADAMS. (Uniform with BREWER'S "Reader's Handbook.") Crown 8vo, half-bound, 12s. 6d. [In preparation.

Dramatists, The Old. Cr. 8vo, cl. ex., Vignette Portraits, 6s. per Vol.
Ben Jonson's Works. With Notes Critical and Explanatory, and a Biographical Memoir by WM. GIFFORD. Edit. by Col. CUNNINGHAM. 3 Vols.
Chapman's Works. Complete in Three Vols. Vol. I. contains the Plays complete, including doubtful ones; Vol. II., Poems and Minor Translations, with IntroductoryEssay by A. C. SWINBURNE; Vol.III., Translations of the Iliad and Odyssey.
Marlowe's Works. Including his Translations. Edited, with Notes and Introduction, by Col. CUNNINGHAM. One Vol.
Massinger's Plays. From the Text of WILLIAM GIFFORD. Edited by Col. CUNNINGHAM. One Vol.

Dyer. — The Folk-Lore of Plants. By Rev. T. F. THISELTON DYER, M.A. Cr. 8vo, cloth extra, 6s.

Edgcumbe. — Zephyrus : A Holiday in Brazil and on the River Plate. By E. R. PEARCE EDGCUMBE. With 41 Illusts. Cr. 8vo, cl. extra, 5s.

Edwards.—Words, Facts, and Phrases: A Dictionary of Curious, Quaint, and Out-of-the-Way Matters. By ELIEZER EDWARDS. Crown 8vo, cloth extra, 7s. 6d.

Early English Poets. Edited, with Introductions and Annotations, by Rev. A. B. GROSART, D.D. Crown 8vo, cloth boards, 6s per Volume.
Fletcher's (Giles, B.D.) Complete Poems. One Vol.
Davies' (Sir John) Complete Poetical Works. Two Vols.
Herrick's (Robert) Complete Collected Poems. Three Vols.
Sidney's (Sir Philip) Complete Poetical Works. Three Vols.

Edwardes (Mrs. A.), Novels by: A Point of Honour. Post 8vo, illustrated boards, 2s.
Archie Lovell. Crown 8vo, cloth extra, 3s. 6d.; post 8vo, illust. bds., 2s.

Eggleston.—Roxy: A Novel. By EDWARD EGGLESTON. Post 8vo, illust. boards, 2s.

Emanuel.—On Diamonds and Precious Stones: their History,Value, and Properties ; with Simple Tests for ascertaining their Reality. By HARRY EMANUEL, F.R.G.S. With numerous Illustrations, tinted and plain. Crown 8vo, cloth extra, 6s.

Englishman's House, The: A Practical Guide to all interested in Selecting or Building a House ; with full Estimates of Cost, Quantities, &c. By C. J. RICHARDSON. Fourth Edition. With Coloured Frontispiece and nearly 600 Illustrations. Crown 8vo, cloth extra, 7s. 6d.

Ewald (Alex. Charles, F.S.A.), Works by:
The Life and Times of Prince Charles Stuart, Count of Albany, commonly called the Young Pretender. From the State Papers and other Sources. New and Cheaper Edition, with a Portrait. Crown 8vo, cloth extra, 7s. 6d.
Stories from the State Papers. With an Autotype Facsimile. Crown 8vo, cloth extra, 6s.

Eyes, Our: How to Preserve Them from Infancy to Old Age. By JOHN BROWNING, F.R.A.S., &c. Eighth Edition (Fourteenth Thousand). With 70 Illustrations. Crown 8vo, cloth, 1s.

Familiar Short Sayings of Great Men. By SAMUEL ARTHUR BENT, A.M. Fifth Edition, Revised and Enlarged. Cr. 8vo, cl. ex., 7s. 6d.

Farrer (J. Anson), Works by : Military Manners and Customs. Crown 8vo, cloth extra, 6s.
War: Three Essays, Reprinted from "Military Manners." Crown 8vo, 1s. ; cloth, 1s. 6d.

Faraday (Michael), Works by:
Post 8vo, cloth extra, 4s. 6d. each.
The Chemical History of a Candle:
Lectures delivered before a Juvenile
Audience at the Royal Institution.
Edited by WILLIAM CROOKES, F.C.S.
With numerous Illustrations.
On the Various Forces of Nature,
and their Relations to each other:
Lectures delivered before a Juvenile
Audience at the Royal Institution.
Edited by WILLIAM CROOKES, F.C.S.
With numerous Illustrations.

Fin-Bec. — The Cupboard
Papers: Observations on the Art of
Living and Dining. By FIN-BEC. Post
8vo, cloth limp, 2s. 6d.

Fireworks, The Complete Art
of Making; or, The Pyrotechnist's
Treasury. By THOMAS KENTISH. With
267 Illustrations. A New Edition, Revised throughout and greatly Enlarged.
Crown 8vo, cloth extra, 5s.

Fitzgerald (Percy), Works by:
The World Behind the Scenes.
Crown 8vo, cloth extra, 3s. 6d.
Little Essays: Passages from the
Letters of CHARLES LAMB. Post
8vo, cloth limp, 2s. 6d.
A Day's Tour: A Journey through
France and Belgium. With Sketches
in facsimile of the Original Draw-
ings. Crown 4to picture cover, 1s.
Fatal Zero: A Homburg Diary. Cr.
8vo, cloth extra, 3s. 6d.; post 8vo,
illustrated boards, 2s.

Post 8vo, illustrated boards, 2s. each.
Bella Donna. | Never Forgotten.
The Second Mrs. Tillotson.
Seventy-five Brooke Street
Polly. | The Lady of Brantome.

Fletcher's (Giles, B.D.) Com-
plete Poems: Christ's Victorie in
Heaven, Christ's Victorie on Earth,
Christ's Triumph over Death, and
Minor Poems. With Memorial-Intro-
duction and Notes by the Rev. A. B.
GROSART, D.D. Cr. 8vo, cloth bds., 6s.

Fonblanque.—Filthy Lucre: A
Novel. By ALBANY DE FONBLANQUE.
Post 8vo, illustrated boards, 2s.

Frederic (Harold), Novels by:
Seth's Brother's Wife. Post 8vo,
illustrated boards, 2s.
The Lawton Girl. With a Frontispiece by F. BARNARD. Crown 8vo,
cloth extra, 6s. [*Shortly.*

French Literature, History of.
By HENRY VAN LAUN. Complete in
3 Vols., demy 8vo, cl. bds., 7s. 6d. each.

Francillon (R. E.), Novels by.
Crown 8vo, cloth extra, 3s. 6d. each;
post 8vo, illust. boards, 2s. each.
One by One. | A Real Queen.
Queen Cophetua. | King or Knave?
Olympia. Post 8vo, illust. boards, 2s.
Esther's Glove. Fcap. 8vo, 1s.
Romances of the Law. With a Frontispiece by D. H. FRISTON. Crown
8vo, cloth extra, 3s.; post 8vo, illustrated boards, 2s.

Frenzeny.—Fifty Years on the
Trail: The Adventures of JOHN Y.
NELSON, Scout, Guide, and Interpreter,
in the Wild West. By HARRINGTON
O'REILLY. With over 100 Illustrations
by PAUL FRENZENY. Crown 8vo, picture
cover, 3s. 6d.; cloth extra, 4s. 6d.

Frere.—Pandurang Hari; or,
Memoirs of a Hindoo. With a Preface
by Sir H. BARTLE FRERE, G.C.S.I., &c.
Crown 8vo, cloth extra, 3s. 6d.

Friswell.—One of Two: A Novel.
By HAIN FRISWELL. Post 8vo, illustrated boards, 2s.

Frost (Thomas), Works by:
Crown 8vo, cloth extra, 3s. 6d. each.
Circus Life and Circus Celebrities.
The Lives of the Conjurers.
Old Showmen and Old London Fairs.

Fry's (Herbert) Royal Guide
to the London Charities. Showing
their Name, Date of Foundation,
Objects, Income, Officials, &c. Edited
by JOHN LANE. Published Annually.
Crown 8vo, cloth, 1s. 6d.

Gardening Books:
Post 8vo, 1s. each; cl. limp, 1s. 6d. each.
A Year's Work in Garden and Green-
house: Practical Advice to Amateur
Gardeners as to the Management of
the Flower, Fruit, and Frame Garden.
By GEORGE GLENNY.
Our Kitchen Garden: The Plants we
Grow, and How we Cook Them.
By TOM JERROLD.
Household Horticulture: A Gossip
about Flowers. By TOM and JANE
JERROLD. Illustrated.
The Garden that Paid the Rent.
By TOM JERROLD.

My Garden Wild, and What I Grew
there. By F. G. HEATH. Crown 8vo,
cloth extra, 5s.; gilt edges, 6s.

Garrett.—The Capel Girls: A
Novel. By EDWARD GARRETT. Cr. 8vo,
cl. ex., 3s. 6d.; post 8vo, illust. bds., 2s.

Gentleman's Magazine (The)

for 1890.—1s. Monthly.—In addition to the Articles upon subjects in Literature, Science, and Art, for which this Magazine has so high a reputation, "Table Talk" by SYLVANUS URBAN appears monthly.

₊ *Bound Volumes for recent years are kept in stock, cloth extra, price* 8s. 6d. *each; Cases for binding,* 2s. *each.*

Gentleman's Annual (The).

Published Annually in November. In picture cover, demy 8vo, 1s.

German Popular Stories. Col-

lected by the Brothers GRIMM, and Translated by EDGAR TAYLOR. Edited, with an Introduction, by JOHN RUSKIN. With 22 Illustrations on Steel by GEORGE CRUIKSHANK. Square 8vo, cloth extra, 6s. 6d. ; gilt edges, 7s. 6d.

Gibbon (Charles), Novels by:

Crown 8vo, cloth extra, 3s. 6d. each; post 8vo, illustrated boards, 2s. each.

Robin Gray.	The Braes of Yar-
What will the	row.
World Say ?	A Heart's Prob-
Queen of the	lem.
Meadow.	The GoldenShaft.
The Flower of the	Of High Degree.
Forest.	Loving a Dream.
In Honour Bound.	

Post 8vo, illustrated boards, 2s. each.

The Dead Heart.
For Lack of Gold.
For the King. | In Pastures Green.
In Love and War.
By Mead and Stream.
A Hard Knot. | Heart's Delight.
Blood-Money.

Gilbert (William), Novels by:

Post 8vo, illustrated boards, 2s. each.

Dr. Austin's Guests.
The Wizard of the Mountain.
James Duke, Costermonger.

Gilbert (W. S.), Original Plays

by: In Two Series, each complete in itself, price 2s. 6d. each.

The FIRST SERIES contains — The Wicked World—Pygmalion and Galatea — Charity — The Princess — The Palace of Truth—Trial by Jury.

The SECOND SERIES contains—Broken Hearts—Engaged—Sweethearts— Gretchen—Dan'l Druce—Tom Cobb— H.M.S. Pinafore—The Sorcerer—The Pirates of Penzance.

GILBERT (W. S.), *continued*—
Eight Original Comic Operas. Written by W. S. GILBERT. Containing: The Sorcerer—H.M.S. "Pinafore" —The Pirates of Penzance—Iolanthe — Patience — Princess Ida — The Mikado—Trial by Jury. Demy 8vo, cloth limp, 2s. 6d.

Glenny.—A Year's Work in

Garden and Greenhouse: Practical Advice to Amateur Gardeners as to the Management of the Flower, Fruit, and Frame Garden. By GEORGE GLENNY. Post 8vo, 1s.; cloth, 1s. 6d.

Godwin.—Lives of the Necro-

mancers. By WILLIAM GODWIN. Post 8vo. limp, 2s.

Golden Library, The:

Square 16mo (Tauchnitz size), cloth limp, 2s. per Volume.

Bayard Taylor's Diversions of the Echo Club.
Bennett's (Dr. W. C.) Ballad History of England.
Bennett's (Dr.) Songs for Sailors.
Godwin's (William) Lives of the Necromancers.
Holmes's Autocrat of the Breakfast Table. Introduction by SALA.
Holmes's Professor at the Breakfast Table.
Hood's Whims and Oddities. Complete. All the original Illustrations.
Jesse's (Edward) Scenes and Occupations of a Country Life.
Leigh Hunt's Essays: A Tale for a Chimney Corner, and other Pieces. With Portrait, and an Introduction by EDMUND OLLIER.
Mallory's (Sir Thomas) Mort d'Arthur: The Stories of King Arthur and of the Knights of the Round Table. Edited by B. MONTGOMERIE RANKING.
Pascal's Provincial Letters. A New Translation, with Historical Introduction and Notes by T. M'CRIE, D.D.
Pope's Poetical Works.
Rochefoucauld's Maxims and Moral Reflections. With Notes, and Introductory Essay by SAINTE-BEUVE.

Golden Treasury of Thought,

The: An ENCYCLOPÆDIA OF QUOTATIONS from Writers of all Times and Countries. Selected and Edited by THEODORE TAYLOR. Crown 8vo, cloth gilt and gilt edges, 7s. 6d.

Gowing. — Five Thousand

Miles in a Sledge: A Mid-winter Journey Across Siberia. By LIONEL F. GOWING. With a Map by E. WELLER and 30 Illustrations by C. J. UREN. Large crown 8vo, cloth extra, 8s.

Graham. — The Professor's Wife: A Story. By LEONARD GRAHAM. Fcap. 8vo, picture cover, 1s.

Greeks and Romans, The Life of the, Described from Antique Monuments. By ERNST GUHL and W. KONER. Translated from the Third German Edition, and Edited by Dr. F. HUEFFER. With 545 Illustrations. New and Cheaper Edition, large crown 8vo, cloth extra, 7s. 6d.

Greenaway (Kate) and Bret Harte.—The Queen of the Pirate Isle. By BRET HARTE. With 25 original Drawings by KATE GREENAWAY, reproduced in Colours by E. EVANS. Sm. 4to, bds., 5s.

Greenwood (James), Works by: Crown 8vo, cloth extra, 3s. 6d. each. The Wilds of London. Low-Life Deeps: An Account of the Strange Fish to be Found There.

Greville (Henry), Novels by: Nikanor: A Russian Novel. Translated by ELIZA E. CHASE. With 8 Illusts. Crown 8vo, cloth extra, 6s. A Noble Woman. Translated by ALBERT D. VANDAM. Crown 8vo, cloth extra, 5s.

Habberton (John), Author of "Helen's Babies," Novels by: Post 8vo, illustrated boards, 2s. each; cloth limp, 2s. 6d. each. Brueton's Bayou. Country Luck.

Hair (The): Its Treatment in Health, Weakness, and Disease. Translated from the German of Dr. J. PINCUS. Crown 8vo, 1s.; cloth, 1s. 6d.

Hake (Dr. Thomas Gordon), Poems by: Crown 8vo, cloth extra, 6s. each. New Symbols. Legends of the Morrow. The Serpent Play. Maiden Ecstasy. Small 4to, cloth extra, 8s.

Hall.—Sketches of Irish Character. By Mrs. S. C. HALL. With numerous Illustrations on Steel and Wood by MACLISE, GILBERT, HARVEY, and G. CRUIKSHANK. Medium 8vo, cloth extra, 7s. 6d.

Halliday.—Every-day Papers. By ANDREW HALLIDAY. Post 8vo, illustrated boards, 2s.

Handwriting, The Philosophy of. With over 100 Facsimiles and Explanatory Text. By DON FELIX DE SALAMANCA. Post 8vo, cl. limp, 2s. 6d.

Hanky-Panky: A Collection of Very Easy Tricks, Very Difficult Tricks, White Magic, Sleight of Hand, &c. Edited by W. H. CREMER. With 200 Illusts. Crown 8vo, cloth extra, 4s. 6d.

Hardy (Lady Duffus). — Paul Wynter's Sacrifice: A Story. By Lady DUFFUS HARDY. Post 8vo, illustrated boards, 2s.

Hardy (Thomas).—Under the Greenwood Tree. By THOMAS HARDY, Author of "Far from the Madding Crowd." Post 8vo, illustrated bds., 2s.

Harwood.—The Tenth Earl. By J. BERWICK HARWOOD. Post 8vo, illustrated boards, 2s.

Haweis (Mrs. H. R.), Works by: Square 8vo, cloth extra, 6s. each. The Art of Beauty. With Coloured Frontispiece and numerous Illusts. The Art of Decoration. With numerous Illustrations. Chaucer for Children: A Golden Key. With Eight Coloured Pictures and numerous Woodcuts.

The Art of Dress. With numerous Illustrations. Small 8vo, illustrated cover, 1s.; cloth limp, 1s. 6d. Chaucer for Schools. Demy 8vo, cloth limp, 2s. 6d.

Haweis (Rev. H. R.).—American Humorists: WASHINGTON IRVING, OLIVER WENDELL HOLMES, JAMES RUSSELL LOWELL, ARTEMUS WARD, MARK TWAIN, and BRET HARTE. By Rev. H. R. HAWEIS, M.A. Cr. 8vo, 6s.

Hawley Smart. — Without Love or Licence: A Novel. By HAWLEY SMART. Three Vols., crown 8vo. [*Shortly.*

Hawthorne (Julian), Novels by. Crown 8vo, cloth extra, 3s. 6d. each; post 8vo, illustrated boards, 2s. each.

Garth.	Sebastian Strome.
Ellice Quentin.	Dust.
Fortune's Fool.	Beatrix Randolph.
David Poindexter's Disappearance.	
The Spectre of the Camera.	

Post 8vo, illustrated boards, 2s. each.

Miss Cadogna.	Love—or a Name.

Mrs. Gainsborough's Diamonds. Fcap. 8vo, illustrated cover, 1s. A Dream and a Forgetting. Post 8vo, cloth, 1s 6d.

Hays.—Women of the Day: A Biographical Dictionary of Notable Contemporaries. By FRANCES HAYS. Crown 8vo, cloth extra, 5s.

Heath (F. G.). — My Garden Wild and What I Grew There. By FRANCIS GEORGE HEATH, Author of "The Fern World," &c. Crown 8vo, cloth extra, 5s. ; cl. gilt, gilt edges, 6s.

Helps (Sir Arthur), Works by :
Post 8vo, cloth limp, 2s. 6d. each.
Animals and their Masters.
Social Pressure.

Ivan de Biron: A Novel. Crown 8vo, cloth extra, 3s. 6d.; post 8vo, illustrated boards, 2s.

Henderson.—Agatha Page: A Novel. By ISAAC HENDERSON. Crown 8vo, cloth extra, 3s. 6d.

Herrick's (Robert) Hesperides, Noble Numbers, and Complete Collected Poems. With Memorial-Introduction and Notes by the Rev. A. B. GROSART, D.D., Steel Portrait, Index of First Lines, and Glossarial Index, &c. Three Vols., crown 8vo, cloth, 18s.

Hesse-Wartegg (Chevalier Ernst von), Works by :
Tunis: The Land and the People. With 22 Illusts. Cr. 8vo, cl. ex., 3s. 6d.
The New South-West: Travelling Sketches from Kansas, New Mexico, Arizona, and Northern Mexico. With 100 fine Illustrations and Three Maps. Demy 8vo, cloth extra, 14s. [In preparation.

Hindley (Charles), Works by :
Tavern Anecdotes and Sayings: Including the Origin of Signs, and Reminiscences connected with Taverns, Coffee Houses, Clubs, &c. With Illustrations. Crown 8vo, cloth extra, 3s. 6d.
The Life and Adventures of a Cheap Jack. By One of the Fraternity. Edited by CHARLES HINDLEY. Crown 8vo, cloth extra, 3s. 6d.

Hoey.—The Lover's Creed. By Mrs. CASHEL HOEY. Post 8vo, illustrated boards, 2s.

Hollingshead—NiagaraSpray: Sketches. By JOHN HOLLINGSHEAD. Post 8vo, picture cover, 1s.

Holmes (O. Wendell), Works by :
The Autocrat of the Breakfast-Table. Illustrated by J. GORDON THOMSON. Post 8vo, cloth limp, 2s. 6d.—Another Edition in smaller type, with an Introduction by G. A. SALA. Post 8vo, cloth limp, 2s.
The Professor at the Breakfast-Table; with the Story of Iris. Post 8vo, cloth limp, 2s.

Holmes. — The Science of Voice Production and Voice Preservation: A Popular Manual for the Use of Speakers and Singers. By GORDON HOLMES, M.D. With Illustrations. Crown 8vo, 1s. ; cloth, 1s. 6d.

Hood (Thomas):
Hood's Choice Works, in Prose and Verse. Including the Cream of the COMIC ANNUALS. With Life of the Author, Portrait, and 200 Illustrations. Crown 8vo, cloth extra, 7s. 6d.
Hood's Whims and Oddities. With all the original Illustrations. Post 8vo, cloth limp, 2s.

Hood (Tom).—From Nowhere to the North Pole: A Noah's Arkæological Narrative. By TOM HOOD. With 25 Illustrations by W. BRUNTON and E. C. BARNES. Square 8vo, cloth extra, gilt edges, 6s.

Hook's (Theodore) Choice Humorous Works, including his Ludicrous Adventures, Bons Mots, Puns, and Hoaxes. With Life of the Author, Portraits, Facsimiles, and Illustrations. Crown 8vo, cloth extra, 7s. 6d.

Hooper.—The House of Raby : A Novel. By Mrs. GEORGE HOOPER. Post 8vo, illustrated boards, 2s.

Hopkins—" 'Twixt Love and Duty :" A Novel. By TIGHE HOPKINS. Post 8vo, illustrated boards, 2s.

Horne.—Orion : An Epic Poem, in Three Books. By RICHARD HENGIST HORNE. With Photographic Portrait from a Medallion by SUMMERS. Tenth Edition. Crown 8vo, cloth extra, 7s.

Horse (The) and his Rider : An Anecdotic Medley. By "THORMANBY." Crown 8vo, cloth extra, 6s.

Hunt.—Essays by Leigh Hunt : A Tale for a Chimney Corner, and other Pieces. With Portrait, and Introduction by EDMUND OLLIER. Post 8vo, cloth limp, 2s.

Hunt (Mrs. Alfred), Novels by :
Crown 8vo, cloth extra, 3s. 6d. each;
post 8vo, illustrated boards, 2s. each.
Thornicroft's Model.
The Leaden Casket.
Self Condemned.
That other Person.

Hydrophobia: an Account of M. PASTEUR'S System. Containing a Translation of all his Communications on the Subject, the Technique of his Method, and the latest Statistical Results. By RENAUD SUZOR, M.B., C.M. Edin., and M.D. Paris, Commissioned by the Government of the Colony of Mauritius to study M. PASTEUR'S new Treatment in Paris. With 7 Illusts. Cr. 8vo, cloth extra, 6s.

Indoor Paupers. By ONE OF THEM. Crown 8vo, 1s.; cloth, 1s. 6d.

Ingelow.—Fated to be Free: A Novel. By JEAN INGELOW. Crown 8vo, cloth extra, 3s. 6d.; post 8vo, illustrated boards, 2s.

Irish Wit and Humour, Songs of. Collected and Edited by A. PERCEVALGRAVES. Post 8vo, cl. limp, 2s.6d.

James.—A Romance of the Queen's Hounds. By CHARLES JAMES. Post 8vo, picture cover, 1s.; cl., 1s. 6d.

Janvier.—Practical Keramics for Students. By CATHERINE A. JANVIER. Crown 8vo, cloth extra, 6s.

Jay (Harriett), Novels by: Post 8vo, illustrated boards, 2s. each.
The Dark Colleen.
The Queen of Connaught.

Jefferies (Richard), Works by: Nature near London. Crown 8vo, cl. ex., 6s.; post 8vo, cl. limp, 2s. 6d.
The Life of the Fields. Post 8vo, cloth limp, 2s. 6d.
The Open Air. Crown 8vo, cloth extra, 6s.; post 8vo, cl. limp, 2s. 6d.
The Eulogy of Richard Jefferies. By WALTER BESANT. Second Ed. Photo. Portrait. Cr. 8vo, cl. ex., 6s.

Jennings (H. J.), Works by: Curiosities of Criticism. Post 8vo, cloth limp, 2s. 6d.
Lord Tennyson: A Biographical Sketch. With a Photograph-Portrait. Crown 8vo, cloth extra, 6s.

Jerome.—Stageland: Curious Habits and Customs of Its Inhabitants. By JEROME K. JEROME, Author of " Idle Thoughts of an Idle Fellow." With 64 Illusts. by J. BERNARD PARTRIDGE. Fourth Edition. Fcap. 4to, cloth extra, 3s. 6d.

Jerrold (Tom), Works by: Post 8vo, 1s. each; cloth, 1s. 6d. each.
The Garden that Paid the Rent.
Household Horticulture: A Gossip about Flowers. Illustrated.
Our Kitchen Garden: The Plants we Grow, and How we Cook Them.

Jesse.—Scenes and Occupa- tions of a Country Life. By EDWARD JESSE. Post 8vo, cloth limp, 2s.

Jeux d'Esprit. Collected and Edited by HENRY S. LEIGH. Post 8vo, cloth limp, 2s. 6d.

Jones (Wm., F.S.A.), Works by: Crown 8vo, cloth extra, 7s. 6l. each.
Finger-Ring Lore: Historical, Legendary, and Anecdotal. With over Two Hundred Illustrations.
Credulities, Past and Present. Including the Sea and Seamen, Miners, Talismans, Word and Letter Divination, Exorcising and Blessing of Animals, Birds, Eggs, Luck, &c. With an Etched Frontispiece.
Crowns and Coronations: A History of Regalia in all Times and Countries. One Hundred Illustrations.

Jonson's (Ben) Works. With Notes Critical and Explanatory, and a Biographical Memoir by WILLIAM GIFFORD. Edited by Colonel CUNNINGHAM. Three Vols., crown 8vo, cloth extra, 18s.; or separately, 6s. each.

Josephus, The Complete Works of. Translated by WHISTON. Containing both " The Antiquities of the Jews " and " The Wars of the Jews." Two Vols., 8vo, with 52 Illustrations and Maps, cloth extra, gilt, 14s

Kempt.—Pencil and Palette: Chapters on Art and Artists. By ROBERT KEMPT. Post 8vo, cloth limp, 2s 6d.

Kershaw.—Colonial Facts and Fictions: Humorous Sketches. By MARK KERSHAW. Post 8vo, illustrated boards, 2s.; cloth, 2s 6d.

Keyser.—Cut by the Mess: A Novel. By ARTHUR KEYSER Cr. 8vo, picture cover, 1s.; cloth, 1s. 6l.

King (R. Ashe), Novels by: Crown 8vo, cloth extra, 3s. 6d. each; post 8vo, illustrated boards, 2s. each.
A Drawn Game.
"The Wearing of the Green."
Passion's Slave. Three Vols. Crown 8vo.

Kingsley (Henry), Novels by: Oakshott Castle. Post 8vo, illustrated boards, 2s.
Number Seventeen. Crown 8vo, cloth extra, 3s. 6d.

Knight.— The Patient's Vade Mecum: How to get most Benefit from Medical Advice. By WILLIAM KNIGHT, M.R.C.S., and EDW. KNIGHT, L.R.C.P. Cr. 8vo, 1s.; cloth, 1s. 6d.

Knights (The) of the Lion: A Romance of the Thirteenth Century. Edited, with an Introduction, by the MARQUESS of LORNE, K.T. Crown 8vo c oth extra. 6s.

Lamb (Charles):
Lamb's Complete Works, in Prose and Verse, reprinted from the Original Editions, with many Pieces hitherto unpublished. Edited, with Notes and Introduction, by R. H. SHEPHERD. With Two Portraits and a Facsimile of a page of the "Essay on Roast Pig." Cr. 8vo, cl. extra, 7s. 6d.
The Essays of Elia. Both Series complete. Post 8vo, laid paper, handsomely half-bound, 2s.
Poetry for Children, and Prince Dorus. By CHARLES LAMB. Carefully reprinted from unique copies. Small 8vo, cloth extra, 5s.
Little Essays: Sketches and Characters by CHARLES LAMB. Selected from his Letters by PERCY FITZGERALD. Post 8vo, cloth limp, 2s. 6d.

Lane's Arabian Nights.—The Thousand and One Nights: commonly called in England "THE ARABIAN NIGHTS' ENTERTAINMENTS." A New Translation from the Arabic, with copious Notes, by EDWARD WILLIAM LANE. Illustrated by many hundred Engravings on Wood, from Original Designs by WM. HARVEY. A New Edition, from a Copy annotated by the Translator, edited by his Nephew, EDWARD STANLEY POOLE. With a Preface by STANLEY LANE-POOLE. Three Vols., demy 8vo, cloth extra, 7s. 6d. each.

Larwood (Jacob), Works by:
The Story of the London Parks. With Illusts. Cr. 8vo, cl. ex,, 3s. 6d.
Anecdotes of the Clergy: The Antiquities, Humours, and Eccentricities of the Cloth. Post 8vo, printed on laid paper and hf.-bound (uniform with "The Essays of Elia" and "Gastronomy as a Fine Art"), 2s.
Post 8vo, cloth limp, 2s. 6d. each.
Forensic Anecdotes.
Theatrical Anecdotes.

Leigh (Henry S.), Works by:
Carols of Cockayne. A New Edition, printed on fcap. 8vo hand-made paper, and bound in buckram, 5s.
Jeux d'Esprit. Collected and Edited by HENRY S. LEIGH. Post 8vo, cloth limp, 2s. 6d.

**Leys.—The Lindsays: A Romance of Scottish Life. By JOHN K. LEYS. Post 8vo, illustrated boards, 2s.

Life in London; or, The History of Jerry Hawthorn and Corinthian Tom. With the whole of CRUIKSHANK'S Illustrations in Colours, after the Originals. Cr. 8vo, cl. extra, 7s. 6d.

Linskill.—In Exchange for a Soul. By MARY LINSKILL, Author of "The Haven Under the Hill," &c. Post 8vo, illustrated boards, 2s.

Linton (E. Lynn), Works by:
Post 8vo, cloth limp, 2s. 6d. each.
Witch Stories.
Ourselves: Essays on Women.
Crown 8vo, cloth extra, 3s. 6d. each; post 8vo, illustrated boards, 2s. each.
Patricia Kemball.
The Atonement of Leam Dundas.
The World Well Lost.
Under which Lord?
"My Love!" | Ione.
Paston Carew, Millionaire & Miser.
Post 8vo, illustrated boards, 2s. each.
With a Silken Thread.
The Rebel of the Family.

Longfellow's Poetical Works. Carefully Reprinted from the Original Editions. With numerous fine Illustrations on Steel and Wood. Crown 8vo, cloth extra, 7s. 6d.

Long Life, Aids to: A Medical, Dietetic, and General Guide in Health and Disease. By N. E. DAVIES, L.R.C.P. Cr. 8vo, 2s.; cl. limp, 2s.6d.

Lucy.—Gideon Fleyce: A Novel. By HENRY W. LUCY. Crown 8vo, cl. ex., 3s. 6d.; post 8vo, illust. bds., 2s.

Lusiad (The) of Camoens. Translated into English Spenserian Verse by ROBERT FFRENCH DUFF. Demy 8vo, with Fourteen full-page Plates, cloth boards, 18s.

Macalpine (Avery), Novels by:
Teresa Itasca, and other Stories. Crown 8vo, bound in canvas, 2s. 6d.
Broken Wings. With Illusts. by W. J. HENNESSY. Cr. 8vo, cloth extra, 6s.

McCarthy (Justin H., M.P.), Works by:
The French Revolution. 4 Vols., demy 8vo, 12s. each.
[Vols. I. & II. *in the press.*
An Outline of the History of Ireland, from the Earliest Times to the Present Day. Cr. 8vo, 1s.; cloth, 1s. 6d.
Ireland since the Union: Sketches of Irish History from 1798 to 1886. Crown 8vo, cloth extra, 6s.
England under Gladstone, 1880-85. Second Edition, revised. Crown 8vo, cloth extra, 6s.
Hafiz in London: Poems. Choicely printed. Small 8vo, gold cloth, 3s. 6d.

McCarthy (Justin H.), *continued—*
Harlequinade: Poems. Small 4to,
Japanese vellum, 8s.
Our Sensation Novel. Crown 8vo,
1s.; cloth, 1s. 6d.
Dolly: A Sketch. Crown 8vo, picture
cover, 1s.; cloth, 1s. 6d.
Lily Lass: A Romance. Crown 8vo,
picture cover, 1s.; cloth, 1s. 6d.

McCarthy (J., M.P.), Works by:
A History of Our Own Times, from
the Accession of Queen Victoria to
the General Election of 1880. Four
Vols. demy 8vo, cloth extra, 12s.
each.—Also a POPULAR EDITION, in
Four Vols. cr. 8vo, cl. extra, 6s. each.
—And a JUBILEE EDITION, with an
Appendix of Events to the end of
1886, complete in Two Vols., square
8vo, cloth extra, 7s. 6d. each.
A Short History of Our Own Times.
One Vol., crown 8vo, cloth extra, 6s.
—Also a CHEAP POPULAR EDITION,
in post 8vo, cloth extra, 2s. 6d.
A History of the Four Georges. Four
Vols. demy 8vo, cloth extra, 12s.
each. [Vols. I. & II. *now ready.*
Crown 8vo, cloth extra, 3s. 6d. each;
post 8vo, illustrated boards, 2s. each.
Dear Lady Disdain. | A Fair Saxon.
The Waterdale Neighbours.
Miss Misanthrope.
Donna Quixote. | Maid of Athens.
The Comet of a Season.
Camiola: A Girl with a Fortune.
Post 8vo, illustrated boards, 2s. each.
Linley Rochford.
My Enemy's Daughter.
"The Right Honourable:" A Ro-
mance of Society and Politics. By
JUSTIN McCARTHY, M.P., and Mrs.
CAMPBELL-PRAED. Cr. 8vo, cl. ex., 6s.

MacDonald.—Works of Fancy
and Imagination. By GEORGE MAC-
DONALD, LL.D. Ten Volumes, in
handsome cloth case, 21s.— Vol. 1.
WITHIN AND WITHOUT. THE HIDDEN
LIFE.— Vol. 2. THE DISCIPLE. THE
GOSPEL WOMEN. A BOOK OF SONNETS,
ORGAN SONGS.—Vol. 3. VIOLIN SONGS.
SONGS OF THE DAYS AND NIGHTS.
A BOOK OF DREAMS. ROADSIDE POEMS.
POEMS FOR CHILDREN. Vol. 4. PARA-
BLES. BALLADS. SCOTCH SONGS.—
Vols. 5 and 6. PHANTASTES: A Faerie
Romance.—Vol. 7. THE PORTENT.—
Vol. 8. THE LIGHT PRINCESS. THE
GIANT'S HEART. SHADOWS.— Vol. 9.
CROSS PURPOSES. THE GOLDEN KEY.
THE CARASOYN. LITTLE DAYLIGHT.—
Vol. 10. THE CRUEL PAINTER. THE
WOW O' RIVVEN. THE CASTLE. THE
BROKEN SWORDS. THE GRAY WOLF.
UNCLE CORNELIUS.
The Volumes are also sold separately,
in Grolier-pattern cloth, at 2s. 6d. each.

MacColl.— Mr. Stranger's
Sealed Packet: A Story of Adven-
ture. By HUGH MACCOLL. Second
Edition. Crown 8vo, cloth extra, 5s.

Macdonell.—Quaker Cousins:
A Novel. By AGNES MACDONELL.
Crown 8vo, cloth extra, 3s. 6d.; post
8vo, illustrated boards, 2s.

Macgregor. — Pastimes and
Players. Notes on Popular Games.
By ROBERT MACGREGOR. Post 8vo,
cloth limp, 2s. 6d.

Mackay.—Interludes and Un-
dertones; or, Music at Twilight. By
CHARLES MACKAY, LL.D. Crown 8vo,
cloth extra, 6s.

Maclise Portrait-Gallery (The)
of Illustrious Literary Characters;
with Memoirs—Biographical, Critical,
Bibliographical, and Anecdotal—illus-
trative of the Literature of the former
half of the Present Century. By
WILLIAM BATES, B.A. With 85 Portraits printed on an India Tint. Crown
8vo, cloth extra, 7s. 6d.

Macquoid (Mrs.), Works by:
Square 8vo, cloth extra, 7s. 6d. each.
In the Ardennes. With 50 fine Illus-
trations by THOMAS R. MACQUOID.
Pictures and Legends from Nor-
mandy and Brittany. With numer-
ous Illusts. by THOMAS R. MACQUOID.
Through Normandy. With 90 Illus-
trations by T. R. MACQUOID.
Through Brittany. With numerous
Illustrations by T. R. MACQUOID.
About Yorkshire. With 67 Illustra-
tions by T. R. MACQUOID.

Post 8vo, illustrated boards, 2s. each.
The Evil Eye, and other Stories.
Lost Rose.

Magician's Own Book (The):
Performances with Cups and Balls,
Eggs, Hats, Handkerchiefs, &c. All
from actual Experience. Edited by
W. H. CREMER. With 200 Illustrations.
Crown 8vo, cloth extra, 4s. 6d.

Magic Lantern (The), and its
Management: including full Prac-
tical Directions for producing the
Limelight, making Oxygen Gas, and
preparing Lantern Slides. By T. C.
HEPWORTH. With 10 Illustrations.
Crown 8vo, 1s.; cloth, 1s. 6d.

Magna Charta. An exact Facsimile of the Original in the British
Museum, printed on fine plate paper,
3 feet by 2 feet, with Arms and Seals
emblazoned in Gold and Colours, 5s.

Mallock (W. H.), Works by:

The New Republic: or, Culture, Faith, and Philosophy in an English Country House. Post 8vo. picture cover, 2s.; cloth limp, 2s. 6d.

The New Paul and Virginia; or, Positivism on an Island. Post 8vo, cloth limp, 2s. 6d.

Poems. Small 4to, parchment, 8s.

Is Life worth Living? Crown 8vo, cloth extra, 6s.

Mallory's (Sir Thomas) Mort

d'Arthur: The Stories of King Arthur and o the Knights of the Round Table. A Selection. Edited by B. MONTGOMERIE RANKING. Post 8vo, cloth limp, 2s.

Man - Hunter (The): Stories

from the Note-book of a Detective. By DICK DONOVAN. Post 8vo, illustrated boards, 2s.; cloth, 2s. 6d.

Mark Twain, Works by:

Crown 8vo, cloth extra, 7s. 6d. each.

The Choice Works of Mark Twain. Revised and Corrected throughout by the Author. With Life, Portrait, and numerous Illustration·.

Roughing It, and The Innocents at Home. With 200 Illustrations by F. A. FRASER.

The Gilded Age. By MARK TWAIN and CHARLES DUDLEY WARNER. With 212 Illustrations by T. COPPIN.

Mark Twain's Library of Humour. With numerous Illustrations.

A Yankee at the Court of King Arthur. With 220 Illustrations by DAN BEARD.

Crown 8vo, cloth extra, (illustrated), 7s. 6d. each; post 8vo (without Illustra ions), illustrated boards, 2s. each.

The Innocents Abroad; or, The New Pilgrim's Progress: "MARK TWAIN'S PLEASURE TRIP."

The Adventures of Tom Sawyer. With 111 Illustrations.

The Prince and the Pauper. With nearly 200 Illustrations.

A Tramp Abroad. With 314 Illusts.

Life on the Mississippi. With 300 Illustrations.

The Adventures of Huckleberry Finn. With 174 Illustrations by E. W. KEMBLE.

The Stolen White Elephant, &c. Crown 8vo, cloth extra, 6s.; post 8vo, illustrated boards, 2s.

Marlowe's Works. Including

his Translations. Edited, with Notes and Introductions, by Col. CUNNINGHAM. Crown 8vo, cloth extra, 6s.

Marryat (Florence), Novels by:

Post 8vo, illustrated boards, 2s. each.

A Harvest of Wild Oats.

Fighting the Air | Written in Fire.

Open! Sesame! Crown 8vo, cloth extra, 3s. 6d.; post 8vo, picture boards, 2s.

Massinger's Plays. From the

Text of WM. GIFFORD. Edited by Col. CUNNINGHAM. Cr. 8vo. cloth extra, 6s.

Masterman.—Half a Dozen

Daughters: A Novel. By J. MASTERMAN. Post 8vo, illustrated boards, 2s.

Matthews.—A Secret of the

Sea, &c. By BRANDER MATTHEWS. Post 8vo, illust. bds., 2s.; cloth, 2s. 6d.

Mayfair Library, The:

Post 8vo, cloth limp, 2s. 6d. per Volume.

A Journey Round My Room. By XAVIER DE MAISTRE. Translated by HENRY ATTWELL.

Quips and Quiddities. Selected by W. DAVENPORT ADAMS.

The Agony Column of "The Times," from 1800 to 1870. Edited, with an Introduction, by ALICE CLAY.

Melancholy Anatomised: A Popular Abridgment of "Burton's Anatomy of Melancholy."

The Speeches of Charles Dickens.

Literary Frivolities, Fancies, Follies, and Frolics. By W. T. DOBSON.

Poetical Ingenuities and Eccentricities. Selected and Edited by W. T. DOBSON.

The Cupboard Papers. By FIN-BEC.

Original Plays by W. S. GILBERT. FIRST SERIES Containing: The Wicked World — Pygmalion and Galatea— Charity — The Princess— The Palace o' Truth—Trial by Jury.

Original Plays by W. S GILBERT. SECOND SERIES. Containing: Broken Hearts — Engaged — Sweethearts— Gretchen—Dan'l Druce—Tom Cobb —H.M.S. Pinafore — The Sorcerer —The Pirates of Penzance.

Songs of Irish Wit and Humour. Collected and Edited by A. PERCEVAL GRAVES.

Animals and their Masters. By Sir ARTHUR HELPS.

Social Pressure. By Sir A. HELPS.

Curiosities of Criticism. By HENRY J. JENNINGS.

The Autocrat of the Breakfast-Table. By OLIVER WENDELL HOLMES. Illustrated by J. GORDON THOMSON.

Pencil and Palette. By R. KEMPT.

Little Essays: Sketches and Characters by CHAS. LAMB. Selected from his Letters by PERCY FITZGERALD.

Forensic Anecdotes; or, Humour and Curiosities of the Law and Men of Law. By JACOB LARWOOD.

Mayfair Library, *continued—*
Post 8vo, cloth limp, 2s. 6d. per Volume.
Theatrical Anecdotes. By Jacob Larwood.
Jeux d'Esprit. Edited by Henry S. [Leigh.
Witch Stories. By E. Lynn Linton.
Ourselves: Essays on Women. By E. Lynn Linton. [Macgregor,
Pastimes and Players. By Robert Macgregor.
The New Paul and Virginia. By W. H. Mallock.
New Republic. By W. H. Mallock.
Puck on Pegasus. By H. Cholmonde-ley-Pennell.
Pegasus Re-Saddled. By H. Cholmondeley-Pennell. Illustrated by George Du Maurier.
Muses of Mayfair. Edited by H. Cholmondeley-Pennell.
Thoreau: His Life and Aims. By H. A. Page.
Puniana. By the Hon. Hugh Rowley.
More Puniana. By Hon. H. Rowley.
The Philosophy of Handwriting. By Don Felix de Salamanca.
By Stream and Sea By William Senior.
Leaves from a Naturalist's Note-Book. By Dr. Andrew Wilson.

Mayhew.—London Characters and the Humorous Side of London Life. By Henry Mayhew. With numerous Illusts. Cr. 8vo, cl. extra, 3s. 6d.

Medicine, Family.—One Thousand Medical Maxims and Surgical Hints, for Infancy, Adult Life, Middle Age, and Old Age. By N. E. Davies, L.R C.P. Lond. Cr. 8vo, 1s.; cl., 1s. 6d.

Menken.—Infelicia: Poems by Adah Isaacs Menken. A New Edition, with a Biographical Preface, numerous Illustrations by F. E. Lummis and F. O. C. Darley, and Facsimile of a Letter from Charles Dickens. Beautifully printed on small 4to ivory paper, with red border to each pa e, and handsomely bound, price 7s. 6d.

Mexican Mustang (On a), through Texas, from the Gulf to the Rio Grande. By A. E. Sweet and J. Armoy Knox, Editors of "Texas Siftings." With 265 Illusts. Cr. 8vo, cl.extra, 7s.6d.

Middlemass (Jean), Novels by:
Post 8vo, illustrated boards 2s. each.
Touch and Go. | Mr. Dorillion.

Miller. — Physiology for the Young; or, The House of Life: Human Physiology, with its application to the Preservation of Health. With numerous Illusts. By Mrs. F. Fenwick Miller. Small 8vo, cloth limp, 2s. 6d.

Milton (J. L.), Works by:
Sm. 8vo 1s. each; cloth ex., 1s. 6d. each.
The Hygiene of the Skin. Rules for the Management of the Skin; with Directions for Diet, Soaps, Baths,&c.
The Bath in Diseases of the Skin.
The Laws of Life, and their Relation to Diseases of the Skin.

Minto.—Was She Good or Bad? A Romance. By William Minto. Cr. 8vo, picture cover, 1s.; cloth, 1s 6d.

Molesworth (Mrs.), Novels by:
Hathercourt Rectory. Post 8vo, illustrated boards, 2s.
That Girl in Black. Crown 8vo, picture cover, 1s.; cloth, 1s. 6d.

Moore (Thomas), Works by:
The Epicurean, and Alciphron. A New Edition. Post 8vo, printed on laid paper and half-bound, 2s.
Prose and Verse, Humorous, Satirical, and Sentimental, by T. Moore; with Suppressed Passages from the Memoirs of Lord Byron. Edited, with Notes and Introduction, by R. Herne Shepherd. With Portrait. Crown 8vo, cloth extra, 7s. 6d.

Muddock (J. E.), Stories by:
Stories Weird and Wonderful. Post 8vo, illust. boards, 2s.; cloth, 2s. 6d.
The Dead Man's Secret; or, The Valley of Gold: Being a Narrative of Strange and Wild Adventure. With a Frontispiece by F. Barnard. Crown 8vo, cloth extra, 5s.
The Man from Manchester. With a Frontispiece. Crown 8vo, cloth extra, 6s. [*Shortly.*

Murray (D. Christie), Novels by. Crown 8vo, cloth extra, 3s 6d. each; post 8vo, illustrated boards, 2s. each.
A Life's Atonement. | A Model Father.
Joseph's Coat. | Coals of Fire.
By the Gate of the Sea. | Hearts.
Val Strange. | Cynic Fortune.
A Bit of Human Nature.
First Person Singular.
The Way of the World.

Old Blazer's Hero. With Three Illustrations by A. McCormick. Crown 8vo, cloth extra, 6s.; post 8vo, illustrated b ards, 2s.

Murray (D. Christie) & Henry Herman, Works by:
One Traveller Returns. Cr.8vo, cloth extra, 6s.; post 8vo, illust. bds., 2s.
Paul Jones's Alias, &c. With Illusts. by A. Forestier an' G. Nicolet. Crown 8vo, cloth extra, 6s. [*Shortly.*
The Bishop's Bible. Three Vols. crown 8vo, [*Shortly.*

Murray.—A Game of Bluff: A Novel. By HENRY MURRAY, joint-Author with CHRISTIE MURRAY of "A Dangerous Catspaw." Post 8vo, picture boards, 2s.; cloth, 2s. 6d.

Novelists. — Half-Hours with the Best Novelists of the Century: Choice Readings from the finest Novels. Edited, with Critical and Biographical Notes, by H. T. MACKENZIE BELL. Crown 8vo, cl. ex., 3s. 6d. [*Preparing.*

Nursery Hints: A Mother's Guide in Health and Disease. By N. E. DAVIES, L.R.C.P. Cr. 8vo, 1s.; cl., 1s. 6d.

Oberammergau.—The Country of the Passion Play, and the Highlands of Bavaria. By L. G. SEGUIN, Author of "Walks in Algiers." With a Map and 37 Illustrations. Third Edition, with a new Preface for 1890. Cr. 8vo, cloth extra, 3s. 6d.

O'Connor.—Lord Beaconsfield: A Biography. By T. P. O'CONNOR, M.P. Sixth Edition, with a New Preface. Crown 8vo, cloth extra, 5s.

O'Hanlon (Alice), Novels by: Post 8vo, illustrated boards, 2s. each.
The Unforeseen.
Chance? or Fate?

Ohnet (Georges), Novels by: Doctor Rameau. Translated by Mrs. CASHEL HOEY. With 9 Illustrations by E. BAYARD. Cr. 8vo, cloth extra, 6s.; post 8vo, illustrated boards, 2s.
A Last Love. Translated by ALBERT D. VANDAM. Crown 8vo, cl. ex., 5s.

Oliphant (Mrs.), Novels by: Whiteladies. With Illustrations by ARTHUR HOPKINS and H. WOODS. Crown 8vo, cloth extra, 3s. 6d.; post 8vo, illustrated boards, 2s.

Post 8vo, illustrated boards, 2s. each.
The Primrose Path.
The Greatest Heiress in England.

O'Reilly.—Phœbe's Fortunes: A Novel. With Illustrations by HENRY TUCK. Post 8vo, illustrated boards, 2s.

O'Shaughnessy (A.), Poems by: Songs of a Worker. Fcap. 8vo, cloth extra, 7s. 6d.
Music and Moonlight. Fcap. 8vo, cloth extra, 7s. 6d.
Lays of France. Cr. 8vo, cl. ex., 10s. 6d.

Ouida, Novels by. Crown 8vo, cloth extra, 3s. 6d. each; post 8vo, illustrated boards, 2s. each.

Held in Bondage.	Pascarel.
Strathmore.	Signa.	Ariadne.
Chandos	In a Winter City.
Under Two Flags.	Friendship.
Cecil Castle-	Moths.	Bimbi.
maine's Gage.	Pipistrello.
Idalia.	In Maremma
Tricotrin.	A Village Com-
Puck.	mune.
Folle Farine.	Wanda.
Two Little Wooden	Frescoes. [ine.
Shoes.	Princess Naprax·
A Dog of Flanders.	Othmar.

Guilderoy. Crown 8vo, cloth extra, 3s. 6d.

Position. Three Vols., crown 8vo.

Wisdom, Wit, and Pathos, selected from the Works of OUIDA by F. SYDNEY MORRIS. Sm. cr. 8vo, cl. ex., 5s. CHEAPER EDITION, illust. bds., 2s.

Page (H. A.), Works by:
Thoreau: His Life and Aims: A Study. With Portrait. Post 8vo, cl. limp, 2s. 6d.
Lights on the Way: Some Tales within a Tale. By the late J. H. ALEXANDER, B.A. Edited by H. A. PAGE. Crown 8vo, cloth extra, 6s.
Animal Anecdotes. Arranged on a New Principle. Cr. 8vo, cl. extra, 5s.

Parliamentary Elections and Electioneering in the Old Days (A History of). Showing the State of Political Parties and Party Warfare at the Hustings and in the House of Commons from the Stuarts to Queen Victoria. Illustrated from the original Political Squibs, Lampoons, Pictorial Satires, and Popular Caricatures of the Time. By JOSEPH GREGO, Author of "Rowlandson and his Works," "The Life of Gillray," &c. A New Edition, crown 8vo, cloth extra, with Coloured Frontispiece and 100 Illustrations, 7s. 6d. [*Preparing.*

Pascal's Provincial Letters. A New Translation, with Historical Introduction and Notes, by T. M'CRIE, D.D. Post 8vo, cloth limp, 2s.

Patient's (The) Vade Mecum: How to get most Benefit from Medical Advice. By W. KNIGHT, M.R.C.S., and E. KNIGHT, L.R.C.P. Cr. 8vo, 1s.; cl. 1/6.

Paul Ferroll: why he Killed his Wife Post 8vo, illustrated boards, 2s.

CHATTO & WINDUS, PICCADILLY. 19

Paul.—Gentle and Simple. By
MARGARET AGNES PAUL. With a
Frontispiece by HELEN PATERSON.
Cr. 8vo, cloth extra, 3s. 6d.; post 8vo,
illustrated boards, 2s.

Payn (James), Novels by.
Crown 8vo, cloth extra, 3s. 6d. each;
post 8vo, illustrated boards, 2s. each.

Lost Sir Massingberd.
Walter's Word.
Less Black than we're Painted.
By Proxy. | High Spirits.
Under One Roof.
A Confidential Agent.
Some Private Views.
A Grape from a Thorn.
The Talk of the Town.
From Exile. | The Canon's Ward
Holiday Tasks. | Glow-worm Tales.
The Mystery of Mirbridge.

Post 8vo, illustrated boards, 2s. each.
Kit: A Memory. | Carlyon's Year.
A Perfect Treasure.
Bentinck's Tutor.|Murphy's Master.
The Best of Husbands.
For Cash Only.
What He Cost Her.| Cecil's Tryst.
Fallen Fortunes. | Halves.
A County Family. | At Her Mercy.
A Woman's Vengeance.
The Clyffards of Clyffe.
The Family Scapegrace.
The Foster Brothers.| Found Dead.
Gwendoline's Harvest.
Humorous Stories.
Like Father, Like Son.
A Marine Residence.
Married Beneath Him.
Mirk Abbey.| Not Wooed, but Won.
Two Hundred Pounds Reward.

In Peril and Privation: Stories of
Marine Adventure Re-told. With 17
Illustrations. Crown 8vo, cloth extra,
3s. 6d.
The Burnt Million.   Three Vols.,
crown 8vo.   [Shortly.

Pears.—The Present Depres-
sion in Trade: Its Causes and Reme-
dies. Being the "Pears" Prize Essays
(of One Hundred Guineas). By EDWIN
GOADBY and WILLIAM WATT. With
an Introductory Paper by Prof. LEONE
LEVI, F.S.A., F.S.S. Demy 8vo, 1s.

Pennell (H. Cholmondeley),
Works by:
Post 8vo, cloth limp, 2s. 6d. each.

Puck on Pegasus. With Illustrations.
Pegasus Re-Saddled. With Ten full-
page Illusts. by G. DU MAURIER.
The Muses of Mayfair. Vers de
Société, Selected and Edited by H.
C. PENNELL.

Phelps (E. Stuart), Works by:
Post 8vo, 1s. each; cl. limp, 1s. 6d. each.
Beyond the Gates. By the Author
of "The Gates Ajar."
An Old Maid's Paradise.
Burglars in Paradise.

Jack the Fisherman. With Twenty-
two Illustrations by C. W. REED.
Cr. 8vo, picture cover, 1s.; cl. 1s. 6d.

Pirkis (C. L.), Novels by:
Trooping with Crows. Fcap. 8vo,
picture cover, 1s.
Lady Lovelace. Post 8vo, illustrated
boards, 2s.

Planché (J. R.), Works by:
The Pursuivant of Arms; or, Her-
aldry Founded upon Facts. With
Coloured Frontispiece and 200 Illus-
trations. Cr. 8vo, cloth extra, 7s. 6d.
Songs and Poems, from 1819 to 1879.
Edited, with an Introduction, by his
Daughter, Mrs. MACKARNESS. Crown
8vo, cloth extra, 6s.

Plutarch's Lives of Illustrious
Men. Translated from the Greek,
with Notes Critical and Historical, and
a Life of Plutarch, by JOHN and
WILLIAM LANGHORNE. Two Vols.,
8vo, cloth extra, with Portraits, 10s. 6d.

Poe (Edgar Allan):
The Choice Works, in Prose and
Poetry, of EDGAR ALLAN POE. With
an Introductory Essay by CHARLES
BAUDELAIRE, Portrait and Fac-
similes. Crown 8vo, cl. extra, 7s. 6d.
The Mystery of Marie Roget, and
other Stories. Post 8vo, illust.bds.,2s.

Pope's Poetical Works. Complete in One Vol. Post 8vo, cl. limp, 2s.

Praed (Mrs. Campbell-).—"The
Right Honourable:" A Romance of
Society and Politics. By Mrs. CAMP-
BELL-PRAED and JUSTIN McCARTHY,
M.P. Crown 8vo, cloth extra, 6s.

Price (E. C.), Novels by:
Crown 8vo, cloth extra, 3s. 6d. each;
post 8vo, illustrated boards, 2s. each.
Valentina. | The Foreigners.
Mrs. Lancaster's Rival.

Gerald. Post 8vo, illust. boards, 2s.

Princess Olga—Radna; or, The
Great Conspiracy of 1881. By the
Princess OLGA. Cr. 8vo, cl. ex., 6s.

Proctor (R. A.), Works by:

Flowers of the Sky. With 55 Illusts. Small crown 8vo, cloth extra, 3s. 6d.

Easy Star Lessons. With Star Maps for Every Night in the Year, Drawings of the Constellations, &c. Crown 8vo, cloth extra, 6s.

Familiar Science Studies. Crown 8vo, cloth extra, 6s.

Saturn and its System. New and Revised Edition, with 13 Steel Plates. Demy 8vo, cloth extra, 10s. 6d.

Mysteries of Time and Space. With Illusts. Cr. 8vo, cloth extra, 6s.

The Universe of Suns, and other Science Gleanings. With numerous Illusts. Cr. 8vo, cloth extra, 6s.

Wages and Wants of Science Workers. Crown 8vo, 1s. 6d.

Rambosson.—Popular Astronomy. By J. RAMBOSSON, Laureate of the Institute of France. Translated by C. B. PITMAN. With numerous Illustrations and a Coloured Chart of Spectra. Crown 8vo, cloth extra, 7s. 6d.

Reade (Charles), Novels by:

Crown 8vo, cloth extra, illustrated, 3s. 6d. each; post 8vo, illust. bds., 2s. each.

Peg Woffington. Illustrated by S. L. FILDES, A R.A.

Christie Johnstone. Illustrated by WILLIAM SMALL.

It is Never Too Late to Mend. Illustrated by G. J. PINWELL.

The Course of True Love Never did run Smooth. Illustrated by HELEN PATERSON.

The Autobiography of a Thief; Jack of all Trades; and James Lambert. Illustrated by MATT STRETCH.

Love me Little, Love me Long. Illustrated by M. ELLEN EDWARDS.

The Double Marriage. Illust. by Sir JOHN GILBERT, R.A., and C. KEENE.

The Cloister and the Hearth. Illustrated by CHARLES KEENE.

Hard Cash. Illust. by F. W. LAWSON.

Griffith Gaunt. Illustrated by S. L. FILDES, A.R.A., and WM. SMALL.

Foul Play. Illust. by DU MAURIER.

Put Yourself in His Place. Illustrated by ROBERT BARNES.

A Terrible Temptation. Illustrated by EDW. HUGHES and A. W. COOPER.

The Wandering Heir. Illustrated by H. PATERSON, S. L. FILDES, A.R.A., C. GREEN, and H. WOODS, A.R.A.

A Simpleton. Illustrated by KATE CRAUFORD.   [COULDERY.

A Woman-Hater. Illust. by THOS. Singleheart and Doubleface: A Matter-of-fact Romance. Illustrated by P. MACNAB.

READE (CHARLES), *continued*—

Good Stories of Men and other Animals. Illustrated by E. A. ABBEY, PERCY MACQUOID, and JOSEPH NASH.

The Jilt, and other Stories. Illustrated by JOSEPH NASH.

Readiana. With a Steel-plate Portrait of CHARLES READE.

Bible Characters: Studies of David, Nehemiah, Jonah, Paul, &c. Fcap. 8vo, leatherette, 1s.

Reader's Handbook (The) of Allusions, References, Plots, and Stories. By the Rev. Dr. BREWER. With an Appendix, containing a COMPLETE ENGLISH BIBLIOGRAPHY. Fifteenth Thousand. Crown 8vo, 1,400 pages, cloth extra, 7s. 6d.

Riddell (Mrs. J. H.), Novels by:

Crown 8vo, cloth extra, 3s. 6d. each; post 8vo, illustrated boards, 2s. each.

Her Mother's Darling.

The Prince of Wales's Garden Party.

Weird Stories.

Post 8vo, illustrated boards, 2s. each.

The Uninhabited House.

Fairy Water.

The Mystery in Palace Gardens.

Rimmer (Alfred), Works by:

Square 8vo, cloth gilt, 7s. 6d. each.

Our Old Country Towns. With over 50 Illustrations.

Rambles Round Eton and Harrow. With 50 Illustrations.

About England with Dickens. With 58 Illustrations by ALFRED RIMMER and C. A. VANDERHOOF.

Robinson Crusoe. By DANIEL DEFOE. (MAJOR'S EDITION.) With 37 Woodcut Illustrations by GEORGE CRUIKSHANK. Post 8vo, handsomely half-bound (uniform with Lamb's "Elia"), 2s.   [*Shortly*.

Robinson (F. W.), Novels by:

Crown 8vo, cloth extra, 3s. 6d. each; post 8vo, illustrated boards, 2s. each.

Women are Strange.

The Hands of Justice.

Robinson (Phil), Works by:

Crown 8vo, cloth extra, 7s. 6d. each.

The Poets' Birds.

The Poets' Beasts.

The Poets and Nature: Reptiles, Fishes, and Insects.   [*Preparing*.

Rochefoucauld's Maxims and Moral Reflections. With Notes, and an Introductory Essay by SAINTE-BEUVE. Post 8vo, cloth limp, 2s.

Roll of Battle Abbey, The ; or, A List of the Principal Warriors who came over from Normandy with William the Conqueror, and Settled in this Country, A.D. 1066-7. With the principal Arms emblazoned in Gold and Colours. Handsomely printed, 5s.

Rowley (Hon. Hugh), Works by:
Post 8vo, cloth limp, 2s. 6d. each.
Puniana: Riddles and Jokes. With numerous Illustrations.
More Puniana. Profusely Illustrated.

Runciman (James), Stories by :
Post 8vo, illustrated boards, 2s. each ; cloth limp, 2s. 6d. each.
Skippers and Shellbacks.
Grace Balmaign's Sweetheart.
Schools and Scholars.

Russell (W. Clark), Works by:
Crown 8vo, cloth extra, 6s. each; post 8vo, illustrated boards, 2s. each.
Round the Galley-Fire.
In the Middle Watch.
A Voyage to the Cape.
A Book for the Hammock.
The Mystery of the 'Ocean Star."
The Romance of Jenny Harlowe.

On the Fo'k'sle Head. Post 8vo, illustrated boards, 2s.
An Ocean Tragedy: A Novel. Three Vols., crown 8vo.

Sala.—Gaslight and Daylight.
By GEORGE AUGUSTUS SALA. Post 8vo, illustrated boards, 2s.

Sanson.—Seven Generations of Executioners: Memoirs of the Sanson Family (1688 to 1847). Edited by HENRY SANSON. Cr.8vo,cl.ex.3s 6d.

Saunders (John), Novels by:
Crown 8vo, cloth extra, 3s. 6d. each; post 8vo, illustrated boards, 2s. each.
Guy Waterman. | Lion in the Path.
The Two Dreamers.

Bound to the Wheel. Crown 8vo, cloth extra, 3s. 6d.

Saunders (Katharine), Novels by. Cr. 8vo, cloth extra, 3s. 6d. each; post 8vo, illustrated boards, 2s. each.
Margaret and Elizabeth.
The High Mills.
Heart Salvage. | Sebastian.

Joan Merryweather. Post 8vo, illustrated boards, 2s.
Gideon's Rock. Crown 8vo, cloth extra, 3s. 6d.

Science-Gossip for 1890 : An Illustrated Medium of Interchange for Students and Lovers of Nature. Edited by Dr. J. E.TAYLOR, F.L.S.,&c. Devoted to Geology, Botany, Physiology, Chemistry, Zoology, Microscopy, Telescopy, Physiography, Photography,&c. Price 4d. Monthly ; or 5s. per year, post-free. Vols. I. to XIX. may be had at 7s. 6d. each ; and Vols. XX. to date, at 5s. each. Cases for Binding, 1s. 6d. each.

"Secret Out" Series, The :
Cr. 8vo, cl.ex., Illustrated, 4s. 6d. each.
The Secret Out: One Thousand Tricks with Cards, and other Recreations; with Entertaining Experiments in Drawing-room or " White Magic." By W. H.CREMER. 300 Illusts.
The Art of Amusing: A Collection of Graceful Arts,Games,Tricks,Puzzles, and Charades By FRANK BELLEW. With 300 Illustrations.
Hanky-Panky: Very Easy Tricks, Very Difficult Tricks, White Magic, Sleight of Hand. Edited by W. H. CREMER. With 200 Illustrations.
Magician's Own Book: Performances with Cups and Balls, Eggs, Hats, Handkerchiefs, &c. All from actual Experience. Edited by W. H. CREMER. 200 Illustrations.

Seguin (L. G.), Works by :
The Country of the Passion Play, and the Highlands and Highlanders of Bavaria. With Map and 37 Illusts. and a NEW PREFACE for 1890. Crown 8vo, cloth extra, 3s. 6d.
Walks in Algiers and its Surroundings. With 2 Maps and 16 Illusts. Crown 8vo, cloth extra, 6s.

Senior.—By Stream and Sea.
By W.SENIOR. Post 8vo,cl.limp, 2s.6d.

Seven Sagas (The) of Prehis- toric Man. By JAMES H. STODDART, Author of " The Village Life." Crown 8vo, cloth extra, 6s.

Shakespeare :
The First Folio Shakespeare.—MR. WILLIAM SHAKESPEARE'S Comedies, Histories, and Tragedies. Published according to the true Originall Copies. London, Printed by ISAAC IAGGARD and ED. BLOUNT. 1623.—A Reproduction of the extremely rare original, in reduced facsimile, by a photographic process—ensuring the strictest accuracy in every detail. Small 8vo, half-Roxburghe, 7s. 6d.
Shakespeare for Children: Tales from Shakespeare. By CHARLES and MARY LAMB. With numerous Illustrations, coloured and plain, by J. MOYR SMITH. Cr. 4to, cl. gilt, 6s.

Sharp.—Children of To-morrow: A Novel. By WILLIAM SHARP. Crown 8vo, cloth extra, 6s.

Shelley.—The CompleteWorks In Verse and Prose of Percy Bysshe Shelley. Edited, Prefaced and Annotated by R. HERNE SHEPHERD. Five Vols., cr. 8vo, cloth bds., 3s. 6d. each.

Poetical Works, in Three Vols.

Vol. I. An Introduction by the Editor; The Posthumous Fragments of Margaret Nicholson; Shelley's Correspondence with Stockdale; The Wandering Jew (the only complete version); Queen Mab, with the Notes; Alastor, and other Poems; Rosalind and Helen; Prometheus Unbound; Adonais, &c. Vol. II. Laon and Cythna (as originally published, instead of the emasculated "Revolt of Islam"); The Cenci; Julian and Madda'o (from Shelley's manuscript); Swellfoot the Tyrant (from the copy in the Dyce Library at South Kensington); The Witch of Atlas; Epipsychidion; Hellas. Vol. III. Posthumous Poems, published by Mrs. SHELLEY in 1824 and 1839; The Masque of Anarchy (from Shelley's manuscript) and other Pieces not brought together in the ordinary editions.

Prose Works, in Two Vols.

Vol. I. The Two Romances of Zastrozzi and St. Irvyne; the Dublin and Marlow Pamphlets; A Refutation of Deism; Letters to Leigh Hunt, and some Minor Writings and Fragments. Vol. II. The Essays; Letters from Abroad; Translations and Fragments, Edited by Mrs. SHELLEY, and first published in 1840, with the addition of some Minor Pieces of great interest and rarity, including one recently discovered by Professor DOWDEN. With a Bibliography of Shelley, and an exhaustive Index of the Prose Works.

Sheridan(General).—Personal Memoirs of General P. H. Sheridan: The Romantic Career of a Great Soldier, told in his Own Words. With 22 Portraits and other Illustrations, 27 Maps, and numerous Facsimiles of Famous Letters. Two Vols. of 500 pages each, demy 8vo, cloth extra, 24s.

Sheridan (Richard Brinsley): Sheridan's Complete Works, with Life and Anecdotes. Including his Dramatic Writings, printed from the Original Editions, his Works in Prose and Poetry, Translations, Speeches, Jokes, Puns, &c. With a Collection of Sheridaniana. Crown 8vo, cloth extra, gilt, with 10 full-page Tinted Illustrations, 7s. 6d.

Sheridan's Comedies: The Rivals, and The School for Scandal. Edited, with an Introduction and Notes to each Play, and a Biographical Sketch of Sheridan, by BRANDER MATTHEWS. With Decorative Vignettes and 10 full-page Illusts. Demy 8vo, half-parchment, 12s. 6d.

Sherard.—Rogues: A Novel. By R. H. SHERARD. Crown 8vo, picture cover, 1s.; cloth, 1s. 6d.

Sidney's (Sir Philip) Complete Poetical Works, including all those in "Arcadia." With Portrait, Memorial-Introduction, Notes, &c., by the Rev. A. B. GROSART, D.D. Three Vols., crown 8vo, cloth boards, 18s.

Signboards: Their History. With Anecdotes of Famous Taverns and Remarkable Characters. By JACOB LARWOOD and JOHN CAMDEN HOTTEN. With 100 Illustrations. Crown 8vo, cloth extra, 7s. 6d.

Sims (George R.), Works by: Post 8vo, illustrated boards, 2s. each; cloth limp, 2s. 6d. each.
Rogues and Vagabonds.
The Ring o' Bells.
Mary Jane's Memoirs.
Mary Jane Married.
Tales of To-day.

Cr. 8vo, picture cover, 1s.ea.; cl., 1s.6d.ea.
The Dagonet Reciter and Reader: Being Readings and Recitations in Prose and Verse, selected from his own Works by G. R. SIMS.
How the Poor Live; and Horrible London. In One Volume.

Sister Dora: A Biography. By MARGARET LONSDALE. Popular Edition, Revised, with additional Chapter, a New Dedication and Preface, and Four Illustrations. Sq. 8vo, picture cover, 4d.; cloth, 6d.

Sketchley.—A Match in the Dark. By ARTHUR SKETCHLEY. Post 8vo, illustrated boards, 2s.

Slang Dictionary, The: Etymological, Historical, and Anecdotal. Crown 8vo, cloth extra, 6s. 6d.

Smart.—Without Love or Licence: A Novel. By HAWLEY SMART. Three Vols., cr. 8vo.

Smith (J. Moyr), Works by: The Prince of Argolis: A Story of the Old Greek Fairy Time. With 130 Illusts. Small 8vo, cloth extra, 3s.6d.
Tales of Old Thule. With numerous Illustrations. Cr. 8vo, cloth gilt, 6s.
The Wooing of the Water Witch. With Illustrations. Small 8vo, 6s.

Society in London. By A FOREIGN RESIDENT. Crown 8vo, 1s.; cloth, 1s. 6d.

Society in Paris: The Upper Ten Thousand. A Series of Letters from Count PAUL VASILI to a Young French Diplomat. Trans. by R. L. DE BEAUFORT. Crown 8vo, cl. ex., 6s.

Society out of Town. By A FOREIGN RESIDENT, Author of "Society in London." Crown 8vo, cloth extra, 6s. [*Preparing.*

Somerset.—Songs of Adieu. By Lord HENRY SOMERSET. Small 4to, Japanese vellum, 6s.

Spalding.-Elizabethan Demonology: An Essay in Illustration of the Belief in the Existence of Devils, and the Powers possessed by Them. By T. A. SPALDING, LL.B. Cr. 8vo, cl. ex., 5s.

Speight (T. W.), Novels by:
The Mysteries of Heron Dyke. With a Frontispiece by M. ELLEN EDWARDS. Crown 8vo, cloth extra, 3s. 6d; post 8vo, illustrated bds., 2s.
Wife or No Wife? Post 8vo, cloth limp, 1s. 6d.
A Barren Title. Crown 8vo, cl., 1s. 6d.
The Golden Hoop. Post 8vo, illust. boards, 2s.
By Devious Ways; and A Barren Title. Post 8vo, illust. boards, 2s.
The Sandycroft Mystery. Crown 8vo, picture cover, 1s. [*Shortly.*

Spenser for Children. By M. H. TOWRY. With Illustrations by WALTER J. MORGAN. Crown 4to, cloth gilt, 6s.

Stageland: Curious Habits and Customs of its Inhabitants. By JEROME K. JEROME. With 64 Illustrations by J. BERNARD PARTRIDGE. Fourth Edition. Fcap. 4to. cl. th extra, 3s. 6d.

Starry Heavens, The: A Poetical Birthday Book. Square 8vo, cloth extra, 2s. 6d.

Staunton.—Laws and Practice of Chess. With an Analysis of the Openings. By HOWARD STAUNTON. Edited by ROBERT B. WORMALD. Small crown 8vo, cloth extra, 5s.

Stedman (E. C.), Works by:
Victorian Poets. Thirteenth Edition. Crown 8vo, cloth extra, 9s.
The Poets of America. Crown 8vo, cloth extra, 9s.

Sterndale.—The Afghan Knife: A Novel. By ROBERT ARMITAGE STERNDALE. Cr. 8vo, cloth extra, 3s 6d.; post 8vo, illustrated boards, 2s.

Stevenson (R. Louis), Works by:
Post 8vo, cloth limp, 2s. 6d. each.
Travels with a Donkey in the Cevennes. Eighth Edition. With a Frontispiece by WALTER CRANE.
An Inland Voyage. Fourth Edition. With Frontispiece by WALTER CRANE.

STEVENSON (R. LOUIS), *continued—*
Cr. 8vo, buckram extra, gilt top, 6s. each.
Familiar Studies of Men and Books. Fifth Edition.
The Silverado Squatters. With Frontispiece. Third Edition.
The Merry Men. Second Edition.
Underwoods: Poems. Fourth Edit.
Memories & Portraits. Third Edit.
Virginibus Puerisque, and other Papers. Fifth Edition.

Cr. 8vo, buckram extra, gilt top, 6s. each; post 8vo, illust. boards, 2s. each.
New Arabian Nights. Eleventh Edit.
Prince Otto: Sixth Edition.

Stoddard.—Summer Cruising in the South Seas. By CHARLES WARREN STODDARD. Illustrated by WALLIS MACKAY. Crown 8vo, cloth extra, 3s. 6d.

Stories from Foreign Novelists. With Notices of their Lives and Writings. By HELEN and ALICE ZIMMERN. Frontispiece. Crown 8vo, cloth extra, 3s. 6d.; post 8vo, illust. bds., 2s.

Strange Manuscript (A) found in a Copper Cylinder. With 19 full-page Illustrations by GILBERT GAUL. Third Edition. Cr. 8vo, cl. extra, 5s.

Strange Secrets. Told by PERCY FITZGERALD, FLORENCE MARRYAT, JAMES GRANT, A. CONAN DOYLE, DUTTON COOK, and others. With 8 Illustrations by Sir JOHN GILBERT, WILLIAM SMALL, W. J. HENNESSY, &c. Crown 8vo, cloth extra, 6s.; post 8vo, illustrated boards, 2s.

Strutt's Sports and Pastimes of the People of England; including the Rural and Domestic Recreations, May Games, Mummeries, Shows, &c., from the Earliest Period to the Present Time. Edited by WM. HONE. With 140 Illustrations. Cr. 8vo, cl. extra, 7s. 6d.

Suburban Homes (The) of London: A Residential Guide to Favourite London Localities, their Society, Celebrities, and Associations. With Notes on their Rental, Rates, and House Accommodation. With Map of Suburban London. Cr. 8vo, cl. ex., 7s 6d.

Swift (Dean) :—
Swift's Choice Works, in Prose and Verse. With Memoir, Portrait, and Facsimiles of the Maps in the Original Edition of "Gulliver's Travels." Crown 8vo, cloth extra, 7s. 6d.
A Monograph on Dean Swift. By J. CHURTON COLLINS. Crown 8vo, cloth extra, 8s. [*Shortly.*

Swinburne (Algernon C.), Works by:

Selections from the Poetical Works of A. C. Swinburne. Fcap. 8vo, 6s.
Atalanta in Calydon. Crown 8vo, 6s.
Chastelard. A Tragedy. Cr. 8vo, 7s.
Poems and Ballads. FIRST SERIES. Cr. 8vo, 9s. Fcap. 8vo, same price.
Poems and Ballads. SECOND SERIES. Cr. 8vo, 9s. Fcap. 8vo, same price.
Poems and Ballads. THIRD SERIES. Crown 8vo, 7s.
Notes on Poems and Reviews. 8vo, 1s.
Songs before Sunrise. Cr. 8vo, 10s 6d.
Bothwell: A Tragedy. Cr. 8vo, 12s. 6d.
George Chapman: An Essay. (See Vol. II. of GEO. CHAPMAN'S Works.) Crown 8vo, 6s.
Songs of Two Nations. Cr. 8vo, 6s.
Essays and Studies. Crown 8vo, 12s.
Erechtheus: A Tragedy. Cr. 8vo, 6s.
Songs of the Springtides. Cr. 8vo, 6s.
Studies in Song. Crown 8vo, 7s.
Mary Stuart: A Tragedy. Cr. 8vo, 8s.
Tristram of Lyonesse, and other Poems. Crown 8vo, 9s.
A Century of Roundels. Small 4to, 8s.
A Midsummer Holiday, and other Poems. Crown 8vo, 7s.
Marino Faliero: A Tragedy. Cr. 8vo, 6s.
A Study of Victor Hugo. Cr. 8vo, 6s.
Miscellanies. Crown 8vo, 12s.
Locrine: A Tragedy. Crown 8vo, 6s.
A Study of Ben Jonson. Cr. 8vo, 7s.

Symonds.—Wine, Women, and Song: Mediæval Latin Students'
Songs. Now first translated into English Verse, with Essay by J. ADDINGTON SYMONDS. Small 8vo, parchment, 6s.

Syntax's (Dr.) Three Tours:
In Search of the Picturesque, in Search of Consolation, and in Search of a Wife. With the whole of ROWLAND-SON'S droll Illustrations in Colours, and a Life of the Author by J. C. HOTTEN. Crown 8vo, cloth extra, 7s. 6d.

Taine's History of English Literature. Translated by HENRY
VAN LAUN. Four Vols., small 8vo, cloth boards, 30s.—POPULAR EDITION, Two Vols., crown 8vo, cloth extra, 15s.

Taylor's (Bayard) Diversions
of the Echo Club: Burlesques of Modern Writers. Post 8vo, cl. limp, 2s.

Taylor (Dr. J. E., F.L.S.), Works
by. Crown 8vo, cloth ex., 7s. 6d. each.
The Sagacity and Morality of Plants: A Sketch of the Life and Conduct of the Vegetable Kingdom. Coloured Frontis. and 100 Illusts.
Our Common British Fossils, and Where to Find Them: A Handbook to: Students. With 331 Illustrations.
The Playtime Naturalist. With 366 Illustrations. Crown 8vo, cl. ex., 5s.

Taylor's (Tom) Historical
Dramas: "Clancarty," "Jeanne Darc," "'Twixt Axe and Crown," "The Fool's Revenge," "Arkwright's Wife," "Anne Boleyn," "Plot and Passion." One Vol., cr. 8vo, cloth extra, 7s. 6d.
₊ The Plays may also be had separately, at 1s. each.

Tennyson (Lord): A Biogra-
phical Sketch. By H. J. JENNINGS. With a Photograph-Portrait. Crown 8vo, cloth extra, 6s.

Thackerayana: Notes and Anec-
dotes. Illustrated by Hundreds of Sketches by WILLIAM MAKEPEACE THACKERAY, depicting Humorous Incidents in his School-life, and Favourite Characters in the books of his every-day reading. With Coloured Frontispiece. Cr. 8vo, cl. extra, 7s. 6d.

Thames.—A New Pictorial His-
tory of the Thames. By A. S. KRAUSSE. With 340 Illustrations. Post 8vo, picture cover, 1s; cloth, 1s. 6d.

Thomas (Bertha), Novels by:
Crown 8vo, cloth extra, 3s. 6d. each; post 8vo, illustrated boards, 2s. each.
Cressida. | Proud Maisie.
The Violin-Player.

Thomas (M.).—A Fight for Life:
A Novel. By W. MOY THOMAS. Post 8vo, illustrated boards, 2s.

Thomson's Seasons and Castle
of Indolence. With Introduction by ALLAN CUNNINGHAM, and over 50 Illustrations on Steel and Wood. Crown 8vo, cloth extra, 7s. 6d.

Thornbury (Walter), Works by:
Crown 8vo, cloth extra, 7s. 6d. each.
Haunted London. Edited by ED-WARD WALFORD, M.A. With Illustrations by F. W. FAIRHOLT, F.S.A.
The Life and Correspondence of J. M. W. Turner. Founded upon Letters and Papers furnished by his Friends and fellow Academicians. With numerous Illusts. in Colours.
Post 8vo, illustrated boards, 2s. each.
Old Stories Re-told.
Tales for the Marines.

Timbs (John), Works by:
Crown 8vo, cloth extra, 7s. 6d. each.
The History of Clubs and Club Life in London. With Anecdotes of its Famous Coffee-houses, Hostelries, and Taverns. With many Illusts.
English Eccentrics and Eccen-tricities: Stories of Wealth and Fashion, Delusions, Impostures, and Fanatic Missions, Strange Sights and Sporting Scenes, Eccentric Artists, Theatrical Folk, Men of Letters, &c. With nearly 50 Illusts.

Trollope (Anthony), Novels by:
Crown 8vo, cloth extra, 3s. 6d. each ;
post 8vo, illustrated boards, 2s. each.
The Way We Live Now.
Kept in the Dark.
Frau Frohmann. | Marion Fay.
Mr. Scarborough's Family.
The Land-Leaguers.

Post 8vo, illustrated boards, 2s. each.
The Golden Lion of Granpere.
John Caldigate. | American Senator

Trollope(Frances E.),Novelsby
Crown 8vo, cloth extra, 3s 6d. each;
post 8vo, illustrated boards, 2s. each.
Like Ships upon the Sea.
Mabel's Progress. | Anne Furness.

Trollope (T. A.).—Diamond Cut
Diamond, and other Stories. By
T. ADOLPHUS TROLLOPE. Post 8vo,
illustrated boards, 2s.

Trowbridge.—Farnell's Folly:
A Novel. By J. T. TROWBRIDGE. Post
8vo, illustrated boards, 2s.

Tytler (C. C. Fraser-). — Mis-
tress Judith: A Novel. By C. C.
FRASER-TYTLER. Cr. 8vo, cloth extra,
3s. 6d.; post 8vo, illust. boards, 2s.

Tytler (Sarah), Novels by:
Crown 8vo, cloth extra, 3s. 6d. each ;
post 8vo, illustrated boards, 2s. each.
What She Came Through.
The Bride's Pass. | Noblesse Oblige.
Saint Mungo's City. | Lady Bell.
Beauty and the Beast.
Buried Diamonds.
The Blackhall Ghosts.

Post 8vo, illustrated boards, 2s. each.
Citoyenne Jacqueline.
Disappeared. | The Huguenot Family

Van Laun.—History of French
Literature. By H. VAN LAUN. Three
Vols., demy 8vo, cl. bds., 7s. 6d. each.

Villari.—A Double Bond. By L.
VILLARI. Fcap. 8vo, picture cover, 1s.

Walford (Edw., M.A.),Works by:
Walford's County Families of the
United Kingdom (1890). Containing
Notices of the Descent, Birth, Mar-
riage, Education, &c., of more than
12,000 distinguished Heads of Fami-
lies, their Heirs Apparent or Pre-
sumptive, the Offices they hold, their
Addresses, Clubs, &c. Twenty-ninth
Annual Ed. Royal 8vo, cl. gilt, 50s.
Walford's Shilling Peerage (1890).
Containing an Alphabetical List of
the House of Lords, Scotch and
Irish Peers, &c. 32mo, cloth, 1s.

WALFORD (EDWARD), *continued—*
Walford's Shilling Baronetage(1890).
Containing List of the Baronets of the
United Kingdom, Biographical Not-
ices, Addresses, &c. 32mo, cloth. 1s.
Walford's Shilling Knightage (1890).
Containing an Alphabetical List of
the Knights of the United Kingdom,
short Biographical Notices, Dates of
Creation, Addresses,&c. 32mo,cl.,1s.
Walford's Shilling House of Com-
mons (1890). Containing List of all
Members of Parliament, their Ad-
dresses, Clubs, &c. 32mo, cloth, 1s.
Walford's Complete Peerage, Baron-
etage, Knightage, and House of
Commons (1890). Royal 32mo,
cloth extra, gilt edges, 5s.
Walford's Windsor Peerage, Baron-
etage, and Knightage (1890).
Cr. 8vo, cloth extra, 12s. 6d.
William Pitt: A Biography. Post 8vo,
cloth extra, 5s.
Tales of our Great Families. A New
and Revised Edition. Crown 8vo,
cloth extra, 3s. 6d. [*Shortly.*
Haunted London. ByWALTERTHORN-
BURY. Edited by EDWARD WALFORD,
M.A. Illusts. by F. W. FAIRHOLT,
F.S.A. Cr. 8vo, cloth extra 7s. 6d.

Walton and Cotton's Complete
Angler; or, The Contemplative Man's
Recreation. By IZAAK WALTON; and In-
structions how to Angle for a Trout or
Grayling in a clear Stream, by CHARLES
COTTON. With Memoirs and Notes by
Sir HARRIS NICOLAS, and 61 Illusts.
Crown 8vo, cloth antique, 7s. 6d.

Walt Whitman, Poems by.
Selected and Edited, with an Introduction, by WILLIAM M. ROSSETTI. A
New Edition, with a Steel Plate Portrait. Crown 8vo, printed on hand-
made paper and bound in buckram, 6s.

Wanderer's Library, The:
Crown 8vo ,cloth extra, 3s. 6d. each.
Wanderings in Patagonia; or, Life
among the Ostrich-Hunters. By
JULIUS BEERBOHM. Illustrated.
Camp Notes: Stories of Sport and
Adventure in Asia, Africa, and
America. By FREDERICK BOYLE.
Savage Life. By FREDERICK BOYLE.
Merrie England in the Olden Time.
By GEORGE DANIEL. With Illustra-
tions by ROBT. CRUIKSHANK.
Circus Life and Circus Celebrities.
By THOMAS FROST.
The Lives of the Conjurers. By
THOMAS FROST.
The Old Showmen and the Old
London Fairs. By THOMAS FROST.
Low-Life Deeps. An Account of the
Strange Fish to be found there. By
JAMES GREENWOOD.

WANDERER'S LIBRARY, *continued*—

The Wilds of London. By JAMES GREENWOOD.

Tunis: The Land and the People. By the Chevalier de HESSE-WARTEGG. With 22 Illustrations.

The Life and Adventures of a Cheap Jack. Edited by CHARLES HINDLEY.

The World Behind the Scenes By PERCY FITZGERALD.

Tavern Anecdotes and Sayings. By CHARLES HINDLEY. With Illusts.

The Genial Showman: Life and Adventures of Artemus Ward. By E. P. HINGSTON. With a Frontispiece.

The Story of the London Parks. By JACOB LARWOOD. With Illusts.

London Characters. By HENRY MAYHEW. Illustrated.

Seven Generations of Executioners: Memoirs of the Sanson Family (1688 to 1847). Edited by HENRY SANSON.

Summer Cruising In the South Seas. By C. WARREN STODDARD. Illustrated by WALLIS MACKAY.

Warner.—A Roundabout Journey. By CHARLES DUDLEY WARNER, Author of "My Summer in a Garden." Crown 8vo, cloth extra, 6s.

Warrants, &c. :—

Warrant to Execute Charles I. An exact Facsimile, with the Fifty-nine Signatures, and corresponding Seals. Carefully printed on paper to imitate the Original, 22 in. by 14 in. Price 2s.

Warrant to Execute Mary Queen of Scots. An exact Facsimile, including the Signature of Queen Elizabeth, and a Facsimile of the Great Seal. Beautifully printed on paper to imitate the Original MS. Price 2s.

Magna Charta. An exact Facsimile of the Original Document in the British Museum, printed on fine plate paper, nearly 3 feet long by 2 feet wide, with the Arms and Seals emblazoned in Gold and Colours. 5s.

The Roll of Battle Abbey; or, A List of the Principal Warriors who came over from Normandy with William the Conqueror, and Settled in this Country, A.D. 1066-7. With the principal Arms emblazoned in Gold and Colours. Price 5s.

Weather, How to Foretell the, with the Pocket Spectroscope By F. W. CORY, M.R.C.S. Eng., F.R.Met. Soc., &c. With 10 Illustrations. Crown 8vo, 1s. ; cloth, 1s. 6d.

Westropp.—Handbook of Pottery and Porcelain; or, History of those Arts from the Earliest Period. By HODDER M. WESTROPP. With numerous Illustrations, and a List of Marks. Crown 8vo, cloth limp, 4s. 6d.

Whist. — How to Play Solo Whist. With Specimen Hands in red and black, and Revised Code of Laws. By ABRAHAM S. WILKS and CHARLES F. PARDON. Crown 8vo, cloth extra, 3s. 6d.

Whistler's (Mr.) Ten o'Clock. Crown 8vo, hand-made paper, 1s.

Williams (W. Mattieu, F.R.A.S.), Works by:

Science In Short Chapters. Crown 8vo, cloth extra, 7s. 6d.

A Simple Treatise on Heat. With Illusts. Crown 8vo, cloth limp, 2s.6d.

The Chemistry of Cookery. Crown 8vo, cloth extra, 6s.

Wilson (Dr. Andrew, F.R.S.E.), Works by:

Chapters on Evolution: A Popular History of Darwinian and Allied Theories of Development. 3rd Ed. With 259 Illusts. Cr.8vo, cl. ex., 7s.6d.

Leaves from a Naturalist's Notebook. Post 8vo, cloth limp, 2s. 6d.

Leisure-Time Studies, chiefly Biological. Third Edit. With numerous Illustrations. Cr. 8vo, cl. ex., 6s.

Studies In Life and Sense. With numerous Illusts. Cr. 8vo, cl. ex., 6s.

Common Accidents, and How to Treat them. By Dr. ANDREW WILSON and others. With numerous Illusts. Cr. 8vo, 1s. ; cl. limp, 1s. 6d.

Winter (J. S.), Stories by :

Post 8vo, illustrated boards, 2s. each.

Cavalry Life. | Regimental Legends.

Wood.—Sabina: A Novel. By Lady WOOD. Post 8vo, illust. bds., 2s.

Wood (H.F.), Detective Stories by :

Crown 8vo, cloth extra, 6s. each ; post 8vo, illustrated boards, 2s. each.

The Passenger from Scotland Yard.

The Englishman of the Rue Caïn.

Woolley.—Rachel Armstrong ; or, Love and Theology. By CELIA PARKER WOOLLEY. Post 8vo, illustrated boards, 2s ; cloth. 2s. 6d.

Wright (Thomas), Works by :

Crown 8vo, cloth extra, 7s. 6d. each.

Caricature History of the Georges. (The House of Hanover.) With 400 Pictures, Caricatures, Squibs, Broadsides, Window Pictures, &c.

History of Caricature and of the Grotesque In Art, Literature, Sculpture, and Painting. Profusely Illustrated by F.W. FAIRHOLT, F.S.A.

Yates (Edmund), Novels by :

Post 8vo, illustrated boards, 2s. each.

Land at Last. | The Forlorn Hope.

Castaway.

THE PICCADILLY NOVELS.

Popular Stories by the Best Authors. LIBRARY EDITIONS, many Illustrated, crown 8vo, cloth extra, 3s. 6d. each.

BY GRANT ALLEN.
Philistia.
The Devil's Die
This Mortal Coil.
The Tents of Shem.

BY REV. S. BARING GOULD.
Red Spider. | Eve.

BY WALTER BESANT & J. RICE.
Ready-Money Mortiboy.
My Little Girl.
The Case of Mr. Lucraft.
This Son of Vulcan.
With Harp and Crown.
The Golden Butterfly.
By Celia's Arbour.
The Monks of Thelema.
'Twas in Trafalgar's Bay.
The Seamy Side.
The Ten Years' Tenant.
The Chaplain of the Fleet.

BY WALTER BESANT.
All Sorts and Conditions of Men.
The Captains' Room.
All in a Garden Fair.
Dorothy Forster. + Uncle Jack.
Children of Gibeon.
The World Went Very Well Then.
Herr Paulus.
For Faith and Freedom.

BY ROBERT BUCHANAN.
A Child of Nature.
God and the Man.
The Shadow of the Sword.
The Martyrdom of Madeline.
Love Me for Ever.
Annan Water. | The New Abelard
Matt. | Foxglove Manor.
The Master of the Mine.
The Heir of Linne.

BY HALL CAINE.
The Shadow of a Crime.
A Son of Hagar. | The Deemster.

BY MRS. H. LOVETT CAMERON.
Juliet's Guardian. | Deceivers Ever.

BY MORTIMER COLLINS.
Sweet Anne Page. | Transmigration.
From Midnight to Midnight.
MORTIMER & FRANCES COLLINS.
Blacksmith and Scholar.
The Village Comedy.
You Play me False.

BY WILKIE COLLINS.
Antonina. | Basil.
Hide and Seek.
The Dead Secret
Queen of Hearts.
My Miscellanies.
Woman in White.
The Moonstone.
Man and Wife.
Poor Miss Finch.
Miss or Mrs. ?
New Magdalen.
The Frozen Deep. |
The Two Destinies
The Law and the
Lady.
Haunted Hotel.
The Fallen Leaves
Jezebel'sDaughter
The Black Robe.
Heart and Science
" I Say No."
Little Novels.
The Evil Genius.
The Legacy of
Cain.
A Rogue's Life.

BY DUTTON COOK.
Paul Foster's Daughter.

BY WILLIAM CYPLES.
Hearts of Gold.

BY ALPHONSE DAUDET.
The Evangelist; or, Port Salvation.

BY JAMES DE MILLE.
A Castle in Spain.

BY J. LEITH DERWENT.
Our Lady of Tears.
Circe's Lovers.

BY M. BETHAM-EDWARDS.
Felicia.

BY MRS. ANNIE EDWARDES.
Archie Lovell.

BY PERCY FITZGERALD.
Fatal Zero.

BY R. E. FRANCILLON.
Queen Cophetua.
One by One.
A Real Queen.
King or Knave ?
Prefaced by Sir BARTLE FRERE.
Pandurang Hari.

BY EDWARD GARRETT.
The Capel Girls.

BY CHARLES GIBBON.
Robin Gray.
What will the World Say ?
In Honour Bound.
Queen of the Meadow.
The Flower of the Forest.
A Heart's Problem.
The Braes of Yarrow.
The Golden Shaft.
Of High Degree.
Loving a Dream.

BY JULIAN HAWTHORNE.
Garth.
Ellice Quentin.
Sebastian Strome.
Dust.
Fortune's Fool.
Beatrix Randolph.
David Poindexter's Disappearance.
The Spectre of the Camera.

BY SIR A. HELPS.
Ivan de Biron.

BY ISAAC HENDERSON.
Agatha Page.

BY MRS. ALFRED HUNT,
Thornicroft's Model.
The Leaden Casket.
Self-Condemned.
That other Person.

BY JEAN INGELOW.
Fated to be Free.

PICCADILLY NOVELS, *continued—*

BY R. ASHE KING.
A Drawn Game.
"The Wearing of the Green."

BY HENRY KINGSLEY.
Number Seventeen.

BY E. LYNN LINTON.
Patricia Kemball.
The Atonement of Leam Dundas.
The World Well Lost.
Under which Lord?
"My Love!"
Ione.
Paston Carew.

BY HENRY W. LUCY.
Gideon Fleyce.

BY JUSTIN McCARTHY.
The Waterdale Neighbours.
A Fair Saxon.
Dear Lady Disdain.
Miss Misanthrope.
Donna Quixote.
The Comet of a Season.
Maid of Athens.
Camiola.

BY AGNES MACDONELL.
Quaker Cousins.

BY FLORENCE MARRYAT.
Open! Sesame!

BY D. CHRISTIE MURRAY.
Life's Atonement. | Coals of Fire.
Joseph's Coat. | Val Strange.
A Model Father. | Hearts.
By the Gate of the Sea.
A Bit of Human Nature.
First Person Singular.
Cynic Fortune.
The Way of the World.

BY MRS. OLIPHANT.
Whiteladies.

BY OUIDA.
Held in Bondage. | TwoLittleWooden
Strathmore. | Shoes.
Chandos. | In a Winter City.
Under Two Flags. | Ariadne.
Idalia. | Friendship.
Cecil Castle- | Moths.
maine's Gage. | Pipistrello.
Tricotrin. | A Village Com-
Puck. | mune.
Folle Farine. | Bimbi.
ADog of Flanders | Wanda.
Pascarel. | Frescoes.
Signa. | In Maremma
Princess Naprax- | Othmar.
ine. | Guilderoy.

BY MARGARET A. PAUL.
Gentle and Simple.

PICCADILLY NOVELS, *continued—*

BY JAMES PAYN.
Lost Sir Massing- | A Grape from a
berd. | Thorn.
Walter's Word. | Some Private
Less Black than | Views.
We're Painted | TheCanon'sWard.
By Proxy. | Glow-worm Tales.
High Spirits. | Talk of the Town.
Under One Roof. | In Peril and Pri-
A Confidential | vation.
Agent. | Holiday Tasks.
From Exile. | The Mystery of
| Mirbridge.

BY E. C. PRICE.
Valentina. | The Foreigners.
Mrs. Lancaster's Rival.

BY CHARLES READE.
It is Never Too Late to Mend.
Hard Cash. | Peg Woffington.
Christie Johnstone.
Griffith Gaunt. | Foul Play.
The Double Marriage.
Love Me Little, Love Me Long.
The Cloister and the Hearth.
The Course of True Love
The Autobiography of a Thief.
Put Yourself in His Place.
A Terrible Temptation.
The Wandering Heir. | A Simpleton.
A Woman-Hater. | Readiana.
Singleheart and Doubleface.
The Jilt.
Good Stories of Men and other
Animals.

BY MRS. J. H. RIDDELL.
Her Mother's Darling.
Prince of Wales's Garden-Party.
Weird Stories.

BY F. W. ROBINSON.
Women are Strange.
The Hands of Justice.

BY JOHN SAUNDERS.
Bound to the Wheel.
Guy Waterman. | Two Dreamers.
The Lion in the Path.

BY KATHARINE SAUNDERS.
Margaret and Elizabeth.
Gideon's Rock. | Heart Salvage.
The High Mills. | Sebastian.

BY T. W. SPEIGHT.
The Mysteries of Heron Dyke.

BY R. A. STERNDALE.
The Afghan Knife.

BY BERTHA THOMAS.
Proud Maisie. | Cressida.
The Violin-Player.

BY ANTHONY TROLLOPE.
The Way we Live Now.
Frau Frohmann. | Marion Fay.
Kept in the Dark.
Mr. Scarborough's Family.
The Land-Leaguers.

PICCADILLY NOVELS, *continued—*

BY FRANCES E. TROLLOPE.
Like Ships upon the Sea.
Anne Furness. | Mabel's Progress.

BY IVAN TURGENIEFF, &c.
Stories from Foreign Novelists.

BY C. C. FRASER-TYTLER.
Mistress Judith.

PICCADILLY NOVELS, *continued—*

BY SARAH TYTLER.
What She Came Through.
The Bride's Pass. | Saint Mungo's City.
Beauty and the Beast.
Noblesse Oblige.
Lady Bell. | Buried Diamonds.
The Blackhall Ghosts.

CHEAP EDITIONS OF POPULAR NOVELS.
Post 8vo, illustrated boards, 2s. each.

BY EDMOND ABOUT.
The Fellah.

BY HAMILTON AÏDE.
Carr of Carrlyon. | Confidences.

BY MRS. ALEXANDER.
Maid, Wife, or Widow?
Valerie's Fate.

BY GRANT ALLEN.
Strange Stories.
Phillstia. | The Devil's Die.
Babylon. | This Mortal Coil.
In all Shades.
The Beckoning Hand.
For Maimie's Sake.

BY REV. S. BARING GOULD.
Red Spider. | Eve.

BY SHELSLEY BEAUCHAMP.
Grant'ey Grange.

BY WALTER BESANT & J. RICE.
Ready-Money Mortlboy.
With Harp and Crown.
This Son of Vulcan. | My Little Girl.
The Case of Mr. Lucraft.
The Golden Butterfly.
By Celia's Arbour
The Monks of Thelema.
'Twas In Trafalgar's Bay.
The Seamy Side.
The Ten Years' Tenant.
The Chaplain of the Fleet.

BY WALTER BESANT.
All Sorts and Conditions of Men.
The Captains' Room.
All In a Garden Fair.
Dorothy Forster.
Uncle Jack.
Children of Gibeon.
The World Went Very Well Then.
Herr Paulus.

BY FREDERICK BOYLE.
Camp Notes. | Savage Life.
Chronicles of No-man's Land.

BY BRET HARTE.
An Heiress of Red Dog.
The Luck of Roaring Camp.
Californian Stories.
Gabriel Conroy. | Flip.
Maruja. | A Phyllis of the Sierras.

BY HAROLD BRYDGES.
Uncle Sam at Home.

BY ROBERT BUCHANAN.
The Shadow of | The Martyrdom
the Sword. | of Madoline.
A Child of Nature. | Annan Water.
God and the Man. | The New Abelard.
Love Me for Ever. | Matt.
Foxglove Manor. | The Heir of Linne
The Master of the Mine.

BY HALL CAINE.
The Shadow of a Crime.
A Son of Hagar. | The Deemster.

BY COMMANDER CAMERON.
The Cruise of the "Black Prince."

BY MRS. LOVETT CAMERON
Deceivers Ever. | Juliet's Guardian.

BY MACLAREN COBBAN.
The Cure of Souls.

BY C. ALLSTON COLLINS.
The Bar Sinister.

BY WILKIE COLLINS.
Antonina. | My Miscellanies.
Basil. | Woman in White.
Hide and Seek. | The Moonstone.
The Dead Secret. | Man and Wife
Queen of Hearts. | Poor Miss Finch.
Miss or Mrs.? | The Fallen Leaves.
New Magdalen. | Jezebel'sDaughter
The Frozen Deep. | The Black Robe.
The Law and the | Heart and Science
Lady. | "I Say No."
TheTwo Destlnies | The Evil Genius.
Haunted Hotel. | Little Novels.
A Rogue's Life.

BY MORTIMER COLLINS.
Sweet Anne Page. | From Midnight to
Transmigration. | Midnight.
A Fight with Fortune.

MORTIMER & FRANCES COLLINS.
Sweet and Twenty. | Frances.
Blacksmith and Scholar.
The Village Comedy.
You Play me False.

BY M. J. COLQUHOUN.
Every Inch a Soldier.

BY MONCURE D. CONWAY.
Pine and Palm.

BY DUTTON COOK.
Leo. | Paul Foster's Daughter.

CHEAP POPULAR NOVELS, *continued—*

BY C. EGBERT CRADDOCK.
The Prophet of the Great Smoky Mountains.

BY WILLIAM CYPLES.
Hearts of Gold.

BY ALPHONSE DAUDET.
The Evangelist; or, Port Salvation.

BY JAMES DE MILLE.
A Castle in Spain

BY J. LEITH DERWENT.
Our Lady of Tears. | Circe's Lovers.

BY CHARLES DICKENS.
Sketches by Boz. | Oliver Twist.
Pickwick Papers. | Nicholas Nickleby

BY DICK DONOVAN.
The Man-Hunter.
Caught at Last!

BY MRS. ANNIE EDWARDES.
A Point of Honour. | Archie Lovell.

BY M. BETHAM-EDWARDS.
Felicia.

BY EDWARD EGGLESTON.
Roxy.

BY PERCY FITZGERALD.
Bella Donna. | Never Forgotten.
The Second Mrs. Tillotson.
Polly. | Fatal Zero.
Seventy-five Brooke Street.
The Lady of Brantome.

BY PERCY FITZGERALD, &c.
Strange Secrets.

BY ALBANY DE FONBLANQUE.
Filthy Lucre.

BY R. E. FRANCILLON.
Olympia. | Queen Cophetua.
One by One. | King or Knave.
A Real Queen. | Romances of Law.

BY HAROLD FREDERIC.
Seth's Brother's Wife.

BY HAIN FRISWELL.
One of Two.

BY EDWARD GARRETT.
The Capel Girls.

BY CHARLES GIBBON.
Robin Gray. | In Honour Bound
For Lack of Gold. | The Flower of the
What will the | Forest.
  World Say? | Braes of Yarrow.
In Love and War. | The Golden Shaft.
For the King. | Of High Degree.
In Pastures Green | Mead and Stream
Queen of the Mea- | Loving a Dream.
  dow. | A Hard Knot.
A Heart's Problem | Heart's Delight.
The Dead Heart. | Blood-Money.

BY WILLIAM GILBERT.
Dr Austin's Guests. | James Duke.
The Wizard of the Mountain.

BY JOHN HABBERTON.
Brueton's Bayou. | Country Luck.

BY ANDREW HALLIDAY.
Every-Day Papers.

CHEAP POPULAR NOVELS, *continued—*

BY LADY DUFFUS HARDY.
Paul Wynter's Sacrifice.

BY THOMAS HARDY.
Under the Greenwood Tree.

BY J. BERWICK HARWOOD.
The Tenth Earl.

BY JULIAN HAWTHORNE.
Garth. | Sebastian Strome
EllieQuentin. | Dust.
Fortune's Fool. | Beatrix Randolph.
Miss Cadogna. | Love—or a Name.
David Poindexter's Disappearance.
The Spectre of the Camera.

BY SIR ARTHUR HELPS.
Ivan de Biron.

BY MRS. CASHEL HOEY.
The Lover's Creed.

BY MRS. GEORGE HOOPER.
The House of Raby.

BY TIGHE HOPKINS.
'Twixt Love and Duty.

BY MRS. ALFRED HUNT.
Thornicroft's Model.
The Leaden Casket.
Self-Condemned. | That other Person

BY JEAN INGELOW.
Fated to be Free.

BY HARRIETT JAY.
The Dark Colleen.
The Queen of Connaught.

BY MARK KERSHAW.
Colonial Facts and Fictions.

BY R. ASHE KING.
A Drawn Game.
"The Wearing of the Green."

BY HENRY KINGSLEY.
Oakshott Castle

BY JOHN LEYS.
The Lindsays.

BY MARY LINSKILL.
In Exchange for a Soul.

BY E. LYNN LINTON.
Patricia Kemball.
The Atonement of Leam Dundas.
The World Well Lost.
Under which Lord? | Paston Carew.
With a Silken Thread.
The Rebel of the Family.
"My Love." | Ione.

BY HENRY W. LUCY.
Gideon Fleyce.

BY JUSTIN McCARTHY.
Dear LadyDisdain | MissMisanthrope
The Waterdale | Donna Quixote.
  Neighbours. | The Comet of a
My Enemy's | Season.
  Daughter. | Maid of Athens.
A Fair Saxon. | Camiola.
Linley Rochford.

CHEAP POPULAR NOVELS, *continued—*
BY AGNES MACDONELL.
Quaker Cousins.

BY KATHARINE S. MACQUOID.
The Evil Eye. | Lost Rose.

BY W. H. MALLOCK.
The New Republic.

BY FLORENCE MARRYAT.
Open! Sesame. | Fighting the Air.
A Harvest of Wild | Written in Fire.
Oats. |

BY J. MASTERMAN.
Half-a-dozen Daughters.

BY BRANDER MATTHEWS.
A Secret of the Sea.

BY JEAN MIDDLEMASS.
Touch and Go. | Mr. Dorillion.

BY MRS. MOLESWORTH.
Hathercourt Rectory.

BY J. E. MUDDOCK
Stories Weird and Wonderful.

BY D. CHRISTIE MURRAY.
A Life's Atonement | Hearts.
A Model Father. | Way of the World.
Joseph's Coat. | A Bit of Human
Coals of Fire. | Nature.
By the Gate of the | First Person Sin-
Val Strange [Sea. | gular.
Old Blazer's Hero. | Cynic Fortune.
One Traveller Returns.

BY HENRY MURRAY.
A Game of Bluff.

BY ALICE O'HANLON.
The Unforeseen. | Chance? or Fate?

BY GEORGES OHNET.
Doctor Rameau.

BY MRS. OLIPHANT.
Whiteladies. | The Primrose Path.
The Greatest Heiress in England.

BY MRS. ROBERT O'REILLY.
Phœbe's Fortunes.

BY OUIDA.
Held in Bondage. | Two Little Wooden
Strathmore. | Shoes.
Chandos. | Ariadne.
Under Two Flags. | Friendship.
Idalia. | Moths.
Cecil Castle- | Pipistrello.
maine's Gage. | A Village Com-
Tricotrin | Puck. | mune.
Folle Farine. | Bimbi. | Wanda.
A Dog of Flanders. | Frescoes.
Pascarel. | In Maremma.
Signa. [ine. | Othmar.
Princess Naprax- | Ouida's Wisdom,
In a Winter City. | Wit, and Pathos.

BY MARGARET AGNES PAUL.
Gentle and Simple.

BY JAMES PAYN,
Lost Sir Massing- | A County Family.
berd. | At Her Mercy.
A Perfect Treasure | A Woman's Ven-
Bentinck's Tutor. | geance.
Murphy's Master. | Cecil's Tryst.

CHEAP POPULAR NOVELS, *continued—*
Clyffards of Clyffe | Mirk Abbey.
The Family Scape- | Less Black than
grace. | We're Painted.
Foster Brothers. | By Proxy.
Found Dead. | Under One Roof.
Best of Husbands. | High Spirits.
Walter's Word. | Carlyon's Year.
Halves. | A Confidential
Fallen Fortunes. | Agent.
What He Cost Her | Some Private
Humorous Stories | Views.
Gwendoline's Har- | From Exile.
vest. | A Grape from a
£200 Reward. | Thorn.
Like Father, Like | For Cash Only.
Son. | Kit: A Memory.
Marine Residence. | The Canon's Ward
Married Beneath | Talk of the Town.
Him. | Holiday Tasks.
Not Wooed, but | Glow-worm Tales
Won. | The Mystery of Mirbridge.

BY C. L. PIRKIS.
Lady Lovelace.

BY EDGAR A. POE.
The Mystery of Marie Roget.

BY E. C. PRICE.
Valentina. | The Foreigners
Mrs. Lancaster's Rival.
Gerald.

BY CHARLES READE.
It is Never Too Late to Mend.
Hard Cash. | Peg Woffington.
Christie Johnstone.
Griffith Gaunt.
Put Yourself in His Place.
The Double Marriage.
Love Me Little, Love Me Long.
Foul Play.
The Cloister and the Hearth.
The Course of True Love.
Autobiography of a Thief.
A Terrible Temptation.
The Wandering Heir.
A Simpleton. | A Woman-Hater.
Readiana. | The Jilt.
Singleheart and Doubleface.
Good Stories of Men and other
Animals.

BY MRS. J. H. RIDDELL,
Her Mother's Darling.
Prince of Wales's Garden Party.
Weird Stories. | Fairy Water.
The Uninhabited House.
The Mystery in Palace Gardens.

BY F. W. ROBINSON
Women are Strange.
The Hands of Justice.

BY JAMES RUNCIMAN.
Skippers and Shellbacks.
Grace Balmaign's Sweetheart.
Schools and Scholars.

CHEAP POPULAR NOVELS, *continued—*
BY W. CLARK RUSSELL.
Round the Galley Fire.
On the Fo'k'sle Head.
In the Middle Watch.
A Voyage to the Cape.
A Book for the Hammock.
The Mystery of the "Ocean Star."
The Romance of Jenny Harlowe.
BY GEORGE AUGUSTUS SALA.
Gaslight and Daylight.
BY JOHN SAUNDERS.
Guy Waterman. | Two Dreamers.
The Lion in the Path.
BY KATHARINE SAUNDERS.
Joan Merryweather. | The High Mills.
Margaret and Elizabeth.
Heart Salvage. | Sebastian.
BY GEORGE R. SIMS.
Rogues and Vagabonds.
The Ring o' Bells.| Mary Jane Married.
Mary Jane's Memoirs.
Tales of To-day.
BY ARTHUR SKETCHLEY.
A Match in the Dark.
BY T. W. SPEIGHT.
The Mysteries of Heron Dyke.
The Golden Hoop. | By Devious Ways.
BY R. A. STERNDALE.
The Afghan Knife.
BY R. LOUIS STEVENSON.
New Arabian Nights. | Prince Otto.
BY BERTHA THOMAS.
Cressida. | Proud Maisie.
The Violin-Player.
BY W. MOY THOMAS.
A Fight for Life.
BY WALTER THORNBURY.
Tales for the Marines.
Old Stories Re-told.
BY T. ADOLPHUS TROLLOPE.
Diamond Cut Diamond.
BY ANTHONY TROLLOPE.
The Way We Live Now.
The American Senator.
Frau Frohmann | Marion Fay.
Kept in the Dark.
Mr. Scarborough's Family.
The Land-Leaguers.| John Caldigate
The Golden Lion of Granpere.
By F. ELEANOR TROLLOPE.
Like Ships upon the Sea.
Anne Furness. | Mabel's Progress.
BY J. T. TROWBRIDGE.
Farnell's Folly.
BY IVAN TURGENIEFF, &c.
Stories from Foreign Novelists.
BY MARK TWAIN.
Tom Sawyer. | A Tramp Abroad.
The Stolen White Elephant.
A Pleasure Trip on the Continent
Huckleberry Finn.   [of Europe.
Life on the Mississippi.
The Prince and the Pauper.

CHEAP POPULAR NOVELS, *continued—*
BY C. C. FRASER-TYTLER.
Mistress Judith.
BY SARAH TYTLER.
What She Came Through.
The Bride's Pass. | Buried Diamonds.
Saint Mungo's City.
Beauty and the Beast.
Lady Bell. | Noblesse Oblige.
Citoyenne Jacqueline | Disappeared.
The Huguenot Family.
The Blackhall Ghosts.
BY J. S. WINTER.
Cavalry Life. | Regimental Legends
BY H. F. WOOD.
The Passenger from Scotland Yard.
The Englishman of the Rue Cain.
BY LADY WOOD.
Sabina.
BY CELIA PARKER WOOLLEY.
Rachel Armstrong; or, Love&Theology.
BY EDMUND YATES.
The Forlorn Hope. | Land at Last.
Castaway.
ANONYMOUS.
Why Paul Ferroll Killed his Wife.

POPULAR SHILLING BOOKS.
Jeff Briggs's Love Story. By BRET HARTE.
The Twins of Table Mountain. By BRET HARTE.
A Day's Tour. By PERCY FITZGERALD.
Esther's Glove. By R. E. FRANCILLON.
The Professor's Wife. By L. GRAHAM.
Mrs. Gainsborough's Diamonds. By JULIAN HAWTHORNE.
Niagara Spray. By J. HOLLINGSHEAD.
A Romance of the Queen's Hounds. By CHARLES JAMES.
The Garden that Paid the Rent. By TOM JERROLD
Cut by the Mess. By ARTHUR KEYSER.
Our Sensation Novel. Edited by JUSTIN H. McCARTHY, M.P.
Dolly. By JUSTIN H. McCARTHY, M.P.
Lily Lass. By JUSTIN H. McCARTHY, M.P.
Was She Good or Bad? By W. MINTO.
That Girl in Black. By Mrs. MOLES-WORTH.
Beyond the Gates. By E. S. PHELPS.
Old Maid's Paradise. By E. S. PHELPS.
Burglars in Paradise. By E. S. PHELPS.
Jack the Fisherman. By E. S. PHELPS.
Trooping with Crows. By C. L. PIRKIS
Bible Characters. By CHAS. READE.
Rogues. By R. H. SHERARD.
The Dagonet Reciter. By G. R. SIMS.
How the Poor Live. By G. R. SIMS.
The Sandycroft Mystery. By T. W. SPEIGHT.
A Double Bond. By LINDA VILLARI.

J. OGDEN AND CO. LIMITED, PRINTERS, GREAT SAFFRON HILL, E.C.